Philippa Gregory is an established writer and broadcaster for radio and television. She holds a PhD in eighteenth-century literature from the University of Edinburgh. She has been widely praised for her historical novels, including *Earthly Joys* and *A Respectable Trade* (which she adapted for BBC Television), as well as her works of contemporary suspense. *The Other Boleyn Girl* won the Parker Romantic Novel of the Year Award in 2002 and it has recently been adapted for BBC Television. Philippa Gregory lives in the North of England with her family.

Visit www.PhilippaGregory.com for more information and www.AuthorTracker.co.uk for exclusive updates about Philippa Gregory.

PHILIPPA GREGORY

Fallen Skies

Set in Fournier

Printed and bound in Great Britain by
Clays Ltd, St Ives plc

HARPER

This novel is entirely a work of fiction.
The names, characters and incidents portrayed in it are
the work of the author's imagination. Any resemblance to
actual persons, living or dead, events or localities is
entirely coincidental.

Harper
An imprint of HarperCollins*Publishers*
77–85 Fulham Palace Road,
Hammersmith, London W6 8JB

www.harpercollins.co.uk

This paperback edition 2006
5

First published in Great Britain by
HarperCollins*Publishers* 1993

A catalogue record for this book is
available from the British Library

ISBN-13: 978 0 00 723306 9
ISBN-10: 0 00 723306 X

A
re
i
ph
e
d,
'
or

This book is dedicated to
Private Frederick John Carter
of the 11th Scottish Rifles
who died at Salonika,
12th September 1917,
aged twenty-four

Ours is essentially a tragic age, so we refuse to take it tragically. The cataclysm has happened, we are among the ruins, we start to build up new little habitats, to have new little hopes. It is rather hard work: there is now no smooth road into the future: but we go round, or scramble over the obstacles. We've got to live, no matter how many skies have fallen.

D. H. LAWRENCE, *Lady Chatterley's Lover*, 1928

Chapter One

Stephen's mouth was filling with mud, wet slurry pressed on his eyelids, slid into his nostrils like earthworms. He flailed helplessly against the weight of it on his face, on his body, in his hair. He felt the silty terrible power of it pinning him down. When he opened his mouth to scream it poured into his throat, he could taste its wetness: the terrible non-taste of earth.

He choked on it, retching and heaving for breath, spitting and hawking. He was drowning in it, he was being crushed by its weight, he was being buried alive. His hands like paddles, he scrabbled against it, trying to claw a space for his face, and then he grabbed linen sheet, woollen blankets, counterpane, and he opened his eyes, clogged only by sleep, and saw the white ceiling of his home.

He whooped like a sick child, gasping in terror, rubbing his face roughly, dragging his palm across his lips, across his tongue where the dead taste still lingered. He whispered 'Oh God, oh God,' pitifully, over and over again. 'Oh God, oh God.'

Then he turned his head and saw her. In the doorway was his mother, her dressing-gown pulled on over her thick cotton nightdress, her tired face set in lines of fear and . . . something else. He stared at her, trying to read the expression on her face: disapproval.

His bedside table was overturned, the ugly pottery electric lamp broken, his jug of water spilling into a puddle on the carpet. 'I'm sorry,' he said. He was humble, ashamed. 'I was dreaming.'

7

She came into the room and lifted up the table. She set the empty jug and the pieces of the bedside light on it in mute accusation. 'I wish you'd let me call Dr Mobey,' she said. 'You were having a fit.'

He shook his head quickly, his anger rising. 'It was nothing. A bad dream.'

'You should take one of my sleeping tablets.'

Stephen dreaded deep sleep more than anything else. In deep sleep the dream would go on, the dream of the collapsed dug-out, the dream of scrabbling and suffocating, and only after a lifetime of screaming horror, the bliss of feeling the earth shift and tumble and Coventry's gentle hands scraping the soil from his face and hearing his voice saying, 'You're all right, Sir. I'm here now. We'll have you out in a jiffy.' Stephen had wept then, wept like a baby. There had been no-one but Coventry to see his coward's tears, and he had wiped them away with dirty bleeding hands. Coventry had dug bare-handed, refusing to put a spade in the earth. He had scrabbled in the mud like a dog for its master and then they had both wept together; like new-found lovers, like reunited twins.

'I'll go downstairs and make myself a brew,' he said. 'You get to bed. I don't want any tablets.'

'Oh, go to sleep,' Stephen's mother said irritably. 'It's four in the morning. Far too late for tea.'

He got out of bed and threw his dressing-gown around his shoulders. When he stood, his height and maleness could dominate her. Now he was the master of the house, not a sick man screaming with nightmares. 'I think I'll have a brew and a cigarette,' he said with the upper-class drawl he had learned from the senior officers in the trenches. 'Then I'll sleep. You toddle off, old lady.'

She turned, obedient but resentful. 'Well, don't make a mess for Cook.'

He shepherded her out of the room and she shied away

8

from him as if fear were contagious, as if terror were catching.

'I wish you'd let me call Dr Mobey,' she said again, pausing on the landing before she turned into her bedroom. 'He says it's very common. They have all sorts of things to cure nervous troubles. It's just hysteria.'

Stephen smoothed his moustache, his broad handsome face regaining its confident good looks. He laughed. 'I'm not a hysteric,' he said. His voice was rich with his male pride. 'Not me,' he said, smiling. 'I just get the odd bad dream.'

He turned away from her and loped down the stairs. The hall was dark but the fanlight above the front door showed him the green baize door that separated the domestic quarters in the basement from the rest of the house. He opened the door and went quietly down the back stairs.

The kitchen was light; it was warm from the kitchen range. Coventry was at the stove, warming a teapot. He looked up when Stephen entered and took him in, took him all in, with one comprehensive glance. Stephen sighed with relief at the sight of him. 'Had a bit of a dream,' he said. 'Fancied a cup of tea, and here you are. Ministering bloody angel.'

Coventry smiled his slow crooked smile. As Stephen watched, he spooned five heaped spoonfuls of tea from the caddy into the teapot, adding them to the old dregs left in the pot. He poured boiling water on the stale brew and stood the pot on the range for a few moments, then took up the two mugs. He put four spoonfuls of sugar into each mug and poured a dark stream of tea from the pot. It tasted stewed, and sour from the old tea, as strong as poison and teeth-grittingly sweet. It was how it had tasted in the trenches. It was that taste which told you that you were alive, that you had come back, against all odds, from a night patrol, from a dawn attack, from a lonely dangerous sniper's mission. The strong sweet taste of tea was the taste of survival. The taste of mud was death. Stephen sank into one of the chairs before the range and put his slippered feet against the warm oven door.

'Good Christ, Coventry! I wish you would speak again,' he said. 'I wish I could stop dreaming.' He sipped a taste of tea, the strong sour brew rinsing his mouth clean of the taste of dream-mud. 'I wish it had never happened,' Stephen said with rare bleak honesty. 'I wish to Christ it had never happened at all.'

Stephen Winters first saw Lily on the stage of the Palais music hall on the opening night of the first show, 5 May 1920: her debut. He missed her solo song – he was at the bar and then in the gents. But in the can-can finale his cousin David Walters, on a flying visit to Portsmouth, had nudged him and said: 'See that girl? Can't half kick. Bet she's French.'

'Damn the French,' Stephen said automatically. 'Beer at five francs a glass and then someone's peed in it.'

'See that girl?' David persisted. 'Pretty girl.'

Stephen had looked, blearily, through the glass window of the bar and seen Lily dive down into the splits and then fling her head up, beaming. She looked ready to laugh for joy.

'Oh yes,' Stephen said, surprised. 'Oh yes.'

'Pretty girl,' David repeated drunkenly.

They watched while the orchestra galloped into the walk-down and the artists came downstage and took their bows. There was something about Lily's face that appealed to Stephen. Something he could not name.

'I know what,' he said suddenly to David. 'She looks like the girls used to look – before.'

'No! She's got short hair. None of them had short hair before.'

'She does, she does,' Stephen persisted. 'She looks like the girls used to look. She looks . . .'

David was cheering the star, Sylvia de Charmante, who was curtseying deeply, like a debutante at court.

'She looks like there had never been a war,' Stephen said slowly. 'She looks like there had never been a war at all.'

'Go backstage!' David said with sudden abrupt determination. 'If you like the look of her, take her out!'

'D'you think she would come?' Stephen asked. The curtain had dropped and now rose. Lily was at the end of the line; he could see her blush at the applause and her frank grin.

'Oh yes,' David said cheerily. 'Heroes we are. Bloody heroes. We should have worn our medals.'

'I didn't think you'd *got* any medals. I didn't know they gave medals for pushing papers in London.'

'We can't all be you,' David said pleasantly. 'Charging around, blowing your whistle and massacring Huns single-handed.' He slapped Stephen on the back. 'Let's have a little bracer and ask the girl out,' he said. 'She can bring along a friend for me. They're all tarts, these girls. She'll come like a shot.'

He shouldered his way back to the bar and shouted for two single whiskies. Stephen downed his in one thirsty gulp.

'Come on, then,' David said cheerily. 'There's usually a stage door around the back somewhere.'

The two men pushed through the crowd spilling out of the little music hall and then linked arms to stroll down the dark alley at the side of the theatre. Further down the alley a couple were locked in each other's arms; the woman's hat was pushed back as they kissed passionately.

'Dirty bitch,' Stephen said with sudden venom. 'I hate tarts.'

'Oh, you hate everybody when you've had a drink,' David said jovially. 'Bang on the door!'

A hatch in the stage door opened at once. George, the stage door porter, looked out.

'Please send our compliments to the dancers,' David said with assurance. 'We were wondering if you could tell us the name of the little blonde one.'

The porter looked blankly at them. A shilling found its way from Stephen's pocket to gleam in the gaslight. George opened the door and the shilling changed hands.

'The young one, with the fair bobbed hair.'

'Miss Lily Valance, gentlemen.'

'We wanted to ask her to dinner. Her and a friend.'

'She can bring the plump dark one who was on with the conjuror,' David interrupted.

'Miss Madge Sweet, gentlemen.'

'Ask them both. Shall I write a note?'

The porter nodded.

Stephen took out his card case. It had a small silver propelling pencil inside. On one of his cards he wrote in small spidery script: 'My cousin and I would be honoured if you would come to the Queens Hotel for dinner with us. We are at the stage door.'

'We'll wait for a reply,' he said to the porter.

The porter nodded and was about to go inside when a middle-aged woman, drably dressed, came down the alley behind the two men, quietly said 'Excuse me', and stepped between them and through the open door.

'These gentlemen are asking for Lily,' the porter told her.

Helen Pears turned and looked at them both. 'My daughter,' she said quietly.

Stephen had to remind himself that she was only the mother of a chorus girl and therefore she could not be a lady. There was no need to feel abashed. She was a tart's mother, she was probably an old tart herself.

'I am Captain Stephen Winters,' he said, invoking his wartime status. 'This is Captain David Walters. We were wondering if Miss Valance and Miss Sweet would like to have dinner with us.'

The woman did not even smile at him, she had the cheek to look him straight in the eye, and she looked at him coldly.

'At the Queens,' he said hastily to indicate his wealth.

She said nothing.

'We can go in my car, my driver is waiting,' he added.

Helen Pears nodded. She did not seem at all impressed. 'I will tell Miss Sweet of your invitation,' she said levelly. 'But my daughter does not go out to dinner.'

She went inside and the porter, raising sympathetic eyebrows, shut the door in their faces.

'That's that then,' David said disconsolately. 'What a harridan!'

'You go on, I'll meet you at the Queens.'

'You've got no chance here, not with her ma on sentry-go.'

'I'll give it a try,' Stephen said. 'Go on.'

'Forlorn hoper!'

Stephen walked with David down to the end of the alley and waved across at Coventry, waiting in the big Argyll limousine in front of the music hall.

'Bring the car up here,' he called.

Coventry nodded, and drove the car up to the end of the alley. Half a dozen of the cast looked at it curiously as they went past. Stephen stood by the rear passenger door and waited.

He could see the streetlight glint on Lily's fair hair, only half-covered by a silly little hat, as she walked down the shadowy alley, her hand tucked in her mother's arm. They

13

were laughing together. Stephen was struck at once by the easy warmth between them.

'Excuse me, Mrs Valance, Miss Valance,' Stephen said with careful politeness. 'I must apologize for my behaviour. I was in Belgium for too long, and I've forgotten my English manners.'

Lily beamed at him with her open friendly smile. Her mother stood waiting. Stephen felt a frisson of irritation. The woman showed no respect for a gentleman. He opened the car door. 'I quite understand that it is too late for dinner,' he said smoothly. 'But may I, at least, see you home? It is so difficult to get a cab at this time of night.'

Stephen saw the quick movement as Lily pinched her mother's arm. Helen Pears hesitated for only a moment and then she nodded. 'Thank you very much,' she said. 'We live in Highland Road.'

Helen went in first, Lily next. Stephen climbed in after them and spoke into the tube that ran from the back seat to the driver.

'Highland Road.'

'It's the grocery shop on the corner. Pears Grocers.'

'My family is a Portsmouth family too,' Stephen said, desperate for some common ground. 'We are Winters the lawyers.'

Helen nodded. 'I know.'

'Do you? I beg your pardon! I did not recognize you.'

'We've never met. I saw your photograph in the *Hampshire Telegraph*.'

There was a short awkward silence.

'I thought the porter said your name was Miss Valance,' Stephen said gently to Lily.

She glanced up at him from under her eyelashes. Stephen felt desire like hunger. She was hardly a woman yet, she was still a girl with skin like cream and hair like honey.

'Valance is my stage name,' she said. Her voice was clear, her speech elocution-pure. 'My real name is Lily Pears.'

The car drove slowly down Marmion Road; Stephen felt he was no further forward.

'I wonder if you would like to come to dinner tomorrow night?' he said nervously to Helen. 'You and Miss Pears. And Mr Pears too, if he would like to come?'

'I am a widow. There is no Mr Pears.' Helen paused. Stephen saw again the quick secret movement of Lily's gloved hand on her mother's arm. 'Yes, Captain Winters, thank you. That would be very nice.'

'Shall I pick you up after the show?'

'Thank you,' Helen said again.

The big car slowed and stopped. Lily and her mother got out on to the pavement, and Stephen followed them.

'I'll say goodnight then, and look forward to dining with you both tomorrow,' he said.

Helen held out her hand and Stephen shook it, and then turned to Lily.

He took her gloved hand in his and felt the warmth of her palm through the white cotton. She looked up at him and smiled. She smiled as if she had some secret assurance, some private conviction, that nothing bad could ever happen to her. Stephen, looking down into that bright little face, felt again the potent magic of young confidence. He had not seen a face like that since the early days, the first days of the war. The young subalterns from public schools looked like that – as if life were one easy glorious adventure and nothing would ever disappoint them.

'Goodnight, Miss Pears,' he said. 'I will see you tomorrow.'

'Goodnight, Captain Winters.' Her voice was light and steady with an undercurrent of amusement, as if she might giggle at any moment at this game of being grown-up.

He let go her hand with reluctance, and waited by the car until the poky little door of the shop doorway had shut behind them. 'Goodnight,' he said again.

Coventry drove him in silence to the Queens Hotel, where he dined with David, and then got royally drunk at half a dozen of the worst pubs in Portsmouth.

Chapter Two

The dinner was not a success. Lily was overawed by the gold and crimson grandeur of the Queens Hotel dining room, Stephen was awkward in the company of women and had little to say to Lily under these formal circumstances. They had discussed the eclipse of the moon a few nights earlier; Stephen had speculated about British chances at the Antwerp Olympics; then he had fallen silent. He had nothing to say to Lily. If she had been the tart that he first thought, then he would have taken her to some cheerful bar and got her so drunk that she would go to an alleyway at the back of the pub and let him take her, with deliberate roughness, against a brick wall. But with the two women masquerading as ladies, Stephen did not know how to deal with them. He could not resist his desire for Lily, nervous as a child in the formal dining room, wary of waiters and wide-eyed at the other diners. She was cheaply pretty in her little blue cocktail dress and her frivolous feather of a hat. Her mother was as dignified as a duchess in a beaded black gown and gloves.

The waiter, sensing another hiatus in a stilted evening, removed the pudding plates and replaced them with small coffee cups, cream, sugar, and a large silver coffee pot. Mrs Pears turned her attention from the band and the dancers and poured coffee into the three cups.

'Jolly good dinner,' Stephen said, seeking thanks.

Mrs Pears nodded.

'I expect it makes a change for you, from rationing.'

Mrs Pears shook her head. 'The only good thing about running a shop is that you never go short.'

'Oh, really, Ma!' Lily exclaimed, thinking of the dried ends of ham joints and day-old bread.

Stephen had flushed a deep brick-red. 'I thought . . . I thought . . . that things were dreadfully short,' he said. 'Th . . . th . . . that was what they t . . . t . . . told us.'

Mrs Pears's smile was sardonic. 'Yes,' she said. 'They would have told you that. But there would have been enough for everyone if people had shared. As it was, those who could afford it never did without.'

'You s . . . s . . . sold from under the counter?' Stephen demanded. 'P . . . p . . . profiteered?'

'I saw that Lily had shoes on her feet and food on the table. I bought her ballet lessons and singing lessons. I made my money from rich and selfish people who would rather pay a little more than do without. If you call that profiteering, Captain, then I'm a wartime profiteer. But you'd best look around at the company you're in before you point an accusing finger at me.'

Lily's fair head was bowed over her coffee cup. The feathers in her hat trembled with embarrassment. 'Hush, Ma,' she said softly.

Mrs Pears pointed one black-gloved finger at the next-door table. 'That man is Councillor Hurt, cloth-maker. Ask him how much khaki and serge he ran off in the four years. Ask him about the greatcoats and trousers like paper. The other is Alderman Wilson, scrap metal. Ask him about the railings and saucepans and scrap given free for the war effort but then sold by him for thousands. And that's Mr Askew, munitions. Ask him about the girls whose skins are still orange and about the shells which never worked.' She paused. 'We were all profiteers from the war except those that died. Those who didn't come back. They were the mugs. Everyone else did very nicely indeed.'

Stephen's hands were trembling with his anger. He thrust them beneath the tablecloth and gripped hard.

'Let's dance!' Lily said suddenly. 'I adore this tune.' She sprang to her feet. Stephen automatically rose with her.

She led him to the dance floor, his arm went around her waist and she slipped her little hand in his. Their feet stepped lightly in time, gracefully. Lily's head went back and she smiled up at Stephen, whose face was still white with rage. Lily sang the popular song softly to him:

> If you could remember me,
> Any way you choose to,
> What would be your choice?
> I know which one I would do . . .

Above them the winking chandelier sparkled as they turned and circled the floor. Stephen's colour slowly came back to his cheeks. Lily sang nonsense songs, as a mother would sing to a frightened child:

> When you dood the doodsie with me,
> And I did the doodsie with you.

The music stopped and Lily spun around and clapped the band. They bowed. The band leader bowed particularly to Lily.

'Miss Lily Valance!' he announced.

Lily flushed and glanced at her mother. The older woman nodded her head towards the bandstand. Lily obediently went up to the band leader, her hand still on Stephen's arm.

'Miss Lily Valance, the new star of the Palais!' the band leader announced with pardonable exaggeration.

'Wait there,' Lily said to Stephen and hitched up her calf-length dress and clambered up on to the bandstand.

'"Tipperary!"' someone shouted from the floor. 'Sing "It's a Long Way to Tipperary!"'

Lily shook her head with a smile, and then stepped to the front of the stage. 'I'll sing "Danny Boy".'

The band played the overture and Lily stood very still, listening to the music like a serious child. The dining room fell silent as Lily lifted her small pale face and sang.

She had a singing voice of remarkable clarity – more like the limpid purity of a boy soprano than a girl singer from a music hall. She sang artlessly, like a chorister practising alone. She stood with both her hands clasped loosely before her, not swaying nor tapping her feet, her face raised and her eyes looking outwards, beyond the ballroom, beyond the dockyard, beyond the very seas themselves, as if she were trying to see something on the horizon, or beyond it. It was not a popular song from the war, nor one that recalled the dead – the mugs who had gained nothing. Lily never sang war songs. But no-one looking at her and listening to her pure poignant voice did not think of those others who had left England six years ago, with faces as hopeful and as untroubled as hers, who would never come home again.

When the last note held, rang and fell silent the room was very quiet, as if people were sick of dancing and pretending that everything was well now, in this new world that was being made without the young men, in this new world of survivors pretending that the lost young men had never been. Then one of the plump profiteers clapped his hands and raised a full glass of French champagne and cried: 'Hurrah for pretty Lily!' and 'Sing us something jolly, girl!' then everyone applauded and called for another song and shouted for the waiter and another bottle.

Lily shook her head with a little smile and stepped down from the stage. Stephen led her back to their table. A bottle of champagne in a silver bucket of ice stood waiting.

'They sent it,' Mrs Pears said, nodding towards the next-door table. 'There's no need to thank them, Lily, you just bow and smile.'

Lily looked over obediently, bowed her head as her mother had told her and smiled demurely.

'By jove, you're a star!' Stephen exclaimed.

Lily beamed at him. 'I hope so!' Her cheeks were flushed, her eyes sparkling. 'I really hope so!'

The waiter brought the round flat glasses for champagne and filled one for each of them. Lily raised her glass to the neighbouring table and dimpled over the top of it.

'That'll do,' her mother said.

Stephen grinned at Mrs Pears. 'I see you keep Lily in order!'

She nodded. 'I was a singer on the halls before I met Mr Pears. I learned a thing or two then.'

'Ma goes with me everywhere,' Lily said serenely.

'Nearly time to go home,' Mrs Pears said. 'Lily's got a matinée tomorrow. She needs her sleep.'

'Of course!' Stephen nodded to the waiter for the bill. The two women stood up and drifted across the dance floor to fetch their wraps from the cloakroom while Stephen paid.

He waited for them outside, on the shallow white steps under the big glass awning. Coventry drew up in the big grey Argyll motor car, got out, walked around to open the back door and stood, holding it wide. Stephen and Coventry looked at each other, a long level look without speaking while Stephen lit a cigarette and drew in the first deep draw of fresh smoke. Then the doorman opened the double doors and the women came out, muffled against the cool of the May evening. The men broke from their silent communion and stepped forward. Stephen licked his fingers and carefully pinched out the lighted ember of his cigarette, and raised his hand to tuck it behind his ear.

Coventry shot a quick warning glance at him, saying nothing. Stephen exclaimed at himself, flushed, and dropped the cigarette into one of the stone pots that flanked the steps.

He helped Lily and her mother into the luxurious grey-upholstered seats of the car and got in after them. Coventry drove slowly to the Highland Road corner shop and parked at the kerb. Mrs Pears went into the dark interior of the shop with a word of thanks and goodnight as Lily paused on the doorstep, the glazed shop door ajar behind her. Stephen thought Lily was herself a little commodity, a fresh piece of provender, something he might buy from under the counter, a black-market luxury, a pre-war treat. Something he could buy and gobble up, every delicious little scrap.

'Thank you for a lovely evening,' Lily said, like a polite child.

'Come out tomorrow,' he said. 'Coventry can drive us along the seafront.'

'Can't. I've got a matinée.'

'The next day then, Sunday?'

'If Ma says I can.'

'I'll call for you at three.'

'All right.'

Stephen glanced shiftily towards the darkened shop. He could not see Mrs Pears in the shadowed interior. He leaned towards Lily. Her pale face was upturned to look at him, her fair hair luminous in the flickering gas lighting. Stephen put his hand on her waist. She was soft under his tentative touch, unstructured by stiff corsets. She reminded him of the other girl, a girl long ago, who only wore corsets to Mass on a Sunday. On weekdays her skin was hot and soft beneath a thin cotton shirt. He drew Lily towards him and she took a small step forward. She was smiling slightly. He could smell her light sweet perfume.

He could feel the warmth of her skin through the cheap fabric of her cocktail dress.

'Time to come in, Lily,' said her mother's voice immediately behind them.

Stephen released her at once.

'Goodnight, Captain Winters. Thank you for a lovely dinner,' said Mrs Pears from the darkness inside the shop.

The door behind Lily opened wide, and with a glance like a mischievous schoolgirl, she waved her white-gloved hand and went in.

Stephen sat beside Coventry for the short drive home, enjoying the open air of the cab.

'Damned pretty girl,' he said. He took a couple of cigarettes from his case and lit them both, holding the two in his mouth at once. The driver nodded. Stephen passed a cigarette to him. The man took it without taking his eyes from the road, without a word of thanks.

'Pity about the mother,' Stephen said half to himself. 'Fearfully respectable woman.'

The driver nodded, exhaled a wisp of smoke.

'Not like a showgirl at all, really,' Stephen said. 'I could almost take her home for tea.'

The driver glanced questioningly at Stephen.

'We'll see,' Stephen said. 'See how things go. A man must marry, after all. And it doesn't matter much who it is.' He paused. 'She's like a girl from before the war. You can imagine her, before the war, living in the country on a farm. I could live on a little farm with a girl like that.'

The cool air, wet with sea salt, blew around them. It was chilly, but both men relished the discomfort, the familiar chill.

'There are plenty of girls,' Stephen said harshly. 'Far too many. One million, don't they say? One million spare women. Plenty of girls. It hardly matters which one.'

Coventry nodded and drew up before the handsome

red-brick house. In the moonlight the white window sills and steps were gleaming bright.

'You sleeping here tonight?' Stephen asked as he opened the car door.

The driver nodded.

'Brew-up later?'

The man nodded again.

Stephen stepped from the car and went through the imposing wrought-iron gate, through the little front garden, quiet in the moonlight, and up the scoured white steps to the front door. He fitted his key in the lock and stepped into the hall as his mother came out of the drawing room.

'You're early, dear,' she said pleasantly.

'Not especially,' he said.

'Nice dinner?'

'The Queens. Same as usual.'

'Anyone I know?'

'No-one you know, Mother.'

She hesitated, her curiosity checked by their family habit of silence and secrecy. Stephen went towards the stairs.

'Father still awake?' he asked.

'The nurse has just left him,' Muriel said. 'He might have dozed off, go in quietly.'

Stephen nodded and went up the stairs to his father's bedroom.

It was dark inside, a little nightlight burning on the mantelpiece over the fireplace. The fire had died down, only the embers glowing dark red. Stephen stood inside the door waiting for his eyes to get used to the darkness. Suddenly, he felt his chest constrict with terror and his heart hammered. It was being in the darkness, waiting and straining to be able to see, and knowing he had to go forward, half-blind, while They could watch him, at their ease, in safety; watch him clearly against the pale horizon, and take Their time to put the cross-sight neatly in the centre of his silhouette, and gently, leisurely, squeeze the trigger.

He put his hand behind him and tugged the door open. The bright electric light from the landing flooded into the room and Stephen shuddered with relief. He loosened his collar and found his neck and his face were wet with the cold sweat of fear. 'Damn.'

He could see now that his father was awake. His big head was turned towards the door and his sunken eyes were staring.

'I hate the dark,' Stephen said, moving towards the bed. He pulled up a low-seated high-backed chair and sat at his father's head. The sorrowful dark eyes stared at him. The left side of the man's face was twisted and held by the contraction of a stroke. The other half was normal, a wide deeply lined face.

'Took a girl out to dinner,' Stephen said. He took his father's hand without gentleness, as if it were a specimen of pottery which had been handed to him for his inspection. He hefted the limp hand, and let it fall back on the counterpane. 'Music hall girl,' he said. 'Nothing special.'

With an extended finger he lifted one of his father's fingers and dropped it down again. There was no power in any part of the man's body.

'You're like a corpse yourself, you know,' Stephen said conversationally. 'One of the glorious dead you are. You'd never have been like this but for Christopher, would you? Mother told me – she handed you the telegram, you took one glance at it and fell down like you were dead.'

There was complete silence in the room except for the slow ticking of the mantelpiece clock.

'You wouldn't have dropped down half-dead for me,

would you?' Stephen said with a hard little laugh. 'Not for me! One of the white feather brigade?' He raised his father's hand, casually lifting the limp index finger with his own. Then he dropped it down again. 'Who would ever have dreamed that I'd come home a hero and Christopher never come home at all?' He smiled at the wide-eyed, frozen face. 'You do believe I'm a hero?' he asked. 'Don't you?'

Stephen heard his mother's footsteps on the stairs and he got up from the chair and smoothed the counterpane. 'Sleep well.' He went quietly out of the room.

'Goodnight, Mother,' he said.

She was going to her bedroom opposite. 'Are you going to bed now?'

'I'm having a brew with Coventry,' he said.

She smiled, containing her irritation. 'You two are like little boys having feasts after lights out. Don't leave cigarette ends around, Cook complains and it's me who has to deal with her – not you.'

He nodded and went down the stairs, through the baize door at the head of the basement stairs and down to the warm, sweet-smelling kitchen. It was the only place in the house that smelled of life. His father's bedroom smelled like a hospital, the drawing room smelled of cold flowers and furniture polish. But down here there were mingled smells of cooking and soapsuds, tobacco smoke and ironing. The range was still hot and Coventry had a kettle on the top. On the wide scrubbed kitchen table drawn up before the range was a battered tin teapot and two white enamelled mugs. Coventry poured the tea, added four spoonfuls of sugar to each cup and stirred them each ritually, five times, clockwise. The two men sat in comfortable silence, facing the kitchen range. They hunched up their shoulders, they wrapped their hands around their mugs. They sat close, shoulders, forearms and elbows just touching, huddled as if they were still in a dug-out. They did not speak; their faces were serene.

Lily, dressed in cotton pyjamas, leaned against the window frame and watched the moonlight reflected on the shiny slates of the roofs opposite.

'He's ever so handsome,' she said.

Helen Pears, turning down the bed and slipping a hot water bottle between the cold sheets, grunted non-committally.

'Don't you think he's handsome?'

'Get into bed, Lil. You'll catch your death of cold.'

Lily left the window unwillingly. Helen drew the thick blackout curtains on the lingering yellow moon.

'He was a hero in the war,' Lily claimed. 'One of the girls had read about him in the newspaper. He captured a farmhouse and killed all the Huns.'

Helen held up the covers, Lily slid into bed reluctantly and Helen tucked her up like a child.

'Did I sing well?'

'Like a bird.'

'They liked me, didn't they?'

'They loved you.'

'Will you sit with me till I'm asleep?'

'I've got a bit of sewing to do, I'll sit in my chair.'

Helen fetched her sewing and sat in the basketweave nursery chair under the gaslight. She was darning Lily's stockings, her face screwed into tired lines. When Lily's dark eyelashes closed, Helen put her work away and turned down the light. She paused for a moment in the darkness, watching her sleeping daughter, as she had done for the long years of Lily's babyhood and childhood. 'Goodnight,' she said very quietly. 'Goodnight, my dearest. Sweet dreams.'

Chapter Three

Lily had been stage-struck from babyhood when she would drape herself in her mother's old feather boa and traipse around the little flat above the shop, singing in her true little voice. Against all the odds Helen Pears had forced the corner shop into profit and saved the money to send Lily to ballet school and to a singing teacher. Scrimping on the household bills and hiding money from her husband, she had managed to get Lily a training which had been good enough to win her a place in the chorus of the Palais, owned by the Edwardes Music Halls of Southsea, Bournemouth and Plymouth. It was not what Helen Pears had wanted for her daughter, but it was the best she could provide. And it was the first step in moving the girl away from the narrow streets and narrow lives of Portsmouth.

Lily might have been a dancer in the chorus line for ever, if she had not caught the eye of the musical director, Charlie Smith, in the first week of rehearsals.

'Here, Lily, can you sing?' he asked during a break in one of the sessions. The dancers were scattered around the front seats of the darkened theatre, their feet up on the brass rail that surrounded the orchestra pit, drinking tea out of thermos flasks, eating sandwiches and gossiping. Charlie was picking out a tune on the piano.

'Yes,' Lily said, surprised.

'Can you read music?'

Lily nodded.

'Sing me this,' he said, tossing a sheet of music at her.

Charlie started the rippling chords of the introduction. Lily, her eyes still on the song sheet, walked to the orchestra pit, stepped casually over the brass rail and leaned against the piano to sing.

There was a little silence when she had finished.

'Very nice,' he said casually. 'Good voice production.'

'Back to work everybody, please,' the stage manager called from the wings. 'Mr Brett wants to see the greyhound number. Just mark it out. Miss Sylvia de Charmante will be here this afternoon. Until then please remember to leave room for her.'

Charlie winked at Lily. 'Buy you lunch,' he said.

The girls climbed the catwalk up to the stage and got into line, leaving a space in the middle for the soloist.

'She's got a dog,' the stage manager said dismally. 'A greyhound thing. Remember to leave space for it. Madge, you'll have to move stage left a bit. Lily, give her a bit more room.'

'What does the greyhound do?' Charlie demanded.

'Bites chorus girls, I hope,' Mike, the SM, said without a flicker of a smile. 'From the top, please.'

They ate lunch in a working-men's café in one of the little roads near the Guildhall Square. Charlie drank tea and smoked cigarettes. Lily ate a bread and dripping sandwich and drank milk.

'Disgusting,' Charlie said.

Lily beamed and shamelessly wiped her mouth on her sleeve.

'Would you like to be a singer?' Charlie asked. 'Want to be a star?'

'Course,' Lily said. 'Who doesn't?'

'Not very old, are you?' Charlie asked. 'Seventeen? Eighteen?'

'I'm seventeen and a half.'

Charlie grinned. 'I could get you a spot. We're an act short. We need a girl singer. But something a bit different. Want to do it?'

Lily gaped for a moment, but then shot him a quick suspicious look. 'Why me?'

Charlie shrugged. 'Why not? Someone's got to do it. Who else is there?'

'Madge Sweet, Tricia de Vogue, Helena West.' Lily ticked the names of three of the other five dancers off her fingers. 'They can all sing.'

'Yes, yes, yes,' Charlie said. 'I've heard them all. They all sound like someone else. They're all "in the style of" ... I've got something else in mind. An idea I've had for a while. D'you want it or not?'

Lily grinned at him. 'I told you already,' she said. 'I want to be a star. Course I want it.'

'Bring your ma here to see me this evening,' Charlie said. 'I have my tea here too.'

Back at the theatre, Charlie found the director talking on the stage door telephone, dictating a telegram to Miss Sylvia de Charmante at the Variety Theatre, London, due on the eleven o'clock train from Waterloo and still not arrived. Charlie took him gently by the elbow. 'Lily Pears, in the chorus, I want her to try the song I told you about,' Charlie said persuasively. 'You said we could give it a go. There's no-one else available and a big gap in the second half.'

William Brett flapped an irritated hand and said, thank God there were still some people who wanted work – and what more could he do to get that overpaid spoiled damned prima donna out of her hotel bed and down to Southsea for rehearsals?

Charlie nodded and drifted across the stage and down the steps to the orchestra pit to play a few soft chords.

'Places please, dancers,' the stage manager said with

infinite patience from the prompt corner. 'I shall walk Miss Sylvia's steps and you can dance around me.'

'Will you sing soprano as well?' Charlie asked.

The SM scowled at him. 'Like a bleeding canary if that's what it takes to get this show on the road,' he said dourly.

Lily waited till the afternoon tea break to tell the girls that she was to have a song in the show and then smiled smugly as they fluttered around her and kissed their congratulations. Her smile was as false as the kisses and the cries of delight. They were a company bonded by work and riven with jealousy. Lily's luck was declared to be phenomenal.

'I'm just so envious I am sick!' Madge Sweet said, hugging Lily painfully hard.

'How will you do your hair? And what will you wear?' Helena asked. 'You don't have anything to wear, do you? This is your first show?'

'I expect my ma will get me something,' Lily said. 'She was in the business. There's all her old costumes in a box at home.'

The girls burst into high malicious laughter. 'A hundred-year-old tea gown is *just* what Mr Brett wants, I don't think!' Tricia said.

'Moth-eaten fan!'

'Bustle and crinoline!'

Lily set her teeth and held her smile. 'I'll think of something.'

'You could wear your hair long,' Madge suggested. She pulled the pins at the back of Lily's head and Lily's thick golden hair tumbled from the roll at the nape of her neck and fell down. It reached to her waist. 'You could wear it with a hair band and sing a girl's song. Alice in Wonderland type.'

'Little Lily Pears, the child star!' Tricia suggested sarcastically.

31

'I shan't be Pears,' Lily said with sudden decision. 'I'll use my ma's stage name. She was Helen Valance. I'll be Lily Valance.'

'Lily Valance! God 'elp us!' Tricia said.

'Dancers, please,' the SM called. 'The flower scene. *Please* remember that in front of you is a conjuror who will be taking flowers out of your baskets and coloured flags and ribbons and God knows what else. The conjuror isn't here yet either. But leave a space for him centre stage. We don't have the baskets yet, but remember you've got to hold them up towards him so he can do the trick. Have we got the music?'

'Music's here,' Charlie said from the pit.

'One out of three isn't bad, I suppose,' the SM said miserably. 'When you're ready, Mr Smith.'

Helen Pears shut the shop early to meet Lily at the stage door and walk her home. She knew her daughter was old enough to walk home alone, and there would be no men at the stage door until the show was open. But Lily was her only child and, more than that, the only person in the world she had ever loved. Helen Pears's life had been one of staunchly endured disappointments: a failed stage career, an impoverished corner shop, a husband who volunteered in a moment of drunken enthusiasm for a ship which blew up at sea before it had even fired a shot in anger. Only in the birth of her fair-headed daughter had she experienced a joy unalloyed by disappointment. Only in Lily's future could she see a life that might, after all, be full of hope.

Lily said nothing to her mother until they were crossing the road before the music hall. Then she breathlessly announced that she was to sing a solo. Helen stopped in the middle of the tram tracks and squeezed Lily's hand so hard that she cried out.

'This is your first step,' Helen said. 'Your first season and you're further ahead than I ever got. This is your big chance, Lily. We'll make it work for you.'

Lily smiled up at her mother. 'As soon as I can earn enough we'll sell the shop,' she promised. 'As soon as I earn enough I'll buy you a house in Southsea, on the seafront, somewhere really nice.'

'I'll talk to this Charlie Smith,' Helen said with decision. 'And to Mr Brett too, if needs be.'

'Charlie said to meet him for tea,' Lily said, leading the way. 'He wants to talk to you.'

Charlie was sitting at the window. He half-rose to greet them and shook hands with Helen. The woman behind the counter brought them thick white mugs of tea.

'We can go back to the theatre and try something out,' Charlie said. 'I'm working late tonight anyway. Sylvia de Charmante's music has arrived and I have to adapt it for our orchestra. We can try out Lily's song. I've got an idea for it.'

'Nothing tasteless,' Helen stipulated.

Charlie met her determined gaze across the scrubbed wood table. 'Your daughter has class, Mrs Pears,' he said. 'We don't want to lose that.'

The theatre was very cool and quiet and empty, smelling hauntingly of stale beer and cigarettes. The rows of seats stretched back from the stage until they vanished into the darkness. The pale balcony floated in the dusty air. There was a hush in the theatre like that in an empty church, a waiting hush. Charlie's little green light in the orchestra pit was the only illumination. Lily and Helen, crossing the darkened stage, were like ghosts of old dancers moving silently towards an audience that had vanished, called up and gone.

On the left of the stage was the rickety catwalk and

steps. Helen walked gingerly down and sat in the front row near Charlie's piano.

'Can we have some lights?' Charlie called to a technician working somewhere backstage.

A couple of houselights came on, and one working stage light.

'Sit down,' Charlie said to Helen. 'I have an idea for her.'

Lily stood at her ease in the centre of the stage. She smiled at her mother.

'D'you know this?' Charlie handed a sheet of music up to her.

Lily gave a little gasp of surprise and then giggled. 'I know it!' she said. 'I've never sung it!'

'Try it,' Charlie suggested. He played a few rippling chords and nodded to Helen. 'Just listen,' he said.

The beat of the music was regular, like a hymn. Helen knew the clear simple notes but could not think of the song. Then Lily on the stage, half-lit, threw back her head and sang Bach's 'Jesu, Joy of Man's Desiring'. Helen felt tears prickle behind her eyes as the sounds arched upwards into the bell-shaped ceiling, and the piano accompaniment formed a perfectly paced symmetry with the rhythm and cadence of the song. It was a holy moment, like the sound of a blackbird singing in no-man's-land. When Lily was silent and the last chord had died away, Helen found her cheeks were wet.

'That was lovely,' she said. She fumbled in her handbag for her handkerchief. 'Just lovely,' she said.

'It's hardly music hall!' Lily complained. She dropped to one knee to speak to Charlie in the pit. 'I can't do that in front of an audience.'

Charlie grinned at her, turned and spoke to Helen. 'Just wait a moment,' he said. 'Think of Lily in a chorister's outfit. Red gown and a white surplice, white ruff.'

'Blue,' Helen said instantly. 'Brings out the colour of her eyes.'

'Blue gown,' Charlie agreed. 'She comes out. No-one knows what to expect. She sings like that. Just simply. Like an angel. Everyone cries. All the old ladies, all the tarts, all the drunks. They'll weep into their beer and they'll love her.'

'They'll laugh themselves sick,' Lily said.

Charlie shook his head. 'I know them,' he said. 'I've been doing this a long time, Lily, and I know what tickles their fancy. They like their ta-ra-ra-boom-de-ays and they like a class act. They like something that makes them feel pious. They love a good weep.'

Helen nodded. 'You're right,' she said. 'But if they heckle . . .'

Charlie shook his head. 'Not here,' he said. 'London maybe. Birmingham maybe. Glasgow, certainly. But not here. And not anywhere on tour. They want a good time, a good laugh and a good weep. They'll adore her.'

'I'm a chorus girl!' Lily protested. 'Not a choir girl!'

'Not a choir girl,' Charlie agreed. He nodded to Helen. 'Keep thinking the ruff and the white surplice. Keep thinking Christmas cards and carols and weddings.' He climbed out of the pit and strode up the catwalk.

'Let your hair down,' he said to Lily. He stood behind her and folded her sheet of music into a little fan. 'Hold this under your chin,' he said. He nodded to Helen. 'Think of a spotlight, very white, and no make-up at all. Perhaps a little pale powder. No lipstick.'

He scooped up Lily's mass of blonde hair and folded it so that it was as short as a bob.

'Choir *boy*,' he said. 'Ain't I a genius?'

There was a full minute of silence from the auditorium. 'You'd never cut her hair,' Helen said finally, outraged.

'Bob it,' Charlie said. 'So it's the same length all around.

35

She has a side parting and it comes down to the middle of her ears both sides. We oil it back a little bit, off her face. Nothing shiny, nothing slick. Just a newly washed boy. A well-scrubbed choir boy. A little angel from heaven.'

Lily giggled irrepressibly, but stood still as Charlie had ordered her, holding her folded sheet music under her chin while Charlie held her hair in handfuls off her neck.

'A young Vesta Tilley,' Helen said incredulously.

'Delicious,' Charlie said.

'Tasteful,' Helen conceded.

'And hidden oomph,' Charlie said, looking over Lily's shoulder. 'She's just gorgeous. There isn't a public school boy in England that wouldn't fall down and die for her. Ain't I right?'

Helen nodded. As he sensed her agreement Charlie dropped Lily's hair and took the mock-ruff from under her chin. 'What d'you think, Lily?' he asked.

She shrugged and grinned. 'I've wanted my hair bobbed for ages,' she said.

He laughed. 'As easy as that?'

'Ma said I had to keep it long,' Lily said. 'If I can have my hair bobbed I'll sing whatever you like!'

They never rehearsed Lily's song again. She tried it through once more with Charlie that night and he gave her the score and told her to learn the words and practise with her singing teacher. Mr Brett the director was resigned to the experiment. Charlie had been batting on for years about a choir boy number and with the conjuror drunk in Swansea and Miss Sylvia de Charmante still in London, he had neither time nor energy for an audition and an argument. Besides, Charlie Smith was rarely wrong.

'So what are you singing?' the girls asked in the crowded dressing room. The costumes, hung on hangers on hooks on the wall, bulged out into the room, shrouded in cotton sheets to keep them clean. Lily, as the youngest and newest dancer, had her hairbrush and comb perched on the inconvenient corner of the table, nearest to the door and overwhelmed by hanging gowns.

'It's a classical song,' Lily said. 'Charlie Smith's idea.'

'He's off his rocker,' Madge said. 'You should speak to Mr Brett and tell him you won't do it.'

'I couldn't do that.'

'You ought to,' Helena said. 'It's not fair making you sing something no-one wants to hear. You should try "Blue-eyes".' She sang the chorus in a hard nasal tone, nodding at Lily.

'Or "Walking my Girl",' one of the other dancers suggested. She sang the first verse.

'No!' someone else exclaimed. 'That wouldn't suit Lily, she ought to have something saucy!'

There was a gale of sarcastic laughter.

'I can see your ma letting you do something saucy and tying your garter during the chorus!' Susie said. 'What are you wearing anyway?'

'A long blue gown,' Lily said mendaciously. 'Charlie told Ma what I should have and she's making it for me.'

'You're not going to set the town alight,' Madge said, without troubling to conceal her pleasure. 'A classical song and a home-made dress! Not so lucky as you thought then, Lily.'

'Probably be dropped after the Southsea opening anyway,' Susie said. 'We're running hours too long.'

Lily kept her head down and her mouth shut.

The night before the dress rehearsal Lily and her mother took a tram up to Commercial Road, Southsea, the best part of town, for Lily to have her hair cut.

'Not a woman. No woman in the history of the world

37

has ever known how to cut hair,' Charlie decreed. 'You're to go to David's, on Commercial Road. I've told him you'll be there at seven. He's keeping open just for you so there won't be any men around. You can be quite private.'

Helen had frowned.

'Come on, Ma!' Lily had urged. 'It can't hurt.'

David's shop was closed for the night as Charlie had predicted. The blinds were discreetly down.

'Charlie Smith told me you wanted a straight bob,' David said. Lily sat in the comfortable barber's chair, her feet tucked up on the foot rail, looking at herself in the mirror.

'No fringe, just the same length all around,' she said. 'Like a boy's.'

David nodded and took the pins from her hair. The tumble of gold silky hair fell down. He glanced at Helen. 'Are you sure?'

'Don't ask me, I could weep,' Helen said grimly. 'Just do it.'

Helen looked at the floor but she heard the snipping of the scissors and the soft fall of heavy hair. The floor was a patterned linoleum, smart and easy to keep clean. Out of the corner of her eye Helen could see a fallen lock of deep gold.

'Take a look,' David said after a while.

Helen glanced up.

Lily was stunning.

Firstly she noticed Lily's long neck and the way she held her head. She could see the shape of her little head, her small ears. Helen walked slowly around to the front of the chair. Lily's hair was combed smoothly to one side, just long enough to tuck behind her ears. Helen had never seen her daughter's features so clearly, she stared at her as if she were a stranger. The clear lines of her face were exposed, the bones of her cheeks, her forehead, her nose.

The curve of her mouth and her huge dark-lashed deep blue eyes. She was a beautiful androgynous object of desire. A tomboy, a romantic poet, a St Joan.

David was watching Helen's face with a half-smile. 'Charlie's a clever man,' he said quietly. 'I think you have something a bit special here.'

Helen nodded, her eyes still on Lily's rapt self-absorbed beauty. 'What d'you think, Lily?'

'What a lark!' Lily breathed adoringly at her reflection. 'What a giddy lark.'

Chapter Four

There were shrieks and screams in the dressing room the next day when Lily took her cloche hat off her newly bobbed head but the girls were too busy with their own worries to interrogate her. The technical rehearsal in the morning went as badly as everyone expected. The backdrops and props had been kept to the bare essentials of a touring set which would be loaded and unloaded all along the south coast; but even so there was a problem with a quick change of scene which had to be done over and over again until the crew could do it quickly and noiselessly while the comedian told jokes in front of the curtains and the dancers raced down the stone steps backstage to their cramped dressing room to change their costumes.

'I'll break me bloody neck on these stairs,' Madge cursed as she scurried down the steps in her silver high heels.

They worked through the dinner break, snacking on sandwiches and tea while William Brett, with infinite and weary patience, went through the lighting cues again. One of the stage lads went out and bought hot meat pies for everyone at three in the afternoon. Lily went to eat hers in the dressing room.

'Not in here! Not in here!' Susie screamed. 'Mike'll kill you if he sees you taking hot food into a dressing room.'

Lily froze on the threshold, backed rapidly into the corridor and demolished the pie in three giant bites. They took their dinner break at four.

'Total run through at six o'clock. I want everyone here at five thirty,' William said. 'And we'll run through as if for real. I'm not stopping for anything. We open tomorrow and I want to see it as for real. No changes, no accidents.'

They went out for their tea in a dismal group to Charlie's café. Sylvia de Charmante, who had arrived that very day from London in a gentleman's car and a cloud of apologies, came with them, and the drunken conjuror as well. Miss de Charmante was graciousness itself, promising the woman behind the counter a complimentary ticket to the show if she could make her a cup of tea just as she liked it. Charlie sat in his usual seat like a sardonic pixie and kept quiet.

'D'you like my hair?' Lily finally prompted him.

He nodded briefly. 'It's how I thought it would be.'

Lily waited for him to say something more but Charlie only drank his tea and smiled at her. 'Scared?' he asked finally.

'Petrified!' Lily said with a quavery laugh.

Charlie grinned. 'You'll do,' he said. 'I've got a bet running on it, Lily. I've got a guinea on you.'

Lily's face lit up. 'Have you?'

'It's time we went,' Charlie said to everyone generally.

The conjuror extracted a silver hip flask from his pocket and splashed a measure of dark treacly rum into his tea cup. 'Bloody Southsea,' he said in his rich plummy voice. 'My God, I hate the seaside.'

Lily watched him, fascinated, as he downed a mixture of cold tea and rum. 'Do you?' she asked.

He glanced at her with brief interest and looked away. 'I just said so,' he replied with massive dignity.

The chorus girls opened the show with a charleston number, then they changed into long gowns while the comic was on, and strolled in a slow languid walk from one side of the tiny stage to the other while Sylvia de Charmante sang her first song, a mournful ballad.

Two of the girls assisted Arnold the conjuror's first appearance and came back to the dressing room giggling about his fumbling and Mr Brett's silent white-faced anger in the front row. Then there was a juggling act – a brother and sister team who had arrived only that morning from Dover – and then the interval.

Lily was on after the opening song from the chorus. She took her choir boy gown to the ladies' toilet. She did not want to change in front of the other girls and endure their ribaldry when she was already sick with nerves. She sat on the toilet with her cotton camiknickers rolled up and her fists pushed into her churning stomach.

'Oh God,' she said miserably.

She stood up and unwrapped the precious gown from its white sheet, then the snowy surplice and ruff. She had tried them on at home and she knew she could do the fastenings. But now her fingers were trembling with nerves and she could not hook the back at all. In the end she twisted the whole gown around and did most of the hooks in front and then pushed it around to the back. The surplice was just thrown over the gown and her mother had put a single popper on the starched ruff which Lily could see in the broken triangle of mirror shoved behind a water pipe on the wall. Her face was pale, even her lips were white.

'Oh God,' Lily said.

She could hear the dancers clattering up the steps to the stage and then she heard the thump of the orchestra for their number. Lily's stomach suddenly contracted with nausea and she had to pull up her gown and undo her knickers again.

Nothing came but a trickle of urine. Lily wiped herself and pulled the chain. The cistern was slow to fill. It would not flush. Lily bundled the robe to one side and put both hands down to try to button her knickers. By the time she managed it her face was flushed and the gown crumpled. 'Oh God, I look awful.'

At least her hair was perfect. Lily smoothed it flat again, pushed it just a little more off her face. She felt as if she had been waiting in the cold evil-smelling toilet for days and days.

She heard the SM's boy coming up the stairs and his knock on the door. 'You in there, Lily?'

'Yes.'

'Are you sick?'

'No.'

'Three minutes.'

Lily turned to the mirror again, straightened the ruff, smoothed the surplice. She turned to the door with absolute reluctance. Suddenly she needed to pee again.

'Oh God,' Lily said miserably. 'I can't. I mustn't! There isn't time!'

She opened the door and peered out. There was no-one in the corridor. She tiptoed down the stairs and through the door to the wings of the stage. The girls were near the end of their number, banging out the beat. Lily went and stood behind the stage manager's desk, trying to blend into the shadows. He glanced behind at the movement and then gave a double-take.

'My God, you scared me to death. I thought you were a ghost. What the hell are you supposed to be?'

'Choir boy.'

'Charlie Smith must have gone off his head,' the SM said bluntly. 'Has Mr Brett seen you?'

'Not yet.'

The man buried his face in his hands as if he could not stand the prospect.

43

'You're dead,' he said. 'We're all dead. But you especially are dead and buried.'

'I feel it,' Lily said, quite without sarcasm. 'I wish I was.'

The girls clattered to a standstill.

'Applause applause,' came the weary voice from the dark auditorium. 'No announcement at all now. Lily comes straight on.'

The girls, clearing the stage, pushed past Lily as she stepped forward. She just heard Madge say, 'Wait a minute, what're you wearing?' and then she was under the dazzling hot lights and she could see nothing but Charlie's face and his raised hand, and a quick bright nod to her and the regular sweet notes of the start of 'Jesu, Joy . . .'

Lily, her mouth dry and her throat so tight that she knew she would be mute for the rest of her life, stood still with her hands clasped before her and longed for a pee.

She opened her mouth on cue, knowing no sound would come, and then she heard, as if it were someone else singing, the sweet steady notes in their ordered simplicity. 'Jes-u, joy (wait) of man's desir-ing (wait wait wait) holy wis-dom, lo-ve most bright . . .'

'Golly,' Lily thought. 'It's all right.' It was as if her own stage-fright had moved her to a place where she could feel neither nerves nor her own body. She sang clearly and simply and her ears could hear the rightness of the sounds, and even enjoy them, as if they were being sung by another girl. As if it were not Lily Pears, sick with fear, under a burning hot spotlight, with all the Palais Dancers crowded in the wings behind her, waiting to laugh.

She sang as she had been taught, simply and clearly, and held the last note. The final chords died away like ringing bells.

'You win a guinea, Charlie. Very nice indeed. Applause, applause, weep, weep. Next,' William said from the darkness.

44

Charlie threw a grin at Lily and the drum rolled.

'Come off,' the SM hissed behind her. 'Come on! Clear the stage. You've had your moment of glory, duckie. It's someone else now.'

Mesmerio the hypnotist, splendid in a black tie and tails, pushed past Lily and stepped on to the stage. Lily, still dazzled by the lights, stepped into the wings and went slowly down the stairs to the dressing room. The girls, silenced by a glower from the SM, went with her like a patrol with a prisoner in their midst.

'Well!' Madge said, outraged, as soon as the dressing room door was shut. 'I never saw such a performance in my life!'

'Pie!'

'I thought she was sweet! You were sweet, Lily!'

'She looked more like a boy than a girl!'

'Charlie must be off his head!'

'Too scared to hang around the dockyard more like!'

'What d'you mean?'

'I always thought Charlie Smith liked boys – now look what he's done to Lily!'

Lily undid her ruff and pulled her surplice off over her head, hardly hearing them.

Helena undid the hooks of the gown for her. 'They're all crooked. You should have got someone to help you.'

'I will tomorrow,' Lily said vaguely.

'Where did you learn to sing like that – proper singing?'

'With my teacher.' Lily felt a deep sleepy weariness, as if all the excitement and nervousness had drained out of her body, leaving her empty and exhausted. 'I've had singing lessons since I was little.'

'You ought to be a proper singer, opera or something.'

Lily smiled, shook her head. 'I'm not good enough,' she said.

She hung her gown with the surplice and the ruff on

the hanger and then wrapped the sheet around them. Helena thrust her next costume towards her. It was a scarlet froth of tulle with a black tightly-laced boned bodice for the finale – a can-can. Lily stepped into it and Helena spun her around and did up the hooks at the back.

'You all right? You're very quiet.'

Lily's little face was pale against the harsh cherry-red of the gown. 'I'm fine.'

The boy knocked on the door. 'Finale. Five minutes.'

There was a rush towards the mirror. Madge screamed for someone to do her up quick! and then the six of them burst out of the dressing room and clattered up the narrow stone steps to the wings.

Sylvia de Charmante was singing her final song. It was 'Keep the Home Fires Burning'. Lily – last of the line in the wings – leaned back against the cold wall and gritted her teeth. She hated the song. She hated all the war songs. She hated their sentimental lushness, she hated the stupidity of men whistling them as they marched to the Front. She had taken her father's death as an act of folly, not heroism. Alone of all the kids in the street, Lily hated the war, and disliked and blamed Kitchener when everyone else worshipped him. Lily never knitted socks and balaclavas, she never joined a gang to collect scrap paper. A solitary rebel, she pretended that the war, which overshadowed her childhood and drained it of joy, did not exist.

'Applause, applause, weep, weep. Very nice, Miss de Charmante,' William said from the front row. 'Now, Sylvia, step forward. Gauze down. Lights down. Can-can backdrop down. Sylvia, you're still bowing, taking flowers. Then you walk slowly slowly slowly across the stage and you're gone. And we should be ready . . . now.'

Absolutely nothing happened.

'Mike!' William said very quietly through his teeth.

46

The SM waved frantically to the stage hands. 'Clear the stage, we're going up!' he hissed. 'Go!'

The drummer gave a long exciting roll on the drums and Charlie at the piano with the trumpeter and the two violins burst into a spirited thumping rendition of the 'Thunder and Lightning Polka' – the traditional can-can music.

Lily, with Helena's hand firmly clutching her boned waist, and her hand behind Helena's back gripping Madge's wrist, started marking the steps as the first girl on the stage – Susie – danced out sideways. Lily's head went up; she loved the can-can. She grinned at the morose SM as she danced out under the hot lights, matching her kick to the others, then keeping the rhythm of the music with the low half-kicks as the line folded in on itself and Lily and Susie were face to face and then pairing off, dancing around, in pairs through the middle and into the line of the can-can again.

It was a short number. Can-can was spectacular, but exhausting. Charlie played it at the edge of safety – as fast as he dared. The girls' screams as they kicked, or cartwheeled, or jumped into the splits, were screams of protest, not excitement. But Lily loved it. The relief at her song being over, her simple delight at being on stage and the absolute fun of the music and the dancing, and Charlie's darkened face in the orchestra pit, kept her feet pounding on the stage. The final dance step and dive into the splits came too soon for her. Lily stayed in the splits, her head up, her face radiant.

'Applause, applause, rapturous applause,' William said miserably. 'Walk down.'

The chorus girls stepped smartly up, walked forward in time to Charlie's brisk march, took a bow and then fell back either side of the stage. In order of increasing importance the stars entered from the rear of the stage, strode forwards, took a bow and stepped to one side. Arnold the drunken magician stood in front of Lily and she could see nothing more than his back and his outflung hand inviting applause.

The curtain fell, throwing the stage into twilight. The cast formed themselves into two straight lines facing the curtain, waiting for it to rise again. They bowed. The curtain fell. The music reached a closing phrase and stopped.

It was as if the strings of puppets had been snapped. All the smiles were switched off and everybody slumped, ostentatiously weary.

'That fool on the light had me in blue,' Sylvia de Charmante exclaimed.

'Darling girl, if you don't hold your basket steady I'll be taking ribbons off your tits, not out of your basket,' Arnold said to Madge. 'I can't run around the stage after you.'

'We were too bunched up in the can-can,' Helena complained. 'I was squashed in the middle.'

'I can't spread out any more,' Susie replied. 'I was half in the wings as it was.'

The curtains rose slowly, as if to signal this was work, not performance.

'Get changed and then out here for notes in five minutes,' William said. 'All of you. Five minutes only.'

Lily looked towards the orchestra pit to Charlie. He was checking his sheet music and did not look up.

'Come on, Lily,' said one of the girls. 'We've only got five minutes.'

The 'notes' were William's final chance to make corrections. He had a sheaf of papers in his hand. The stars he spoke to individually. Sylvia de Charmante was soothed and complimented until she consented to sit down and

48

listen to the general comments. She even agreed to speed up 'Keep the Home Fires Burning'.

'It can sound like a dirge otherwise,' William said tactfully. 'It's the song. It's draggy. I love the way you do it, but it needs to move along.'

He was not so tender with the feelings of the dancers, nor the jugglers, nor the conjuror.

'Arnold, get yourself sorted out,' he said. 'We could see the ribbons in the baskets. It needs to be quicker.'

'The girl must hold the basket still,' Arnold said, looking reproachfully at Madge.

'She will,' William said with quiet menace. 'Now, jugglers – I know it's difficult on a stage raked as steeply as this one; but you're hired to catch the bloody things, not fling them past each other into the wings.

'Hypnotist – very nice. Lily – very nice. Tumblers – very nice. Can you speed up the final position a bit? It's slow.'

The tumblers nodded.

'The walk-down.' There was a brief depressed silence. 'Do it again,' William said. 'I'm sorry, but we'll do it again and again until it goes march-march-march. You're trailing down like you're off to the Somme. I want a bit of briskness. I want a bit of life. Back up on stage and don't wander off. You're all going to the right places but you're taking too long. I want it quick. I want it catchy. I want you to run if you have to. Gentlemen – you can certainly run. Ladies – an elegant scuttle please. March-march-march. Let's get a move on.'

There was a general murmur of irritation and boredom and then the cast went back up the catwalk to the stage and took their places.

'Chorus girls, you're in your line, in the splits. Don't bunch up. Spread out. There's only six of you, there's no need to advertise it. Spread out and look like twenty.'

Lily wriggled over sideways.

'Now, Charlie! Can we have the whole thing quicker?'

'You can do. But it'll be more of a gallop than a march.'

'Gallop the bloody thing then. Let's have the Charge of the Light Brigade, not an advance up the Menin Road. I want it to move!'

Charlie nodded to the orchestra. 'One, two-three, four,' he said quickly. 'That speed. Off we go. One, two-three, four.'

The drum rolled. The chorus line leaped to their feet, stepped briskly forward and bowed. Lily found herself almost running backwards, trying to keep time to the music and get to her place.

The stars stormed down the centre of the stage, bowed, and dashed to their positions. Only Sylvia de Charmante swayed down, serene and unruffled, at the same speed as before, smiling.

'Thank you,' William said. 'Hold it there.'

Lily waited with malicious anticipation for Sylvia de Charmante to receive one of William's pithy criticisms.

'Much, much better,' he said. 'That's the speed. That's fine. Sylvia, you were gorgeous. Just a tiny bit faster to the front and the audience will have longer to see you. You're lost at the back of the stage, we don't know you're there. Come downstage quicker and you have all the time in the world in the spotlight taking your bow.'

Lily eyed William with growing respect.

'OK then, we're done,' William said. 'Over to you, Mike.'

The SM came out from the wings, his shirt blotchy with sweat. 'Tea matinée tomorrow at three,' he said. 'Everyone here by two thirty. Any problems with costumes, see Mary in wardrobe straight away. Two thirty tomorrow. Goodnight everybody. Well done.'

Lily went back to the dressing room and found her hat

and coat. The hat had fallen off the peg to the floor and was dusty. Lily brushed it absent-mindedly and pulled it on her head. She wanted to see Charlie.

She went back up the stairs to the stage. The crew were tidying up and the SM had gone from his corner. Lily stepped out on to the stage and looked out into the darkness. With the stage lights dimmed she could see the auditorium. Immediately below the stage were the stalls. Each seat had a little bracket where a tray for drinks or tea could be clipped. Lily tried to imagine the seats filled with people talking, laughing, drinking and flirting.

At the back of the theatre was the bar with a half-glass partition to separate the drinkers and promenaders from the seated audience. Lily would have to sing clearly and loudly enough to be heard over their chatter and the shouting of orders. Above them was the circle, and behind the circle seats, the circle bar with waiter service. Lily looked up at the vaulted ceiling painted blue with white and pink clouds and a yellow sunburst in the middle. She breathed in the smell of the theatre – stale cigarette smoke, cold air, the smell of emptiness where there had been a crowd. It smelled of magic. Anything could happen here.

Lily stepped forward, holding out her arms as she had seen Sylvia de Charmante do, as if to embrace an adoring crowd. She bowed with immense dignity as if she were overwhelmed with praise. When she came up she was smiling for a shower of bouquets.

Chapter Five

Helen walked Lily to the theatre for her debut at the tea matinée and then went around to the front of the house and treated herself to a ticket in the circle. Lily had been weepy with nerves and Helen had smiled calmly and told her to fear nothing. Only now that the stage door was closed behind her daughter could she acknowledge how anxious she was feeling. She sat in the little seat and ordered tea. She had not treated herself to such an outing in years but when the tea tray came, and the sandwiches, and the slice of cake, she found her mouth was so dry that she could taste nothing.

Charlie Smith came out with the orchestra, looking handsome and young in his black tie and tails. Helen smiled down at him, knowing he could not see her, willing him to help Lily in performance as she knew he had helped her in rehearsal. So much depended on the girl doing well. Not just the financial investment – all those saved shillings and pennies through all the hard years – but Lily's whole future. Helen could not see a way for Lily to escape from the backstreets of her home unless her talent could carry her away, far away, to distant music halls and perhaps even theatres. Lily might be one of the prettiest girls in Portsmouth but that was not enough. She had to be seen, she had to be perceived as a talented girl, an exceptional girl. If this chance did not work for her she would be behind the counter of the Highland Road grocery shop for life. Helen put her tea tray to one side. She could not bear to think of Lily working a twelve- or fourteen-hour day, six days a week, to earn a wage that would barely feed her.

The first half of the show passed with frightening speed. Helen stayed in her seat for the interval, then the houselights went down, Charlie slipped into his place at the front of the orchestra and opened the second half with the chorus girls' number. Helen barely saw them. The girls dashed off stage and then there was a brief silence and the measured beautiful beats of 'Jesu, Joy of Man's Desiring' started and the spotlight shone down on Lily.

At the first note Helen relaxed. It was flawless. Lily's pale gold hair and pale face were luminous in the spotlight, her voice as clear as an angel's. Helen let the music wash over her, freeing her from anxiety. When the last note came and Lily held it clearly, without a quaver of nerves, Helen found that she was shaking with sobs, crying very softly for joy in her daughter's talent, and pride.

Helen went backstage after the performance with her face calm and powdered. She gave Lily a swift hug at the stage door and promised to collect her after the evening show. She did not think Lily would need a chaperone, the song was not one likely to attract the rougher sort of man, nor even an idle gentleman. But that night, at the stage door, waiting for Lily, were Stephen and David. Helen Pears realized then that Lily's choices for her future were wider and more hopeful than she had ever imagined.

For the next week Stephen divided his time between his work at the family legal practice, and thinking of Lily. He went to see the show twice more. He liked her singing 'Jesu, Joy of Man's Desiring', but he hated her dancing the can-can. When she was on the stage he did not look at her or at any of the girls but glared around the bar at other men. If anyone had passed a comment about her, he would have hit him.

After the show he would wait beside the big Argyll with Coventry at the wheel for Lily and her mother and drive them home. He took them out to dinner a second time, at the fish restaurant just off the seafront. He persuaded Lily to try oysters – which she thought disgusting. He ordered lobster in hot butter for her.

Helen let him take Lily for a drive along the seafront in the afternoon, but not out into the countryside. The early May weather was promising. Stephen wanted a picnic. He wanted to sit with Lily in a hayfield and watch larks in the sky. He wanted to lie back on a tartan rug and sleep for once without dreams. He wanted to look from Portsdown Hill across half of Hampshire without planning in his mind where he would put a machine gun post to defend the summit, or calculate how long it would take to dig a good deep trench across those quiet fields.

The hayfields were pale watery green, starred with thousands of wildflowers, rich with butterflies and busy with nesting birds. It was a different world, a different countryside from the lands that had been his home for two and a half years. He could not believe that fields could sprout such different crops as purple vetch and white clover here, and shell cases and dead men over there. The long flat Flanders plain must have been green and growing once. He could not imagine the Menin Road verged with primroses, wet with bluebells. It was another world. There could be no connection between that place which he had left far, far behind him, and this Hampshire, in this spring of 1920 when Stephen fell in love.

He did not know how to court her. Lily's bright light was for everyone. She smiled with equal radiance on him, on Coventry, on Charlie Smith, on a passer-by who asked her for directions to Clarence Parade. The joyous expectancy of Lily's smile was a universal currency. Anyone could buy. Stephen longed to ration her.

She loved his car. She learned to enjoy the comfort of a ride home instead of the walk to the tram stop and then the cold wait. She liked to walk into a restaurant on his arm. But the smile she gave a waiter for pulling out her chair was no less grateful than the smile she gave Stephen for paying the bill. She had no sense of money; he could not buy her. If he gave her a bouquet of hot-house roses, sugar pink in tight sweet buds, she would exclaim with pleasure; but she would be just as delighted with a primrose in a pot from Charlie Smith.

She had no sense of status either, and Stephen was uncomfortable with Lily's blithe belief that the only reason she had not met his mother and visited his house for tea was because his father was so ill that they never entertained.

Mrs Pears understood the situation perfectly, and Stephen feared her dark knowledgeable glance. She knew very well that he was using Lily to amuse himself while he settled to the urgent peacetime tasks of repairing the family business and choosing a girl from his own class for marriage. Mrs Pears held the line against him like a veteran gunner at a salient point. He feared that she would poison Lily against him, abuse him behind his back even though she ate his dinners. But then he realized that Lily was not someone whose mind you could poison. If you said something disagreeable or spiteful, Lily would look at you, rather wide-eyed and surprised. If it was a funny piece of malice – and he had heard Charlie Smith compare Sylvia de Charmante to a Jersey cow in season – then Lily would scream with laughter and then cram her palm against her mouth to muffle helpless giggles. But if she heard spiteful talk, without the sugar of wit, Lily looked somehow anxious – as if it were her own reputation under attack. And then she would look puzzled and ask one of her frighteningly candid questions – 'Do you dislike him then?'

Stephen learned that Mrs Pears would not oppose him

directly. She would bide her time and watch him. When he escorted them home he could hold Lily's hand in the shadowy darkness of the car. But always Mrs Pears waited in the shop while he said goodnight to Lily on the doorstep. In the ten days while he drove Lily home, and out along the seafront, and paid for expensive dinners, he never even kissed her goodnight.

It was Lily who brought matters to a head. 'I shall miss you, Stephen,' she said easily. They were taking tea at a café in Palmerston Road. Mrs Pears had unbent so far as to allow Stephen to take Lily out to tea without a chaperone. Lily had eaten a hearty tea: sandwiches, tea-cakes, scones and a handsome wedge of chocolate cake. 'Oh, that was divine!' she said.

'Don't they feed you at the theatre? Go on, you can have another slice.'

'D'you think I dare? No! The waitress is looking at me. She'll think I'm a starving Belgian. I won't! But I'll have another cup of tea.'

As she poured her tea, her earlier sentence suddenly struck Stephen.

'Why should you miss me? I'm not going away.'

Lily beamed at him. She had a little smudge of chocolate cake at the corner of her mouth. Stephen longed to lean forwards and wipe it off with his napkin. 'No, but I am. This is a touring show. We go to Southampton next Monday.'

For a moment he felt nothing, as if her words were the whine of a bomb which would rock the ground with a dull terrifying thud a few moments after the incoming shriek. 'Going? But when will you be back?'

Lily gazed upwards in thought. 'Um. July,' she said finally. 'We're touring the south coast from here to Plymouth. Misery, misery! How will I ever get enough to eat in Plymouth without you!'

Stephen said nothing. He could imagine only too well how Lily would be wined and dined in Plymouth.

'Is your mother going?'

Lily shook her head. 'She can't get anyone to mind the shop. Well, she could get Sarah. But she doesn't really trust Sarah to manage on her own. So she has to wait until she can get Clare – but she's a school teacher, so she can't come until the school holidays and even then . . .'

'Never mind that now! How will you manage, on your own?'

'I'll be all right! I'll be with the other girls in digs. The company books ahead for us, you know. It'll be just like being here. Same show. Same work. The only thing that will be different is I shan't have you to buy me lovely teas!'

Stephen could feel a shudder starting up through him. He felt very cold. He felt like smashing the table and shouting at Lily, or at the waitress, or at damned Helen Pears for her careful – no, her suspicious – chaperonage of *him* and then her feckless way of letting her daughter draggle off all around the south coast with God knows who.

'You'll be lonely.'

'Oh no.' Lily had been looking out of the window at the people walking by. 'Stephen! D'you see that woman in that most extraordinary hat! I hope it's not a new fashion. It's enormous!' She glanced back at him and noticed his dark glower. 'Oh, sorry! No, I won't be lonely. Some of the girls are nice, and Arnold is all right when you get to know him, and the jugglers are really good fun. Charlie Smith is quite wonderful. It's a nice company. It'll be fun going from one town to another, all together. We'll travel by train, you know. Arnold is going to teach me how to play poker. And Henry – that's Mesmerio – says he'll teach me how to hypnotize people! It'll be good

57

fun. And who knows, someone might see me and like me!'

'What?'

'A producer or a director or a manager. Someone might be on holiday and spot me! It could happen. Charlie says it could happen. And then I'd be off to London!'

Stephen nodded slowly. 'So I won't see you until July,' he said.

Lily smiled at him happily. 'No.'

Stephen nodded at the waitress and paid the bill. 'Let's drive back along the seafront,' he said.

Coventry was parked on the other side of the road, watching for them. But as Stephen took Lily's arm to guide her across the road a man shuffled forward on a ramshackle home-made wheelchair, a tea chest on little castors.

'Sir!' he cried. 'Captain! D'you remember me?'

Stephen turned. The man was a pitiful sight. His legs had been amputated at the thighs and his trousers were pinned neatly over the stumps. He was wearing an army greatcoat which had been roughly cut to blazer-length to keep his chest and shoulders warm. Around his neck he had a large placard reading: 'Old soldier, Portsmouth Battalion, wife and three children to support. Please help.'

'Captain! I can't remember your name but you were in command of us at Beselare. D'you remember, Sir? I lost my legs there. We got stuck in the shellhole and couldn't get out? D'you remember we were there all night with the shells going from one side to another like bleeding birds? And Corporal Cray bit through his tongue to stop himself screaming?'

Stephen had shrunk back against Lily. His mouth was working but he could get no words to come. 'D . . . d . . . d . . .'

'D'you remember you gave me morphine from my field

pack and joked with me? And we had nothing to drink. D'you remember how hot it was that long day?'

Stephen was blanched white. He stared at the crippled man as if he were a ghost.

'Oh, go away!' Lily said roughly.

Stephen swallowed his stammer in surprise.

'Go away!' Lily said brusquely. 'Go down to the British Legion and get some work you can do with your hands. You should be ashamed of yourself, begging in the street.'

'I can't get work, missis . . .' the man said. 'There's no work for men like me.'

'Then your wife should work and you could keep house,' Lily said swiftly. 'You've no right to clutter up the shops with your stupid little trolley and your horrible stories.'

'They're not stories,' he blustered. 'They're true. Every damned word! And if you think they're horrible you should have been there yourself. There were things I saw over there which would make your dreams a terror to you for the rest of your life.'

'I'm too young,' Lily said sharply. 'It wasn't my war. I was too young. So don't tell me about your nightmares because it's nothing to do with me!'

She pulled Stephen towards the car away from the veteran.

'You've got no pity!' he shouted at her back. 'No pity! We died for you and your sort. Out there in the mud. We died for you!'

Lily turned back. 'I don't care!' she shouted. A tram rang its bell and came rumbling between them. 'I don't care!' Lily yelled over the noise of the tram. 'It wasn't my war, *I* didn't ask you to go, *I* didn't ask anyone to die, and I don't want to know anything about it now!'

Coventry was holding the door. Lily flung herself inside and Stephen followed her.

'Just drive!' Stephen forced the words out. Coventry

nodded and set the big car in motion. Stephen looked out of the back window. The crippled soldier had gone. He turned to Lily as if he could scarcely believe her.

'My G . . . God, Lily, you were angry.'

'I hate the war,' Lily said fiercely. 'All the time, all the time I was a girl if there was anything I wanted to do, or anything I wanted to have it was always "no" – because there was a war on.

'I was twelve when it started. My dad went rushing off the first moment he could and got himself killed. And now, all the time people want to hear the war songs, want to go on and on about what it was like before, and how it was better then. Well, it's *my* time now. And if it isn't as good as it was then – well, at least it will be as good as I can have.

'I'm sick of all the old soldiers and sailors and the charities. I'm sick and tired of it. All my childhood we were fighting the war, no-one would talk about anything else, and now it's over people still want to go on and on about it. I want to leave it behind. I want to forget it!'

Stephen said nothing. Coventry drew the Argyll up at the edge of Southsea Common and the seafront promenade. Coventry got out of the car and stood by the bonnet. He lit a cigarette and smoked it slowly, looking out to sea.

The silence went on.

'D'you think I'm selfish?' Lily asked suddenly.

'I think you're wonderful,' Stephen burst out. He felt a great wave of relief. 'I've never heard anyone talk like that before. It wasn't my war either, you know. I felt as if I never knew why I was there. But I just had to stay and stay and stay there. Whatever it was like. My brother, Ch . . . Ch . . . Christopher – he *wanted* to go. He volunteered.' He took a breath. 'But I l . . . left it to the very l . . . last moment. They'd have con . . . conscripted me if I hadn't gone. They called me a c . . . a c . . . a coward.

Someone sent me a f . . . a f . . . a feather.' His stammer had escaped his control. He bared his lips, straining to make the words come. Lily watched him with wide scared eyes. Stephen struggled and then shrugged. 'I can't talk about it,' he said.

Lily shook her little head. 'Well, I don't want to know. I don't know whether it should have happened. I don't know whether you should have been there. I don't care. It's over now, Stephen. You don't have to think about it any more.'

Stephen reached into his pocket and lit a cigarette. His hands were shaking slightly.

'You d . . . don't want to know about it?'

Lily shook her head. 'Why should I?' she asked coldly. 'It's past. It's long gone. I want to live my life now. I don't care about the past.'

Stephen exhaled a long cloud of smoke. The tension was draining away from his face. He was staring at Lily as if she had said something of extraordinary importance. As if she had the key to some freedom for him.

'It's over,' he repeated as if he were learning a lesson from her.

Lily smiled. 'It doesn't matter any more,' she said. 'It's finished and gone. You'll never have to go back there. You don't have to even think about it. I never want to hear about it from you or anybody else.'

Stephen drew a deep breath. 'Let's have a look at the sea.' He opened the door and got out. Coventry dropped his cigarette and opened the door for Lily.

'We'll just walk for a little,' Stephen said.

Lily's hat lifted off her head precariously with the offshore breeze. They walked along the promenade and then stepped off the low wall on to the shingle of the beach. Ahead of them was the short white fist of the pier extending out into the sea. The little theatre and amusement parlour at the end of the pier were being repainted white for the summer season of Vaudeville shows. They could see the ladders and the workmen. Lily pulled off her hat and held it in her hand as they walked. Stephen slid his arm around her waist, Lily leaned against his shoulder, comfortable with his closeness.

'I shall miss you,' she said as if it were a new thought. 'I shall miss you while I am away.'

Stephen paused, turned her towards him, leaned down and kissed her on her smiling lips, held her body close to his for the first time and sensed her slightness, the roundness of her breasts against his chest, the warmth of her face against his. He smelled the warm clean female smell of her, the scent of her hair. He kissed her, pressing his lips on hers and then licking the corner of her mouth, tasting that little provocative smudge of chocolate. He was excited by her rejection of the war; he felt elated as if she could set him free from his nightmares, free from his sense that the war could never end while he, and all the men scarred like him, fought it and re-fought it in their dreams. And she was warm like that other girl had been, and soft, like that other girl had been. And her skin smelled of desire.

Lily stayed still, her feet shifting slightly on the shingle for a few moments, struggling with her discomfort. She felt stifled and claimed and overpowered. She let him hold her for a little while with a sense of confused courtesy, as if she should not rebuff him, not after their sudden slide into intimacy. He had trusted her with a confidence; she could not pull her body away roughly. So she let him hold her, resenting the weight of his body against hers, tense against the insistent closing of his arms. Then she felt the disgusting touch of his tongue on the corner of her lips, and the smooth scented brush of his moustache, and she shuddered with instinctive revulsion, and stepped back, her gloved hand up at her mouth rubbing her lips. 'Don't!' she said breathlessly. 'You shouldn't . . .'

Stephen smiled. He felt very much older and more experienced than Lily, who had been a little girl at school when other women had forced him to war. 'Was that your first kiss?' he asked.

'Yes!'

He chuckled. 'I will give you very many more than that, Lily, my lovely Lily.' He drew a breath. He felt daring. He saw himself through Lily's eyes, handsome, wealthy, powerful. He gave a little excited laugh, freed by Lily's rejection of the past, by Lily's hatred of the war. 'I will give you many more kisses,' he promised recklessly. 'Many, many more. I will marry you. I am prepared to marry you, Lily. So what d'you say to that?'

Lily's face was blank with surprise. Her hand fell to her side and the little smudge of chocolate was very dark against the whiteness of her skin. 'Oh no,' she said. 'I couldn't possibly. I never thought of you like that. I'm very sorry. I must have been very silly. But I'm much too young. And you're much too old, Captain Winters. I am sorry.'

They said nothing, staring at each other in mutual incomprehension. Stephen flushed slowly, a deep dark red. He felt deeply, horribly snubbed by Lily. All of their days together and their treats together were shaken and remade into a new, offensive pattern. He had been a sugar daddy, a patron – while he had thought himself an acknowledged lover.

'Lily,' he said and he reached out his hand to draw her back from her sudden enmity, from her sudden girlish rejection.

Wobbly on the shingle in her little shoes, Lily stepped quickly back, out of his reach. The sea, a few yards away, washed in and out, sucking at the pebbles of the foreshore, a nagging ominous sound, like distant gunfire. Lily looked frightened, ready for flight. Stephen was filled with a bullying desire to smack her. She had led him on with her prettiness and her provocative respectability and now she shrank like some virgin child from his touch. She did not understand that she was compromised by his dinners, that she had been bought by his little treats. She was cheating on the sale. He wanted to grab her and pinch her. He wanted to hold her with one arm and rummage inside her pretty jacket. He wanted to rub her breasts and pinch her nipples. He wanted to strip away Lily's delicacy and thrust his hand up her skirt. She was not a lady, whatever she might like to pretend, she was a chorus girl. If it had been dark he would have grabbed her and slapped her face. Frustrated by daylight and chaperoned by the people walking on the promenade, Stephen stared at Lily with a desire very near to hatred.

'I should like to go back to the theatre now, please,' Lily said in a very small voice. 'I should like to go.'

Chapter Six

Stephen was not waiting at the stage door to drive Lily home after the last show that night. Helen Pears, accustomed to the silver gleam of the Argyll under the lights at the end of the alley, hesitated and glanced around for it.

'I don't think he'll be here,' Lily said quietly.

Helen tucked her daughter's hand under her arm and they walked to the tram stop. Charlie Smith loped up behind them, droplets of water from the sea mist like sequins in his black curly hair. 'Lost your beau, Lily?'

'Looks like it,' she said.

Charlie cocked an eyebrow at Helen to see how she was taking the news. 'Small loss,' he offered.

'He asked me . . .' Lily was driven to speech by sheer indignation. 'You'll never believe what he asked me! You'll never believe what he thought I would do!'

Helen and Charlie exchanged a shocked glance.

'Don't look at me, I had him down as a gentleman,' Helen said defensively. 'They were only ever alone at tea. I was always with them in the evening. I would have sworn he knew the line.'

Charlie shrugged. 'Belgium,' he said shortly. 'The gentlemen died first.'

'He asked me to marry him!' Lily said angrily. 'Actually, he didn't even ask me! He said: "I am prepared to marry you", as if he was doing me a favour. As if I should be grateful! And he kissed me too, and it was horrid. And if

65

it's going to be like that I shan't ever spoon with anyone. I think it's quite beastly!'

They had reached the empty tram shelter. Helen put her arm around Lily's shoulders but Lily shook her off. 'You'd have thought he'd know better at his age!' Lily said, still indignant. 'You'd have thought he'd know I didn't think of him like that! He's old enough to be my father!'

Charlie chuckled. 'He's about the same age as me, Lily,' he said. 'Not quite old enough to be your father.'

Lily flushed scarlet from the collar of her coat to the brim of her hat. 'You're different,' she said, muffled. 'You don't seem old. You weren't a soldier like him.'

Charlie shrugged his shoulders. 'I was actually. I went over in the first wave. It was my luck that I took a bullet in the first week. I was invalided out for the rest of the war. It didn't damage me like those men that were there for all that long time.'

Lily turned her face away. 'You're different from him,' she insisted. 'You understand me. He should have known that I didn't think of him like that.'

Charlie glanced at Helen. She was watching Lily's rosy face.

'Men don't always see things that clearly, Lil,' he said gently. 'A man sees someone who takes his fancy, and he tries it on. And a lot of girls would have thought themselves lucky to catch your Captain.'

'Charlie's right,' Helen said. 'When you said that he'd upset you, I thought he'd asked you to be his girl – to set you up in little rooms somewhere. I didn't think he'd propose marriage. I never thought he was that serious. I'd never have dreamed his family would allow it.'

Lily said nothing.

'It's a compliment,' Charlie pursued. 'He's a big name in this town, Winters. Good family, plenty of money, handsome house by the Canoe Lake. A lot of girls would be glad to catch him, Lil.'

Lily shook her head, crossly. 'He's miles too old,' she said. 'And he's funny. He stammers when he talks about the war. And his driver never speaks at all. He's nicknamed Coventry because he's silent. He and Stephen just look at each other as if they can tell what the other is thinking. It's creepy. I *never* liked him like that. I never gave him reason to think I liked him like that.' Her voice quavered slightly. 'I didn't lead him on. He's too old. How was I to know that he didn't know that he was miles too old?'

Helen tucked Lily's little hand under her arm. 'Now that's enough,' she said firmly. 'You're getting yourself all upset over nothing. As you say, he's old enough to look after himself. He's made you an offer. You've said "no". That's an end to it.'

The wires above them hummed and the tram clattered around the corner and stopped beside them. It rocked as they clambered on and sat on the scratchy seats.

'You wouldn't have wanted me to say yes?' Lily turned to her mother. '*You* don't think he's a catch?'

Helen Pears hesitated. Charlie smiled knowingly at her, enjoying her dilemma before Lily's open-faced honesty.

'He *is* a good catch,' she said cautiously. 'If you were a girl without talent then you couldn't do better, Lily, and that's the truth. If you didn't have me behind you, and the shop, and Charlie here to help you with your work, then you'd have done well to have him. He's not a bad sort. He's a gentleman and his wife would be a lady wherever she came from.

'But you don't need to marry, not while you've got me.' She took Lily's gloved hand in her own and squeezed it. 'Why, you're just starting out,' she said. 'Who knows how far you'll go?'

'We're off to Southampton next week anyway,' Charlie

said. 'And I want you to try a new song. Not in the show, but I want you to rehearse it with me while we're on tour. There might be an opening in Portsmouth when we get back and I've got an idea.'

'What do I have to do now?' Lily demanded. 'Go bald? Scalped?'

'Worse than that!' Charlie winked at Helen. The conductor came towards them and chinked the large brown pennies in his dirty hand.

'Fares please!'

Charlie paid for them all. 'I'll tell you later,' he said. 'This is my stop. I'll see you at the matinée, Lil. Sleep well, and don't bother about it.'

He leaned forward and patted her face. Lily looked up at him and smiled like a trusting child. On impulse Charlie bent and gently kissed her forehead. 'Little Lil,' he said tenderly.

The tram stopped and he jumped down to the pavement. Lily raised her hand to him in farewell. Her face was scarlet.

Neither woman saw the car parked in the shadows at the end of the street. It had followed the tram on its short journey.

Coventry turned to Stephen sitting beside him in the passenger seat.

Stephen shrugged as if in answer to a question.

'I just wanted to see her safe home, I suppose,' he said. 'I'm a damn fool, I know.'

Coventry went back to his silent contemplation of the dark street.

'Can we go to your place?' Stephen asked suddenly. 'Go and have a brew? It's early yet.'

Coventry nodded and started the engine. They took the eastern road out of town, past the lounging heap of

Eastney Barracks, an ominous pile of heavy red brick with two marines guarding the gates. Stephen's hand went up to the salute out of habit, and then he checked himself with a laugh.

Beyond the town the car picked up speed. They drove on a low flat road alongside the harbour. The tide was out, and over the mudflats the reflection of the moon chased alongside them. There was a mist rolling in from the sea and somewhere out in the Solent a foghorn called into the lonely darkness. The road raced over a low wood bridge built on piles driven into the chocolate-coloured mud. Stephen glanced inland and saw the black outline of the roofs of Portsmouth houses against the dark sky. There were concrete gun emplacements all along the coast road, and ugly tangles of barbed wire still despoiling the beach. Stephen looked at the mat of wire with a hard face.

'She's like water,' he said suddenly. 'She's like a cold glass of clean water. She'd take the taste of mud out of my mouth.'

They turned right on the main coast road, driving east towards the rising moon. It was nearly full, a blue-silver moon, very close to the earth, the craters and pocks on the asymmetric face very clear. The light was so bright that the yellow lamps of the Argyll barely showed on the road ahead. On the right of the road were the flat marshes of Farlington running down towards the sea, and a pale barn owl quartering the sedges and rough grass. On the left was a patchwork of little fields growing vegetables and salty hay.

'Very bright,' Stephen said uneasily. 'Very bright tonight.' Then he shook his head. 'Doesn't matter now,' he reminded himself.

They drove a little way, and then turned right, south to the sea. There was a small village and then a darkened water mill. Coventry slowed the Argyll and drove past an old toll-gate pub. The inn sign creaked in the wind, the paint all blistered away from the picture of a sailing ship. The mist was coming inshore, rolling in from the sea. Ahead of them was a low narrow bridge joining the island to the mainland. Beneath the mist, the sea, closing from both sides, washed and sucked at the wooden piles of the bridge. Coventry slowed and drove carefully over. Stephen watched the wet mudflats on either side of the car where they gave way to sedge and shrubs and reeds. A sea bird, disturbed in its sleep, called once, a lingering liquid call, and then fell silent. The mist batted against the headlights, fluttered in ribbons on the windscreen.

'Can you see?' Stephen asked.

Coventry nodded. He had lived on Hayling Island all his life. He had known this road before the summer visitors came, when it was a mud track for the fishermen and there was no bridge to the mainland, only a ferry. He drove unerringly through the flickering mist to the south of the island where it jutted out into the sea and the waves broke all day and all night on the ceaselessly shifting shingle beaches. They turned right along the seashore. Only one road, a sand track, ran west. At the westernmost point of the island was a solitary inn where you could take the ferryboat which plied across the narrow harbour from Southsea. In summer, people took pleasure trips to Hayling Island for the day, to picnic on the wide beaches and play in the sandy dunes. In the evenings the ferries crossed from one side to another in a constant stream, the women's sunshades and pretty dresses reflected in the harbour water and in the quiet evening air you could hear people laughing.

The foghorn moaned. Sand from the high dunes on their left had drifted over the road and Coventry leaned forward to see his way in the mist. The road was pot-holed and the Argyll lurched when one wheel dropped into a rut. Stephen and Coventry were smiling, enjoying the darkness and mist, the bad road, the discomfort.

On the right of the road was an inlet of still water, a little harbour off the main tidal reach. Dimly in the mist loomed the outlines of houseboats – three of them – pinned in the shallows by little white-painted staircases stretching from the shore. One was a pretty holiday home: there were empty pots waiting for geraniums on the steps. Furthest out, and the most ramshackle, was a grounded houseboat stained black with marine varnish and with no lights showing. It was Coventry's. He had gone from it in a dull rage when he had been conscripted, knowing that his father could not survive without his earnings, knowing that the houseboat was icily cold in winter and damp all the year round. His father had died in the winter of 1917 and they had not allowed Coventry home in time to be with him. The old man had died alone, wheezing with pneumonia. Coventry had arrived for the funeral and then returned to the Front to serve as Stephen's batman.

He parked the car alongside the houseboat and followed Stephen up the rickety gangplank. The houseboat had been long grounded. Its main structure was boat; but a permanent roof had been built on top, and what had once been the engine room and below decks was now a two-roomed cabin. Stephen went in first; the unlocked door opened directly into a small living room. There was one dining chair drawn up to a little table before the fire and one easy chair at the hearthside. Through the doorway beyond was the other room, Coventry's bedroom, with a box for his clothes and a camp bed, as they had used in the *estaminet* behind the lines.

Coventry came in behind Stephen and drew down the blinds and shut the door before he struck a match to light the oil lamp. Stephen sniffed at the smell of burning oil with relish. There was a little coal-burning range and a kettle filled with water set beside it. The fire was laid with newspaper twists and driftwood sculpted into pale monstrous shapes by the ceaseless working of the sea. The two rooms were cold and damp with the tang of the sea fret. Coventry set a match to the bleached wood and shook half a scuttle of coal on top. Stephen sat in the easy chair and watched as Coventry moved silently around the room, fetching the mugs, the teapot, the tea caddy and the sugar.

'Got any biscuits?' Stephen asked.

Coventry reached into a cupboard and brought out a tin. Stephen beamed as if his own home – luxuriously equipped, warm and carpeted, and filled with delicacies – were a lifetime away. 'Oh, good show!'

While the kettle boiled, both men bent down and unlaced their shoes and put them to one side. The weather had been dry for days and both Stephen and Coventry rode in a car, walking only for pleasure. But they felt their socks with anxious attention, and put their shoes alongside the range so that they could warm through. Stephen undid the belt from his trousers and carefully put it within reach, over the back of his chair.

'There now,' he said. 'That's comfortable.'

The kettle whistled and Coventry made the tea. Once again he made fresh tea on top of the dregs of the old, and the brew was sour and stewed. Stephen watched him as he measured four spoonfuls of sugar into each mug, poured the tea, stirred it vigorously clockwise and then passed the mug to Stephen. They each took a stale biscuit and ate in silence.

'She's like water,' Stephen said thoughtfully. 'I feel as if I could wash in her and I'd be clean. I feel that if I had her, if she loved me, I would be like I was before it all. I can get back to the world that I had – if I can have Lily.'

*　　*　　*

'You were late last night,' Stephen's mother said pleasantly at breakfast. 'It was midnight before I heard you come in. Did you have a good time?'

'I went over to Hayling Island and had a brew with Coventry,' Stephen said from behind his paper. 'Drove myself home. But if you want to go anywhere this morning Coventry can drive you. He'll be in at nine to take me to the office. He's coming over on the ferry.'

'I'm going to the hairdresser at eleven,' Muriel said. 'I don't need the car before then. Will you be home this afternoon?'

Stephen put down the newspaper and buttered a second slice of toast. 'I've got a client at three but I should be home by four,' he said. 'Another wartime marriage on the ropes. Should be fairly straightforward.'

'I'm having some people round for tea. I thought you might like to meet them.'

Stephen grimaced. 'A hen party? I'd rather not!'

Muriel looked at her son across the table. 'I should like you to be here, dear,' she said. 'You're not meeting anyone nice of your own age. Lady Philmore is coming with her daughter, and Mrs Dent with Sarah, and Mr and Mrs Close with their two girls. You won't be the only man. Mr Close is very pleasant. You've met him before. He edits some kind of defence journal in London, I believe.'

'Lots of girls,' Stephen observed neutrally.

Muriel smiled at him serenely. 'There *are* lots of girls. And they don't all dance in the chorus at the Palais. You should meet some of them.'

Stephen raised an eyebrow. 'Has David been gossiping?' he asked.

Muriel's smile remained bright. 'Never you mind. My staff work has always been excellent. I shall expect you home at half past four.'

Stephen finished his cup of tea and stood up, tossing

the linen napkin down beside his breakfast plate. 'I shall report for duty, as required,' he said. 'Is Father awake?'

At Muriel's nod he left the room and went up the stairs to the master bedroom. The old man was having his breakfast. The nurse was spoon-feeding him boiled egg. At every spoonful she gently wiped the twisted side of his face where the runny yolk spilled out and ran down his chin. Stephen looked without emotion at the wreck of what had once been his father. 'I'm off to work,' he said clearly.

The nurse rose and went to take the breakfast tray away.

'Don't bother, this is just a flying visit.' He went closer to the bed and leaned towards his father. The grave eyes stared at him. 'Business is good,' Stephen said. 'I'm interviewing for a new clerk today, an extra one. There's a lot of buying and selling of houses going on, plenty of conveyancing work. Endless divorce work.'

One dark eye blinked like a roguish wink.

'I'll give them your best,' Stephen said. 'They ask after you every day. I always tell them you're as well as can be expected.' He turned to the nurse. 'That's what you're supposed to say – isn't it? "As well as can be expected"? Or do you say "doing nicely"?'

The nurse smiled. 'He's doing very nicely,' she said. 'Very nicely indeed, aren't you, Mr Winters?'

'That's good,' Stephen said with a cold smile. 'I'll remember to tell them that he's doing nicely. I'll tell them that he's lying there like a corpse with his breakfast running down his face and doing nicely.' He left the room and went downstairs.

Coventry was waiting at the foot of the stairs with his peaked chauffeur's hat under his arm.

'To the office then,' Stephen said. 'And then come back and take Mrs Winters to the hairdresser for eleven.'

Coventry nodded, opened the front door and followed Stephen out down the steps.

'If she were here with me I don't think I'd be so damn cruel,' Stephen said thoughtfully as he got into the back of the car and Coventry walked around to the driver's door. 'If she were here with me I wouldn't feel so bloody. When I'm with her I feel like it's all over. I feel it's finished at last. Sometimes I even feel as if we might have won.'

He broke off as Coventry slammed the door and started the car. 'It would be fun to send back the car for her to go to the hairdressers,' he said. A smile lit up his face and made him seem boyish for a moment. He could not think of any other reason for a woman wanting a car than to go to the hairdressers. 'It would be fun to see her riding around in it on her own,' he said. 'Lily in the back of my car with some decent clothes and a ring on her finger, going to the hairdressers. That would be a sight to see!'

Stephen's working day was slow and tedious. He had his father's office – a tacit acknowledgement that his father would never come back to work. His father's partner in the firm, John Pascoe, had the office opposite. He was an elderly man, nearing retirement. He would have been replaced by his son Jim three years ago, but Jim had gone over the top at Loos in 1915 and run into that acrid gaseous mist and never come back. After months of delay and false hopes and bureaucratic muddles over Paskoe or Pascoe or Paske the War Office had regretfully decided that Jim Pascoe would never sit behind his father's desk. John Pascoe had grown more grey and stooped since Jim had been missing. He once had the bad form to ask Stephen if it was not – really now – not *too* bad out there. 'The conchies now, and the pacifists, they make it out as seven sorts of hell. But it wasn't like that really – was it?'

Stephen had looked at him with silent hatred. But the public school, officer code of never complaining, never telling tales, kept him dumb.

75

'Jim wouldn't have suffered,' Mr Pascoe asserted. 'In an attack you scarcely know what's going on, do you? The excitement of it? And everything?'

Stephen thought of the first day at Loos when the British poisonous gas had been fired into a clear beautiful autumn morning and drifted slowly slowly back on the wind, like the veil of a whorish bride, to sink into the British trenches and blind and choke the soldiers who were waiting for the order to run forward into barbed wire, which was still perfectly intact, towards guns, which were still expertly manned. Everyone had known that the weather was wrong for the attack, that the wind would blow the gas back towards the British. Everyone had known that it was morally wrong to use gas, that gas was banned from warfare. Everyone knew that the attack would fail and that men would die for nothing. But the HQ staff let it go ahead because they wanted to see the gas, and because the chain of command was so slow and unwieldy that it was almost impossible to cancel an advance even though it was bound to fail. A thousand deaths here or there made little difference – and anyway, that is the nature of war.

Stephen started to say that Jim died a hero. That he would not have suffered. That when you run forward, stumbling through the churned earth towards the bright flashes of cracking fire with the shells whining above you and the sudden earth-shaking crump of them landing near you, then you go joyfully: for your country, for freedom, for your God. But his stammer choked on the lies and all he could do was to shake his head, shake his head like a broken doll and say: 'He d ... he d ... he d ...'

'I'm sorry,' John Pascoe had said quickly. 'I beg your pardon. I shouldn't have mentioned it.'

They never spoke of the war again.

'Busy day?' Pascoe asked now, opening his door at Stephen's footstep on the stairs. The office was a twisted old building in Old Portsmouth, the most ancient part of the town. The streets were cobbled, they glowed an eerie shadowy blue from the gas lighting at night. The office floors went up and down and there were little turns and extra stairs in every corridor. It was not an efficient building but it suited the firm's Dickensian style.

'Not very busy,' Stephen said. 'Anything I can do for you?'

John shook his head. 'I've got a paternity suit you might like to look at,' he said. 'I think we've got a good case. She's a respectable girl, and the man sounds a bit of a cad.'

'All right,' Stephen said. 'Shove the file over later on.'

He worked on letters all the morning, dictating replies to his clerk. They would be typed and posted in the afternoon. The clerk had only one arm. Stephen kept his eyes turned away from the pinned sleeve. The man's job had been done by girls while he was away at the Front, but Stephen had insisted that men take the jobs when they returned, though they were not paid at the pre-war rate. Stephen kept the cheaper women's wages and gave jobs back to men. He did not like women in the office. He did not like their high frivolous voices answering the telephone. He thought it unsuitable that a spinster should read the divorce cases with their detailed adulteries and abuses, and he would never have employed a married woman whose place was at home.

In the afternoon, after a leisurely lunch with John Pascoe at their usual table at the Dolphin Hotel on the High Street, he saw Mrs Shirley Walker, whose husband had beaten her, buggered her, and finally run off. She had no evidence and no witnesses either for the beatings or buggery.

'Did you tell no-one?' Stephen asked gently.

77

She was pale with distress at having to tell the secret, and to a stranger. She was as guilty as if she had been the abuser. She shook her head.

Stephen stayed silent for a few moments, hoping the quiet of his room and the measured judicial tick of the clock would calm her. He was sleepy and quiet himself. On Tuesdays at the Dolphin Hotel it was stew with dumplings and he felt full and satisfied.

'May I ask,' he said softly, 'is there any especial reason why you wish to divorce your husband? Do you wish to remarry?'

She shook her head again and blew her nose into a damp scrap of plain handkerchief. Stephen assessed her looks. She would have been a pretty girl at her marriage in 1914. Since then she had given birth to one child and watched it die in the flu epidemic at the end of the war, and then her soldier-husband had come home and knocked the hope out of her. She was pale, underweight and miserable. In these competitive times she would not be remarrying. There were thousands and thousands of widows far prettier than her, looking for men to replace those who still lay in the mud.

'What I suggest is that we note that your husband has abandoned you and that you divorce him for desertion in seven years from now.'

Her pink-rimmed eyes leaped to his face. 'Why can't I divorce him right now?'

Stephen hesitated. 'I am sorry to say that you have no grounds for divorce.'

She looked dumbfounded. She gestured to the notes Stephen had made of her stilted account of her marriage. 'But he hit me, and he did . . . that.'

Stephen nodded. 'Unfortunately we have no proof. If he were to deny it in court then it would simply be your word against his.'

'But he's been with other women!' She was becoming angry now, there were red spots on her cheeks.

Stephen sighed. 'Adultery by the husband is not grounds for divorce.'

'I thought it was.'

'If a *wife* is adulterous, then that is a ground for divorce. But if a husband is adulterous then there has to be some offence to aggravate his adultery. And we have no evidence of anything else against your husband.'

'It doesn't seem right, that.' She was dissatisfied. She got up from the chair. She had a small brown handbag, worn at the seams, and an umbrella with an ugly synthetic handle. Stephen thought of Lily's light grace. 'I'm no further on than I was.'

'You cannot have an immediate divorce as the law stands,' Stephen said. 'But we can get you a divorce in seven years' time if Mr Walker does not return.'

'That's not right,' she said. 'That's not fair. All through the war I worked in the dockyard. I painted the ships. I was a painter. Long hours I worked and precious little pay. What do I get for serving?'

Stephen looked at her with sudden dislike. 'I don't think anyone came out of the war very well,' he said sharply. 'But the women did better than most! They stayed at home in perfect safety after all!'

He saw the rebellion in her face flare, and then bank down. 'Thank you very much, Sir,' she said.

He saw her from the room with as much courtesy as if she had been a lady and then took his hat and his soft tailored greatcoat from the coatpeg in the corner and ran down the stairs to where Coventry was waiting for him by the car. Stephen's earlier calm had deserted him and did not return on the short journey home. He felt rattled by the woman's ugliness and her sordid story, and he did not want to attend his mother's tea party which was in full swing when he entered the drawing room.

'What's wrong, Captain Winters?' Marjorie Philmore said blithely. 'A penny for your dark thoughts!'

They had trapped Stephen between two girls, Marjorie and Sarah, on the sofa, a small table before him with his tea cup and plate and a napkin on his knee.

'Just business worries. A poor woman came to see me today to divorce her husband. He's a bit of a brute.'

'How horrid!' Sarah exclaimed, opening her eyes very wide. 'How absolutely horrid!'

'Can't she dump him?' Marjorie asked. She was 'fast', Stephen noticed. She wore an outrageously short skirt and silk stockings. He knew, with weary prescience, that after tea she would take a cigarette holder out of her sequined clutch bag and insist upon smoking a cigarette in his mother's drawing room. Stephen, who never smoked except in his own room, or in his study, would have to watch her puffing ostentatiously, but not inhaling, while his mother tried to look as if she were not anxious about the smell on the curtains.

'I think divorce is possible,' he said dryly. 'I am advising her.'

'How horrid!' Sarah said again. 'Do you have to do all sorts of ghastly things, Captain? As a lawyer? All sorts of horrid quarrels?'

'Some.'

'Oh, do tell!' Marjorie said. 'Really steamy divorces with shocking evidence? Do you employ private detectives or do you snoop around hotels yourself?'

'Marjorie darling . . .' Lady Philmore said indulgently. 'She's such a flapper,' she said to Muriel. 'Such high spirits!'

'I rarely take cases of that nature,' Stephen said icily. 'We are an old-established and very respectable firm. We choose our clients rather carefully.'

'Stuffy of you!' Marjorie exclaimed. 'I should simply adore to be a lawyer and stand up in court and say, "May I assist your memory?" and "Would you call yourself a respectable woman, Mrs Bloggs?" Are you really vile to witnesses, Captain? Or do you look at them with your lovely smile and get them to tell you everything?'

'Unfortunately, although women are now admitted to the bar, it would be some years before you could qualify. I don't think you would make a good lawyer, Miss Philmore.'

'Call me Marjie! Everybody does!'

'Thank you.'

'More tea, Stephen?' Muriel asked.

'No thank you, Mother. I am sorry but I have to leave you. I promised to drop some papers around to John Pascoe. Will you excuse me, Mother? Ladies? I have so enjoyed meeting you.'

Stephen rose from his seat on the sofa and the parlour maid had no choice but to move the heavily laden table and let him escape. Marjorie put a hand on his arm.

'Come back after you've played postman and we'll go out for drinks,' she invited. 'I know a quite wonderful place round the back of Palmerston Road. A real dive!'

'I am sorry, I have an appointment for dinner. Perhaps another time.'

Stephen closed the door behind him and leaned back against it. 'Lily,' he whispered.

Chapter Seven

Mike, the SM at the Palais music hall, was quieter and more morose than ever at the close of the second week in Southsea. He would work all night loading the scenery, the props and all the costumes into the big lorry which would drive to Southampton and unload at the Southampton Palais, ready for the show to open on Monday night, and then he would be responsible for the whole company on tour.

Lily watched the girls packing their make-up and their bags, their lucky charms and their dried flowers with a sense of excitement. 'What's Southampton Palais like?' she asked Madge, who was the only one who had worked the tour before.

'Same as this one. Except there are sinks in the dressing rooms which is nice. And sometimes if they forget and leave the boiler on, there's hot water to wash in. Digs are all right too, if we go to the same ones. The landlady is a good sort. Bit of a sport. She used to be an actress in her younger days, there are pictures of her all over the house. She'll turn a blind eye if you're late in. And if she takes a fancy to you, she'll let you sit in her front room and you can have visitors.'

'No-one's going to visit me at Southampton,' Lily said unwarily.

'What's happened to the Captain in his big car then?' Madge demanded. 'Did he try it on?'

The entire dressing room fell silent and everyone looked at Lily. 'No, he didn't!' she said indignantly. 'He wouldn't do such a thing.' She felt the need to defend Stephen against mass female suspicion. 'He's just ... busy,' she said lamely. 'He's a lawyer, you know. He works in his family's law firm. They've been lawyers for four generations. And he's very busy right now.'

Susie said something under her breath and the girl next to her laughed.

Helena put her arm around Lily's shoulder and gave her a hug. 'Plenty more fish in the sea,' she said. 'And the big ones are always the hardest to catch.'

'I didn't try and catch him!' Lily said indignantly. 'And if I'd wanted to catch him ...'

'You what?' Susie asked. 'If you'd wanted him – what then?'

'I could have had him,' Lily said lamely.

There was a ripple of sceptical amusement.

'Never mind,' Helena said again. 'Better luck next time, eh, Lil?'

Lily nodded; there was no point trying to convince them that Stephen had proposed and been rebuffed. But as she packed her comb and the little pot of hair cream which Charlie had given her into her vanity bag, she could not resist imagining the uproar it would have caused if she had strolled into the dressing room with a large diamond on her finger and the news that she was to be Mrs Stephen Winters. Lily smiled at the thought. They would have screamed the place down and Sylvia de Charmante would have died of envy.

It would have been fun to be engaged to Stephen. Not married of course; but it would have been fun to be engaged. He would certainly have bought her a large diamond ring. It would have been nice to have been taken out to dinner from the Southampton lodging house in the big grey car and see the curtains twitch as the girls watched her drive away. It was tiring to walk to the tram stop at the end of the day. The Argyll had been comfortable, and the dinners had been fun, and Stephen had been very pleasant when he had held her hand in the darkness and smiled at her.

But the kiss on the beach had been shocking. And Lily's pride as well as her youth had recoiled from Stephen's declaration that he was prepared to make her his wife. She threw in her flannel and her towel and slammed the dressing case shut.

'I'm packed,' she said.

'See you Monday!' Madge called. 'Town station, ten o'clock, Monday morning. Don't be late!'

'I won't! See you then!' Lily called.

Stephen was at the stage door with a bouquet of creamy golden roses. Helen Pears was waiting discreetly halfway down the alley.

'I couldn't let you go away like that,' Stephen said. His face was anxious, he looked like a boy in trouble, not an experienced older man.

Lily took the flowers automatically and said nothing.

'I'm sorry,' Stephen said. 'I startled you. I startled myself actually! I like you awfully, Lily, and I'd like you to consider being my wife. I'd do my best to make you very happy. I'd give you everything you want, you know. I'd like you just to give it a thought. Don't say "no" outright.'

Lily started walking towards her mother, her arms full of roses. 'I don't think I can,' she said.

'Leave it for a while then. Put it out of your mind. It was an idea of mine but you're probably right, you're too young to be thinking of marriage. We'll be friends, shall we, Lily? Like we were before?'

Helen Pears was beside them, glancing from her daughter's face to Stephen's anxious expression.

'Captain Winters?' she said coolly.

84

Stephen glanced at her. 'I've made a bit of a fool of myself, Mrs Pears,' he said. 'I asked Lily to marry me and of course, she's too young to be thinking of such things yet. I like her awfully, you see, and I just thought I'd ask. But if she wants, and if you permit, we'll consider ourselves friends again. Just friends.'

'It's up to Lily,' Mrs Pears said gently. 'She's much too young to marry and she's got her career to think of as well.'

'Oh yes, her career,' Stephen said dismissively. 'But can we be friends again, Lily?'

Lily's good nature was too strong to withstand Stephen's anxious look. And besides, the Argyll was waiting, and the roses were nice. The girls would be coming out of the stage door at any moment and then they would see who had failed to land a big catch. It would be fun if Stephen drove over to Southampton and took her out for dinner and anyway, Coventry was holding open the door and smiling at her, as if he was pleased to see her again. And there was nothing creepy about Coventry at all – she had imagined that. Charlie Smith had said that Stephen was no older than him; and Charlie Smith was certainly not too old.

'All right!' Lily said. 'I'd like that.' She freed one hand from holding the roses and held it out to Stephen. 'We'll be friends again.'

Stephen shook her hand firmly, as if she were a young clerk at his office. 'That's grand,' he said. 'And now – would you like a farewell dinner, Mrs Pears? Lily? To say goodbye to the Queens Hotel before you conquer the south of England?'

Lily glanced at her mother and then nodded. 'Divine!' she said, using Sylvia de Charmante's favourite word of praise. 'Too, too divine!'

* * *

Stephen called for her at the grocery shop on Sunday morning. Mrs Pears had agreed that they might all go out for a picnic. Coventry had a large hamper in the boot of the Argyll, and a spirit stove, a tea kettle, a silver teapot, and a complete tea service.

'On a Sunday, darling?' Muriel had asked her son. 'Such an odd day for a picnic. I don't think it's quite the thing.'

'She's going away tomorrow, Mother, if she doesn't come now I don't know when she'll be free again. And I've longed for a picnic in the country for weeks. The forecast is good for tomorrow. And if you don't tell anyone – who's to know?'

Muriel had sighed and said nothing more. The tea party to introduce Stephen to young women of his own class had been a total failure. He had hated them all. And Muriel, watching them over her tea cup as they postured and pre-ened, had hated them too. Marjorie had obviously studied the magazines to learn how to be a Modern Girl and was both shocking and vulgar. Sarah had been sickeningly sentimental. Stephen, trapped on the sofa between two versions of post-war womanhood, had looked uncomfortable – even angry. He must wonder, Muriel thought, what it was all for – those long two and a half years away – when he comes home and finds girls like Marjorie and Sarah as the best that Portsmouth can offer, his father a cripple, and the house silent with grief. She sighed.

She was still grieving for her oldest son, their heir. Christopher had marched off to war believing that it would be an adventure like a *Boys' Own* story. They had all thought that then. It sounded like madness now. But in the first heady days of 1914 there had been a sort of wild carnival atmosphere as if the boys were going away on some delightful crusade. The newspapers had been full of pictures of handsome young men smiling and waving, and the journalists had written that England would reclaim her power and her strength with the British Expeditionary Force. There had not been a war since the Boer war – and the faraway privations of that struggle were quickly forgotten. The Germans were behaving like animals in Europe and should be abruptly stopped. Everyone knew that the British soldier – Tommy Atkins – was the finest in the world.

People were bored of peace. All the rumblings and discontent in the country, all the eccentricities and oddness of the young men and women would be blown away when they had their chance to be great. The newspapers said it, the clergy blessed it in the pulpits. Everyone believed that a war – a good romp of a quick war – would somehow set them up, would unite the nation, cleanse it. The country needed a war, they told themselves. They were a fighting nation, an imperial nation. They needed to prove themselves again.

Christopher had been in the Officer Training Corps at school and joined the Reserve Army after school. He believed it was his duty to go and – more than that – he had thought it the finest adventure possible. He had volunteered and been commissioned at once. His father and he went down to the tailors Gieves, on the harbourside, and ordered his uniform in a joyous male shopping trip which had ended in the Dolphin Hotel with a bottle of champagne for the hero. He had looked wonderfully handsome in khaki. He had been very fair with clear pale skin and light blue eyes. He looked like a boy off to boarding school when he leaned out of the train window and waved his new cap with the shiny badge and shouted goodbye.

He died within seven weeks, during the first disastrous battle that they would later call the first battle of the Somme, when they had to distinguish it from the second, then the third and then the fourth: battles fought again and again, over the same ground, now layered with dead like some strange soft shale rock.

Muriel learned to be grateful that Christopher had died early. He had never known trench warfare and the souring of courage and hope that seemed to happen in the mud. She was glad that her fair-headed son had never come home alive with lice and shaking with nerves. She was glad, afterwards, that it had been quick for him, that she had never had to listen to him screaming from nightmares or found him huddled under his bed, soaked in sweat, keening with terror. Christopher had ridden out like a hero and was gone for ever, before she had time to miss him. She had not even finished knitting his gloves.

Stephen had been totally different. He had resisted recruitment to the very last moment. The news of Christopher's death had come and his father had dropped where he stood, as if a bullet had found his heart. But still Stephen would not go. His father had been able to move his hand then, his right hand, and he had written Stephen a note, the only thing he ever wrote. It read: 'Now, your turn.' Stephen had completely ignored it.

His godfather had written to him that it was his duty to go, and that he would be cut from the old man's will if he did not volunteer. It was no empty threat. The old man had a large house in Knightsbridge. Stephen had secretly enjoyed the knowledge that it would one day be his ever since Christopher's death had left him as sole heir. But even that threat did not move him from his refusal to go. One painful evening after dinner Muriel had told him that she was convinced that it was her duty to let him go, and his to leave. She had read in the paper that a woman's service to her country meant sacrifice. She was ready to sacrifice him. A popular daily paper was minting medals for women who sent their sons to war. Muriel recognized the rightness of the award. A woman could do nothing, could give nothing – but she could let her son go. Muriel had tears in her eyes when she told Stephen that she was convinced that he must leave. But nothing would make him go.

It was only when it became apparent to him that conscription was coming, and that no fit young man would escape, that he could either volunteer as an officer or be conscripted as a soldier, that he went down to the town hall and signed on. He went without telling his mother of his intention, and he came back with a face like a servant.

There was no joyous backslapping trip to Gieves with his father. His father's hand had lost its strength; he could not write. He nodded at the news, but Stephen had no praise from him. There was no singing on the train which took him and the other surly late volunteers to London. There were no optimistic promises about being home by Christmas.

When she was clearing out his room, after he had gone, Muriel found an envelope tucked at the back of the drawer for his socks. There was no letter, but it was not empty: there was a white feather in it. Someone had posted a white feather to her son. She looked at the postmark. It was posted in Portsmouth, their home town where they had been well-known and respected for generations. Someone had troubled themselves to discover Stephen's home address and post him a white feather. Someone had seen his reluctance to fight and named him as a coward.

Muriel had thought then that Stephen would never forgive any of them. When he had come home on leave with his face white and tight, slept for days and wallowed in the bath, eaten as if he were starving, but never once smiled at her nor at his father, she knew she was right. She asked him in the new humble voice that she was learning to use to him, measuring the extent of her misjudgement, 'Is it very, very bad, Stephen? I've seen photographs and it looks . . .'

He had looked at her with his broad handsome face hardened and aged to stone. 'You have sent me to my death,' he said simply, and turned away.

Muriel moved restlessly around the sitting room. Stephen had been proved wrong. He had not died, he had come home; and now he had a new life to make. He had his work to do, and he would find a suitable wife, he should have a child, a son to continue the family. It was Muriel's job to find a girl who would bring some life into this quiet house where the old man upstairs lay in silence and grieved for his brightest lost son.

The girl, the right girl, must be somewhere among Muriel's many acquaintances. Muriel would make the effort, she would give tea parties, lunch parties and even dinner parties. She would put aside her grief and her longing for silence and fill the house with women and girls so that Stephen could take his pick. He would meet a girl and like her, and the threads of life could be picked up and knitted on like one of those interminable khaki mufflers which everyone had made so badly for four years. The tight cruel look that crossed Stephen's face sometimes would go. His stammer would fade away and be forgotten. And the nightmares, when he woke the whole house with his screaming – these too would stop. Stephen's wife would turn him back into a civilian. Stephen's wife would pick up the pieces left by the war and mend him into a whole man again.

The girl from the Palais and this picnic in the country could not be prevented. Muriel had lost her power over Stephen when she sent him to his brother's graveyard. He had thought then that if she had loved him at all she would have fought to keep him safe, at home. Her betrayal had opened a wide gulf between them that Muriel alone could not bridge. But Muriel still had authority. The chorus girl from the Palais would never set foot in number two, The Parade.

Lily lay on her back, a stem of grass in her mouth, hat askew, watching the blue sky and the small pale clouds drifting across it. Stephen was leaning back against the Argyll's polished mudguard, hardly daring to breathe for fear of harming his sense of peace.

'This is nice,' Lily said carelessly.

Stephen nodded. There were no words for how he felt, watching Lily's face turned up to the sky, her long body stretched seductively over a tartan rug, her little feet in white stockings and white sandals, demurely crossed. On the corner of the rug Mrs Pears repacked the picnic basket. Coventry sat on a log a little way off smoking a cigarette.

There was a lark going upwards and upwards into the blue. Lily's eyes – as blue as the sky – watched it soaring, listening to its call. 'Funny little bird,' she said. 'What's it doing that for?'

'For joy,' Stephen said softly. His heart felt tight in his chest. Lily's profile, as clear and exquisite as a cameo, burned into his mind. He thought he would see her face, blanched by the bright colours of the tartan rug, for ever. He thought this one picture of a pretty girl on a summer day might drive all the other pictures from his mind.

'How lovely,' Lily said wonderingly. 'I never thought they sang because they were happy. I thought they just sang because they had to.'

Stephen smiled. He could feel laughter bubbling inside him like an underground spring, blocked for too many years. 'Like a paid choir?' he asked.

Lily giggled at her own silliness. 'Like the chorus line,' she said. 'Whether they feel like it or not. Up at dawn and in a line, twitter twitter twitter. You, sparrow, you're flat!'

'And the stars come on later,' Stephen suggested. 'The blackbird. And the nightingale only comes for command performances. And the cuckoo has a really short season!'

'Does it? Why?'

Stephen was puzzled by her ignorance. 'It's only here in spring,' he said.

Lily turned to look at him, one casual hand shielding her eyes from the sun. Stephen drank in the crook of her elbow, her short hair spilling out from her hat.

'Is it?'

'You know the song – "April come she will, May she will stay, June she change her tune . . ."'

Lily giggled gloriously. 'No,' she said. 'Sing it to me!'

Stephen laughed, a croaky unfamiliar feeling. 'I can't sing!'

'Sing!' Lily commanded.

Stephen glanced across at Coventry and Mrs Pears, embarrassed. Both of them were deaf and blind to him and Lily. Coventry was slowly smoking, looking out over the hills. Mrs Pears had taken some sewing out of her bag and was concentrating on her stitching.

> April, come she will,
> May she will sing all day,
> June she will change her tune,
> July she will fly,
> August go she must.

Lily sat up, clasping her knees, to listen.

'Sing it again!' she commanded.

This time she joined in with him, her clear steady voice hesitating around the tune and stumbling on the words.

'Again,' she said when they had finished. 'Please, Stephen. It's so pretty.'

He sang it again with her, watching her mouth shaping the words and the unwavering concentration on her face.

She was very young still. He thought of Marjorie and Sarah at his mother's tea party with their affectations and tricks. Lily was like a child beside them. Like a child or like a woman of extraordinary purity. As if she lived in a different country altogether from post-war England with its greed and compromise. She was like the other girl, when he first saw her in Belgium, a simple girl who worked on the land and knew only the seasons and crops. A girl who trotted her donkey cart past a line of silent marching men and looked at them with pity in her eyes.

'I've got it,' Lily said. She gestured him to be quiet and then sang the song through to him. 'Is that right?' she asked.

Stephen felt his heart move inside him as if it had been frozen and dead for years.

'Oh Lily, I do love you so,' he said.

And Lily, with the sun on her back, too content to demur, reached forward and put her hand to his cheek in a gesture that silenced and caressed him, at once.

On the drive home Stephen hesitated about asking permission to visit Lily in Southampton or elsewhere on tour. But Lily's smiling contentment throughout the long sunny day had made him more confident.

'I should like to visit Lily next week, while she is in Southampton,' he said, speaking across her to Mrs Pears. 'I have to go to Southampton for business on Wednesday. If you would give your permission I should like to take Lily out to dinner and take her back to her lodgings later.'

He watched for the slight movement which was Lily's nudge and her nod. Mrs Pears hesitated. 'Lily's still very young, Captain Winters,' she said. 'I don't want her talked about. Girls gossip and there's more gossip talked in the theatre than you would imagine. I think it's perhaps better for Lily if she goes home with the other girls after the show.'

'Oh, Ma!' Lily remonstrated.

Helen Pears shook her head, addressed herself to Stephen. 'I don't want to make one rule for you and a different one for everyone else,' she said frankly. 'Lily's bound to get asked. The answer should always be the same. She doesn't go out to dinner without me. If I can't be there, then she can't go.'

Lily hunched her shoulders but she did not appeal against her mother's decision.

'What about taking her out for tea, between the shows? As I have done in Portsmouth?' Stephen asked. He could feel his anger rising that Helen Pears should stand between him and Lily. Like all women, he thought, very quick to sacrifice someone else for their own ends.

Helen nodded. 'If it is not inconvenient for you when you are working,' she said. 'Lily may certainly go out to tea with you in Southampton.'

Lily peeped a smile at him from under her hat. 'On Wednesday?' she asked.

'Wednesday,' he said.

'You keep Captain Winters at arm's length,' Helen observed to Lily as she watched the Argyll drive off from the upstairs sitting room window. 'He's very much in love with you. And if he asks you out to dinner again, you remember I said no.'

'He's nice though,' Lily said. 'He's nice to take us out like that. I haven't had such a lovely day ever, I don't think. And did you see the china? And the teapot? It was solid silver, wasn't it?'

Helen nodded. She had felt the weight of the pot as she had repacked the hamper.

'Plenty of money there,' she observed. 'But not for you.

You don't have to marry, you don't have to make a choice for years. You can be free, Lily, with your talent. You've got your career ahead of you and all sorts of opportunities.'

Lily came away from the window, immediately diverted. 'I wonder what Charlie has in mind for a new act,' she said. 'Has he told you?'

Helen shook her head. 'No,' she said. 'But you can do what he says. He's got a wonderful eye. He'll go far. I heard some gossip when I was waiting for you the other day that he's applied for the post of musical director at the Kings Theatre, Southsea. A proper theatre – not just music hall. That'd be a big step for him! I wouldn't be surprised if he got it either.'

Lily nodded. 'He can play anything,' she said proudly. 'If you just sing it to him once he can play it straight away. I'm going to sing him the cuckoo song. I think it's really pretty.'

'Cuckoo song!' Helen said indulgently. 'You'd better get yourself packed for tomorrow. I'll make us some supper. I've got some nice ham in the shop which won't last another day. I've got some biscuits and tea for you to take with you. Don't forget to eat properly, Lil. And your washing is on the landing, all ironed.'

Lily moved to the door and stopped to put her arms around her mother. 'Will you be all right without me?' she asked. 'You've never had to manage without me before.'

Helen patted her on the back. 'I'll be fine,' she said. 'It's a big start for you. I'd rather see you do it than anything else in the world. I wouldn't stand in your way, Lil. You go off and I'll be proud of you.' She hugged her daughter tight for a moment, and quickly blinked the tears from her eyes before she let her go so Lily would not see what it was costing her. Lily was her creation, made of finer stuff than the other children of their street. Every spare penny had been poured into Lily's singing, into Lily's dancing, into her elocution. It was only sense, now that the girl had her chance, for her mother to send her out to the wider world, and be proud. But it was only natural that she should feel deeply bereft, as if Lily were still her baby taken from her too early.

She gave Lily a little push. But the girl hesitated at the door. 'D'you think Charlie Smith likes me? I mean as a girl, not just as a singer?'

Helen looked at her daughter. 'It doesn't matter, does it? He's really old, according to you. As old as Captain Winters. And injured in the war too.'

Lily nodded, unconvinced.

'You can go out to dinner with him, if he asks you, while you're on tour,' Helen said. 'You'd be perfectly safe with him, Lily.'

'Because he's not in love with me and Stephen is?'

'Something like that,' Helen said. 'And he knows the line.'

'I like him awfully,' Lily confided.

Helen smiled. 'I know,' she said. 'He's a good friend to you, Lily, you wouldn't have got this far without his help. You keep him as a friend and bide your time. You've got years ahead of you for love.'

Chapter Eight

Helen did not go with Lily to the station. She ordered a cab for her and waved her off from the shop doorway. There were customers in the shop and they had no time for any farewell more than a hurried peck on the cheek.

'Write to me if you need me,' Lily said hastily as her mother thrust her into the cab. 'You know I'll come home if you need me.'

'Stuff and nonsense,' Helen said brusquely. 'You go and have a lovely time, Lily. Be sure you eat properly and get enough sleep.' She slammed the car door. 'And remember what I said – no dinners out.'

Lily nodded and waved, turning around to watch her mother's indomitable figure recede as the car drove away. Helen stood in the road, her arm raised, waving and waving until the cab was out of sight. Then she wiped her face roughly on her white apron and strode back into the shop. 'Who's next?' she said crossly. 'And there's no credit, so don't ask for it.'

Lily, gripping her handbag tightly on her lap, with her vanity bag on the seat beside her, rode on her own to the station, tipped the driver and called the porter for her suitcase all by herself, and then merged joyously with the company waiting on platform two for the Southampton train.

Charlie was there, supervising the trunks going into the luggage wagon. Sylvia de Charmante was being driven to Southampton by a gentleman friend and would meet them at the theatre.

'I'd have thought you'd have got Captain Winters to drive you,' Madge said. 'Is he back on the scene for keeps?'

Lily smirked. 'He took me and Ma out for the day yesterday. In the Argyll. We had a picnic. He has a real silver teapot. And really good china. Just for a picnic!'

The train drew in, snorting smoke and hissing steam. The stoker leaned out over the curved panel of the cab and winked at the girls, his face shiny with sweat and streaked with coal dust. Porters opened the doors and the company piled into adjoining carriages. Charlie found himself seated beside Lily.

'So, are you planning your wedding, then, Lily?' he asked with a smile under cover of the noise of the girls getting settled and piling their hatboxes into the overhead shelves.

Lily giggled. 'No, I told him not, and he's not going to ask me again. Ma won't let him take me out to dinner on my own but I can have tea with him. He's coming to Southampton on Wednesday.'

'Well, watch your step,' Charlie advised. 'If your ma is happy with it then I suppose it's all right. But watch your step with him, Lily.'

Lily turned her candid blue gaze on him. 'What d'you mean?'

Charlie flushed a little and shifted in his seat. 'Oh dammit, Lil, you know what I mean!'

'D'you mean he might want to kiss me and spoon even though I told him we wouldn't get married?'

Charlie nodded.

'He won't do that!' Lily said decidedly. 'He's a gentleman after all.'

The engine hissed a cloud of white steam and the doors slammed down the length of the train.

'Shut the window! Shut the window! We'll all get covered in smuts!' the girls cried.

They pulled the window up, and fastened it with the big leather strap on the brass hook. The station master blew a loud blast on his whistle, raised the green flag and dropped it. The engine started forward and there was the exciting thump as the carriages moved too, and then with a rattle the whole train eased forward and wheels rolled into their regular clatter.

'Well, that's all right, then,' said Charlie ironically. 'A gentleman!'

Lily had thought the show would be different in another theatre, but it was reassuringly the same. There was less of a panic in the quick costume changes because the girls' dressing room was nearer the stage. It was a bigger room and Lily had a proper place at the mirror, and her own peg for her costume. Charlie Smith complained about a draught in the orchestra pit and wore a vest and then a ludicrous pair of combinations under his immaculate white shirt and black bow tie. One of the scene changes was too much for the Southampton crew, and after they had fluffed it for two successive nights it was dropped entirely. But apart from small alterations, the show was up and running, and Lily found the familiar songs and scene changes and the acts made the theatre feel like home in a strange city.

The lodgings were fun. They were all living together in the same house and Lily loved supper after the last show, when Charlie Smith sat at the head of the table and Mike the SM sat at the foot, and the girls gossiped and told jokes and stories of theatre life. Lily felt the proud glow of being one of the elite. There were other lodgings in Southampton, there were other dinner tables. But *this* was the table for the cast at the Palais. They were all noisy and exhibitionist even when the curtains had closed and they were home for the night.

Sylvia de Charmante's gentleman friend took her out to

dinner at night and she rarely spent time with the rest of them. The other acts ate with the chorus girls, or picnicked in their rooms. There was always someone going shopping who wanted company, or someone who had to stay home and sew her stockings who wanted Lily to sit with her.

There was a piano at the digs and Charlie would play every morning and sometimes call Lily into the room to sing with him. She would sing for as much as a couple of hours at a time until she was tired. 'Slower,' Charlie would say. 'More oomph, Lily. A little more slur there and raise your eyes and smile, really slowly. Attagirl! That's it!'

And Lily would lean, as he commanded, against the piano and sing leisurely, as if the audience would wait all night for the next note.

'Keep 'em guessing!' Charlie said. 'You're a queen and they're your subjects. Don't ever let them think they know what it's all about. You've got to be the boss.'

Lily's teacher at home had been a singer trained in the classical tradition. She had taught Lily to sing standing upright with her eyes fixed on a distant horizon. Charlie taught her to drape herself over a piano and introduced her to ragtime.

Not that ragtime was particularly easy. 'Count, for God's sake, Lily!' he said impatiently. 'Don't guess it!'

'I did count!' Lily protested. 'I came in on the third beat!'

'You rushed it. It's syncopated. You sing it like a march. Leave it slow, Lil. Do it one-two-and-three this time.'

Lily sang it again and was rewarded by one of Charlie's dark-eyed beams. 'Angel,' he said. 'Do it again, and really hit it this time.'

On Wednesday Stephen came as he had promised. The Argyll was waiting outside the Southampton Palais stage door. Charlie chanced to be going out as Lily met Stephen on the doorstep.

'Hello, Captain Winters,' Charlie said easily. 'Taking Lily out to tea?'

Stephen nodded, his eyes never leaving Lily's face, pink under Madge's cream cloche hat.

'The Raleigh Tea Rooms are very nice,' Charlie observed.

'We're going to the Grand,' Stephen said. 'There's a band there, and dancing. I thought you might like it, Lily.'

'Divine!' Lily said.

'Back at six,' Charlie said impartially. He glanced at Coventry, holding the passenger door open for Lily. He smiled at him. Coventry looked at him and slowly put a finger to his cap.

'See you at six,' Charlie said again and sauntered down the street.

Lily enjoyed the tea dance. Stephen was relaxed and more amusing when they were alone. He could dance well and Lily liked being held by him. His arm was warm and firm around her waist and she felt that her hand in his was held as if it were precious. She enjoyed the feeling of being dainty, special. She liked how Stephen rested his cheek softly against her hat. He was close without being oppressive. His touch on her was light, a caress, not an embrace.

The Grand was expensive. Lily was the youngest woman there, and certainly the only girl in a borrowed hat and without a little fur stole. She liked the waiters' deference to Stephen, and the shining service for the tea. She liked the little cakes and the good china.

'I wish Ma could be here. She'd love it.'

'Shall I take her a message from you? Would you like me to go and see her?'

'That'd be nice of you,' Lily said. 'I write to her every couple of days. She's only got a delivery lad to help in the shop and it's a lot of work for one. Especially on Thursdays when the wholesalers' lorries deliver.'

'I could go and see her on Thursday evenings and telephone you,' Stephen said. 'I could keep an eye on her for you.'

Lily giggled. 'I don't think she'd like that! But you could pretend you were passing. You could go in and buy some cigarettes or something, couldn't you?'

'And then I'll phone you,' Stephen said. 'If you give me the number of all of the places on your tour I could call you every Thursday to tell you that she's all right.'

The dance ended and Lily beamed up at him and clapped the band. 'You're lovely. Thank you. I'd like that.'

Stephen returned Lily to the stage door at six o'clock on the dot. Charlie Smith was leaning against the door smoking a cigarette and watching girls walk past.

'Hello again, you're very prompt.'

'Army training,' Stephen said with a grimace. 'Were you over there?'

'Briefly,' Charlie said. 'I took a piece of shell at Arras and ended up training conscripts in Wales for the rest of the war.'

'One of the lucky ones.' There was an edge to Stephen's voice.

'I know it.'

'I was there till the bitter end.'

Lily put out her gloved hand to Stephen. 'Thank you for a lovely tea,' she said formally. 'I will write to you with the telephone numbers.'

Stephen took her hand and held it. He glanced over her head. Charlie smiled blandly at him from the doorway.

'Goodbye, Lily.' Stephen yielded to yet another chaperone. 'Have a lovely time and come home to us soon.'

Lily patted his cheek and then vanished inside the stage door.

'Bye,' Charlie said.

Stephen got into the passenger seat beside the driver and the big Argyll eased away.

'Bye,' Charlie said again to the empty street.

In the following weeks Stephen missed Lily more every day. In her absence he could forget the way her speech sometimes grated on him and the occasional cheerful twang of her Portsmouth accent. He forgot Lily's vanity and her ambition to succeed in a vulgar profession in a vulgar age. He forgot how much he disliked the determined gentility of Mrs Pears, and the way she looked at him as if he were not to be trusted. He forgot his dislike of Charlie Smith who had seemed to linger at the stage doorway to see Lily safely in. He forgot his jealousy of Lily's bright promiscuous smile. All he remembered was the light in Lily's face, the exact shade of blue of her eyes, her silky cap of fair hair. He remembered her at the picnic sprawled out on the rug, at once wanton and demure with her little white-stockinged feet in the white sandals crossed at the ankles. He adored her hats — frivolous little pots which fitted her head like a bluebell on the head of an elf in a children's picture. And he felt that enjoyable half-painful ache of desire when he thought of her against the red curtain in her blue choir boy's gown with her pale face upraised and her voice as clear and pure as a ringing bell from heaven.

He drove past the corner shop every day. He did not care whether Helen Pears was well or ill. But if she were to be taken sick then someone would have to contact Lily and fetch her home. Stephen wanted to snatch her from the music hall tour. Stephen wanted to draw up in his big car and take her away from the noisy, reckless crowd of them. He wanted to take her away from the chorus line, from the men who would drink at the bar and watch the girls' legs, from Charlie Smith. But every day the sign on the door was turned to 'Open' at seven thirty promptly, and Helen did not turn it around to 'Closed' until seven or eight o'clock at night.

Stephen's work continued around him in its slow routine. Women seeking to escape husbands married in a hurry in the excitement of the war came to his office and wept, registered their complaint and left thinking Stephen sympathetic and kindly. An officer who had married a nurse in a spasm of wounded despair, and then learned that she was the hospital cleaner, an unmarried woman with three children at home, found Stephen worldly and understanding. A woman charged with theft, a man charged with violence, a drunkard, a wartime profiteer making his will, an officer whose estate had to be managed by a trust now that he vomited in crowds and screamed at night, all these victims of the war traipsed through Stephen's office and told their stories, and thought him compassionate.

Not one of them touched him. Muriel Winters, watching her son who had gone to the war in despair and come back stricken, thought that her firstborn was mouldering to Flanders clay, and her second was calcifying to stone. Stephen's head would nod, and his hand would move slowly, accurately across the page, but he was as distant from the pain of the people who came to him for help as Muriel had been from the battle when she had heard the rumble of guns like a faraway thunderstorm one still sunny day in Kent and said innocently, 'Listen! What's that noise?' and then been unable to imagine what it must be like to be under shellfire in Belgium so savage that the noise of it could be heard in an English garden.

Muriel gave a dinner party. She knew the house was

too quiet. The silent man upstairs, Stephen walled inside himself, Coventry neurasthenic and mute. Muriel wanted noise in the house which was not the thin hidden cry of a woman who has lost both sons. She invited the Dents and Sarah. It was another failure. Sarah was huge-eyed and trembling with sensitivity. Stephen's work, his father's health, even the weather drew from Sarah a little shiver of compassion and an earnest nod. She put her hand on Stephen's hand and whispered to him that she knew the war had been awful – too dreadfully awful. Muriel saw Stephen hold his hand still under the insult of the woman's pity. But after dinner, when the guests had gone, Muriel saw Stephen slip through the baize door to the kitchen and knew that he would sit late with Coventry that night in the silence which was their last and most secure refuge.

Stephen's best moment in the week was when he went into the corner shop on Thursday to buy his cigarettes and ask after Lily. Helen Pears seemed pleased to see him. The second time he came she made tea for them both and they perched on stools on either side of the counter in the empty shop and Helen read to him from Lily's letter. She had written from Bournemouth of the grandness of the hotels and the wonderful long sandy beach. They were playing at a music hall near the Winter Gardens and Lily went out in the afternoons and sat in a deck-chair by the bandstand to listen to the band play and watch the people walking by. She never mentioned a man's name. She never asked her mother to send her good wishes to Stephen, though she knew he was calling. Her letters were full of the summer gardens, and hats, the lengths of skirts which were being worn and the fun they had on their day off when the entire cast went down to the beach and paddled. Lily had bought a swimming costume and was teaching some of the other girls to swim. Stephen thought of Lily's long pale legs stretched out on the sand and felt his throat contract with a feeling as potent as fear, which he had come to know as desire.

Once a week he spoke to Lily. He timed his call so that she would be off stage at the end of the performance. He telephoned the numbers she had sent to him, ticking each stage door off the list as she moved steadily away from him: from Southampton to Bournemouth, to Poole, further and further away, travelling westwards down the coast. Behind her voice, on the crackly line, he could hear doors banging and people calling to each other. He knew she was only ever half-attentive. Once he found himself talking to one of the other girls as they teased Lily about his phone call. All day Stephen would plan what to say when he spoke with her, but then he would find Lily morose and quiet after a bad performance, or bubbling with joy after a good evening and a delivery of flowers. She was out of his control. Stephen hated her being beyond his control.

'Is Ma well?' was the only question Lily would always ask. And after he had told her that Helen was well and busy he knew that he would lose her attention, and that however long he tried to spin out their talk Lily's mind was no longer with him. She was, he thought, too frivolous, too light and above all too young to be trusted far from home. If he had not loved her so much Stephen thought he would have hated her.

On the fourth Thursday of Lily's absence there was a change. The shop was shuttered and dark when Stephen called at seven o'clock in the evening. He knocked on the door for some moments and stepped back to look up at the little flat. The windows were all in darkness, and no light came on at his knock.

'She's poorly,' a woman volunteered from the red brick doorway beside the shop. 'She's got the flu and they've taken her to the Royal. Proper poorly she is.'

Stephen stepped forward eagerly. 'Very bad? Should her daughter be sent for?'

The woman nodded. 'Yes, but none of us know where she is. She's on tour with one of the music halls. And Helen's mind was wandering with the fever. She kept asking for her but we didn't know where to send.'

'I know.' Stephen found his hands were shaking. 'I know where she is. Should I fetch her?'

The woman nodded. 'The doctor said she'd best come home. But none of us knew where to send. We didn't even know which town she was in. And Helen couldn't tell us. It's the Spanish flu, you know, she'll be lucky if she pulls through.'

Stephen turned away and strode to the Argyll. 'The Royal Hospital,' he said shortly to Coventry. 'My luck's turned at last.'

He was not allowed to see Helen. The ward sister spoke to him in the corridor outside the ward. She said that the daughter should certainly be sent for. The mother was sick, but not in immediate danger. She was asking for her daughter and the girl should be there.

Stephen drove home and found Muriel while Coventry packed for them both.

'I have to go to Sidmouth, I'll take the car and Coventry.'

Muriel dropped her sewing into her lap. 'Sidmouth? But why, Stephen? What has happened?'

'The girl I was seeing, Lily Pears, her mother is ill and asking for her. I'm going to fetch her. I should be back late tomorrow night, or early Saturday. Depends on the roads.'

Muriel followed Stephen out into the hall. Coventry was holding his coat out for him. 'Stephen . . .'

He turned and she saw his face was alight with a kind of wild excitement. Coventry too had the same keen expression, as if something at last was about to happen. As if all the long months of the peace had been wasted time. As if they were both only half-alive during the peace, as if sudden action were the only joy they could feel.

'She's not the sort of girl you want to get involved with,' Muriel said rapidly and softly. She put her hand on Stephen's arm to draw him back to the sitting room. 'Send her a telegram, my dear, that's all you need to do. You shouldn't go and fetch her. It's not right.'

Stephen brushed her hand off his arm. He hardly even saw her. 'I love her,' he said simply. 'I hope she'll marry me. Of course I'm going to fetch her.'

He turned abruptly away from her and ran up the stairs, taking the steps two at a time. His father's room was in half-darkness, lit only by the light from the dying fire, but his father was still awake. He looked towards the door as Stephen burst in and his dark gaze focused on Stephen's sudden vitality.

Stephen stepped up to the bed. 'I'm going away for a couple of days. I'm going to fetch a girl I know. Her mother's sick and she should come home.' Stephen's smile was radiant. 'I like her awfully, Father. I'll bring her to see you. I think you'd like her too.'

He moved towards the door. 'I've got to go now,' he said. Then he suddenly checked himself and came back into the room. He picked up his father's limp hand from its place on the counterpane. He held it and looked into his father's immobile face. 'I've been a bastard. I've been a bastard to you. If Lily will have me, it'll all be different. I'll be different.'

Stephen swung from the room. His mother, waiting at the foot of the stairs, watched him run down and thought, for the first time since he had come home, that he moved with the grace of a young man, that he was still a young man, one who could fall in love and flirt and chatter and laugh. He kissed her on the cheek as he went past, hardly checking his stride, and then he and Coventry were down the front steps and out through the garden gate. Coventry slung the suitcases into the boot of the car and Stephen got into the front passenger seat beside him. As the car moved away she caught a glimpse of their faces, as excited as boys.

'Coast road,' Stephen said, consulting the map book. 'D'you know it? Southampton, Bournemouth, Weymouth, Sidmouth. Quite a run.'

Coventry nodded.

'We'll do it in watches,' Stephen decided. 'You drive for four hours now, wake me at midnight. I'll take twelve till four and then wake you. What about petrol? Are there cans in the boot?'

Coventry nodded again, watching the road as they drove along the front, careful of summer visitors in their best clothes returning to their hotels after admiring the sunset over the sea.

'Provisions?'

Coventry jerked his head to the rear seat. There was a picnic basket half-shut on a loaf of bread and a ham, a flask for a hot drink and some apples. Coventry had raided the kitchen as casually as an invading army.

'Should get there around midday, maybe earlier,' Stephen said, scanning the map. 'Catch her before she goes to the theatre anyway. Pack her bags, bring her home. Home by midnight or so.'

He stretched luxuriously in his seat and shut his eyes. 'Wake me at midnight,' he ordered, and he fell instantly asleep.

Chapter Nine

Lily loved Weymouth even more than Bournemouth. The town was smaller and the audiences less smart but the countryside around the little resort was spectacularly beautiful with wide sheep-grazed fields interlinked with winding hedged country lanes and scatterings of prosperous grey stonebuilt villages. Charlie borrowed a motorbike and sidecar from one of the stage crew and on their day off, Sunday in the first week of June, drove Lily out along the coast. Lily, very daring, wore a pair of slacks lent to her by Madge.

'Keep your legs in the sidecar, you'll cause a riot, you hussy,' Charlie said tolerantly.

Lily had hesitated. 'D'you like them? I'm not sure if they're all right to wear out of doors.'

'We'll go down secluded lanes, all you will frighten is cows.'

They took a picnic with them. Lily, remembering the Argyll and the grand picnic set, laughed when she saw Charlie's doorstep sandwiches of cheese and pickle in brown paper bags, and a bottle of lemonade for them to drink.

'You're a good deal too choosy.' Charlie spread his feast on Lily's outspread head scarf. They had stopped at the crest of a cliff, looking out to sea. Below them a little white chalk path wound down to a bay. The waters were a clear light-filled blue, so clean that Lily could see the shadows of seaweed shifting in the currents and sometimes the flicker of a school of dark fish.

'The trouble is you've been spoiled,' Charlie pronounced.

'I have not! I like cheese and pickle. I can like posh things and ordinary things. I can like both.'

Lily took a sandwich and bit into it. Beside them, at clifftop level, a kittiwake gull riding the thermals from the beach below them wheeled inland, its bright black eyes on Lily and her sandwich. Lily took a piece of crust and flung it upwards.

'There you go, wasting good food!' Charlie said instantly.

Lily chuckled easily. 'I didn't waste it, I gave it to a seagull. Seagulls have a right to be fed I suppose.'

Charlie unstoppered the lemonade and took a swig from the bottle before wiping the mouth and handing it to Lily. 'Forgot cups.'

'That's all right.'

Lily drank and handed the bottle back to him. 'D'you think Sylvia de Charmante is really good? I've watched and watched her and I can't see what she does that is so much better than anyone else.'

'Better than you, you mean?'

Lily flushed and shot a shy look at Charlie. 'Well yes, actually. I know I've got loads to learn and everything but . . .'

He nodded. 'She's no better than you, in fact her voice is weaker and she's much less musical. But she got herself a name during the war and she'll trade on that for the rest of her life. I saw her once, she did one of those recruitment shows with a film of the Western Front and free beer at the bar, and some songs and a kiss for the lads who went up and signed on. Poor fools.'

'Did many go?'

Charlie shrugged. 'A dozen or so, I suppose. It made little difference in the end. Once conscription came in everyone had to go. It just made the difference to what time you got there.'

'I'm glad you weren't there for long,' Lily said. 'I don't like to hear about it. It spoiled everything for me when I was a girl. The streets had to be kept dark, and it was always cold. Everyone's dads and brothers went away. Everyone was short tempered and there was never enough money.'

Charlie nodded. 'Poor Lily,' he said mockingly.

Lily threw the rest of the crust to the gull and lay back on the short springy turf. 'I know,' she said. 'I'm supposed to think I was lucky because I was a girl, and my dad died quickly and didn't come home a cripple, and my ma had the shop. But she never thought there was any point to the war. Not from the very beginning. And so I never thought it was so wonderful either. And when the kids in the streets did pageants, or the girls did knitting, or collected newspapers or cloths or whatever, I always thought that it was a great big lie. And I thought Kitchener was a bully, I hated his face on the posters everywhere you went. He used to give me nightmares.'

Charlie chuckled. 'You're preaching to a convert, Lily, I never liked the man either. I volunteered to go because I thought it was a good cause and that Germany had to be stopped. I bought it almost at once –'

'Where were you hurt?'

'Lungs.'

'Did it hurt very bad?'

'Ohhh.' Charlie flapped his hand at the memory. 'Pretty bad. And then I came home and trained more poor fools in a dismal camp at the back of beyond in Wales for the rest of the war.' Charlie lay back and closed his eyes. 'Rhyll. It feels like a long, long time ago now.'

'And Sylvia de Charmante made her name out of it,' Lily pursued.

Charlie chuckled. 'Yes. You won't have a chance like that, but I've got an idea for you, Lil. When we get back to Portsmouth I may have a new job. I may get the post of music director at the Kings.'

Lily sat up at once. 'Golly.'

Charlie smiled. 'Yes indeed. You may call me Mr Smith. I'll see if I can get you an audition as an act. They'll put a show together, like this one, and then do a two- or three-theatre tour with it. It's a different group of theatres and it's Variety – not old-fashioned music hall. So you'll have a chance to do a little bit more.'

'Was that your idea? That you told Ma and me about?'

Charlie nodded.

'Why are you so nice to me?' Lily burst out. 'You picked me out of the chorus line and asked me to sing, and then you tried out your choir boy idea using me, so I've got an act of my own now and billing on the posters. And now you're thinking about something new. Why are you so good to me?'

Charlie's arm was over his eyes, blocking out the overhead sun. He raised it slightly and squinted at her. 'Because,' he said equably.

'No, why?'

He grinned. 'Because I choose to.'

Lily leaned over him and put her hand, tentatively, on his chest. 'Because you like me?'

Charlie took his arm from his face and put his hand on top of Lily's.

'Yes, I like you a lot.'

There was a long silence. The gull, weaving back over them, cast a fleeting shadow and cried a short mournful cry.

Lily dropped her fair head to Charlie's upturned, passive face. The sleek bob of her hair fell forward and brushed both his cheeks. Lily hesitated, her lips an inch above his. Charlie made no gesture at all. Lily bent a little lower and kissed him.

Charlie's other hand came behind Lily's waist and held her gently. Lily raised her head and sighed, scanning his dark face. Charlie smiled up at her, still unmoving.

'Charlie . . .'

He put his hand up and covered her lips. 'Don't chatter, Lil. You'll only say things that you'll regret.'

Lily shot a puzzled look at him as he sat up. She leaned towards him, expecting him to put his arms around her, but he got to his feet and put out his hand and pulled her up.

'Let's go and have a paddle,' he said.

He led the way down the little path, Lily slipping and breaking into a little run with an affected shriek of alarm behind him. She wanted him to turn to catch her and hold her in his arms but Charlie strode on, hands determinedly in his pockets, down the steep zig-zag path to the sea. He reached the water's edge while Lily was still hopping and limping over the stones in her little shoes. He picked up some flat stones from around his feet and skimmed them across the waves.

Lily came up beside him and put her hand on the small of his back as he stood, watching the waves.

'Charlie . . .'

He gave a sudden wordless exclamation and then turned and caught her into his arms, crushing her against him, her face into his shoulder, his cheek pressed against her fair head. Lily, unable to move, hardly able to breathe, stood motionless, half-dizzy with sudden desire.

As soon as he slackened his grip, Lily flung her arms around his neck and raised her face but Charlie did not kiss her. He held her gently, scanning her face. Lily was flushed, her eyes bright.

'I thought you said spooning was beastly and you were never going to do it with anybody?'

Lily caught her breath. 'This is different, I feel . . .' She broke off. 'Charlie, will you kiss me?'

His smile down at her eager face was very rueful. 'I suppose I will,' he said with mock reluctance, then he bent his dark head and his lips met hers.

Lily felt herself melt with rising desire. Her conscious mind noted that her legs felt suddenly weak and her whole body was longing for the touch of Charlie all over. She tightened her arms around his neck, pressing his mouth still harder down on hers. She heard herself make a tiny noise, a little moan, and suddenly understood what her mother had meant about getting carried away. Lily felt that Charlie could have carried her away in a handcart and she would not have objected. More than anything else in the world she wanted to lie down and feel the weight of Charlie along the length of her body. She bent slightly at the knees.

Charlie stayed determinedly upright. After a few minutes he released her, and then put his arm around her waist to steady her. Lily's eyelids fluttered open slowly. She looked around at the blue moving sea, the shingle beach and Charlie's tight smile.

'And that's our lot,' Charlie said gently. 'Your ma would skin me alive if she knew I'd brought you out into the country and then kissed you.'

'No she wouldn't, she likes you.'

'She might like me when she sees me taking care of you at the theatre. She'd like me a lot less if she knew I took advantage of you when we're away on tour.'

'But you didn't.' Lily, finding her legs still a little unsteady, sat on the shingle and looked up at Charlie. 'I took advantage of you.'

'Well, you're a forward hussy,' Charlie said pleasantly.

'And you won't catch me in a weak moment again.'

He turned his back to Lily and stooped and picked out another flat stone. 'Watch this,' he said. He threw it with a smooth sideways lob at the tops of the waves and the stone skipped. 'Four! Four jumps. Bet you can't do better than that!'

'Bet you I can. I spent my childhood on Southsea beach, remember.'

Lily scrambled to her feet and picked a stone. Feet astride, frowning as she took aim, she threw it at the waves. It skipped along from crest to crest. 'Three, four, five!' Lily yelled, diverted. 'Beat five if you can!'

Charlie picked another stone but it sank on four. Lily's next was too heavy and dropped down at three. They threw for a few more moments.

'It's hot,' Lily said. 'I wish I'd brought my swimming costume.'

Charlie shot a quick look along the cliff. The skyline was deserted for miles in both directions, the only access to the cove was down the little zig-zag path. 'You could swim in your camiknickers,' he said. 'I've got a towel in the sidecar.'

Lily was unbuttoning her shirt. 'Will you swim?'

Charlie grinned. 'Why not? I'll get that towel first.'

He set off up the cliff path as Lily stepped out of Madge's trousers and folded them carefully, laying them on the shingle. She picked her way down to the water's edge over the knobbly stones. Charlie, climbing up the path, heard her shriek as a wave splashed her thighs. He turned and looked back.

Lily was wearing old-fashioned cotton camiknickers. They clung to her slim long back and as a wave splashed her he could see the smooth lovely outline of her buttocks. He watched her for a little while, saw her confident plunge into a wave and the strength of her stroke. When he turned to walk the last few yards to the motorcycle, his face was grim.

Lily was a small dot heading out to the horizon when Charlie arrived back at the beach with a large stripy towel. He shouted to her, and when she turned, waved her inwards. He stripped down to his shorts and waded into the sea and swam out towards her.

'Going for France, Lil?'

Lily pointed to a tiny island, weed-covered, which stood in the centre of the bay. 'I was going to that.'

Charlie shook his head. 'Too far,' he said firmly. 'You will keep an old man happy and stay within your depth.'

Lily made a face at him and duck-dived. He saw the gleam of greenish fair hair underwater and then felt a tickle around his toes. When Lily burst up out of the water she was laughing so much that she choked. She turned and swam away from him and Charlie gave chase.

For an hour they played in the deep water and then they swam inshore and lazed in the shallows. The receding tide had uncovered a little shelf of sand studded with small pink shells. Lily, rolled over and back by the incoming waves, collected a handful, and then got up.

'You can have first go with the towel,' Charlie said. 'I'll have another quick swim.'

He turned his back on her and went out to sea and swam until he judged she would be dressed. When he came back inshore she was waiting for him with the towel spread out as if she would wrap him up in it. Charlie took it from her hands, fending her off, and skipped over the pebbles to his clothes. Lily openly watched him as he dried himself and pulled on his shirt and trousers.

'You've got lovely skin.' Her voice was lazy. Charlie sensed her desire as sweet as perfume.

He grinned. 'Smooth as a baby's bottom.'

'My dad was hairy all over. I don't like that. But you've got a lovely smooth back.'

'I want a cup of tea,' Charlie announced. 'Did you see a tea shop at any of those villages we came through?'

Lily thought. 'Wasn't there one at the post office, in that last little place?'

'Excellent,' Charlie said. 'You may race me up the cliff.'

Lily started out at a good pace but stopped halfway up, panting and holding her side. Charlie, at a steady jog, trotted past her and overtook her. He slowed and they reached the top neck and neck.

'An honourable draw,' Charlie said.

He scrunched the paper bags, put the empty lemonade bottle in the sidecar and shook the crumbs from Lily's headscarf. 'Sidmouth tomorrow. Have you ever been there, Lil?'

She shook her head. 'I've never been anywhere but day-trips from home. I just love it. Is Sidmouth pretty – like here?'

Charlie nodded and helped Lily into the sidecar. 'It's pretty all along here,' he said. He kickstarted the engine and it roared into life.

'Tea for two!' he yelled.

The motorbike swung out into the lane and cruised along. Charlie relished the smell of the hedges in bloom and the flowers on the roadside. Over the noise of the engine he could hear Lily singing: '. . . a boy for you, a girl for me . . .'

She looked up and smiled at him with her whole heart in her eyes. Charlie, despite himself, winked at her and smiled back.

The theatre in Sidmouth was the smallest they had played on the tour. The bar at the back of the theatre was open to the auditorium. If they were rowdy in the bar then the audience would turn around in their seats and yell at them. Sometimes fights broke out. Lily was in a state of utter terror at going before them to sing a sacred song but Charlie had been right when he had judged the deep sentimental streak in the most unruly English crowd. And Lily did not realize how captivating she was as a choir boy.

They listened to Lily with attention and they clapped warmly and long at the end of her song. Sylvia de Charmante, on the other hand, received whistles and catcalls and loud indecent suggestions. She rode the wave of noise like an old trooper. Nothing upset her. Lily, waiting in the wings, found that she had her hands up over her mouth in horror at the lewdness of the shouts from the bar at the back but Sylvia swayed in time to the music and sang a little louder to drown out the heckling.

'She doesn't answer them,' Charlie pointed out to Lily. They were between shows, sitting at the bar at the back of the theatre drinking lemonade. 'Sometimes you can go downstage and give as good as you get. I've seen people do that with a really sticky house. But generally you do better just to sing over the top of the noise and leave it to the audience whether they listen to you or not.'

'I should never have the nerve.'

'You'd better learn to have the nerve. You've got to be able to sing for the drunks at the bar as well as the ladies in the dress circle, Lil. If you're a performer you have to grab them whoever they are.'

Lily nodded. 'I'll learn.'

'Let's try out that new act for you,' Charlie said. He led the way through the darkened auditorium. A cleaning woman was sweeping under the seats, grunting with the effort. She straightened up to let them pass, watching them without interest. Charlie opened the little door to the orchestra pit and waved Lily up to the stage.

'D'you know "Burlington Bertie", Lil?'

'Yes, of course.'

'I want you to do it. We'll dress you in a gent's morning suit, flower in your pocket, umbrella, all the props. Just sing it through for now. See how it sounds.'

Charlie shuffled through some music in his case. 'Here's the words,' he said, handing up a sheet. 'Off you go. Just sing it. No actions.'

Lily stood still as he instructed and sang the little song, 'I'm Burlington Bertie, I rise at ten thirty...', concentrating only on the tune and the light syncopation of the rhythm.

'Ever see Vesta Tilley do it?' Charlie demanded when they reached the end of the song.

Lily shook her head.

'She did it like a man. She walked like a man, she moved her hands like a man. She had this big bust on her, and her waistcoat stretched over it and then she went on stage and sang and moved exactly like a man. People loved it. It was really...' Charlie flapped his hand, seeking the right word. 'Contradictory. Entertaining.'

'I don't know I can do that.'

Charlie shook his head. 'No! No! It's been done! You never do what's been done already. You don't want to be the second Vesta Tilley, you want to be a wholly original Lily Valance. You do the song differently. How would you do it?'

Lily thought. 'It'd have to be in boy's clothes. It's a song about being a man. I'd have to do it in man's clothes.'

Charlie nodded, waited for more.

'It's almost a sad song,' Lily suddenly said. 'I don't know how to do it but in a way it's a song about someone pretending to be something he isn't. Someone with nothing to do. It comes over funny, but if you actually think about his life – it's lonely.'

Charlie snapped the fingers on both hands. 'Jackpot! You try it!'

He played the introductory notes, Lily took a fold of her blouse in each hand, as a man holds the lapels of his coat, and strolled across the stage. She sang with a sort of lingering wistfulness, her clear voice very sweet on the simple tune.

'Magic,' Charlie said softly to himself over the keyboard. 'Burlington Bertie as one of the lost generation. No real friends, no-one who knows what it was like. One of the ones who came back, who's learning to envy those who won't ever come back. A young man who has buried young men. Magic.'

Lily stood downstage, looking down at Charlie in the pit. 'It felt really sad,' she said. 'But I don't know how to do it.'

'That'll do nicely for a try-out.' Charlie hid his delight. 'That's all I wanted for today. Just to hear it through.'

Madge stepped out on to the stage. 'Would you hear something through of mine?'

'All requests graciously received,' Charlie said with patience. 'What did you want to do, Madge?'

'It's a ragtime song. I want to have it as an audition piece. It's called "Red Hot Baby".'

'"Red Hot Baby",' Charlie repeated. 'Can you count, Madge? Can you count beats to a bar?'

'Not really,' Madge said cheerfully. 'But if you play it over to me and sing it to me then I can remember it.'

Charlie took the music and set it in the stand. He counted Madge in. She missed the introduction. He played it through again and nodded her when to start. This time she hit the beat and stayed with it, more or less, till the end of the song. She had a thin little voice but she could keep a tune, and she danced with a lot of energy, swinging her hips and winking at the empty auditorium.

The cleaning woman wasted one glance on all of them and carried on with her work. Charlie clattered into the finale and did a mock drum-roll with the bass notes.

'Not bad!' he said. 'Have you ever heard coon-shouting, Madge?'

Madge shook her head.

'You don't worry about the tune at all, you just shout as though you are hoarse over the top of the music and dance like you do – only more so.'

Lily widened her eyes. 'She'll get arrested.'

Madge gurgled. 'Divine!'

'Once more?' Charlie offered. 'Try it without singing the tune, Madge, try just talking it. Leave the tune to me, but make sure you hit the rhythm of it. You've got to get the beat of it – the rest can look after itself.'

Madge took a couple of steps upstage and cakewalked her way to the front. Her speaking voice was lower than her singing, huskier. At once the song became compelling, sexual. Madge winked at Charlie and went into a few dance steps, wiggling her bottom with a swing of her hip on each beat. At the end of the song she stretched out her arms and frankly jiggled her breasts and then finished with her arms upflung and her head thrown back.

Lily applauded with her mouth open. Charlie roared with laughter.

'A star is born, Madge! That's the way to do it! You want an exotic kind of set, like a speakeasy or a club, and some kind of tight dress with a big slit up the front. You'll be a huge hit!'

'Will you suggest it to Mr Brett?' Madge asked breathlessly. 'He listens to you. He let you put Lily in even though he didn't think it would work.'

'If someone drops out and makes a space, I'll mention it to him. And it'd be a good audition piece for you, Madge. It's a real knock 'em dead number.'

Madge beamed. 'Will you rehearse me again sometime? Like you do with Lily?'

Charlie smiled. 'I have no favourites, ladies. Of course I will.'

Madge blew him a kiss for thanks and then slipped her hand through Lily's arm and led her off the stage. 'Liar,' she said under her breath. 'He does have favourites. You.'

They went to their dressing room. It was empty, the other girls had gone out for tea. Lily dropped into the broken-springed armchair, the only furniture in the room. Madge sat before the mirror and scowled at her reflection.

'Are you courting?' she asked. 'I can't tell with you two. He takes you out a lot and you went out for the day on Sunday but then he treats you like he treats the rest of us when we're all together.'

Lily slung her legs over the arm of the chair and picked at the frayed edge of the loose cover. 'I don't know,' she said. 'I think he's wonderful. Sometimes I feel like he really likes me, and then other times I don't know. He makes a big fuss of my singing and he's really taught me a lot. But he'd do the same for you, I think.'

'He doesn't take me out for a day in the country,' Madge observed. 'Did he kiss you?'

Lily flushed. 'Sort of. Actually, Madge, I don't know what to do. I've never had a proper boyfriend and Charlie is so . . .'

'So what?'

'When he looks at me,' Lily said slowly. 'When he looks at me and smiles and his eyes are so dark and his smile is so . . .'

'Well?'

'I just want to take all my clothes off and crawl all over him!' Lily said defiantly. 'I do! When he smiles at me I don't care what I do. And I don't care what anyone thinks.'

Madge shrieked with laughter. 'Lily!' she said. 'Your ma would go mad!'

Lily's face was alight with mischief and desire. 'I don't care! I don't care what she would think. I don't care what anyone thinks. I must be in love with him. I must be. This must be what it feels like.'

Madge nodded. 'Head over heels,' she said.

Lily looked at her wonderingly. 'D'you think so? Is this it? I'm in love?'

Madge nodded.

'Just think of that!' Lily said. 'I'm in love with Charlie Smith.'

'But what about him?'

Lily frowned and picked at the threads of the armchair cover again. 'I don't know,' she said. 'He kissed me on the beach and he held me really tight. But then he said we shouldn't. That my ma would be angry. And then he didn't touch me for the rest of the day.'

'He thinks of you as a little kid,' Madge advised. 'He knows your ma and he dressed you up in the choir boy costume. He thinks of you as a little girl still. You'll have to show him you're a woman if you want him to take you seriously.'

Lily's dark blue eyes were huge. 'How?'

Madge shrugged and then giggled. 'If I felt like you do I'd wait till everyone had gone to bed and then I'd sneak down the corridor and just get into his bed.'

Lily gave a short delighted scream and clapped her hand over her mouth. 'I'd never dare!' she said. 'What if he threw me out? What if he was angry?'

Madge shook her head. 'He wouldn't be angry. There isn't a man in England who would be angry! He might say you were too young or that your ma wouldn't like it but at least you'd be there – wouldn't you? And he'd have to do something!'

'He might tell me he doesn't like me,' Lily said.

'He won't say that,' Madge replied. 'Anyone can see that he's crazy about you. But he won't say so. You want to move him on a bit, Lil. Get him going. There's only a fortnight left of the tour and then you might never work with him again. If you want him, you'd better catch him while you can.'

Chapter Ten

L ily walked her way through the evening performance and was white and silent at supper at the digs. Even the conjuror noticed it. 'Have you got a gyppy tum, darling?' he asked. 'I can let you have a drop of brandy if it would settle it. I happen to have a little bottle in my room.'

Lily flushed scarlet while Madge snorted on a laugh. 'No, no, I'm fine,' Lily said. 'Just a bit tired.'

'Better go to bed early then,' Madge said with a wealth of meaning.

Lily shot a reproachful look at her. 'I'm fine,' she said again.

After dinner had been cleared away and the teapot served and Madge had poured everyone a cup, the cast started drifting off to their rooms. In the first weeks of the tour they had often gone out after supper, to clubs or late-opening pubs. But as they had moved further and further west the towns had become smaller, and even in June at the start of the holiday season there were few late-night bars. They would still go out on a Saturday night, booking a table for all of them and going out as a gang. But in the middle of the week even the chorus girls would go to bed after the late supper and sleep in until midday.

Lily lay wakefully in her bed. She shared her bedroom with Susie, who had sat at the mirror for ten minutes, creaming her face, and was now fast asleep. She had a little travelling clock by the bed and Lily could see it in the moonlight if she leaned up. She had promised herself that she would go to Charlie's room at midnight. The clock said five minutes past and Lily still had not found the courage to make a move.

The minute hand clicked to six minutes past and Lily sat up in bed. From there she could see her own reflection in the dressing table mirror: the smooth bobbed hair, her big dark eyes and the prosaic candy-stripe of her pyjamas. Lily thought with envy of Sylvia de Charmante's lace-trimmed negligee. Charlie would probably take one look at her in her faded hand-me-down pyjamas and laugh aloud. Lily grimaced at the mirror and swung her bare feet to the cold oilcloth floor.

On the dressing table was Susie's turquoise and gold bottle of eau de cologne. With a guilty glance at the girl fast asleep in her bed, Lily put a generous dab behind each ear, down her neck, and then tipped a chilly rivulet which ran down between her breasts under her pyjama jacket. She screwed the little metal cap back on, and tiptoed for the door.

It creaked as it opened and Lily froze, expecting Susie to wake and call out. Nothing happened. Susie turned over in her bed and stayed asleep. Lily shut the door cautiously behind her and crept down the corridor.

There was a narrow strip of red and blue patterned carpet over the stained wood floorboards. Lily slid her bare feet cautiously down the carpet runner, flinching from boards which creaked as they received her weight. Charlie's room was at the back of the boarding house, near the bathroom. If anyone should open their door and see her, Lily could say that she was going to the toilet. Only her intent face and the strong waft of eau de cologne would deny her story.

Lily reached Charlie's door and put her hand on the door knob. It turned easily under her touch. 'Oh blimey,'

Lily said miserably and stepped into the room and shut the door behind her.

The curtains were drawn open and the room half-lit by moonlight. Lily could see Charlie lying on his back, one hand behind his head, the other hand outflung. He was wearing pyjamas but the buttons of the jacket were undone. Lily could see his pulse beating steadily and unhurried at his throat, and the smooth skin of his chest. She felt her longing to touch him rise up like a fever and obliterate her nervousness. As she watched his eyelids flicker as he dreamed, and his chest rise and fall with his steady confident breathing, she knew that whatever it cost her in embarrassment or even shame, she had to feel the skin of his chest against her face. She had to lie beside him. Even if it were only for a moment. Even if it were only once.

Lily untied the cord of her pyjama trousers and dropped them to the floor, undid the buttons of her jacket and shrugged it off. Then she lifted the bedclothes and slid into bed beside Charlie.

He did not wake at first. He moved over to the far side of the bed as if to make room for her and he smiled in his sleep as if he welcomed her. He stretched out a hand and touched her shoulder, and, as if he had been shaken awake by the sense of that smooth skin under his fingertips, his eyes flew open and he said at once: 'Oh my God, Lil! You'd better go.'

Lily didn't move. She lay on her side, her head on his pillow, her eyes fixed on his face, and said nothing.

Charlie flinched away to the far side of the bed and gathered his pyjama jacket around his body. 'Lily, you must go!' he said again. He passed a hand quickly over his face, to rub his sleep away. 'I can't believe you're here.'

Lily extended a hand cautiously, like someone reaching out to touch a strange animal. She put her fingers on the base of his throat where she had seen his pulse beating steadily as he slept. Under her touch she could feel his pulse speeding up. Lily smiled. She no longer felt like a young girl, a silly girl, with an infatuation for a man who cared nothing for her. She felt his pulse thudding faster at her touch and she knew he desired her.

'I love you,' she said wonderingly. 'I couldn't bear for you not to know it. I've loved you from the moment I first met you.'

Charlie sat up in the bed, drew up his knees, and rested his head on his crossed arms, his whole body armouring itself against her. 'Lily, this is crazy,' he said. 'You must get out of my bed and go back to your own room and we'll talk about it in the morning.'

Lily shook her head. 'No,' she said simply. She sat up beside him. The sheet slid away from her and Charlie could see the smooth pale skin of her shoulders and the curve of her breasts.

'This is very unfair.'

Lily chuckled irresistibly. Charlie felt himself smiling in response.

'Put your arm around me,' she commanded.

He put his arm around her and she leaned her fair head on his shoulder. He could feel the warmth of her skin through his thin pyjama jacket, he sensed her nakedness and he felt the start of the long ache of his pain.

'Don't you care for me at all?' Lily asked.

Unconsciously his grip tightened. 'Don't think that,' he said softly. 'I do care for you.'

Lily turned her face up to him. 'I don't mean like a friend, or a pupil. I want you to love me. Like a lover.'

Charlie's face was dark with tension. 'You don't understand,' he said softly. 'You're too young, Lil. You don't know what you're asking. And I cannot . . .'

Lily tipped her head back. In the moonlight the smooth

column of her neck was pale, her breasts emerged from the rumpled bedclothes. Charlie, despite himself, put a hand to her cheek, her chin, stroked down the sensuous line of her neck, cupped her breast in his hand. Lily put her arm around his neck and drew his head down to kiss her. They slid down into the pillows together and Charlie kissed her face hungrily, like a man snatching at a meal; kissed her lips and her closed eyelids, kissed her ears and her neck, kissed her breasts and then lipped tenderly, and then more roughly, at her nipples. Lily moaned very quietly and arched her back, reaching up for his touch. Charlie's arms held her close. Lily buried her face in his neck. She could smell the clean smell of his hair, the tang of his sweat, she could smell the overpowering scent of warmed eau de cologne. Charlie sighed and then rolled on top of her, Lily opened her legs and wrapped them around his thighs, tightened her arms around his back and arched her body upwards to meet him.

'Oh yes,' she said.

As if that word of assent broke a spell, Charlie wrenched himself away from her and flung himself to the edge of the bed. He threw back the covers and got out of bed, not even looking at Lily.

'It's not possible, Lil,' he said tightly. 'Please believe me. This is not possible.'

He picked up her pyjamas from the floor and thrust them at her. 'Put these on. Get them on, Lil, I won't speak to you until you're dressed.'

'I . . .'

'Get dressed!' he ordered angrily.

He flung himself to the hearthrug before the gas fire and fumbled with matches. He turned the brass tap for the gas and with a little pop-popping the flame rippled along the base of the fire and the white spiky bones grew pink and then orange and then glowed a steady red.

Lily fastened the buttons of her pyjama jacket with shaking hands. She slid out of bed and pulled on the trousers. She was scarlet with shame. Then she sat on the edge of the bed like a naughty child sent to her room as a punishment, with nothing to do but to wait for adult forgiveness.

'I'm dressed,' she said in a small voice.

Charlie turned around and saw her stricken face.

'Oh, come here,' he said, holding one arm out to her. Lily tumbled off the bed to the hearthrug and into his arms. He held her firmly, affectionately. He patted her back as if he were consoling her for some little hurt. Then he seated her in the chair beside the fire and sat back on the hearthrug, at a little distance from her so that he could see her face.

'I'll have to tell you something which I prefer to keep private,' he said. 'Will you promise to tell no-one?'

Lily nodded.

'It's about my injury, from the war.'

Lily thought of half his lung missing, and then remembered the smooth skin of his back, the silky warmth of his chest, his run up the cliff path when he had raced her to the motorbike, and how he had reached the top without being breathless. 'You said you were injured in the lungs.'

Charlie shook his head. 'I was injured in the groin,' he said precisely. His face was stiff, the words forced out. 'Castrated. I'm not a proper man, Lily. I couldn't ever be your husband. I took a piece of shell across my thighs. It took out my balls and half my penis.' His face was grim, he was forcing the words out. 'We were trapped in a shellhole, heads down into the earth. Half of the men took wounds in their legs and buttocks. It was a pitiful day – a long, long day. We were on a night patrol which went wrong, we were pinned down in no-man's-land from dawn till twilight. They couldn't get stretchers out to us till dark.'

131

He was silent for a moment then he shook his head at the memory.

'It's a common injury,' he said. 'Fighting over that ground with no shelter. There were a lot of men injured low. It's your instinct to get your head down, to shelter your face. We must have been a funny sight.' His smile was as bitter as gas. 'Our heads ducked down and our bums left out. We must have been a funny sight,' he said again.

Lily put her hand out gently and rested it on the sleeve of his pyjama jacket.

Charlie gave her a brief unhappy smile. 'So I can't give you children, and I can't give you pleasure, normal pleasure,' he said. 'I thought that I might be able to be your friend. But I can offer you nothing more than my friendship.'

Lily said nothing. The fire made a little popping noise and the flames flickered and jumped from orange to yellow. Charlie reached behind Lily's chair and put another sixpence in the meter from a little pile balanced on top of the metal box. The gas flowed steadily again and the bones of the fire glowed.

'I don't care,' Lily said, scarcely taking in what he was saying. 'I love you. Do you love me, Charlie? That's all I want to know.'

He shrugged with a hard smile as if none of it mattered very much at all. 'Oh yes, I love you, Lily. I utterly and absolutely adore you.'

She reached forward at once but he fended her off. 'It doesn't matter – don't you see? It doesn't make any difference. You should marry a man who can give you all the things you deserve. I wouldn't want anything less than that for you. You should have the best. I want the best for you. I don't want you married to a cripple, to half a man.'

Lily shook her head.

'It *does* matter,' Charlie insisted. 'You think now that you love me enough to overlook it. That we could be happy together in spite of it. But you would want children. And you are young and beautiful and passionate. You need a lover, Lil, not half a man. I am not the man for you. I am of no use to any woman.'

He had been looking at the prosaic flicker of the fire but now he glanced up at Lily's face. She was very still but her face was shiny with the wetness of many tears. He pulled her down beside him on the hearthrug and held her close.

'If I loved you any less, then I would marry you and make you stay with me,' he said softly into her hair. 'If I loved you any less I would marry you and keep you and try to convince you that children don't matter, that making love doesn't matter. But I love you so much that I won't do that to you.' He took a breath. 'I made up my mind when I was first injured. I wouldn't do that to any woman. I'll even play ragtime at your wedding.'

Lily shook her head and turned to argue but Charlie kissed her into silence. Her mouth was wet and salty. He took the sleeve of his pyjamas and wiped her face very gently.

'I'm not a child,' Lily said.

He nodded. 'I know it. You're a beautiful and desirable woman, Lil. And I wish to God that my luck was different. There have been times when I've wished that the shell had killed me outright; but I don't think that any more. Not even now – with you in my arms and nothing I can do for you. There are things that I have had to put from me and forget, and there are things which I can still have and enjoy. I cannot be your lover but I'm damned if I'll spend my whole life regretting that. I didn't come out of that shellhole and on to that stretcher and through that bloody dressing station where young men – children – were dying all around me, to spend the rest of my life wishing it away. I *won't* grieve, Lil. Don't you grieve either.'

Her young bright courage rose at that, as he had thought it would. She pushed back her hair. 'But you *do* love me?'

He smiled. 'Oh, you're a woman all right! Yes. I love you, and I will never love anyone else like I love you tonight. Will that do for you? I never *have* loved anyone as I feel for you. And I have never told anyone else about this – my injury. I love you and I trust you, Lil. And I'll help you with your career when I can, and sometimes we'll work together and we'll always be friends. Will that do?'

Lily nodded, and tried to smile.

'But I won't stand in your light. I won't overshadow you. You have to go forward. You'll meet other men and you'll like them and one of them you will love. You'll love him even more than you love me now. That's how it has to be, that's how I want it. I want you to promise me that you'll love and marry when you wish. Don't hold back for me. Because I won't thank you for it.'

Lily nodded forlornly, her face strained, dark shadows under her eyes.

'You look all in,' Charlie said. 'That's enough for tonight. We'll talk more tomorrow if you want, sweetheart. But you go now. Off to bed with you.'

'Can't I stay here? Just for a few moments? Can't we cuddle up together and just hold each other?'

He pulled her to her feet and settled her into his bed. He got in beside her, careful that their bodies did not touch. He put his arm around her shoulder and she rested her head on his chest. He lay very still until the steady rhythm of her breathing told him that she was asleep. Only then did his face relax and he felt the warmth of his tears on his own cheeks as he acknowledged the ache in his body where his balls had been, and the pain of his heart, still thudding too fast from impotent desire.

They both jumped awake at the hammering on the front door. Charlie, with an old trained response, was out of his bed and at the bedroom door before he was fully awake.

'Damn. That's torn it,' he said.

Lily slipped out of bed and came to his side.

They could hear the landlady opening the door and the flush of the cistern from the next door bathroom.

'Miss Pears?' the woman said to the caller. 'I think all the girls are still asleep.'

Lily shot a quick anxious look at Charlie. 'You'll have to make a run for it,' he said. 'Try and look as if you're coming out of the bathroom.'

He half-opened the door but then pulled her back behind it as the conjuror's partner saw the door open and said jovially, 'Morning, Charlie! What's all the damned noise about so early?'

'Miss Pears,' said the man clearly from the doorstep. 'It's an emergency.'

'That's Stephen Winters,' Lily hissed. She paused for a moment and then realized. 'My God! It must be my ma.'

She slipped from Charlie's restraining hand, tore open the door and ran to the stairs.

'Stephen!' she called, running downstairs towards him, careless of her striped pyjamas and her rumpled hair. 'Is Ma ill? What's happened?'

Charlie followed to the head of the stairs to listen.

'She's very ill, Lily,' Stephen said. Charlie could hear the triumph in the man's voice, his self-importance. 'She's got Spanish flu. She's at the Royal Infirmary. I drove all night to come and fetch you. I'll take you home to her now.'

Lily turned away from him and looked up the stairs to

Charlie. Stephen followed the direction of her gaze and saw Charlie, dark-jawed and weary, standing at the head of the stairs.

'What should I do?' Lily asked him.

He nodded at Stephen. 'You'd better get dressed and pack, Lil. You'd better go at once.' He spoke past her to Stephen. 'Are you fit to drive back? There are trains.'

Stephen gleamed at him. Despite driving all night he looked glossy with health. Charlie felt rumpled and dissolute, blinking in the late-morning brightness, still aching from the distress of last night.

'I shared the driving with my man,' Stephen said. 'I'll trouble your landlady for some bread and cheese to take with us and we'll be off as soon as Miss Pears is ready.'

Charlie nodded. 'Please, both of you, come in. Mrs Harris will make you some tea and some breakfast. Lil had better have something to eat before she goes as well.'

He waved Stephen into the dining room and retreated to his bedroom, pulled on a pair of trousers and a shirt. He felt better once he was dressed. He went next door to the bathroom and splashed water on his face. His deep-set dark eyes looked at him from the mirror. His face was grim.

Downstairs two of the chorus girls were fluttering around the dining room in their dressing-gowns. Mrs Harris brought in tea and chunky bacon sandwiches thick with butter and dripping with fat. Stephen sat quietly in the midst of all the confusion and excitement and ate hungrily. Coventry ate standing up beside the sideboard. Lily came into the room with her handbag and vanity case. Charlie went up to her bedroom to fetch her suitcase and put it by the front door.

In the dining room the girls were pressing Lily to eat, but all she would have was a slice of bread and butter and a cup of tea.

'Telephone from Portsmouth as soon as you know

what's happening,' Madge instructed. 'Let us know how she is.'

Lily nodded, chewing bread without being able to swallow. She sipped tea. Charlie felt his heart wrenched for her white-faced fear.

'D'you want me to come with you?' he said suddenly, offering the impossible.

Lily looked at him while Stephen covertly watched them both.

'No,' she said gently. 'I know you can't. It's all right. I'm a grown-up now.'

He smiled at her, the tender intimate smile of lovers who have spent the night in each other's arms. 'You are indeed,' he said. 'Be brave, Lil.'

She nodded and ate the last of the slice.

'Time to go,' Stephen said. He pressed his napkin to his moustache and threw it down. Mrs Harris had given him the best linen, Charlie noticed. He drained his tea cup and went towards the door. Coventry loaded the suit-case into the boot of the Argyll and opened the door for Lily. Mrs Harris bustled up from the basement kitchen with a bag of sandwiches and a couple of bottles of ginger beer. Stephen took them with a word of thanks and got into the back seat beside Lily. Coventry slammed his door and started the engine. The girls screamed good wishes to Lily who leaned forward and waved. Charlie met her eyes. She mouthed 'I love you' to him and he nodded and raised a hand in acknowledgement, as the big car drew away from the kerb.

'Isn't he *the dreamiest* man in the world?' Madge demanded as they went back into the house. 'Isn't he just the best?'

'Oh yes,' Charlie agreed. 'Smug bastard.'

137

Chapter Eleven

Stephen did not speak much to Lily during the first part of the drive. After he had told her all he knew of her mother's health they sat in silence, watching the countryside roll by as Coventry drove as quickly as the curving country roads allowed. Stephen's nose prickled. He could smell scent on Lily. He had never smelled perfume on her before. She smelled cheap, like a chorus girl, like a tart. The clarity of his decision, when he had told his mother that he loved Lily, faded away at the girl's real presence, at her smell. She had been warm and rumpled when she had run downstairs. There had been something domestic and repellent about her cheap pyjamas and her ruffled hair and her sleepy face. Stephen wanted Lily as she was when she was on stage as a choir boy, flawless as a china doll. When she had come down the stairs to the front door she had been a warm sleepy sensuous female. It was not just the smell of cheap perfume he disliked, it was the smell of warm skin.

Stephen shook his head. He had not liked the digs, he had not liked Mrs Harris. And most of all he had disliked how Charlie Smith had been at once a part of that world – he had the same dreamy tranced expression as Lily, he too was still warm from a comfortable bed – and at the same time he had been commanding. Stephen had envisaged himself ordering Lily. But she turned at once to Charlie to ask him what she should do. And Charlie somehow had taken control of the whole situation.

Charlie had looked like an enlisted man, a common

man, barefoot, unshaven and scruffy, but even so he had told Lily to pack and sent Stephen and Coventry in for breakfast. Stephen scanned his memory of the man and saw him coming in to the dining room, hastily washed, and saw the long level look exchanged between him and Lily.

He glanced across the back seat at her. Lily was asleep, her head thrown back, her little hat askew. There were dark blue shadows in the delicate skin under her closed eyes. Her face was white, a sprinkling of freckles over her nose showing brown against her pallor. Stephen stared at her, torn between longing and anger. He loved her, he desired her, he wanted to hold her and protect her. He wanted to serve her and keep her. Especially he wanted to keep her well away from that hugger-mugger intimate domesticity that he sensed when she and Charlie had looked at each other and Charlie had decided what she should do.

Stephen shuddered, shook his head. He slid back the glass panel between the rear seats and the driver. 'We'll go back the same way,' he said. He wanted to hear the normality of his voice giving orders. He did not want to think of Lily and Charlie. He could not believe that she would allow such a man, a common man, to be intimate with her. He did not want to see Charlie's pale dark-jawed face or Lily looking up the stairs, up to him. 'It was a good road,' he said to Coventry. 'We made good time.'

Coventry nodded his alert attentive nod. Coventry always listened, never changed. He had been allocated to Stephen as his batman when Stephen had arrived at the Front and had stayed with him ever since. He had spoken very little, even in those days. But his smile was as reassuring as an older brother. Whenever there had been an attack and they had been pinned down in the trenches, sometimes for hours, Coventry always managed to make a brew and bring Stephen a mug of hot tea and a slice of bread and cheese. When they had to advance, Coventry was always at Stephen's side. Stephen knew that if he was hit, then Coventry would stop and drag him to safety. All the others would go on, obeying orders and ignoring the wounded even if they screamed for help. But Coventry would stop for Stephen, and while he had morphine in his pack Stephen would never be left, screaming with pain, waiting for the stretcher bearers to reach him, knowing they might never come at all.

Once Stephen had taken an order on the field telephone to advance and the fool at the other end would not listen when Stephen told him that the wire ahead of them had not been cut. He tried and tried to tell him that they could not advance for against them was a sprawl of ragged razor-sharp barbed wire and behind that were the Huns with six machine gun emplacements, and behind the Hun soldiers was their artillery which had the range of the British trenches and would see them as they stumbled across the waste ground. They would snipe at Stephen and his men, with their trained deadly accuracy, and they would mow them down with the easy spray of machine gun fire. Shelling them with big heavy artillery shells would be as easy as range practice for them. Stephen had been screaming, trying to tell that bland voice that it could not be done, when Coventry had leaned over Stephen's shoulder and snatched the telephone wire from its connecting point, so the phone went suddenly dead. 'Bad connection,' he had said. 'Sorry, sir. Rotten connection. I doubt you could hear him, could you?'

Later that day, while Coventry was leisurely repairing the telephone, a runner arrived to tell them that the attack was cancelled because the weather was too bright and there had been some muddle and there were no reserve forces in place. They would never have cancelled it just because some junior officer at the front line had said that he would die, and all his men would die, if they obeyed.

Stephen had often protested in those days, his early days at the Front in 1917. In those days Stephen had felt anger at his entrapment in the killing grounds of the Flanders plain, had felt an urgent longing to live. In those days Coventry could speak.

Stephen glanced at Lily; her face was turned away, her eyes were shut. He reached through the panel and put his hand on Coventry's shoulder. He felt the comfort of the good wool material of Coventry's grey uniform jacket. He felt the reassuring meatiness of Coventry's muscled shoulder.

'Four hours,' he said. 'I'll take over driving in four hours,' and fell asleep.

Lily's eyes were shut but she was not asleep. She felt trapped in a nightmare of her worst fear. The moment Stephen had told her of her mother's illness she had felt as if she had stepped into a cold shady morass. Even now, in the comfort of the car with the warm morning sun gilding the upholstery and the veneered wood, Lily could feel herself chilled inside. She could hardly imagine her mother ill in bed. Helen had been remorselessly fit for all of Lily's life. She was a powerful woman, she could shift crates of lemonade bottles, stack boxes of dried goods. She had risen at six every morning of her life and worked until nine or ten every night. Lily could not imagine her mother with that core of physical strength drained from her. She could hardly imagine her tired – it was impossible to imagine her sick.

Lily turned her face into the sunlight as it flickered through the windscreen. Coventry was driving into the sun, his eyes screwed up against the glare, his hat pulled down so that the peak of the cap shaded his eyes. On the windscreen the splattered bodies of insects glowed like little specks of gold. 'Please, Jesus, no,' Lily whispered. 'Please make her well. Please make her well.'

At midday Coventry pulled over to an open gateway to a field. Stephen awoke as soon as the car stopped.

'My shift?' he asked. 'Where are we?'

In answer Coventry opened the driver's door and spread the road map on the warm bonnet of the Argyll. Stephen got out of the back seat and stretched. The midday sun was hot on the back of his neck, his dark business suit was crumpled, the shirt dirty at the collar. 'By God, I'd be a lot more comfortable in uniform. I never thought I'd say that.'

Coventry smiled grimly and pulled a packet of cigarettes from his jacket pocket, lit two in his mouth and passed one to Stephen. They looked at the map, their heads close together.

In the back seat Lily stirred and opened her eyes. Through the windscreen the two men looked as if they were embracing like brothers.

'We're making good time,' Stephen said, pleased. 'We'll take a pee-break and I'll drive.'

He went to the rear door of the car and then suddenly hesitated. He did not know how to tell Lily that she could urinate in the field. Lily looked up at him and got out of the car. She stretched.

'I slept well,' she lied. 'Are we stopping for lunch?'

'We'll eat as we drive,' Stephen said. 'I'll drive now. If you want a ...' He broke off. All the euphemisms his mother used at tea parties were hopelessly inappropriate in this thick hayfield. How could he ask Lily if she wanted to powder her nose or wash her hands? Stephen flushed a deep mortified red. He did not know the common forms of speech between men and women. He could not deal with ordinary life with Lily. She was a lady to him, and thus a whole world of experience was taboo, unmentionable.

'Coventry and I are going to stretch our legs for a moment,' he said awkwardly. 'We'll be five minutes.'

Lily turned her puzzled face to him and Stephen backed away from her, and touched Coventry's arm. 'Pee in the next field,' he said in a low voice. 'Come on.'

Coventry followed him. Lily, still not understanding, watched the two men go. They climbed over a five-barred gate and then Lily saw the top of Stephen's brown head and Coventry's cap line up side by side and stand still. She gave a quick embarrassed giggle. 'Bloody fool,' she said. She stepped a little way from the Argyll so that the hedge hid her from the road and squatted to relieve herself. She watched the clear trickle of urine soak into the ground and smelled the damp sweet smell of wet earth and the musky aroused smell of her own body with innocent animal relish. Then she straightened up and pulled down her tailored summer skirt. 'Damn fool,' she said again.

Stephen and Coventry stood in the other field staring into the distance until Stephen checked his watch to ensure that he had given Lily the full five minutes, and then they clambered awkwardly over the gate. Stephen was still blushing.

'Ready to go on?' he asked Lily.

'Yes.'

Stephen got behind the wheel with Coventry sitting beside him, leaving Lily alone in the back seat.

'You eat all you want from the picnic basket,' Stephen said as he started the engine. 'Then Coventry will take it from you and we'll have the rest. We had a good breakfast, so make sure you have all that you want.'

Lily unbuckled the leather straps on the hamper and opened the lid. She was too unhappy to be hungry. She took a slice of bread and a piece of cheese and an apple and one of the bottles of ginger beer. 'That's all I want.'

Coventry kneeled up on the front passenger seat and

leaned into the back to take the picnic hamper from Lily. Then he sat back into his seat with the hamper on his lap. 'Cheese sandwich and a piece of that ham in with it too,' Stephen said, glancing over.

Coventry deftly sliced bread, cheese and ham with his pocket knife and passed a bulky sandwich over to Stephen. He ate nothing himself until Stephen had finished, and he held the ginger beer bottle while Stephen drank. Only when Stephen said, 'I'm done now', did Coventry choose his own food and eat. Lily, watching the two men in their monosyllabic communion, sensed long days and nights of working and keeping watch and resting together when there had been nothing to say except a brief order or an assent.

She dozed, lulled by the swaying of the car, and when she awoke it was mid-afternoon and the sun was behind them instead of ahead.

'Where are we?'

'Just outside Southampton,' Stephen said, glancing over his shoulder. 'Not long now. We'll go straight to the Royal Infirmary.'

Lily nodded. She watched the wide green fields of Hampshire without seeing them. She still could not believe that her mother was ill. She still could not believe that the little shop which had opened every week day for ten years was shut today and would not open tomorrow.

Stephen drove swiftly and well. A hay cart pulled out in front of him, towed by an old slow tractor. He waited until the road straightened and then pulled out to the right and swept past it. The driver waved amiably, Coventry raised a hand in reply. Lily watched for the familiar landmarks of Portsmouth, the ugly suburbs of Hilsea and Portsdown. Stephen turned right off the coast road and headed south down the Fratton Road to the hospital. The Argyll swept through the gateway and up to the entrance. Lily was out of the car and running through the hospital door before Stephen had brought the car to a complete halt.

'Damn! I wanted to go in with her,' he said. He opened his door. 'Drive home at once and tell Mother that I am back and that she must make up the spare bedroom for Lily. We'll come home when we're finished here. Come back here and wait for me. Quick as you can.'

There was no sign of Lily in the shadowy entrance hall. She must have found her way to the right ward at once. Stephen said 'Damn' again and ran up the stone steps to the women's medical ward on the first floor. A nurse was in the corridor. Stephen nodded at her in his authoritative way. 'Helen Pears?' he asked.

'She's in there,' the nurse said. 'I'll tell Sister you're here.'

She threw a quick flirtatious look at Stephen from under her eyelashes but he was already turning away and going into the side room.

Lily was leaning over her mother's bed, her face wrenched with pain. She had her mother's hand held to her heart. Helen Pears was barely conscious. Her face was waxy and white, the skin of her eyelids and her lips pale yellow. Every breath came unwillingly in a deep rattling sigh. When she opened her eyes they were misty as if they were filming over already. Stephen nodded. He had seen enough men die to know the signs.

'Ma? Can you hear me? Ma?'

The hand Lily was pressing to her heart tightened slightly.

'Lily,' the dying woman said softly.

As her mother said her name Lily gave a little gasp and the tears tumbled down her face. 'Oh, Ma! You're all right, aren't you? You're going to be well?'

The door behind Stephen opened and the Ward Sister came into the room. 'Are you the daughter?' she asked.

Lily nodded without taking her eyes from her mother's face. 'I should like to have a word with you,' the Sister said. 'Would you step outside, Miss Pears?'

Lily glanced up at her with sudden impatience. 'Not now.'

She pulled up a chair to her mother's bedside and sat leaning towards her so her head was nearly on her mother's pillow. 'I've missed you so much,' she whispered. 'I've had a wonderful time but I've missed you so much, Ma. I thought of you every day. And I so wished you could have come too.'

A small weary smile went across the pale face.

'But after this season I might get work in town,' Lily said encouragingly. 'Charlie may be MD at the Kings! Think of that, Ma! And he has worked on an audition piece for me and wants me to try for an act there! You get well and you'll be able to see me up on that lovely stage!'

'Miss Pears,' the Sister interrupted again. 'I have other patients to attend to. Please come outside for a moment.'

Lily glanced up at the woman and Stephen realized that although she had heard the harshness of the tone and the irritation in the voice she had not taken in the words at all. Her whole awareness was focused on her mother. She had forgotten that Stephen or the Sister were even there.

He took the Sister's arm. 'I'm a friend of the family,' he said. 'I've just fetched Lily from Sidmouth to see her mother. Please tell me the news. I'll tell Lily later.'

He drew her from the room. 'She should prepare herself for the end,' the Sister said bluntly. 'Mrs Pears has an acute form of Spanish influenza and she has not responded to any treatment. It has developed into pneumonia. We don't think she will last the night.'

Stephen nodded. 'I thought so,' he said. 'Is she in pain?'

The Sister shook her head. 'We are giving her morphine

to control the pain,' she said. 'But of course it makes her rather vague. If her daughter wants to speak to her we could stop the morphine for a little while. I had not thought she was so young.'

Stephen shook his head decisively. 'Mrs Pears should not suffer pain,' he said firmly. 'Lily needs no words of advice. She has friends who will care for her. They both know that. She would not want to see her mother suffer.'

The Sister nodded. 'I'm afraid there's nothing more we can do,' she said.

Stephen smiled slightly and touched her arm. 'I am sure you have been wonderful,' he said. 'I wonder, could you obtain a cup of tea for Miss Pears? It has been a long and worrying day for her.'

The Sister nodded and sent a junior nurse scurrying. Stephen stayed outside the room in the corridor, watching Lily through the little porthole window in the door. For a long while she stayed with her head close to her mother's head on the pillow. When the junior nurse came in with the tea she took it without thanking her and drank it almost as if she did not know what she was doing. She stroked her mother's hair off her face, she smoothed the coarse cotton of the pillow slip. She held her hand. She talked to her constantly. Stephen watched her animated face through the window and knew that she was trying to push death away with the force of her will, to summon her mother back to life. She was trying to build a bridge between life and the drowsy half-coma that held Helen Pears. She sang to her. Stephen saw Lily's face uplifted and the tears on her cheeks and heard, muffled through the door, her silver longing voice.

It nearly worked. It very nearly worked. She nearly succeeded. Helen's grip on her daughter's hand tightened and her primrose-coloured eyelids flickered open once. She stared at her for one moment with a curious intensity as if she wanted to convey a whole lifetime of wisdom and experience in one look. And then there was a deep gurgling rattle in her throat and she spewed a lungful of yellow slime on to the pillow, and she closed her eyes and died.

Stephen was in through the door in a moment, drawing Lily away from the bed, shouting for the nurses. They came in and bundled the two of them out of the room while they cleaned her up. Stephen held Lily close while they stood together in the corridor outside. He watched through the porthole window over her head. He was unemotional. Stephen had seen too many deaths to be moved by one more, and that of a civilian and a woman. When they had changed the pillow slip and the dead woman was clean they let them in again. Stephen stepped back and let Lily say goodbye to her mother alone.

Lily had no idea what she should do. She had seen the rituals of mourning on her street but never been present at a death. She had some vague memory of an Irish family whose child died and they had opened the window to let the soul fly to heaven. Stephen, watching through the door, saw Lily bend over her mother and kiss her cold still lips. Then she went to the window and tried to open it. It was an old sash window, the cords had broken and it had been painted shut with successive layers of thick magnolia gloss. It would never move. Lily tugged and tugged at it, her fingers thrust through the handles at the foot of the window. It would never move. Stephen watched her. Lily banged against the frame, trying to loosen it. Stephen watched her in case she smashed the glass with her bare hands but although she had the intensity of an anxious child she was not hysterical.

Lily turned from the window. He could see she was not crying though her face was very pale. She went back to her mother, lying so still and cold in the bed, and he saw her nod and say something to the dead woman. Then, still whispering, she came towards the door.

She opened the door and held it open, in an odd gesture as if she were calling someone to follow her. She went past Stephen without a glance at him. 'Come on,' he heard her say. 'Come with me. Come with me. I'll set you free.'

She went swiftly past him to the head of the stairs, her high heels clattering lightly down the stone steps and he could hear her still saying, 'Come on, come with me. Come on,' as she ran down to the entrance hall.

He quickly went after her, watched her as she held the swinging entrance door open with that odd gesture again, as if waiting for someone to follow behind her. 'Come on,' she said to the empty air and the deserted hall. 'Come on.'

Outside at the head of the hospital steps she paused. Stephen stood in the doorway, waiting to see what she would do next.

'There,' she said and her voice was as desolate as a bereaved child's. 'There. You can see it now. You can see the sky. You can go straight up to heaven now. And I'm letting you go, Ma, I'm letting you go. Good luck. God bless. Goodbye.'

She was shaking now as if the words were being forced from her when really she wanted to hold her mother beside her for ever. She even raised her hand in a little helpless wave like a child when a parent leaves for the first time. 'Goodbye,' Lily whispered.

Stephen, watching her, thought of the other dead he had seen. The thousand thousand thousands of them, dead in dug-outs, buried in shellholes, blown into fragments, cut by bullets, gassed, smashed, spitted on bayonets. He turned and nodded to Coventry and the waiting car. Another death made little difference. Lily would get over it, he thought.

She got into the car without realizing where she was. Coventry raised an eyebrow at Stephen and Stephen shook his head in that old familiar gesture which meant that someone, a friend, a colleague, a beloved comrade had bought it. Dead. Coventry shrugged, which meant acceptance of the news. The two men, and all the other survivors, had learned a code for death which was now so familiar as to be unconscious. Of course, they would never grieve for any loss ever again.

Coventry drove to the front door of Stephen's home and held the passenger door open for Lily. She stepped out of the car and took Stephen's arm without looking around her. On the Canoe Lake behind them a swan chased a seagull and the bird squawked and flew off. Lily did not turn her head. She did not hear it.

The tweeny had been waiting for them, the door swung open. Muriel Winters came out of the drawing room, her face stiff with anger. Stephen guided Lily past her into the handsome room and thrust her into an armchair. 'Sit here. I'll get you some tea, and then you must have a lie down,' he said. 'We've got a room ready for you here. Don't worry about a thing.'

He took his mother firmly by the arm and drew her from the room across the hall into the dining room opposite.

'Stephen, I simply cannot . . .'

'Lily's mother has just died. She has nowhere to go. She is to stay here until she has decided what she wants to do.'

'She must have family or friends of her own.'

'She has no-one.'

Muriel looked at her son in open disbelief. 'She must have someone. A neighbour who would take her in.'

'She has no family and no close friends, and anyway, I want her to stay here.'

'It's most unsuitable,' Muriel said. 'For how long is she to stay here? And what am I to say about her? I am sure that I'm very sorry about her bereavement, Stephen; but surely you see that she cannot possibly stay here.'

'She will stay here. And you may tell everyone that we are engaged to be married. That makes it all right, doesn't it? I will post a notice in the *Telegraph* tomorrow. That makes it quite all right, doesn't it, Mother?'

Muriel fell backwards and then steadied herself with a hand on a dark wooden table. 'Oh no, Stephen. Not marriage. Not to a singer. Not to a chorus girl!'

'Yes, marriage. And she is not a chorus girl any more. She will retire from the stage of course. She will become my wife and she will never sing in public again. You can tell your friends that she is a local girl whose parents had a small retail business. I suppose *that* is suitable?'

Muriel could feel her whole face trembling. 'Stephen, I beg you to reconsider.' Her voice shook with her distress. 'This is because of the war, I know. You think that none of the girls of your sort can understand how you feel. But they can, my dear, we all suffered. We all put a brave face on it. You don't have to pick up some little nobody because you think you can teach her to suit you. There are so many girls, nice girls. Of course Miss Pears can stay while she makes other arrangements. She can stay as long as she wishes. But let's not be hasty, Stephen. Don't announce an engagement. Let's not say anything to anyone.'

Stephen gave a harsh laugh. 'I've made up my mind, Mother. Nothing you can say will change it. But you are right, you're damnably right, I give you credit for seeing that. It *is* to do with the war. It is because you and the nice girls packed me and every one of those p . . . p . . . poor devils into a place that none of you could ever imagine. You sent me like a child to p . . . p . . . play on a tram track. You, and all the nice girls, sent me with a handful of white feathers and then posted me a parcel of c . . . c . . . cake and a pair of mittens. I don't think I'll *ever* forgive you! Any of you! Not just you, but all the p...p... pretty harpies. You and all the nice girls marching under b... banners and singing p... patriotic songs. All of you women who b... believe in war, and send others to do the fighting.'

Muriel was trembling, her face was pale. 'I knew you felt like this, Stephen.' Her hand was at her throat, gripping her pearls. 'I knew you were angry with me and your father for making you go. But don't punish me by marrying an unsuitable girl. If you marry a girl who is no good, a girl from the stage, then you'll have misery ahead of you. The war's over and thank God you came through safely. I want you to have a good life now, Stephen, not some dreadful struggle with a bad wife.'

Stephen turned on her a face with so ghastly a gleam that Muriel recoiled, fell back until she was against the heavily polished sideboard. The rattle of expensive china stopped her.

'I came through safely, did I?' Stephen repeated. His smile was like the wide grin of a naked skull. 'Safely, is it, Mother! Safely with the dreams I have, and the sudden panics. A chauffeur who can't speak and a life that is unbearable to me? Filled with hatred for the old m... men. F... filled with hatred for the young women. Hating the men who survived like me, wondering who they b... betrayed, where they skulked to miss the killing shells. Hating the ones who d...d... died because they are the saints and now I will always live in their shadow. And this is safety?'

Muriel gave a little cry and put her hand up to her mouth to stifle the sound.

'I tell you Lily is my saviour! She is free of the smell of it, free of the sound of it, free of the knowledge of it. How it happened I don't know but it hasn't touched her or spoiled her or corrupted her. When she's beside me I feel clean again. I can't tell you how or why. But if I don't marry her and have her for ever, for ever, Mother, then I will go m . . . m . . . m . . .' He snatched a deep breath to say the word. 'Mad.'

There was a short terrible silence.

Stephen went on very quietly. 'I know it. I know it. I feel half mad already at times. I dream – I dream – but you don't want to know my dreams.

'You kept your distance from the reality and you don't want to know the taste of it as it comes back to me. I wake vomiting sometimes, Mother. I dream of something I found in my mess tin. We were shelled while eating dinner, and a new officer, a young lad, was sitting beside me one moment, and the next, he was gone . . . but in my mess tin, and on my spoon halfway to my mouth, and on my face, on my lips so that I tasted it, was his blood and his bits of flesh, against my lips, in my mouth . . .' Stephen gagged on his words and turned away. Muriel held on to the sideboard with both hands. Her knees were trembling, she would have fallen if she had let go. Stephen pulled out a chair from the table and flung himself down with his head in his hands, breathing deeply until the sweat on his neck cooled and his stomach stopped churning.

'I b . . . beg your pardon, Mother,' he said with careful politeness. 'I c . . . c . . . can't think what I was saying. I have had too little sleep over the past few days. Please forgive me.'

Muriel rubbed her slack mouth. 'My dear,' she started. 'I knew you felt . . .'

'You really must excuse me,' Stephen said icily. 'I don't know what I was thinking of, dragging all that old weary stuff up. I p . . . p . . . p . . . prefer not to talk of it.'

Muriel stared at him hopelessly as he got to his feet and turned a cold shut face towards her. 'But I hope you will be glad for me,' he insisted tonelessly. 'I hope you will be happy for me, Mother, and that you will learn to love Lily in time.'

Muriel looked up at him imploringly. 'Of course,' she said quietly. 'If that is what you truly wish.'

'I'll go to her now,' Stephen said. 'She's had the devil of a day. She should go to bed, I think. Did you have the blue room made ready for her?'

Muriel nodded and stood aside as Stephen went towards the door. 'Stephen . . .' she started. Her eyes were filled with impotent tears, she stretched her hand towards him.

He turned to her his dead cold face. 'Yes?'

'Nothing, my dear. Nothing, my dear. My dear . . . nothing.'

Chapter Twelve

Lily went through the days of the following week blank-faced and blank-eyed. Muriel Winters, facing her over the lunch table, could not think what Stephen had seen in this dull silent girl unless it was the very appeal of her emptiness – a plain page on which he could prescribe his ideal. She had thought that the girl might have been grieving, and she was prepared to be sympathetic and supportive. But when she had said, laying a hand on Lily's cold fingers: 'You must try not to grieve too much for your mother. I am sure she would not have wanted that,' Lily had looked at her with her dull blue eyes and said only: 'I am not grieving too much.'

The girl was useful, Muriel had to allow her that. As it happened, the nurse who usually cared for Mr Winters during the day had given her notice. An agency nurse came and dressed him in the morning, changed him during the day and undressed him at night, but there was no-one to sit with him or to keep him company. On the second day of her visit Lily was taken by Stephen to see his father, and after he had left for the office she had crept upstairs and sat at the old man's bedside for most of the morning. It was Muriel's Women's Empire League meeting so she knew nothing of it until Lily came down for lunch and said that she had been sitting with Mr Winters.

'With Rory? Whatever for?' Muriel said unguardedly.

'I thought he might be lonely. All alone, in such a big house.'

Muriel hesitated. 'We don't know he even hears us. We

don't know he even knows we're there. He's like someone who is dead really.'

Lily shook her fair bobbed head very definitely. 'No he isn't. Someone dead is gone. Gone for ever.'

Muriel nodded at the parlourmaid to clear the plates; she was embarrassed. 'Well, if you like to sit with him I am sure I appreciate it very much. If you like to do it.'

When Stephen came home in the evening he was not pleased. 'Whatever did you let her go in there for? I took her in for common courtesy, just so she knew her way around the house. It's not right that she should sit with him. She's not here to nurse him, for God's sake. It's unhealthy for her. It's positively m . . . morbid.'

'I can hardly stop her. You introduced them. If she wants to sit with him rather than sitting in her bedroom or in the drawing room then I suppose she must be allowed to do as she wishes. She's clearly not used to life in a large house. She creeps around the drawing room as if she were afraid of being told not to touch. If she feels comfortable with Rory then I can hardly forbid her to be with him.'

'It's unhealthy,' Stephen persisted. He hardly knew what he meant by the words. He had a certainty that it was too close to death for Lily. He wanted her in the sunshine, even in the limelight. He did not want her in the darkened shadows of the sickroom. He did not want her with a tang of antiseptic in her hair or the smell of decay and death on her hands.

Muriel shrugged. 'Then you must tell her,' she said.

She was biding her time. The threatened announcement of the engagement had not gone in the *Telegraph*. Lily wore no ring. Stephen's attitude to her was proprietary, protective. But Lily seemed deaf to his tone and blind to the lingering touch of his hand on her sleeve. She moved from one strange room to another in this strange house like the little automated dolls that had come from

Germany before the war. Her legs took her from bed-room to dining room to drawing room and up the stairs to bed again, and her little fair head moved from side to side. But there was nothing inside her but little clockwork workings – and a most terrible emptiness.

Muriel thought that Stephen would weary of Lily. She no longer had the bright glamour of being a stage girl. She was no longer a challenge to convention. She was a shabbily dressed quiet little doll who walked – tick-tock – from room to room as she was bid. Her face was an even greyish pallor, her home-made summer dresses were pastel prints which seemed to fade daily. Her hair seemed to be losing its brightness and becoming pale and limp. Even Stephen, with his longing for peace and stillness, could not desire this little drab, Muriel thought. She was as quiet and as humble as a housemaid without a character. Stephen might pity her, but surely he could not continue to be in love with her. She was not a girl who could inspire any emotion but pity.

After dinner they took coffee in the drawing room. The long curtains were pulled around the sections of the octagonal tower windows but even so they could hear the sea. A foghorn out in the Solent blew dismally at irregular intervals and they could hear the wind blowing the waves uneasily against the shingle of the beach.

'High tide,' Stephen said. 'I shouldn't like to be out at sea tonight.'

Lily held her coffee cup on her lap and looked blankly at the dried flower arrangement in the fireplace. She did not even seem to hear him.

'Lily, my dear,' Stephen said. She turned her pale face slowly towards him. 'I have made arrangements for your mother's funeral for the day after tomorrow. I thought you might need some clothes. A black dress perhaps, and shoes and a hat of course. We have an account at Handleys, which you may make use of. I wonder, Mother, if you would go with Lily and help her choose whatever is necessary and charge it to the account?'

'I'm free all day tomorrow.'

'In that case I shall send Coventry back with the car after he has driven me to the office. Perhaps you would both like to join me for lunch at the Dolphin? I generally lunch there.'

Muriel waited for Lily to consent but the girl said nothing. There was an awkward silence. Muriel wondered if Lily had heard, and looked to Stephen for guidance, raising her eyebrows slightly.

He put down his coffee and crossed the room to stand before the fireplace as if he were warming the seat of his trousers.

'You would want to show proper respect for your mother's funeral, wouldn't you, Lily?' he said encouragingly. 'You would want a black dress and a jacket or coat. Some new black shoes and a black hat. A proper hat! Not one of your little flowerpots!'

Lily suddenly stood and put down her cup and saucer with such force that the coffee tray rattled. 'No!'

Muriel jumped. It was the first time she had heard Lily speak louder than a whisper.

'My mother had no time for any of that nonsense. When my father died at sea she didn't even chip in to a fund for a memorial for the men who were lost. She said life was for living and money was for spending on living people. She never wore black and she never put me in black either. And I don't think it would be respectful to her – or to myself – to go to her funeral in clothes which a stranger had bought me.'

'Lily!'

Muriel slipped from her chair and stole from the room, the very model of maternal tact. She wanted Lily to feel no restraint. She wanted Stephen to hear every word of backstreet abuse which Lily must have at her tongue's end. She closed the door behind her and was too much of a lady to listen. She walked quietly up the stairs to Rory Winters's bedroom and drew up a chair beside his bed and held his hand in silence.

In the drawing room Stephen was on his knees before Lily. 'I asked you before, and you said no; but you're all alone now, Lily, and you need someone to look after you. You wouldn't be at her funeral in stranger's clothes, Lily. You would be dressed as you should be, out of respect to your mother. And of course I would buy your clothes. Now and always. I want you to be my wife, Lily. I want to take care of you.'

Lily let Stephen hold her hands, she looked down on him as if he were an importunate dog, pawing for attention. 'Oh don't. Don't, Stephen. Not now.'

'Yes, now,' Stephen said, getting up. 'You have to accept things from me, Lily, you have no money of your own.'

'There's the shop, and Ma had some insurance.'

'I've checked, and it is bad news, my dear.' Stephen spoke with concealed relish. 'You must be brave. The shop was a tenancy and in fact the rent is owing from the last quarter. There are no buildings or assets to come to you, my dear. Your mother had cashed in her insurance policy during the war. I imagine she found it difficult to make ends meet. And her illness has left her estate with some bills which will have to be met. If I can sell the stock in the shop and the goodwill to an incoming tenant I imagine you will make some thirty or forty pounds. But you will have no more than that.'

'I can go back to work. I can get a job.'

'You can. But I doubt you feel much like getting up on a stage and doing the can-can now, do you, Lily? I really don't think you could do it. And I don't think your mother would want you going around the music halls, looking for work, having to take whatever was offered and mixing with all sorts of people without her caring for you. Why, I remember the very first time we went out to dinner you told me that she went everywhere with you. How could you cope in that world alone, Lily? I don't think she'd want you out in that world on your own.'

Lily's face was wretched, her lower lip was red and sore where she had bitten at the skin. Her face was ugly with strain. 'I don't care what I do. I don't care what becomes of me. I am lost without her. I've heard people say that and I never knew what they meant but I know now. I am lost without her.'

Stephen let the silence go on. He could see Lily's pain naked on her young face. He had seen that look before, on young children in Belgium and France, when they had lost both parents and their home in one night of shelling. They were blank-faced but in their eyes was deep terror and deep despair. Lily, robbed of the only person in the world who had ever cared for her, was as lost as a Belgian refugee.

'Marry me. I'll take care of you. Marry me and you'll have no financial worries, you'll be well looked after. She liked me. She knew I would care for you. She said you could come out to tea with me – d'you remember? She trusted me to care for you. I think if she could advise you now she would tell you to marry me.'

Lily looked at him with that dark-eyed look of blank despair. 'I don't know.'

Stephen took her hands again. 'I know,' he said firmly. 'You don't have to think about it, Lily. I will take care of everything.'

Lily sighed. She was too weary to care one way or another. 'All right.'

Stephen hesitated for a moment in his persuasive murmur.

'What?'

'I said, all right.'

Stephen tightened his grip on her hands and leaped to his feet. He put his arms around Lily and felt her ungiving stiffness. 'Lily, my darling –'

'Don't. I can't hear it now. I've said all right.'

'Of course, of course.' Stephen was placatory.

'But I'm going to the funeral in my own dress.'

'Whatever you say, Lily, whatever you say.'

He released her and waited. He thought that she would turn to him for comfort. He expected some kind of reward for his proposal and for releasing her when she asked. But Lily walked past him, opened the drawing room door and went out of the room. He heard her going up the stairs to her bedroom and the door softly closing. He wanted to feel triumphant – a man who has won the woman he desires. Instead he felt a worm of irritation, as if Lily had given herself and yet retreated to an even more impenetrable place. It was like winning the first trench but then finding that there is another trench behind, and another behind that, and that you will never reach the end; you will never finish the struggle.

Lily lay on her bed in the blue room, facing the ceiling. She was hardly aware that she had agreed to be Stephen's wife. His voice came to her thickly, dully, like someone speaking through water. She lived in a bubble of pain and loss which nothing seemed to penetrate. She could not believe that her mother was not alive, she could not believe that her present life was real. Every morning on waking she would keep her eyes tight shut, willing the ceiling to be her old bedroom at home. Every morning she willed herself to hear her mother's voice calling: 'Time to get up, Lily.' But the voice never came.

161

She blamed herself, in the guilty way of all survivors. She thought that if she had never left Portsmouth then her mother would never have taken ill. She thought her mother had been overworked, in the shop on her own. She imagined her skipping meals, she imagined her sliding into bed at night too weary to make a proper supper. She imagined her opening the shop at half past six prompt every morning while her flu got worse and worse, until she collapsed. Lily was sure that if she had been there she would have made her mother rest; she somehow believed that the flu germs would not even have taken hold if she had been there, encircling her mother with her young strong love. Lily was too young to bear tragedy. She had turned her face from the war and refused to be touched by it. She was unprepared for a death which came so close to her that now she even wished that she had died too, rather than survive and feel this excessive pain.

She was sick to her heart with grief. She could marry Stephen or throw herself under a tram – they were equally attractive options. Lily, lying on her bed, dozing in her cheap dress with her worn shoes on the silk coverlet, knew herself to be adrift in life. She had lost the mother who was her anchor and her harbour. Nothing else mattered.

That night, when the house was dark and asleep and it was quiet in every room, Stephen walked noiselessly through the baize door and down the back stairs to the kitchen.

Coventry was making toasted cheese. The rich strong aroma floated up the kitchen stairs to Stephen as he came quietly down in his slippers and dressing-gown.

'Good show,' he said.

Coventry turned and gave him a slow comfortable smile. It was a recipe of his own invention. First he toasted a slice of white bread on one side and then folded it, toast side in, over a slice of cheese. With the folded side down-wards so there were no drips he then toasted both sides. He put the toasting fork prongs down on to a cheap china plate and pushed the sandwich off the tines of the fork with his broad clean hand, and handed the plate to Stephen. Then he poured the tea and added four spoonfuls of sugar to each mug. Then, when Stephen had everything he needed, Coventry made his own sandwich.

The men sat in silence, savouring the smoky crunch of the fire-toasted bread and the hot strong taste of the melted cheese.

'Any more tea in the pot?' Stephen asked, knowing there would be.

Coventry poured another two mugs. Stephen felt in his dressing-gown pocket for his cigarettes and said lazily, 'Oh damn.' Coventry reached back to where his jacket was spread over his chair and took a packet from the pocket. He took two, lit them both, and handed one to Stephen.

'Good,' Stephen said contentedly.

There was a long silence.

'She's agreed to marry me. She said so tonight.'

Coventry raised an eyebrow and nodded, examined the tip of his cigarette and then drew a deep breath of smoke.

'I'll hold her to it,' Stephen said coldly. 'She's in shock now – I should know, I've seen it often enough. D'you remember Tommy Patterson? Straight over the top and walking towards the Hun as if he was strolling down Palmy Road on a Saturday. Someone had died – I can't remem-ber. Was it his brother? It was nasty, I remember that. All his face was blown off.'

Coventry shook his head firmly.

Stephen sighed with contentment. 'No. All right. Neither do I. I can't remember a thing either. It's all gone. I can't remember any of it. But I do remember Tommy Patterson taking his walk. He was shocked. She's like that

163

now. Same eyes. A kind of blankness. She doesn't care what happens to her right now. She even said so. She'll marry me and by the time she wakes up, it'll be all signed and sealed, and I'll have her.'

Coventry glanced sideways at Stephen as if he were only partly convinced.

'No,' Stephen said certainly. 'It's the right thing to do. There's no future for her except hanging around music halls until she becomes tarty and shop-soiled like the rest of the girls. I won't let that happen to her. And I have to have her. I've known it for weeks. When she is my wife it will all be different for me. Everything about me will be different. This house, my work, my d...d... damn dreams. Everything will come right when she marries me – you'll see.'

Coventry hefted the teapot to judge its weight, topped it up with the water from the kettle and poured another two mugs. The brew had stewed and was darker and stronger. Stephen smacked his lips on it. 'My God, it's got a kick like rum,' he said. 'But I never liked it when they put rum in the tea. You always knew you were for it when they put an extra tot of rum in the tea. The men didn't like it either. They knew damn well what it meant. D'you remember?'

Coventry smiled at the embers of the fire in the open grate and slowly shook his head. He looked like an old man casting his mind back years and finding everything mercifully forgotten.

'No,' Stephen sighed. 'I don't remember it very well. It all seems such a long time ago now. And such a long way away. And anyway, it was a dirty war on both sides. W...w... whatever we did was no worse than them, eh?'

Coventry shook his head again. He could remember nothing. He could see nothing in the grate but warm red embers and soft grey ashes and a little sizzling stalactite of dropped cheese dripping off one of the bars.

'No.' Stephen rested himself on Coventry's amnesiac serenity. 'And when I have Lily I shall forget all of it, all of it, too.'

Lily wore her blue striped skirt and a white shirt to her mother's funeral. She wore a little straw cloche hat trimmed with a blue ribbon. The funeral was first thing in the July morning and there was a cold wind blowing in from the sea. Muriel came to Lily's room in her dressing-gown and offered to lend her a jacket. Lily looked into Muriel's substantial wardrobe and rejected both a dark jacket and a very suitable black linen summer coat. She chose instead a little white blazer with bright blue piping at the edge and the cuffs. 'It's rather gay,' Muriel commented neutrally.

Lily nodded. 'I am sorry if I offend you,' she said in her careful voice. 'But my ma hated funerals and people dressing in black. She never even wore a black armband during the war. Even though she lost my dad and her only brother. I don't want to go against her today. And anyway, I've already said my goodbye to her. I can do my mourning inside, I don't have to show it off.'

Muriel suddenly felt a wave of pity for Lily. 'As you wish. Who will see us, anyway?'

Lily disengaged herself. 'Are you coming?'

'I assumed you would want me there.'

Lily shook her head. 'No. Not you, nor Stephen. Thank you for thinking of it. But Ma didn't know you. I don't think you would even have liked her very much. I'd rather it was just me and anyone from our street. People who really knew her. Not people who are there only for good manners.'

Muriel had been taught as a child that nothing in the

world was more important than good manners. 'As you wish,' she said again. 'But you must let Stephen take you to the church and go in with you.'

Lily suddenly shrugged, the fight gone from her. 'Yes. Yes. I am sorry to be so difficult.'

'I understand.' Muriel did not understand at all.

'The car's ready,' Stephen called up the stairs. Muriel and Lily went down together.

'I am not coming with you,' Muriel told Stephen. 'Lily wishes to go alone.'

Stephen scowled, his handsome face suddenly darkening. 'I shall be with you, Lily,' he said. 'You will need me there.'

Lily made a little gesture with her hand as if the weight of their combined wills was too much for her. 'Oh, all right.'

The service was held in the small church opposite the depressing Highland Road cemetery. Stephen was surprised to see that it was full. Very few people were wearing black, he noted, but there were a number of stiff Sunday best suits and at least most of the women had hats. He glanced along the pew while others were praying and saw the calloused red hands clasped in prayer. These were working people, Helen Pears's customers, residents of the small terraced houses of Highland Road, tenants of the rented rooms over the cheap shops. No wonder Lily had not wanted her future mother-in-law to see the sort of people she had grown up with, Stephen thought sympathetically. She would be ashamed of them, no doubt. Half of them probably had guilty consciences – Helen Pears had died with a week's wages from each family on the slate. She'd been foolishly generous with credit. They'd never pay now.

They shuffled to their feet and then sat while the vicar addressed them. He seemed to know Helen Pears personally. He spoke of her courage when she lost her husband and her struggle to bring up Lily and to run the little business. Stephen heard someone sob from the back of the church and tried to look around to see who was crying without fully turning in his seat. Probably some woman getting over-emotional about nothing, he thought. Lily, at least, was dry-eyed and self-possessed. She still had that white blankness which Stephen remembered from men in shock from shellfire. Odd, he thought irrelevantly. When he had first met Lily he had liked her chatter and her easy spontaneous giggle. Now she was to be his wife and she was as silent as himself. 'She'll brighten up,' he told himself as they rose for the final hymn. 'It's not as if anything really bad has happened to her.'

The coffin bearers were the skimpy undersized men typical of poor homes. They looked like conscripts – the last batch to come out when the recruiting sergeants were scraping the barrel and men were ordered to the Front when they were underweight, underheight, pallid with TB and murmuring hearts, limping on dropped arches and damaged feet. Stephen shook his head disapprovingly. One man had only one arm, another had the thick cough of a gas attack survivor. They all wore campaign medals and had the recognizable brittle nerviness of men who had been at the Front. Stephen turned his head away from them, he didn't want to look like an inspecting officer – but my God, what a motley crew. Stephen took Lily's little hand under his arm and led her out into the sunlight.

It had become a hot brilliant morning. The sky was a bright July blue, with not a cloud in sight. A little breeze flapped the vicar's white surplice as he read the words of the burial service at the graveside. Lily's face was as pale as his linen. He paused and nodded to her after the coffin was lowered into the ground and Lily took a handful of earth and threw it in. Stephen had expected tears but Lily's face was set and still. Someone at the back of the crowd sobbed.

Stephen, used to the brisk rolling of canvas-shrouded corpses into mass graves and a quick gabble over the bundles in lots of twenties or forties, or after an especially bad night, hundreds of bodies, found the service tediously long for just one woman. The headstone, which he had ordered and paid for from his own pocket, seemed expensive and ostentatious compared with the hastily nailed wooden crosses made from packing cases. God alone knew how many men were buried as they dropped, in a shower of mud, to be resurrected in gruesome glimpses by the next trench-digging party or by a hard shower of rain.

Stephen turned away and led Lily to the car. She went slowly, unwillingly. As they walked people came towards Lily, ignoring Stephen, to take hold of her hands. Badly dressed women hugged Lily and whispered quick comforting words to her. Men came up and wrung her hand. 'One of the best, really one of the best, your ma,' one of them said. One fat woman with her gloves splitting along the seams held Lily and rocked her while the tears coursed down her red cheeks. 'Bloody hell, Lil,' she said. 'What'll we do without her?'

Lily's composure broke at that. She let out a little cry and flung her arms around the woman's waist. Her hat fell off and Stephen stooped to pick it up. Lily was at once surrounded by people, men and women muttering, 'Poor little duck.' 'She looks about done in.' 'Such a loss for her.' 'Not many girls have a mother like that.'

'You come home with me,' the big woman said. 'I've boiled a ham all ready. I thought it was the right thing to do.'

Stephen stepped forward. 'I will take Lily home,' he said pleasantly. 'She will be well looked after, I assure you.'

The woman looked uncertainly at him. 'We were going

to have a bite to eat. You're very welcome to come too, Sir.'

Stephen put his hand out to Lily. 'Thank you very much but I think Lily should come home with me and rest.'

Lily did not obey him as he had expected. She kept her arm around the big woman's waist and her head laid on the fat shoulder. 'I'll go and have my dinner with Betty. I'll come home this afternoon.'

Stephen was too wise to argue. 'Of course. I'll send the car around for you at three, shall I?'

Lily nodded. 'Tell Coventry to come to the shop,' she said.

Stephen stepped back and let Betty and the rest of them pass. They smelled faintly of mothballs from the Sunday suits. Stephen watched them walk out of the church gate and down the road. Then he went across the road to where Coventry waited with the car.

'Go and collect Lily from the corner shop at three,' he said. 'Drop me at the office now. I might as well do some work for what's left of the day.'

Lily was glad to be in Betty's house. Betty had bought a bottle of sweet cheap sherry and everyone drank to Helen's memory and Betty made a speech reminding everyone of Helen's generosity with tick, and her fairness. Then the men went out and brought back a jug of beer and they carved the ham and ate it with white bread and butter and wilting tasteless lettuce. Dick Sharp had brought some of his tomatoes from his allotment and they were small and sweet. Lily's Aunt Mary had made a summer pudding with gooseberries, redcurrants, blackcurrants and a handful of raspberries from her precious raspberry canes. Lily ate well, for the first time in days, and some colour came back into her cheeks.

'What are you going to do, Lil?' Betty asked, bringing

her a strong sweet cup of tea to finish the meal. 'The shop's no good for you, I take it?'

Lily shook her head. 'I'm promised to Stephen Winters,' she said. 'The gentleman at the church.'

'Get away!' Betty was enormously impressed. 'Your ma told me about him and I said he'd be up to no good. But she told me he was a real gentleman. Fancy you marrying up, Lily! You'll be so grand. Here!' she called over to Mary. 'Lil's going to marry that gentleman at the church. Stephen Winters. What d'you think of that!'

Mary came over and kissed Lily on both cheeks. 'Well, that is good news. And there was me, lying awake at nights, worrying what would become of you left all alone in the world while you are set up with a handsome man and a good fortune. He's a lawyer, didn't your ma tell me? And a hero too? Didn't he get a big medal or something in the war?'

Lily nodded.

'That's right,' Betty said. 'Helen was telling me. There was a farmhouse which the Jerries had captured and they had killed the women who had been hiding inside it – and done worse to them too. There was a baby there as well – savages they were. That was killed too. But your gentleman rushed up to it, captured it, and killed the Jerries. They gave him a medal.'

'He never talks about the war,' Lily said.

'Well, he wouldn't, would he?' Mary demanded. 'That sort never do. It's the ones who were twenty miles behind the line who won't stop talking about it, like my George who won it single-handed if you listen to him. But your young man, Lily, why, he'd never say a word.'

Betty nodded. 'It was in all the papers,' she said. 'All of them were killed, our boys and the Jerries, everyone except your young gentleman and his batman or whatever they call them.'

'Coventry?' Lily asked. 'Was Coventry there too?'

Betty nodded. 'Is that his name? Your ma looked it up while you were away and she showed it to me, in the papers. Ten of our boys went into the attack on the farmhouse. It was called one of those funny names, Pullyers, something like that. And of the ten, only two came back. They killed all the Germans. But all the women and the baby inside were dead.'

'Raped, I suppose?' Mary said out of the corner of her mouth.

'Dreadful,' Betty confirmed. 'Raped and stabbed, and the little baby! Stabbed on bayonets where they lay. Devils they are, the Germans. They got all that was coming to them and if I had my way we'd have turned the lot of them over to the Russians. Let 'em sort each other out. Bloodthirsty savages, all of 'em.'

Lily moved away and looked out through the net curtains to the corner shop opposite where she had spent her childhood. There was an agent's 'To Let' sign up outside.

'I'll come over and help you pack up tomorrow,' Betty said behind her. 'Past is past, Lil. Your ma wouldn't want you to grieve.'

Lily nodded. 'I know.'

'When's the wedding?' Betty demanded. 'Have you set a date?'

'I only agreed the day before yesterday,' Lily said. 'We haven't decided.'

'And you live at his house with his mum and dad, do you? That must be cosy.'

Lily gave a little laugh. The cold silent house was anything but cosy. 'It's all right,' she said. 'His father is bedridden. He's had a stroke. His mother is nice.'

'She'll take the place of Helen,' Betty assured her. 'A girl your age, about to marry, needs a mother.'

Lily shook her head. 'No-one could take her place.'

'But she'll take you around and show you the ropes. You'll meet their friends and get to know the nobs. And you'll buy wonderful clothes. I expect you'll have a proper trousseau and go away!'

'I expect so.'

'You don't look too thrilled,' Mary said, coming up on the other side of Lily. 'Are you sure you're doing the right thing, Lil? Don't you go rushing into it and making a mistake. They're one thing when they're courting and another when they're married.'

Lily turned on her that blue blank gaze. 'I don't know,' she said simply. 'Ever since Ma died I feel like nothing matters. It doesn't matter if I marry him or not. It doesn't matter if I ever sing again or not. Everything I did, really, was to please her. All of my singing, going on tour, getting a job. I wanted her to be proud of me. Now she's gone I can't see the point of it. I can't see the point of anything.'

Mary and Betty exchanged a glance. 'I know it,' Mary said. 'That could be me speaking. I lost my mother when I was twenty. The doctors told her it would kill her to have another baby but what could she do? They didn't tell her how to not get one. They were right. She swelled up when she was six months gone. Kidneys, they said. I thought my world had ended. It took me years and years to get over it.'

Lily looked at her blankly. 'I can't imagine ever feeling right.'

'No,' Mary said. 'Just get through each day, Lil darling. Just take a day at a time and get through each one.'

'Could I come and live with you?' Lily asked, turning to Betty. 'Just stay here till I get back to work again?'

'Oh, bless you!' Betty folded Lily in her arms. 'I wish to God I could say yes, but I can't. There's my old man coughing his guts up every day and funny in his ways ever since the war, and I've got my two big girls at home and four children under five. You could have a couple of nights here, darling, if that's any help, but you'd have to share a bed with Millie and Clare. I don't think you'd like it – she brought you up so nice in your ways. And nothing for supper but bread and dripping.'

'Your ma brought you up too nice,' Mary said. 'She brought you up to be a lady. You don't really know what it's like, Lil.'

Lily nodded. 'It was just an idea. Seeing the shop made me want to be here again.'

Mary looked distressed. 'I'd offer you a bed with me but you know how George is. And he's back from prison next weekend.'

'No,' Lily said. 'It wouldn't work.'

'Don't look back,' Betty said. 'You've got your whole life to look forward to. A nice place to live and a gentleman. You're better away from here, Lil. Your ma was one of the best but she was never really happy here. She wanted better than this for you. She'd want you well married and away from here.'

Lily turned her large-eyed look on her. 'Are you sure?' she asked urgently. 'Are you sure she'd want me to marry him? She always told me not to marry young, to work at my career. But then she was there to care for me. What d'you think she'd tell me to do now?'

Betty and Mary exchanged one anxious glance. It was clear to them that Lily was incapable of running her own life, and there was no-one in the world to take care of her.

'She'd say marry him,' Betty said determinedly. 'Any mother would. The stage is no life for you, Lil, when you've not got her and the shop to fall back on. She wanted you to get ahead but she thought she'd always be there when you were out of work. Now she's gone you have to look after yourself. Marry him, Lil. He's a gentleman and he'll keep you handsome. Your ma would tell you the same if she was here. I know she would. And *I'm* telling you – and I loved your ma like she was my own sister. Marry your gentleman, Lil. There's nothing else for you to do.'

Lily nodded. She looked grim rather than relieved. 'I s'pose I'll have to, then,' she said.

Mary slid an arm around her waist and hugged her. 'It's your only choice,' she said. 'And there's very few marriages start as well. You'll get accustomed to his ways, and you'll never want for anything. He's head over heels for you, and when you're feeling better about your ma you'll be glad to be a married woman and have a nice home.'

Lily nodded. 'I will, then,' she said.

Coventry was outside the corner shop promptly at three and took Lily straight home. Stephen was still at the office but Muriel had ordered afternoon tea in the drawing room at a quarter to four. Lily went upstairs to take off her hat and called in to Rory Winters's room on her way down to the drawing room.

The room was shady, the curtains had been drawn for his afternoon sleep, but Lily could see his eyes were open. 'Shall I open the curtains?' she asked.

They were on cords and swished back easily when she pulled the heavy knobs. Golden sunlight spilled into the room. Lily looked out from the tower window over the Canoe Lake where people boated in little rowboats. Beyond them was the seafront road and the sea wall. The tide was out and there was a long smooth stretch of sand busy with children building castles and spooning fishing nets into the shallows. It was Alexandra Rose Day and Lily could see a long-skirted woman in a picture hat with a tray half-full of wilting roses walking slowly down the promenade.

'It's a lovely day,' Lily said. 'It really couldn't be nicer.' She came away from the window and stood at the foot of the bed. 'Perhaps we should see if you couldn't get into a wheelchair. I could wheel you along the front and you could see the sea and the children playing. We could go along to the pier. You'd like that, I expect.'

Rory Winters's twisted face was still. His dark eyes watched her intelligently like a man peeping through thick prison bars.

'We'll have to find things to do,' Lily said. 'You and me. Both of us in this house with nothing to do and no feelings in us. Perhaps we could walk by the sea.'

Chapter Thirteen

Stephen had decided that they should be married at the register office by special licence. By these means he overruled his mother's objections that Lily could hardly have a full formal white wedding in church while she was in mourning, and that waiting for the correct six months was clearly impossible while Lily was living in the same house.

Muriel took coffee with Jane Dent, Sarah's mother. 'It seems so rushed. But when I say anything to Stephen he's so impatient with me.'

'You would think she would want some time to get her things together,' Jane suggested.

Muriel sighed. 'What things? I mean, *what* things? She brought all her clothes from her mother's house in one suitcase. If she's to have any trousseau at all Stephen will have to buy it. And I will have to shop for it with her.'

'Can't she be trusted?'

'The only mercy, as far as I can see, is that she does have excellent taste. Whatever her mother was, she gave the girl as good a start in life as she could manage. No Portsmouth accent, thank God. She sent her to acting classes and they cured that. And she carries herself like a lady because of all the dancing classes.'

'No tendency to staginess?'

'She's just crushed,' Muriel said. 'I can't help but feel for her, even if I'd rather she'd never have been born. She goes around the house like a little white ghost. Stephen tells her what they are going to do and she just nods like a little doll. She's in no fit state to marry. She's in no fit state to take any decision. But if they don't marry what on earth can be done?'

'Can't you ship her off to friends? Family? She must have cousins or someone.'

'The mother seems to have been one of only two, and both her brother and Lily's father died in the war. Lily has friends in Highland Road.'

Jane gave a little ripple of horrified laughter.

'Exactly. And nowhere suitable for her to stay. She really is utterly alone in the world and she is very young. I can see that Stephen feels we should care for her.'

'Is it just chivalry then?'

Muriel shook her head. 'Not Stephen. If it had been Christopher now . . .' She broke off. She still could not mention her first son's name without the weight of her grief silencing her. 'Christopher was the one for chivalry,' she said, recovering. 'He was always rescuing things. Wounded seagulls, stray dogs, he brought a cat home once, I remember . . .' She broke off once more. The picture of Christopher's bright face above a mottled tabby kitten was unbearably vivid. 'Not Stephen. He's far too hard-headed. If he says he loves her and wants her to be his wife then I can't argue with him.'

'And is she happy that you should live all together in the same house?'

Muriel shrugged. 'She's never expressed an opinion on the matter one way or another as far as I know. Stephen seems to think there is no difficulty. If he wants to buy them a house then of course he has the funds to do so. But she fits very well into our lives. She sits with Rory, you know, every morning.'

Jane poured another cup of coffee into the delicate china cup. 'Honestly, my dear, if she had come from a good family I would be congratulating you. There aren't many girls today who would tolerate living with their in-laws. Let alone sitting in a sickroom.'

Muriel nodded. 'I suppose so. And no-one cares as much about families as they did before the war. Everything is changed. But you know, Jane, I wanted a lively girl. I wanted someone who would bring a little life into the house. Not parties all night of course, nothing fast. But I wanted a girl who would bring a little fun into Stephen's life. In the evenings it's like drinking coffee in a library. It's totally silent. Stephen reads the paper and Lily sits in the window seat with the curtain half-open and looks out at the sea.'

'When they're married it'll be different,' Jane said comfortingly. 'And when you have a little grandchild there will be enough noise in the house then, I should think!'

Muriel's face lit up. 'That's what we need,' she said. 'A child in the house again.'

'It's only a matter of time. And that will take her mind off the loss of her mother.'

Muriel nodded. 'A grandson,' she said wistfully. 'A little boy like Christopher. He was such a perfect baby. D'you remember how fair he was? He had blond curls from birth. Lily is fair, she might well have a fair-headed boy.'

'Bring her to tea,' Jane said. 'If she chooses not to be in mourning she might as well be out and about. She can meet Sarah. Bring her on one of my days. Bring her this Thursday.'

'Thank you, I will.' Muriel hesitated. 'And you will keep this between you and me, won't you, dear? I shouldn't like it to get around that I'm not especially thrilled with Stephen's choice. And I'd rather no-one knew about the corner shop. I tell anyone who asks that her parents had a small retail business. It's not a lie but it sounds better, don't you think?'

'Oh, trust me! I shan't tell a soul!'

'No,' Muriel said uncertainly, knowing she had been indiscreet. 'Heavens, is that the time? I must go, Coventry will be waiting.'

'Oh, do you have him still? I'd have thought you'd have got rid of him by now. It must be so inconvenient having a mute for a chauffeur.'

'Stephen would never let him go.'

Jane rang the bell and waited. Then she rang again, louder and more impatiently. 'I don't think anyone ever imagined what the war would do to girls,' she said irritably. 'During the war I couldn't get a girl to work in the house for love nor money because they all wanted to work in the dockyard or be landgirls, and now they charge the earth, they want countless days off and they simply don't know their jobs.'

'They just don't care.'

'You would have thought with a million people unemployed that they would want the work!'

'They were spoiled during the war. Ridiculous wages and too much freedom. We'll never get the old days back again.'

'Stephen must wonder what he fought for, he really must.'

'Yes,' Muriel said, suddenly descending from indignation. 'I am afraid he does. It is not the England he left in 1917. Nor the sort of world he thought he would come home to.'

The maid burst into the room, holding Muriel's summer jacket. 'Beg pardon, m'm. I was out the back.'

Muriel took the jacket.

'He should have what he wants,' Jane said. 'He was a hero, after all.'

Muriel nodded. 'Yes,' she said. 'I'll bring Lily to see you on Thursday. She is quite presentable, really, you'll see.'

*   *   *

179

Lily and Stephen were shopping together in Palmerston Road, Southsea. It was an attractive street, busy with trams running up and down and horse-drawn delivery wagons, boys on bicycles with big iron baskets and the occasional private car. A band of crippled ex-soldiers played a ragged march with a collecting bucket placed before them. A label propped against it read: 'Veterans of the Great War. Please give generously. No work, no pensions, no hope.' Lily and Stephen crossed the road to avoid them without comment. They were going to buy Lily's engagement ring.

'A sapphire, to match your eyes,' Stephen said.

Lily remembered her daydream of swanning into the dressing room with a large and expensive ring on her finger. She summoned a smile. 'That would be nice,' she said.

The jeweller was expecting them. Stephen's clerk had telephoned from work to say they would be coming. 'It's better that way,' Stephen explained. 'Then they know who they're dealing with. It saves time and you get better service.'

The man had a tray of sapphires ready. Stephen picked out the largest at once. It was a big square-cut stone, set on its own in a claw setting on a thin band of gold. 'That's a beauty.'

The jeweller manifested intense surprise. 'Captain Winters, I had no idea you had any experience with gems.'

Stephen smiled and smoothed his moustache. 'A man of the world has a certain eye . . .'

'A very certain eye if I may say so. Would the young lady like to try?'

Lily put out her hand. The ring slid on, the band was far too big. 'It's too big.' She felt it drowned her hand, the big stone and the bright blue of the colour.

'We can alter it to your size, Madam. Any one of these

can be altered to your size. Don't let that distract you from your choice.'

Lily pointed to a smaller stone set either side with white diamonds. 'That's pretty.'

'Charming,' the jeweller said. 'A charming choice. A modest little ring which suits a small hand.' He slid it on.

'Paltry,' Stephen declared. He picked up the ring with the big stone again.

'Nothing to compare with that beauty of course. But a very pretty ring and exquisitely set. You certainly know craftsmanship when you see it, Madam.'

'Try this one.' Stephen indicated another.

Lily slid it on. It was another large stone, only a little smaller than the first. It bumped against her knuckle and weighed heavy on her hand.

'It feels heavy.'

'You'll get used to it. You'll have to get used to a wedding ring as well, Lily, remember!'

Lily nodded. She spread her hand and moved it under the lights, making the stone sparkle. It covered the whole of the lower joint of her finger from knuckle to the first joint. Under the smart electric lights it glowed like a blue flame.

'Either this one, or the bigger one,' Stephen decided. 'Don't you think, Lily? It's your choice of course.'

'Whichever you prefer.' Lily could feel a deep weariness spreading through her. She had felt tired for days, ever since the funeral. She wondered if she had caught her mother's flu.

Stephen chuckled. 'It's not which I like best, my little darling. It's which you like best.'

The jeweller stepped discreetly back from the counter, out of earshot, keeping his eye on the tray of rings.

'You're the one that will wear it, dearest.'

Lily looked up at Stephen; her pale face was quite indifferent. 'But you're the one who will see it.'

'You'll see it, little goose! It will be on your hand!'

She shook her head. 'I won't see it any more than I see my fingernails or my face in the mirror. I shall get accustomed to it. I shall get accustomed to everything in time.'

'I shall never get accustomed to you.'

They were silent for a moment.

'Which one do you really prefer?' Lily asked politely.

It struck Stephen that they were jointly incapable of taking a decision. Lily was too young and her tastes were still unformed. For instance, she had chosen the small sparkly ring in preference to the large stone which was clearly more valuable.

Fortunately she had the good sense to give way to him in all decisions, and it would be his duty as her husband to guide and form her taste. Consultation was a courtesy and he would never neglect it. But you couldn't run a regiment democratically. In any relationship there was a leader and the led. In his relationship with Lily he would lead her and guide her, and, if needs be – order her. She was to be his wife after all. Not an equal but a helpmeet.

In any case Lily and Stephen had no language for ordinary conversation. In the days of their brief courtship Lily had chattered and he had listened. Now Lily was silent there were no patterns of speech between them that could be adapted to making decisions. Even important decisions about the wedding and their future life had been made by Stephen; Lily only ever consented.

'We'll have the big one. Damn the expense.'

'Is it very expensive?'

Stephen chuckled indulgently. 'And what if it is? I can afford it, and you deserve it.'

The jeweller measured Lily's finger and promised that it would be altered at once.

'Could you send it round when it's done? We'd want it at once.'

'Of course, Sir.'

Stephen passed him a card. The man noted the select address. 'I could probably have it ready for this evening. I will deliver it myself. With a jewel of this quality I wouldn't trust it to anyone else.'

'We'll have it safely on your finger in no time,' Stephen said, smiling at Lily.

'Yes.'

Coventry had been ordered to meet them after driving Mrs Winters home. 'Let's stroll towards home and window shop,' Stephen suggested. 'You'd better get your skates on, Lily, and buy some clothes. When people know we're married you'll be invited everywhere.'

Lily nodded.

'You used to be mad for clothes. Every time I took you out for tea or dinner you would be looking at ladies' clothes. Don't you want to shop? We could have a dress-maker round, have her run some things up for you? Or London, now? We could go up to town and you could take your pick. I bet you'd like Harrods, eh, Lily?'

Lily smiled. She hardly heard him. She felt as if she were at the bottom of a thick glass jug. A cider jug with narrow finger-sized handles at the neck, for carrying. A narrow, narrow neck through which she would never escape and a wide echoing body. Lily felt she would roll round and around inside the empty jar while people's voices boomed and rang around her. But they could never hear her reply. And she could never quite distinguish what they said. She was as incapable of speech, of speaking truly and openly to Stephen, as she was incapable of tears.

Lily's grief had stunned her. All she could hear was the

echoing booming of speech. All she could see was a curiously shrunken distant world, lacking in colour or interest. All she could feel was the cold lost confusion of a little doll swirling round and around in the bottom of a deep glass jar.

'Come on, dear!' Stephen said. 'Wouldn't Harrods be fun? Actually, I've a better idea! Let's leave it all until after we are married and then go up to London for a couple of days. We could stay at a hotel. We could go to some shows. We could have a bit of a lark, Lily – you'd like that. Dancing, sightseeing, a real trip. And you could buy your clothes and come back to Portsmouth with a whole set of London outfits and turn a few heads, eh? What d'you think of that?'

Lily looked up at Stephen. She saw his bright eager face smiling at her. She remembered a time when he had seemed terribly old, and terribly battered from the war. Now she felt years older than his boyish enthusiasm. Years older, and so weary that she ached with tiredness.

'That would be great fun, Stephen. Thank you. I should like that.'

'And if you liked, we could . . .'

'There's the car,' Lily interrupted.

Stephen stepped forward into the road and hailed Coventry with a stentorian shout. Coventry pulled up on the opposite side of the road and held the door open for Lily. Stephen got in the back beside her.

'Home,' he ordered.

Coventry drove down Clarendon Road, past East Southsea station to the seafront, and drew up outside the house. He opened the door for Lily but Stephen got out only to escort Lily to the front door and to open it for her. 'I'll go on to the office, my dear,' he said. 'Tell Mother I'll be home for tea.'

Lily nodded and went slowly inside. She did not notice

184

that Stephen had leaned forward to kiss her cheek and she parted from him without touching him. She had forgotten to thank him for the ring. The door closed behind her. Stephen, thrown off balance by his step forward and his rejected kiss, turned and strolled down the steps to the car.

'Let's go to that pub down by the Hard,' he said, getting into the passenger seat beside Coventry. 'I'm damned if I'm going into the office this morning. They don't expect me until after lunch anyway.'

Coventry drove carefully down the seafront. Stephen stared at the people promenading beside the sea. The women were wearing light summer dresses cut very short with thin white stockings. Many of the men had taken off their blazers and loosened their ties. 'Trippers.'

Children were playing at the edge of the sea. The tide was half in, and the sandy bars of the beach were covered. There were bathing machines rolled down to the water, some ready for hire further up the beach. The new clubhouse for the Southsea swimming club was busy. Men were standing around the steps in boaters and long bathing suits.

They drove past the pier, past the signs advertising boat trips. They drove beside the common where a space had been allocated for an impressive war memorial which would commemorate the names of all of Portsmouth's sons who had died on land and sea in the Great War.

'Bloody Christopher,' Stephen said aloud.

Coventry drove into Old Portsmouth under the shadow of the old harbour walls, built like the outer walls of a castle, two storeys high. He parked the car at some distance from the pub. Stephen cocked an eyebrow at him. 'I daresay you're right,' he said. 'We don't want anyone getting funny with us. I can't start fighting at lunchtime half a mile from my office.'

185

The pub was a rough working-men's drinking room, catering mainly to dockers coming off shift, to sailors on shore leave and to anyone prepared to risk being caught drinking out of hours, the new restrictive hours which had come in with the wartime regulations, and never been phased out.

Stephen knocked on the door and stepped into the shadowy room. Coventry was close behind him. The landlord behind the bar looked up quickly when they came in but then relaxed as he recognized the two of them.

'What'll it be, gentlemen?'

'Two pints and two whiskies.'

Stephen paid and they took their drinks to a table in the corner. Next to them were two men bent over a cribbage board. At the bar was the only other customer, an ex-boxer. He drank slowly and cautiously, but every now and then his head would twist, and he would throw himself back, once, twice, three times, ducking from imaginary hits. His hands were balled in permanent fists.

Stephen watched him curiously, a man who carried his battles with him, who could never be free of the fighting he had done. Coventry drank from his pint glass and sipped from his whisky alternately with quiet thoroughness.

'I love her,' Stephen offered suddenly. 'No doubt about that. No doubt at all. But I made no allowances for the amount of work she creates. The inconvenience.'

Coventry took a cigarette, took two to light them together, recollected where he was and instead offered the packet to Stephen. Stephen took his own and lit it. 'She's not very gay. I know her mother's only been buried a few days but how long is she going to mope? She sits in Father's bedroom with him and you know, there's little to choose between the two of them. I wanted her because she was so untouched. You only had to look into her face to know that she had never been afraid, she had never

186

been hurt, she had never seen death. But she's different now.'

Coventry leaned forward and knocked the ash from his cigarette into his cupped palm and then dropped it on the floor. He gave Stephen a long level look.

Stephen paused on a thought. 'No,' he said slowly. 'I won't pull out. I'll marry her. She'll perk up when she's married. She's still shocked. I can still see that white shocked look about her. Some of them, d'you remember? stayed shocked for days. Not the really bad cases, but if you had a bit of a fright you'd be a bit shaky for a week or so. You'd b . . . be a bit shaky for a w . . . w . . . week or so.'

Stephen leaned forward and took a large mouthful of whisky to still his stammer.

'I want her,' he said. 'This changes nothing. I want her as she was before she went away, before her mother died. She'll change back. She's the girl I want. I knew the moment I saw her that she was the right one for me; and she will be. She can make it all come right for me. She can if she wants to. She can make it all come right for me if she wants to.'

Lily hesitated in the hall listening to the car drive away. The house was quiet. Muriel was upstairs waiting for the gong for lunch. The nurse was feeding Rory Winters. Lily could hear her bright meaningless words of encouragement. She turned to go up the stairs as the tweeny came through the baize door.

'Oh Miss Pears, there's a letter for you, came on the second delivery. Did you see it?'

Lily hesitated.

Sally picked up the letter from the hall table, placed it on the little silver tray and offered it to Lily. It was a pink envelope, liberally sprayed with Devon violets perfume –

the show had reached Plymouth. Lily could smell it at arm's length. She grinned at Sally. 'A bit strong!' she said.

'Would that be one of your theatrical friends, Miss?'

Lily nodded. 'Madge Sweet, I should think. They're on tour, working their way home along the coast.' She took the letter and ran up the stairs to her room. She cast off her hat and slung it towards her dressing table, dropped forwards on to her bed like a girl and tore open the envelope. Madge had not stinted with scent on the letter either.

'Phew!' Lily waved the letter in the air, half-laughing.

Dear Lil,

Thank you for your note though it was v. short. I am sorry to hear about your ma. What a shock. Everyone here says they are very sorry too. That flu is a real killer, my aunt had it and they nearly lost her but she has very strong lungs on account of having been in the busness too as a singer.

You missed out on some good fun. Plymouth was a lark. Packed out every night and the place crawling with sailors. Jones the Magic was in his element as you can imajine. He nearly had us thrown out of the digs – you can imajine why. Mike smoothed it all down but he was furius. I fell completly in love for two days but then found that he was maried. Anyway I have a nice handbag to show for it so can't complain.

Guess who has your spot? Yes me! Not as a choir-boy thank you very much. I do that number you saw me practise with darling Charlie – red hot baby. I wear the red can-can bodice with a pair of frilly red shorts like a bathing costume. Indesent! Charlie desined it, of course. For a man who never seems to do anything more, he does a lot of looking!!!

Which reminds me that I never heard what happened to you that night! What a shame you had to dash off before you could tell us All About It. And what does your Captain say now?

Charlie says absolutely zero like the gent. he is. I told him straight that I had put you up to your midnight visit and he looked down his nose and said I was a trumpet!

Anyway. You're not at all welcome back since I've got your spot! But we do all miss you so you can come and fight me for it. Actuly the show would run better if they dropped Sylvia de Charmante altogether – but don't say I said so. She was drery as ditchwater in Plymouth. If she goes any slower they'll fall asleep. She sings Keep the Home Fires like it was a funral march.

Let us know what is going on. When are you coming back? Got to dash – it's tea time. Will post this at once.

Love Madge (The red hot baby!)

PS Charlie says he will add a page and then seal up the envelope and post it for me. Wonder what he'll say? Do write and tell me!

There was one more page in a different hand.

Dear Lily,

I am so grieved for you in your loss. I know how much your mother meant to you and how much you must miss her now. She was a fine brave woman. There are no adequate words.

I hope you will come back to us when you feel able – and not before. If you can't come back before the end of the tour that will be all right. I'll straighten it out with William. And you can still audition for the Kings when I come back.

I have thought of you, and missed you. It was painful for me after you left, having to part so quickly like that, without a chance to talk. I hope it was easier for you.

Even though I can never be anything more, I am your very good friend. Let me know if there is anything you need.

With my love as I promised,
Charlie Smith.

Lily read and re-read Charlie's letter. Then she put her face deep into her pillow so that her sobs would not be heard in that quiet empty house, and she cried and cried and cried.

That afternoon she walked down to the post office and asked for a telegram form. She addressed it to Charlie Smith at the digs, copying the address carefully off Madge's letter. She wrote: 'I AM MARRYING STEPHEN WINTERS ON SATURDAY UNLESS I HEAR FROM YOU STOP.'

She paid with the last pound note in her purse and then she walked back to the silent red-brick house with the white windows overlooking the Canoe Lake.

Charlie's reply came the next day while Muriel and Lily were finishing their breakfast. Stephen's broken eggshells and empty cup were still at the head of the table. Lily was moving her hand in the sunlight, watching her ring sparkle with its deep blue colour.

'A telegram!' Muriel exclaimed as she saw the boy's peaked cap pass the dining room window to the front door steps. Her colour drained from her face, her hand was up at her pearls, pressing them against her throat. 'A telegram!'

'It's all right,' Lily said quickly. 'It's probably from Plymouth. I wrote to my friends that I was getting married. It's all right, Mrs Winters.'

The colour began to return to Muriel's cheeks. 'How silly of me.' She was still trembling. 'It was just that during the war everyone dreaded the telegram boy. I remember watching him biking down the road and praying that he wasn't coming here. And then one day it was for us.'

Lily went to the door to take the telegram from Sally.

'Silver tray,' Muriel said sharply. 'All letters, even telegrams, must be put on the silver tray before you bring them in. I will not tolerate this kind of post-war sloppiness.'

'Sorry, M'm,' Sally whispered. She snatched the telegram back and disappeared into the hall. Lily had to wait until she brought it back on the silver tray.

As Muriel watched, Lily took it and opened it. It was from the Midsummer Madness company. 'HEARTIEST CONGRATS STOP WILL THINK OF YOU SAT STOP MUCH FUTURE HAPPINESS STOP WHAT A BREAK STOP. MIDSUMMER MADNESS, PLYMOUTH.'

'Bad news?' Muriel asked, looking at Lily's shocked face.

Lily turned with a thin little smile. 'No. It is congratulations for Saturday. I telegraphed them yesterday that I was marrying Stephen.'

She held out the telegram to Muriel. Muriel flinched a little when she came to the bright vulgarity of 'WHAT A BREAK STOP'.

Lily took the telegram back.

'What a shame none of them will be in Portsmouth for your wedding. Will your friends from Highland Road come to the register office?'

'No. Stephen and I want to be very quiet.'

'And have you chosen your dress? Did you see anything when you were out buying your ring?'

Lily shook her head. 'Could we go shopping today or tomorrow?'

'Of course. What d'you have in mind? A little dress and jacket? Or a coat dress outfit?'

Lily tried to smile but her whole face was trembling. 'I don't know. Let's see what there is. I don't know really.'

'Are you all right, Lily?'

'Yes! Oh yes!' Lily crumpled the telegram into a ball and tossed it into the waste paper basket. 'Quite all right,' she said.

Chapter Fourteen

Lily's July wedding was sunny. Her dress was yellow linen – low-waisted with a pleated skirt, and matching coat. Her hat was a little panama straw cloche trimmed with a matching yellow ribbon. Muriel thought she did them all credit, under the circumstances. Stephen wore a plain light grey summer suit. He refused to wear his medals. The witnesses were Muriel and John Pascoe from Stephen's office. The only hitch in the smooth and unemotional proceedings came when Lily's Aunt Mary and Betty appeared without warning and threw rice and kissed Lily, loud smacking sentimental kisses outside the register office and in full view of anyone who might be passing. Lily flushed rosy red and threw her arms around them and kissed them back. Muriel scowled at Coventry, who was holding open the car door and grinning, and then shot an angry look at Stephen.

'Would you ladies like to join us? We have booked a table for luncheon at the Dolphin Hotel before we leave for London.'

Betty and Aunt Mary recoiled at once from Stephen's icy politeness.

'Not at all!'

'So sorry, we can't.'

Lily giggled. For a moment in her new yellow dress and little hat, she looked like a pretty girl, a bride.

'Oh, go away, you two!' she exclaimed. 'Coming up to town and making a lot of fuss! I told you it was going to be a quiet wedding!'

Betty hugged her again. 'You look a picture. A picture!'

She turned to Muriel. 'I'm glad to meet you, Mrs Winters, you couldn't have a better daughter-in-law than our Lil.'

Muriel frigidly proffered a white gloved hand. 'Thank you, Mrs . . . er . . .'

'Betty Hoskins. And this is Lil's Aunt Mary.'

Aunt Mary leaned forward. 'She's not had it easy, little Lil,' she confided. 'But she's not one of those flighty types and for all she was on the stage she knows where to draw the line. Her ma – God rest her soul – kept her in line. You can ask anybody.'

Muriel prompted Stephen with another speaking glance.

'Lily, we must go,' he said.

Lily hugged Betty and Aunt Mary again. 'You're a pair of ducks to come!' she said. 'An absolute pair of ducks. But I've got to go now. I'll come and see you when we get back.'

Aunt Mary held her close. 'She'd have been glad to see you settled, Lil,' she whispered. 'She wanted the stage for you but it was only to see you make your own living. She wanted you to be set up for life. She'd be pleased to see you settled and with a man with a steady income.'

Lily blinked rapidly. 'I know.'

'Lily . . .' Stephen said, a hint of irritation in his tone.

Lily stepped back and got into the Argyll. Muriel got in beside her and Stephen and John Pascoe took the little fold-down seats facing the ladies. Lily leaned forward to wave. Betty threw handfuls of rice as they drew away. More by luck than judgement it pattered against the half-open window and spilled over the floor. Stephen tutted at the mess. 'My hat, Lily, what an awful pair!'

Lily looked at him, unsmiling. 'What d'you mean?' she asked.

Stephen shook his head and put his hand to his moustache to hide his smile. 'Nothing, my dear. Nothing at all.'

Lunch was a restrained affair. They had a private dining room and they ate roast beef, Yorkshire puddings, roast potatoes, carrots and overcooked sprouts. John Pascoe ordered a bottle of warm champagne and drank a toast to the happy couple. Lily ate very little and hardly tasted the champagne.

'Sugar lump!' Stephen said. He reached over to Lily's glass and dropped a lump of sugar in it. He smiled at John Pascoe and his mother. 'We had a young lad in our battalion. Never drunk wine or beer in his life. Methodist family; I think he signed the pledge when he was a child. We had him taste some champagne – we got hold of a case – and he hated it. We put a sugar lump in it and told him it was lemonade and he couldn't get enough of it. Taste it, Lily!'

Lily took a cautious sip and then smiled and drank. 'I like it better sweet,' she said.

'How on earth did you have a case of champagne in the trenches?' Muriel asked.

Stephen winked at John. 'Spoils of war. Spoils of war.'

'And what happened to the teetotaller?'

Stephen laughed a cracked laugh. 'That was funny. He got the most dreadful taste for it and we couldn't stop him drinking. He'd drink as soon as he got up in the morning and he'd try and buy the men's tots of rum off them. Every time we went behind the lines he'd be dead drunk!'

Lily was shocked. She had lived in a class where a drinking husband was a death sentence for a family. 'That's dreadful. What happened to him?'

Stephen shrugged. 'It didn't matter so much, really. He d . . . d . . . died a few weeks later.'

'Because he was drunk?' Lily pursued.

'B . . . b . . . b . . . because he was there,' Stephen snapped.

'What time is your train?' Muriel asked, filling the silence.

Stephen checked his watch. 'Not long. I'll pay the bill and we'll go. You'll see us off, won't you, John?'

'Of course! It's not every day I get a chance to celebrate a wedding between two such delightful young people.'

Lily grinned at him and for a moment even Muriel could see Lily's unconscious easy charm.

The two women went to the cloakroom and straightened their hats.

Muriel put her hand out on Lily's arm to delay their return to the men. She was blushing furiously. 'Lily, did your mother tell you about men, about men as husbands, I mean?'

Lily turned her wide blue eyes on Muriel. 'No,' she said. 'She didn't think I'd be getting married for years.'

Muriel took her hat off again and turned towards the mirror, pushed her waved hair into place, and replaced her hat. 'Then you should know, my dear, that a man has to take his pleasure with his wife. And that the wife has to consent. But I expect you knew that?'

Lily nodded slowly.

'It hurts a little the first time, but it is not "done" to complain,' Muriel said rapidly. She took off her hat again. Lily watched her, saying nothing.

'You may bleed a little.' Muriel's voice was scarcely more than a whisper. 'There is no need for alarm. You may feel some pain. Just ignore it.'

Lily had a sudden vivid thought of Charlie's warm bed and the smell of his skin and the soft stubbly scratch of his growing beard as he kissed her. She thought of his lean body against hers and how she had felt herself swirling and spinning as he held her.

196

'Isn't it nice? Isn't it nice at all?'

Muriel suddenly lost her embarrassment and became disapproving. 'Certainly not,' she said. 'Not for a lady. A lady always behaves with restraint.'

Lily looked at her uncertainly. What Muriel was telling her was confirmed by her own mother's reluctant acceptance of her husband's drunken kisses and the belief among the Highland Road women that men demanded their rights and that women avoided them where possible. But it made no sense with the memory of Charlie's warm kisses.

'But men enjoy it,' Lily suggested.

'A lady is not like a man,' Muriel said stiffly. 'A man gets pleasure from it, and the lady's pleasure is in giving in to him. It is how children are conceived and those are true joys of marriage. Stephen is a gentleman, of course. You have nothing to fear, Lily. I just thought I should make sure you knew that something will happen.'

'But when girls go wrong . . . they must do it because they like it?'

Muriel jammed her hat on her head and scowled in the mirror at Lily. 'Those are bad girls,' she said fiercely. 'A lady does not enjoy it. A well-brought-up girl does not enjoy it. Bad girls are the same as prostitutes. They are like men. We do not think about them. We do not mention them. Stephen would not want a bride like that.'

'I'm not like that!' Lily said, stung.

Muriel turned from the mirror and gave her a hard look. 'I trust not, my dear. No girl who felt those kind of feelings would have any business marrying into a family such as ours. I trust indeed that you have the feelings of a lady. Leave it all to Stephen, he'll know what to do. He wants nothing from you but your innocence.'

Lily faced her mother-in-law for a few cold moments and then she nodded. The two women left the cloakroom and joined the men. The bill had been paid, the car was waiting. Coventry had swept out the back seat but Lily could still see little grains of rice trapped in the corners.

Stephen had reserved seats for them on the train and their first-class compartment was empty. Stephen and Lily waited on the platform as Coventry stowed the bags, then got into the train and smiled from the window at Muriel and John waiting for them to leave.

Lily suddenly thought of the fuss and the noise on the platform when Midsummer Madness was on tour, the girls screaming instructions about their cases and Charlie smiling across the carriage at her. It was a painful contrast between the carefree scramble on tour and this stiff solemn ritual which was her honeymoon.

'Are you all right, Lily? You're pale.'

Lily shook her head at Muriel. 'I'm fine.'

The guard blew a whistle, unfurled a green flag. 'Bye!' Stephen called. He was looking beyond his mother and his business partner to where Coventry stood at the ticket gate at the end of the platform. Coventry raised a hand in a gesture like a half-salute, or even a blessing, a benediction. Lily waved at Muriel and John and the train jolted forward, throwing her against Stephen. He caught her, and so the last Muriel saw of them was Lily in Stephen's arms and both of them laughing as the train drew away.

'They looked happy,' she said doubtfully to John as they turned and walked slowly to the car.

He threw her a sideways look. 'If anyone knows how bad these post-war marriages can be it would be Stephen,' he said. 'Day in and day out he is doing divorce work. He knows his own mind. Don't fret. And she is a lovely, lovely girl.'

'I don't understand him any more,' Muriel said. 'Ever since the war . . .'

'Oh, the war,' John sighed. Coventry held the door of the car and Muriel got in, John beside her. 'Nothing is the same now. Nothing ever will be the same again. Who would have thought that just four years could have changed so much?'

Stephen had booked them into the Russell Hotel in Russell Square. When the cab dropped them at the imposing red-brick doorway he had been pleased to see Lily look up and up at the high building and then jump nervously when the doorman stepped forward and opened the door for them.

Stephen registered their names at the reception desk while Lily gazed around the imposing lobby. There was a bright crystal chandelier hanging from the high painted ceiling, and a massive flight of shallow stairs edged with what looked like a marble balustrade. There was a cocktail bar to the right of the entrance and they could hear laughter and the chink of glasses. To the left was another bar and the dining rooms.

'Room twenty-four, Mr Winters,' the clerk said, handing him a key. He struck the bell on the counter top and two porters came forward to carry the suitcases. Lily and Stephen followed them up the stairs. Stephen liked how Lily looked all around her and how her ring, now matched with the new broad gold band, sparkled as her hand trailed up the bannister.

Their room was large, dominated by a double bed, furnished with heavy gilt furniture upholstered in green velvet. The carpet was green and the curtains at the tall windows were green, swagged back with heavy tie-backs of green and gold lace. There was even a bathroom attached to the room. Stephen had spared no expense. He tipped the porters sixpence each, and they left, shutting the door behind them.

'I bet you've never been anywhere like this in your life before!' Stephen crowed.

Lily's little face was quite aghast. 'Stephen, it must have cost a fortune. Can you afford it?'

He laughed confidently. 'I think we can run to a little luxury just this once. Now, what would you like to do first? The British Museum? The shops? A drive around the park? The Tower of London?'

'I want to unpack.'

Stephen chuckled indulgently. 'Ring for a maid, she can do it for you.'

Lily laid hold of the lid of her suitcase. 'No! No! I want to do it!'

'Funny girl. Go on then, I'll wait for you. No hurry.'

He went to the telephone by the bed and rang down for a whisky and soda. He did not offer a drink to Lily. He did not think of it. When the waiter came with the drink Stephen settled himself into an armchair by the window, lit a cigarette, and watched Lily moving quietly around their bedroom unpacking her few dresses, and putting her toothbrush and her flannel and her little piece of soap in the bathroom which he would share.

'Lily,' he said softly. He was aroused by this quiet domestic preparation.

Lily looked towards him, warned by his tone.

'Come here.'

She glanced at her empty suitcase and towards the bathroom door. There was no reason to refuse him. She stepped slowly, awkwardly, the three or four steps across the room. She stood before him.

Stephen made no move to touch her. He eyed her over the top of his whisky glass, his cigarette in his other hand. 'Have a taste,' he said, holding out the glass to her. Lily took a quick instinctive step backwards, whipping her hands behind her back. 'No!' she said.

'Why, you're like a little girl, a little girl, Lily.' He was smiling. He got to his feet, bringing the glass with him.

'Try a little whisky. You might like it. You tried lobsters. D'you remember when we were out at dinner in Southsea? And oysters? I should make you eat lots of oysters, Lily, even though you hate them. D'you know why?'

Lily stepped back again and then felt the double bed against the back of her legs. She did not know why she felt this rising fear. This was not like Stephen, not courteous gentlemanly Stephen. This was like some kind of stranger, the sort of man who once stopped her on the street and offered her sweeties. Lily, with a shopful of sweets at home, had been instantly suspicious and ran away. But she remembered the mixture of fascination and fear. What did Stephen want of her that he spoke so softly and yet why was his voice also so menacing?

He brought the glass up to her face. Lily, trapped by the bed behind her, stood still and bent her lips to the glass. He tipped it and she took a good mouthful. She gulped it down and coughed, her eyes watering. 'It's horrible!' she exclaimed. 'Ugh! It burns! It's really nasty!'

Stephen put down the glass and put a gentle hand under her chin to turn her face up to him. 'I don't like to see a girl drink spirits,' he said. 'I'm glad you don't like it, Lily.'

He bent his head closer. Lily remembered the time he had kissed her on the beach and her sense of suffocation and fear. She moved slightly backwards, and again felt the edge of the mattress against the back of her knees. She could not move away from him now. She could not demand to be taken to the theatre now. She could not refuse to see him again. She had married him.

Stephen's mouth came down on hers. Lily tasted whisky and the stale taste of cigarette smoke. She stayed absolutely still, her face upraised. She let him kiss her cool lips and she let his arm go around her waist and press her closer to him. She felt a sense of enormous detachment, as if her real self had retreated to a corner of her mind, curled up, and was watching Stephen's hand as it slid down over the curve of Lily's buttock and clenched it tight.

Stephen's tongue touched the corner of her mouth. Lily found she was holding her breath and breathed out with a sigh, relaxing her lips. At once his other arm came around her and his grip tightened. His tongue probed into her mouth. Lily froze, enduring the sense of invasion. She was afraid she would gag.

He pushed her gently back on the bed. Lily stiffened as if she were going to struggle and then suddenly the fight went out of her and she sat, and then, obedient to his hand on her shoulder, she lay back. She thought for a second, for nothing more than a second, of the night she had spent in Charlie Smith's narrow single bed, and the warmth, and the popping light of the gas fire, and a man whose body she had longed to touch all over, who had lain silent and smiling, holding her close.

The green silk counterpane was cold, slick against the nape of her neck. Stephen was pressing down on top of her, his knee driving in between her legs, forcing her to open them, and then he was lying between her legs and his hand was fumbling down between them.

The clock on the mantelpiece gave a whirr, and then struck. The little silvery bells rang one – two – three – four – Lily gave a gasp. 'Four o'clock!' she exclaimed. Her voice was high with panic. She snatched a breath and brought it under control. She could act her way out of this. She knew she could act her way through this horror. She thought of her ma saying, 'You're a born actress, Lily,' and the lessons where she had been taught to mimic a thousand emotions – fear, anger, shock, terror, grief. She had never been taught to sound like a lady, like an upper-class virgin on her way to tea. But Lily was gambling that she could do it.

Stephen's hand was under her skirt, fumbling at her

thighs, the cool bare stretch of thigh between stocking top and camiknickers. 'Four o'clock,' Lily said calmly. 'Tea time, Stephen.'

As he hesitated she slid up the bed away from him, pulling down the yellow linen skirt, and smiling at him. She felt her lower lip tremble with her fear, and she reassembled the smile at once. 'Tea time,' she said.

Stephen got up at once from the bed, turned his back to her, adjusted his trousers and turned back. 'You must forgive me,' he said with a throaty chuckle. 'Broad daylight too. I can't imagine what I was thinking of.'

Lily crossed to the mirror and combed her hair. Her face was absolutely serene. The room was reflected behind her and she was watching Stephen closely. He looked half-abashed and half-proud.

'You must forgive me. I have waited to be alone with you as my wife for a very long time. I feel very passionate. A man has feelings like this. Urgent feelings. They cannot be denied. It is bad for the health to deny these feelings for too long.'

Lily nodded and put down her comb. Unconsciously she was reproducing precisely the gestures and the well-born confidence of Stephen's mother. 'Of course,' she said smoothly. She had not listened to one word that he had said. But she had heard, attentively, the voice of a man bringing himself back under control. She would be safe from Stephen until tonight. She would be safe until the strict conventions of his class sanctioned the act of inter-course. Stephen thought it wrong to make love at tea time. The time for lovemaking between a respectable man and his wife was night-time and in the dark. Anything else, by daylight, or anywhere else but the marital bed, was the behaviour of a whore and a client.

Lily put on her hat and took up her gloves and they went downstairs to the residents' lounge for tea.

It was gay downstairs. There was a little quartet playing music from light operas and Strauss waltzes and there were a number of well-dressed women and attractive men taking tea together. Lily looked around her with interest. She could see now that her yellow dress and coat were badly cut and ordinary compared with the London fashions. It had stood out in the Portsmouth department store, but here they were using lighter materials, double-lined even treble-lined for decency but which still floated out when the woman walked or moved, and fell in loose folds and pleats when she sat still. Lily could not see the secret of the cut of the fabric but she could see that the dresses flowed in a shimmer of material while hers stayed obstinately stiff. Her hat, she noted with relief, was entirely all right.

'I should like to go to the shops,' she said with sudden decision. Stephen had lit another cigarette, but when the waiter came with the tea things and a tray of scones and another tray of little cakes he put it out.

'I am longing to buy some clothes,' Lily said. 'D'you know where we should go, Stephen?'

'I should think Harrods would be the place to start,' he said. 'Mother jotted down some names for me. I have them in my diary. But she hasn't been up to town for clothes for years. If we go now, we should catch them before they close, and you can ask the girls there where they would recommend.'

Lily nodded. Her face over the teapot was bright. She looked like the old Lily that Stephen had desired as his saviour from his fear of war. She was experiencing a rush of elation at having got away from the bedroom so easily and so well. Lily set aside the thought of the coming night. She had been forced down by Stephen, and she had felt the panic of weakness; but then she had talked herself out of trouble. Lily beamed at him and drained her cup of tea.

Stephen smiled back. 'Well, Mrs Winters,' he said. 'You look as if you were enjoying married life, I must say.'

'What a lark!' Lily said. Her voice shook slightly with fright, but then she got it under control. 'What a huge lark!'

The shopping trip was a success. Stephen loved being waited on and treated with unctuous respect. They fetched him a little gilt chair in the women's dress department and he sat at the glass showcase for gloves smoking a cigarette and watching while Lily changed from one fashionable frock to another. Now and then Stephen would wave a hand authoritatively at one of the three women who were serving them and say: 'She must have that one! We'll take it!'

Lily was feeling very bright and modern surrounded by beautiful dresses and watched by a handsome man, her new husband. She had never before had more than one new dress at a time, and since all her clothes were made by either her mother or her Aunt Mary she had seen them at every stage of their making – from the cloth, to the cut-pieces, to the final dress. By then the dress had lost its gloss of newness and Lily had lost her excitement over it. After it had been fitted half a dozen times and Lily had been co-opted to sew the seams and the hem it felt like an old dress, certainly a familiar one.

But these beauties came from some mysterious store room at the back of the shop. The shop assistant eyed Lily with a flattering gaze as if she could hardly believe how young and pretty she was. Then she turned to Stephen and shrugged her shoulders. 'Everything we have would look ravishing on Madam,' she said simply. Then she raised one finger. 'But I do have something which I think is extra-special.'

She snapped her finger and one of the sales girls rushed

to fetch another dress which was a full-length evening gown of the sheerest blue silk. It draped Lily like water pouring over a naked statue. One small brooch held it at one shoulder, a scarf of the material was tossed over the other. It was too long but they offered to take up the hem at once, that very evening.

'Madam is too beautiful in it,' the senior sales woman said. 'I knew it would be so. She can wear anything, but the pure classical line is hers to perfection.'

Stephen stroked his moustache and winked over the top of his gloved hand at Lily. 'I say, you do look rather the thing, Lily,' he said with careful casualness. 'You really do look the very thing indeed.'

And Lily, looking at herself in the long pier glass, with a view of her slim back encased in shimmery blue silk provided by another mirror held by yet another sales girl, thought how much she wished that Charlie could see her, looking so lovely. Then she turned to Stephen with a bright smile on her face and said: 'I am so happy I could just die!'

And they all laughed, indulgently, at the pretty bride's extravagance.

Two dresses had to be altered, but one cocktail dress, a lovely peach bead-encrusted gown ending daringly short on the knee but with a train at one side all the way down to ankle length, they took back to the hotel with them in the smart Harrods box.

'You are to wait downstairs while I change!' Lily announced gaily as Stephen emerged from the bathroom tying his bow tie. 'I want to sweep down those stairs in my new gown while you watch!'

Stephen had been thinking that he would sit in the chair and watch Lily get dressed in her new clothes, watch a parade of cream silk stockings and silken underwear. He had taken the sales lady at Harrods to one side and given her to understand that they were shopping for a honeymoon trousseau. He thought that the size of the bill indicated that Lily's underwear was no longer plain cotton knit.

'I will only be a few minutes,' Lily commanded. 'But it cost you so much I want you to have the full effect.'

Stephen hesitated. 'I wanted to watch it go on! It cost me so much I want to have the full effect of the underwear too!'

Lily hesitated and for a moment he was afraid he had offended her. At once he felt a sudden rush of excitement. She was such a young thing, such a little girl and yet, like it or not, she was his wife and there were certain things which would have to be done. He felt two contradictory emotions at once: a fearful respect for her which he had learned from his mother and from the code of his class who held women to be angels, far above carnal desires; and a demanding lust which he had learned in Belgium from girls no older than Lily who had serviced the British troops. Stephen feared and longed to know whether under Lily's cool exterior there was a whore like the Belgian whores. If she were wanton he would desire her and despise her. If she were frigid he would respect her and rape her.

Lily pushed him imperiously towards the door. 'We'll be late for the theatre if you wait here, silly! You must go!'

Stephen went. He strolled down the arching staircase, meeting the eyes of fashionable women who watched him as he crossed the lobby. He felt a bit of a dog. He had a beautiful new wife upstairs making herself pretty to come out to the theatre with him, and a long night ahead of him when he would be giving the orders and Lily would see that the dresses and the silk underwear and even the handsome large stone on her finger carried a price after all.

Chapter Fifteen

L ily sang as they drove back to the hotel in the cab. They had been to a musical and the tunes were haunting. Lily hummed over the words she did not know and sang the tune to Stephen in her sweet silvery voice.

'What about a nightcap?' Stephen suggested as the doorman held open the door.

'Lovely,' Lily said. 'I'll have a lemonade.'

Stephen chuckled fondly. 'No you won't! I'll get us a little bottle of bubbly,' he said. 'It's our honeymoon night, Lily. You should have something to drink to our good health.'

Lily smiled. She could feel her throat drying a little from nerves. It was not as bad as waiting in the wings, she told herself. She knew that she had felt fear worse than this. It was apprehension, nothing more. After all, even though she knew little about it, nothing could be too bad. If there were any marital secrets that were too bad to bear someone would have told her. People would not stay married if it were too awful. Women would not remarry when they had free choice.

Whatever Muriel might have said in that horrid cloakroom, Lily knew at least one girl who had found herself in trouble with a baby and she was not a prostitute. Lily's tough common sense asserted itself. She could not be frightened into frigidity as upper-class girls usually were. Lily had seen prostitutes – a couple worked near the Palais music hall and they were pleasant girls who would call good evening to Lily and wish her luck. And Trixie, who was married in a dress the size of a billowing tent over her swelling belly, said privately that she had been nothing worse than unlucky, and that hundreds of women had got married from the same state as her and never regretted it. Lily thought briefly of Charlie on the beach in Dorset and how his kisses had felt. If married life were anything like that then it was nothing to fear at all. Lily resolutely put Muriel's whispered warnings from her mind.

'Here we are,' Stephen said cheerfully. A waiter wound through the tables towards them, bringing an ice bucket with a bobbing bottle and two chilled glasses.

'And some sugar,' Stephen said. He met the waiter's surprised look with a cold stare. 'Some lump sugar,' he ordered again. 'Don't you have such a thing in the kitchen?'

'Yes, Sir, of course, Sir,' the waiter said disdainfully.

Lily giggled as he went away. 'Is it a bad thing to do? To put sugar in champagne?'

'It's only allowed if you are very, very beautiful,' Stephen said tenderly. 'And very young and quite adorable, and on the first night of your honeymoon.'

Lily laughed and her voice shook only a little. 'I qualify!' she said brightly. 'I shall have sugar in my champagne!'

The waiter brought a silver sugar bowl with tongs. 'Sugar, Sir,' he said, his tone perfectly neutral. 'Shall I open the champagne now?'

Stephen nodded, frowning slightly, waiting for the man to make a mistake so that he could complain. The waiter poured two glasses; nothing was spilled. He placed them down on the table and stepped back. Stephen, seething inwardly, was left with nothing to say. It was Lily who scored the point for them. She leaned forward and picked up the sugar bowl and smiled at Stephen. 'One lump or two, Vicar?' she asked in a chirpy Pompey accent.

The waiter bowed and retreated, Stephen and Lily dissolved into laughter. Lily dropped a cube of sugar into her champagne and they clinked glasses, still laughing. They drank the whole bottle in perfect accord.

It was midnight before the bottle was empty. Stephen rose and extended a hand to Lily. 'Come on, Mrs Winters, we've a big day sightseeing tomorrow!'

Lily let him pull her to her feet but then she staggered slightly.

'My God, you're tight!' Stephen chuckled. 'Tight as a tick. My word, Lily, you'll have a headache tomorrow.'

Lily beamed at him. 'I don't care,' she announced. 'I don't care two hoots. Two hoots. What are two hoots?'

Stephen steered her towards the stairs. 'Upsadaisy,' he said. They walked carefully upstairs, taking one step at a time. Lily held the long heel-length train of her gown carefully out to the side. Stephen, looking down to watch her feet, could see the seductive movement of Lily's knees under the short skirt.

'My God, Lily, you're a lovely piece,' he said.

They reached their bedroom door and Stephen opened it. A chambermaid had been in and turned down the bed, drawn the green curtains against the darkness outside and lit the lamps. The room looked luxurious and welcoming.

'Pretty,' Lily said with deep approval. She turned and went into the bathroom.

Stephen undressed quickly and got into his pyjamas. After a moment's thought he took the jacket off; then he put it on again but left it undone. On the side of the bed away from the window was Lily's new silk nightdress, folded carefully by the chambermaid. Stephen put out a finger and touched it. It was smooth and seductive.

'Come on, Lily,' he called. 'Are you all right?'

Lily had her back against the locked bathroom door. Her earlier elation had gone. She had exaggerated the effect of the wine, thinking perhaps she could pretend to be sick, or pretend to fall instantly asleep. She did not want to leave the bathroom and face Stephen.

'Lily?' he asked. He got up from the bed. Lily heard him coming towards the bathroom door. He knocked. 'Are you all right?'

Lily looked around her. If there had been a window in the bathroom she might have climbed out even wearing her new evening dress and high heels. But there was no way out except through the bedroom. There was no way out without facing Stephen.

'Lily!' Stephen sounded irritated.

Lily looked at herself in the bathroom mirror. Her face was pale, there were shadows under her eyes. She shrugged at her reflection and then she took a deep breath and unlocked the bathroom door.

Stephen took her in his arms as the door opened and carried her over to the bed. Lily lay back with her eyes shut. Stephen had no idea whether she was sick from the wine, or weary, or too afraid to look at him. He was beyond caring. He laid her down on the bed and he unfastened the gown. It had a row of fiddly hooks under the arm. He remembered how much the garment cost and he undid each one patiently, then he pulled the dress carefully over Lily's head. She held up her arms to help him, and she sat up a little to slide the dress off, but she did not open her eyes.

She was hopelessly beautiful. She was wearing peach silk camiknickers with tiny pearl buttons and trimmed with peach lace. She had a tiny lace suspender belt under the camiknickers and the elasticated straps of the suspender belt peeped out, fore and aft, to hold up peach silk stockings. Stephen slipped her peach slippers off her little feet and stared at her motionless body.

Lily lay as if she were dead, her eyes tight shut. She

guessed Stephen was looking at her, she had heard him sigh when her dress had come off. She was not thinking about him, about herself, about anything. She lay with her eyes tight shut and her mind held to a determined blank. Silently she heard the silly song 'If you knew Suzie, like I know Suzie, oh! oh! oh what a girl' playing in her mind. She concentrated on it, trying to remember all the words. Trying to remember precisely the tune. Trying to remember the harmonies and the key and the tempo.

Stephen moved up the bed towards her. He put his hand down to the crutch of the camiknickers and he fumbled with the little buttons. Lily, her eyes still shut, flinched a little at the touch of his hand probing at her secret, private parts. 'If you knew Suzie, like I know Suzie . . .'

Stephen had the buttons undone at last. Lily felt the bed sink as he moved over her. She felt him fumble to free his penis from his pyjama trousers. She kept singing in her head, determinedly holding the tune, as if someone else were singing a different song in her ear, trying to distract her.

Stephen was pushing against her. Lily felt something hard and rubbery and horrible at her thigh, at her belly, at the crutch of her body and then he stabbed her suddenly, without warning, and Lily pulled away from him and screamed. He had his hand over her mouth in a moment. 'Sssh, Lily,' he said urgently. 'Don't cry, it's all right, I'll be as gentle as I can. It always hurts a bit, you know. You mustn't shriek though!'

Lily lay still again, searching for the song she was singing in her mind, hunting for the tune. 'If you knew Suzie . . .'

Stephen lay still for a few moments and nothing hurt too much except the sense of being suffocated and crushed. Lily felt horridly filled by him, an extraordinary sensation, as if she were being stuffed like a helpless Christmas turkey. 'Oh! oh! oh what a girl . . .'

Stephen started moving. His hand tightened over Lily's mouth to muffle her cry. Her vagina was quite dry and at every movement Stephen rubbed against her dryness, pulling the delicate skin. She was bleeding now and the feel of the warm wetness excited him, and made his movements more rapid and easier. He arched his back to push further inside her. Lily found that she had moved on to Madge Sweet's song, 'I'm a Red Hot Baby, try-ing to get along . . . a Red Hot Baby . . . never done no wrong', and somewhere in her mind she noted the incongruity of that song at that moment.

Stephen plunged deeper inside her. Lily gasped at a new level of pain, and then Stephen said, 'Oh God! oh God!' and tore himself away from her and fell at her side, groaning in pleasure as his seed, stained red from the blood on his penis, spurted against Lily's pretty camiknickers.

They lay very still for a little while. Lily drew her legs together and noted, as a dancer, that though she was stiff and sore that no muscles were torn. She felt dry-mouthed and weary. The headache from the champagne and from the fatigue of the day was closing on her neck and on the back of her head. She felt neither resentment nor anger. It had been a good deal worse than she had imagined but it had been over quicker than she had thought, and she had not disgraced them by crying or screaming.

She was surprised, though, that the experience was so thoroughly nasty. She thought of Charlie and the moment of utter delight when he had lain on her and she had wrapped herself around him, pressing him closer and closer. She could hardly understand that the same move-ment with Stephen had made her feel smothered and sick. She did not understand his desire, his insistent eager burrowing into her flesh. She did not understand the sud-den tearing away from her and the hot disgusting wetness at her side. She thought of Charlie and the smooth hairless skin of his crutch, criss-crossed with scars where his male body had been shot away and they had stitched him and patched him, and saved his life but made him into a strange sexless being, almost like a girl. Then she turned her thoughts away from Charlie, because he had written to her that he could be nothing more than a friend. And now she understood what he meant. He could not do this with her. Now she was a married woman. She would have to do it with her husband whenever he wanted, and it would be easier if she did not think of Charlie at all.

'Are you hurt?' Stephen asked softly. His hand came up to stroke her hair, and Lily flinched from the smell of it. A deep rich smell like sweat, only riper.

'A little.'

'Lie still, I'll fetch a towel.'

He went, not to the bathroom, but to his suitcase. He had brought an old towel from home, planning to wipe Lily's blood with it and then throw it away. Lily watched him as he took it from his suitcase and dabbed at her thighs and at the bottom sheet. She found his preparedness insulting, he was too knowing. He had planned ahead and he had known she would bleed for him.

'There we are, dear. Are you in much pain?'

Lily looked carefully at him. She heard her cue and saw the curious elation on Stephen's face.

She smiled at him wanly and let her lower lip tremble a little. 'It doesn't matter. If it was what you wanted then it doesn't matter.'

He bent over her and kissed her. 'You're the first lady I've ever been with,' he said. 'I didn't know what it would be like. We used to hear such stories – you know – from the other chaps. About what girls liked and what girls would do. You never really know where you are.'

Lily was listening carefully, gathering clues of what Stephen wanted from this painful intrusive experience, urgent to get the information she needed to manage him.

'You didn't like it at all, did you, Lily?'

Lily shook her head tentatively, it seemed to be the proper response. It was what his mother had said, it was what he wanted.

Stephen leaned over and put out the light. His sigh was deeply contented. He gathered her to him and rested her head on his shoulder. 'That's how it should be. I won't trouble you often, there is no need to be concerned.'

In a few moments he was deeply asleep.

Lily lay awake. The bright lights of the London streets shone through the curtains. On the ceiling the curtain rings let in little circles of light and when a cab went past, its motor rumbling, the little circles of light moved along the ceiling from one end of the curtain pole to the other.

Stephen started to snore.

Lily held up the blankets and slid noiselessly out of bed. She dropped the camiknickers from her shoulders. They were stained with her blood and with the pallid cream of Stephen's semen. Lily put them, unhesitatingly, in the waste paper bin. She felt that the cost of them was a legitimate fine which Stephen should pay.

The suspender belt was tight around her waist. She undid it, and undid the clips on her stockings and rolled them down. She put them in the dressing table drawer with the belt and then pulled on the new silk nightdress. The light fabric felt as cold and slick as snow against her skin. Lily shivered. There was nowhere warm in the room. There was nowhere for her to go but back to bed beside Stephen. She sat for a little while in the armchair, watching him sleeping in the half-light which came through the curtains, watching the big shadow of the bed leap and flicker in the quickly moving light from passing cars. Somewhere near the hotel there was a party going on. Cars

215

came and went, people were dancing, drinking, having fun. Women were in the arms of men they liked and when they kissed they did not feel a suffocating repulsion but instead that melting feeling of desire which Lily had known once. Lily sat in the darkness, watching her husband sleep, knowing that she must make the best of this marriage which she had undertaken in shock and in grief, and must now live with for the rest of her life.

It was hot in London in July, not a good time to go sightseeing around a crowded city. The parks were dusty and the flower beds drying out. The hotel was filled with visiting Americans and Stephen complained that the waiters were surly and slow from being constantly over-tipped. Stephen and Lily went to another show, they took a pleasure boat up the Thames. They visited the Houses of Parliament, they went to London Zoo. Lily was amazed at the energy Stephen had for visiting places. Left to herself she would have wandered aimlessly along some interesting streets and then rejoiced in the idleness of sitting in restaurants, and cafés, doing nothing. But Stephen woke them early each morning with an itinerary that had to be completed by tea time. Lily was forced to learn history: at the Tower of London he bought a book on the kings of England and expected her to know one from another. She was forced to study architecture – he constantly pointed out buildings to her. Lily had never thought of churches or bridges or houses except in terms of their function. But Stephen went on and on about how they looked and who had built them, and how old they were. They looked around the Palace of Westminster, quiet in the long summer recess, and Stephen lectured her on the meaning of democracy and why the British system was superior to any other in the world. He took her down to the Inns of Court and explained to her the legal system of which he was a part. Lily was exhausted, overworked, and bored beyond belief.

And she was grieving still. When she was tired, or in the honesty of early morning hours when she could not sleep, she would think of her mother. When she slept, she dreamed that the little corner shop was still open and her mother behind the counter. She dreamed that she could go home at any time she wanted and her mother would greet her in the old way, would hold out her arms to her and enfold her in that warm capable hug. When she woke, Lily would lie for a little while in the dark, puzzled by the unfamiliar shape of the room. Then she would recognize Stephen's bulk beside her and hear his measured steady breath and know that her girlhood was over, that her mother was dead, and that she was married for life to this stranger. Her obedience to Stephen's whims of sight-seeing, of education, was made possible by her grief. For Lily, in those long hot summer days, nothing mattered. In the back of her mind, in the foreground of her dreams, she grieved for her mother constantly. Nothing else mattered at all.

One morning, on the third day of the visit, they were walking away from a long wearying visit to the British Museum, looking for a restaurant to have lunch, when a car on the opposite side of the road suddenly backfired with a gout of smoke and a smell of oil. It was so loud and so startling that Lily jumped and dropped her handbag, but Stephen dived without a moment's hesitation towards the pavement and rolled over and over, in his best suit, with his hands over his ears, his arms around his face.

Lily shot a quick horrified look up and down the road. People were staring at them. A woman gave a little sound, halfway between a scream and a laugh, and pointed. Stephen did not move. Lily knelt beside him, put her hand on his shoulder and shook him. 'Stephen, it's only a car, get up.' His shoulders were shaking, his whole body was shaking. Lily thought he must be having some kind of fit. She stood up helplessly and looked around again. A man came out of the shop doorway and stared at her.

Lily knelt down on the pavement beside her husband again. Stephen was compressed like a foetus, he was kicking out with his feet, as his whole body shook in convulsive little thrashings, dirtying his suit on the pavement. Lily put her hand on the nape of his neck where the short haircut left him bare and vulnerable.

'Shellshocked?' the man in the shop doorway asked her. 'Need a hand?'

'I don't know, I don't know,' Lily said.

Slowly Stephen stopped shuddering. His long legs unfolded. He sat up, and gazed around him with blank unseeing eyes. He rose up to stand as slowly and unwilling as if someone were bawling orders at him. His arms were still wrapped around his head one on top of the other, his hands over his ears.

'Stop it!' Lily hissed. 'Everyone is staring at us.'

She put an impatient hand on the crook of his arm and tugged it down from his face. Stephen stood with both hands dangling like a scolded child. His face was blank and white.

'Get us a cab,' Lily said to the man in the doorway.

She took Stephen's hand. It lay limp in hers, icy cold and unattractively damp. A taxi drew up beside them. Lily got in and the shopman pushed Stephen gently in beside her.

'Poor devil,' he said. 'You should get him to a doctor, Missis.' He spoke to Lily across Stephen's stony shiny face. 'They give them electric. Poor devils.'

He slammed the door. Stephen did not flinch at the noise, he did not seem to hear it. He had gone somewhere in his mind where nothing could touch him.

Lily gave the name of the hotel and sat back beside Stephen. He was staring straight ahead but his eyes were not moving. He did not even blink.

They were very close to the hotel. Lily paid the driver and tugged Stephen out of the cab. He followed her with the obedience of a beaten child. She took him up the front steps and the doorman held the door for them with an expression of professional uninterest. People stared at them as they went past, Lily pulling Stephen along by the hand. Suddenly Stephen jerked his hand from her grasp and gripped her shoulder. He walked behind her, with his eyes staring open but unseeing, gripping her shoulder, with his white mad face swinging from one side to the other. He made Lily lead him, like a blinded gas casualty, through the lobby of the fashionable London hotel, and up the elegant sweep of the marble stairs. As they went he muttered tunelessly, very quietly, 'It's a long way to Tipperary, it's a long way to Tipperary, it's a long way to Tipperary,' over and over, never more than the first line. People turned and stared at the two of them, Lily walking before him, her face scarlet with shame, and Stephen shambling behind her, one arm slack at his side, his other hand clamped on her shoulder and his eyes staring sightlessly before him.

The chambermaid was in the room making the bed. 'Oh, get out!' Lily said, enraged, and slammed the door on her. Stephen sat on the edge of the bed with his hands dangling, his head drooped.

'Are you ill?' Lily demanded.

Slowly he shook his head. 'Tired. Very, very tired.'

'Then lie down and sleep,' Lily said through her teeth. She pushed his shoulder and he sank back against the pillows and closed his eyes. Lily turned to the mirror and dragged off her hat. Her face was burning with colour, there were tears of anger and humiliation in her eyes.

'Kill her,' Stephen said softly. 'Kill the whore.' And then he slept.

He did not wake until the afternoon. Lily let him sleep. She curled up in the armchair and watched him. His eyelids flickered in his sleep and his hands twitched. Sometimes he strained his head up towards the ceiling and his mouth moved as if he were trying to shout orders. Saliva drooled from the corner of his mouth. He dropped back to the pillow again. Lily shrank away. She thought him ugly. She thought his behaviour was unforgivable. She sat in the armchair and listened to the distant rumble of other people going out to lunch parties and having fun and she watched her husband sleep and twitch and dream.

Her stomach rumbled with hunger and she was chilled in her light summer dress. But Lily did not move. She sat in the chair, hugging her knees, staring at Stephen as if he were an enemy.

At half past three he stirred and opened his eyes.

'Lily!' he said contentedly. 'How lovely it is to wake up and see you there!' He smiled at her, as sunny as a little boy.

'Are you all right now?' Lily asked icily.

He blinked at her tone, not understanding her. 'I'm fine, fine.'

'Good.'

There was a silence. Stephen frowned, trying to recall what had happened, trying to comprehend Lily's bottled-up fury.

'I can't remember,' he said finally. 'How did we get home?'

'A car backfired,' Lily said through her teeth. 'You fell down on the pavement and rolled around. You wouldn't get up. A man, a stranger, had to help me get you into the cab and get you home. You made me lead you through the lobby with your hand on my shoulder in front of hundreds of people. You sang "It's a long way to Tipperary", over and over. Everyone saw us. And then you slept.'

Lily looked at the little gold watch he had bought her. 'You have slept for four hours,' she said spitefully. 'Dreaming and saying things.'

A shuttered look closed down over Stephen's face. 'Saying what?' Lily said nothing. She found she could not repeat 'kill the whore' even though she longed to batter Stephen with the evidence of his abnormality. 'You're sick,' she accused.

Stephen swung his feet to the floor and went to the bathroom. He shut the door without replying. Through the thin dividing wall Lily could hear the stream of his urine, the clank and flush of the cistern, and then the taps running into the sink. She heard him thrust his face under the water and splash, blowing out heavily. He opened the door, drying his face and hands on the white fluffy hotel towel.

'You're not to say that,' he said.

It was as if a gulf had opened up on the floor between them. Stephen's face was fixed, he stared at Lily unforgivingly. 'You are never to say that again.'

Lily moved her little hands as if to push his determination away from her. 'It's only what the man in the street said. He said you were shellshocked, and that doctors could help. They give you electricity.'

Stephen came further into the bedroom. His step was heavy. 'You are never to suggest such a thing. Not to me, not to anyone else.'

Lily looked mutinous.

'I am not shellshocked,' he said carefully. 'There is no such thing as shellshock. Cowards and conchies pretend to have shellshock. But there is no such thing. I was decorated for my courage. I was mentioned in dispatches. No-one calls me a coward, least of all you.'

'But if you're sick . . .'

'I am not sick.'

'What were you doing on the ground then?' Lily demanded. 'Rolling on the ground when the car backfired?'

Stephen put down the towel and turned to the mirror. His shirt had been creased while he sweated in his deep sleep. He took off his jacket, tossed his tie to one side and stripped to the waist. Formidably half-naked, he brushed his hair with his two silver-backed brushes, as if he were grooming a glossy horse. The muscles across his broad chest and in his forearms rippled with the movement. He looked powerful. He looked triumphantly male. Lily could smell the sweat on him. 'Who says?'

'Who says what?'

'Who says I was on the ground?'

'Well, I saw you . . . and so did all the other people who were there!'

Stephen shrugged. 'You are to say nothing. We agreed that. And the other people do not matter. They did not give their names, you will never see them again. They are not witnesses. No-one of any importance saw anything. And I shall deny it.'

Lily grasped the arms of the chair as if she were falling. 'Now hang on a minute,' she said.

Stephen shook his head and smiled at his handsome reflection. He crossed to the wardrobe and took out a fresh, perfectly ironed shirt and pulled it on. He unbuttoned his fly, facing Lily, and half-dropped his trousers to tuck in his shirt. Lily saw the silk of his underpants and the bulge of his penis. He was half-erect. He stood before her like that for a moment. Lily fell silent at once.

Stephen tucked in his shirt and did up his trousers with a smile. He chose a new tie from the dressing table drawer.

'Poor darling, you must be starving,' he said in a quite different voice. 'No lunch! I tell you what – let's go mad and splash out. I'll take you to tea at the Ritz! They probably have some dancing. Let's go and have tea at the Ritz!'

Lily hesitated.

'I'll wait downstairs while you change,' Stephen offered. 'Wear your very best frock, Lily. You look rather crumpled.'

Lily got to her feet. Her pretty summer dress was soiled where she had knelt on the pavement. The heel of her shoe had kicked out the hem and the skirt was bedraggled. Stephen gave a little loving chuckle. 'You look like a mad thing. No-one would believe a word you said,' he told her. 'A mad little waif and stray. Smarten up, darling, you're not fit to go anywhere like that!'

He went from the room and shut the door behind him. Lily could hear his confident step marching down the corridor. Obediently, she opened the wardrobe and changed her dress for a blue linen outfit with a matching jacket and a little flowery hat. She looked at herself in the mirror as if only her own prettiness could be trusted in this world of shifting evidence.

Downstairs Stephen was chatting with the concierge, leaning against the man's polished desk. He said something that made the man laugh and then passed him a coin. The man palmed it and threw Stephen a half-salute.

'He says there's a wonderful show at the Lyndhurst,' Stephen said, joining Lily. 'Let's go on to it after tea.'

Lily looked at the concierge, at the receptionist clerks who had seen Stephen stumbling into the hotel like a blinded soldier. None of them glanced towards her, no-one hid a smile. Stephen, offering her his arm, guiding her confidently across the marble floor, was glossy with well-being. Anyone looking from his smooth confident smile to Lily's strained pallor would see a charming worldly man with a nervous young wife.

The doorman held the door for them and whistled for a cab. Stephen slid him a coin, the doorman tipped his hat with a smile. Lily sat beside Stephen in the cab and watched the streets and the faces of people sliding past the window. Nothing was real; not the busy streets, not Stephen's glowing confidence. Lily longed for her mother and the old world of certainties where her mother had kept her safe.

Tea at the Ritz was a success. Lily regained her colour and she and Stephen danced. The show was good and they had dinner at a restaurant on their way home. In the night Stephen reached out for Lily, while he was half-asleep. Lily rolled over to the extreme edge of the bed to avoid his touch. Stephen settled on his back and slept deeply. Lily lay awake, watching the lights moving along the ceiling.

Stephen dreamed. He was at the start of it once more. They disembarked at Calais but under the bright lights of the dockside Stephen had no sense of foreign soil. There was too much to do – the men to order to the waiting railway carriages, the stores, the equipment, the roll call. It was not until he climbed over the legs of his fellow officers to his window seat that he had a chance to look out into the darkness and try to sense this strange country where his brother had died.

It was dark and quiet. A thick honey moon skimmed the tops of trees, highlighted hedges. The train clattered swiftly through the backs of darkened villages. Stephen caught a glimpse of station names, of small back gardens trimmed into bare tidiness. When they moved into the open countryside he saw fields and hedges, the broad gleam of a river. The road, running alongside the railway, was as straight as the railway track. A Roman road, Stephen thought sleepily, going to Rome. Running far away from the destination of the railhead, at the end of the line. 'How I wish I was on it,' he said aloud carelessly.

'Do what, old man?' someone asked drowsily.

'Nothing.'

It was nothing, the wish to be walking down the road with a light holiday pack on his shoulders and that jolly amber moon laying a striped shadow across the road from one slim poplar tree to the next. It was nothing, his dream of going into a little roadside bar and drinking a cold beer, sitting outside at a little metal table and watching some old man ride by on a wagon full of straw pulled by a plump spoiled horse. Nothing.

Stephen dozed with his face against the cold hardness of the window, his teeth juddering when the train crossed points. He was not yet soldier enough to sleep through everything.

The train went too fast for him. He wanted it to travel slower, to take time for the dawn to catch up with them so that he could see the quiet fields and the grazing cows showing palely through the morning mist. He wanted to idle along the embankments and see the flowers growing in the coarse grass. He wanted to travel at walking pace so that he and the men could drop down from the high wagons and stroll beside the train, picking flowers, picking fruit, winding bindweed into garlands.

Someone kicked his foot. 'You're groaning, old man,' he said. 'Keeping me awake.'

'Sorry.'

Stephen wanted the train to ride forever under the round sovereign moon across the pale landscape intersected with dark hedges and high etched trees and dotted with dark contented farmhouses. He wanted to sit forever gazing out of the window as the landscape loomed close and then slid by. He wanted never to arrive. He wanted never to arrive.

A few hours later and he was awakened by a dark raw rumble which sounded like thunder very low and very close. And he knew that he had been asleep and dreaming. And that they were at St Omer station, and that his war had begun.

He awoke with a jerk and with that familiar falling feeling in his belly – terror. For a second he lay, his eyes raking the room from one corner to another, with no idea where he was. There had been so many rooms in his two and a half years. So many billets, so many little corners where he had slumped and slept, his exhaustion overwhelming his fear. He put his hand out and there was Lily, quiet and warm beside him.

Stephen sighed as his terror bled away from him. It was over. He need never dream of that quiet journey again. He would never again travel home on leave and then back to the Front thinking each time that this would surely be his last. This time he would surely die. This time, if nothing else, his sheer choking terror would block his throat and kill him.

He moved closer to Lily's sleeping warmth. He need fear nothing, he told himself. The war was over. He would never make that journey again. No-one would ever make him go.

But it was no use. Stephen had no faith in the future. They broke his will when they sent him to the Front, and then again when they released him to go home and then again sent him back. He learned, in some deep and frightened place, that he could not stop them from sending him where they wished. They could send him to the trenches. They could send him forward into uncut barbed wire to face skilled machine gunners. Nothing he could do would stop them. He could not even say 'no'. His face twisted,

Stephen gathered Lily into his arms, put a firm hand over her mouth, and plunged himself without warning into her body, battering himself against her inert dryness, forcing himself inside her. Only when he reached release did he tear away from her and let her go. Only then could he sleep again. He slept without dreams.

'I don't know about you, but I'd like to leave,' Stephen said baldly the next morning at breakfast.

Lily waited.

'It's the noise, and everywhere so crowded. It's not like it used to be, I'm sure. Before the war I can remember coming up to town and parking the car outside the theatre and just strolling in. It's so rushed now, and crowded everywhere.'

Lily buttered a slice of toast.

'Even here –' Stephen broke off and looked around the dining room with dissatisfaction. 'How long have we been here? Three days? Four? They don't remember our name, they don't give us the same table every time. I tell you, Lily, before the war we would have had a table reserved with flowers on it after the first meal, and a waiter who greeted us by name. It's not like it used to be.'

An American tourist came into the dining room and a table of Americans yelled and hooted in greeting. Stephen scowled. 'I'm not a spoil sport, I like a bit of fun like the rest of them. But I tell you, Lily, before the war people wouldn't kick up larks before breakfast, not in a good hotel.'

'D'you want to go home?' Lily asked, as if it were no business of hers whether they went home early or stayed the whole week.

Stephen's hand holding out his tea cup shook slightly so the china cup rattled. 'Yes,' he said. 'I want to see . . .'

He hesitated. Lily looked up, wondering what he would say.

'I want to see Coventry,' he said.

Coventry met them with the car at the town station. He loaded the bags on to the luggage rack of the Argyll. Lily got into the back seat and leaned against the cushions. The porter took a tip from Stephen, touched his cap and wheeled his barrow away. Coventry and Stephen did not greet each other with words. They exchanged one long unspeaking look, like lovers, parted for a prolonged painful absence.

'Everything all right at home?'

Coventry nodded, and then jerked his head to where Lily sat in the back of the Argyll. He raised an eyebrow.

'All right,' Stephen said. 'London was dreary. Full of Yanks. They win Wimbledon, they win the Americas' Cup and they think they own the place. Noisy. Not what it used to be.'

Coventry smiled gently and held open the door for Stephen. As Stephen got in he brushed slightly against Coventry's shoulder and put his hand momentarily on Coventry's hand.

Coventry looked at him in comfortable silence.

'Good to be home,' Stephen said.

Chapter Sixteen

M uriel was waiting for them in the hall. At the sound of the car drawing up she threw the front door open herself and met them on the doorstep.

'How good to see you back! Lily! What an exquisite hat! I can't wait to see the rest of your clothes. What a lovely jacket!'

She led them into the drawing room and they sat in their usual places.

'Nothing much has happened here at all,' Muriel said, pouring tea. 'Your father seems a little better, Stephen. We have a new nurse, her name is Nurse Bells – just like the whisky! She seems to think that he is improving. She's here now, I'll introduce you later.'

Muriel nodded to the parlourmaid, who passed Lily a plate of sandwiches. Lily took one and left it on the side of her plate. Stephen took several and ate heartily.

Muriel talked easily of Portsmouth gossip: the increase in cyclists around the Canoe Lake, tomorrow's baby show in Victoria Park and the news of her friends, while stealing covert glances at Stephen and Lily. Lily was pale and looked strained. Stephen had never looked better. In the four days he seemed to have filled out and tanned. His moustache seemed thicker, darker. His eyes were bright, his face shiny with well-being. He was like a groomed horse at the peak of fitness, Muriel thought. She nodded to the maid, who passed him more sandwiches. Stephen ate like a hungry boy on his first day home from boarding school.

Lily's yellow hat made her face sallow. There were dark smudges of fatigue under her eyes and her smile was strained.

Honeymoon nerves, Muriel thought. She didn't think Lily would have the spirit to stand up to Stephen but if they ever quarrelled his wife would find Stephen a hard man to challenge. Muriel remembered the fights between Stephen and Christopher when they were little boys. Christopher, two years older, was only slightly bigger and heavier. He would always win a scrap with Stephen and Muriel would hear his polite over-educated voice demanding: 'D'you submit? D'you say pax?'

Stephen, grounded beneath his brother, would cry 'Pax! Pax!' and Christopher would get up off him and turn away, thinking that the quarrel was fairly ended. Then Stephen would fling himself against his brother's unsuspecting back and push his face into the rose bushes or, even more unfairly, wait until they were going to bed and push him down the stairs. Stephen could bide his time all day until he saw an opportunity for revenge.

Muriel did not envy his wife their natural conflicts. There would be nothing for Lily to do but to submit to Stephen's will.

Muriel nodded to Browning the parlourmaid to refill the teapot. Lily's new suit was charming and the hat – though hardly a hat at all, just a slice of straw and ribbon – was pretty. Stephen must have spent a large sum on his new bride, and this had to be a good sign, Muriel assured herself. She did not ask why they had come home early. There were so many unasked questions in the house already that Muriel was accustomed to discreet silence. Under the comfortable pretext that the young people needed their privacy, and that if Lily wished to confide in her, she would make the first move, Muriel let her son return early from his honeymoon with the girl he had insisted on marrying without demanding an explanation.

Besides, whatever had passed between them, Stephen had won. You only had to look at him to see that. Muriel was disinclined to know what battle had been fought, on what ground, and how badly Lily had been hurt. She told herself that she was showing commendable delicacy in not probing. In truth she rather feared this newly prosperous newly confident Stephen. She wanted to believe that his handsome veneer came from satisfied love. She did not want to hear anything from Lily that contradicted the picture of Stephen's new happiness.

'Now I've a surprise for you,' she said when tea had finished. 'I hope you like it. I have moved you two into the bedroom above your father's. It's a lovely room with the tower window that you like so much, Lily. I've had it redecorated as well!'

'That's very good of you, Mother!' Stephen said.

'The little room opposite I thought you could have as a dressing room,' Muriel suggested. 'And the other bedroom I thought we might convert to another bathroom. You could have your own suite of rooms up there.'

Mother and son said nothing, waiting for Lily to speak. 'Thank you,' she said.

'That's a jolly good idea, Mother,' Stephen said. 'But I imagine it'll be an awful lot of bother.'

'I've spoken to two plumbers and they both think they can do the majority of the work within a week. It shouldn't be too bad.'

'Excellent,' Stephen said. 'Let's see it.'

The three of them went towards the stairs. Lily glanced at the letter rack in the hall. In it was one of Madge's pale purple envelopes with Lily's new name written boldly across it in purple ink. Lily started to reach for it.

'Do you want your post now?' Muriel hesitated.

'We'll look at it later, when we come down,' Stephen decreed.

Lily obediently turned to the stairs and went up ahead of them. Stephen smiled a satisfied little smile at his mother and stood back for her.

They went past the sickroom on the first floor without stopping and up the stairs to the matching room above it. It had been Christopher's room. When he had died Muriel had taken the advice of her friends and cleared the room at once. Too many women she knew had left the cricket bat in the wardrobe and the pictures of school football teams on the wall. When a dead son's goods were sent home from France and unpacked on his cold bed his mother clung to the small collection of trivial things. A kind letter from the commanding officer, his kit bag. A bundle of letters in which he lied about his fear and the censor blacked out whole sentences which he now would never explain. A book, a souvenir German bullet, some Belgian lace found in his pocket, perhaps bought to send home. A handful of francs. The mothers left with this boxload of rubbish found they could throw away nothing. It was all they had left of their sons. The school reports, the silver cup for rifle shooting, a couple of small-sized snaps of him at school, a drawing he had done when he was six. They kept everything, and the bedrooms of the missing boys became their shrines.

Muriel had cleared the room on the very day that the letter confirmed Christopher's death. While the family doctor called in specialists to see her husband, Muriel boxed up all Christopher's clothes, his outgrown school uniform, his school books, his reports, his letters home requesting money and cakes. She ordered one of the maids – they had three in those days – to take them all down to the garden and tell the gardener to burn them. A thin column of smoke went up from the little garden at the back of the house as if Muriel were burning up the last of her joy. As if everything that was normal and right about their life should be destroyed in one day on a pyre which burned from midday till dinner time. And when it was all gone a wind got up from the sea. When Muriel went out to see that the work had been done, even the ashes had been blown away and scattered. Christopher's body was never found. He had been blown away, just like his things.

Since then it had not been Christopher's room but the best spare bedroom. No-one had stayed in it. The house was too quiet and too unwelcoming for anyone but day visitors. Stephen had thought of moving into it when he came home out of uniform. But he was used to his smaller room which overlooked the back garden and the dark moving slab of sea which filled the tower windows disturbed him.

Muriel had made it into a pretty room, a feminine room in pale butter yellow and blue. The wallpaper was sprigged flowers, the curtains a yellow and blue glazed chintz, were swagged back with wide ribbons. The bedcover and the cushions on the bed were decorated in matching fabric as were the window seat cushions. Lily went at once to the window. 'Perfect,' she said. She smiled at Muriel and there was a glimpse of the old joyful Lily in her smile. 'Divine,' she said. The floorboards were still bare and the bed was the only furniture in the room except a large dark wood wardrobe.

Stephen looked around in satisfaction. 'Very nice indeed, Mother,' he said. 'You have been busy!'

'I had it well planned! The cushions and carpets were ordered as soon as you said you were marrying. I had to rush the decorators through, but I knew exactly what I wanted and I wouldn't take any excuse. I counted on having at least three more days . . .' Muriel broke off. There was a little silence. No-one wanted to acknowledge that

Stephen and Lily had come home from their honeymoon early.

'It looks finished,' Stephen offered.

'There's a dressing table with a little stool to come,' Muriel said. 'And the carpet fitters are due tomorrow. I've ordered a blue carpet, I think it'll match.'

'Lovely!' Lily said. 'It's a lovely room. Thank you.'

Muriel went towards the door. 'I'll leave you to get settled,' she said. 'Shall I send Sally to unpack for you?'

'I can manage,' Lily said.

'Dinner at seven then.'

She shut the door behind her. Stephen and Lily were alone.

'Jolly nice of her to go to all this trouble.'

Lily nodded.

'You like the colours and everything?'

'Oh yes.'

'And I know you like looking out at the sea. Just like a little mermaid.'

'Yes.'

There was a silence between them.

'It's good to be home.'

Lily nodded.

'I tell you what, we'll take a run out in the car tomorrow. Drive over and have lunch at Chichester or somewhere. I don't have to be back at the office until next week – we could have a couple of jaunts out and about.'

'That would be nice.'

'I'll leave you to unpack,' Stephen said. 'Or get the girl to do it.'

'I like to do it,' Lily said. 'I like to deal with my own things. I want to look at them again.'

Stephen chuckled. 'I'll go down and sit with Father for a bit, meet this new nurse.'

He put a hand on Lily's shoulder as he went towards

the door. It was the first time they had touched in daylight since he had collapsed outside the British Museum. Lily stayed very still and looked steadily at him, her face showing nothing. She was a little basilisk. Stephen's confident smile never flickered. He bent and kissed her lips. Lily felt the brush of his moustache and the touch of his full lips on her mouth and forced herself not to pull away. She stood quite still, her lips cold and uninviting.

Stephen sighed with pleasure. 'What about trying out the bed, Mrs Winters?' he asked gently. 'Trying out the new bed? We'll be sharing it for a good few years!'

Lily moved away from him and sat in the window seat, looking out towards the sea, the beach, the calling gulls and the holidaymakers packing up and going back to their hotels and boarding houses.

'Stephen, really!' she said. Her voice was balanced precisely between reproof and mild shock.

Stephen flinched at her tone. 'I'm sorry, Lily,' he said. He looked at her apologetically. Lily sat like a little yellow statue of indifference with the blue sky behind her. 'You're so damned lovely. I keep wanting to . . .'

Lily looked at him coldly and his words dried in his mouth. He smiled awkwardly. 'I'll go and visit Father,' he said.

Lily nodded. She sat without moving until the door had closed behind him and only then did she exhale deeply, as if she had been holding her breath with fear.

When she heard the door of his father's room close, Lily slipped from their bedroom and stepped quietly down the stairs. They were carpeted with a faded red and blue runner held in place with brass stair rods and rings. By stepping on the edge of the carpet where it was thickest, Lily could get downstairs unheard.

Madge's letter was at the front of the post rack. There was one other letter for Lily with a typewritten envelope and a Southsea postmark. Lily took them both and slipped upstairs again.

She sat on the window seat to look at them. She opened Madge's letter first.

Darling Lil,

How does it feel to be a maried woman then? I bet your not so keen now you know all about it! Make sure you don't get into trouble – you know what I mean. When I see you again I'll tell you a few things you should know. Idoubtanyoneelsehas putyouwise!

Your the luckiest girl that ever was catching your Captain. Hes a real peach and absolutely rolling in it. Charlie was telling me about the family the other night. So you'll be living in that lovely house unless you get your own I suppose? I'd hold out for my own place actualy. What about a nice little flat overloking the seafront? Or London? Cant you get him to move?

Were working our way home again. Im writing this from Sidmouth again on the return trip and we'll be home in four weeks. Its going well. No news really. Ill phone you when we get into Southsea and you can invite me round for tea, duches! Posh!

As you can guess, I didn't really want to write. Charlie made me write to you and he's going to inclose a page. By the by Sylvia de Charmante made a huge pass at him and he turned her down flat. She was sick. It was divine. Charlies leaving the show to take up his new post at the Kings almost at once. We've got some drery replasement starting tomorrow.

See you when we get home,
Love
Madge.

Lily read through Madge's letter quickly and then turned to Charlie's.

Dear Lily,

Congratulations on your marriage. I hope you will be very happy. It's obvious that Captain Winters was very much in love with you from the start. I am sure you have made the right decision in marrying him.

I am writing to tell you that they will be auditioning for the Kings from the middle of July and if you wish I can put your name forward. There is also the pantomime which might suit you in the winter season, especially as it would not take you from your new home.

Yours sincerely,
Charlie Smith.

There was a postscript, as if Charlie knew that his letter to Lily must be something that her husband could read, and yet at the moment of putting it into the envelope he had heard the coldness of his tone, and remembered her despairing telegram the day before her marriage which he had left unanswered.

I should like to see you if Captain Winters permits.
Your friend, as ever,
Charlie.

Lily read and re-read the letter. Then she folded it up and put it carefully in a pocket in her new handbag. She sat for a moment looking towards the sea where the families playing on the beach had been replaced by people dressed in their evening clothes, strolling along the sea wall. Somewhere in the distance there was a brass band playing waltzes. Lily remembered the night in Charlie's room and the irresistible longing, as powerful as pain, that she had felt for his touch. She could not relate the arid painful struggles with Stephen to her easy melting desire for Charlie. The night with Charlie seemed like a dream now, one of the strange romantic dreams of her girlhood. Charlie's scarred wounded body was like a girl's dream: sensual, warm, unthreatening. The reality was a nightmare. Lily could not think of Stephen's aggressive maleness as part of the same species.

She remembered her second letter and opened it. She gave a little gasp of delight. It was work. It was from the manager of the Kings Theatre offering her a date for an audition to be held at the theatre under the supervision of their new musical director, Charlie Smith, on 21 July. Lily leaped to her feet and walked around the room, too excited to sit still. On the bare floorboards her shoes echoed loudly. Lily did not care, she had the offer of work as a professional singer in her hand.

The sound of Rory's bedroom door opening and Stephen's step on the stairs startled Lily. She thrust the letter in the pocket of her jacket and threw open the lid of her suitcase.

'Not unpacked?' Stephen said, coming into the room.

Lily stared. He had not knocked. She realized that he would never have to knock. He had an absolute right to walk into her bedroom any time of day or night. She would never again have a room that was exclusively her own.

'I was daydreaming,' Lily excused herself. 'And watching people walk by the sea.'

'I must dress for dinner,' Stephen said.

'I want a bath,' she said. 'I'll go now. Will there be hot water?'

Stephen smiled. 'We always have enough hot water. It's something I insist on.'

Lily took her sponge bag and her dressing-gown, and then, on second thoughts, took her evening dress and stockings and underwear from her open suitcase. Stephen did not notice. She slipped from the bedroom with her evening clothes bundled in her hands. She did not want to dress in front of him.

They met for sherry in the drawing room before dinner. Muriel admired Lily's dress and noticed how much brighter the girl looked. She must have been just tired, Muriel thought. Tired and perhaps a little shocked by the honeymoon. But now she is home she is blooming. She must be happy with Stephen. She would not look so well if she were not happy with Stephen.

With more confidence than she had felt earlier, Muriel asked them how they had liked London. Stephen told her it was much changed from the days of his wartime leaves. Changed for the worse.

'The war . . .' Muriel shrugged. 'You won't believe the rates I have to pay for the new nurse. None of them want to nurse a civilian. They all want a glamorous wounded officer who will marry them!'

'Ghastly thought,' Stephen said lightly. 'I told you, didn't I, of the chap who came in to see me having married his nurse and found himself lumbered with the hospital cleaning woman?'

Lily gurgled with laughter. 'No! But surely he couldn't divorce her just for that?'

Stephen tapped the side of his nose with his finger. 'You be warned, Mrs Winters, a clever lawyer can get you in or out of a marriage in a moment. There is no telling how fast an undesirable wife can be shot out the door. Women's movement or no!'

'You're an old tyrant,' Muriel said good-humouredly. 'In my day you married for life, and that was that.'

Stephen reached out and touched Lily's hand as it lay on the table. She did not move away, she let his hand rest heavily on hers and smiled steadily at him. 'That's the way it is for us,' Stephen said confidently. 'Married for life, eh, Lily?'

It is all right then, Muriel thought to herself, seeing Lily's beautiful clear smile. He does love her and she will learn to love him. It couldn't have been a worse-looking marriage but if Stephen loves her and she has the sense to respond, then they will settle together. And when there are children they will be tied together by that strongest of all bonds. Who could ever have left a home where Christopher was growing up?

When Stephen prompted her later in the evening, Lily agreed that she was tired from the journey. She went up the stairs to their bedroom with him. She undressed while he was in the bathroom and was in bed with her eyes shut and her bedside light off by the time he came into the bedroom.

He said 'Lily' softly and she did not stir at all.

He got into bed beside her and turned off his bedside light.

The room was very dark. Lily, still and quiet in the darkness, could hear the sea.

Stephen's heavy hand came out of the darkness on to her shoulder.

'Lily,' he said.

Lily stayed silent for a few more moments.

His hand moved down to her breast, gripping her flesh through the thin silk of her nightgown.

Lily stirred as if she had just woken. 'Stephen,' she said softly. 'You must excuse me. After the journey I feel so tired. I really must sleep.'

Stephen said nothing. Lily froze, wondering if he would insist, if she could get away with a refusal, wondering what the rules were.

He sighed. 'Of course, my dear.'

The sea sounded loud in the darkness. Lily could feel

Stephen wakeful and threatening in the bed beside her. She forced herself to breathe slowly and noisily. She knew that any movement, any sound that betrayed she was awake would serve as an excuse for him to touch her, to insist on his rights, this first night in his home.

They lay side by side in silence for long minutes.

'I'm just popping downstairs,' Stephen said quietly. 'You go to sleep. I'll be a little while. I think I'll have a brew.'

The bed rocked as he got out and Lily heard the whisper of his silk dressing-gown as he put it on, heard him fumble with his bare feet for his slippers. Then the door opened and closed behind him and he was gone.

Coventry was in the kitchen, the kettle boiled and keeping hot on the stove. He was smoking a cigarette. An earlier cigarette butt smouldered in the grate. He looked up when Stephen came down the kitchen stairs.

Stephen made a grimace at him. 'Tired,' he said as if in explanation. 'Tired from the journey! Sitting in a train for what – little more than an hour? Remember the march from the railhead to the bivouac at St Omer? Travelling all day and all night and then a ten-mile march to a barn?'

Coventry smiled non-committally and spooned more tea into the dregs in the pot.

Stephen pulled up a chair and helped himself to one of Coventry's cigarettes. 'This is good,' he said. 'London was bloody awful. Might as well have been Paris. Packed out with Yanks and foreigners. Noisy as hell. Cars everywhere. Rotten service. Everything overpriced.'

Coventry poured the tea. Stephen took his mug and breathed in the reassuring acrid smell of strong stewed tea.

'Nobody knew me from Adam,' Stephen complained. 'I didn't even want to go to my club. Who's going to be there, after all? Old men, just old men!'

Coventry nodded and opened a tin of biscuits. Stephen

took one and dipped it in his tea and sucked the tea from it. Bits of biscuit crumbled wetly and sweetly in his mouth, some dropped into the mug.

'I don't know anyone who lives in London any more,' Stephen said. 'Charles Hollingbury did – remember Major Hollingbury? But he got the shakes with the noise and bought a farm in Wiltshire somewhere.'

Coventry nodded.

'I'd like a farm,' Stephen said. 'A farm like that little place in Belgium. A farm where Lily and I could be together. Charles had the right idea.'

Stephen fell silent at last and the two men sat together, saying nothing, watching the red embers glow in the little grate.

'I had a bit of a turn,' Stephen said quietly. 'Lily made a fuss about it – she can't understand. There was a bang, from a car, and I . . .' He broke off. 'I h . . . h . . . I h . . . h . . .' he panted, trying to manage the 'h' sound. 'I had a bit of a turn.'

Coventry said nothing. Stephen tightened his grip on his mug and dipped his head and drank deeply of the sour sweet hot tea. 'I didn't say anything. N . . . n . . . nothing to fear.'

Coventry reached to the stove and took the teapot. He topped up Stephen's mug and then his own.

Stephen's whole face quivered. 'J . . . j . . . just a little turn,' he said. 'D'you know – I can hardly remember a damn thing about it? J . . . just the bang, and then Lily in the hotel room and she was r . . . r . . . really mad.'

'Mad,' he repeated. 'M . . . mad.'

There was a long silence. 'She can't say anything,' Stephen said harshly. 'Sh . . . she was all but h . . . h . . . hysterical.'

Coventry, not looking at him, reached out a hand, put an arm along Stephen's shoulders.

'I didn't tell,' Stephen said. 'I w ... wouldn't trust her.'

Coventry's grip tightened. 'But – oh God! I dreamed again!' Stephen said in sudden pain. 'I started the dream again. Arriving, and the train journey, and the march ... what if I dream every day of it? What if I dream of the farmhouse?'

Coventry's grip on his shoulder was painfully hard. Stephen froze for a moment. Then with a harsh sob he turned to Coventry and thrust his twisted face into Coventry's neck. Coventry held him very tightly. In the steady mild light from the fire the two men clung to each other as if they were still in the mortal danger of the long rolling plains of Flanders.

The sun woke Lily in the morning. Stephen was already gone. The octagonal tower window faced south but curved from west to east. The sun pouring in the east windows made the yellow curtains glow. Lily woke smiling and stretched wide in the freedom of the big bed on her own. 'Divine! Too, too divine!'

She gazed upwards at the newly painted ceiling for a little while, too contented to stir, then with a sudden movement she threw back the covers and pattered over to the window. She drew back the curtains and the sun streamed into the room. Motes of dust danced in the bright light, the unpolished pale wood floorboards gleamed pale. Lily, like a classical nymph on a vase, spread her flimsy nightgown and danced in the sunlight.

A knock at the door sent her flying into bed, the covers snatched up to her chin. 'Come in!'

It was Sally with a large tray with teapot and tea cup, two boiled eggs, toast and a butter pat stamped with a little thistle flower. There was a single rose in a silver vase. Sally was grinning broadly. 'Captain Winters said you should have breakfast in bed, Miss Pears – I mean,

Mrs Winters. He went for a walk by the sea but he said if you would be ready at eleven then you could go out for the day.'

Lily sat up in bed and received the tray on her knees. 'Thank you,' she said with careful nonchalance.

Sally scanned the tray. 'Is there anything else you'd like, Ma'am?'

Lily took up the rose and inhaled the perfume as well as the 'Ma'am' as incense to her new class position. She had gone to school with girls like Sally. The parents of girls like Sally had patronized the little shop and talked down to Lily's ma and patted Lily on the head and given her a ha'penny for sweets on wages day. Now Sally put a tray carefully on Lily's bed and tucked the curtains back behind the swags, and waited for orders.

'That's all, Sally,' she said graciously. 'Thank you.'

Sally nodded and went out of the door, closing it carefully behind her. Lily waited until she heard the girl going downstairs before she let herself grin. Then she ate her eggs and her toast and drank her tea. It tasted infinitely better than anything she had ever made for herself. It tasted infinitely better than anything she had ever paid for.

She was ready for Stephen promptly at eleven, wearing a summer dress of wild silk in a rich pink-peach colour. The silk was slightly rough to the touch, the surface marked with little bobbles of thread. Lily had pointed them out in the shop. 'That's not right,' she had said. 'Silk ought to be smooth.'

The shop assistant had shaken her beautifully marcelled head. 'This is *wild* silk, Madam,' she had said. 'Very exclusive. This is the proper texture of wild silk.'

Lily had nodded, committing two words to memory – 'wild' silk and 'exclusive'. They had altered the dress so that it fitted perfectly. It was cut square across the neckline with two broad straps over the shoulders. It came with a little jacket with broad shoulders and neat square lapels. Lily glowed in it like a peach herself.

'By jove, Lily, you are a lovely thing,' Stephen said as he met her in the hall. 'Got a hat? It's quite a scorcher.'

Lily had a sun hat of woven white straw.

'And I've ordered a picnic,' Stephen said. He was wearing white flannel trousers and a white shirt with a cravat at his neck. Lily looked at him with approval. He looked younger when he was not wearing his dark office suits. 'Something rather special,' Stephen said, indicating the hamper. 'Cook has done us proud.'

Lily suddenly remembered the doorstep sandwiches and shared bottle of lemonade on the picnic with Charlie. Stephen's treats were always planned ahead, he was like an adult planning excursions and amusements for a child. Charlie and she had been like two children, run away for the day together. Even Stephen's play was constrained. At his most easy he was always formal.

Lily beamed at him. He was her husband and Charlie was far away. 'Divine!' she said firmly. 'Too, too divine.'

Coventry was waiting at the car. He came up the steps and took the hamper from Stephen. He loaded it into the boot and then shut the passenger door on Stephen and Lily.

'Take us down the Chichester road,' Stephen said. 'Keep an eye open for somewhere nice to stop. If you don't see anywhere, take us to Bosham. It's a pretty little village,' he said to Lily. 'Right on the water's edge. When there's a high tide they get sea water in their sitting rooms! Ever been there?'

Lily shook her head, enjoying the sunlight and the bright colours of Southsea Common rolling past the car window. 'It sounds lovely.'

'And then we'll go on to Chichester and have a look

round the cathedral. Maybe get a cup of tea before we come home.'

Lily nodded.

Stephen put his hand confidently on her knee. Lily did not move. She had a private certainty that his hand was damp and would mark the delicate silk, or crush it and take the desirable new stiffness from it. She remained silent for as long as she could, but then she could bear it no longer. 'Mind my skirt,' she said, lifting his hand a little.

With a slow challenging look Stephen lifted the fabric of the skirt up out of the way, and then put his hand back on her knee, moist and warm against her stocking. Lily flushed scarlet and glanced towards Coventry in front of them, his eyes on the road.

'All right,' Stephen said pleasantly. 'I'll mind the skirt.'

Chapter Seventeen

Lily and Stephen looked around Chichester cathedral for a little while until Stephen grew gloomy over the memorial stones.

'Such a fuss,' he said irritably. 'Such a fuss about death.'

'Tea!' Lily declared. 'I am longing for tea!' She was learning to manage him. More importantly, she was learning that she must manage him to secure her own comfort.

Stephen's face cleared. 'I know the very place!'

They left the cathedral by the main west door. It opened on to a little green edged with large trees. Beyond them was the street, the shops and hotel of the little market town. Lily liked the way that the cathedral was part of the buildings of the town, as if you might purchase or pray depending on which door you entered. She was learning to like cathedrals and museums and art galleries. Before her marriage she had never so much as inspected the outside of a public building. She had been amazed in London at how much arduous sightseeing they had done. She was beginning to learn that the problem for Stephen's class was how to fill their empty leisure time. They had no labour to exhaust them, they had no education left incomplete. They had to take up sports, and drive aimlessly around. They had to change for different times of the day, several times a day, and make a fuss about the timing of different meals and different drinks. There was nothing else for them to do.

In Lily's childhood everyone she knew had worked so hard that when they had days off, they rested. It was a rare family that even bothered to take the short bus ride to the sea. Only children had the energy for play, the adults were in a permanent state of weariness. It was strange for Lily suddenly to be within a class where getting tired was the purpose of half of their activities.

'Here we are,' Stephen said.

The Dolphin and Anchor hotel faced the cathedral, and was painted white on the outside, dark and cool inside. Stephen and Lily sank into deep leather armchairs in the hotel foyer and Stephen ordered tea, sandwiches and cakes.

Lily waited until he had eaten and she had poured him a second cup. Only then did she open the subject that had been on her mind since she had woken in smiling confidence in the morning. 'I've had a letter from my friend in the Midsummer Madness company, Madge Sweet.'

'I saw you had a letter. What did she want?'

'Nothing. Only to tell me that there is a show being put together at the Kings, Southsea. She thought I could try for a part.'

Stephen's eyebrows snapped together. 'Why?'

Lily looked at him inquiringly. 'Because it would be a good show . . .'

Stephen's moustache moved with his smile but his eyes were stern. 'I hardly think my wife need hop about the stage for a pittance of a wage.'

Lily replaced her tea cup in the saucer. 'I know I don't need to. But I never thought that I would stop work just because I was married.'

'You'd better think it now then. I have no intention of seeing my wife high-kicking in the chorus line on stage.'

There was a silence. Lily was measuring Stephen's determination.

'It wouldn't be the chorus line, it would be a solo. I am a soloist.'

'Makes no difference.'

248

Lily fell silent again. 'I didn't know you felt like this,' she started. 'I had thought that I would go back to work as soon as we came home.'

Stephen shook his head.

'My ma was very proud of me,' Lily said. There was a slight quaver in her voice. 'She thought that I would be a star. The Midsummer Madness tour was just the start. And she was right. I've had a letter from the Kings offering me an audition.'

'No,' Stephen said shortly.

'Wait!' Lily said. She could feel her rising irritation. 'You don't even know what kind of show it is, or what kind of part I could get. I wouldn't be a chorus girl, I'd be a singer. There are many married women who are singers. I wouldn't necessarily go on tour even. And I thought you liked my singing?'

'I *do* like your singing. But my wife does not give public performances, Lily. It's simply not on.'

Lily gritted her teeth. 'It's a wonderful chance for me, Stephen. If I don't take it I might never get another.'

Stephen smiled. 'You're right on both counts. You won't take this and you won't take another. You are my wife now, Lily, not a chorus girl. The two roles are entirely separate. You cannot do both.'

'You don't understand – you keep saying chorus girl. But I wouldn't be a chorus girl. I wouldn't be in the chorus. What we should do is let me try for it, and, if I get it, you can see what I would be doing, and see if you like it.'

'No.'

'Stephen . . .'

'No.'

Lily picked up her tea cup, her hands shaking with anger, her face blazing. 'You are ruining my career,' she said angrily.

'You have no career. You are my wife.'

249

'What d'you want me to do? Stay at home all day? Knit?'

Stephen shrugged. 'I expect you will find pastimes suitable for your position.'

'I am a singer,' Lily said, her voice shaking with tears and anger. 'That is my career.'

Stephen shook his head. He was outwardly calm but he could feel his anger building inside him. The taste of anger in his mouth made him sick. It tasted like blood. It smelled like the sweet dangerous smell of violets, of gas. 'For the last time, Lily, you will not go back to the stage. That is my final decision.'

There was a silence. A waitress came to clear the tea things and wondered at the two of them sitting woodenly opposite each other, Lily flushed and trembling, Stephen icy white.

'Those two are having a row,' she whispered to the other waitress. 'A scorcher.'

'I thought you would look after me,' Lily eventually whispered. 'Not ruin my life!'

'You over-dramatize everything. You are hysterical. I am not ruining your life. I am ensuring that you behave in the way you ought. You are my wife. You owe a certain behaviour to my position.'

Lily said nothing. She thought of telling him that she would leave him. She thought of sweeping from the tea room and never coming back. But though Lily was young and angry, she was realistic. She had nowhere else to go and she had no money of her own.

'Let's go home,' Stephen said. 'You've spoiled the whole day anyway.'

Coventry watched them in his wing mirror on the drive back to Portsmouth. He saw Lily's head turned determinedly away from Stephen, looking out over the fields. Once or twice she put her gloved hand up to her cheek and blotted a tear with her fingertip. Stephen was leaning back with his eyes half-closed. Coventry knew the signs of his anger – the flexing of the muscles in his jaw and the skin white around his mouth. Coventry pursed his lips in a silent whistle, following tunes in his head. He drove a little quicker to get them home sooner.

The quarrel was not resolved over dinner. Stephen sat one end of the table and Muriel the other. Lily bent her head over her plate between them. Muriel inquired after their day and received polite but monosyllabic replies from each of them. She launched into a detailed description of her own day which took them from the first course past the steak pie and on to dessert, which was fruit salad and thin cream. Neither of them spoke.

'Will you be going out for the day tomorrow?' Muriel inquired of Stephen.

'No,' Stephen said shortly. 'I shall go to the office.'

So the honeymoon was over, Muriel thought. Please God the rest of the marriage goes better than this first week. Home early from London, home early from a day trip. If he cannot get on with her, then why did he marry her in the first place? Muriel shot a look at Lily's downcast profile. A girl so very beautiful ought to be blissfully happy in her first weeks of marriage. Blissful, Muriel repeated to herself. Stephen married for love, the girl of his choice. Why could the two not get on?

Lily excused herself when they took their coffee in the drawing room. 'I have a headache. I think I'll have an early night.'

'Oh, poor dear!' Muriel said. 'D'you have everything you need? Aspirin?'

'Yes,' Lily said. 'I have everything. Goodnight.'

Muriel said 'goodnight'. Stephen nodded. He watched the door close behind her, saying nothing.

Muriel hesitated. It would be most natural to ask Stephen what was wrong with Lily. What was there between the two of them that was souring these early days? But the habit of silence between her and her son was very heavy. Muriel could not break it unaided. She glanced towards Stephen and he smiled at her. His face was quite impassive.

'More coffee, Mother?'

Muriel sighed. 'No thank you, dear.'

'I think I'll take mine upstairs and drink it with the old man.'

Muriel nodded. It was not her place to suggest that Stephen would do better to climb the next flight and try to settle matters with his young wife.

Stephen went heavily up the stairs. Muriel heard the door of Rory's bedroom open, and then the quick exchange of words as the nurse went out.

Stephen shut the door behind her. 'Hello, Father,' he said.

The figure on the bed lay as still as ever.

'Rum sort of day,' Stephen said. 'Hot as ever. The garden wants rain.' He sat beside his father's bed and put his coffee cup down on the bedside table. His father's dark eyes watched him.

'We took the car over to Chichester for the day,' Stephen said. 'Had a look around the town. I showed Lily the cathedral. We had tea at the Dolphin and Anchor hotel.'

There was a silence in the room. Rory's loud breathing rasped as he inhaled and then breathed out again.

'We had a bit of a spat,' Stephen volunteered. 'Silly really.'

Rory's face never changed. Stephen shrugged his shoulders. 'She's young,' he said. 'And highly strung. She gets overwrought very easily. She doesn't understand how we live yet. The kind of family she's married into. Mother will have to show her the ropes, show her the way around.

She'll learn. She'll pick it up. She's young enough to break in, after all!'

He gave a little laugh, and reached for his coffee cup.

His father lay in silence.

'Oh, I know,' Stephen said disagreeably. 'You're thinking that if Christopher had lived he would have married a baronet's daughter at the very least.'

He put his coffee cup down with a rattle of cup on saucer. 'Well, he didn't live. He's gone. All you have left is me. And all I could fancy was Lily. However she is, however she behaves, she's still better than those damned harpies which were all that Mother could find for me.'

He broke off and went to the window, twitched back the curtain and looked out. It was a clear star-filled night. The moon stretched a silver path out over the sea. The waves moved like gleaming muscles on the body of the water.

'Bright,' Stephen said anxiously. 'Bright as day out there.'

He dropped the curtain and turned back into the room. 'She's so clean,' he said. 'Even now. Even now we're married I look at her and she's like a girl that you might dream about. She's like the girls were before they learned to be modern and smoke. Even in the short skirts she wears she's not like a modern girl. She's young and she's clean and it's as if none of the war ever happened when I'm near her.'

He sat back beside the bed again and took his father's limp cold hand. 'They're all whores,' he said confidentially. 'Every single one of them. All of them, except for Lily. You can tell just by looking at her. She's not like the rest of them. She's clean and she's young. We might have a bit of difficulty – well, everyone has a bit of difficulty in the early days of a marriage. But she is the only English girl I ever met that I could look at and know for sure that she's not like the rest of them. She's not a whore.'

He patted his father's hand and laid it to rest on the counterpane. Rory stared at him as if he could hear, as if he had something to say in reply to his son.

'There was a girl in Belgium like her,' Stephen said softly. 'A farmer's daughter, a country girl. A real old-fashioned girl.' He smiled for a moment, his whole face softening at the memory. 'Goodnight,' he said abruptly, and went quietly from the room.

Upstairs he found Lily lying in bed with the light out. He undressed in the bathroom to avoid disturbing her and then he slid into the bed beside her.

The tide was high, he could hear the sound of waves on the shingle beach. It was full moon; the yellow curtains glowed in the darkness of the room. Stephen knew from Lily's careful stillness that she was awake.

He smiled to himself. She was young, she would learn. It was funny that he had mentioned that Belgian girl Juliette Perot to his father. She would have been even younger than Lily if she had lived, but they both had that same purity. She had been taught by the nuns at Ypres convent, and then come home to help her mother and father on the farm when her brothers were called up to fight. Juliette would have made a good nun, Stephen thought. When she brought eggs or meat or cheeses to sell she carried herself with that serene confidence. She drove a little pony and cart – he smiled suddenly at the memory of the little pony and cart. Along those little lanes, behind the lines of the trenches, far enough away, so that people could pretend that life was still normal, Juliette trotted her pony delivering her father's produce to the little cafés.

Every day they heard guns like thunder and saw the lines of reserves marching northward. Every day they saw the commandeered buses and wagons and stretcher carriers slogging south with loads of dying men. But Juliette would trot her little pony about her business as if the world had not gone to war on her doorstep.

Stephen nodded. *That* was where she resembled Lily. That same gritty determination not to acknowledge the war. The refusal to see it, to be touched by it, which was so infinitely better than either sympathy or enthusiasm.

He reached out a hand to touch Lily on the shoulder. It occurred to him for the first time that she might be distressed. He had banned her from her work and from her friends, she had eaten virtually nothing at supper and complained of a headache. Her mother was dead and she had no friends. She might have been weeping. The poor little thing was kicking against the traces, but she would have to be broken in.

His hand brushed the warmth of her skin. Tenderness swelled in Stephen, he was ready to make up.

'If you lay one finger on me,' Lily said clearly and icily, 'I will scream the house down.'

Lily did not get up for breakfast, although Stephen ensured that she was awake by briskly drawing the bedroom curtains and stamping around the room, his shoes very noisy on the bare floorboards, looking for his cufflinks.

Lily lay back on the pillows and watched him. She made no effort to get out of bed and help him look for them. When he found them left in the bathroom she showed no interest.

'I'm going down for breakfast,' he prompted.

Lily did not move. 'Ask Sally to bring me up some coffee and a slice of toast,' she said. 'I'll get dressed later.'

Stephen hesitated. He wanted to tell her that breakfast in bed was a luxury which had been offered to her yesterday as a treat, as part of their honeymoon. Today was a working day when she should be dressed before him, and downstairs in the dining room ready to pour his cup of tea while they breakfasted together.

'Are you not having breakfast with me?' he asked pointedly.

Lily smiled at him pleasantly. 'No,' she said simply. 'I don't have any work to go to, I don't have any friends to meet. There is nothing for me to get up for. I'll have a bath and get dressed later.'

'If you're still sulking . . .'

Lily shook her fair head. Her smile was imperturbable. 'No,' she said. 'I'm not sulking. But if I am to be a lady of leisure I might as well enjoy it.'

Stephen crossed the room and pecked her cheek. 'I'll see you this afternoon then,' he said. He was still dissatisfied but he could find no reasonable grounds for complaint.

Lily nodded. She sat up in bed and smoothed the covers to her liking. 'Have a nice day at work,' she said.

Muriel poured Stephen's tea and sat at the opposite end of the table while he ate his breakfast and read *The Times*. If she expected Lily to come downstairs and have breakfast with her new husband and see him off to work, she did not say. She heard Stephen order Sally to take a tray upstairs to Mrs Winters and she said nothing. When Stephen went to work Muriel sat in the drawing room on the window seat, watching the children playing at the Canoe Lake for a long time. The swans, which had been banished during the war to prevent people wasting bread on them, sailed serenely on the glassy water, breast to breast with their own reflections.

Muriel did not want to go upstairs to see if Lily were ill, if she needed anything. She did not want to invite Lily's confidences. She found that she had no inclination to advise, to intervene into Stephen's marriage. She found that she wanted to know nothing about it at all.

There was not a sound from Lily's room until eleven when the bedroom door banged open and Lily pattered down the stairs. She called in to Rory's sickroom to say good morning and then she came downstairs. Muriel, emerging from the drawing room, met her in the hall and saw with some alarm that she had on her hat and gloves.

'Are you going out?'

Lily smiled. 'Just for a little walk, along the front, perhaps up to the shops.'

'Coventry will drive you. He is in the garden, but I can send for him in a moment.'

Lily shook her head. 'No need. I want a walk. It's a lovely day.'

'I am going for tea to Mrs Frost. Her daughter will be there and some other people. Will you come too, Lily?'

'Lovely!' Lily said. 'What time?'

'We'll leave here at half past three,' Muriel said. 'Coventry can drop us and then fetch Stephen. We can all come home together.'

'Lovely,' Lily said again. 'See you later.'

She opened the door herself and stepped outside. 'Lunch at twelve,' Muriel called.

Lily opened the door again and stuck her head round. 'Not for me,' she said cheerily. 'I'll be back in time for tea.' And then she was gone before Muriel could protest.

She walked along the seafront until she was out of sight of the house. It was a surprisingly long way. The house was tall, three storeys high, and the octagonal tower commanded a wide view of the promenade. Lily glanced over her shoulder. When all she could see was the red tiled roof of the tower she crossed the council flower gardens and walked briskly towards Palmerston Road until she came to a tram stop. She waited for a little while and then the tram came, half-empty on a weekday morning.

Lily looked in her purse when she paid for her ticket.

She had a few shillings and some coppers but she had spent her last pound on the telegram to tell Charlie that she was marrying. Stephen had spoken of giving her an allowance but, as yet, he had given her no money. Lily grimaced. It would be embarrassing to ask him for money when he bought all her clothes and had opened accounts for her in the major Portsmouth stores, but without money in her pocket she might as well have stayed Lily Pears with at least a weekly wage to spend.

She leaned forward to see out of the front window. The boat-like prow of the Kings Theatre was ahead of them. There were posters up for the summer variety shows. There was a sticker pasted over the posters: 'And the Kings Orchestra', it said. 'Conductor Charles Smith.' Lily beamed.

The tram stopped and she jumped down from the wooden slatted steps. The glass swing doors of the theatre were shut, except for one entrance where you could go in to buy advance tickets. A cleaning woman was laboriously washing the marble floor of the foyer. A thick green carpet ran up the steps leading from the foyer into the heart of the theatre.

Lily had been to shows at the Kings with her mother ever since it had opened in 1907, but they had sat in the gods, the highest seats in the theatre, which had a separate entrance and separate box office at the side of the theatre. They had been strictly segregated from the ladies and gentlemen who entered by the front entrance and walked on carpet. Lily smiled. She was Mrs Winters now. If she came to the theatre it would be through those doors and up those stairs and into the deep green and gilt and cream auditorium to sit in comfortable cushioned seats. She turned from the front entrance. She would rather be Lily Valance and enter at the stage door.

The theatre had been squeezed into a block of land

tucked between terraced houses. Lily had to walk along the white-painted side of the building and then turn the corner and walk along the street at the back of the theatre to the stage door. On the other side of the road were small two-storey terraced houses. Children played in the street and one, spotting her hat and her expensive yellow dress and jacket, came running up to her with his hands out asking for a penny for sweets. Lily scowled at him, fearing his dirty hands on her skirt. 'Shove off,' she said abruptly.

She paused before the stage door and pulled a hand mirror from her purse. Her hair was smooth, the little slice of straw and flowers which served as her hat was on straight. Her lipstick was discreet. She looked as pretty as she had when Charlie had first seen her, but now, shadowed with sadness, her face had a new maturity which was growing towards beauty. Lily smiled at herself with absolute satisfaction. She raised her hand and tapped on the door.

A man opened it. 'Lily Valance,' Lily said, waving the letter from the theatre. 'For an audition.' She was gambling that he would not read it and see that the date was wrong and that she was a day early.

'All right,' he said. He pushed the door towards her and Lily slipped inside. On her left was the little glass-fronted office, like a booking office, where the doorman sat and brewed tea for the actors and crew, and ran a good business taking bets, selling newspapers, carrying messages and spreading gossip. Ahead of her was a flight of concrete steps which led directly to the stage. Dressing rooms ran off to the left, and there was another floor of dressing rooms up the flight of steps on the next level. The largest room, up a few steps and to the right, convenient for the door and the doorman, was the star dressing room.

'D'you know your way?' the doorman asked. 'Who d'you have to see?'

'Charlie Smith,' Lily said. She found she was breathless.

'He's rehearsing the band,' the man said. He nodded towards the steps which led upward to the darkness. 'Go on up.'

Lily turned and climbed the short flight of stone steps. At the top was a large echoing space. Lily had never been on such a big stage. It was the size of a warehouse, a barn. Enormous slices of scenery leaned against the back wall, as high as houses. Three men, dirty as tramps, were painting a flight of stairs which led nowhere. They winked at Lily as she glanced at them. She smiled and walked on. She was afraid of being challenged and thrown out before she could find Charlie.

She could hear the orchestra, they were playing a charleston number. Lily heard Charlie's voice say wearily: 'No! No! No! We'll start again. I'll count you in and then you keep the beat. It *has* to be crisp. Two, three, four, and . . .'

The band came in raggedly and Charlie tapped the music stand of his piano again. 'No,' he said. 'Try again. Two, three, four . . .'

This time they hit the beat like a sledge-hammer. *Charle*ston *Charle*ston. Lily grinned as the familiar tune made the boards of the stage beneath her feet throb. She had a sudden sense of coming alive again, coming home. She felt herself beaming. Suddenly free of nerves, she went swiftly up the side of the stage and stepped out of the wings on to the stage itself.

It was in darkness, except for the houselights of the theatre and the musicians' lights over their stands. Lily looked out. It was a superb theatre, the most wonderful she had ever seen, as good as the London ones. It was richly coloured. Two bulging boxes were stacked two deep on the right and left of the stage. A confident sweep of the balcony showed the generous space of the upper circle, the same wide curl was the balcony of the stalls above. The upper stalls, above that, were raked like a ship heeling over, crammed into the roof space.

Lily looked from the extravagant painted roof of the theatre, hung with fat glassy chandeliers, to the first row of seats upholstered in green velvet beneath her feet, and thought that she would never be able to reach all those people with her voice. She would never learn, as Charlie had taught her, to be a queen to them, to keep them waiting, to keep them guessing.

Charlie, glancing up from the score, saw a movement out of the corner of his eye. He looked up to the darkened stage and there was Lily, radiant in her yellow summer dress, her face lifted to the empty gallery, the smooth lovely line of her neck, her shoulders, her body, inviting applause from the empty seats.

'Well, look what the cat brought in,' he said. 'Welcome back, Lil.'

Chapter Eighteen

At his voice Lily looked down and beamed at him. She hurried downstage and scampered down the make-shift gangway to the auditorium floor. Charlie swung his legs over the brass rail which divided the orchestra pit from the audience and, as the band raggedly stopped playing to watch, Lily flung herself into his open arms and was thoroughly kissed.

Her hat fell off, her arms tightened around his body and Lily smelled his warm familiar male smell, as good as baked bread. She buried her face in his neck and felt the warmth of his skin against her face. For the first time since her mother's death she felt safe.

'Oh Charlie . . .'

'That'll do,' Charlie said. He glanced behind him at the open interest of the members of the orchestra. 'All right,' he said. 'Show's over. You can take a ten-minute break.' He checked his watch. 'Back at twenty past twelve and no later.'

He guided Lily to the front row and sat down beside her. 'Well!' he said. 'How's the girl?'

Lily, suddenly bashful, could think of nothing to say. She bent forward and picked up her hat. 'Oh, I'm fine,' she said. 'Thank you for your letter.'

Charlie nodded.

Lily put her hat on again and pushed it vaguely into place. 'Madge wrote to me,' she said. 'Twice. Oh! Of course you know.'

Charlie nodded again, his eyes never leaving her face. 'I am sorry about your ma,' he said gently.

Lily looked at him quickly and then looked away. 'Yes,' she said.

Charlie looked at the perfect profile beside him and sighed at his own sense of frustration. There was nothing he could say to comfort Lily for the death of her mother. She had suffered an absolute loss – her guardian, protector, chaperone and manager gone in one moment. He shook his head. Although he had been a witness to the disappearance of a whole generation, and confronted the deaths of many of his own friends, he knew that each death is an individual tragedy. Each of the little white graves which they were starting to arrange so carefully in France was separately named. A whole regiment might have died to hold a little wood on the top of a little hill. But that meant heartbreak in hundreds of individual homes, hundreds of notices in a hundred local papers, hundreds of black arm bands, and more than a million women had learned that their boy would not be coming home again. Lily's grief, one little death amongst these many, was the greatest loss of her young life. He noted the shadows under her eyes. It would take her a long time to finish grieving.

'So what's new?' he asked. 'Have you come to audition? Does the Captain let you work?'

Lily turned her face to him, her blue eyes guileless. 'Yes,' she said simply. 'As long as I'm back for tea when he comes home, he won't mind.'

Charlie shook his head. 'You can do that during rehearsal, but not when we're in performance. The tea matinée finishes at four thirty and then the evening show opens at seven thirty. You'd have to be here for six thirty.'

Lily shrugged. 'So? I'll have dinner with him instead of tea. His mother can pour his tea. She's always in.'

'You live in her house?' Charlie asked. 'Aren't you getting a place of your own?'

Lily shook her head. 'Why should we?'

Charlie closed his lips on a dozen reasons. 'And *she* doesn't mind you being on the stage?'

'Not at all,' Lily said airily.

Charlie hesitated, scenting the lie. 'And what about Captain Winters's dad? Doesn't *he* mind?'

'I do wish you'd stop nagging on about Stephen's family! Anyone would think you were his favourite aunt!' Lily exclaimed petulantly. 'Nobody minds what I do, or where I go – all right? And stop calling him Captain. He's not a captain any more, he's a lawyer. It's stupid keeping war titles when the war is over and everyone has forgotten all about it.'

'Have they?'

'Yes,' Lily said sharply. 'Now what's the show and who's in it?'

Charlie grinned at Lily's new confidence. 'Well, Madame, the show is Summertime Variety and the star is George Tyler. We're auditioning the cast but we've got a magician and an animal act, a comedian and a memory man. The chorus line is picked and marking out steps in the circle bar, and I was working with the band when you swanned in.'

'Can I have an audition now?'

'Why didn't you come tomorrow, when you were due?'

Lily shot him a fleeting sideways glance. 'I was in a temper,' she confessed. 'I wanted to get out of the house and into the theatre. And I wanted to see you. I'll come back tomorrow if you can't see me today.'

Charlie dropped his hand along the back of the seat to take her shoulder in a quick hug. She was as slight as a child, he could feel her shoulder light and bony through the thin fabric of her dress. He felt a sudden longing to take her and hold her and love her, to comfort her hidden grief, to steal her from the husband who had left her in a temper this morning, only a week married. He took his hand away at once, and when Lily turned her bright face up to him for a kiss he was looking away and his face was shuttered.

'Today's fine,' he said. 'Richard Rice is the director. He's coming in at twelve thirty. You can sing for him then. What d'you want to do? "Burlington Bertie"?'

Lily nodded. 'Can I do it without a costume? Will he see what it should be like?'

'Take your hat off.'

Lily pulled her hat off and shook her head. The bobbed hair had grown and was brushing her shoulders. She had changed from the girl on the *Midsummer Madness* tour. There was a reserve about her that was new, a gravity which the old well-mothered Lily had never shown. She looked steadily back at Charlie, not smiling or coquetting. She took in his face and his body in the half-darkness of the auditorium as he was reading her. They stared at each other with the open intensity of reunited lovers, without self-consciousness, without any facade. They faced each other and looked and looked.

He thought Stephen had probably hurt her. He thought she was probably here without his permission, perhaps defying a specific ban. Charlie wanted to caution her, but then he stopped himself. Lily had married of her own free will and he had not cautioned her then. His lips moved into a painful little smile. He had been impotent in every sense of the word. He had taken a decision to set Lily free and keep her free. He had loved her and let her go to another man. There was no point in trying to make her marriage run smoothly, interceding for her happiness. Stephen and Lily would have to work things out for themselves, there was no place for him in their shared life.

'What is it? You look sad.'

Charlie shrugged and grinned at her. 'Nothing,' he said. 'I was worrying about the bother you're getting yourself into, but I suppose you can look after yourself. A smart girl like you. I suppose you can wind Mr Winters around your little finger?'

Lily looked at him thoughtfully. 'Not yet.'

'A clever woman can generally manage a man who is in love with her,' Charlie commented. 'You don't have to get your head down and fight your way through. You can smile and charm and ask for favours. And of course, you can get his mother on your side. If she supports you, you're home and dry.'

The orchestra were coming back to their places, coughing loudly to display their discretion. Charlie grinned at them.

'Right, lads, this is Lily Valance who was with me on the Midsummer Madness tour. She's going to do "Burlington Bertie" as an audition piece for Mr Rice when he gets here. We'll run through it now. Has everyone got the music?'

There was a scuffle while the musicians hunted for the score on their stands and in their cases. The violinist had no copy but he could stand behind Charlie at the piano and see his.

'Up you go, Lil,' Charlie said. 'And remember, nice and slow and mournful.'

While she was making her way up the gangplank to the stage he turned to the band. 'She does it very slow,' he said. 'We'll take one and two and three and four – that slow. It sounds funny at first but I've seen her do it, and it works. It's like a ballad, a sad Irish ballad.'

Lily was waiting at the back of the stage. 'OK,' Charlie said, counting again. 'One and two and three and four . . .'

The refrain played through once and then Lily stepped

266

forwards. Her voice was strong and clear and simple. She had tucked her hair behind her ears and she looked like an orphaned boy. She held the lapels of her little jacket and sauntered like a street urchin. In her clear steady voice the song became the story of the survivors of the war, who came back to find that their place in the world was gone, that their friends were missing, that their joy was lost.

When she finished Charlie found that he had a lump in his throat. He swore loudly and thoroughly.

'Now sit somewhere out of the way,' he said disagreeably. 'We've got work to do. When Mr Rice comes he'll listen to you.'

Lily backed off meekly to the prompt corner, perched on the stool out of sight in the darkness and listened to Charlie rehearsing the band.

They stopped after a few more minutes and Lily peeped around the open curtain. Richard Rice was talking to Charlie. He was a tall man, with a fringe of blonde curly hair around a large bald dome of a head, twinkling blue eyes and a look of complete unconcern.

'Of course I'll listen,' he said pleasantly. 'Miss Valance!'

Lily stepped forward, shading her eyes against the working lights. 'I'm here.'

'Charlie tells me you're something special,' he said with a smile. 'Is that right?'

'He says that to all the chorus girls,' she said roguishly.

Richard laughed and slapped Charlie on the back. 'Let's hear it then,' he said.

'She does it in costume,' Charlie explained rapidly while the musicians turned back to the 'Burlington Bertie' music. 'Either morning dress – but I thought, what about uniform? You know, officer's khaki?'

'For "Burlington Bertie"?' Richard queried.

'Well, just bear it in mind,' Charlie suggested, turning

to the band and giving them a nod. 'One and two . . .'

Lily sang easily. She had the sense of the stage now, and had felt the acoustics of the theatre. She knew she could be heard clearly and easily. She knew she would not have to strain her voice. When the music finished she stayed in the centre of the stage and waited for Richard Rice's comments.

'Mmmm,' he said. He nodded at Charlie. 'Can she dance?'

'Loves dancing.'

'Sing something a bit risqué?'

Charlie shook his head. 'It's not her style. She's too young for it. She sings ballads very well and she can do ragtime like no-one you've ever heard. She's got the rhythm and she's been taught to count.'

'Can you do something else for me, dear? Can you do "Alexander's Ragtime Band"?' Richard called up to the stage.

Lily glanced at Charlie; he nodded.

'Yes,' she said. The hours in the lodging house drawing rooms with Charlie playing the piano came back to her. He had made her count beats to the bar, clap the rhythm, tap the rhythm, count it silently and come in eight bars later after eight bars of silence, and hit the beat precisely. 'I can do ragtime,' she said certainly.

She went to the back of the stage. She had never sung ragtime on stage, she had always leaned against the piano and sung to Charlie. She thought of Madge's outrageous vamping and Sylvia's elegant drifting. Somewhere between the two there must be a style that Lily could manage. She walked as slowly as she could to her position, racking her brains.

Nothing came. She would just sing the song pure and simple, trusting to the beat and the happy-go-lucky tune to take her through. Lily paused. That was it. Ragtime was more than anything else happy. It was joyful. And *that* was the style that Madge could not manage because she was a vamp, and Sylvia could not do in her style of an elegant English lady. It was a toe-tapping street dance, a song for errand boys to whistle.

'Wait a minute!' Lily hissed at Charlie and darted to the prompt corner. Hanging up on the pegs were three or four hats and among them a straw boater. Lily grabbed it and rushed back on to the stage. She turned herself sideways to the audience, tipped the boater low down over her nose, stuck her hands in the pockets of her jacket and crossed one foot over another.

'Attagirl!' Charlie said softly. 'Pretty quick, eh, Lil?' he said aloud.

'Very slow to start,' she replied without moving from her pose, 'and then very quick.'

'Tricky,' Charlie commented. 'One, two, three, four!'

Lily froze motionless, like a tableau of an errand boy, and started the catchy song as if it too were a haunting ballad.

'Come on and hear, come on and hear, Alexander's Ragtime Band . . .'

Slowly she speeded up as Charlie just picked out chords with his left hand so that he could conduct the band with his right, keep them following Lily precisely on a steadily increasing beat. The excitement of the song was infectious. Lily, her face radiant, whipped the hat off her head and spun it on her finger. When she forgot the words in the middle she whirled around and tap-danced and Charlie cut off the band with a sharp gesture to let her tap in silence and then brought them in to a thundering final chorus without missing a beat.

'Yes indeed!' Richard Rice called. He clapped, walking down the aisle to the orchestra pit. 'That was stunning.

Miss Valance, you're in. Third billing. Start Monday, eleven o'clock.'

Lily flung the boater in the air. 'Yippee!'

There was an uneasy truce between Lily and Stephen at dinner. Muriel kept a flow of small talk steadily through tomato soup, liver casserole and apple crumble. Lily ate hardly any meat.

'I don't like liver,' she said when Muriel asked if she was unwell. 'I never eat it.'

'How unusual,' Muriel said frostily. The meals at number two, The Parade were planned on a monthly basis. Liver casserole occurred twice a month. She did not know what Cook would say if she were told that it was to be banned.

'We often have it,' Stephen said. 'It's one of my favourites.'

Muriel looked from Stephen's determined heavy face to Lily's pale stubbornness. 'Shall we have coffee in the drawing room?' she asked, as if they did not have coffee there every night. 'Lily dear, would you wind some wool for me?'

Lily sat before the dried flower arrangement in the cold hearth with her arms upraised like a little doll. Muriel draped the yarn of wool over both Lily's hands and then wound it off into a ball. 'What are you knitting?' Lily asked.

'A little matinée coat and boots. My niece, Sarah-Louise, is expecting a baby. She lives in Scotland so we hardly ever see them, but I like to keep in touch.'

Lily nodded.

'She's only been married two months,' Muriel said, watching the downturned face for any expression. 'She always said she wanted a large family. She might as well start as soon as possible.'

Lily looked up and smiled at Muriel. 'I don't,' she said simply.

Stephen wandered around the room, his coffee cup in his hand. The tide was down and they could not hear the sea.

'I think I'll pop out,' he said. Muriel and Lily looked at him. 'I'll take a run over to Hayling Island with Coventry. I've been cooped up in that office all day. I feel like a breath of air.'

'As you like, dear,' Muriel said placidly. 'Lily, would you like to go too?'

'No thank you,' Lily said sweetly. 'I was going to sit with Mr Winters for an hour.'

Stephen nodded. Muriel noticed that he did not press Lily to go with him. 'I'll be late,' he said. 'I'll drive myself home. Don't wait up.'

Muriel and Lily nodded. 'Don't forget your key,' Muriel said.

Stephen patted his pocket and went from the room. 'Goodnight,' he said at the door. Lily stayed at her seat before the empty fireplace, her arms raised, the yarn stretched ready for Muriel to roll the ball of wool. Muriel reached forward to take the wool from her, so that she would be free to go to the door and bid Stephen goodnight, but she checked the movement. Lily sat quietly serene.

The two women heard Stephen call down the back stairs, 'Coventry!' and then Coventry's footsteps up the stairs.

'Night patrol,' Stephen said to him. The front door slammed and the two men were gone.

Muriel wound the ball of wool, Lily moving her hands to the right and to the left, obligingly keeping rhythm with Muriel. They heard the car start and drive away, and then the summer night outside the drawn curtains was silent.

'I hope you're happy,' Muriel said abruptly.

Lily looked up at her. Lily's lovely face was like a mask to Muriel, she could not imagine what the girl was feeling. Her sapphire eyes were empty. 'Why not?' she asked.

The last of the yarn was wound into a plump ball. 'Thank you, my dear,' Muriel said, trying to inject some warmth into her voice.

'That's all right,' Lily said politely. 'Shall I go and sit with Mr Winters now?'

'If you want to,' Muriel said awkwardly. 'You know you don't have to. We don't know for sure that he even knows we're there.'

'Oh, I think he does,' Lily said. 'I think he knows everything that's going on. He hears all the secrets as well. Stephen talks to him, and I talk to him, and you do too, don't you, Mrs Winters?'

Muriel flushed slightly. 'The doctors seemed to think it was a good idea. It might make him want to respond, they thought.'

'It'll be a surprise for us all when he does respond then,' Lily said brutally. 'All the secrets will be out then, won't they?'

Muriel stared at her. 'Goodnight,' Lily said pleasantly and went from the room closing the door quietly behind her.

Muriel sat in silence beside the puffy brown heads of the dried hydrangea in the fireplace vase, the ball of wool in her hands. Stephen was driving in the darkness away from his home to some pub or club or rough gambling place with Coventry. Lily, his vulgar child-wife, was sitting in the half-light beside a half-dead man. Only Christopher was untouched, unchanged. He was smiling as the train drew out of the station, smiling and waving his hat as the band played 'Tipperary'. The sunlight very bright on his golden head, his smile as radiant as a boy off to a party. 'Home by Christmas!' he had shouted.

Muriel pictured each of her family one by one; but only Christopher seemed truly alive. Christopher, who had promised to be home by Christmas and had never broken a promise in his life.

Stephen and Coventry drank heavily and well at half a dozen public houses in Havant, Bedhampton, and finally Hayling Island. Then with a quart of whisky in a brown paper bag they drove carefully down the track to Coventry's houseboat.

It was as dark and cold and unwelcoming as ever. The tide was coming in and as Stephen got from the car and climbed the rickety steps to the black door he could hear bubbles popping in the mud and the whisper and suck of incoming waves. The highest of the spring tides might wash up all around the houseboat but it would never float again. Coventry's fisherman father had grounded it with boulders in the keel and wedged it into the estuary bed with sacks of sand. An ordinary high tide, like the one creeping steadily in, never came higher than halfway up the black-painted belly of the boat, never did more than lay a reef of flotsam under the gangplank for Coventry to collect for firewood in the morning.

'Good,' Stephen said at the flickering light of the oil lamp. Coventry trimmed the wick and put the glass chimney over the flame. He put a match to the newspaper sausages in the grate and they twisted and burned and flamed under the white scraps of driftwood. As the kindling caught, Coventry added larger pieces of wood until the fire was burning well. He took the kettle and went out into the darkness for a few moments and came back with fresh water from the standpipe on the quay.

Stephen already had his dry shoes set in the grate, and

four mugs down from their hooks – two for tea, two for whisky. 'Good,' he said again.

Coventry put the kettle on the stove, put the teapot and the tea caddy and sugar on the table, and then took off his own perfectly dry shoes, and set them against the stove. They both took off their socks and laid them side by side over the brass rail at the front of the stove. They acted as if they had no choice in the matter. They acted without thinking. The little gestures – housekeeping, protecting themselves against trenchfoot, seeking warmth and dryness and comfort – seemed to assert themselves, quite independently of the two men's will, despite the peace and ease of life which they could both now command. It was as if the habits of survival had been ingrained so deeply by those two and a half years of living under sentence of death that no peace, and no life, would erase them.

'That's good,' Stephen said with immense satisfaction as the fire glowed and the kettle steamed.

Coventry made the tea, added four spoonfuls of sugar, stirred clockwise, and then they took sip for sip of scalding tea and cheap whisky.

'It's not as easy as you think,' Stephen said after a long contented silence. 'This marriage business. You see a girl and you think – she's the one – but when you actually have her it's not just dinners and dances and nights out. It's different when you're married. She doesn't try so hard. She doesn't look the same.'

Coventry nodded and blew on his tea. His hands were locked tight around the scalding mug.

'She's a good girl,' Stephen said judicially. 'But she doesn't know the rules. She doesn't come from my part of town. She can't help it; but she's going to have to learn.'

Coventry said nothing. He raised an eyebrow at Stephen when Stephen turned to him.

'I know. I could have married one of Mother's friends,'

he agreed. 'But I was crazy for Lily. I thought she would set me free of it – free of it all.'

He paused for a moment, sipped his tea, sipped his whisky. 'The last thing I thought was that she would make it worse.'

There was a shocked silence.

Stephen nodded. 'Worse,' he repeated. 'The thing in London was worse than it has ever been before. She made it sound like bally madness. She exaggerates of course, all girls do. And she's inclined to be hysterical, of course. But the dreams I get . . .' He broke off. 'And I thought with her in bed beside me, I wouldn't dream any more. I was rather counting on that.'

Coventry was watching the fire, his long pale face sad and tired.

'It hasn't worked,' Stephen said resentfully. 'I seem to be dreaming more and more clearly. And the dreams are in order. I've dreamed as far as the first posting. D'you remember? I've dreamed arriving in France, and disembarking, and the train journey and then the first time I ever went to the trenches. It was just outside Boezing. That was when you were attached to me. When we met. It was summer, 1917. D'you remember?'

Coventry shook his head. Nothing would ever make him remember.

'Well, I wish to God I didn't remember either,' Stephen said bitterly. 'I couldn't have got there at a worse time. The third battle of Ypres had just started, and we went forward and back in mud so deep that if you stumbled and fell you would drown! Christ! I remember! I remember it all! And now with Lily lying beside me I'm dreaming it all through again, every day, every night. Every inch of that ground. It's the last thing in hell I want to do.

'It's as if she's so free of it, so untouched by it, that I want to dream it out on to her pillow. She draws it out

275

of me. It's like I want to tell her. I want to get it out.'

He gave a shaky little laugh and took a deep swig of whisky from the mug. 'Don't worry,' he said unhappily. 'I'm not such a fool. I won't ever tell about it. We'll always be heroes. No-one will ever know.'

Coventry turned and looked at him. His dark unremembering eyes were filled with tears for all that he had forgotten.

Stephen did not work at the weekend and Muriel had promised that he and Lily would attend a garden fete with her in aid of the Portsmouth War Wounded Fund.

'I hate this sort of thing,' Lily said in the hall as Muriel gathered up her gloves and hat and hurried down the stairs.

'I'm sure you do,' Muriel said reassuringly. 'But we really have to do it. And it's a very good cause.'

'I think Lily is a bit of conchie,' Stephen said, but his tone was affectionate; he had recovered his patronizing affection for his little wife, who was looking very sleek and pretty. 'I think she's a bit of a radical. Look at that bobbed hair, Ma! I think we've got a Votes for Women type in the bosom of the family.'

Lily made a face at him. 'I just don't like war charities,' she said.

'Oh, get along with you,' Muriel said, enjoying the lighter atmosphere. 'You need only go round the stalls and say hello to a few people. It's not much to ask. And then you can disappear as long as you send the car back for me at six.'

'We will,' Stephen said. 'And tonight I shall take Lily out on the town. We'll go to the Theatre Royal, Lily. There's a play on: *The Three Wise Fools*, transferred from London, no less!'

Lily's face lit up. 'Wonderful!' she said.

So that's all right after all, Muriel said to herself as she walked to the car and nodded to Coventry, who held the door for her. The front seat was filled with roses from the garden, cut for the flower stall, and the car was heady with their sweet fruity perfume. Whatever differences they had yesterday, they're all gone today. I worry too much. And I know too much. I should just leave them to get on with their lives and not fret.

'Got a head, Coventry?' Stephen asked jovially.

Coventry gave him a slow easy smile.

'Were you drinking together?' Muriel asked, trying to keep the disapproval from her voice.

'Oh no, Ma,' Stephen said with a giggle. 'We were visiting the war wounded.'

Lily giggled too and Stephen slid his hand around her shoulder and hugged her.

So that's all right, Muriel thought. I shouldn't worry so much.

Chapter Nineteen

Lily and Stephen accepted congratulations on their wedding from Muriel's friends at the garden fete and glowed as if they had found in their marriage the answers they had sought. Stephen, with Lily's little hand tucked in the crook of his elbow, felt that he had made the right choice for a wife. However inadequate she was proving as an antidote to his nightmares she was, none the less, an attractive asset during the day.

He enjoyed the night out with her as well. Lily wore the beaded peach dress they had bought in London to the Theatre Royal and Stephen had the pleasure of seeing men eyeing him with visible envy. Coventry drove them home in the early hours of the morning after they had stayed late at the Queens Hotel dancing.

Lily, feeling joyous and confident, knowing that Charlie Smith was back in Portsmouth and that she would see him again on Monday, enjoyed the evening, drank champagne and staggered a little as she went upstairs to the bedroom. While Stephen was in the bathroom she undressed and got into bed, but she did not put out her bedside light and feign sleep.

That was a mistake. Stephen's urbane, attractive charm fell away from him when he got into bed beside Lily. He put his hand firmly on her shoulder and drew her towards him.

'I'm a little tired,' Lily said instantly.

'You're a little liar,' Stephen said baldly. He reached

278

over and turned off his bedside light. 'Turn your light off,' he commanded.

Lily moved away from him and pressed the switch that plunged the room into darkness. For a moment she thought of slipping from the bed and running to the bathroom to lock herself inside. But she knew it was no use. She was married to Stephen and he had rights, legal rights, to use her body when he wished.

She heard the rustle of him pulling down his pyjama trousers and then she smelled the warm male scent of him. She felt the muscles of her face lock with distaste.

Stephen heaved himself awkwardly upon her and pulled her nightgown up to her waist. His face was pressed against her neck, his body was heavy on her. 'Oh, Lily,' he said softly. 'Please love me.'

Just as she was about to reply she felt the familiar stabbing pain and gasped instead.

'I'll be gentle,' Stephen promised. 'I'll really be gentle, Lily. Just lie still.'

He thrust himself inside her again and again. Lily put her fist in her mouth and bit hard on her fingers. The bed rocked with a sickening rhythm and Lily felt herself submerged and half-drowned under Stephen's selfish uncaring weight. She moaned very softly against her fist and then gasped as the rhythm suddenly speeded. Then with a groan Stephen tore himself away from her and dropped on his back. Lily could feel the hot spurting semen against her thigh while Stephen twitched uncontrollably, his breathing hoarse.

Lily took her hand from her mouth and rubbed her face.

There was silence for a few moments.

'You will become accustomed to it,' Stephen said.

'Will we have a baby?'

Stephen reached out and clicked on the bedside light

again. Lily flinched from his warm flushed face, his satisfied glow. Stephen tapped the side of his nose, smiling knowingly at her. 'I learned a trick or two in Belgium. We won't have a baby until we're good and ready. Don't worry about it, Lily. I can control myself. I'm not an animal.'

Lily understood none of what he was saying. 'I thought we would have a baby.'

'Little Lily,' he said caressingly. 'We would have a baby if I came inside you. A chap in Belgium explained it all to me. He had a book too – a damned disgusting book written by a woman who is just a disgrace, a disgrace . . .' Stephen's anger made him break off, then he shrugged. 'Anyway, there are things you can do which are wicked, acting like animals. Things no lady would do. And then there is taking care, having a bit of self-control. I can do that. I'll always do that. We don't want children, Lily. We don't want children in the house with the noise and the trouble.'

Lily said nothing. She did not completely understand, but she did not want Stephen to explain. She shrank from the intimacy of an explanation.

'Damned disgusting things,' Stephen said, still thinking about the book. 'Things that a decent woman would never do. Would never even know about. Things that whores do.'

He broke off. Then: 'I hate whores,' he said. 'I hate whores. All the Belgian women were whores. They served in brothels behind our lines, and d . . . d . . . d'you know when the lines m . . . moved they s . . . served G . . . Germans t . . . t . . . too.' His stutter was overwhelming his speech. His breath was coming short. 'D . . . d . . . damn whores!'

Lily said nothing, watching him warily in the soft bedside light.

'You c . . . c . . . can't tell with whores!' he said, angry

280

and plaintive at once. 'You can't tell what they're thinking! You think they're on your side. You think you're doing them a favour, r . . . r . . . risking your life for their d . . . damn country. You th . . . think they l . . . l . . . like you. And th . . . th . . . then you find it c . . . c . . . could be anyone! Anyone! A b . . . b . . . b . . . bloody Hun and they'd s . . . s . . . sit on his lap . . .'

His stutter and his breathless anger suddenly overwhelmed his speech. He rolled towards Lily, taking her by surprise. He clamped his hand over her mouth as she gasped, and thrust inside her again. Lily froze underneath him, her eyes tight shut. Stephen lurched and pushed against her, bumping painfully on her, grinding his pelvis into the delicate skin of her crutch. He flung himself from her after a few moments but kept his hand on her mouth and the other on her neck. As he groaned with pleasure Lily felt his tears wet against her breast. 'D . . . damn whores,' he sighed. 'All of them. Every woman.'

When he was still and sleeping Lily slipped out from under him. She went to the newly plumbed bathroom and locked the door. She ran a deep, deep hot bath, careless of the clanking of the water pipes which might wake Muriel or Rory. She poured into it half a jar of the expensive bath crystals, which were for show, not for use, then she stood up in it, scalded pink with the heat, and scrubbed herself all over, first with soap and then with a nail brush. Then she lay down in the water and let the scented heat wash over her. She felt filthy; even after all the washing. She felt as if her skin itself, her scrubbed scalded skin, was rank. She felt as if Stephen's randy hatred of women was a fault of hers. She stayed in the bath as it cooled and then she topped it up again with hot water. She did not drag herself from the water and dry herself for hours. When she came back into the bedroom there was daylight around the edge of the curtains and it was Sunday morning. When

Lily looked at herself in the mirror her face was white and haggard. She had not known that a man could think of women with that perverse combination of hatred and desire. She had not known that Stephen thought of her like that.

Muriel insisted that they all attend church together at ten o'clock. Lily did not arrive downstairs until the perilously late time of half past nine. Muriel and Stephen were waiting at the foot of the stairs, Coventry was outside holding open the door of the car. Muriel thought of lightly teasing Lily for her pallor, and suggesting she had stayed out dancing too late. But she saw the grimness of Lily's young face, and remembered the noise of a bath running at three in the morning; and she chose to see nothing, and say nothing.

Sunday lunch was tomato soup, roast lamb, roast potatoes, peas and carrots, with Cook's watery trifle for pudding. They drank a thin red wine, and Stephen fell asleep in the study with the Sunday paper over his head.

He woke at tea time and took Lily for a spin in the car. He let Lily steer and work the gear lever and promised to teach her how to drive. They came home in smiling accord and Muriel poured them tea.

Dinner was mushroom soup, cold lamb sandwiches and fruit salad because Sunday was Cook's night off and the parlourmaid Browning could not be trusted to prepare anything hot.

'I feel like a stuffed turkey,' Lily said to Stephen as she drew the curtains back from the window and got into bed. 'If I see another slice of lamb I shall bleat.'

'Well, get ready,' Stephen said unsympathetically. 'Because it will be lamb hot-pot or cottage pie with lamb mince tomorrow to finish up the joint.'

'Why not buy a smaller joint and then we wouldn't have to eat it for half of the week?'

Stephen frowned at Lily over the top of the Sunday paper which he was reading in bed. 'That's Mother's department,' he said. 'Mother and Cook decide the menus. I should think you've rocked the boat enough already by refusing to eat liver.'

'If it was my house I should eat what I want,' Lily said, climbing into bed. 'I'd have thought that if I'm old enough to get married I'm old enough not to eat liver if I don't want to.'

'Well, you're not eating liver, are you? You made it very clear that you don't like liver. So now none of us, even those of us who like it very much, will eat liver.'

'I don't like lamb either. I certainly don't like lamb for three meals running. I certainly don't like roast lamb for dinner and roast lamb sandwiches for tea and minced roast lamb for dinner the next day and probably lamb bone soup the next day as well.'

'Lunch and dinner,' Stephen corrected. 'Not dinner and tea.'

'Whatever.'

Stephen rattled the paper and read ostentatiously, implying that menus are women's work and that men have to be informed about world affairs.

Lily clicked off the light on her side of the bed and shut her eyes.

Lily was awake at six, trembly with excitement, but she made herself lie still beside her sleeping husband until she could see by the little alarm clock on his bedside table that it was seven. Then she slid from the bed and went to the new bathroom opposite their bedroom. She ran herself a deep bath with bath crystals and perfume poured into the water. She soaped herself thoroughly with the gardenia guest soap which was kept in a little wickerwork basket. The three scents clashed deliciously and fought for supremacy in the hot steamy room. Lily washed her hair with the bath soap for the benefit of the perfume and then lay back, pink and sighing with contentment in the water.

There was an abrupt knock at the door. 'Are you in there, Lily?'

She raised her wet head. 'Yes, of course I am. Who did you think it was?'

'Well, come out. I have to have my bath before work.'

Lily surfaced quickly, a tidal wave of water from the overfilled bath washing up to the taps and then back, slopping water over the side. She pulled out the plug, hopped down to the sodden bathmat and then wrapped one bath towel around her and the other around her head. 'I'll just be a minute,' she called.

'What are you *doing* in there?'

'Having a bath,' Lily said irritably. 'What d'you think I'm doing? Ballroom dancing?'

'God in heaven,' Stephen said to himself in a suppressed monotone on the other side of the door. 'One week she won't get up for breakfast and the next she's bathing at dawn.'

'All right, all right.' Lily threw open the door and Stephen recoiled as powerfully scented steam billowed out of the little room. Pools of water stood on the new blue lino. The bathmat was a sodden mess of towelling. There were only face towels left on the rack. The ebbing bathwater was leaving a thick rim of suds and blonde hairs. In the middle of this chaos Lily was wrapped in the only two decent-sized towels and radiant.

'Well, really!' Stephen said. 'What a mess! I shall go and use Mother's bathroom. I don't know what you think you are doing!'

He tightened his dressing-gown cord around him and stamped down the stairs to the next landing. Lily heard him tap on the door to his mother's bedroom. 'Excuse me, Mother, but may I take my bath in your bathroom this morning? Lily is using ours.'

'Of course, dear,' Muriel called back. 'I have quite finished.'

Stephen came back upstairs to collect his shaving brush and mug. He looked around the bathroom in disbelief and then at Lily, who was towelling her hair. 'I think it's easier for us all if you *do* stay in bed half the morning,' he said unpleasantly. 'I can hardly tolerate this mayhem every Monday morning.'

He turned and went downstairs again. Lily heard the bolt shoot across on the other bathroom door. 'Mayhem,' she said with pleasure at a new word. 'Mayhem every Monday morning. Midsummer Mayhem.'

Stephen was stoically bad-tempered at breakfast. Lily had taken all the hot water and he had washed and shaved in cold.

'Worse things happen at sea!' Lily said brightly.

Muriel looked at the two of them. Stephen was deep in bad humour but Lily looked like a child about to go on holiday. She was wearing one of her London outfits, a white sun dress with wide shoulder straps which crossed at the neck in front and at the back, leaving her arms and shoulders bare. A little white jacket completed the outfit. Too smart, Muriel thought, for a morning's shopping in Palmerston Road. Too smart for a morning at home. Where was Lily off to this morning that got her out of bed three hours before her usual time, dressed before breakfast, and as excited as a child before a picnic?

'What are your plans for today, Lily?' she asked, buttering toast.

Lily beamed at her. 'None,' she said. 'Are there any errands I can do for you?'

Muriel hesitated with the slice halfway to her mouth

and then put it carefully on her plate. Lily had never offered any assistance in the house before. 'Nothing, thank you,' she said. 'Unless you are going near the library. I have some books to take back.'

'I can go for you,' Lily said agreeably.

Stephen folded the newspaper with ostentatious care. 'I'll be off,' he said.

Muriel reminded herself to stay seated and let Lily follow him out to the hall. Browning was there with his hat and umbrella and briefcase. Lily leaned against the newel post at the foot of the stairs with the air of one observing some bizarre foreign ritual, and watched him take his things from the parlourmaid.

When Stephen had his hat at the correct angle, his briefcase in one hand and his umbrella in the other he stepped forward and kissed Lily on the cheek. Browning held open the door, Coventry, waiting outside by the Argyll, opened the passenger door, Stephen strolled down the steps, inhaled the sea air, looked up at the cloudless sky and got into the car. Lily waved from the doorstep.

Muriel said nothing while Lily lingered over breakfast and then disappeared upstairs. When she came down again it was ten o'clock and she had been curling her hair. The sleek bob fell straight to her shoulders and then curled under. She had her tiny hat placed far at the back of her head. She had a light scarlet lipstick painted on her lips and she was undoubtedly wearing rouge.

'Bye,' she said, tripping to the front door.

'Shall I see you at lunch?' Muriel asked, hurrying from the dining room.

'I'll be home for tea!' Lily shouted from the doorstep and slammed the door before Muriel could ask any questions. Watching from the window Muriel saw her swoop down the front steps, fling open the garden gate and dance across the road, past the Canoe Lake, and down the seafront in the direction of town. She was carrying a small vanity case in one hand and her handbag in the other. She had forgotten all about Muriel's library books.

'Oh, Lily,' Muriel said anxiously to herself. 'Where are you going?'

It was all different for Lily at the Kings Theatre. On the Midsummer Madness tour she had shared a dressing room with the chorus girls, now she shared with only one other girl who assisted the magician. The list of dressing rooms was pinned up on the notice board by the steps up to the stage. 'Miss Valance and Miss White room six,' it said. Lily went up the few steps and then along the corridor past doors numbered three, four and five, till she came to dressing room six. Her name was on the door in a little metal card holder. She tapped on the door, and when there was no reply, she went in.

Lily scanned the empty room from the doorway, pleased that she was first to arrive. On her left was a row of hooks, a large full-length mirror and one armchair with the stuffing oozing from the seat. Before her was a high window with opaque panes and below it another make-up mirror with a workbench table before it. In the corner was a little sink and two taps. 'Hot water!' Lily said. On her right was another long table before another long mirror. This one had electric lights on either side of the mirror and two on a wooden block along the top. There were two rickety bentwood chairs, one before each mirror.

Lily at once claimed the workbench on her right, with the lights and the mirrors, by opening her vanity case and spreading her things on the worktop.

She had taken one of Muriel's best hand towels which she laid like a tablecloth along the workbench and then unpacked her other things, spreading them out to take up as much space as possible. The pot of hair oil Charlie had given her, her hairbrush, a little posy of dried flowers her mother had given her for luck, two postcard views of the Dorset coastline, a playbill for the Midsummer Madness tour, a pot of rouge, a pot of powder, a powder puff, rather grubby she noticed. A pot of wetwhite which she had never yet used. Two different lipsticks, one very pale and one bright scarlet. A small pot of eyeblack and a blackened teaspoon to hold it in, a stub of candle to heat it, and a box of matches to light the candle. Lily's mother had given her a small watercolour brush to apply the eyeblack as either eyeliner or mascara. She also had a cake of Muriel's gardenia guest soap, a face flannel, some talcum powder which Stephen had bought in London and a glass bottle of perfume with a squeezy ball vaporizer in knitted pink silk which had belonged to her mother.

There was a tap on the door. Lily called 'Come in!' The door burst open and Madge Sweet flung herself into the room and into Lily's arms.

'Well, here's a surprise!' she said. 'And you number three on the bill, a married woman and looking as if butter wouldn't!'

'What are you doing here?'

' "Red Hot Baby" of course! And chorus. So if you don't want to talk to me, you needn't.'

'Of course I do! Who else will I know?'

Madge threw herself into the broken armchair and cocked her legs over the side. 'Not a soul, I don't think. It's an entirely new cast. I shouldn't even *be* here. I had a falling-out with the Midsummer tour at Weymouth and I packed my bags and walked out.'

Lily gasped. 'You didn't!'

'I did! Mind you, I wouldn't have been so quick if I hadn't known there'd be work for me here! But Charlie said he'd get me a solo and the MD who took over from him on the Midsummer Madness tour was a brute! So I walked out night before last, and here I am with a solo spot!'

'I'm to do "Burlington Bertie", and maybe ragtime as well.'

Madge nodded. 'Fast worker,' she said without heat. 'I suppose that's lover boy putting in a good word for you.'

'D'you mean Charlie?' Lily queried.

'How many lovers do you have?'

Lily smiled and shrugged. 'He got me the audition but Mr Rice himself heard me sing.'

'Oh, hell!' Madge said. 'I suppose you *do* have a voice. But I thought that hubby would keep you home. What does he think about it all?'

Lily glanced to see that the dressing room door was shut. 'He doesn't know I'm here.'

Madge looked blankly at her. 'Come again?'

'He doesn't know!' Lily said. There was a quaver of laughter in her voice. 'I'm going to see him off to work in the morning and then come here, and I'll be home by the time he gets home for tea.'

'Not once the show starts you won't.'

'I'll have told him by then. He can't stop me once we're into performance.'

'The hell he can't!' Madge exclaimed. 'You must be mad, Lily Pears. You made your choice, girl, and you chose to be Mrs Winters. You can't have it both ways.'

Lily hesitated. 'Oh, come on,' she said. 'I thought you'd be on my side.'

'I *am* on your side. But I'm not blooming mad. You can't live in that posh house and take tea with all the lords and ladies and then come out and sing on stage.'

'Vesta Tilley did . . .' Lily started.

'Vesta Tilley's husband said she could! You can't carry on like this without Stephen's say-so. You can't do it, Lily.

You'd better tell Mr Rice, here and now, that it's no good and leave.'

Lily turned her back to Madge and sat before the mirror. 'I can't,' she said. Her defiance collapsed and Madge saw her mouth quiver. 'Honestly, Madge, you don't know what you're saying. It's like being buried alive in that house. Stephen's out all day, every day. His ma has a hundred things to do, none of them worth doing. His dad lies upstairs like a dead man, and no-one goes to see him unless they have to. Nobody talks, nobody laughs. Nobody ever sings. Nobody ever has any fun. I can't live there. I have to have *something* to do. I'm a singer. I have to sing. I have to be on stage. I can't just die on my feet. I'm eighteen! What am I going to do for the rest of my life?'

Madge shrugged. 'You should be running the house.'

'His ma does everything. I'm not allowed even to choose what I eat.'

'You'll have a baby.'

'I don't *want* a baby. Stephen doesn't want a baby. He makes sure we don't have one.'

'You should visit your friends.'

Lily simply shrugged her shoulders in reply.

Madge thought of Lily's mother dead before her daughter was a woman, of the corner shop and the noisy vulgar women who would not be welcome at number two, The Parade, of Lily's hopeless loneliness. 'Well, you surely can't get away with not telling him,' she said pragmatically. 'He'll have to know.'

'When we open,' Lily said. 'That's when I'll tell him. When it's too late for him to do anything about it. I'll tell him then.'

Charlie was running rehearsals. The stage manager was miserable with summer flu and had handed everything over to him. Richard Rice was in an office tucked away high up in the dress circle and had left Charlie to organize things. Charlie decided to run through all the soloists and all the acts in the morning and early afternoon and leave the chorus till mid-afternoon, either side of the tea break. All morning the chorus worked in the circle bar with the choreographer.

'So you get home on time,' Madge said spitefully to Lily as the dancers came into the theatre for their practice with the band. 'Nice to have friends in high places.'

'Oh, hush,' Lily said. 'It makes sense to have the acts on stage first, and he won't keep you late.'

'The acts can go now,' Charlie said from the pit. 'All except anyone who has a number which they have rehearsed with the chorus girls. We'll do those now. The rest of you can go. Tomorrow, same time, eleven o'clock.'

Lily smiled at him. It was just four. She would have plenty of time to get home before Stephen returned from the office. 'Goodbye,' she called to Charlie. He barely looked up from his notes. 'Goodbye, Lil,' he said. 'See you tomorrow.'

Lily slipped out of the stage door and walked briskly around the building to the main road. The tram stopped outside the Kings. She had to wait only a few minutes before it came. It rattled down the Palmerston Road, then on down the Clarendon Road and terminated at East Southsea station. Lily walked the little way up Granada Road and tapped on the front door of her home at twenty past four. No-one had given her a door key.

Browning let her in. Muriel came forward out of the drawing room. 'Lily, my dear,' she said. 'I was just going to have tea.'

'Lovely,' Lily said easily. 'I'll go and take my hat off.'

She washed her face and hands, rubbing the lipstick away with her flannel. She combed her hair. She beamed at herself in the mirror. The carpet men had come, as

Muriel had promised they would, and there was a deep blue carpet on the bedroom floor which matched the blue trim of the curtains.

'Lovely,' Lily said with satisfaction. She was on her way downstairs for tea when she heard the noise of Stephen's key in the lock. She had timed it to perfection. Stephen was surprised, when he came into the hall, that Lily came down the stairs and kissed him. She had obviously forgotten the morning's conflict over the bathroom. Stephen, receiving her into his arms, decided to forget about it too.

'I don't know what to do,' Muriel confided on the telephone to Jane Dent. It was the second week of rehearsals. 'The wretched girl goes out every day, dressed to the nines, and gets back minutes before Stephen is home, and she looks at me and smiles as if she *knows* that I daren't say a thing.'

'Why don't you just tell him?' Jane asked.

'How can I! They've been married less than a month. I can hardly say to him that his wife is having an affair with another man. I've no evidence. I know nothing for sure.'

'Speak to her?' Jane suggested. She was filing her nails while she listened to Muriel. This was not the first telephone call on the subject. She was losing interest.

'She just smiles at me, and she's so pleasant, and Stephen is so happy. I hardly want to drop a bombshell into the middle of all that.'

'Leave it alone then,' Jane advised. 'If it *is* a bombshell it'll go off anyway. Someone will plough it up and lose a leg. He'll catch Lily out sooner or later. You need have nothing to do with it.'

'But what will happen then?' Muriel wailed. 'If it goes on so long and he catches her out too late?'

'He's a lawyer,' Jane said levelly. 'If she's ready to run

off with the greengrocer then he'll divorce her. Stephen won't suffer. You shouldn't worry.'

'I just want him to be happy,' Muriel said miserably.

Jane shrugged and put her nail file back in the little box. 'I think they forgot,' she said. 'I think they forgot how to be happy in France. All the young men Sarah sees now, they know how to drink and they know how to smoke and they can dance like dervishes, charleston, ragtime, the shimmy, all sorts. But I don't see any one of them who knows how to be happy. They're all jumpy. They all know they're lucky to be alive and none of them know how to deserve it. We lost the happy ones in France, Muriel.'

'My Christopher.'

'And all the other boys.'

It was at the end of the second week of rehearsals that Charlie took Lily out for coffee break. His favourite café for this theatre was little more than a private house opposite the stage door, with the front door open to customers and a hatch knocked through from the kitchen to the sitting room and a handful of plywood chairs and tables.

'Have you told your husband you're working?' Charlie asked abruptly.

Lily was wearing a peach coat and dress with a large picture hat and gloves to match. Her skin under the shadow of the peach hat was glowing with warmth. She was almost edible. Charlie stirred his tea to avoid looking at her. 'Have you told him?'

Lily shook her head.

'Well, you have to. We open next Monday, Lil, he's going to notice you're not at home. God knows how you've covered up so far.'

'Rehearsals seemed to finish on time,' Lily said mischievously.

'Well, I'm an idiot to help you,' Charlie said frankly.

'God knows why I did. Because now we're going to open, and now's the time that he tells you not to work, and we'll be an act down and all the posters will have to be reprinted. I should have made you tell him at the start. I *did* tell you that you could manage him if you handled him right. I didn't want to interfere.'

'I listened to what you said. I've been sweet as pie.'

Charlie grunted, wrapped his hands around the mug and sipped his tea.

'It'll be all right,' Lily reassured him. 'Now I've had a fortnight in rehearsal I can show him that it'll be all right. He can see that it works. It was a good idea to leave it a while before telling him. He didn't like the idea, but he can see that it fits in well to our lives. I'll talk him round.'

'I hope to God you do,' Charlie said. 'Richard is going to go mad if you drop out at this late stage.'

'I won't drop out,' Lily said.

'If you drop out, you'll never work here again,' Charlie warned.

'I won't drop out.'

Charlie nodded. 'All right then,' he said.

They sat for a while in silence, Lily sipping her tea, Charlie scowling into the middle distance.

'D'you remember that day when we went out on the motorcycle?' Lily asked suddenly. 'It was so sunny, and we swam, and we had a picnic, and then we had tea in that little village shop on the way home. Just outside Bournemouth, wasn't it? In Dorset? D'you remember?'

Charlie looked up at her and his eyes were very dark. 'I remember,' he said tightly.

'Were you in love with me?' Lily asked gravely. 'I was in love with you. I was – oh – madly in love with you.'

'I expect so,' Charlie said. He could feel a hard hot compression in his chest which later on, probably tonight, he would know as pain. Pain from a war wound, he thought.

'Were you?' Lily insisted. 'Were you in love with me then?'

Charlie scanned her face; if she were seeking flattery she could go elsewhere. But there was no vanity there. She was as innocent as the girl he had taken to the country that day. The girl who had wanted to be kissed, and had thrown her sandwich to the seagull, and had come to his bed like an innocent desirous animal.

'Yes,' he said unwillingly. 'I was in love with you that day. I was in love with you for the whole tour. And I am in love with you now. As far as I know, I will be in love with you for ever. But for all the difference it is going to make to your life and to mine I might as well not bother. I cannot be your lover, I cannot be your husband. I do love you – but it hardly matters. I love you, but there is nothing I can *do* with that love. It's just there.'

Lily said nothing but her face under the wide peach brim glowed. 'It matters to me,' she said with dignity. 'It matters to me that the first man that I ever loved – loved me back.'

They sat in silence for a little while, then Charlie glanced at his watch. 'Time we were getting back,' he said.

Lily nodded and picked up her bag and her gloves. Charlie held the door for her as they went out into the bright street. 'If you have a quarrel,' he said tightly, 'don't let him hurt you, Lil. I can't bear the thought of you being hurt.'

She turned back to face him. 'He can't hurt me,' she said with certainty. 'Only the people that you love can hurt you. Stephen can't hurt me at all.'

Chapter Twenty

Lily meant to tell Stephen that she was in the new show at the Kings Theatre on Friday evening. But Muriel had invited the Dents around for dinner and there was no time. In the night, Stephen moved towards her and Lily pushed his hand away.

'I cannot, I am unwell,' she said.

Stephen moved back to his side of the bed without speaking, and lay still, without touching her.

Lily listened to the sea and thought that she should have let him do what he wanted and then he would have felt obliged to her on Saturday. She thought she would leave it until Saturday evening, when they might be happy again, and tell him then.

On Saturday morning, Rory's wheelchair arrived. Lily had suggested to Muriel that they buy a wheelchair and take Rory out, and the family doctor had been enthusiastic. Muriel had said nothing more, hoping that Lily would forget. But on one of her trips along the Palmerston Road she had stopped in a shop and ordered, on account, one of the new lightweight wheelchairs that were so popular with crippled officers.

'I will *not* have that thing in the drawing room,' Muriel said to Stephen in a passionate whisper at the foot of the stairs. Coventry and Nurse Bells were manhandling Rory Winters's slack body from bed to wheelchair and then Coventry was going to bump it gently down the stairs. 'I know Lily is thinking of Rory's good and I know her intentions are the best; but I will *not* have that chair in my drawing room.'

'Good God, no!' Stephen said. 'He can be walked by Nurse Bells and then come in the back door and Coventry can take him upstairs again. I don't want to walk with him, I don't see why you should walk with him. Do we want all our friends to see him? All his old colleagues? You should have stopped Lily ordering the chair, Mother. She's been much too interested in him from the start, it's morbid and unhealthy.'

'She thought it would be good for him, and when I asked Dr Mobey he said it would be an excellent idea. I couldn't really say no. How could I say that I didn't want him downstairs? How could I say that I didn't want him taken out?'

Stephen made a muffled exclamation and turned away. At the top of the stairs he heard the wheelchair bump gently down the first step.

'Careful!' Lily exclaimed from the first floor landing, behind Coventry. 'Do hold on tight, Coventry! Can you manage? Stephen! Come up!'

Unwillingly Stephen went up the stairs to help. His father was dressed. Stephen had not seen him properly dressed in six years, not since Christopher's death. He was wearing a pale summer suit. Someone had cut his hair and he had been properly shaved, the little unattractive tufts of hair that the nurse usually missed had been smoothly shaved away. His skin was pink and healthy. He had a white panama hat with the colours of the Southsea cricket club on the hat band. He looked distinguished, he looked alive.

'You look very smart, Father,' Stephen said in surprise.

His father's dark eyes looked at him. Stephen thought they held some inner twinkle, as if his father had heard him, had understood.

'I bought him a new cravat to celebrate the day out,' Lily said. 'And a new carriage rug so he'll be warm. Isn't this a lark?'

With Coventry holding the handles and Stephen holding the bottom of the chair, they carried it carefully downstairs and set it on its wheels in the hall. Muriel, rather pale, was standing by the front door, watching.

'Isn't this a lark?' Lily demanded of the old man. She leaned forward and straightened his hat and kissed his cheek.

Stephen recoiled and looked at his mother. They exchanged one swift look like conspirators.

'Get your hat then, Stephen!' Lily exclaimed. She turned to Muriel. 'Are you ready, Mrs Winters?'

Muriel, with neither hat nor gloves, was clearly not ready. She hesitated. 'I'm not coming,' she said baldly. She looked at Stephen.

'Neither of us is coming. None of us is going,' he corrected himself. 'Nurse Bells can manage the chair perfectly well on her own. Coventry can help her up and down the steps.'

Lily looked from her husband to her mother-in-law in surprise. 'But why not?' she asked. 'I thought we would all go with him. I thought it would be fun.'

'Hardly!' Stephen said. He turned and went into the drawing room and shut the door behind him. Muriel and Lily faced each other in the shadowed hall.

'Don't you *want* to come for a walk with Mr Winters?' Lily asked, genuinely surprised. Muriel could see her looking from the firmly shut door, to Muriel's flushed face, and then to Rory. 'Don't you want to come?'

Muriel shook her head, speechless, turned and pushed past Lily, past Nurse Bells and Coventry and went up the stairs without speaking. Her bedroom door slammed shut.

There was a silence in the hall. Lily turned to Nurse Bells and to Coventry. 'I don't understand,' she said simply.

Coventry said nothing.

'I'll go on my own,' Nurse Bells said briskly. 'Do me good to get out in the fresh air. I've always been a one for my own company.'

'Go on slowly,' Lily said. 'I'll catch you up. I promised I'd walk with him.'

The nurse nodded and opened the door for Coventry to manhandle the chair down the front steps. Lily opened the door to the drawing room and went in.

'Stephen?' she said.

He was standing by the fireplace. As she came in he turned to her and she saw his face was crumpled with distress.

'Oh Stephen!' she said and went towards him.

He flung himself on her and she staggered under his weight. He held her breathlessly tight and she felt his body shake with deep sobs. Lily put her arms around him and patted his back with her little hands. 'It's all right,' she said helplessly. 'It's all right.'

The weight of him was bearing her down, she felt smothered by his need. 'Do stop it,' she said gently. 'Stephen, do stop.' She felt a half-disgusted pity for him, but she did not understand. 'Shush,' she said gently. He was leaning heavily on her. 'Do stop,' Lily said.

Slowly he recovered, pushed her away and pulled out his handkerchief from his jacket pocket and wiped his face. 'I don't want to see you with a bath chair!' he said, speaking very low. 'I don't want to see you with a half-dead man. I don't want to see him myself. He's one of the war dead! Can't you see? Can't you see how obscene it is to get him dressed up and wheel him around like a big rag doll? I don't want you near him! I married you because you were

299

young and alive and not like any part of the war. I don't want you wheeling a wheelchair!'

'He's your dad,' Lily said simply. 'And the doctor said it would do him good.'

'He's nothing to me!' Stephen said passionately. 'No-one is anything to me except Coventry and you. You two. Everyone else is part of the war. Mother who sent me off to it. John Pascoe who sent his son. The Dents who did very well out of it, thank you. All the women who stayed at home in comfort and let us do the fighting for them. They're all part of it. I look around and everyone I see has been part of it.' He broke off on a racking sob, and then drew a deep breath, rubbing his face. 'Except you,' he said. 'You, because you were too young to know anything, and because you hate it as much as I do. And Coventry, who has forgotten it all.'

Lily went closer to Stephen and took his hand. She was frightened by his earnestness. She didn't know what to say to reassure him, she did not know what to do with the power he thrust on her when he wept in her arms. 'I don't like you like this,' she said uneasily. 'Don't be like this, Stephen. Come out for a walk. We can walk in front of him if you like, or behind him. I won't push the chair. But I promised him, I've been promising him for weeks that I'd take him out for a walk by the sea.'

'He can't hear you!' Stephen shouted in frustration. 'It doesn't matter what you say to him, what you promise him. He can't hear a thing and he can't feel a thing. He's dead. He's dead except that he eats and breathes. You want to walk out with a corpse, Lily. You've been talking to a dead man. You should leave him alone, Lily, leave him to the nurse. You should be thinking about *me* – about the promises you made to me.'

'He's not dead . . .' Lily started.

'I married you so that I could forget about pain,' Stephen

interrupted. 'I married you so that I could be free of the war. And now you want me to push a wheelchair, and my dreams are worse than ever before.'

'Your dreams?'

Stephen put his face close to her and spoke as if he hated her, as if he blamed her for his nights. 'Dreams,' he said quietly. 'Dreams that you would rather die than see. Bodies bobbing up out of the mud, friends blown away in a storm of red and wet. A whore spread out against the kitchen wall with bullets stitched through her. A baby . . . a baby . . .'

His arm held Lily's waist. He thrust his face so close to hers that she could smell his warm breath. She leaned away from him as far as she could go. 'Why don't you see a doctor?' she asked.

Stephen abruptly released her and Lily staggered back and nearly fell.

'See a doctor! See a doctor!' Stephen mimicked. 'What for? Can he make it so the war never happened? That's all I need. Can he make it so I was never there, so I never saw, so I never did?'

Lily shook her head, saying nothing.

They were silent.

'I was counting on you to make things better here,' Stephen said. His voice was businesslike, as if he had a legitimate complaint. 'I married you to make things better.'

'I'm sorry,' she said. 'I do try.'

Stephen gave a hard little laugh and turned towards the window. '*Now* she can't manage the steps up to the promenade,' he said irritably, watching the nurse and Coventry helping her. 'They've got themselves stuck.'

'I'll go,' Lily said. 'I promised him.'

Stephen rounded on her. 'I'll fetch my hat,' he said savagely. 'I suppose I'll have to go or see my father tipped out like a guy on the road.'

301

He slammed out of the door and fetched his hat from the cloakroom. Lily waited for him by the front door and then took his arm in silence as they went down the white scoured steps.

On the skyline of the promenade they could see Nurse Bells, her cape blown back by the sea breeze, pushing the wheelchair. She had managed the steps with Coventry's help and she was strolling along, pushing the lightweight chair. Lily and Stephen crossed the road, walked around the Canoe Lake and then on to the promenade. They caught up with the wheelchair in a few moments. They walked ahead of it, Stephen eyeing people carefully, hoping that they would meet no-one they knew. Lily's hand was tucked into his arm and he held her tight without affection.

'This will bring the colour to our cheeks,' Nurse Bells said cheerfully. 'And give us a good appetite for our dinner! What a nice change of scene! How thoughtful of Mrs Winters to buy us a wheelchair! What a lovely treat for us all this is!'

Muriel did not come down at tea time, though she must have heard the bumping of the wheelchair going up the stairs to Rory's bedroom. When she came down to dinner she said nothing about the walk and the atmosphere was silent and strained.

'I have to see Pascoe about a case,' Stephen announced when they were drinking coffee in the drawing room. 'I'll pop over now and be back late. Don't wait up for me.'

Muriel looked at Lily to see if she had registered the lie. Lily was sitting in the window seat, looking at a magazine, not reading the words, just looking at the pictures, flicking forwards and back and then examining very carefully the detail on a skirt or a dress.

'At this time of night?' Muriel asked, trying to alert Lily

302

to the fact that Stephen was going out alone, and that it was extremely unlikely that his destination was the Pascoes' quiet house.

'Yes,' Stephen said. 'Is nine o'clock so very awful? Coventry can drive me.'

Lily looked up from her magazine and smiled at her husband. 'Goodnight then,' she said pleasantly.

Stephen kissed her on the top of her head and left the room. Coventry came up the back stairs without being called – so they had arranged to go out, Muriel thought. The women heard the front door slam, and then the car doors. They heard the engine start. Lily opened the curtains a crack and looked out. Stephen was sitting in the front seat of the car, one arm along the back of Coventry's seat, the other hand holding two cigarettes in his mouth. As she watched, he passed one over to Coventry. Coventry let in the clutch and they drove off.

Muriel opened her mouth to speak to Lily, to tell her that she doubted very much that John Pascoe was working at nine o'clock on a Saturday night. Lily smiled her untroubled smile. Muriel said nothing.

Stephen and Coventry drove around the darker streets of Portsea and then parked the car under a gaslight. They walked to a cheap music hall which played behind a pub near the docks. The hall was full of sailors on shore leave drinking heavily and looking for a fight. The show was just ending; the chorus girls came off the stage and drank with the men at the bar.

Stephen and Coventry sat in a dark corner, drinking their favourite beer with a whisky chaser, watching the rumbling irritability of the drunk group. It was only a little while and then someone spilled another man's drink and trouble flared. With a sigh like a man moving towards his lover, Stephen downed his whisky and put the table to one side. He stepped towards the half a dozen jostling men and tapped one on the shoulder and when he turned, threw a punch precisely and pleasurably behind his ear.

Behind Stephen, Coventry tripped another man, and when the fight became general they were active on the fringes, a punch thrown at a man's head, a knee in his groin. They fought without passion, their faces showed the same detached venom. When Stephen landed a fist smack in the centre of a youth's face and felt the cartilage of the boy's nose collapse beneath his knuckles he smiled very slightly and stepped back as the boy howled and fell to the floor, his nose gushing blood. Coventry and Stephen stayed near to each other, almost back-to-back, never getting deep into the centre of the fight where men were clubbing wildly around them with chair legs and there was the dangerous sound of smashing glass. They cruised the periphery of the fight, sometimes working together, picking on an individual and flooring him with a trip and then kicking together in smooth balletic unison with their hard feet into his belly, into his back, at the delicate point of the kidneys. The man groaned and tried to roll away and Stephen snatched up a bottle of beer from one of the tables, knocked the end off it with one swift movement and grabbed the man's hair, dragging his head back and baring his throat. The bottle's jagged edge was seconds away from the thin white neck when Coventry stepped forward and gently put his hand on Stephen's arm. They looked at each other for a moment, a deep blank gaze, and then Stephen smiled and tossed the bottle aside and let the man go. A few minutes after it had started, but before the police arrived, Stephen and Coventry slid quietly away and walked, arms around each other's shoulders, to where the car was parked, under the gas lamp, some streets away.

'A good fight,' Stephen sighed with satisfaction. His face was flushed, all the petulance and disappointment smoothed away. He was rosy. His arm on Coventry's shoulder was heavy.

Coventry nodded, his face impassive.

'Let's go somewhere and have another drink. Let's have a lot of drink.'

Coventry unlocked the driver's door and leaned over and let Stephen into the front seat. 'D'you think that's all we can do now?' Stephen demanded suddenly. 'Do you? Break heads? Cut throats? Cause pain?'

Coventry turned and looked at him, a long dark sorrowful stare.

'Yes,' Stephen whispered. 'So do I.'

Stephen woke late on Sunday morning, his head thick and his mouth sour. He could not remember where he had been drinking. He had one clear memory of a fight in some dive, a broken nose, a throat ready for cutting. No-one had hurt him. Stephen smiled at the memory. He did not go down to breakfast, but he was washed and shaved and in his best suit by quarter past nine, in time for the cathedral service at ten.

Muriel said nothing about his absent place at breakfast. She kept her mouth buttoned tightly on her disapproval. Lily, who was not familiar with ordinary life at number two, The Parade, did not know that for Stephen to go drinking on a Saturday night and not to come home till dawn was unknown before his marriage. Muriel, of course, could not tell her.

The service lasted until half past eleven and then Muriel, Stephen and Lily walked from the cathedral down the High Street to the sea walls of the old town. It was a sunny day and already there were holidaymakers settling rugs and sunshades on the little patch of pebbly beach before the town walls. Stephen laughed shortly. 'The tide comes up there,' he said. 'They'll get wet.'

Many of Muriel's friends were also walking around the ramparts, watching the warships in the harbour and the yachts tacking skilfully between them. Muriel stopped often and introduced Lily to people who had not yet met Stephen's wife.

Lily was at her best at these times, Muriel thought. She might be only acting the part of a young lady newly married, but she did it superbly well. She was wearing the peach coat and dress with the peach broad-brimmed hat. Stephen, with his head clearing in the fresh air, looked debonair and handsome, and Lily held his arm and kept her other hand on her hat. They were an attractive couple. Muriel took pride in their appearance and tried to forget Stephen's late night and Lily's missing days.

Lunch was pea soup, roast beef, roast potatoes, sprouts and peas, with apple snow for dessert. Cook had been distracted by the Sunday paper when she was cooking the vegetables and they had boiled over. The sprouts were drenched and soft as rotting rosebuds. Lily picked at her food.

'I can't eat a roast dinner when it's so hot,' she said. 'Couldn't we have salad sometimes?'

Muriel looked astounded. 'On a Sunday?'

'We always have a roast for Sunday lunch,' Stephen said. 'We have something cold in the evening.'

'Oh,' Lily said mutinously. 'I didn't know it had to be that way.'

There was an awkward silence. 'Perhaps you would like to discuss menus with me when Cook and I next meet,' Muriel offered. 'We plan the menus for a month at a time. Then you could tell me if there are any things you particularly like.'

'Thank you,' Lily said. 'But I don't want to interfere . . .'

'It's not an interference, I should like you to be there.

306

Monday morning at eleven o'clock. Unless you are going out as usual?'

Lily met the challenge without wavering. 'I'm not going out in the morning.'

Muriel took her knitting and went upstairs to sit with Rory after lunch. Stephen took the local paper with him into his study. Lily idled on the window seat. She hated Sundays even worse than other days in this house. There was a weight to them that no other day had. Freighted by over-large meals, the hours dragged from breakfast to lunch to tea time to dinner. Lily had nothing to do but wait for Stephen, and see if he would take her out for a drive again. She pulled at the fringe of the curtain. Stephen might read his newspaper and then doze until tea time and then she would not have been out all day except to go to church. She thought of her mother and how Sunday in the little flat above the shop was a special day for them, the only day when they did not have to rise at six for the deliveries, a glorious lazy morning when they did not wake until ten. They would cook breakfast in their dressing-gowns, using up the ends of bacon and bruised tomatoes. Supper would be a delicious picnic of everything that needed eating up – cakes, fruit, jam, cheeses, chocolate.

She thought of Sundays on the Midsummer Madness tour when she had slept like a diver going into deep water until noon, and then picnicked and played with the others. She thought of the noise of the lodging houses with the chorus girls shrieking at each other and larking in the corridors. She thought of the Sundays when they had gone to the beach at Bournemouth and danced in the little waves on the wrinkled sand beach and people had pointed to them and known that they were the chorus girls from the Midsummer Madness tour. One time they had linked arms and done a can-can and a photographer from the local paper had taken their picture. She thought of that sunny quiet day when Charlie had borrowed the motorbike and taken her out into the country.

She picked idly at the curtain fringe. She did not want to sleep, she was irritable with restlessness, bloated with roast dinner, headachey with the Sunday lunch wine. And she knew that either this afternoon or this evening, she would have to tell Stephen that she was working at the Kings Theatre.

Muriel, knitting upstairs at Rory's bedside, thought that he was looking better. There was a faint flush on his cheeks from yesterday's sunshine. Nurse Bells had propped him upright and he looked alert and interested. He could not turn his head but Muriel was sure he was watching her and listening to her.

'She *is* a lovely girl,' she said. She glanced over her shoulder to check that the door was shut and Nurse Bells had gone downstairs to the kitchen for her Sunday lunch. 'Pretty, of course. And she has a pleasant nature. She's never said one word to me that was out of turn.'

Muriel broke off and consulted the pattern. She counted stitches. She was knitting the back of the matinée jacket in the delicate soft wool.

'But she's up to something,' she said grimly. 'She has been out all day, every day for a fortnight. She scuttles into the house at twenty past four, and then she floats down the stairs as Stephen comes in the door. I'm longing to ask her – but I don't dare. What if she's seeing someone? What if she's having an affair?'

A look of horror suddenly crossed Muriel's face and she dropped the knitting and put her hand to her neck to hold her pearls. 'Oh my God, Rory!' she said. 'What if she's gone back to the shop? What if she's serving in the shop?'

Rory's dark eyes never moved.

'No,' Muriel said. 'She can't have done that. She wouldn't do anything as bad as that.' She nodded, remem-

308

bering Lily's smart clothes. 'She wouldn't dress up like that for the shop,' she said. 'And besides, it's been sold. Someone else has it. She wouldn't go to work for anyone else. It must be something else.'

She took a deep breath of relief, and waved her hand before her face. The room was stuffy, the hot August sunshine beating against the drawn curtains. Muriel picked up her knitting and started another row. 'I can't ask,' she said finally. 'I can't ask. And I can't tip the wink to Stephen. They'll have to resolve their differences in their own way. I can't interfere.'

Suddenly, from the floor below they heard the study door slam and Stephen's quick step towards the sitting room.

They heard him shout, 'What the *hell* does this mean?' but Lily's reply was too faint for them to catch.

Muriel dropped her knitting to her lap. 'Oh dear.'

There was silence from the sitting room. Muriel's hand crept to her neck to hold her pearls. 'Oh dear.'

The sitting room door was flung open and they heard footsteps on the stairs. 'Not another word,' they heard Stephen say as he forced Lily up the stairs to their bedroom. 'Not here. Not now. Upstairs. You can explain upstairs.'

'But Stephen . . .' Lily said quickly.

'Up!' They heard the bedroom door slam and then a high panicky voice – Lily's – talking very rapidly. Stephen interrupted her once, twice, and then they heard him shout at her. 'It's in the paper, your name is in the paper, you bloody little whore!'

'Oh dear,' Muriel said. 'This is awful.'

Lily was shouting back, the door too thick for them to hear the words. But they could sense her defiance, and it was that which triggered Stephen's deep rage.

They heard him bellow at her and then the ceiling shook

as he ran across the room, grabbed her, and threw her on the bed. Then they heard Lily scream. It was a single scream of pure terror.

Muriel leaped to her feet and took two swift paces to the door, then she stopped and returned to her seat again. Her face was white. 'I can't interfere,' she said in a frightened whisper. 'I mustn't interfere. It's nothing to do with me. They're in their own room. I can't interfere.'

She glanced at Rory. He was moving. For the first time in six years he was moving the muscles of his jaw. The slack disused muscles in his neck tightened, as he tried to heave himself upwards.

'Rory!' Muriel said, frightened. 'What is it?'

There was another scream from upstairs, a raw scream of pain. Rory heaved himself to one side and looked at Muriel. His slack mouth, twisted and useless from the stroke, was moving, working. 'Help,' he said in a voice croaky with disuse. 'Help.'

'Oh my God! I'll get Nurse,' Muriel said, then she stopped at the door. 'But I can't! I can't call her. She can't come upstairs while this is going on! She'll hear!'

'Help.' Rory groaned on the word, saliva drooled from his mouth at the effort of speaking.

Muriel turned from the door. 'I *can't* get help,' she snapped. 'In a minute, Rory, in a minute. You'll have to wait.'

Upstairs they could hear Lily crying out. 'No! No! No! No!' They could hear the noise of the bedsprings.

'He's raping her,' Muriel said to herself in horror. 'He's up there now, raping her.'

Rory's idle muscles could not be forced to obey him. He opened his mouth, gasping with the effort but no sound came. Then, in a sudden convulsive jerk, he heaved himself to the edge of the bed. *'Help her!'* he bellowed and then he flung himself headlong towards the floor.

There was a terrible damaging thud. Rory went face down into the floor, his slack arms helpless to protect him. Blood from his nose gushed into the carpet. Muriel tore open the door and shouted up the stairs. 'Stephen! Stephen! You must come! Your father has had an accident! Stephen, come down!'

There was a sudden silence from upstairs and then the bedroom door was torn open. Stephen came running down the stairs, glowing with energy. His flies were undone and his shirt torn. Muriel could see a long scratch from his eye running down his cheek. Lily had fought all the way from the door to the bed. He was sweating, his face and his chest were shiny with sweat, and he was radiant. He was alive in a way that Muriel had never seen before. He looked like a young savage god called away from a feast. There was a trickle of blood at the corner of his mouth and he licked it with unconscious relish.

Muriel recoiled. 'Stephen!'

Stephen shook his head as if re-entering the normal world. 'What's the matter?' he said, his voice too loud.

'Your father's had another stroke. He's fallen. Help me!'

Stephen came down the stairs two at a time, tucking his shirt into his waistband and buttoning his flies. Muriel stood well back to let him go into his father's room. She could smell sex on him like a poisonous musk. She could smell the hot aroused smell of a man, a dangerous man. She put her hand over her mouth, covering her nose. She found she was shivering as if she were icy cold. She was afraid of him.

'Call the nurse,' Stephen said over his shoulder. 'And then telephone the doctor.'

He kneeled beside his father on the carpet. Rory was crumpled head-down into the floor, his feet, above his head, still tangled in bedclothes. He was bleeding from the nose and a dark bruise was starting to show on the crown of his head. He looked up at Stephen and his dark eyes were shielded and secretive.

'Still alive anyway,' Stephen said spitefully as his mother went downstairs out of earshot. 'Still hanging on, eh?'

He put his hands under his father's arms and heaved his body on to the bed and then pushed his legs over. Rory was jumbled like a guy in an urchin's barrow. Stephen pushed him into the centre of the bed.

Nurse Bells, her hair awry and her face flushed from a large lunch and a bottle of Stephen's wine, burst into the room. 'Leave it to me, Mr Stephen,' she said. 'I'll get us sorted out. Your mother is telephoning the doctor. D'you know what happened?'

'No,' Stephen said. 'Mother just called that he was having another stroke and had fallen out of bed.'

Nurse Bells nodded. 'Don't you worry,' she said kindly. 'Leave him to me. I'll get him comfortable again.'

Stephen nodded and went towards the door. 'What's that?' Nurse Bells demanded. Very softly they could hear the sound of Lily crying. She was crying like a beaten child, quietly, without hope of answer.

'My wife's upset,' Stephen said. 'A death in her family.'

'I'm sorry to hear that,' Nurse Bells said politely. She pulled back the bedclothes and heaved Rory back into his usual sitting position. Stephen turned back at the door. He found he could not meet Rory's black unseeing stare.

He closed the door behind him.

Chapter Twenty-one

S tephen sat downstairs drinking tea, leaving Lily crying quietly in their bed while Dr Mobey examined Rory. His nose had bled and his forehead and face were badly bruised from his fall; but he was not seriously hurt. The doctor thought it was not another stroke but that something more interesting might have taken place. Rory might be trying to break through his silence. He asked Muriel if anything had happened to stimulate Rory, if he had been trying to get out of bed, or move. Had he been disturbed or angered by anything?

Muriel, holding to the family standard of silence, even at the cost of her husband's health, said that nothing had disturbed Rory, she had come into the room to see him thrashing on the bed and then fall on his face. Rory could not contradict her, but Muriel felt his dark eyes on her while she spoke.

After the doctor left Muriel ordered tea in the drawing room. She said not one word to Stephen about the screams from his bedroom. She poured tea for him without meeting his eyes, and then took her cup upstairs to sit with Rory. Stephen nodded. The no-man's-land between his mother and himself would not easily be crossed. He did not want it crossed. He stayed in the drawing room in moody silence, sitting in his favourite chair by the cold grate. At seven o'clock as the sky outside the tower window was turning primrose-coloured in the west, Stephen rang for Browning to make a fresh pot of tea for one, on a pretty tray for him to take upstairs to Lily. Browning went into the garden and picked a rose and put it in a little glass vase. There was a round of dainty sandwiches and three small dry cakes left over from Cook's Friday baking session. Stephen took the tray with a word of thanks and carried it upstairs to Lily.

He opened the bedroom door with caution but Lily had stopped crying. She was lying on her back on the crumpled bedclothes. She had pulled down her skirt, but her blouse was torn from collar to waist. She had a bruise on her cheekbone and a cut on her lip. She looked at her husband as he came through the door, proffering his pretty tray, as if he were her mortal enemy.

'Feeling better?' he asked pleasantly. He put the tray down on her bedside table. Lily sat up, pulled her shirt together, set a pillow behind her back and took the cup of tea he handed to her.

Stephen watched her approvingly. 'Father's quite all right,' he said conversationally. 'The doctor said that he may recover the use of his muscles. It was a little spasm. He might even learn to speak again. It's quite a miracle.'

Lily looked straight ahead of her as if she could neither hear nor see him.

'Mother's very pleased,' Stephen said. 'Very pleased indeed. She's sitting with him now.'

There was silence. Stephen strolled over to the window and pulled back the lace curtains. The sky was turning rosy and the lights on the pier were coming on, one by one. There were people dressed in gay bright clothes walking on the promenade. There were horse-drawn cabs with the hoods let down, and cars going by. Lily heard with dull resentment the noises of the outside world going about joyful business.

'Will you get dressed and come down for dinner?' Stephen asked.

Lily said nothing.

'Or shall I bring you up a tray if you're not feeling quite up to it?' He paused. 'A little tray of something nice?' He smiled. 'Not cold beef, I promise.'

Lily shook her head and lay back on the bed, her face turned away from him.

Stephen watched her for a few moments, trying to gauge her mood.

'It's no use sulking,' he said quietly. 'You'll have to come downstairs sooner or later. You've got nowhere else to go. You can spend this evening up here on your own, though Mother will think it very odd; but you'll have to come down tomorrow, or the next day.'

Lily turned her bruised face to him. 'I'll come down,' she said tightly.

Stephen smiled. 'Good.'

Lily's eyes were dark with anger. In the face of her rage he could not maintain his easy smile.

'Good,' he said again uncertainly.

Lily got off the bed and slipped her feet into her shoes. She pulled the blouse around her shoulders and went for the door.

'Are you going to the bathroom?' Stephen asked.

'I'm going downstairs,' Lily said.

Stephen crossed the room in one rapid stride and had her by the arm before she could reach the door. 'Not like that you're not.'

She looked at him with her blank insolent stare. Stephen felt the palm of his hand itch to slap her face.

Instead he took her gently by the shoulders. Beneath his touch her skin cringed away. 'Now look, Lily,' he said. 'We've started off all wrong. I see that. I shouldn't have been rough with you like that. But I'm gentleman enough to say sorry when I'm in the wrong. So I'm sorry.'

Lily's face never changed.

'You did very wrong,' Stephen said. 'Very wrong indeed.

You'll go to the Kings Theatre in the morning and tell them you withdraw from the show. They can pay you any money owing you, and if they talk about breach of contract or anything like that you'll give them my card and leave it to me to deal with.' He gave her a slight shake to make sure that she was attending to him. 'Understood?'

Lily shook her head.

'And then we'll put this behind us,' he said. 'Put it behind us and start our life all over again. I shall forgive you for your deceit and you will forgive me for being a bit heavy-handed. It's over. It's forgotten.'

Lily shook her head again.

'You keep shaking your head. Are you unwell? What d'you mean?'

'I won't resign from the show,' Lily said through her teeth. 'I want to do the show and I'll do it. It's at the Kings for two weeks, and then at Southampton for two weeks, and then back for two weeks. Alternate weeks till the end of the summer. I'll never spend a night away from home. I'll get up and see you off to work every morning. I'll eat everything that's put in front of me. And I won't complain about what you just did. I'll keep it secret. But I am going to do the show, Stephen. Nothing will stop me.'

She looked like a Portsmouth mudlark, her cheek bruised and turning blue, her cut lip, her rumpled hair. She looked boyish and defiant, like a fag at school who has suffered a well-earned beating. Stephen felt tenderness rising up in him. 'Oh, Lily,' he said softly. 'Why did you make me do it? You know I wouldn't hurt you for the world.'

There was no answering warmth in her face at all. 'I'm going to do the show,' she said. 'You cannot stop me.'

Surprised by a sudden sentimental warmth he released her shoulders and folded her into his embrace. The top of her head came under his chin. He bent and kissed the fair hair and felt the delicacy of her body in his arms. He could have snapped her neck with one hand, he thought pityingly. He loved the vulnerability of her bruised face. If he hit her too hard he would break the bones of that perfect profile, he thought. She had to have a little leeway, a little permission from him. And if she overstepped the line, he could always smack her. Stephen felt his desire rise at the thought of smacking Lily, at the thought of taking her against her will and then kissing her hurts better.

'I think I want to spoil you,' he said tenderly. 'You're a thoroughly bad girl but I'll let you get away with it this time.' He held her chin and forced up her bruised face so that he could kiss her. He pressed his mouth on hers. Holding her tightly, he could feel her breath coming quicker from her fear. At least there was no danger that she was a tart, he thought comfortably. She might be on the stage, but she was a lady through and through. No-one would overstep the line with his wife; she was frigid.

'If you're a good girl, you can do the show,' he said.

He slid his tongue between her lips and felt her flinch away from him. He tightened his grip. Lily would have to pay for her permission. He licked her lips, her skin was salty with her tears; the taste of them excited him and he pressed her closer. He thought he would have her again, push her back on the bed again and have her twice, just to teach her who was master. He bared his teeth in the kiss and he nipped at her mouth. Then he tasted the richer salty taste of blood, where the cut on her mouth had opened up. At once he recoiled and pushed her away from him.

'Ugh,' he said. 'Go and wash, Lily, your mouth is bleeding.'

She turned slowly and went towards the door.

'I hate the taste of blood,' he said. He spat into his hand

and rubbed his hand on his torn shirt. 'I hate it.' He put his shirt up to his mouth and scrubbed at his tongue. 'Oh God! It's vile, it's really vile.' He rubbed at his tongue, and then his mouth, and then his hands went all over his face, scrubbing away imaginary blood. 'Oh God! It's vile!' he said again. He spat wildly on the new blue carpet. 'No,' he said pitifully. 'No.' The pale yellow walls of the room wavered and swirled, for a moment he was back in the trench, his mess-tin held to his chest, and bobbing in the stew was skin and bone and blood, and on his uniform and all over his face ... 'No,' Stephen cried.

Lily took his plucking hands from his shirt, from his face. 'Hush,' she said gently. 'It's gone now, Stephen.'

'I j ... j ... just hate it so ...'

'I know,' she said softly. 'It's gone now, Stephen.'

With a sob he took her little hand and pressed it against his face. She smelled sweet, not of mud nor blood nor cordite.

'All gone now,' she said, as one speaking to a child.

'Thank you,' he said. He stilled his hands with an effort and then took off his ripped shirt and threw it into the bin. He shrugged. 'B ... b ... bad memories,' he said.

'Forget them,' Lily advised simply.

Stephen looked at her intently. 'Help me forget them,' he said. 'Help me. It's what I married you for.'

Lily glanced at the rumpled bed and the blood on the pillow where he had hit her and then raped her. 'If I can,' she said dully. 'If I can. Perhaps we shouldn't have married at all.'

Stephen turned towards her and put his arm gently around her shoulders. Lily rested her head against his chest as if she were very weary and there was nowhere else in the world for her to go.

'It's too late now to regret it,' Stephen said. 'I'll try to be a better husband to you. That won't happen again if you promise you'll never lie to me again.'

Lily hesitated for only a moment. 'Yes,' she said. 'I won't lie again.'

'We'll start afresh,' Stephen promised. 'Maybe leave here, start again in a new house. A little farmhouse perhaps, somewhere in the country.'

'Maybe,' Lily said, thinking 'no'.

'I'd like to live in the country. A little farm, and you and me, happy together.'

Lily smiled weakly at the fantasy.

'Will you be all right to come down to dinner?'

'I need to wash,' she said, and went to the door. He heard her cross the landing and then shoot the bolt on the bathroom door. He heard the noise of her running a bath. He smiled indulgently; she would be in there for hours. Muriel had already spoken to Stephen about Lily's expensive taste in soap. She was using the best guest soap every day instead of the coal tar soap which was to be used by family. Stephen shrugged. Lily should have her little bit of luxury, he thought. She was a lady. No-one could question it.

Coventry drove Lily to the theatre for the Monday matinée though she made him drop her two streets away from the theatre. She thought it ironic that only a little while ago she had longed for a car to deliver and collect her from the theatre like Sylvia de Charmante. Now she had the car she did not want the envy of the other girls. Now she knew the price she had to pay. It was not an enviable bargain.

She was early. She tapped on Madge Sweet's dressing room door at half past one.

'What d'you want?' Madge came to the door in a bedraggled dressing-gown, her hair twisted up in curl

319

papers, her face shiny with cold cream. 'My God, Lil! What's he done to you?'

'He thumped me,' Lily said indifferently. 'I didn't have anything to put on it at home but powder. I was hoping it wouldn't show.'

'I've got some cream,' Madge said. 'Come in.' She drew Lily into the dressing room and tipped her face up to the light. 'Bastard,' she said. 'What did he want to do that for?'

'He saw a playbill in the *Evening News*,' Lily said. 'I was going to tell him Sunday night, but he saw it in the afternoon. He went mad. He took me upstairs and we had a fight.'

Madge hissed under her breath. She sat Lily in the bentwood chair and smoothed back her hair. 'Hurt bad?' she asked.

Lily shook her head. 'Not too bad,' she said.

Madge poured some of the pink cream on to a piece of cotton wool and dabbed it on the bruise on Lily's cheek. Slowly, as the layers of pink built up, the bruise faded and disappeared. Lily was left with a noticeable blob of pink.

'Lots of powder all over and that'll blend in,' Madge said uncertainly. 'Let's have a go at the lip.'

Lily's lip was swollen but the cut was a little red scab against the redness of her lip. 'Can't do anything about the swelling,' Madge said. She smeared a little of the pink cream on the bottom of Lily's lip. 'Paint your lipstick over the top of it,' she said. 'Deep red. Have you got one?'

Lily nodded.

'You won though,' Madge said. 'Since you're here. He's going to let you do the show?'

Lily leaned forward and stared at herself in the mirror. 'Yes,' she said. 'As long as I don't tour. And *that* means that I can audition for the panto in the winter too.'

Madge shook her head in admiration. 'You're a caution,

you are,' she said. 'You look as if butter wouldn't melt in your mouth and yet you're a real fighter. What do you have to do?'

Lily was patting the cream into her cheek, watching the effect in the mirror. 'How d'you mean? What do I have to do?'

'You never get something for nothing from men. What do you have to do for him?'

Lily smiled awkwardly – her lip hurt. 'Nothing much,' she said. 'I don't complain about this to his ma, and I don't stay out late at night. Nothing more. I'm going to try a bit harder though. I married him, after all. We've got to try and make a go of it.'

Madge sat on one of the chairs before the mirror and started untwisting her curls. 'You can try,' she said doubtfully. 'You've got no choice really, have you? You can't divorce him – you've got no grounds; and you can't leave him – you've got nowhere to go. Might as well have a try at being decent, I suppose.'

'Can I borrow the cream?'

Madge nodded. 'I don't use it except when I've got spots. You can keep it till the bruise fades.'

'Thanks,' Lily said and went out into the corridor. All around there was the electric atmosphere of first night excitement. As Lily went down the stairs to her dressing room three of the chorus girls came up chattering and laughing. 'Hello, Lil,' they said.

Lily put up her hand to hide her bruised cheek. 'Hello!' she said.

'Are you nervous?' one of the girls asked. 'I'm dying!'

'Dying!' Lily agreed.

The girls went on up but on impulse Lily turned away from the dressing rooms and went towards the stage.

It was busy, work had started hours ago. The great back wall of the stage was crowded with scenery which would be used for other productions. A grand staircase went to nowhere. There was a cottage with a window above a front door. There was a tree with a massive convincing trunk, a wide branch, and then no top at all.

There was a space between the scenery wide enough to take a horse and cart, and then there were the black curtains which hid the brick wall at the back of the stage. Lily went forward to the wings and looked at the set.

It was nearly ready for the first act. The chorus girls did a French café number, sitting at little tables and chairs. The backdrop was a gay red and white awning over a little blue-painted restaurant. Lily did not know that the scene painter had lain on a stretcher facing the original of his picture for four hours one hot summer's day in 1915. The ambulances had been overcrowded and his stretcher had been put out in the sun of Bilbéque square. A piece of shrapnel had torn into his belly and the blood had soaked through the field dressing and was attracting flies. He was nineteen, and he was very much afraid that he was a coward because he could feel himself shuddering, shaking and shivering all over, and he thought that only cowards trembled with fear.

He was in too much pain to move. He was paralysed with the pain of the wound which pulsed in time to his heartbeat. When he thought that he would die, under that unkindly hot sun, with the ceaseless hammer-hammer-hammer of guns, he heard himself whimpering like a hurt animal. It was then that he opened his eyes and stared ahead of him at the façade of the café.

One of the tricks of this war was that nothing ever stayed the same, he thought. You joined the army to save Belgium from the dreadful Hun and then you got to Belgium and found that it was you who were wrecking their fields, destroying their villages and eating their food. And the dreadful Hun was a man within calling distance in the

322

opposite trench. After the battle of Loos the Germans had held their fire while the English stretchered their dead and wounded from the open deathfield of no-man's-land into the safety of the trench. They were not brutal savages, they had played the game. They had been fair, even merciful. They had let the English rescue their wounded, which was something the Allied high command would never allow. The Germans had been kinder than the English. It didn't make any sense.

The Bilbeque café was another thing that was an illusion. The glass windows were undamaged, not even cracked. The lettering *Café Bilbeque* in gold paint was perfect. The little red and white awning fluttered in the breeze. There was a pot of red geraniums at the upstairs window. And behind the charming facade there was nothing. The café had taken a direct hit and had crumbled inside. The proprietor, his wife and their three children had suffocated under the rubble. No-one had yet had time to dig them out and bury them. But their café, their pretty summertime café, had a brave face for the world. A brave face and no body.

Lily stepped on to the stage to admire the set. She thought it quite delightful. She sat on one of the chairs, she leaned her elbows on the table and dreamed that she might be there in – she turned around and looked at the name – Café Bilbeque, where everything was always delightful.

'Auditioning for the chorus, Lily?' Charlie asked from the pit. He was checking the music in his stand.

'Daydreaming,' Lily said. 'What's the time? I'm not late, am I?'

'You've got an hour yet,' Charlie said. 'It's not two.' He played a chord on the open piano and glanced up at Lily.

'What's that on your face?'

Lily's hand went to the bruise. 'Nothing,' she said. 'I

bumped myself.' She thought rapidly. 'In the bath,' she said. 'I slipped and bumped myself on the tap.'

'Wait there,' Charlie said and stepped over the brass orchestra rail and went around to the door that led back-stage. Lily met him in the concealing darkness of the wings.

Charlie took her face in his hands and turned it so the working lights on stage shone full on her. 'He hit you,' he said. His voice was very soft.

'Yes,' Lily said shortly. 'He found out I was working. We've sorted it out. He's letting me work. That's the end to it, Charlie.'

Charlie let her go and turned away from her so that she wouldn't see the impotent rage on his face. He took a breath and then spoke softly. 'Leave him. If he's hit you once, he'll do it again. Leave him tonight, Lil. You can come to my digs, I'll fix you up with a room.'

'No.'

He swung back. 'This isn't a request, this is an order. You're to leave him. You can get a divorce for this. I'll take you to a lawyer tomorrow morning.'

'No.'

Charlie took her hands. 'Please, Lil,' he said. 'Don't let him do this to you. He's bound to win in the end. You're not sorted out now just because he lets you do one little show – but belts you before you go on. It's no good.'

Lily shook her head.

Charlie exclaimed in exasperation. 'Why the hell do you want to put up with it? D'you admire him for thumping you? D'you think he's manly or something? Is he so bloody potent that he can thump you and make love to you and you let him do it? Do you like it? Is that how you are? A woman who takes a blow in her face and then a kiss to make up and thinks this is true love?'

'Oh, shut up,' Lily said in sudden repulsion. 'Is that all you can think about? Is that all you ever think about?

About Stephen making love to me? I stay with him because I've nowhere else to go. I stay with him because I've no money except for what I earn here week by week and this is a short-term contract. And, actually, though you don't want to believe it, I stay with him because I married him and because he *does* love me, and I belong there now. I love his father, and his mother's kind to me. Stephen's funny from the war. I can't blame him for that. I can help him with it.'

'God in heaven!' Charlie exclaimed. 'Funny from the war, and you love his dad. You can't stay with a man for those reasons!'

Lily pulled her hands out of his tightening grip. 'Oh, leave me alone,' she said. 'You're too late, Charlie. I telegraphed you before I married and gave you the chance to stop it then. If you had sent me *one word* I wouldn't have gone through with it. I didn't know where I was nor what I was doing. I was out of my head with Ma's death and I didn't know what to do. But you didn't do a thing. You sent me that telegram from everyone saying "Good Luck"! You made your choice then, Charlie. You can live with it. And I made my choice. And I'll live with it too. I married Stephen and I'm going to be a good wife to him. If you don't like it then hard luck! You swore you'd never interfere; well, don't!'

She turned on her heel and ran from the wings down the dressing room stairs. Charlie heard her high heels rattle down the stone steps.

He walked slowly over to the prompt corner and sat on the prompter's stool. He laid his arms carefully on the desk and then put his face deep in the crook of his arm. 'God almighty,' he said slowly. 'I could wish I'd not made it. I could wish I'd never got through it. I could wish I'd never come back.'

*   *   *

Stephen was waiting with Coventry in the big grey Argyll outside the Kings Theatre when Lily came out from the evening show.

'Can we give Madge a lift?' she asked.

Stephen smiled. 'Of course, hop in.'

He held the door for the two girls and then got into the back with them.

'I have digs in Silver Street,' Madge said, a little breathless at the sight of the soft grey upholstery and Coventry's uniform. 'Down Kings Road, left at Kings Terrace and I'll get out on the corner.'

'Nonsense,' Stephen said warmly. 'We'll take you to your door. It's too late for you to be walking home alone.'

Lily shot Madge a small superior smile.

'Good show?' Stephen asked. 'I would have got a ticket but they were sold out! That's got to be good, hasn't it, Lily?'

'They give away a lot of tickets for the first night. It's tomorrow that they want to see a full house.'

'But it went well,' Madge volunteered. 'Lily was lovely. You couldn't see the bruise under the make-up at all.'

Stephen's eyes narrowed for only a second. 'What bruise?' he asked. He turned to Lily. 'What bruise, my darling?'

'I slipped in my bath this morning and banged my cheek on the tap,' Lily said wearily. 'Madge gave me the lend of some cream for my cheek.'

'Lent me.'

'Lent me.'

'Poor darling,' Stephen continued. 'Let me see.'

Lily turned her face to him and he gently touched the bruise with his finger. 'Poor little cheek,' he said. 'But it will soon heal. It's only a little bump.'

Madge swelled beside Lily in the seat. Lily dug her

elbow into Madge's ribs, commanding her silence. 'Left here,' was all she said.

They drew up outside Madge's lodging. A curtain twitched at the window and was drawn frankly back so the landlady could stare at Madge getting out of an Argyll with a chauffeur holding the door. Stephen and Lily watched Madge till she stepped in the opening front door.

'Drive on,' Stephen said.

Coventry let in the clutch and they went quietly forwards. 'Cook left you a little supper,' Stephen said. 'I didn't know how hungry you would be.'

Lily shook her head. 'I'm so tired I could drop,' she said. 'I'm not hungry at all.'

'Well, you must have a little something,' Stephen said. 'And then a lie-in tomorrow. There's no need for you to come downstairs for breakfast. Not while you're working so late at night.'

'Thank you,' Lily said.

The car drew up before the darkened house. 'Mother's gone to bed already,' Stephen said, glancing up at the windows. He let them into the house while Coventry drove away.

'Isn't he parking round the back?' Lily asked.

'No, he wanted to go home tonight. Some nights he likes to go to his home.'

Lily wastefully switched on all the lights as she went into the house: the chandelier in the hall and the lights on the walls. She switched on the lights for the drawing room on her right though she did not go into the room. She went further down the hall to the dining room and switched on the wall lights and the lights over the dining room table. There was one place laid, with a glass of milk beside it and, in the breakfast chafing dishes, a dish of bubble and squeak – Lily recognized the Sunday dinner vegetables in their second incarnation. Sliced thickly on another plate were tough cold wedges of beef from the Sunday joint.

Lily helped herself to the two smallest slices and a generous portion of the crispy brown bubble and squeak. Cook had put a pickle jar of her own green tomato chutney on the sideboard so Lily guessed that you were allowed pickles with bubble and squeak. She had once asked for pickle with steak and kidney pie and had seen Stephen and his mother both look deeply shocked. Since then she had learned that pickle or sauce was a very rare treat. Mustard though, a horrible yellow slimy mustard, you could eat with anything.

Stephen came through the house turning off the lights and then drew up a chair to sit with Lily.

'What about the things?' she asked, gesturing to the dishes. 'Should we clear them?'

'Oh no,' Stephen said. 'Browning will do it.'

'Hasn't she gone to bed?'

'She'll get up early in the morning to do it. I've told them. The house has to be run to your convenience while you are working. They all know.'

Lily blinked. 'Thank you,' she said again.

'You look surprised?'

'I didn't think that you were very happy about me working,' Lily said tentatively.

Stephen smiled. 'I don't like it at all,' he said frankly. 'But since you insist, it doesn't help us much if we fight every day of your season, does it? We might as well agree to differ and get along as well as we can. Don't you think, Lily?'

Lily nodded. 'Yes,' she said. 'Thank you. Of course.'

'Bed for you,' Stephen said tenderly. 'Want an apple?'

Lily shook her head. Stephen switched off the dining room lights and then put on one light for the stairs. He slid the bolts on the front door and put the safety chain across. He followed Lily up the stairs to their bedroom.

There was a thermos flask and a cup and saucer by the bed with some arrowroot biscuits. 'Browning's left you a nightcap,' Stephen said. 'Hot milk and cinnamon. She always used to do it for Christopher and me if we were out late somewhere. It's her treat.'

Lily smiled and opened the flask. It smelled rather strongly of old tea. The milk inside was tepid, pale brown from the cinnamon powder and speckled with floating pieces of skin stained beige.

'Lovely,' Lily said. 'I'll drink it while I'm washing my face in the bathroom.'

She took the cup and saucer through to the bathroom and bolted the door behind her. Then she poured it carefully down the toilet and pulled the chain. She washed her face and hands, combed her hair, cleaned her teeth and changed into her nightdress.

Stephen was in bed when she came in, reading a book. When she shut the door behind her he put the marker in place and laid the book carefully on his bedside table. He pulled back the blankets. 'Come to bed, little wife,' he said kindly. 'I bet you're exhausted.'

Lily nodded and climbed into bed beside him, pulling the covers up. 'Good night,' she said, turning her back to him and closing her eyes. Stephen waited and then put out his bedside light. They were both asleep in moments.

In the early hours of the morning, at about three, Stephen jerked awake from a nightmare. He had been running westwards down a well-built zig-zagging trench, four paces north, four paces west, four paces south. He knew that there was some vital message he had to get through. There would be an attack but his brigade did not have to advance. He had to get the message through that they must *not* advance. They must stay in the safety of the trench while someone else's lot did the work. Someone else's friends could get shot to pieces, or snagged and torn by the wire, or bombed.

On and on Stephen ran until he started wondering about the message he carried. What if it were a message ordering an advance? What if it had been some kind of trick from those devils, those mad devils at headquarters? What if they had lied to him and told him that the message said *not* to advance, knowing he would run like a deer; when in fact the message said 'advance and take the brunt of the counter-attack.' Suppose it said, as some insane officer had said last week, 'we have been ordered to hold the trench at all costs. I expect you to die beside me, men.' Stephen's legs went slower and slower and then he stumbled and finally stopped. He undid his breast pocket and took out the message. It was written on the standard officer memo pad from CO to Brigadier Wentworth, the time 1400 hrs. It was only two lines. It said: 'This messenger is not a hero, he is a murderer. When he arrives, shoot him.'

In his dream Stephen screamed 'No!' and it was this that flung him into his waking world.

The room was very quiet, wrapped in a deep blue darkness. Lily at his side was sleeping deeply, breathing softly. She had rolled over in the night and was sleeping on her back with one arm flung above her head. She was smiling in her sleep.

Stephen shifted the bedclothes slightly and then fumbled with his pyjama trousers and took out his erect penis. He moved on to her and thrust himself steadily and slowly inside her.

Lily's eyes flew open and she opened her mouth to scream as his hand came down, gagging her.

'Please let me,' he whispered very softly, his mouth furred with sleep, his nightmare still driving him. 'Please let me, Lily. It takes the bad dreams away. Please let me, I won't hurt.'

Lily closed her eyes to shut Stephen's flushed determined face from her mind. She felt her bruised body being hurt again. She bit her lip and turned her face away as Stephen, as gently as he could, pushed himself inside her uninviting body and took his relief. But he did not pull away as he used to do. Lily felt him gasp and then grow limp inside her.

It was minutes before he rolled over to his side of the bed and, purged of his fears, fell asleep at once.

Lily lay on her back as he had left her, looking at the ceiling which grew paler as the sun rose over the quiet ebb sea.

Chapter Twenty-two

The next day marked the start of a new routine for Lily and the household which now revolved around her work – as before it had revolved around Stephen alone.

Breakfast was still at eight thirty sharp for Mr Stephen but now the house had to go on tiptoe until ten thirty, when Browning would take a pot of tea and two slices of toast to the young Mrs Winters's bedroom. Only after eleven could noisy housework commence. The young Mrs Winters had to have her sleep.

Stephen took to coming home for lunch to be with Lily before she went to the theatre so Cook had to be warned that the skimpy little omelettes and reheated left-overs, which had sufficed for the women lunching alone, now had to be expanded to suit the man of the house. Cook managed by the inventive strategy of exchanging dinner menus with luncheon menus so that poor Lily's hated parade of oversalted soups, overcooked meat and damp vegetables was now served at midday, and she went to the afternoon matinée with the weight of Cook's cuisine heavy in her stomach. The food seemed even more indigestible at noon, with the sunshine beating through the dining room windows, and Lily wilted in the heat before her well-stocked plate.

Muriel ate lunch with them and then took her dinner at the usual time of seven, when she was served Cook's lighter offerings of a boiled egg, soufflé, omelettes, veal and ham pie, or overcooked fish. Stephen and Lily, late home after the theatre, would have soup left hot for them, or sandwiches or a limp salad. As often as not, as the weeks went on and Stephen and Lily adapted to the new freedom, they went out to dinner after the theatre, sometimes with other members of the cast.

Even Charlie joined them in the second week of the run. He had barely spoken to Lily for a week, but when she included him in the general invitation to dinner he had looked up and given her a grim little smile. 'Yes, I'll come,' he said.

There had been eight of them, a jolly rowdy party in the respectable Southsea restaurant. But much could be forgiven to actors; and when Lily consented to sing a song and Charlie sat at the piano and accompanied her, there was a round of applause from the other diners. They knew of Lily's name, she had been praised in the Portsmouth paper and even one of the national papers had named her as a young singer of promise. Stephen glowed at the praise for his wife and kept a proprietary arm along the back of her chair.

He watched Charlie narrowly for any signs of jealousy. He had not forgotten him, lounging in the stage door at the start of the Midsummer Madness tour, making sure that Lily was back on time. But the man was no threat, Stephen decided. Lily barely looked twice at him and he was relaxed and friendly with everyone at the table. If anything, he was attentive to Madge. When the band started to play again after their break he danced only once with Lily, but twice with Madge. Stephen, holding Lily close as they danced, knew himself to be with the prettiest woman in the room, in unquestioned ownership of her.

When the bill came, he paid for them all – he felt like paying. The chorus girls kissed him on the cheek for gratitude and the men smiled and said thank you. Then Stephen swore that he could drop everyone at their digs in the Argyll. Six of them squeezed in the back, and Lily sat on Stephen's lap in the front. They sang and giggled all their way to every quiet lodging house and noisily whispered goodnight on the pavements. Then Coventry drove Lily and Stephen home to number two, The Parade.

'That Charlie, he was in the show, wasn't he?' Stephen asked, tossing his shirt into the laundry basket in the corner of their bedroom.

'He's musical director,' Lily said from the bed.

'Not your little show,' Stephen said. '*The* show. The war.'

'Yes. Not for long. I think he was a gunner. He was invalided out.'

'A blighty?'

Lily shrugged. 'You know I don't understand soldiers' slang,' she said pettishly. 'What's a blighty?'

'A blighty is a wound which gets you shipped home – back to Blighty. Not so bad that you're in too much pain, but bad enough so they can't patch you up and push you back which, God knows, they did. Half of them shot themselves. Was he one of them? A convenient wound in the knee?'

Lily thought of Charlie's stitched and scarred body, of the secret wound which he had showed to her, and of his hands which had touched her and moved her in a way that a whole man like her husband could not. 'Why?' she asked. 'Isn't that what you had? A blighty? A bullet in your ankle?'

Stephen flinched. 'That's damned insulting, Lily,' he said. 'I got my wound when I was leading an attack against a f . . . f . . . farmhouse. The H . . . H . . . Huns were . . . in there . . . with the v . . . village women . . . they had raped them and then stabbed them, the place was like a b . . . b . . . butcher's sh . . . sh . . . shop . . .'

'Stop it,' Lily said suddenly, with her hands over her ears. 'I don't want to hear about it. Don't think about it!

You'll only give yourself bad dreams. Forget it, Stephen! Pretend it never happened!'

For a moment he was angry, and then his face cleared. 'Yes,' he said. 'Let's pretend it never happened.'

He moved to the bed and Lily could tell by the curiously intent look on his face that he would want her again. He put his arms around her; Lily's skin was icy, as welcoming as cold water. He slid the little straps from her shoulders so that he could see her breasts. 'They were whores,' he said clearly. 'They deserved to die. It wasn't even rape.' He pushed her gently back on the bed and thrust into her.

On Saturday night there was a birthday party for one of the chorus girls and Stephen and Lily went along. It was held after the show in the upper circle bar. There was a piano and Charlie obligingly played dance music so the girls could charleston. They all went on to a nightclub later, piled two deep into the Argyll. One of the chorus girls begged that Coventry should go in with them, so at Stephen's nod he left his cap in the car and went dancing too.

'Don't mention it to Mother, Lily,' Stephen warned.

Lily nodded. Charlie was dancing with Madge again, and with one of the chorus girls called Isabel. They had started a line and other people were joining at the end, a repetitive easy dance step, two forwards, a kick, and two back.

'Come on,' Lily said. She dragged Stephen's arm and broke into the line beside Charlie. When the music changed Charlie caught her up and danced her off, while Madge and Stephen partnered each other.

'All right, Lil?' Charlie said quietly.

'All right,' she said.

Marjorie Philmore strolled on to the floor and tapped

Madge on the shoulder as she danced with Stephen. 'Ladies' Excuse Me,' she said and took her place.

Stephen looked surprised. 'Oh God, don't say you don't even remember me,' Marjorie drawled. She took a puff of smoke from her cigarette holder and blew it out over his shoulder. 'We had tea, at your mother's. My mother was there, and Sarah Dent and her mother. It was the wildest of fun. Don't you remember?'

'Oh yes!' Stephen said. 'Forgive me, I had forgotten. I've been married since then, you know.'

'I heard,' Marjorie said indifferently. 'Chorus girl, ain't she?'

Stephen's teeth went on edge. 'She's a soloist. A singer. That's her over there.' He nodded his head to where Lily and Charlie were dancing together. Lily had dressed up for the party in a turquoise silk dress cut on the bias so that it floated outwards from her whenever she moved. It had a short tightly fitted bodice with two tiny beaded shoulder straps. It was delightfully obvious that she had nothing on under her dress but her pale peachy skin. Charlie had one hand resting lightly on her bare back and his face set in an expression of pleasant indifference.

'A baby!' Marjorie exclaimed. 'You're a cradle-snatcher, Stephen!'

'She's the most beautiful girl in the room. That's good enough for me,' Stephen said levelly.

Marjorie stepped back a little from him. 'Touché,' she said. 'But I've never thought of myself as more than passable so you don't hurt me.'

Stephen flushed with embarrassment. 'I beg your pardon . . . I didn't mean . . .'

Marjorie shook her head and smiled and moved closer to him so that he could feel her down the length of his body. 'I've always relied on being the sexiest girl in the room,' she whispered very softly in his ear. 'I think it's just as effective. And besides, pretty women have such off days, don't they? Whereas a sexy woman is always sexy.'

The music stopped with a flourish and Marjorie abruptly stepped back and clapped. 'Thank you,' she said to Stephen. 'Now I have to go.'

'Won't you come and meet my wife? Have a drink with us?'

Marjorie narrowed her eyes and smiled at him. 'Ask me another time,' she said. 'I don't really go in for wives. Ask me another time when you're alone.'

Stephen let her go, but he watched her threading her way through the tables. She moved with a sensuous self-conscious slink.

Stephen went back to their table and ordered another bottle of champagne. He felt as if he needed it.

On Sunday morning Lily and Stephen had to go to church and take the obligatory walk around the harbour walls. At least one of Muriel's friends snubbed her. A daughter-in-law on the stage was a major social disadvantage. But all the friends who had children of their own, especially those with surplus young daughters, were pleasant enough. The girls thought that Lily was unspeakably glamorous and they nudged their mothers for an introduction. The boys of sixteen and seventeen merely gaped at Lily as if she were a goddess descended to walk on the sea walls between her mother-in-law and her husband by some special dispensation. There were no young men at all.

Lily ate Sunday lunch – cream of mushroom soup, roast chicken, stuffing, bread sauce, roast potatoes, boiled peas strangely dry tasting and limp carrots – with polite enthusiasm. She folded her napkin, put it carefully through the ring and then left it by her place. They would not have clean napkins until Monday. Lily thought that clean linen once a week was simply disgusting. It would have been better to wipe your mouth on both sleeves and change your shirt every other day.

Before Stephen could retreat to his study she said, 'Shall we take Mr Winters for a walk? It's a lovely day.'

Muriel hesitated.

'The doctors *did* say it was doing him good, didn't they?' Lily demanded. 'Nurse Bells has been taking him every day. We could take him today.'

'I don't mind,' Stephen said. 'I'll read the paper for half an hour and then we'll go.'

'I'll go up and tell him,' Lily said.

Rory's face was more alert. When she came in the door his whole head turned to see her and his mouth widened in a slow smile.

'Hello,' Lily said. 'I've come to see if you would like a walk?'

The head on the pillow moved slightly forward indicating 'yes'.

'Stephen and I will take you,' Lily said. 'He's just reading the paper. I'll tell Nurse Bells to get you ready.'

She turned for the door but a little noise from the bed made her turn back. Rory's cavernous face was working, he was trying to speak. Lily came back to his bedside and took his hand.

'Do you want to say something?'

Shaking with effort he put his hand out towards her. Lily at once bent nearer. Gently, like the brush of a feather, he ran the tip of his index finger across her cheek where the bruise was a pale blue shadow.

Lily's face was grim. 'I fell,' she said.

Rory's hand dropped back on the counterpane. Slowly he shook his head.

'Did you hear?' Lily asked directly.

He nodded.

'Was that why you fell out of bed?'

His expressionless imprisoned face turned towards her and she saw his eyes were filling with tears.

She put her fair head down and kissed his cheek. 'Thank you,' she said softly. 'You made him stop. He hasn't hurt me since. He won't hurt me again. He was angry, and it was partly my fault. He won't do it again. We're going to try harder. We're going to make our marriage work.'

The show at the Kings had a second successful week and then packed up for the move to Southampton. It was the tail end of the season and there was no time for a full-scale tour. It had been the failure of a company going bankrupt which had meant that Charlie had thrown a show together at short notice. They played two weeks at the Royal Southampton, to good houses, and then came back for two weeks at the Kings.

Lily slept later while she was working in Southampton but Stephen still met her every evening from the theatre, and Coventry drove her to the theatre every morning. The chorus girls had taken to calling her Duchess, and Stephen they called the Duke. Stephen loved it. At least once a week he treated them all to dinner. Those nights the chorus girls all kissed him goodnight on the cheek. Stephen flushed deep red. 'I say!'

At the start of the first week back at the Kings, Lily felt queasy in the mornings and found her morning cup of tea sour-tasting. She was sick on Wednesday morning and did not get up until midday, to lunch with Stephen. She refused to see a doctor and went in to the afternoon matinée a little early.

'Madge,' she said, walking in to the dressing room.

Madge was creaming her face in front of the mirror, wearing her dressing-gown grown more disreputable than ever and greying with dirt at the hem.

'Madge, I think I'm pregnant.'

Madge paused, her mouth an 'O' of horror, a globule of cream poised on her right hand. 'Oh my God,' she said and scraped her fingers clean on the side of the pot. 'Why? Have you seen a doctor?'

'Not yet,' Lily said. 'I'm a week late with my little visitor and I was sick this morning. I've felt sick every morning since Sunday.'

'Could be a tummy bug,' Madge said hopefully. 'Could be something you ate?'

'And my breasts feel all tender,' Lily said.

Madge gave a little moan and opened her arms to Lily. The two girls hugged each other for a moment and then Lily stepped back. 'You think I am too,' she accused.

'Doesn't make any difference what anyone thinks,' Madge said abruptly. 'If you are, you are. What are you going to do?'

'Is there any way of getting rid of it?' Lily asked, her voice very low.

Madge glanced behind Lily to see that the dressing room door was shut. 'I knew a girl who did it once but she was terribly ill, Lil. You wouldn't want to do it.'

'If I don't, it's the end of my career,' Lily said. 'It's curtains, isn't it? I'll be stuck inside that house forever with a string of babies one after another.'

'It's not safe,' Madge said. 'Some women die, and if you're sick and they have to take you to hospital then it's a police matter and you're in real trouble.'

Lily closed her eyes for a moment and then sat down in front of the mirror with her head in her hands. 'I *have* to get rid of it,' she said. 'What d'you do?'

'There is medicine you can get, but I don't know what it's called,' Madge said. 'It makes you throw up really bad. It makes you so sick that you lose the baby. My sister did it that way but I don't know the name of the medicine. She got her boyfriend's mum to get it for her. She didn't dare get it herself.'

'How can we get some?'

'The girls might know, we could ask around.'

'And then everyone would know,' Lily said. 'And it would get back to Stephen and he would murder me. It's got to be just you and me.'

'There's another way,' Madge said hesitantly.

'Well?'

'It's really dangerous, Lil. You can rupture yourself and bleed to death.'

'For God's sake, tell me! You're like an old hen, Madge! Get on with it!'

'You put a buttonhook up inside you – you know – up your fanny. And you wedge it there with handkerchiefs all rolled up, and you walk around like that for a whole day with it sticking into you. And the hook scrapes round and round inside as you walk – see?'

Lily had gone white. 'I can't do that,' she said.

Madge shrugged. 'That's how it's done,' she said bleakly. 'All day with the hook tearing away at the inside of you. And it can hook on to your stomach or your lungs, or anything.'

'I can't.'

'Well you'd much better not,' Madge agreed. 'It's too dangerous. And anyway, even if you get rid of this one, you're still married, aren't you? Can't do it every month, can you?'

'He used to pull back,' Lily said slowly. 'But then he stopped.'

Madge nodded. 'He wants a baby,' she said. 'He wants a family. He's your husband, Lil. You shouldn't have married him if you didn't want to live with him and have his children.'

'It's not a baby he wants,' Lily said bitterly. 'He wants to keep me at home.'

'You can finish the season at least,' Madge said consolingly. 'You won't show for a month or two.'

'If I can keep it secret from Stephen, I can finish the season,' Lily said. 'And maybe I can come back to work after it's born.'

'Yes,' Madge said without much hope. 'Maybe.'

Lily looked at her pale heart-shaped face in the dressing room mirror and shook her head. 'The chorus girls think I'm the luckiest girl in the world,' she said. 'They should try being me for one day. It's not such a lark then, Madge.'

Three weeks later, almost to the day, Stephen reached for Lily in the night and moved to lie on top of her. Apart from a small half-silenced gasp of discomfort Lily did not refuse him. Stephen stopped at once. 'Are you not unwell?' he asked.

Lily's face, pale in the shadowy dawn light of the room, looked shocked. 'No,' she said.

Stephen smiled. 'Then, if I am right, you have not been unwell for two months.'

Lily saw the trap she was in. She swallowed on a dry throat. 'I am due in a few days,' she said. 'I don't really like to discuss it, if you don't mind, Stephen.'

Stephen smiled more broadly. 'But Lily,' he said cleverly, 'I am your husband. Your health is my concern. I have kept a little diary to assist you in these matters ever since our wedding day. I was concerned at first how often you seemed to have a little visitor so that you were unable to make love. I thought it more gentlemanly if I knew in advance when you would be forced to refuse me, so that I would not press you.'

Lily swallowed again. She felt crushed by Stephen's body and overwhelmed by his courteous authority.

'I see from my little diary that you were due last month, but you made no mention of it. And that you are due now, but you tell me that you are not unwell. My darling, I think you have some news for me, is it not so?'

Lily shook her head.

Stephen's hands were hard on her shoulders, his fingers pinched her.

Lily nodded.

'And what is the news?' Stephen asked.

'I think I am pregnant,' Lily said dully.

Stephen eased gently off her. 'Well, that is wonderful,' he said. 'I can't tell you how delighted I am, Lily. Wonderful news for me and for the whole family. Mother and Father will be thrilled.'

Lily nodded again.

'You must see the doctor tomorrow,' Stephen said. 'He will call here at eleven. I made an appointment yesterday.'

'You knew already?' Lily asked.

Stephen patted her cheek. 'Sooner or later, little Lily, you were bound to be pregnant. I know my duty by you, don't worry. We're going to be happy now. We're going to be very very happy.'

Dr Mobey examined Lily gently and confirmed that she was two months pregnant.

'I want to go on working,' Lily said blankly. She was lying on her bed. She pulled down her skirt and sat up. 'I want to go on working to the end of the season, until October the nineteenth.'

Dr Mobey sat at his ease in the bedroom chair. 'D'you think that's wise, Mrs Winters?' he asked pleasantly. 'Most young ladies I know would welcome the chance to put their feet up and enjoy a bit of fuss.'

Lily smiled an insincere smile. 'I am a singer,' she said.

'I love my work. I do very little dancing now. I would like to finish my contract.'

'Well, we'd better see what Stephen thinks about it, hadn't we? It must be his decision.'

'But there's no medical reason why I should stop work, is there?' Lily pressed.

Dr Mobey hesitated. 'Let's see – October you said – you will be three months pregnant by then – there's no reason why you should stop work. But if you are guided by me you will take things easily, and eat properly.'

Lily gave him her sweetest smile. 'Oh please, Dr Mobey,' she said coquettishly. 'Tell Stephen I can work, and I shall send you a complimentary ticket to a box!'

He chuckled. 'Well, you're a persuasive little thing, there's no arguing with you! I'll tell Stephen you can finish your little season but then there's to be absolute rest and no more work.'

Lily nodded earnestly.

'And if there are any signs, any . . .' He hesitated, embarrassed. 'Any show of blood or discomfort, you are to stop work at once.'

Lily nodded again. She knew that if she saw the least trace of blood she would dance all night and jump down the stairs until dawn.

But it did not happen. Lily took baths as hot as she could bear and inspected her knickers every morning, hoping to see a bright spot of red blood. But the baby was strong and healthy despite her. The supply of tepid cinnamon milk was doubled, and Lily was sent to the theatre every day with two rounds of beef sandwiches for her tea, glistening with fat and chewy with gristle. On fine days Lily walked around the Canoe Lake before Coventry picked her up so that she could feed the sandwiches to the swans. When it rained she gave them to the chorus girls. Of the two, Lily much preferred the swans.

344

Stephen no longer permitted her late nights. Coventry brought her straight home from the theatre, but after he had seen her to bed Stephen sometimes went out again. From sly giggles and odd silences when she came into their dressing room, Lily concluded that Stephen went out to nightclubs with the chorus girls. She could not find any jealousy in her. She could not find any reason to care.

With the show in its two final weeks all the talk backstage was what work was available elsewhere. Two girls had gone for the same audition and would not speak to each other in their dressing room. Madge had work as a fashion model in one of the Southsea shops, she had to walk up and down in the store's dresses while fat women popped eclairs in their mouths and their husbands ogled her.

'Steady money,' she said determinedly. 'And not much else going on.'

There was a season of classical plays coming to the Kings. They would audition actors who could take serious work, but a boisterous vamp like Madge would not be needed until the panto season which would not rehearse until the last week of November. Charlie promised Madge a part.

'What about you, Lil?' he asked. He had come to Lily's dressing room, between the matinée and the evening show, with a pot of tea and two battered mugs. Lily was sitting in the broken armchair with her feet up on the bentwood chair.

She watched him pour the tea and took her cup. 'I'd better tell you something,' she said slowly. 'I won't be auditioning for panto. I won't be working here again.'

Charlie put down his cup and looked at her. 'Stephen,' he said. It was not a question.

'Not exactly.'

'What then?'

'I'm having a baby.'

Charlie caught his breath and a swift expression contorted his face so dramatically that Lily thought he had trapped his finger in the chair leg, or scalded himself with tea. He looked away for a moment and when he looked back at her his face was set. 'Are you pleased?'

Lily shook her head. 'I don't want it,' she said bleakly.

'What a damned mess,' Charlie said softly.

There was a long silence. Lily sipped from her mug of tea and Charlie took up his own cup.

'Does Stephen know?'

'He knew almost as soon as I did. It didn't happen by accident.'

Charlie nodded, his mouth twisted. 'Is he pleased?'

'Like a dog with two tails.'

'When are you due?'

'May.'

Charlie raised his mug to her. 'I wish you very well, Lil. I wish you all the best.'

'Thank you.'

The atmosphere in the little room was full of unspoken longings. Charlie walked towards the barred whitewashed window and rested his head against the coolness of the painted glass.

'I wish to God I could have married you and that this baby was mine,' he said simply.

Lily did not move, she did not even extend her hand to him. She nodded grimly and tipped up her cup so she could sip the dregs of undissolved sugar at the bottom. 'Me too,' she said shortly.

Charlie turned back. 'It's not too late,' he said.

Lily thought of a lad whistling in the dark trying to

pretend he was not afraid. 'Not too late for what?' she asked.

'Not too late for you to run,' he said. 'Get out of that house and that marriage before the baby's born. Come to me, Lil. I'll care for you, and your baby, and when you're ready to move on you'll be free to go, I won't hold you back.'

Lily tipped her head back and rubbed the nape of her neck. 'No,' she said slowly. 'It wouldn't work, Charlie. I don't want your charity. I want to live with you as your wife, nothing less will do. Do you want me to come and live with you as your wife?'

'There'd be a huge scandal...' Charlie said. 'We'd never work in this town again. Stephen would take us both to court. We'd even have trouble finding work in London.'

Lily nodded. 'I'd go through all of that for you. If it's what you want.'

Charlie shook his head. 'Not a hope,' he said forlornly. 'Not a hope in hell, Lil. I could stand the gossip all right, but I couldn't stand living as your lover, and not being your lover. It would kill me to live with you like that. I'll give you every penny of my wages but I can't live in the same house with you. I'd die every moment of the day with longing.'

'That's settled, then,' Lily said calmly. 'I'll only live with you as your wife – I don't care for scandal or for the fact that we can't make love. And you won't live with me at all.'

Charlie turned from the window and sat on the little bentwood chair, took Lily's bare feet in his lap and massaged them gently. 'I couldn't bear to,' he said. 'D'you understand? I'd go mad with you being so close. It would be like being wounded every day, every morning.'

Lily nodded. 'You're the only man I'd ever leave Stephen for.'

Charlie smiled his crooked sad smile. 'And I'm the only man in the world who wouldn't have you,' he finished for her. 'What a mess we've got ourselves into, Lil my little love. What a mess.'

Chapter Twenty-three

The show closed in the first week in October and Stephen agreed that Lily could attend the final party. Everyone cried; two of the chorus girls attached themselves to Stephen's lapels and cried particularly. Charlie, who was standing behind Lily's table, leaned forward and said in her ear, 'Your husband's been out and about a bit lately.'

Lily did not turn her head. 'I know.'

'He's been dancing most evenings with those two.'

Lily nodded.

'And he's been dining on his own with that Marjorie Philmore.'

Lily shrugged. Charlie watched the smooth movement of her shoulders under a pale peach chiffon shawl. 'It doesn't matter to me,' she said. 'How come you know her?'

Charlie grinned. 'Most beautiful women stop and lean on the piano sooner or later,' he said. 'Nothing like a piano to lean on to show off your bum.'

Lily choked on her drink and giggled. 'This is your recipe for success with women, is it?'

Charlie nodded. 'I play 'em soulful music and they come and lean on the piano and tell me their life histories.'

'And what's her life history?'

Charlie shrugged. 'A brother dead in France, a fiancé killed at Gallipoli, a boyfriend wounded and in a wheelchair. Too much money and no sense. No love at all.'

Lily nodded at this harsh précis. 'And what's mine?'

Charlie leaned forward and dropped a kiss on the crown of her fair head. 'Hardly started,' he said tenderly. 'Hardly begun at all. Lots of life history for you to be made yet. A whole lifetime for you, Lil. Let's dance.'

He held her close as they danced, trying to feel against his body the firmness of her rounding belly where the baby was growing. The skin of her bare back under his guiding hand was warm, her breasts swelling with pregnancy pressed against the peach bodice of the dress. 'You're a lovely piece, Lil,' he said with affection as well as desire. 'A lovely piece.'

He danced her over to where Stephen was sitting at a dance floor table and spun her into a seat. 'We must keep her off her feet,' he said pleasantly to Stephen. 'You're going to have real trouble keeping her resting at home.'

'I should say so!' Stephen said.

'She needs a hobby,' Charlie said helpfully. 'Something to keep her busy at home. Next year she'll be busy enough, thank God! But for now she needs something to keep her out of mischief.'

'That's *just* what my mother says,' Stephen exclaimed. 'But Lily doesn't sew or knit, or do flowers, or quilling or painting. She won't learn either, though Mother has offered.'

The two men looked critically at Lily, united in their disapproval. Lily put her chin on her hands and looked back at them without discomfort.

'Singing!' Charlie exclaimed, as if he had just thought of it. 'You have to work on the raw material you have to hand, Captain Winters – remember your training! Improvise with what you have to hand!'

Stephen blinked owlishly. He was quite drunk. 'That's damned clever,' he said, impressed. 'What have I got to hand?'

'A singer,' Charlie explained. 'Get her singing lessons.

Get her piano lessons. All perfectly ladylike, musical evenings in the drawing room, your mother would approve. She's got a good voice, she needn't sing "Burlington Bertie", she could learn to sing Schubert, Mozart.'

'Are they Huns?' Stephen demanded, suddenly belligerent.

'Purcell, Tchaikovsky,' Charlie improvised rapidly. 'English and Russian. Glorious Allies. No Huns at all.'

Stephen nodded. 'We could buy a piano,' he said.

'And Lily could learn to play!' Charlie concluded for him. 'Why, I could come round and teach her myself once or twice a week.'

'You'd do that?'

'I would!'

'Well, that's damned decent of you,' Stephen said. He turned to Lily, who was watching the dancers with her back to them both. 'Here, Lily, Charlie here will come and teach you how to play the piano at home. What d'you say to that?'

Lily smiled at Stephen. 'That would be fun,' she said. 'I'd like that.'

In the months of Lily's pregnancy she slid from resignation to pleasure at the thought of her baby. Her body's changes brought with them a natural weariness but also a new serenity. Stephen no longer reached for her in the night, she was free of his desires. He set up a bank account for her and paid a regular allowance into it. Lily could shop where she wished and she always had the pleasing chink of coins in her purse. She felt well, her fit young body adapting easily to the growth of the baby. Lily found that she was looking forward to the birth, looking forward to having someone to love. The grief, the steady constant grief for her mother which she carried with her always like a shadow, melted and reshaped. She would love her child as her mother had loved her and in that relationship her mother would somehow live again.

The house re-asserted the old rhythms of the days. Breakfast was once more served at eight and Lily was expected to be downstairs and dressed to pour Stephen's tea and to hand him his hat in the hall as he went off to work. Very often, after he had left, Lily would slide upstairs again and climb back into bed. She had joined the Portsmouth library and she had a steady supply of very trashy novels which she read avidly throughout the day. One of Muriel's rules was never resting *under* the bed covers during daylight hours, though a lady could lie down *on* her bed during the day if she were ill. Another of the rules was never reading a novel before midday. Lily, unaware, broke one rule after another. Muriel tightened her lips and said nothing.

When Browning brought her a cup of coffee at about eleven, Lily would go downstairs and sit with Rory Winters until lunchtime. Muriel, writing letters in the drawing room, could hear Lily's bright inconsequential voice going on and on, and Rory's occasional abrupt grunts of replies. She could never think what Lily could find to talk about. Once she had listened at the door and heard Lily wander from weather, to holidays, to Europe, to French fashions, to food, to Cook, to domestic service, to nursing, to votes for women, before Muriel gave up eavesdropping and tiptoed away from the door, no wiser as to why Lily should enjoy talking to Rory, nor why Rory's face should light up when Lily came into a room. Rory and Lily had an unlikely rapport. Muriel could not put her finger on it; but she disliked and mistrusted it.

The two women would lunch together in the dining room at one and then some afternoons Lily would take Rory out for a walk, or she would go shopping, or she would accompany Muriel on her social calls. Three times a week, Charlie would come for Lily's lesson, and he and Lily would sit companionably side by side before the vulgar white baby grand piano which Stephen had bought his bride, and they would play together. Sometimes Charlie would play for Lily to sing and the house would be filled with the haunting sweet sound of Lily's voice.

Charlie played ragtime but he was true to his promise to teach Lily classical music. He taught her Schubert, easy pieces of Mozart, English and Irish folksongs. With an eye to Muriel's silent disapproval, he taught her parlour music, the Victorian music that Muriel's friends would enjoy hearing. Lily, breathing easily from her belly as her pregnancy progressed, found a new power and sweetness to her voice. Even Browning and the tweeny used to pause on the stairs to listen and the clear sweet music percolated upstairs to melt the silence in the room where Muriel sat with Rory.

Muriel disliked Charlie at first because she was unsure of his social status. 'How is one *supposed* to behave?' she demanded of Jane Dent on the telephone. 'He is a piano teacher, which makes him a sort of tradesman, but he is Lily's friend, which makes him drawing room, and he is Stephen's acquaintance, which makes him a gentleman!'

'What is he like?' Jane demanded.

'I don't know,' Muriel confessed. 'I haven't spoken except to say good afternoon.'

'Well, speak to him then,' Jane said simply. 'This *is* the 1920s. No-one seems to care about gentlemen at all any more.'

'Because there are so few left,' Muriel said bitterly. But she took Jane's advice and within a few days was able to report back that at least Charlie had been commissioned during the war, that he spoke with no trace of an accent and seemed to know how to behave. Stephen at any rate was perfectly happy that he should come three times a week to teach Lily to play the piano and sing, and though there was a good deal of chatter and the lessons lasted from early afternoon until the evening when Charlie had to go to work, Muriel was certain there was no hint of impropriety, even though both the man and her daughter-in-law were stage people. Lily's condition must be chaperone enough, and also there was a warmth and a comfort between Lily and Charlie that was nothing like flirtation but more like a deep fraternal affection.

When Muriel mentioned lightly to Stephen that Charlie was coming to tea even on the days when a piano lesson had not been booked, Stephen smiled and patted her hand. 'If it keeps Lily out of that damned theatre we have to be glad,' he said. 'And he's a good chap. He knows how to keep the line. He's got a string of girls of his own, he's just keeping Lily company.' Besides, Stephen thought but did not say aloud, why should any man be interested in the rapidly fattening Lily when he could have his pick of the chorus girls of Portsmouth, and a choice of many society girls too?

During the season of classical plays at the Kings Charlie used his freedom from the theatre to play solo twice a night in a new nightclub, the Trocadero, off Palmerston Road. Marjorie Philmore, Sarah Dent, Constance, Alma, Violet, Diana, a whole crowd of young, single girls, thought him quite divine. Stephen, dropping into the club late one night, was very glad to be called over to Charlie's table to join half a dozen girls and Charlie, lazily smiling, in their midst.

'I say, old boy, you do spoil yourself,' Stephen said in an undertone.

Charlie waved a drunken hand. 'Les Girls,' he said idly. 'All these women hanging around me, and I can't do a damn thing.'

'Drink?' Stephen said understandingly.

'Don't mind if I do,' Charlie replied equably. He was drunk but not so drunk that he could not see the play Marjorie made for Stephen and Stephen's responsiveness.

'Your husband's a bit of a lad,' he said the next day to Lily at tea time. 'Marjorie again.'

Lily was respectably engaged in sewing a nightdress for the baby. 'Doesn't worry me,' she said, biting off a thread.

'Haven't you got any scissors? It sets my teeth on edge when you do that!'

'They're around somewhere,' Lily said idly. 'You're probably sitting on them.'

Charlie exclaimed and cautiously felt in the sofa cushions. He came up with Lily's small embroidery scissors. 'You are a useless girl,' he said. 'You could have mortally injured me.'

'A small loss,' Lily said cheerfully, tossing aside the nightshirt, and pouring them both a cup of tea. 'So where do these assignations take place?'

'At the Troc,' Charlie said. 'It's nothing too serious yet, Lily, but she's a lady, not a chorus girl.'

Lily passed him a cup with a steady hand. 'So?' she said easily. 'I won't break my heart over it. Anyway, what's a man to do?'

Charlie gave her a sharp unsympathetic look. 'Are you suggesting that Stephen's appetites are so irresistible that if you are not available he has to be permitted to make love elsewhere?'

Lily took a large bite of chocolate cake and nodded with her mouth full.

'Bloody slavish, you are,' Charlie said irritably.

Lily shook her head and swallowed. 'Indifferent,' she said shortly.

Charlie sighed. 'I won't queer his pitch then,' he said. 'I thought perhaps you wanted him home.'

Lily shook her fair head. 'Not really.'

Charlie nodded. 'Does having the baby make no difference?' He was thinking of how he would have prized Lily if she were his pregnant wife.

'It makes a difference to me,' Lily said. She was smiling a small inward smile. 'At last I've got something to love. I can't tell you what it's like – knowing that there's a baby growing and growing and getting ready to be born. I think I can feel it moving sometimes, just a little. I lie awake at night and whisper to it. It doesn't really matter about Stephen and me. The baby is much more important.'

Charlie nodded.

'And Stephen will never be better, I don't think,' she said. 'There's a part of him which was made sick in the war and it will always be there. He'll never forget it. It waits for him in dreams or in sudden smells or moonlit nights.' She laughed shortly. 'And of course, the war was the time when he was most happy.'

'Happy?' Charlie exclaimed. He was remembering the terror that had gripped him. The way the ground itself had shaken under the gunfire. How horrible the trees had seemed with their bark hanging in strips and the boughs clawing with broken fingers at dark skies. He could not imagine what it would be to endure that desolate landscape year after year as Stephen had done. 'You must have got it wrong, Lil, he can't have been happy.'

'In a way he was. He wasn't the second-rate son like at home. He was a first-rate officer. He knew where he belonged and what he had to do. Coventry, his batman, was always beside him and they trusted each other. They would have died for each other. There were no women to bother him, there was no boring work, there were no money problems, or demanding parents, or being a gentleman in Portsmouth. There was just the line of the trench, and his men.

'And he had time off. There was a farm where he used

to go and work. There was an old farmer there and his wife and a couple of daughters. He said it was like a little haven, just behind the lines but in a fold of ground so it had never been shelled. A sanctuary. He and Coventry used to go there and help plough and harvest.'

'What happened to the farm?'

Lily shrugged. 'I don't know. Shelled, I suppose. What happened to everything over there in the end?'

They were quiet for a few moments. 'He could see a doctor,' Charlie suggested. 'There are an awful lot of good men dealing with neurasthenia. He could get some help with his nightmares.'

Lily put down her cup and smiled. 'Not Stephen!' she said. 'He employs a chauffeur so shellshocked that he cannot speak and he still says there is no such thing! He deals with it in his own way. He thought I would solve it for him but I can't, I don't know how to.' She shrugged. 'I'd be sorry for him if he wasn't my husband.'

'But they are kind to you here?' Charlie pressed. 'He doesn't hurt you? Your mother-in-law is reasonable?'

'We are *so* polite,' Lily said. 'You don't need love in a house which is as polite as this. We never know what we are all thinking, we never know what we care about. We are so polite that there is no room for anything else.'

Charlie put his hand over hers. 'Oh, Lily,' he said sorrowfully.

She put her other hand on top, holding him, and she looked into his face. 'I'm not lonely now,' she said quietly. 'I thought I would die here when I was first married. My mother gone and the house so silent. But now I've got the baby I don't mind so much. The baby and me – we can live here, we can make our own place here. It doesn't matter that everyone else is silent. We'll have each other.'

Charlie's face was full of pain. 'I wish it were different for you,' he said softly. 'I love you so much, Lily.'

Lily bent her head and took her hand away. He thought he heard her whisper 'I love you too' but it was so faint he might have imagined it. Then Browning came in to clear the tea things and he played for Lily to sing until six o'clock, when Stephen came home and poured them both cocktails before Charlie left to change for the club.

Stephen's driving lessons for Lily had stopped as soon as the weather turned cold in September and they no longer went out into the Hampshire countryside on Sunday afternoons. But Lily had asked if Coventry might teach her and Stephen had agreed. So on the afternoons when Charlie did not come, or in the morning if Coventry was free, Lily would put on her special learner-driver costume, a severely cut blue suit with a little blue felt hat.

Coventry, holding the passenger door open for her, could not wipe the smile off his face before Lily saw it.

'Shut your face,' she said equably. 'I want to look serious.'

Coventry bowed, closed the door, went around to the driver's side and got in himself. Ignoring the drives she had taken with Stephen, Coventry had decided that Lily should be taught from scratch. To Lily's silent seething frustration, Coventry began at the beginning. He made a great pantomime of showing her the retard spark lever and indicating where it should be before she started the engine. He showed her the black ebony start switch, and how to select the gear, and then, gently pressing the accelerator, he eased in the clutch. She could hardly wait until they reached a wide and deserted stretch of the seafront road with a wind whipping in over the mudflats, where Coventry pulled the car over to the side, switched off the engine and changed places with her.

Lily set her hat a little tighter on her head and glowered over the top of the steering wheel at the seagulls riding the autumn winds over the water in the estuary and then gliding down to the mudbanks. The split in the windscreen which enabled the driver to open the top half came directly across her line of sight. Coventry, with a little smile, took off his jacket and indicated to Lily that she should sit on it so that she was higher on the seat. He took her hand gently and unclasped it so that she held the wheel lightly. Then he pointed to the starter switch and nodded.

Lily started the car. Coventry nodded towards the clutch and the accelerator. Lily put her foot on the clutch, revved the engine. She suddenly lifted her left foot from the clutch. The tortured Argyll leaped forward like a released tiger, throwing both of them back in their seats. Lily screamed, the car stalled and stopped.

There was a little silence. Lily looked at Coventry; he was smiling slightly and seemed quite unshaken. He nodded at the starter again. Four times Lily let the car leap forward, each time Coventry let her start again, gesturing with his hand that her foot should come up slowly and steadily. On the fourth try the car moved forward and Lily gave a yell of delight. Coventry let her move a yard down the road, then he gestured to her to stop the car again.

Even though Lily grew mutinous and impatient, he made her stop and start ten times until he was satisfied that she had learned the co-ordination of the movements.

'*Now* can we drive?' Lily demanded.

Coventry shook his head. He pointed to the wing mirror mounted on the driver's side. Lily glanced into it quickly. 'The road's clear,' she said. 'Can I go now?'

Coventry tapped it, indicating that she should keep watching, and then got out and stood behind the car. Lily watched him in the mirror. Slowly Coventry moved from the centre of the road to walk behind the car until its broad back hid him completely. Lily watched the mirror;

he was walking steadily towards her and still she did not see him. When he emerged and was visible in the mirror, he was perilously close. She nodded at him. 'I see,' she said. 'I see what you're saying. You could have been a great big fire engine galloping down the road directly behind me, and I wouldn't have seen you until wallop!'

Coventry nodded emphatically.

'So can I drive *now*?' Lily demanded.

Coventry got back into the car and made a generous expansive gesture with his hand, indicating that he had taught her all she would ever need to know.

Lily started the car, checked the wing mirror, checked over her shoulder, and then moved smoothly forward. Coventry smiled with the quiet satisfaction of a job well done.

Subsequent lessons showed Lily to be a quick learner and Coventry to be a meticulous and critical teacher. He brought a long skewer from the kitchen and he leaned across and tapped the mirror every minute or so to remind Lily to keep checking behind her. She learned how to change gear smoothly in one lesson when he made her drive up and down the deserted autumn coast road, changing up and then down again, up and then down again. It was a four-geared car. Coventry did not attempt to explain the principles of gears, but he would tweak Lily's earlobe to make her listen when the engine noise grew shrill and tortured and it was time for her to change gear.

They nearly came to blows over parking the car. Coventry made her reverse and park at the nearside kerb and then reverse and park on the offside too. Then he took her home and built an obstacle course for her with the dustbins in the back yard and made her reverse and park all around them until she could put the Argyll into the tightest of places.

While Lily grew more and more impatient, Coventry

moved the dustbins around and set her more and more difficult tasks until she had an instinctive awareness of the length and width of the big car. Coventry remained utterly calm and pleasant throughout, despite Lily's rising irritation. But when she misjudged the gatepost and scraped the wing, Lily was aghast. She turned to him like a naughty child caught in some misdemeanour.

'Oh, Coventry, will it have to go to the garage to be repaired?'

He shook his head.

'Stephen will be furious.'

Coventry said nothing.

'I don't think he was wildly keen about me learning to drive. If he thinks I'm going to damage the car he'll never let me have another go.'

Coventry shook his head and mimed a polishing hand.

'You can paint it and polish it so it doesn't show?'

Coventry nodded, smiling.

Lily leaned forward and put her hands on his shoulders and gave him a smacker of a kiss. 'You're an *angel*, Coventry,' she said. 'A proper angel. And thank you for teaching me to drive.'

The man flushed red, he shook his head at her.

'Sweetie,' Lily said. 'Now I must go in. Will you be able to hide the scratch before you fetch Stephen this evening?'

Coventry nodded.

'And you won't tell him?'

Coventry shook his head.

Lily beamed at him. 'You're a real sweetie,' she said. 'A double sweetie.'

Coventry watched her run in at the back door and smiled after her as the door shut.

Stephen had a bed made up in his little dressing room in November, the fourth month of Lily's pregnancy. He said that there was not room for him as well as Lily's growing belly in their bed. Muriel tightened her lips but said nothing. It meant that Stephen was free to come and go as a bachelor. Lily was tired by her pregnancy and never waited up for him. She was always asleep whether he came home at eleven after a show and a dinner, or whether he came home at five in the morning when the milk horse and cart were clopping quietly along The Parade.

Muriel, lying wakeful, would hear the quiet purr of the Argyll as it slipped up the drive at the back of the house and parked. She would hear the two doors slam. Sometimes Stephen and Coventry went to the kitchen together. Cook complained that they had expanded their activities. She now found dirty plates and cutlery as well as stewed tea in the pot and mugs and cigarette ends in the range. When Stephen and Coventry came in at dawn they made cheese on toast and drank a tot of rum with their teas.

'You were very late last night, dear,' Muriel said, driven beyond discretion one morning. Stephen smiled at her over the top of his newspaper. His face was pale and there were dark shadows under his eyes.

'I'm a dreadful dog,' he said frankly. 'I'm in terror of my wife.'

Lily was wearing a white dressing-gown to breakfast, an innovation which Muriel regarded with horror as being un-English and morally unsound. Lily smiled lazily over her tea cup. 'Did you have fun?' she asked.

'I was at the Troc with Charlie,' Stephen said. 'There's a new band, a nigger band. They're quite something. Charlie was sitting in with them and playing jazz. All the girls were practically lying down on the dance floor.'

'American?' Lily asked.

'Nig-wigs anyway. Yes, I think Charlie said they were Yank nig-wigs. They certainly liked Charlie. They would have played all night, I think. David Sweeting had to practically throw them out at the end of the evening.'

'They're going to London, Charlie told me,' Lily said.

'That's right, I remember now, they asked him to go with them.' Stephen nodded. 'Their pianist is sick. We were laughing about whether Charlie would have to black up. They've been hired as a nigger band. They can't have a white man in the middle.'

Lily made an impatient little gesture. 'But he's not going?'

'I think he said he would, actually,' Stephen said vaguely. 'Go with them to London and then a few other places, Europe, I think. Maybe he'll commandeer a trip back to New York with them!'

Lily had gone a little pale, Muriel noticed. 'He has never agreed to go with them?' she demanded.

Stephen folded his paper and glanced at the clock. 'Yes, I think he did,' he said. 'I'll be home early this afternoon, Lily. I'll take you out for a spin if you like. See how you've mastered the driving game. About four?'

He rose from his seat and nodded goodbye to his mother. Lily followed him out into the hall and watched while Browning handed him his hat, his coat and his scarf, and then offered him his umbrella. 'No, it should be fine,' he said decidedly. 'Grand weather for the time of year.'

He suddenly noticed Lily's pallor. 'Are you all right, Lily?' he asked. 'Not squiffy or anything, are you?'

Lily shook her head. 'I'm fine,' she said. 'Fine. Hurry along, you'll be late.' She almost pushed him out of the front door and then when he had gone down the steps and Browning had gone back down to the kitchen, she stood alone and silent in the hall.

Muriel in the dining room made no sound. She sat with her tea cup still in her hand, waiting and listening. She heard the click of the telephone being picked up, she heard

363

Lily's low voice say to the operator: 'Would you get me Portsmouth 214?' Then she heard Lily's hushed moan of anxiety as the phone rang and rang at the other end.

Muriel put her tea cup down on the saucer with microscopic attention. She twisted her napkin in both hands and held it tight.

'Charlie?' Lily said in a soft voice in the hall. 'Oh! I'm so glad you're there!'

There was a momentary pause as he spoke at the other end. 'No, I'm fine. No, I'm well. It's you – I heard you were going. I heard from Stephen that you'd been offered a place in the American band . . .'

Muriel's face muscles were locked rigid. There was a tone in Lily's voice she had only heard before when Lily was talking of her childhood and her mother. It was a warmth, a trustfulness. Muriel thought that the hall of her house had never heard that tone before. It was a tone of confident love. No-one in Muriel's house ever spoke like that.

'And do you want to go?' Lily asked.

There was a pause.

'I do ask,' Lily said hesitantly. 'I am sorry, Charlie. I know I shouldn't. But I *do* ask you not to go.'

There was a silence as Lily listened to Charlie's answer. Muriel found herself perversely wishing against her own interests, that Charlie would obey Lily. That Lily's heart should be given to a man who cared for her. Who cared enough to sacrifice an exciting career for her. Who would stay with her, even if he only saw her four times a week for tea, and that in her mother-in-law's house.

'Thank you,' Lily said in a small voice. 'Oh my darling, thank you.'

Muriel found she had been holding her breath and took a deep sigh.

'I'm very glad,' Lily said softly in the hall. 'I'm sure I'm a selfish pig but . . . oh Charlie . . . I can't be without you. Not now, with the baby coming. I can't live here without you at least sometimes . . .'

Muriel put her hands over her face, but she did not block her ears.

But Lily said no more. She whispered, 'Goodbye,' and then, 'Yes, yes, goodbye.' Then there was the quiet click of the telephone being replaced.

Muriel heard Lily humming as she went up the stairs. It was a Victorian lovesong Charlie had taught her last week:

> And if she cannot come to me
> then I shall wait for ever more.
> For if she cannot come to me
> then I shall wait for ever more.

Muriel rested her face in her hands and found she was weeping.

Chapter Twenty-four

That night at the Trocadero Club the black jazz band played better than ever. Charlie hunched over the keyboard, laughing with pleasure as he tried to follow them, 'jamming'. When they went to a bar for their break, the sweat was pouring off his face. 'God! You've got some nerve!' he said, nodding to the barman for a pint of beer. 'I didn't have the faintest idea what you were doing! I was just following along. Something like two bars behind all the time!'

They laughed and the trumpeter did a hunch-backed mime of Charlie trying to keep up, but always lagging two bars behind, when the door opened and Marjorie Philmore fell into the club. Her dress was ripped and she had a raw graze on her shoulder. Her hair was rumpled and there was a red mark which was turning blue on the side of her cheek.

'Christ, Charlie,' she said. 'Thank God you're here. Can you take me somewhere to clean up? I can't go home like this.'

Her voice was loud, edgy. Charlie threw a quick glance around the club. Everyone within earshot was staring. He gave an apologetic shrug at the band. 'Catch you later,' he said. 'It seems I have to be a white knight.'

'A what?' the trumpeter asked.

'I'll be back in an hour,' Charlie said. He spoke quickly to the barman and borrowed the manager's car which was parked at the back of the club. He slid his dinner suit jacket over Marjorie's shoulders to hide the damage to her dress and the long graze on her shoulder and arm, and he took her firmly by the elbow and led her out of the club.

She was drunk; she walked hesitantly and stumbled once or twice. When the night air hit her she steadied a little and gave a short sob which ended in a hiccough. 'Christ,' she said again.

Charlie pushed her gently into the passenger seat of the car. It was an old Ford and he had to crank-start it. When the engine was running he got behind the wheel. Marjorie was leaning forward, against the dashboard, her eyes shut.

'Who hurt you?' Charlie asked grimly.

She shrugged. 'What does it matter? He won't do it again.'

'You want me to clean you up, you tell me what I want to know,' Charlie said reasonably. 'Who was it?'

Marjorie dropped back in the seat and yawned in his face. 'Stephen Winters,' she said bitterly. 'The bloody war hero.'

Charlie's face was set. 'Why?'

'Because he caught me with one of the band,' she said wearily. 'He's a bit of a prude is our Stephen. He went barmy, frankly. He called me a whore and God knows what else and then he slapped me and when I tried to get away he pushed me against the wall.' Her hand crept inside the jacket to touch the sore graze. 'Not quite the gent we all thought,' she said.

'D'you want to charge him?' Charlie asked levelly. 'Assault? Grievous bodily harm? Shall I take you to the police?'

Marjorie laughed shrilly. 'And tell them I was spooning with a nigger in the alley, and that my married lover caught me and slapped me around? No thanks, Charlie-boy. Just take me to your place and let me have a wash and powder my little nose and then I'll take a taxi home. Chances are, Ma won't even see me.'

Charlie let the clutch in and the little car went forward. 'Stephen's your lover, is he?' he asked.

'Not any more,' Marjorie said. She rested her head on the back of the seat and closed her eyes. 'I'm not that kind of a fool.'

'How long has it been going on?'

Marjorie shrugged and then winced at the hurt on her shoulder. 'Oh, a couple of months. His wife's pregnant – but of course you'd know. You're round there almost every day, aren't you?'

'I teach her the piano, I'm her accompanist,' Charlie said.

'I bet.'

There was a little silence.

'He's a bit free with his fists, isn't he?' Charlie asked, keeping his voice carefully neutral.

Marjorie shrugged. 'He's one of those who hate women at the same time as having them, darling. You know the sort. He calls us all whores but can't keep his hands to himself.'

Charlie turned the car right down his road. 'Is he all right?' he asked. 'I mean, in his head.'

Marjorie smiled. 'Well, he has nightmares and screams about the trenches. If he smells Devon violets perfume he gets down on the floor and covers his mouth with his hands. That's what the gas used to smell of, they say. He dreams about a raid he made on a farmhouse where some women and a baby were found dead. And he cries in his sleep and says the name Juliette. He hates his job, he hates his parents, and he loves and hates his wife.' Marjorie laughed her sexy low laugh. 'In a word – right as rain. You find me a man with the right number of arms and legs and adjacent parts who doesn't cry in his sleep and I'll marry him tomorrow, darling. They're all crazy as coots, or missing essential bits as far as I can see.'

'He hit his wife once,' Charlie said, stopping the car outside his flat.

'So would I,' Marjorie said unkindly. 'Po-faced bitch.'

'I mean, he's violent,' Charlie said. 'D'you think he's dangerous?'

Marjorie opened her wide beautiful grey eyes. 'No more than anyone else,' she said certainly. 'He's quick-tempered and he's spiteful. He's half-mad from the war and he drinks too much. But he's no more dangerous than you or me. We're the jazz age, remember? We're bright young things! We're the mad young things of the twenties! What d'you expect him to be? A vicar?'

'Christ knows what I expect,' Charlie said sharply. 'Whatever it is I expect – I certainly never get it.' He got out of the car and led her to his front door. 'I'll leave you here then,' he said. 'I should get back. Are you sure you can manage?'

Marjorie looked at him sideways, with a little smile. 'Won't you come in and kiss it better?' she asked.

Charlie kissed her cheek and then turned her around and gave her a little push. 'I think you've had enough kissing for one night,' he said.

She paused on the doorway. 'So what is it with you?' she asked. 'Don't you like girls? Is it what the chorus girls say about you – that you go down to the dockyard on a Saturday night for the little apprentices and the midshipmen?'

Charlie's banked-down anger never showed. 'Friday night,' he said easily. 'I always go down on a Friday night. And it's a handsome stoker for me! Leave the key under the mat when you leave. There's a number for a hackney cab by the telephone.'

Marjorie nodded. 'Well, thanks anyway,' she threw over her shoulder and slammed the door.

Charlie walked slowly back to the car, started it and

drove back to the club. 'The jazz age,' he said as he parked and walked under the winking sign which said 'Trocadero'. 'Bright young things. Christ help us.'

Stephen's workload increased noticeably after Christmas. He called in to John Pascoe's office one Friday afternoon in early January to see what the senior partner thought about them taking on another lawyer into the practice.

'I'd been sure that the war divorces would drop off,' Stephen said as the clerk brought them tea, handling the tray awkwardly with one hand. Stephen did not help the man. He watched him carefully as he put the tray down on a small table and then pushed it into the centre. The pinned-up sleeve flapped like the wing of a broken bird. 'But the marriages seem to be as bad as ever. You'd have thought people would have settled down by now.'

'And wardships and trusteeships,' John Pascoe agreed. 'I'm still getting a number of cases of ex-servicemen having to go into hospitals with nerve damage. It really drags on and on. You can sympathize with the distress of the family when the man of the house suddenly finds he can't cope three years after the whole thing ended.'

Stephen nodded. 'I think in most cases you'll find it is men who weren't suited to the war in the first place,' he said. 'That was the problem with conscription. It dragged in people who should never have been there. Even I th ... th ... th ...' He found he had lost the ability to finish the sentence.

John Pascoe waited. Stephen waved the end of the sentence away. 'Any instability and the war would bring it out,' Stephen said instead. 'But it certainly keeps us busy.'

'Where would we get another partner?' John asked.

Stephen said nothing. They were both thinking of Jim Pascoe, who had run into a cloud of British gas on that clear bright morning and never come back to claim the desk that had been waiting for him.

'We've never advertised,' John said dismally.

'Well, we could use another man at least for half the week.'

'D'you have anyone in mind, Stephen?'

'There was a chap I knew at Oxford, he read law and said he was going into the profession. I could drop him a line, I don't know what he's doing these days. I know he survived, he got himself attached to general staff very early on. His family live in the New Forest.'

John Pascoe nodded. 'Your father will never be well enough to come back?'

Stephen shrugged and spread his hands.

'I see they're making a start on the war memorial on the common,' John said, as if it were somehow relevant.

'Jim will be on it. And Christopher.'

'We'll never know the full cost,' John said. 'My son, your brother. But your father as well, and the plans we had. The way this practice was to run. The way the country was going to be. It's all changed, Stephen, without anyone deciding to change it. It's as if, when the boys were away at war, the country changed behind their backs and we can't get it right again.'

Stephen had gone a little pale. 'Ch . . . chaps used to say they felt like ghosts – when they c . . . came home on leave. P . . . place was still the same but they had no part of it. G . . . girls all different, m . . . most of them working. W . . . windows blacked out. No f . . . fruit in the sh . . . sh . . . shops. And no . . . no . . . no . . .' He took a deep breath. 'Nobody understood.'

John Pascoe was listening with painful intensity, trying to hear the voice of his lost son through Stephen's halting speech. 'Understood? Understood what?'

'Wh . . . wh . . . what it was *like*!'

'In the trenches?'

Stephen nodded.

'What was it like?' John Pascoe whispered. 'I want to understand, Stephen. What was it like?'

Stephen shot him a small sideways smile, almost sly. But his brown eyes were glittery with tears. 'I can't say,' he said in a low voice. 'Th . . . th . . . th . . . that's my w . . . w . . . war wound, if you like. I can't say.'

'Because if you *said*, if you told me, you would not be able to bear it?'

Stephen was holding tight to the arms of his chair. His knuckles gleamed white. John Pascoe could see the blue veins bulging on the back of his head and the rising flush in Stephen's face.

'Stephen, we were talking about men cracking up even now,' John Pascoe said very softly. 'Are you sure you are quite well?'

Stephen's head was bent low. John thought irresistibly of a photograph he had seen of a wagon horse bogged down on the Menin Road, where the shell-craters were so deep that they went ten, twenty feet down. The horse was foundering, up to its chest in mud, its back legs kicking deep into slurry, its neck straining against the collar and the gun carriage sinking behind it dragging it down. Stephen's neck was strained forwards in the same way, his neck muscles knotted in a hopeless struggle.

'Are you sick, Stephen? Sick from the war?'

Stephen looked forward under his fair eyebrows. His broad handsome face was contorted with a scowl. He was choking on words that he could not say. John Pascoe knew he had neither the skill nor the courage to summon the words from Stephen so that he need drag the weight of his horrific memories no more.

'Shouldn't you see a doctor, old man? Get some help?'

Stephen's head moved slowly from side to side.

'But how can you bear this?'

Stephen reared up in the chair and John saw him iron the pain from his face. First he unknotted his forehead and settled his eyebrows. He relaxed his cheeks and drew his mouth away from its painful grimace. He forced his shoulders back out of their hunched strain and straightened his back. Only his eyes could not deny the truth. In their blankness John Pascoe saw what he had only feared before, that the war had damaged Stephen Winters more deeply than anyone could have imagined. Stephen's eyes were cold and blank as if they had seen such horrors that they would never look directly at anything again.

'It's not so bad,' he said. 'It's all right if I don't think about it. If I could never think about it at all, I'd be fine.'

The two men sat in silence for a little while. 'Is Lily a help?' John asked softly.

Stephen shook his head. 'Not much.'

'Your parents? Friends?'

Stephen cleared his throat. 'It's not important,' he said distantly. 'Nothing to bother about. A few dreams, a bit of a reaction sometimes. All the chaps have it. We can't *all* be mad!' He said it for a joke but his voice quavered and it sounded more like a defiant hope. 'We can't *all* be mad!' he said again.

That night Stephen had a dream. He dreamed he was back in St Omer, where they used to be sent for short leaves. The men were posted in small farms around the town but the officers stayed in the town itself. There was a club there, and a good little café with chairs and tables outside. In his dream St Omer was as he had first seen it in March of 1917, a grey town of quiet walled houses, a central square and an imposing town hall. Around the square ran blocks of shops: a fruit shop with a richness of goods spread out on the pavement in the early morning sunlight, a woman washing down the steps of her shop before opening, iron gated doorways, cafés steaming with the heat of coffee and fresh bread and croissants, their windows all misty with the warmth inside. It was a cold bright March with hard sunny days.

Later the houses would be picked off like rotten teeth leaving ugly gaps in a familiar smile. Every building of any size would become a hospital or a headquarters building, or a whorehouse. There would be no more fruit and vegetables as everything that could grow was requisitioned for the monster armies which were leaching the goodness from France, from Belgium, from Austria and Germany. There would be no croissants, there would be no coffee. Shopkeepers would not take their own currency, they preferred gold. And there was a ceaseless secretive trade in dreadful things: snub-nosed dum-dum bullets – a collector's item because of their dreadful power to tear open flesh, and because they were illegal but used by both sides; German helmets, especially the old-fashioned type with the spike; Brussels lace embroidered with German names; an Iron Cross cut from a dying man's chest; and, worst of all, blackened fingers, or dried-out ears looking like decayed apricots.

The land around St Omer made Stephen think of Cambridgeshire, wide and naked under a huge arching sky. There was nowhere at all to hide. The land undulated gently, there were no hills, no cover. There were only a few trees, willows, with hair like ill-kempt women, lining drainage ditches and little canals. The road running north and west to the Front sometimes arched over a mud-filled river which had long ceased to flow since the canals and drainage ditches had been shelled into bog. It was wet land, the earth sodden with the water table only inches below the surface.

In his dream Stephen remembered suddenly compre-

hending why the trenches had been built in the first place
– something he had never understood, folding the newspaper in a fury at home. But once he was there, once he
was under that wide exposed sky, he saw immediately that
a soldier, even an unwilling new soldier like himself, would
need no orders to take a spade and dig a hole. There was
no other chance of escaping shots or bombs. There was
nowhere to hide, there was no shelter. No-one could have
withstood the temptation to dig themselves a little hole to
get their vulnerable body off the open ground. A man
would have become serpent and wormed his way into the
earth rather than stand on that open wide blowy plain.

'It's cavalry country,' MacDonald said cheerfully in his
dream. 'Can't wait for the cavalry to come galloping
through, can you, Winters?'

But as Stephen turned to reply he saw MacDonald's
head fly from his body and felt himself thrown from his
feet and coated with warm wetness which he hoped was
mud but knew that it was not.

Stephen rolled in his bed, flinging out an arm in protest,
but he could not throw off the dream.

Now he was in a trench. It was in an awful state. His
men had just been ordered into it and Stephen was in a
rage with the regiment that had left it. The firesteps were
exposed, the duckboards had sunk deep into the mud. The
men had to wade knee-deep to get from one point to
another, there were no adequate dug-outs and they would
have to sleep on little shelves scraped out of the side of
the trench, with no protection from weather or shellfire.
Worst of all, the Huns opposite had the range and location
of all the sniper posts and lobbed occasional, totally accu-
rate, shells.

To order any man to keep watch and to put his head
up to fire a rifle was to condemn him to death – and yet
an officer must order sentries posted. All Stephen wanted

375

to know was the name of the commanding officer who had left the trench in this state. The only man he hated in the whole world was the commanding officer of the previous regiment. He cared nothing for the Germans, he cared nothing for the hard-faced men at home. But the man he wanted dead was back at St Omer on leave. One after another his men were shot or torn to pieces by shells and Stephen strode up and down the trench, his anger transporting him beyond fear, screaming the name of the officer who had left him to do all the work.

He shouted aloud 'Johnson!' and the shout shook him from his dream. Half-awake, he remembered the dream and the day it drew on. The trench had been perilous, the regiment before him had been slack and demoralized. Stephen and his men worked all day digging the trench deeper, widening the sides, laying duckboards. Then at night, when they were weary and wet through and cold and afraid, they had to climb out of the trench, which seemed suddenly desirable and friendly. They had to leave it, their only shelter, and go over the top into no-man's-land on scouting trips for headquarters. Stephen grimaced as he rolled over and dozed, remembering the terror of putting his head slowly, slowly above the parapet, and then easing inch by inch upwards. As each part of his body emerged from the shelter of the trench he imagined a German sniper sighting first on his head, then on his pale frightened face ('Oh please, don't shoot my eyes, don't shoot my eyes!'), then on his throat ('Oh God! Not a bullet in my throat!'), then his chest ('Not my chest!'), then his quivering belly ('Please God, don't let them shoot me in the stomach!'), then his pelvis (an unspeakable prayer this one, Stephen could not even pray for his penis, his horror of castration was too urgent for words), then his legs (a nice clean flesh wound in the thigh, or the foot – 'Yes! yes! yes!'). Stephen grunted with longing and slid back into sleep. A Blighty wound to take him safely home and away from this unending miserable horror.

His final dream was the one that roused him. It started sweetly with the farm, the little farm, and old Perot in his blues, and old Mrs Perot with an enamel basin under her arm feeding the hens. They had two daughters: Nicole, the bad girl who went into St Omer at night and worked in a bar and whored on the side; and Juliette – Juliette, like an English girl, with a pale rose complexion like apple blossom, and pale green eyes like apple skins, and pale long hair like wheat straw.

And the farm was such a miracle. Sheltered by a hill, such a tiny precious hill, just east of St Omer. A tiny fold of ground but just enough to hide the building from the Hun gunners. And far enough behind British lines for them to be safe; safe and grateful. So when Stephen found his way to the farm on a borrowed horse, riding for the fun of it, Juliette came out with a mug of cider and a smile like an English girl in peacetime. He told Madame Perot that he called the farm 'Little England' and she laughed and nodded as if she understood.

It was fertile land. They kept sheep, a few cows, a pig which lived off scraps to be killed for bacon in autumn, and hens. But mostly they grew crops in fields that were broad and scantily fenced: beets and vegetables and clay-loving crops. Perot would curse the soil when he was ploughing and his one skinny horse pulled against the bogged-down weight of the plough. The army had requisitioned his team of plough-horses, even the old pony which Juliette used to ride. All they had left was the old mare who could barely shift the plough along. He was glad when Stephen came with Coventry, and the two men got before the plough and dragged it for him, like a pair of eager geldings. Stephen and Coventry were glad to do the work. It was like a holiday, like a holiday in the old days at home, when you might go and work on a farm for fun and come home and talk all about it, and josh and say you were a farmer's lad at heart.

Stephen smiled in his sleep. The farm – Little England – had a wood where the trees were still sound. The lower branches swept to the ground and grass and small flowers grew in the shade. When he lay back on the grass and looked through the intersecting branches at the sky above he could hear the ground shake with the impact of shells and he could hear the guns like thunder, but know he was far from danger. It was a lovely sound, distant gunfire. Gunfire far, far away, and someone else having to bear it. He loved the branches of the trees, those blessed low branches. Every tree on the Flanders plain within range had been twisted into a corkscrew by shells and fire; but Juliette's trees grew as if there was no war. Juliette would sometimes come and sit beside him and let him take down her hair and hold her hand. One afternoon Stephen fell asleep with his head in her lap and when he opened his eyes and saw her face he thought that the war was over and he was safely home asleep in an English orchard.

His dream shifted; Stephen, in his little bed in his dressing room, gave a muffled groan. His dream pulsed like a heartbeat, thudded like a drum beat. He saw Coventry's intense angry face and his own. He heard himself say – 'God damn them to hell! If they have harmed one hair of her head . . .' He felt the mad joy coming, the mad joy that meant he was unafraid, like being drunk, like being lustful. He pulled his revolver from the holster and secretly, in his other hand, Coventry slipped to him his knife. He was running, running down the road to Little England, running silently as if his boots were light. He was through the German lines, behind their lines in absolute peril as the German advance swept forwards to Paris and the Allies withdrew and then withdrew again.

Stephen did not care; alone of all the English army he was going forward, defying the logic of retreat. And behind him, five of his battalion ran too, from shadow into shade, ran down the road to Little England, already burning for vengeance for what they expected to see. They were losing the war, they knew it. There was nothing to do but to pull back to the coast and hope that the damned Navy did its job and got them off quick. But suddenly, in the middle of ignominious retreat, someone had told Stephen that Germans had gone through to Little England.

If Juliette were hurt, if she were dead – Stephen felt his heart beat quicker and his feet thudded faster on the mud road. His fear, his constant wartime terror was burned up by his rage. He wanted to rescue Juliette, he wanted her to be safe. But more than anything he wanted to kill the man who had harmed her. His breath was coming in gasps as they reached the bolted front door. No-one ever went in that way. He motioned his men to crouch down, to wait. Coldly and reasonably he told himself that when he had his breath, when his heart had stopped its hammering, he would be ready. And then the animals would be sorry they had crawled in here. Then he would cut them down in his righteous anger. And Juliette and her mother and father would be avenged. They were, in the end, the one thing worth fighting for. At last, after two years of war, Stephen could see why he was there. He was there to protect Juliette. He was there to protect her mother, her father, her sheltered lovely farm. And if he were too late to save her, then the man who had hurt her should die.

He gestured to the men to follow him around to the back door. The yard was wet with slurry and they made no noise. The yellow light spilled in bars from the shuttered kitchen window. Stephen paused at the door.

He heard a man's voice, speaking German, and he felt the heat suddenly rush through him in anger, and then he heard a woman laugh. At that sound, as he realized that Juliette and the Perots must be dead and the Germans in occupation with their whores, he kicked in the 'itchen door and stood with his revolver pointing into the room.

Stephen kicked at his bedclothes and then flung himself upright and awake at last, awash with hot sweat. 'Juliette!' he shouted.

'Wake up, wake up.' Lily was standing beside his little bed, shaking his shoulder.

Stephen clawed at her hands and then grabbed on to her. Lily pulled herself away. 'Wake up, Stephen. You are dreaming.'

'Oh God,' Stephen said. 'Oh God, Lily.'

She stepped away from his outreaching hands. 'You were dreaming,' she said severely. 'And screaming. You woke me up through two closed doors.'

Stephen wiped his face and neck with the sheet. 'Thank you,' he said awkwardly. 'I am sorry.' He looked at her hard irritated face. 'Oh God, Lily,' he said miserably. 'Dear God, it is an awful dream.'

Lily moved her hands helplessly. 'Well, it's over now,' she said. 'You're awake.'

'I dreamed I was there again,' Stephen said. 'There.'

He did not need to say where.

He got out of bed and pulled his dressing-gown on. 'I'm glad you woke me,' he said shakily. 'It's a dreadful dream.'

Lily nodded. 'I'm going back to bed,' she said. 'You shouldn't eat cheese after dinner. It's cheese that gives people bad dreams.'

'Cheese?'

Lily nodded. 'If you really want to stop dreaming you should stop eating cheese late at night,' she said.

Stephen gave a trembling laugh. 'You don't even begin to understand,' he said. 'You don't even glimpse what it was like.'

Lily looked at him with no trace of sympathy in her face. 'It was three years ago, whatever it was like. And I am tired. I'm going to bed.'

Stephen put a hand on her arm. 'Don't go,' he said. 'I don't want to sleep again. I'm going down to make myself a brew. I'll have a little brew of tea. Come down with me, Lily.' He saw the refusal in her face and changed his request. 'Or I'll bring you up a cup. I'll bring you up a nice cup of tea in bed. I don't want to be alone. I don't want to sleep again. I don't want to sleep alone.'

Lily looked at him coldly. 'You chose to sleep in here, you can stay here,' she said. 'It's three in the morning. I'm going to bed. I don't want tea in the middle of the night.'

'Lily . . .' he said.

Stephen's young wife turned her pale lovely face to him. Her fair hair gleamed in the moonlight filtering through the curtains, the curve of her belly, rounded with their child, showing clearly in silhouette. 'What?'

'Nothing.' He let her go to the door and then his loneliness called out to her again. 'Lily!'

She turned. 'What?'

'I want to buy a farm,' he said. He was wide awake now, his hair standing up around his head, his eyes alert. 'Lily, I don't want to live here any more, and I don't want to work in the office any more. Let's buy a place of our own in the country, you and me and the baby. Let's buy a lovely little farm in Sussex or Kent and go and live there, you and me. Wouldn't that be wonderful? Wouldn't you like it, Lily?'

She paused with her hand on the light switch. 'I think you're still dreaming,' she said coldly. 'Go to sleep, Stephen.'

She switched off the light and left him in darkness. Stephen put both arms over his head and held his ears and eyes so that he could neither see nor hear anything. 'We'll buy a farm,' he said into his pyjama sleeve. 'I can make it come right for me, I can make it right for us. We'll buy a farm and get away from here, from the office, from the Troc, from the house. We'll start again. I'll buy a farm and call it Little England.'

Chapter Twenty-five

As Lily grew large with her pregnancy in the first months of 1921 she found herself surprisingly frustrated by Muriel's management of the house. She wanted to nestbuild herself, she wanted to plan and decorate a nursery. For the first time in her life Lily was acutely aware of her surroundings. She wanted a place of her own, a place that she could use and furnish as she wished. She was tired of living in another woman's house. Her discontent focused on the nursery that would soon be needed. Even its location in the large empty house was a difficulty. Apparently the only place for the baby was the old nursery, Stephen's old room, a fine sunny room on the first floor overlooking the garden. But then the baby would be within earshot of Muriel and Rory while Lily and Stephen slept on the floor above.

An alternative was that Stephen should move back in with Lily, sharing her bed and her room again, and the baby should have Stephen's dressing room opposite their bedroom as a night nursery. Lily did not want that suggestion to be raised. She could offer no reason why Stephen should not share her bed, except the simple one which must remain unsaid: that she preferred to sleep alone. Stephen had not crossed the divide of the little landing to come to her bed in the long six months of her pregnancy. Lily thought that even when the baby was born, the creaking boards of the landing and her closed bedroom door might still offer obstacles to Stephen's unpredictable desires. She would rather anything than have him sleeping at her side, choking awake on nightmares and spitting imaginary blood from his mouth, or the sudden night-time rising of his lust.

Lily's solution was that Stephen should go back to his bachelor room – the old day nursery – and that she and the baby should live upstairs. This too could not be spoken. It would have exposed the alienation of Lily from Stephen too clearly. He and both his parents would then have been sleeping in the big rooms on the first floor, Lily and the baby above them in a separate suite of rooms. Only the servants slept higher, in the attics.

As with everything in number two, The Parade, the silence had a power of its own, and in that silence nothing that needed words, nor will, nor passion, could take place. The question of where the baby was to sleep was too provocative for speech, and they were accustomed to silences. But Lily longed to buy things – a cot, a white-painted dresser, a nursing chair, a baby bath. One sunny spring morning she asked Coventry to drive her to Palmerston Road.

He came into the department store with her, his cap in his hand, very quick to hold open doors and very quick with a hand under her arm. Lily was carrying the baby high under her ribs and she leaned back against the weight. To Coventry she looked dangerously overbalanced, he found he was always standing behind her as if he feared she would topple backwards. Lily would throw him a smile over her shoulder as she waited at a counter. 'Ready to catch me, Coventry?' The man would smile sheepishly and look around for a chair for her to sit, while she waited.

Lily bought a great number of baby clothes, sitting at the counter while fleecy shawls and fine linen nightshirts were spread before her on the glass top. After she had made her choice, Coventry tapped at a notice which said that the baby's name could be embroidered on the linen at a small extra charge. Lily looked doubtfully at Coventry. 'Isn't it dreadfully expensive?' she whispered while the sales lady was packing the goods.

Coventry beamed at her and shrugged.

'It would be lovely,' Lily said thoughtfully. 'Dead posh!'

Coventry jiggled her chair a little, like a school boy hinting for a treat.

'Oh, what the hell!' Lily sang out, startling the shop woman. 'Keep them, all except two sets, and send them to be embroidered,' she said. 'I'll tell you the initials in May. You can send them round when they are ready.'

Beaming with mutual approval, Coventry and Lily went on to the cots, to the prams, to the baths, to the thick towels and soft fleecy nappies. Lily signed and signed and signed her name to one account after another; never adding the sums in her head, never looking at the prices, drifting in a delightful daze of spending money and saying, 'Please deliver it to me: Mrs Stephen Winters,' as if her own mother had never wrapped half a pound of cheese and popped it in Lily's bike basket for her to take around to a customer while the lad was out.

A river of white cotton, white silk and white lambswool flowed before her. Lily touched and smelled the little clothes in an orgy of innocent sensuality. There was white smocking and white embroidery on every little gown. Someone's hand-stitching was spread before Lily's satisfied stare for approval. There was hand hemming on the little soft white cot sheets. Every little shawl, every little gown, was dense with labour. Lily admired the textures, sniffed at the clean dry smell of perfectly new white goods and revelled in the arduous labour of other women which had brought these dainty perfect things before her.

'I love being rich,' she said to Coventry softly while the saleswoman searched beneath the counter for something

385

especially fine. 'I *love* it. D'you think that's very bad?'

They shopped until midday. Coventry checked his watch and then showed it to Lily. She nodded. 'Bring the car round to the front, there's a darling. I just want to look at the hats and then I'll come straight away.'

Coventry scowled at her with mock seriousness and tapped the face of his watch with emphasis.

'Just *glance*,' Lily said with pretend irritation. 'And anyway, you're a chauffeur, not a nanny. If I want to be late for lunch I damn well can be.'

Coventry grinned, sketched her a deep and humble bow and went to fetch the Argyll with his arms full of little parcels for Stephen's baby.

He waited outside Handley's store, as he knew he would have to; but when Lily came out, a hatbox swinging from one hand, she was with Madge.

'It'll be all right if Madge comes home for dinner, won't it?' she asked Coventry. 'Cook won't mind? Mrs Winters won't mind?'

Coventry shrugged as he opened the door for the two girls. He gave Lily a small reassuring smile. For all her confident spending, for all her claiming of the Winters's accounts, she was still a child in an older woman's house; unsure of the rules and anxious not to offend. When Lily checked with him what she might or might not do, Coventry felt a tenderness that he thought he had lost long ago. She was like an orphan placed in a strict foster-home. She might be Mrs Winters to the saleswomen when she ordered a hundred pounds of embroidery work. But at home she was Stephen's nobody-wife and of negligible importance.

'When's it due then?' Madge asked, eyeing Lily's distended stomach with trepidation.

Lily giggled and leaned back against the seat as Coventry eased the car out behind a horse-drawn delivery van, and then bumped slightly on the tram tracks as he overtook it.

'May,' she said. 'First week in May, only another two months. Golly, I can't wait. I feel like a balloon. I haven't even *seen* my feet for months.'

'And then what? Will you try and get back to work?'

Lily shook her head. 'No. He'll never let me work on the stage while I have a small baby,' she said in an undertone. 'It's all different for me, Madge, I can see that now. I thought at first that I could get my own way, that I could marry Stephen and it would be all right for me. But I can't work. Not when I have the baby. He wouldn't allow it. But what I *can* do is drawing room singing, and concerts in concert halls.'

Madge's eyes widened. 'Proper singing?'

Lily nodded. 'Charlie's been teaching me. He says my voice is good enough. I even sing little bits out of operas now! Think of that! He says I'm good enough to sing in concerts. And concerts are posh. Stephen doesn't object to concerts. Besides, you don't do seasons like theatre. You just do one and then it's over. And I wouldn't tour either.'

Madge nodded enviously. 'And I was pitying you for missing the panto,' she said. 'Precious little money, same show night after night and no work afterwards.'

'Are you out of work now?'

Madge nodded and drew her thin winter coat around her. 'As usual,' she said. 'All the pantos close at the same time, it's too early to start the summer shows, even the clubs don't pick up until after Easter. I hate this time of year. I never have enough money and I'm always afraid I'm never going to work again. I was just looking for a little present for my mum when I saw you. I'm going home to Southampton until they start auditioning for the summer shows. My mum can get me work waitressing in a restaurant.'

'Waitressing!' Lily exclaimed. She put an arm around Madge's shoulder and gave her a hug. 'Poor little Red Hot Baby!'

Madge pulled herself away, bridling at the sympathy. 'Yes,' she said. 'I'll wait tables for two months but then I'll be in a show. I'll be back on the stage and I'll be singing solo. Two months from now and you'll be up to your eyes in nappies. A year from now and you'll be pregnant again. A year after that and you'll be pregnant again and your waist will have gone and you'll have varicose veins. I know who I'd rather be!'

Lily said nothing, but let Madge move away from her.

Coventry, turning the wing mirror to see her face, saw her pallor and the way her bottom lip trembled like a child's.

The last month of Lily's pregnancy passed in a blur of fatigue. She still got up to see Stephen off in the mornings but she went straight back to bed after he had left and only dressed in time for lunch with Muriel. In the afternoons Charlie came and played the piano for her, every afternoon at two o'clock without fail.

'As long as I can hear the piano playing then there's no cause for concern,' Muriel reassured herself as she sat in Rory's room with a small fire of rationed coal burning against the dismal April weather. Rain poured against the octagonal tower windows as hard as sleet. The sea was grey with white heaving crests. Muriel listened to the piano and Lily's faultlessly clear voice, richer in tone and deeper in intensity. When the piano playing stopped for an hour at a time Muriel did not let herself worry. 'A man like that, an attractive man like that, would hardly desire Lily as she is,' she told herself. 'So broad in the beam and so tired, her skin so pale and dark shadows all around her eyes. He comes to sit with her out of sympathy, and because he sees her talent. We should be grateful that he comes to take her out of herself. If it were not for him I think she would spend the whole day in bed.'

Stephen was edgy and bad-tempered with everyone but Charlie for all of April. A national miners' strike was threatening and the government had called on all loyal citizens to volunteer for new units of the regular army. Stephen, reading this, had flung down the newspaper in disgust. 'Volunteer!' he exclaimed to Charlie. 'Again?'

Charlie, seeing the way Stephen's hands trembled and the pallor around his mouth, slapped him on the back. 'Not you!' he said, and his voice was instantly reassuring. 'You've done your share, old man. You'll never have to serve again.'

Stephen had nodded his head. 'I have,' he repeated. 'I *have* done my share. They couldn't make me serve again. Could they?'

'All nonsense anyway,' Charlie said comfortingly. 'Politicians! What do they know?'

'Nothing!' Stephen agreed. He beamed at Charlie with sudden warmth. 'Stay to dinner, old man! A chap gets tired of a houseful of women. Stay to dinner!'

'I've got no dinner jacket!' Charlie protested.

'Oh, what the hell!' Stephen poured them both another whisky. 'We never change for dinner these days, do we, Lily? The days when we would dress for dinner and then go out are long gone!'

So Muriel and Lily ate their dinner in their afternoon dresses – 'So scruffy!', Muriel thought – and Charlie and Stephen in their lounge suits laughed and talked together. They had a wide acquaintance in common from the Trocadero Club, and a whole set of private jokes which neither Muriel nor Lily could understand or enjoy. At nine o'clock

Charlie said: 'Good heavens, I have to run, I'm working tonight,' and Stephen looked like a little boy anxious to be taken out on a treat.

'You coming down tonight, Stephen?' Charlie asked casually as Muriel rang for his overcoat.

'I should say so! I could come with you now, actually.'

Muriel, watching Lily, saw Lily's small patronizing smile. Lily knew that Stephen wanted to enter the Trocadero with Charlie. He wanted to spend the evening at Charlie's table where the girls gravitated to the man who could get them work at the Kings Theatre, and who was, in addition, the most attractive man in Portsmouth.

'I have to go home to change into my black tie,' Charlie warned. 'But if you don't mind waiting you can come with me.'

Stephen jumped up and kissed Lily in passing, on the forehead. 'I'll come at once!' he said. 'Can't keep the audience waiting!'

'Thank you for your hospitality, Mrs Winters,' Charlie said to Muriel. And he winked at Lily and took her hand. 'Go to bed,' he said softly, almost inaudible under the noise of Stephen getting his coat and hat. 'You look exhausted. Go to bed now, I'll see you tomorrow.'

Lily looked up at him, her eyes warm with affection. 'Tomorrow at two.'

The night of 3 May, Lily woke from a deep sleep with a strange wrenching pain in her belly. She lay for a little while, watching the ceiling, thinking nothing. Then it came again. A deep pain, a different pain from the usual aches of pregnancy. 'It's coming,' she said. 'Early.' Then the pain eased and she slept a little more.

She woke again in the early hours of the morning, with her sheets soaked and her belly tight with a hard sharp pain.

'Stephen!' she called. He could not hear her. She glanced at the alarm clock on her bedside table. It was two in the morning, he might not even be home yet.

She heaved herself from the bed and walked awkwardly to the door. Halfway there a pain stabbed her in the belly like a knife and Lily folded over with a gasp. It eased after a little while. 'Stephen!' Lily called, frightened.

She opened the door and looked across the landing. His dressing room door was open; the narrow bed was empty. Lily turned back into her own room and threw on her dressing-gown. She was feeling better now, she had a sense of rising excitement mixed with fear. Her suitcase stood at the door, it had been packed for a week. She was to have the baby in an exclusive and expensive ward of the hospital with Dr Metcalfe, the finest obstetrician in Hampshire. She tied her dressing-gown around her and went down the stairs to wake Muriel.

Just as she was about to tap on her bedroom door she heard the noise of the key turning in the lock of the front door. Lily peered over the bannisters.

Three men came into the hall. Coventry, his hat knocked askew, was supporting Stephen, whose legs were bending under him, dead drunk. On his other side was Charlie Smith.

'Oh, Charlie!' Lily said. She came down the stairs in a rush, her hands held out to him.

Charlie abruptly dropped Stephen who slumped to the floor, only half-supported by Coventry. Charlie caught Lily's outstretched hands. 'Is it coming?' he asked.

Lily's face was radiant. She smiled from him to Coventry. 'It is! It is! Will you take me to the hospital?'

Coventry, holding Stephen's arm as he sank unstoppably downwards, looked from one to another of them.

'I need my bag,' Lily said. 'In my bedroom.'

Coventry heaved Stephen into a wooden carver chair

which stood at the side of the hall and left him there while he ran up the stairs, into Lily's bedroom and brought down the bag in one hand.

'Should we wake your mother-in-law?' Charlie asked.

'I don't know,' Lily said. 'She shouldn't see Stephen like this . . .'

But Muriel's door was opening. She came out on to the landing. 'I heard voices,' she said. 'Is that you, Lily? Is the baby coming?'

'She needs to go to the hospital,' Charlie said, his voice assured. 'Stephen here's a bit under the weather. Shall Coventry and I take her now?'

Muriel peered over the bannisters, clutching her dressing-gown across her nightdress. 'Oh dear,' she said inadequately. 'No, I think I had better get dressed and take her.'

Lily suddenly gave a gasp and clutched to Charlie's hands. 'Oh God!' she said. 'I think I'd better go at once.'

'Come on,' Charlie said. He picked up her bag and Lily turned to the door with him.

'You can't go like that!' Muriel protested ineffectually. 'Lily, you must get dressed! You shouldn't even be downstairs like that! Wait for me! I'll come as soon as I am dressed. We'll leave a message for Stephen. He'll come too.'

Charlie glanced into Lily's face. Suddenly she had gone deathly white and she had her bottom lip gripped between her teeth.

'We daren't wait,' he said tersely.

Coventry nodded and swept Lily up into his arms. He held her carefully and strongly and carried her down the small flight of steps to the garden path. Charlie was holding the gate and then went to the car door to help Lily in. They folded up the arm rest and stretched her along the back seat. Lily's colour had come back to her cheeks. She gave them her cheeky grin. 'Go on then,' she said. 'My heroes.'

Coventry and Charlie jumped into the front seats and Coventry started the engine with a roar. They sped down the road and then turned north, to the hospital. Lily lay on the back seat with her eyes closed, her stomach clenching in painful contractions from time to time. No-one had told her that she could time her pains. No-one had told her of the mechanics of birth. Lily lay, as ignorant as a child, gripped by one hard contraction after another, gasping with pain. But when Charlie glanced back at her he could see she was smiling.

The baby was born at five o'clock in the morning: a small beautiful seven-pound boy. He had a downy head of fair hair and Lily's blue optimistic eyes.

The hospital routine was such that he was taken away from Lily as soon as he was born, before she had even seen him. Lily was washed, offered a cup of tea and commanded to rest.

'But I want my baby,' Lily said, struggling up in the bed against the firm hands of the nurse pressing her down to the pillows.

'Not now, dear,' the nurse said firmly. 'It's time for you to rest.'

'But I want to *see* my baby,' Lily said. 'I hardly caught a glimpse of him. And I want Charlie to see him too, and Coventry, and Muriel.'

'They can see him through the window of the day nursery during visiting hours – four till five o'clock every afternoon except the weekends. Your mother-in-law has been here and we told her all was well and sent her home in her car. Your husband's still here.'

'Stephen?' Lily asked in surprise.

'The gentleman who brought you in,' the nurse said stiffly.

Lily smiled in relief. 'That's Charlie,' she said. 'Will you ask him to come in?'

The nurse frowned. 'We don't have visitors now, Mrs Winters, it is your rest time. Mothers have to learn to do as they are told. We've got far too many mothers to have them running around at all times of the day and night. You go to sleep now like a good girl and we'll bring Baby to you at nine o'clock. We'll take him away then and you rest again, and then we bring him to you at one. And your family can visit at four. I expect you'll give him a bottle, won't you? A modern girl like you?'

Lily's smile never shifted but her blue eyes grew hard. 'I can't sleep until I have seen Charlie,' she said mendaciously. 'I have to give him a message. I *have* to. It's something serious. Can't you let him in for a minute?'

The nurse looked studiedly thoughtful as if she were considering an outrageous life-threatening request. 'I shouldn't allow it really,' she said.

'It's about my husband,' Lily said, improvising rapidly. 'He won't know where his cufflinks are. He won't be able to go to work without them. I have to send a message for him.'

The nurse capitulated at once under the powerful claims of male need. 'Men!' she said, tossing her head. 'Well, he can come in for two minutes,' she said grudgingly. 'And I will be timing him! Mothers and babies have to learn their routine. Rest and feed. Rest and feed. Not chatter and what-not.'

Lily nodded, her dark eyelashes sweeping down and shielding her eyes.

'You can come in,' the nurse said coldly to Charlie who stood in the doorway. 'For two minutes only. She's being very naughty and insistent. She'll have to learn how we do things here. She'll have to do them our way. She's going to be here for a long time, she's going to have to learn to be a good girl.'

'Charlie,' Lily said in her bleakest Portsmouth accent, 'tell this stupid bitch to fetch my baby, I want you to take me home.'

Chapter Twenty-six

They took a motor-cab which had just set someone down outside the hospital; Lily was too angry to wait for Charlie to phone the Winters's house for Coventry and the car. She insisted on leaving the hospital at once with her baby wrapped warmly in the hospital's cot blanket.

The nurse followed them to the front door, remonstrating and scolding in turns. 'But what will Dr Metcalfe say?' she demanded, thinking of that luminary's response to the loss of his fat fees. 'Mrs Winters, you can't just storm out like this! What am I to say to Dr Metcalfe?'

Lily scrambled into the cab, her baby held warm and safe under her coat, nuzzling into the crook of her arm. Her face was alight with excitement and defiance. Charlie swung into the cab beside her, and slammed the door. Lily leaned forward and called out of the window. 'Tell him to bugger off!' she said in her best Duchess voice. 'Give him Mrs Winters's compliments and tell him to bugger off!'

Charlie let out a shout of laughter and pulled Lily back into the cab as they drove off.

'You're a caution, you!' he said, still laughing. 'What did that poor woman do to make you so mad?'

Lily started laughing too as her anger fell away. 'Oh, she was awful, Charlie! She wouldn't let me have my baby, and she wanted to keep you out. And I'm supposed to be in there for a fortnight and then a convalescent home for another fortnight. She wouldn't let me have my baby and she wanted him bottle-fed. And anyway – I can't see what the fuss is about. My ma had me in the front bedroom and was serving in the shop the next day.'

Charlie put his arm around her and held her close.

'Let's see him then,' he said. Lily held her coat back out of the way and Charlie peered into the little face. 'He's so small,' he said in wonder. 'Can I touch him?'

Lily nodded and Charlie extended a cautious hand. He touched the baby's clenched fist. At once the little hand opened like a flower and gripped on his thumb. The tiny fingers, each one with a perfect minute nail, held Charlie's giant thumb with surprising strength. 'I say,' Charlie said, awed. 'He's got a grip, this one. He knows what he wants.'

Lily beamed down at the baby. Charlie looked at her clear lovely profile. 'God, Lily,' he said. 'I wish I was an artist. I wish I could paint you like you are now.'

She turned and smiled at him. 'I wish my ma could see him,' she said. Her eyes were luminous with tears. 'I can't believe that she has a grandson that she'll never know, that he'll grow up never knowing her.'

She blinked quickly and two tears fell on to the baby's blanket. Lily blotted them with a finger. 'But I don't miss her like I used to,' she said softly. 'Now my baby is born I feel like I'm starting a new life, a new life all over again. And to think I didn't want him at first! To think I should have got that so wrong!'

The baby's blue eyes opened and he looked up at Lily with the strange attentive stare of the newborn, as if he were as surprised and delighted with the world as Lily was with him. Charlie swallowed and rubbed his face on his sleeve.

'Are you tired, Lil?' he asked gruffly.

'A little,' she said slowly, still not taking her gaze from her baby. 'I'll sleep when I get home. You'll come in, won't you, Charlie?'

'I won't be able to stay,' Charlie said softly. 'Not the

done thing, Lil. Mrs Winters was unhappy enough about me taking you to hospital, she'd be upset if I hung round too much. I don't want to rock the boat for you, for the two of you.'

Lily nodded. 'Come this afternoon to see me then,' she said. 'You always come for tea.'

Charlie's grip around her shoulder tightened as the cab drew up outside number two, The Parade. 'Yes. I always come for tea,' he repeated bleakly. For a moment he thought of the rest of his life: coming to Lily's for tea and watching her child grow, and knowing that she should have been his wife and the child should have been his boy. He felt one of the quick stabbing pains in his groin which he had learned to curse and ignore, and the longer unstoppable pain beneath his ribs which was heartache and could neither be cursed nor ignored.

He paid the driver and his hand was steady. He opened the door for Lily and held her firmly by the elbow. Then he opened the garden gate and led her up the little path.

The front door swung open and the tweeny stood in the doorway in her working apron. 'Oh Mum!' she said. 'They said you was at the hospital. You ought to still be there, oughtn't you?'

Lily beamed at her. 'No, Sally,' she said brightly. 'I decided to bring my baby home. He's quite well enough to be at home, and I hate hospitals. I hate the smell of them.'

Sally fell back before them and Lily went confidently into the drawing room. 'I should like some tea,' she said. 'And turn my bed down so that I can rest. I'll have the baby's cot in my room for now, so make sure the fire's lit, Sally. We'll need to keep the room warm. I'll want a fire lit in my bedroom all day.'

'Yes'm,' Sally said, dropping a curtsey and backing out. 'I'll tell Browning.'

The news that Lily was home with her baby, just hours instead of a full month after the birth, spread through the house at speed: upwards, to Muriel when she came out of her bathroom, and downwards to Cook, the boot boy, the gardener and Coventry.

Muriel dressed rapidly and came downstairs to the drawing room at once. 'Lily,' she said reproachfully. 'You ought to be in hospital.'

Charlie rose to his feet and guided her to a chair. Muriel sank into it, looking paler and more drawn than Lily.

'I'm going to bed,' Lily said agreeably. 'But I couldn't have stayed in the hospital, Mrs Winters. I'm sorry if it's not convenient. But the nurse there wouldn't let me have my baby. She took him away and she wouldn't let me see him. She wanted him to be bottle-fed and kept in the nursery. And my ma used to say that bottle-fed babies don't do as well. I want to breast-feed.'

Muriel's eyes slid at once to Charlie at this embarrassing intimacy. Charlie assumed an expression of gentlemanly detachment. 'But however did you get home? And what does Dr Metcalfe say?'

Charlie cleared his throat. 'I was just leaving the hospital when Lily sent for me,' he said. 'I thought it better to bring her home to her husband than to leave her there, where she was obviously unhappy.'

'Oh yes,' Muriel said. 'Home to Stephen . . . but he's not up yet. I'll send up Coventry to wake him. It really is most . . .' She went to the door and sent Sally with a message for Coventry to wake Stephen, and then returned to her seat. 'And whatever does Dr Metcalfe say?'

'He wasn't even there!' Lily protested. 'It was just me and the nurse. He didn't even bother to be there! But have a look at the baby! He's so sweet! He's sound asleep. He likes it here.' She pushed back her coat and, cradling her child in her arms, leaned towards Muriel. Automatically

Muriel reached out to take the little baby. Lily let her son go to his grandmother and sat back in her chair with a smile.

Muriel saw the blonde down of hair and the fair smooth skin. She held him close and heard the quiet animal breaths and saw the steady healthy beat of his pulse in the crown of the fair head. 'Christopher,' she said longingly. 'He is *so* like Christopher.'

'Yes!' Lily said delightedly. 'That must be his name. Christopher Charles! Christopher Charles Winters!'

Muriel smiled but did not take her gaze from the baby's face. 'Another Christopher in the house,' she said lovingly. 'Christopher.'

Lily shot a swift covert look at Charlie. He was watching her, his face warm with love and desire.

'Christopher Charles Winters,' Muriel repeated softly. 'It's a fine name. Why Charles, Lily?'

'It was my father's name.' Lily told an easy lie. She glanced at Charlie with a small secret smile that told him that her son was named for him. 'I wanted to call him Charles from the moment I knew he was a boy,' she said.

'A new generation of Winters, a new boy in the house,' Muriel said softly.

The door opened quietly behind Charlie and he turned and saw Stephen standing in the doorway, looking pale and ill. The deep colours of his silk dressing-gown made him sallow. 'I seem to have missed the whole show,' he said, trying for a joke. 'Damned sorry, Lily. I was coming down to the hospital just now to see you; and then up you pop at home.'

'Look, Stephen!' Muriel said. 'This is Christopher.'

A look of immediate anguish at his brother's name went across Stephen's face and was wiped away in a second. He stepped forward and looked at his son's face, touched the edge of his blanket with one clumsy finger. 'He looks fine,' he said softly. 'Nice hair.'

'He has slept ever since we left the hospital,' Lily said. 'We couldn't have stayed there, Stephen, they were hopeless. Charlie was just leaving but I made him bring me home.'

'Good man,' Stephen said, nodding to Charlie. 'And you were the hero last night too?'

Charlie winked at him. 'Coventry and me,' he said. 'You weren't fit for roll-call, old man!'

Stephen shook his head in a pantomime of penitence. 'I should be court-martialled. Lily, d'you forgive me?'

Lily shook her head, smiling. 'Nonsense. What could you have done?' she asked. 'Coventry drove me to hospital and Charlie got me a cab to come home again. And here we are safe and sound! Me and your son, Christopher Charles Winters. Christopher after your brother and Charles after my father. Don't you like it?'

Stephen gritted his teeth on his smile. 'If that's what you want.' He hesitated for a moment, looking to his mother for support. 'But I'd have thought you'd have chosen something a bit more modern.'

Muriel looked up at him. 'He's named after your brother,' she said sharply. 'He couldn't have a better name.'

Only Charlie saw the anger flare in Stephen's face before he banked it down. 'Good show,' he said determinedly. 'It suits him, somehow. Jolly good show.'

There was a short awkward silence. 'I must go,' Charlie said quietly and went to the door.

'Come for tea this afternoon,' Lily reminded him, without looking up. She was watching her sleeping son in Muriel's arms.

'If you're not too tired,' Charlie said, with an eye on

Muriel. He was watching for her disapproval, but the older woman was absorbed in the baby. 'Two o'clock then,' Charlie said, threw a half-salute at Stephen and slipped from the room.

'Let's take him to show your father!' Lily said, suddenly remembering Rory upstairs.

Muriel rose to her feet and held out the baby to Stephen for him to carry upstairs. Lily at once intercepted the gesture and took her son. Stephen stood blinking owlishly and then opened the door as Lily passed through into the hall. Lily could smell the staleness of his breath, he was still half-drunk. The parlourmaid Browning was waiting in the hall to see the baby, Cook, Coventry and the gardener behind her.

Lily beamed with delight at them all. 'Have you all come to see my baby? Look! Isn't he beautiful?'

She held the baby up for them to see. 'Christopher Charles Winters,' she said. 'He's to be called Christopher Charles Winters.' She smiled past Cook at Coventry. 'Isn't he lovely?'

The housemaids cooed and Cook brushed the back of her floury hand to her cheek. 'Christopher,' she repeated softly. 'And as like to young Master Christopher when he was a baby as a little pea in a pod.'

Muriel felt her own tears rising. 'It's time you were in bed, Lily,' she said. 'Up the stairs with you. Can you manage with the baby?'

'Coventry can carry him,' Lily said.

The big man flushed slightly and stepped to Lily's side, his arms out ready. Lily put her baby carefully into Coventry's arms. He looked down into the small sleeping face. 'Hssh hssh sshhh,' he said. It was the first time anyone in the house had heard Coventry make any noise at all. 'Hssh hssh sshh,' he said again, like a groom soothing a restless horse.

'You made a sound, Coventry,' Lily said in amazement. 'Can you speak?'

Coventry shook his head. His gaze met Stephen's warning glare across Lily's head. He gave a small grim smile as if to reassure Stephen that his silence would be unbroken for ever, and shook his head again.

'I bet you can,' Lily said. 'If you can say "sshh" then you can say all sorts of things.'

'Point is,' Stephen interrupted loudly, 'is that he can't. He had an injury, Lily. He can't speak any more. Not really fair to ask different of him, is it?'

'I didn't mean to be unkind . . .'

'Come along,' Muriel said. 'Never mind now. Lily should be in bed.'

'Quite right, Ma,' Stephen said. 'Really she shouldn't be here at all. She should still be at hospital. Let's show the baby to Father and get you into bed, Lily.'

Lily smiled and went up the stairs, followed by Coventry carrying the baby and Muriel and Stephen. Stephen looked down over the bannisters to the staff who gazed upwards. 'Show's over,' he said nastily. 'Suggest you go back to your posts.'

Lily took the baby from Coventry at Rory's bedroom door. Coventry opened the door and she went in. There was a keen alert look about Rory and his hands, pinned at the end of his unmoving arms, flexed and closed with his desire to reach out for the child.

'Yes,' she said, responding to the question in his dark face. 'We're both well. It's a boy.'

She laid the baby on his counterpane, across his immobile thighs. She helped him put one hand on the baby's head and cup the other around his feet.

Rory looked down, his mouth working, trying to frame words. 'Boy,' he said finally.

Lily nodded. 'Yes. A boy. We're going to call him Christopher Charles Winters.'

Rory paused for a moment, searching for the words. 'Chris'opher,' he repeated. 'Like Chris'opher.'

Stephen's face was a mask of polite interest.

'Yes,' Lily said patiently. 'Christopher, named after your son, Christopher. Now you have a grandson Christopher. And when the weather is nice we can go out for walks down to the Canoe Lake and along the prom, you and me and Christopher in his pram.'

Rory nodded, the muscles in his neck flexing slowly.

Lily leaned forward and took up her son. 'I'm taking him upstairs now,' she said gently. 'I'll put him in his new cot. He can sleep in my room for the first few nights, and then we can make Stephen's little dressing room into a nursery.' She spoke with assurance. 'It'll be better for me to have him near me, especially until he sleeps through the nights,' she said. 'But I should rest now.'

Rory nodded. One uncontrolled tear spilled out from the corner of his eye and rolled down his cheek. Lily had been told that his tears meant nothing, that they were a reaction caused by the damaged muscles of his eyes. She never believed it. She took a handkerchief from the pocket of her coat and gently patted his cheek dry.

'There's nothing to cry for,' she said softly. 'Here's a new baby in the house, a new Christopher. We're all going to be very, very happy.'

Stephen held the door open for her and stepped back as she went through, his face rigid.

Upstairs in Lily's bedroom the fire was lit and the bedclothes turned down. The cot with flowing white curtains was in the octagonal turret corner of the room. As Lily put Christopher gently down in his cot she could see the grey waves breaking into white foam on the shingle beach. The May sky overhead was palest blue and the wind was from the east. It was still very early, not yet eight.

'Bed's the best place for us,' Lily said with enormous satisfaction. She was unconsciously echoing her mother's domestic wisdom. 'A cold day like this! Bed is the best place to be.'

Stephen, hearing echoes of Highland Road in Lily's speech to her son, scowled and dropped into the chair before the dressing table. He watched Lily undress and pull on her nightgown without comment. Her belly was as fat as ever, but slack and flaccid. Her breasts were swollen with milk and stained with fat blue veins. Stephen could not recognize the thin androgynous star-struck girl he had married in this confident plump woman. He found her repellent, he was afraid of the rich fertile maturity of her body.

'And what time shall I have your ladyship called?' he asked bitingly. 'After you have taken your rest?'

Lily looked at him in surprise. 'I'll sleep till lunchtime, I expect. If I don't wake for lunch, then they can save me something.'

'And what about the baby? Who is going to care for him?'

Lily plumped up the pillows, lay back against them and drew the covers up to her chin. 'I will, of course,' she said. 'If he wakes I'll just give him a feed and he can go back to sleep again.'

'You make it sound delightfully easy,' Stephen said nastily. 'I think, however, that you will find there is more to it than that. You're rather unprepared, you see. You should have been away from home for a month as we arranged. Then you could have come back and we could have had a nanny ready and waiting. This dash away from the hospital may make things a little inconvenient for you. Don't say I didn't warn you!'

A certain hardness came into Lily's face. 'Stephen, I don't know how much you know about babies, and I don't claim to be an expert; but in this house there are two maids, one cook, one grandmother and one fully trained nurse as well as me. I think we can manage one little sleepy baby between the six of us!'

Stephen reached into his dressing-gown pocket and took out his cigarette packet. 'Neither the maids nor the cook have time to help you. The nurse is paid by me to care for my father. My mother does not work as a skivvy in a nursery.'

'Don't smoke in here.'

'I beg your pardon?' Stephen paused with a cigarette to his lips.

'I don't like the smell of cigarette smoke. And babies should have fresh air. If you want to smoke you must go to your room.'

Stephen glared at Lily and she held his gaze without fear. Then his well-trained manners overcame his anger, and he put the cigarette back in the packet.

'I shall have a bath,' he announced. 'I have a devil of a headache. I shall expect you down for lunch. If you are well enough to march out of hospital you are certainly well enough to come down for lunch.'

Lily nodded equably and waited until he had gone out of the door and it had closed behind him. 'Well, I hope it's not bloody liver,' she said rebelliously.

Chapter Twenty-seven

Stephen's warnings to Lily were swiftly proved wrong. Christopher was a placid easy baby. He slept through the night after only a fortnight of waking at dawn; and in any case, Lily loved taking him into her big bed for a feed and then falling asleep with him in her arms.

'You'll smother him,' Muriel warned. 'You'll lie on him and suffocate him. You'll spoil him too, Lily. He should be put in his cot and left to cry. It's not healthy to hold him so close.'

But Lily would not treat the baby as Muriel wished. She never argued with the older woman, she never contradicted her. But Christopher was picked up the moment he cried and allowed to fall asleep anywhere he wished: in his mother's arms, tucked into the corner of the sofa while she sang with Charlie, on her bed, naked after a bath. 'You'll ruin him!' Muriel warned.

And he was allowed to feed like a savage. Lily had no discipline at all. When he cried in her bedroom, or in the bathroom, she simply undid her shirt and offered him her breast and Christopher would settle at once to loud and sensual sucking which made Muriel colour with embarrassment and leave the room. She had to ask Stephen to make sure that Lily knew that on no account might she ever feed Christopher in the drawing room or in any of the downstairs rooms, or before any of the servants.

'She feeds him in her bedroom, in the bathroom. I even caught her feeding him in front of your father!'

There was a brief disgusted silence. Stephen said, 'For

407

God's sake! I hope you told her that it wasn't the done thing, Mother. She still needs a lot of guidance.'

'How can I?' Muriel demanded. 'I've told her how to care for the baby. I have told her he must be put down and left for four hours between feeds. I have told her that even if he screams she must simply shut the door on him and leave him or he will be spoiled. But she won't do it. Apparently in Highland Road they feed their babies almost continuously, and sleep in the same bed with them all night. Lily seems to think that is the way everyone should behave.'

Stephen pulled gently at his moustache. 'I'll have a word,' he said thoughtfully. 'She's got to learn. Maybe we should get a nanny?'

'A good old-fashioned nanny,' Muriel said with sudden enthusiasm. 'What an excellent idea, Stephen! A sensible firm woman who can show Lily how to go on. Enough of this sloppy spoiling of the baby. A good nanny who can get them both into a routine.'

Stephen did not warn Lily of this decision. He advertised under a box number and then wrote to the best of the replies inviting them to an interview at his office. John Pascoe raised an eyebrow at the office waiting room, filled with half a dozen dark-coated women with overwhelming black hats.

'Nannies,' Stephen said to him on the stairs. 'Lily came out of the hospital in such a rush that I've only now been able to start looking for one.'

'I thought Lily was coping on her own?' John asked.

Stephen shook his head. 'She's having a go,' he said. 'But she really doesn't know which way to start. She's got no mother of her own of course, and she's not got the sense of a kitten. She really needs a sensible woman to get her sorted out.'

John Pascoe nodded. 'Start as you mean to go on with

babies,' he said. 'We always did. Nanny and proper school-room hours from the first week.'

Stephen nodded. 'That's what Mother says,' he said. 'But Lily had to try it her way. She's been overly involved with the baby. Smothering him, y'know.'

'Well, a first child . . .' John said tolerantly.

Stephen shook his head. 'It's not just that,' he said. 'She's hysterical. She won't let it sleep alone. She won't put it down. She feeds it all the time and won't hear of a bottle. She's not quite right where the baby's concerned.'

'Oh,' John said, at a loss.

Stephen smiled. 'We'll get it sorted,' he said. 'A good sensible woman. I'll have her live in. There's a big room on the first floor she can have as a nursery. Then we can all get back to normal.'

He chose the woman that afternoon. She was to be addressed as Nanny Janes. She was to be served all her meals in the nursery. She would do light darning but no laundering. She would provide her own uniform and she was to have every other Thursday afternoon off. She explained to Stephen that she must have absolute control in the nursery. 'I normally like to see Mother,' she said, 'to make sure she understands how we are to go on.'

'My wife is at home with the baby,' Stephen said. 'I thought it would be more convenient for us all if I did the interviews here.'

'I'll take a trial month then, if you're agreeable,' Nanny Janes said. She was a formidable woman, dark-faced and brown-haired. She carried an umbrella despite the warm sunshine outside the window. 'A trial month, seeing as I have not had an opportunity to see Mother. She's a young mother, I take it?'

'Yes,' Stephen said. 'And rather nervous.'

Nurse Janes nodded magisterially. 'I'm familiar with this sort of situation,' she said complacently. 'I think you will find that I can put matters on a proper footing.' She deposited a thick wad of papers from her large handbag on to Stephen's desk. 'My references,' she said. 'You are fortunate in finding me available at once. Owing to a Death.'

'I'm sorry to hear that,' Stephen said, glancing through the letters. There were a number of crested papers, and Stephen felt a frisson of satisfied snobbery. The nanny for his son would have wiped the bottoms of young lords.

'I take it I can contact your former employers?'

Nanny Janes nodded. 'My last place was with the Harcourt family, their address and telephone number is there.'

'You had the care of their baby?'

'Twins,' Nanny Janes said. 'They died in an accident while boating. I did indicate to the father that I thought them too young to be taken out on a yacht. But I was overruled.'

Stephen put down the papers abruptly. 'What happened?'

'They drowned,' Nanny Janes said, without a flicker of emotion across her brown face. 'Aged three years and eight months. Their mother was most distressed. Their father was saved but the boys went under. I was not present at the time.'

Stephen looked at her impassive face and felt his familiar rage building at the woman's detachment. She was like all women. She could see horror and remain untouched. 'How inconvenient for you,' he said spitefully.

Nanny Janes shook her head. 'At the age of four I should have handed them over to a governess,' she said simply. 'I had only four more months with them. And they provided me with an extra remuneration in recognition of my services.'

Stephen felt chilled with an instant powerful sense that he was betraying Lily by handing over their son to this woman who could speak so calmly of the death of two children in her care. He quelled it almost at once. The very thing Lily needed to learn was detachment. This woman would be an excellent teacher.

'Start tomorrow then,' he said briskly.

Nanny Janes rose from her chair and extended her hand to take back her sheaf of references. 'Tomorrow at nine,' she said.

Stephen tried several times to tell Lily that he had engaged a nanny for Christopher. When he came home from work Charlie was at the piano and Lily was leaning against it singing. 'No, no!' Charlie said as Stephen came in. 'More purity, Lily! Deep breath and get that top note and hold it!' He broke off when he saw Stephen. 'Hello, Stephen! Good day at the office?'

Stephen nodded to him. 'Charlie,' he said in greeting. He looked around. Christopher was sleeping on the sofa, wedged in with cushions. He was wearing an exquisite white pin-tucked gown, his fair hair was growing slightly, his eyes were gently closed, his cheeks were rosy. One small hand, clenched in a fist, waved at his dreams from time to time. 'I wonder he can sleep with you singing away in his ear, Lily,' Stephen said.

Lily put a hand on his shoulder as he leaned over their child. 'He'd have heard it in the womb,' she said. 'It must sound quite right to him. He always goes off the moment we start.'

Stephen shifted uneasily at Lily saying the word 'womb' in the drawing room. 'Really, Lily!'

Lily's hand dropped from his shoulder and she did not replace it.

'That was nice, what you were singing,' Stephen said, straightening up and turning to the mantelpiece. 'What is it?'

'It's a lied –' Charlie started to say but he caught himself in time. 'A love song,' he said mendaciously. 'Old English. Lily's been invited to sing at a concert of classical music, in aid of charity. We were just running through the programme in case she wanted to do it.'

'What charity?'

'War-wounded,' Lily said. 'One of your mother's friends is organizing it. The Earl of March will be there, we'll probably have to be introduced,' she added cunningly.

Stephen nodded. 'Oh, very well,' he said. 'It sounds an awful bore.'

Charlie shrugged. 'That's the price you pay for marrying a talented woman!' he said, smiling. 'Lily has quite a few invitations to sing on the concert circuit. She's even been asked to Goodwood House in the summer.'

Stephen could not hide his pleasure. 'Well, I suppose that's virtually a royal command,' he said.

'And useful for your work,' Charlie pointed out. 'You make all sorts of contacts at a place like that.'

Lily crossed to the fireplace and rang the bell for tea. Charlie got up from the piano. 'I must go,' he said.

'Oh, stay for tea,' Stephen said carelessly. 'And then we'll have a drink.'

'Very well,' Charlie said. 'I must tell you the gossip from the Troc, anyway.'

Lily picked up the baby and laid him gently along her knees. He stirred a little in his sleep and opened his eyes. They were a deep luminous blue. 'Hello, Christopher,' Lily said, her voice full of tenderness.

Charlie told Stephen some story about a friend of theirs from the Troc while Lily and her baby, almost nose to nose, communed in whispers from Lily and little gurgles from her child. Charlie never faltered in his anecdote, never took his attention from Stephen, but all the time he was smiling inwardly at Lily's easy contentment.

Browning came in with the tea tray with Muriel behind her. She took in Lily's absorbed play with one glance. 'I suppose I had better pour,' she said irritably.

Lily scarcely glanced up. 'Oh, do.'

Charlie told them about the new shows planned for the summer season at the Kings which would start at once. Madge was to have a solo in the variety show which would then go on tour.

'Will you tour too?' Lily asked, her attention recalled.

Charlie smiled at her. 'No,' he said. 'I'm fixed at the Kings now. We play for the shows while they're with us but they'll take their own touring musicians when they go away.'

'And will you stop working at the Troc?' Stephen asked. 'I hope not.'

'I'll play later,' Charlie said. 'After the show, and only one session. I like working there, it keeps me up to date. They've got all sorts of bands booked this summer. A couple of French singers too.' He and Stephen exchanged a knowing wink.

'I'll take a cup of tea up to your father,' Muriel said. 'Lily, shouldn't Christopher be put down?'

'He's only just woken up.'

'I mean, he shouldn't be played with all the time. You will spoil him.'

Lily smiled vaguely. 'I'll put him down in a moment,' she said. 'But he likes tea time.'

The absurdity of this was too much for Muriel. 'I think you will be sorry for this in a year or two,' she said. 'And when he has to go away at seven to boarding school with no discipline, and no idea how to behave, then he will be sorry too.' She went from the room stiff with indignation.

Lily turned to Stephen. 'Boarding school?'

'Of course,' Stephen said. 'I put his name down the day after he was born. Winchester and Harrow.'

Lily looked completely blank. 'Christopher's not going to boarding school,' she said. 'I thought he'd go to the grammar.'

'Oh really, Lily!' Stephen smiled and looked to Charlie for support. 'I think we can do a little better than that! The grammar school indeed! Well, I suppose that was the wildest dream of Highland Road, but my son will need something a little better. Of course he's going to boarding school.'

'Can you pour me another cup of tea, Lily?' Charlie interrupted. Lily put down Christopher with care at the back of her chair and leaned forward to take up the teapot.

'But . . .' she started.

'Long time to go yet,' Charlie said rapidly. 'Seven years. Not worth worrying about now, Lil.'

Lily closed her mouth and nodded.

'Where did you go to school, Stephen?' Charlie asked.

Stephen flushed. 'Oh, no-one's ever heard of it,' he said awkwardly. 'My father went there and thought it would be a good thing for his sons to go. Christopher won a scholarship to Winchester so he got a decent public school but they sent me to Father's old school. It's called Pitworthy, outside Salisbury. It's a public school all right, but not many people have been there. What about you?'

'Marlborough actually,' Charlie said. 'But I got thrown out.'

Lily gave a delighted giggle. 'What did you do?'

'Played the piano all day and wouldn't play football,' Charlie said. 'Kept dropping my rifle in the OTC and wouldn't drill. Kissed a housemaid and sneaked out at night to play the accordion in a pub. I was a thorough rotter.'

Stephen looked torn between disapproval and envy. 'I say, Charlie,' he said. 'You are a bit of a black sheep.'

'Completely one,' Charlie said easily. 'I can't tell you how nice it is!'

Stephen put down his tea cup. 'I'll drink to that,' he said. 'Anyone for a cocktail?'

Lily shook her head but Charlie nodded. Stephen rang for the tea things to be cleared and then went to the dining room where Muriel insisted that the alcohol be kept locked in the sideboard.

'Is he drinking much?' Charlie asked softly.

Lily shrugged. 'He goes out on a binge once or twice a week.'

'Not at home?'

'He'll have a cocktail before dinner and maybe a whisky afterwards. Nothing more than that.'

Charlie nodded. 'Go upstairs, Lil,' he said gently. 'I'm off after this drink. Muriel wants you to put the baby to bed, and I don't want you fighting with him about schools. It's not worth it. There's a lot can happen between now and 1928. It's not worth you getting upset.'

Lily rose, picked up Christopher and slung him easily over her shoulder, one hand on his back keeping him steady. 'See you tomorrow?'

'Tomorrow,' Charlie said.

They looked at each other for one long moment, in a glance that was as intimate as a goodnight kiss, and then Lily went from the room.

Stephen thought he would tell Lily about Nanny Janes at dinner. But the baby cried twice while they were eating and Lily left the table to go to him and finally brought him down and let him lie smiling in her arms while she ate one-handed.

Muriel was so upset by this that she could hardly speak. They ate fish pie with cabbage in silence. The cabbage was undercooked for once, white and crunchy. Lily ranged the fishbones on the side of her plate. While she was waiting for Muriel and Stephen to finish eating she counted them silently. 'Tinker, tailor, soldier, sailor, rich man, poor man, beggar man, thief.' There were so many bones she went around the rhyme three times and then ended on sailor.

'I don't know what you're smiling at,' Stephen said irritably.

'Nothing!' Lily said. 'Sorry.'

Pudding was rice pudding with a thick brown skin. Cook had been distracted by someone at the back door and brought it out of the oven too early. It was tepid by the time it got to the dining room and it was served on cold plates. Lily scooped out the white rice from under the skin and made herself swallow. Stephen and his mother both ate with relish and had second helpings.

'Shall we take coffee in the lounge?' Muriel asked. 'Surely Christopher should go to bed now?'

'I'll take him up and sit with him till he sleeps,' Lily said. 'Would you ask Browning to bring me my coffee upstairs?'

Muriel nodded with silent disapproval.

'Don't you want to kiss him goodnight?' Lily asked temptingly.

Muriel's face softened. However angry she was with Lily she could never resist an opportunity to touch the baby. 'It's dreadfully unhygienic,' she said. 'My niece won't let anyone handle her baby and she never kisses him.'

'Oh, go on,' Lily said comfortably. 'He's so lovely.'

Muriel took him in her arms and pressed her lips to his sweet-smelling temple. The soft hair on Christopher's firm head was warm and smelled faintly of the expensive gardenia guest soap.

Lily carried him upstairs. As soon as she was past the first landing they heard her singing to her son, her voice

416

growing fainter as she went higher, then they heard her bedroom door shut tight.

'I've engaged a nanny,' Stephen said heavily.

Muriel looked up in surprise. 'Without interviewing her?'

'I interviewed her at the office.'

There was a silence while Muriel took in her son's meaning. Lily had not interviewed the nanny, Lily therefore did not know that a nanny had been engaged. Lily probably had not agreed to having a nanny. There would be a scene when she found out.

'When does she start?'

'Tomorrow.'

'Then you must tell Lily tonight,' Muriel said decisively. 'She can't get up in the morning and find a strange woman here, Stephen. It's dreadfully bad form.'

'It's dreadfully bad form for her to eat dinner with a baby on her knee,' Stephen said. 'It's dreadfully bad form for the child to be dozing off all round the house. He was on the sofa when I came home this afternoon. No wonder he doesn't sleep at night.'

'He does sleep at night.'

'Well, he won't go on sleeping when he can rest all day and play all night.'

Muriel nodded. 'A good nanny would be the very thing,' she said. 'You're sure you made the right choice?'

Stephen smiled. 'One of the old school,' he said. 'She'll knock the two of them into shape. But you're right. I'll tell Lily now.'

He did not go straight upstairs but called down the back stairs for Coventry. 'Brew up later?' he asked when the man came up to him. 'Your place?'

Coventry nodded and raised a curious eyebrow.

Stephen nodded towards the stairs. 'I'm going over the top,' he said. 'I want to secure my line of retreat.'

417

Coventry put out a hand, as if he would stop Stephen.

'No,' Stephen said, correctly interpreting the gesture. 'It's got to be done. The child has to be brought up our way. Lily will have to change.'

Coventry nodded and went back down to the kitchen.

Stephen went slowly upstairs, past his father's room and up to Lily's bedroom. He could hear her singing quietly in the bathroom as she bathed the baby. Stephen sat on the side of the bed and waited for her to come out. They were a long time. He could hear Lily's singing and her chatter, and her occasional chuckle at the baby's splashing. Then the door opened and she came out, pink with heat, her sleeves rolled up to the elbows, and Christopher all warm and gurgling in a bath towel.

She nodded at Stephen and spread out the towel on her bed, and dried and powdered Christopher with minute and loving attention. Every little finger, every toe, every fold of skin was meticulously dried and then patted with powder. Stephen could feel his anger rising, but could not place its source. He knew he should be pleased at his young wife's devotion to their child. It would be worse by far if she were careless or neglectful. But something in Lily's delighted communion with her son set his teeth on edge.

He said suddenly, 'This has got to stop, Lily. You can't go on like this.'

She looked up at him in surprise. She was putting Christopher's towelling nappy on him and securing it with a large pin in the middle. He could see that although she was looking towards him and apparently attending, her whole concentration was on the placing of the pin, and the shielding of the delicate skin of Christopher's stomach with her other hand.

'Oh, for God's sake!' he said irritably.

She sat the baby on her lap and gently pulled the

nightgown over his head. At the hem, white on white, was embroidered CCW. 'For God's sake!' Stephen said again.

Lily looked at him in genuine surprise. 'What's the matter with you?'

'There's nothing the matter with me! It's not me who is hysterical about the baby,' he exclaimed. 'It's got to stop, Lily. My son must be brought up in a normal household.'

She was fastening the buttons at the back of the nightgown with enormous care.

'This is normal,' she said reasonably. Her voice was softened by her child's proximity. 'He's fine. There's nothing to worry about. He's fine – aren't you?'

'It is not normal to have him on your knee at tea time. It is not normal to have him on your knee at dinner. It is not normal to go up to bed at damned half past nine because once it's his bedtime you might as well go too!'

'I get tired,' Lily said defensively.

'Because you're doing too much for him,' Stephen said instantly. 'We need a nanny.'

'No, we don't,' Lily said quickly. 'I'm tired today because I was singing a lot. Usually I'm not tired. And I won't bring him down to dinner if you don't want, Stephen. It just seemed so silly. Him upstairs, and us down. And you don't see him during the day at all. The evening is the only time you can be with him. I brought him down so you could see him.'

'We need a nanny,' Stephen said, sticking to his one point. 'And I have found one.'

There was silence. Lily turned a shocked face to him. 'A nanny?'

'Nanny Janes. She starts tomorrow at nine.'

'Stephen, I . . .'

'She's on a month's trial. She has wonderful references.

She's just what we need. She will have my old room, downstairs, the nursery. Christopher will sleep down there with her. And I shall move back in here with you.'

'No,' Lily said simply.

Stephen got up from the bed and crossed to the window and looked out. It was a cold night. There was a rush of clouds going across a pale distant moon. The sea was uneasy, pitted with scuds of rain.

'I won't argue with you about this,' he said determinedly. 'I will not have my home turned into a bear garden by you and this baby. Nanny Janes starts tomorrow. Christopher will sleep with her in the nursery. That is all.'

'Your mother . . .' Lily started.

'Mother knows. She suggested a nanny. We are none of us happy at the way you have been behaving. You have brought this on yourself, Lily.' He moved to the door. Not since the earliest days of their courtship had he felt so powerful. He felt utterly determined to keep Christopher and Lily in their place, subservient, separated, controlled.

He opened the door, ready to leave.

'Stephen, please . . .'

'No,' he said simply. It was a great pleasure to deny her, before even hearing her request. He could not help smiling. He went out through the door and he shut it quietly behind him. He stood on the landing, silently enjoying his triumph. Lily had defeated him over the theatre, she had taken her beating and then gone on stage. But the balance of power was different now. She had Christopher. She could not even raise her voice with Christopher in her arms.

Stephen ran lightly down the stairs, across the hall and out into the rain without even a coat. The Argyll was waiting for him. Coventry had the engine running.

Stephen flung himself into the passenger seat, slammed the door and laughed aloud.

Coventry let in the gear and moved off. 'Let's get drunk!' Stephen said happily. 'Let's go out and find a couple of whores, and get hugely drunk!'

Chapter Twenty-eight

Stephen and Coventry staggered down the street, their arms around each other's shoulders. A prostitute by a lamp post lounged forward, and then stepped back again into the shadows. She had worked the hard streets of Portsmouth long enough to know men who were too dangerous in drink for safe business. There were plenty of men like that. Sailors hardened out of their humanity on Atlantic convoy work, soldiers who had spent long years in the trenches and would never risk a direct glance at anything again. And men like these two: outwardly well, but sick inside from a cancer of anger or despair. She stayed still and silent in the doorway and let them pass.

They walked until they found the car, parked as usual some distance from the pub where they had been drinking.

'Let's go home,' Stephen said. 'Your home.'

Coventry opened the door for him and then went around to the driver's side. The moon was clear, illuminating the dark terrace streets around them with an eerie unforgiving light. Coventry drove with the headlights turned off, as if a gunner dug in on the Portsdown hills above the city might be watching for a telltale beam.

It was a cold night for June. Stephen had come out without a coat and the air rushing through the half-open cab of the car was cool and damp, blowing in off the sea. Stephen shivered, bunched up in the passenger seat and blew whisky breath on his clenched hands with relish.

'Chilly,' he said. 'But we've known cold that'll never be

matched by any weather in this country. D'you remember the winter of 1917? D'you remember the snow? God! I do! Woke up one morning and the place was white. There were damn great drifts over the tops of the trenches. You couldn't even see them. And chaps wanting to throw snowballs as if we were at some damn kids' party.'

He shook his head. 'That was the morning we lost James Dilke. He just stepped off the road. The mud on either side had frozen on top but it was just a crust covered with snow. He went down like a stone before anyone could get to him. His pack dragged him down on his back and the mud closed over his face while he was screaming.' Stephen paused at the memory of the eighteen-year-old boy, and his face rosy against the whiteness of the snow as he went down. 'Stupid not to make the road wider. Stupid not to mark it out before the snow fell. Stupid to step off.'

Coventry drove with serene concentration as if Stephen was speaking of a time before his birth, before history.

'I . . . I . . .' Stephen stopped to take a breath. 'I . . . I . . . I liked him,' he said. And suddenly his voice was that of a child who cannot understand loss. 'We called him Lucky Dilke. L . . . Lucky Dilke because he took a bullet clean through his helmet and it just parted his hair. And then he st . . . st . . . stepped off the road and drowned before we even knew what was happening. All of us running around and shouting for a rope while he went down.'

Coventry nodded, as if he had never been there. As if this were all news to him.

They had been driving along the line of the coast, and now they turned south down the road to Hayling Island. The tide was in, the waves sucked and pushed against the piles of the little bridge. The moon was silver on the black water. Stephen scanned the sleeping landscape all around them for a flicker of light from a match, or a giveaway reflection of moonlight on polished metal. There was nothing. The island was asleep and the country was at peace.

'Too bright,' Stephen said.

The westbound track along the coast had deteriorated after the winter storms. It was deeply rutted and silted with sand blown in from the dunes at the beach. Coventry eased the Argyll in and out of sand drift and ditch with practised skill.

'I used to like driving to headquarters with you,' Stephen said, watching Coventry's ease with the car. 'Get away from the noise for a bit. The little roads, and even some trees which were still growing. I used to like that.' He sighed.

'It lasted so long,' he said softly. 'So damned long. I think I could have borne a few months of it ... b ... b ... but not years. No-one could have borne years of it.'

The car pulled up at the edge of the creek. Ahead of them the Ferryboat Inn was quiet; the squat ferry waited at its moorings, bobbing up and down. Coventry shut off the engine and the two men got out of the car and went, a little unsteadily, up the rickety ladder at the side of the houseboat.

Inside it was dank and chill. Coventry closed the door and then felt along the shelf for the matches and the lamp. Stephen stood still, letting his eyes grow accustomed to the gloom, feeling again that rush of pure pleasure at being in an enclosed dark place, and not out on the revealing horizon. He had loved the dug-outs in the trenches. They smelled of urine and sweat and fear. But if they were deep, well dug and thickly piled with sandbags then they would withstand anything but a direct hit. Stephen used to creep into the officers' dug-out after an attack, his face grey with terror, shaking as if he had a fever. He used to thrust his face into the dirty blanket and cry silent sobs of relief to be back in the little hole in the ground while the shells still screamed and the flares still exposed the landscape, white as death outside the dark hole.

Stephen never had any notion of a battle plan, rarely hoped that an advance would succeed. From his first day in the trenches he knew it was just a matter of driving himself and forcing the men forward, into the easy swathe of enemy fire, forbidding himself to drop and hide, forbidding himself to crawl. The orders were to march forward, keeping step, firing as you went. Only when he received orders or completed the task could he fumble for the whistle and blow it with a screaming breath and wave the men back, back to the safe little pit in the little trench. And after a while, Coventry would bring tea and rum, and sometimes some biscuits or bread and jam.

Coventry never commented on Stephen's tearstained face. By then, he had lost his voice. They were none of them in very good shape. Stephen's anguished sobbing went virtually unnoticed among men who trembled or winked or drank. The new recruits, underweight and anxious, would stare at them in horror; but within a few weeks those that survived would be shaking too. Coventry would wrap Stephen's hands around his mug and hold them until they were still, and then he would nod gently and leave.

The lamp glowed and the shadows slid back to the corners of the room. Coventry put a match to the newspaper and driftwood in the grate and he and Stephen watched the flames eat along the line of paper, curl around, and then engulf the wood. Coventry lifted the scuttle of coal and shook it on to the flames. Then he took the kettle and went outside to the standpipe.

When he came back he put the kettle on the range and sat in the chair. He and Stephen together slid off their shoes and put them carefully to warm, hung their socks companionably side by side over the rail of the range.

'I don't hate it,' Stephen said suddenly. 'That baby. I hate its goddamned name. But I don't hate it. I'm not trying to separate them for spite. I'm not trying to spite Lily for her damned happiness.'

He broke off. 'In that house,' he said wonderingly, 'with Father upstairs half-dead and half-alive, and Mother with her heart in the grave, Lily can find a way to be happy. And then she brings Christopher back.' He shook his head disbelievingly. 'I married her to make *me* happy. I wanted her to take away the dreams, to put an end to the war.

'But the dreams come worse. Worse and worse. And she just goes on singing, and playing with the baby, and living as if it were all easy. As if she had nothing to fear. As if no-one had anything to fear.'

Stephen leaned forward and felt his perfectly dry socks. 'I thought she would make it as if the war had never been.' He shook his head. 'She has,' he said. 'She's done it for everyone else. She's made the whole house happy; she's brought Christopher back. She's restored him to them. It's as if they never lost him. It's as if they never grieved. And now it's just me. Just me alone, carrying the whole horror of it by myself.'

The kettle boiled. Coventry made fresh tea in a stale pot, as he always did, sugared Stephen's mug with four sugars, stirred it five times clockwise and passed it to him.

'I'll sleep here tonight,' Stephen said suddenly. 'I don't want to be there when that woman arrives and takes Christopher away from Lily. I suppose I shouldn't have done it.'

Coventry gave him a long level look. Stephen met his gaze without fear. They had seen too much together. There was nothing that Stephen could not confess to Coventry. There was nothing that they would not do for each other.

'Had to be done,' Stephen said.

* * *

Nanny Janes was prompt. Browning opened the door to her at three minutes to nine and showed her into the drawing room as the ornate clock on the mantelpiece chimed nine. Muriel rose to greet her.

'I am Mrs Winters,' she said. 'I am afraid my son was away on business last night and is not yet home. You must be . . . ?'

'Nanny Janes,' the woman said briskly, removing her gloves and taking Muriel's limp hand. 'I take it that I am to start my duties today?'

Muriel rang the bell. 'I don't precisely know,' she said uncomfortably. 'My daughter-in-law . . .'

The door opened but instead of Browning, Lily came into the room, holding Christopher in her arms.

'I heard the doorbell,' she said. 'Stephen told me he had engaged a nanny. But I don't want . . .'

'Is this the child?' Nanny Janes stepped forward.

Lily tightened her grip on Christopher.

'A handsome boy,' Nanny Janes said, making no effort to take him. 'Does he suffer much from wind?'

'Only after the night feed,' Lily said, lured into confidences. 'But I walk him rather than use gripe water. I don't like to use it.'

Nanny Janes nodded. 'Have you tried him with a bottle of plain warm water?' she asked. 'It can be very soothing.'

Lily shook her head. 'I didn't know,' she said.

Nanny Janes smiled. 'There are so many little tricks,' she said. 'I've been a nanny all my life! I should know most of them by now.'

'I think he may be teething,' Lily said tentatively. 'I know it would be awfully early but at the back of his mouth there's quite a pale patch on the gum. And sometimes his cheeks are very flushed.'

'The front teeth come first,' Nanny Janes said. 'Always do. The back teeth come later. You'll know when he's

427

teething all right, Mrs Winters! But we'll get through it without difficulty. Are you feeding him yourself?'

Lily nodded.

'And is he gaining well?' The woman held out her arms as if to weigh him. Lily reluctantly relinquished the baby to her, pride overcoming her resentment. Nanny Janes hefted the baby carefully. 'A grand baby boy,' she said approvingly. 'And where is his nursery? Will you show me to it, Mrs Winters?'

'He doesn't have one,' Lily said. 'He sleeps in my room.'

'The old day nursery,' Muriel prompted Lily. 'Show Nanny Janes to Stephen's old room.'

Lily led the way upstairs. 'It's not been prepared,' she said. 'He sleeps in my room. That way I can care for him in the night.'

Nanny Janes, holding Christopher, followed Lily up the stairs. 'Now, now,' she said equably. 'We can't have him being a cry-baby. He needs to sleep through the night. We'll soon have him in a proper routine.'

Lily opened the door to the day nursery. Muriel, looking up from the foot of the stairs, thought that Lily looked younger and powerless already. She looked again like the girl Stephen had brought back from the west country, with no-one to turn to and no-one to trust.

'But I like him being with me,' she said.

The door closed behind the two women. Muriel could hear Nanny Janes's soothing monologue but she could not make out the words. She went back into the drawing room and shut the door.

The car drew up outside and she heard Stephen's footstep and his key in the lock. He put his head around the drawing room door, and, seeing his mother alone, he came into the room.

'Is the nanny here?'

'Really, Stephen! She had no-one to introduce her. I

428

had to go completely by guess. Yes, she's here and upstairs in the day nursery with Lily.'

'No ructions?'

Muriel frowned. 'How should I know? I am only the grandmother. Your wife and your nanny are in the nursery together. Certainly Lily didn't greet her with open arms.'

'I must change my shirt and go to the office.'

Muriel hesitated. She wanted to ask him where he had been last night, and why he had not come home. But those were the recriminations of a wife. Lily had showed no curiosity. She had come down to breakfast and drank a cup of tea with Christopher gurgling on her knee and then gone back upstairs again to dress him. She never even expressed surprise that Stephen was not at home.

'I am surprised at you being late for the office,' Muriel said obliquely.

Stephen nodded. The silence between himself and the household was still holding powerfully even though there was a baby laughing and crying and Lily singing up and down the stairs. The old rules of distance and coldness still held between him and his mother, between him and his father, between him and the servants. Between Stephen and Lily there was opening daily an unbridgeable gulf.

'Well, I shan't be more than an hour late if I go now,' he said lightly and went from the room. He went past the day nursery soft-footed, but he could hear Lily's voice and Nanny Janes's. Christopher's juicy amused gurgle interrupted the two women occasionally. Stephen smiled grimly as he went up the stairs to his little bedroom opposite Lily's room. Christopher's relaxed joy would end very soon. He would learn, as every man had to learn, that pleasure is hardly won and peace exists nowhere. He would not be dandled on his mother's knee for much longer. He would learn loneliness and discomfort – as he should.

Stephen washed himself thoroughly in ice-cold water

and shaved uncomfortably in the same basinful as if he were still in the dug-out and scarce clean water brought to him a bucket at a time. He put on a clean shirt and tie and then took his suit from the wardrobe. When he was dressed he stepped back and looked at himself in the pier glass. He was getting plumper, the waistcoat was tight across his chest and belly, but the broadness of his shoulders could carry the extra weight. His face was square and handsome, a typical Englishman of the middle classes, exuding an air of self-righteous confidence, his brown gaze direct. If you took away the fair glossy moustache and the broadness, he could be a public school prefect, head of games, a hero to the younger boys. 'That's what I am,' Stephen said softly to his reflection. 'A hero. A bloody hero. They can't take it away from me, they can't deny it. Nobody can deny it. It's the truth because I said it was the truth. And now everyone believes it.'

He nodded and smoothed the thick hair of his moustache. He stepped forward and took up the two flat hairbrushes from the little plinth of the pier glass. He brushed his hair, smoothing it back from his face, admiring the shine on it.

'A hero,' he said again softly. 'And now it's over and I'm going to have the life I deserve. The life a hero deserves. My country owes it to me. My family owes it to me. My wife –' He broke off at the thought of Lily's continual intransigence. 'She'll have to learn,' he said. 'She'll have to learn the drill. Good drill can make a man do anything. She'll have to square-bash. She'll have to knuckle down. I'll knock her into shape.'

He nodded at his own reflection, and his mirror-image smiled in agreement at the thought of breaking Lily's independent spirit and remaking her into a wife fit for a hero. 'I've been lax,' he said. 'Damned lax. But it's all going to change.'

He put down the brushes, straightened his tie and went from the room. His heavy confident tread marched down the stairs, pausing outside his father's room. Stephen knocked and put his head around the door of the sickroom.

'Good morning, Father,' he said pleasantly. 'All well?'

Nurse Bells bustled forward. 'Mr Winters!' she said. 'This is a nice surprise! Yes, we're very well this morning. We've had a good breakfast and we may sit up by the window later on.'

Stephen looked past her to the man in the bed. He found his father even more repugnant now the man was recovering speech. He had preferred his corpse-like silence to the continual struggle for movement and the gurgling battle towards expression. The man started now: 'Gl . . . gloo gloo . . .'

'He's saying good morning!' Nurse Bells interpreted confidently. She nodded, beaming at the old man. 'Very good!'

'Got to go to work,' Stephen said clearly. '*I* can't spend all day doing nothing. Someone has to earn the money to keep the house going.' He looked critically at Nurse Bells as if she were an expensive luxury which he might well reduce, but she was beaming at Rory who was struggling to find another word.

Stephen stepped back and shut the door and ran down the stairs to the front door. As he went past the day nursery the door opened and Lily came out. He was pleased to see she was without Christopher. Already Nanny Janes had fractured their unity.

'Good morning, darling,' Stephen beamed. He stopped and brushed his lips against her cold cheek. 'Must dash. I'm late. Coventry's waiting.'

'I don't want her,' Lily said in a swift undertone. She laid hold of Stephen's lapels and looked up at him. 'Please,

Stephen,' she said. 'I'll do anything. Let me keep Christopher. Don't make me give him to her.'

Stephen looked down into Lily's white frightened face. 'But my darling!' he said gently. 'We agreed! Of course he has to have a nanny! You're not losing him! You're just making sure he is brought up properly. You can't care for him yourself, and keep up your singing and see your friends, and get back to normal! Of course he has to have a nanny!'

'I'll give up singing,' Lily said instantly. 'I'll never sing again if you don't want, Stephen. I'll do anything you ask. Anything.' She hesitated and then nerved herself to step closer, to slide one hand inside his jacket to his shirt front. She fingered the buttons of his shirt, intimately, as if she desired him. She looked up, her eyes dark with her fear of losing her son. 'Anything,' she promised.

Stephen, radiant, detached himself from her clinging grasp. 'Of course you must keep up your singing,' he said generously. 'Especially when you are doing so well! Let's just give it a trial period, eh, Lily? And if, after a month, you don't want to keep her on, then she can go. All right?'

Lily followed Stephen downstairs. 'If I don't want her after a month she can go?' she repeated, breathless with anxiety.

Stephen nodded. He rang the bell and Browning brought him his greatcoat and his hat. Lily took them from the parlourmaid and waved her away. Stephen let his wife hold his coat for him and pass him his hat with a sense of delicious triumph. She had never waited on him before. Always she had leaned on the newel post and watched him helped into his coat as if it were some bizarre ritual constructed to serve his vanity. Now she stood as humble as a servant and waited to see if he wanted his umbrella.

'I should like to have my things moved back into my

bedroom,' he said. 'Tell Browning, will you, darling?'

Lily handed him his briefcase with her eyes downcast. 'Of course,' she said obediently.

'And we'll go out tonight,' Stephen said. 'See the show at the Regal, maybe go down to the Troc and listen to Charlie.'

Lily thought of Christopher sleeping in his cot without her to watch over him. She thought of him waking in the night and finding himself in a strange room with a stranger at the side of his bed, strange arms holding him and a bottle forced into his mouth instead of being allowed to nuzzle lazily at the sweet-smelling warmth of his mother's breast.

'Yes,' she said tightly.

Stephen kissed the top of her head, opened the front door, and ran lightly down the steps to the waiting car.

'"Victory is mine, saith the Lord,"' he remarked to Coventry. 'She's well and truly beat.'

The summer month of June – the traditional month for warfare – was the month of Stephen's campaign of reparation against his wife. He was thinking, unconsciously, of the absurd ten million-pound penalty the Allies had sworn that Germany should pay for starting the war, for losing the war. He was thinking of the conversations in *estaminets* behind the lines when men had sworn that all German factories should be packed up and moved wholesale to England and France, that the German prisoners of war should be individually tried as murderers and rapists and hanged for their crimes. That all the German soldiers should be kept in squads of work parties until every piece of shell, every coil of barbed wire had been picked clear from the Atlantic coast to the Mediterranean. Nothing was too bad for a defeated enemy.

In Stephen's battle against Lily he wanted to see her

pay for every little slight he had suffered since his marriage. He wanted her to pay for every light-hearted moment when her natural joy bubbled up. He wanted her to pay for making his house a place where you could hear music, and slamming doors, and running feet on the stairs, and the doorbell ringing with callers. He wanted her to pay for being a child of the peace, while he was still locked in the war. More than anything else, he wanted to punish her for bringing home a baby and calling him Christopher.

But nothing defeated Lily. Stephen kept her away from Christopher every night by insisting that they go dancing, that they dine out, that they go to one theatre after another. Lily danced all night, ate hugely at late supper parties, greeted actress-friends and singers with delight, got up on stage at the Troc to sing ragtime at three in the morning and still was out of bed at six to give Christopher his morning feed.

Stephen started to give long and tedious luncheon parties at home, inviting senior clients and their wives for interminable meals of overcooked meat and heavy puddings which Lily had to arrange. But when the men joined the ladies in the drawing room he would find them clustered around Christopher, who would be kicking his bootees on the sofa, and Lily would laugh and say she had just brought him downstairs for a moment, not more than a moment, but he would stay and stay.

At the weekend Stephen insisted that he and Lily drive out into the country for walks, leaving Christopher in the nursery at home. Lily never demurred. She would put on her hat, kiss her son goodbye and be waiting for Stephen in the hall. He could not fault her. She would walk as long and as far as he insisted. They were caught in a sudden thunderstorm one day three miles from the car and Lily never complained. But the second she was home she skipped up the stairs to the nursery and Stephen heard

Christopher's loud coos of greeting and Lily's delighted half-sung replies.

He had moved into her bedroom as he had promised, but it was Lily who had given the orders that his clothes should be hung in the wardrobe of the big bedroom. Christopher's little toys, his cot, the lingering sweet powdery smell of him, was banished from the room. Lily never complained. Stephen would roll on her in the night, consciously brutish, and Lily would lie still and obedient, and let him do what he wished.

'Will you conceive again?' Charlie asked, coldly frank in the middle of the month.

Lily shook her head. 'Madge got me a thing,' she said. 'There's a doctor who will give them out if you say you're married and you've already got three children. Madge and I went together. It's really expensive, but I won't have another baby until I want.'

Charlie played a ripple of a chord on the drawing room piano. Lily was standing by the window, watching to see Christopher being wheeled back from his walk. Nanny Janes allowed him to come into the drawing room after this. Both Charlie and Lily waited longingly for the door-bell to ring and the bump-bump of Coventry pulling the perambulator up the steps.

'You could always leave,' Charlie said. 'If you took all the work you've been offered you could earn your own living now, Lil. You'd not have to go back on the stage again. You could live off your concert work, or very nearly.'

She shook her head. 'He'd take Christopher from me,' she said simply. 'He'd never let me have him if I left home. I'm here for keeps, Charlie. What I have to do is to keep my side of the bargain and make sure he keeps his. Nanny Janes goes in two weeks, he promised. Then I'll have

Christopher all to myself again.' She smiled across the piano at him. 'As long as I have Christopher I don't really care about the rest. As long as I can have Christopher with me then all the rest of it,' her gesture took in the uncomfortable pretentious house, the paralysed man upstairs, the secret fears of her husband, 'all the rest of it doesn't matter. Marriage, love, nothing matters as much as Christopher.'

Charlie nodded. 'I know,' he said simply. As soon as Christopher had been born he had despaired of Lily ever leaving home. She was right, Stephen would instantly separate her from her child. Stephen knew the law, and the law was designed to protect the family and the children. A part-time singer-actress would have no case for custody against a prominent citizen, a wealthy man, and a war hero.

He played a catchy dance tune. 'Know this one?'

Lily was instantly diverted. 'Is that "Sweet Summer Rag"?'

Charlie nodded. 'The score's in my bag,' he said, still playing. Lily rummaged in his bag and found the words. Charlie started at the beginning again and Lily began to sing. The doorbell rang, Lily moved to answer it, still singing, and caught Christopher up and danced lightly around the room with him, singing softly in his ear. The baby cooed and waved his fists, his eyes never leaving Lily's bright face. Charlie watched them both, smiling.

Chapter Twenty-nine

Lily did not struggle against Nanny Janes any more than she struggled against Stephen during the long month of the woman's trial period. She never argued with her, she never confronted her. She employed the low cunning and street-fighting skills of Highland Road. She smiled at her, she treated her with every courtesy. And she undermined her daily: with the maids, with Cook, with Coventry, with Muriel. She imitated her broad-beamed waddle in hilarious charades in Rory's room. She made faces behind the woman's back. She circumvented her discipline of the nursery whenever she could.

Christopher was to be put out into the garden every day to sleep from nine thirty until midday. Only then could he be brought indoors and changed ready for his midday feed, which was never earlier than one P.M. Lily would watch the pram being wheeled into the garden and then Nanny Janes going indoors to tidy the nursery. At once Lily would throw on a cardigan and go out to smell the roses or to take a breath of fresh air. Nanny Janes, glancing from the nursery window, would see the baby and his mother in silent and mutually absorbing communion as Lily sat on the bench in the garden with the pram turned towards her so that she could see Christopher's face as he smiled at her, and cooed, and then gradually fell asleep.

The first two or three times Nanny Janes surged downstairs and drove Lily indoors, threatening her that the baby would be spoiled or over-stimulated, or over-tired. But each time, as soon as she went away, Lily would steal out again to pick a handful of lavender as an excuse, or taking a slice of cake for the bird table.

While Christopher slept, Lily sat on the seat and guarded his rest. She feared nothing, she was not a nervous mother. She did not think that a cat would scratch him, or that it would suddenly come on to rain and he would catch a chill. She was just drawn to be beside him, as naturally as a mare and a foal move together as one animal. Lily could not be separated from Christopher. Not even Nanny Janes could do it.

Nanny Janes complained to Stephen that Mother was interfering with her running of the nursery. Stephen raised the subject at dinner and pointed out that Nanny Janes had successfully supervised the upbringing of countless children and that Lily would regret any interference in the system. Lily opened her blue eyes very wide and assured Stephen that she *never* interfered. Nanny Janes was with them for a month's trial and Lily had agreed to this. If it so happened that on one morning Lily had been in the garden when Christopher had been wheeled out for his rest it was hardly interference. 'You surely don't want me to *avoid* him?' Lily asked. And Stephen was forced to say 'No, of course not.'

Thursday afternoons were Lily's heaven. Nanny Janes would bring the heavy pram in from the garden at midday, wash and change Christopher, and then begrudgingly hand him over to Lily. Mother and baby were reunited for the whole blissful afternoon and evening. Nanny Janes was not on duty again until nine A.M. Friday morning. On fine days Lily would take Christopher out in his pram along the seafront. Charlie would come with her, pushing the pram along the promenade while Lily strolled beside it, her finger clasped firmly by the child. On other days Coventry would drive Charlie, Lily and Christopher out into the country and Lily would hold Christopher up to the window to show him the countryside. Christopher, pleased at his mother's embrace, watching only her delighted face, cooed like a throaty pigeon. One Thursday it rained and Lily and Charlie had tea in the drawing room, and ordered an unseasonal fire to be lit, then sang and played together while Christopher sprawled on the sofa and beat time with his little fists, and dozed.

On Thursday nights Lily would bath Christopher in her bathroom with extravagant handfuls of bath salts in the water, using the best gardenia guest soap. She would roll him in a big towel before her bedroom fire and sprinkle him thickly with expensive talcum powder. Free from nappies and clothes the baby would kick and gurgle with pleasure. Lily would bury her face in his stomach, press his firm feet to her mouth and nibble at his toes. They played like animals, unconscious of time. When the gong went for dinner, Lily would pretend that she had a headache and forgo her dinner for the pleasure of sitting in the shadowy nursery with her son.

It was a different room now. One end of it was taken up with Nanny Janes's bed, and a large screen for her to hide from the baby's male gaze as she dressed and undressed. Christopher's cot was tucked into the corner by the chimney breast. The landscape pictures by amateur watercolourists had been taken down from the walls as too distracting when he should be sleeping. The curtains were drawn closed all day against the beguiling summer sunshine and only pulled back at night when there was nothing to see except a few pinpricks of stars in the black sky. The window was always tight shut. Nanny Janes believed that night air was cold and unhealthy. The room smelled clean but stuffy, like a well-kept museum.

Lily would put her son to bed on Thursdays at the time she had been ordered, but then she would pull up the nursery chair and sit beside his cot, stroking his plump little stomach until he fell asleep. Muriel and Stephen, eating dinner downstairs in silence, would hear Lily's sweet soft voice singing lullabies to her son.

'Lily's headache can't be too bad then,' Stephen said sarcastically.

Muriel glanced at him. 'She always has a headache on a Thursday.'

Stephen nodded. 'But except for Thursdays, Nanny Janes seems to have the whole thing under control.'

Muriel nodded and swallowed a spoonful of cold pale blancmange. 'Lily will thank us for it in years to come.'

They drank their coffee in the drawing room; Stephen read the evening paper. At ten thirty they heard the front doorbell ring as Nanny Janes returned, and the light footfall as Lily slid from the nursery like a thief, closing the door behind her.

Stephen shook the paper. 'Well, she'll go hungry,' he observed.

But Lily did not go hungry. She had a tin box concealed in Rory's room especially for Thursday nights. She had biscuits and a bar of chocolate. She had apples and a jar of potted meat. She had a wedge of cheese. Charlie, wondering privately at the ways of the middle classes, had given her a little pen-knife with a tin opener, a knife, fork and spoon. While Stephen and his mother sat downstairs in uneasy silence, and Nanny Janes suspiciously inspected the placing of the nursery chair and the sleeping baby, Lily slipped into Rory's bedroom and spread out the goodies on his bedside table.

Rory, who was left to sleep from nine at night until eight in the morning, was always wakeful until the early hours of dawn. He was hungry too, and on Thursdays Lily and he feasted like children raiding a larder on all the things they liked best and then washed it all down with two bottles of stout.

'Good?' Lily asked him, her mouth full of biscuits.

Rory nodded, the muscles of his neck responding more and more easily.

When they had finished their feast, Lily swept up the crumbs and folded up the paper bags to burn on the drawing room fire when no-one was watching. Rory stopped her with a shaking hand.

'All right,' he said very slowly, his mouth working on the words, his throat thick. 'Nurse Bells – good sort.'

'Say again,' Lily commanded.

'Nurse Bells – a good sort.'

'Oh! Good sort!' Lily exclaimed. 'She won't tell that we've been picnicking?'

Rory slowly smiled, the warmth coming to his eyes and then slowly spreading across his face as the recalcitrant muscles moved. 'No,' he said carefully.

Lily beamed. 'We'll do it again, next Thursday,' she promised. She leaned forward and patted his cheek. 'Got everything you want till the morning?'

Rory nodded. 'Goodnight.'

By the time Stephen came up the stairs Lily had washed her face, cleaned her teeth and was in bed with the lights out and her eyes firmly shut.

It was no defence against him. He always took her on Thursday nights without her consent, but without her denial. Stephen's desire was always irritated by Thursdays when Lily radiated confidence and his son had enjoyed free run of the house for the whole afternoon. Lily lay still and let him do what he would without encouragement. She would not even put her arms around his back as he moved on her. Stephen pulled back before his climax and spilled his seed on her nightdress. Lily pulled the wet patch away from her body without even opening her eyes, and went to sleep at once.

She had learned the knack of detachment, she had

learned that skill, which most women of her class and generation knew: of enduring sex with her husband without letting either desire or repulsion arise. She lay as still as a corpse while he took her, she turned her back on him when he had finished. She was never wakeful, she was never distressed. She had learned the knack of going far from him.

It was Stephen who lay awake watching the ceiling. He felt as if in all his life, in the trenches, in shellholes, cradling a dying man and retching himself for fear, that he had never felt as lonely as he did now: with a wife who lay beneath him like a bolster while he made love to her, utterly untouched by him; and a child who had stolen the affections of his home. He watched the moonlight on the white ceiling and listened for the church clock. It struck midnight and then one, then two, before he slept. Then he dreamed.

In his dreams he was far from Portsmouth. He dreamed of a leave that had been granted to his battalion in late May of 1917. They had five days' leave and everyone was going to Paris. Stephen and Coventry were going behind the lines to stay at Little England. Perot was haymaking, scything the hay in the field since the haymaking machine was broken and there was no way to get the spare part he needed. Stephen and Coventry stripped down to their breeches; each took a scythe and worked alongside the man until it grew dark and the big yellow moon came slowly up, and Juliette called to them from the lit doorway of the little farmhouse.

They ate a thick rabbit stew and drank red wine. After dinner Perot shambled up the stairs to his bed and Coventry went to his sleeping quarters in the barn. Stephen and Juliette sat together drinking the last of the wine, either side of the table.

When the bottle was finished Stephen stood and took

her hand. She looked up at him. She had clear honest eyes like an English girl, like the best of English girls. Stephen said, 'Juliette, I love you. I want to marry you,' and watched her smile.

She rose from her seat and he put his arms around her. She was wearing an old skirt and a thin white blouse and he could feel the warmth of her breasts as he held her close. His hand slid up from her waist and nervously touched the underside of her breast. She was still smiling. Stephen bent and kissed her mouth, her neck, and then down to the open neck of the shirt. She smelled deliciously of cooking and haymaking, of the open air and the warm earthy smell of an aroused woman.

His hand cupped her breast and he felt the nipple harden under his palm. Her hand came around his neck and held him close. Stephen, a virgin, trembled with desire; but then his education as an English gentleman held him back. He broke free from her.

'No,' he said gently. He shook his head and touched her cheek. 'No,' he said. 'I would be a very beast if I touched you now, with things so uncertain. Juliette, forgive me . . .' He broke off. She was watching him with a little puzzled smile. She did not understand him at all.

'I want you to be my wife,' he said again. 'I want you to marry me.'

She nodded lightly and reached for him, but he put her hand aside. 'I want it to be right for us,' he said in his school boy French. 'I want us to wait until we are married.'

There was a flash of something, perhaps laughter, in her eyes but she shielded them with lowered lids, nodded solemnly and leaned her forehead against his shoulder.

'When the war is over,' Stephen said, 'you'll come home with me and we'll marry in England and buy a farm in England. Your father and your mother could come too and we could farm it together. I don't want to go into

443

Father's office. I don't want to live in Portsmouth. We'll buy a lovely little farmhouse and it will be just like here. We could buy somewhere in Kent and grow apples and pears.

'They call it the garden of England, it's beautiful there. Or perhaps we could grow vines and make wine.' He sat down on the bench and drew her on to his lap. 'You'll see,' he said. 'There's going to be a big push this summer. But the English will win, we're bound to win, and the war will be over. Then you and I will marry.'

She nodded.

'Or we could marry now!' he suddenly exclaimed. 'The padre could do it. And then if anything happened to me you'd be an Englishwoman. You'd have a pension and the army would take care of you. You could go to my home and Mother would look after you. That's better! We'll marry at once.'

'No,' she said gently.

Stephen broke off and looked at her. 'Why ever not?' he demanded. 'You'd be an Englishwoman then, not a Belgian. Think of that, Juliette!'

She nodded gravely at the thought. 'I want to be married when the war is over,' she said softly. 'In the church. With my friends there.'

'Yes,' Stephen said thoughtfully. 'Of course you do. A proper wedding in peacetime.'

Juliette nodded. She did not tell him of her utter certainty that the Allies would lose the war and that the last thing she wanted was English citizenship under a German occupation. She would have been his mistress while the farm was safely behind English lines, she would never be his wife. If the Germans came forward, as her father and sister were certain they would, then she would take a German husband, as any sensible girl would do, and a strong German man would come and help with the

444

farming and caress her after dinner. She was a survivor, not a patriot.

She smiled and stayed on Stephen's lap until they were both sleepy. Then he kissed her again and she went upstairs to bed. She undressed quickly and slipped between rough cool sheets. She hitched up her nightshirt and slid her hand down between her legs and satisfied herself quickly, gently. She reached orgasm thinking of a man who would take her with confident passion, perhaps without her consent, a man nothing at all like Stephen. She chuckled at the folly of the romantic Englishman who thought he would marry, who thought that his doomed army would win, and fell easily asleep.

Stephen turned over in his marital bed, breaking into his dream, and cuddled closer to Lily's warmth. They had been good days, that leave at the farm which he called Little England. At night they could hear the constant rumble of guns, like a thunderstorm far away. But after a while he blotted out the sounds of death and heard only the birdsong and the noise of the farm animals: clucking hens, the hysterical squeals of pigs at feeding time, and the continuous heartbroken lowing of cows separated from weaning calves. Perot made them work like peasants and Stephen had paid him in gold, the only acceptable currency, for their keep. Stephen and Coventry ate well and the pinched frightened trench look went from their faces. They filled out on fresh food and new-made bread and they forgot the taste of the tinned substandard Maconnoochie stew and stale tea. It was only five days but it seemed like a child's summer holiday. It seemed to stretch for ever.

When they had to return to the line they walked back in a depression so deep that they did not speak for hours. The officers and men home from Paris were pallid from drinking bouts and sick with infections. Stephen thought

445

of Juliette's purity and ignored their coarse teasing. That night they were ordered on a raid across no-man's-land, into the German trench to take prisoners and information. Stephen took only one prisoner. He shot the other German soldiers smack in their faces as they came out of their dug-out with their hands up. He was not even angry. He was gripped with a merciless cold executioner's intolerance. These were the men whose greed and stupidity were standing between him and life with Juliette. He felt bleakly savage towards them.

Stephen grew very popular with the men under his command after they had seen him shoot unarmed soldiers. They preferred the simplicity of war waged without rules. Straightforward murder was much preferable to the complicated combinations of chivalry and massacre which other officers tried to impose. Stephen, watching his men's hatred, their lusts and their terror, knew that all of them were becoming savages. And that when they got home, if they ever got home, they would never live like sane men again.

At the end of the month Lily broached the subject of Nanny Janes. She waited until Muriel had left the breakfast table and Stephen was folding the newspaper and finishing his last cup of tea.

'Nanny Janes's trial month is over,' Lily said lightly. 'How quickly the time has gone.'

Stephen nodded. 'So it has. I'm sure she'll want to stay, she seems quite settled. I must have another go at speaking to the Harcourts – the family where she was before. They were away when I last rang.'

Lily hesitated. 'That doesn't matter, I don't want her,' she said baldly. 'I've given her a fair trial as you wanted, Stephen, and I'm sure she's a very good nanny. But I'd rather look after Christopher myself. The best days for me are Thursdays when she has her afternoon off. I look forward to Thursdays all week. The worst day is Friday morning when I know it's another whole week before I can bath him. Please let her go, Stephen. He's my son. I want to care for him.'

Stephen looked at Lily's pleading face. 'I shall see,' he said magisterially. 'I shall speak with her now, before I go to work. I shall have to see what she thinks.'

He moved towards the door. Lily went with him, putting her hand on his arm. 'Stephen, please,' she said. 'I've not asked you for anything since we've been married. Not one thing. But I am asking you this. Please let me care for Christopher on my own. I can manage perfectly well. If you don't want him in the dining room or downstairs in the evening I will keep him in the nursery. He can go on sleeping there. Sally can sleep in there with him and call me if he wakes in the night. But please send Nanny Janes away and let me look after him.'

Stephen smiled, enjoying his power. 'Why don't you send her down to me?' he suggested. 'I'll see her in the drawing room, before I go to work.'

'It's not her decision,' Lily persisted. 'She's not his mother. I am.'

'Send her down to see me.' He did not even have to answer Lily.

Lily fetched Nanny Janes and then went into the nursery to be with Christopher. She picked him up from his cot and held him close to her heart. She felt as if they were under sentence and Stephen and Nanny Janes would decide whether they could ever be happy again. Christopher let out a small squawk of complaint, she was holding him too tightly. Lily released him at once and sat on the nursery chair and laid him back on her knees and smiled at him. She wiped the tears off her cheeks with the back of her hand. When Nanny Janes came into the room

447

Lily was still there, sitting hunched on the chair. She turned her face to the older woman as meek as a scolded child.

Nanny Janes took Christopher from her without a word. It was time he was out in his pram in the garden. Lily let her son be taken from her arms and slipped down the stairs to the drawing room. 'You kept her on?' she asked.

Stephen was packing papers into his briefcase. 'Of course,' he said. 'You had no actual complaint against her, did you? You did say you were sure she was a good nanny.'

Lily shook her head in silence.

Stephen went past her to the door. Browning was waiting with his overcoat, Coventry was standing by the Argyll. Lily held his briefcase while he shrugged into his coat. Browning discreetly retreated to the back stairs while Lily held the front door open for her husband.

'I shall be master in my own house, Lily,' Stephen said.

He pecked her cheek and went down the steps to the car. Lily shut the door behind him and went slowly up the stairs to her bedroom. She could hear Christopher's gurgles and coos as he was dressed but she made herself go past the nursery. She went into Rory's room instead and laid her head against his hand on the counterpane and rested there for a while, saying nothing.

Chapter Thirty

Lily spent the morning watching Christopher from the nursery window. It was a fine warm morning and Nanny Janes took her knitting out with her and sat in the sunshine while Christopher slept. The pram was turned carefully away from her so that Christopher would not see her face and know that he was not alone. The essence of Nanny Janes's system of childcare was that a baby should spend as much time alone as possible. Gregariousness, affection, spontaneity, were to be feared as signs of vulgarity and weakness. Loneliness and silence were signs of health.

Lily watched Christopher's waving hand and then saw it sink slowly into the pram and relax as he slept. Nanny Janes would sit beside the pram for the rest of the morning, only leaving her post if Christopher woke and cried for hunger or for loneliness. She would not stay within earshot of the nagging sound of a crying baby. It served no purpose to hear him. If he was not due for a feed he would not be fed. If he was not due to be picked up he would not be touched. Christopher could cry from nine till one if he wished; no-one was allowed near him. To pick him up, to respond to his cry, would be to spoil him and to destroy the system of discipline. Christopher would learn, as most babies under this traditional regime learned, to sob himself to sleep or into a state of quiet hopelessness. It was how Stephen had been brought up. It was how Rory had been brought up. It was part of the compulsive mimicry of the

449

upper classes which had always been the rule for the Winters.

Lily left the window and went to Rory's room. A new specialist nurse was with him, teaching him exercises to revitalize the wasted muscles. Rory's damaged body was coming to life. It was learning to work again. 'D'you mind if I come in?' Lily asked.

Rory smiled at her with his attractive crooked smile. 'See the show,' he croaked.

'He's coming on like wildfire,' the nurse said pleasantly. 'And the more practice in talking he gets the better.'

'I can talk with him,' Lily said. 'I am free all week. I am only ever busy on Thursdays.'

The nurse nodded, but Rory's dark eyes scanned Lily's wan face. 'Old bag stays on?' he asked.

'Say again,' Lily said. 'I didn't get it.'

Rory tried again more slowly. 'The old bag,' he said. 'Stays on?'

Lily giggled reluctantly. 'Yes,' she said. 'Stephen spoke to her this morning. She's here for good.'

Rory nodded.

The nurse set him an exercise for his fingers, and then clapping his hands. Rory was clumsy and uncontrolled, he was sweaty with frustration and distress by the time she said: 'That's enough for today.'

'Feel a fool,' Rory said irritably.

'You're coming along fast,' the woman said encouragingly. She turned to Lily. 'He really is,' she said. 'It's a very remarkable recovery.'

Lily nodded and the woman packed her little case. 'Same time tomorrow,' she said cheerily, and left.

'Got a concert?' Rory asked carefully.

'Tomorrow,' Lily nodded. 'Widows and orphans.'

Rory nodded. 'Singing much?'

'Two songs. Charlie's accompanying me. It's in a

church, a concert of sacred music. He'll be playing on the organ.'

Rory smiled. 'A change,' he said.

'Yes. He does all sorts. In a church at tea time, at the Kings in the evening, and in a nightclub at midnight!'

There was a slight very faint sound from the back garden. Lily turned her head to listen. 'That's Christopher,' she said. She glanced at the clock. 'He's only slept an hour. He'll have to be there for three hours now and she won't pick him up.'

The cry was a little louder, penetrating even the front bedroom. The baby was not going to go to sleep again. Rory looked at Lily's pale miserable face. 'He's not allowed inside until one,' she whispered. 'He'll cry and cry.'

They were both silent, listening to the heart-tugging wail from the garden.

'He's out there all on his own, crying for me,' Lily said.

'Fetch him,' Rory said suddenly.

'What?'

'Fetch him.'

'I can't,' Lily said. 'I'm not allowed.'

Rory's crooked smile gleamed at Lily. '*I'm* allowed,' he said impishly. 'Fetch him to me.'

For a moment Lily hesitated, then her face lit up and she slipped across the room and smacked a kiss on Rory's cheek. 'Of course you're allowed!' she exclaimed. 'I'll tell Nanny Janes to bring him in to you.'

She ran from the room and downstairs to the dining room. She opened the French windows on to the balcony. Nanny Janes was rising from the garden seat and collecting up her knitting. She was not going to stay in the garden with her peace disturbed by the irritating noise of a crying baby. She was on her way indoors. Lily waited until the woman had come up the steps to the balcony.

'Oh, Nanny Janes,' she said. She could feel herself

breathless and nervous. She took a deep breath and adopted her Duchess voice. 'Mr Winters wants to see his grandson. If Christopher is awake please take him to his grandfather.'

Nanny Janes paused for a moment as if she wanted to deny that Christopher was awake but his protesting yells were too loud to ignore. 'It's his rest time,' she said unwillingly.

Lily smiled. 'I'm afraid Mr Winters insists,' she said. 'I'll ring for Coventry to bring the pram in.'

She turned and went back inside, up the stairs to Rory's room. When Nanny Janes brought in the baby Lily was sitting in the window seat looking out to sea, indifferent.

Rory held his arms out for the baby. Christopher, still red-faced and sobbing with distress, was settled beside him on the bed.

'That'll be all,' Rory said.

Nanny Janes turned to Lily with studied rudeness. 'I can't understand what he says,' she said.

Lily beamed at her. 'He told you to go,' she said pleasantly. 'You can come and fetch Christopher at lunchtime.'

They waited until the door was firmly shut before they laughed and Lily fled across the room and scooped Christopher up into her arms.

Lily played with Christopher in Rory's room until two minutes before lunchtime, when she handed him over to his grandfather and slid from the room. When Nanny Janes knocked on the door at the stroke of one, and came in, silent with disapproval, the baby was in his grandfather's arms, Lily was not even there. The woman took the baby from the old man without even looking at him and left. Rory, exercising his muscles as his nurse had ordered, poked out his tongue at her back.

*　　*　　*

Stephen signed a pile of letters one after the other, and gazed blankly out of the office window. In the building opposite, a handsome Georgian town house newly converted to offices, he could see a girl tapping away at the keys of a typewriter. She worked slowly, one keystroke at a time, and sometimes there was a long gap between letters. Her hair was bobbed, she was obviously very much a modern girl: short hair, working in an office. She probably did not even live at home, she probably was not even married, thinking herself something special because she earned her own living, putting skilled men out of work. Stephen could remember when his father would dictate letters to male clerks who wrote in perfect copperplate script, and typed letters were regarded as a vulgar novelty, suitable only for ambulance-chasers and litigious companies. Everything was changed. Everything was changed for the worse.

John Pascoe put his head around the door. 'Are you going home for lunch today?'

Stephen nodded. 'My car should be waiting downstairs,' he said.

'How is your father? There's something I wanted to ask him.'

'Still very frail,' Stephen said at once. 'What was it?'

'It's this lady's will. It's our filing system at fault, I'm afraid. It all went to pieces during the war. I could swear she made a new will in about 1917. Lady Seymore, she lived over the water in Gosport. An Admiral's widow. I am *sure* she came in and made a new will. But I don't know where to start looking for it. There are some other papers of that year missing as well. I was hoping your father might have a clue.'

'I shouldn't think so,' Stephen said unhelpfully. 'I should think most of his memory is gone altogether. He's talking a little better now, but I doubt he could help.'

'Mind if I come over and ask him?' John Pascoe opened the door, and Stephen saw that he was carrying his light summer hat. He was obviously determined to come.

'I'll phone ahead and ask them to lay an extra place for lunch,' Stephen said, good manners asserting themselves over his wishes.

'I wouldn't dream of it . . .'

'Mother would love to see you.'

Stephen telephoned home and spoke to Browning before the two men went downstairs. Coventry was waiting with the Argyll at the office door. The two men got in and the car moved off.

'Is it tomorrow the car goes in for service?' Stephen asked.

Coventry nodded.

'All day?'

Coventry nodded again.

'Bother,' Stephen said. 'Lily has a concert. She and Charlie are going to St James's, at Havant. I meant to tell you. We'll have to cancel the service. Do it another time.'

Coventry nodded again.

'You should get her a little car,' John Pascoe said. 'A nice little runabout.'

Coventry nodded emphatically.

Stephen smiled. 'She drives rather well, actually. Coventry taught her. He thinks the world of her. I was thinking of getting her a little Morris.'

'As soon as your boy's up and about you'll need two cars,' John Pascoe warned. 'There'll be cricket matches and school events.'

Stephen smiled.

'What a batsman Christopher was!' John exclaimed. 'D'you remember? Every Wednesday your father would take the day off from the office to drive up to Christopher's school and watch him play. Every Thursday he'd come in, red as a berry from too much sun, and boasting to all the clerks how well Christopher had done. When he made his first century we had a bottle of champagne at lunch!'

Stephen's smile died from his face. 'I remember,' he said. He could remember playing with Christopher in the back garden. The ball had been hard in his little hands. Christopher, a demanding god in white flannels, had sent him fielding into the flower beds and holly bushes. While Stephen searched for the ball he could hear Christopher's excited shrieking of runs: 'Eighty-three ... eighty-four ... eighty-five ... eighty-six.' The ball was nowhere to be found, Christopher would go on running from bails to bundled jacket forever, ignoring Stephen's cries that the ball was missing, that it was not fair. Christopher loved to win. Stephen always lost. He always fielded and there was never time for his turn to bat.

In football he was always in goal while Christopher weaved around the garden, the ball tantalizing inches from his clever feet. When they learned horse-riding Stephen fell off as Christopher cantered triumphantly around the ring. No-one helped him up – Christopher was learning to jump, everyone watched him.

'Christopher won't be playing matches for years yet, if he ever does. Maybe he won't be a sportsman,' Stephen said.

They drew up at the house and the two men went indoors. Stephen glanced back at Coventry as if he would rather have had bread and cheese in the kitchen with him. Coventry looked back at him as if he understood, and then turned to put the car away.

John Pascoe was already in the house, greeting Muriel and Lily and going up the stairs to see Rory. Stephen went into his study without speaking.

John knocked on the door and went in quietly.

Rory was sitting up in bed. When he saw John his eyes

lit up and then slowly, awkwardly, the rest of his face creaked into a smile.

John crossed the room and took his hand. Gently, the grip was returned. 'Well, you're looking better!' he exclaimed. 'Old chap! You really are looking yourself again.'

Rory smiled his crooked smile. 'Well,' he said. 'I'm well.'

John drew up a chair. 'And talking again!' he said. 'I had no idea! What a relief, eh? You must have been going crazy.'

Rory nodded. 'Long time,' he said.

'We're all well at home,' John said. 'Still missing James, of course. Some wounds never heal, do they? You'd know.'

Rory nodded. 'The best,' he said. 'The very best. Went first.'

John cleared his throat and straightened his tie. 'Our boys,' he said softly.

There was a little silence.

'Still, you have a son, and now a grandson,' John said encouragingly. 'How is the baby?'

Rory beamed. 'Bonny,' he said. 'Christopher – again.'

'And that pretty daughter-in-law of yours? Stephen picked a real beauty there.'

'Lovely girl,' Rory said. 'Sings. Sings like a lark.'

'Talent!' John said. 'It's a wonderful thing. Maybe the boy will be musical.'

Rory nodded thoughtfully. 'Chorister,' he suggested.

'Good Lord, yes!' John exclaimed. 'You could get him into Winchester, anywhere, if he can sing. On a scholarship too! That's a good thought, Rory. What a start for the boy! No knowing where he might end up with a start like that! We could see him really rise in the world.'

Rory nodded with satisfaction. 'Bonny,' he said again. He took a breath. 'Good – see them together.'

'Stephen and Christopher?'

Rory shook his head. 'Lily and her son.'

John nodded approvingly. 'A young mother and her baby,' he said. 'Nothing better in the world. Gives you hope in the future, doesn't it? Makes you think it might even have been worth while – all the losses.'

The two men were silent for a minute, then John broke the spell. 'Odd thing at the office, Rory. Can't seem to find one of the files.'

'Which?'

'Lady Seymore's will. The old girl has finally popped off but all I can find is a will dated 1913. I could have sworn she made another. Some time in 1917. She did it with you, I think. But there's no record of it. I've been racking my brains but I can't remember.'

Rory nodded. 'Banked it,' he said.

'Come again?'

'Threat of raids – zeppelins – bombing the dockyard.' Rory spoke in short coherent bursts of speech, the small muscles around his lips straining. 'We decided – put in a vault – all the wills – equities. National Bank.'

John Pascoe slapped his head. 'Good God, I'm a fool!' he exclaimed. 'And then we lost our boys, and you were sick and we stopped doing it, and I forgot all about it. God knows what we put away. We only did it for a couple of months. I must be going dotty.'

Rory grinned crookedly. 'Pop in beside me!'

John laughed. 'Your son will think I'm an absolute fool,' he said. 'There was no note in the file or anything. Thank God you remembered, old boy.'

Rory nodded. 'Nothing wrong with brain,' he said slowly. 'Remember everything. Good and bad. Speech tricky – getting better. Moving hands, arms, head. Legs stuck.'

'Damned good to see you talking again,' John said. 'I've

missed you. Stephen's a bright lad. A hard worker, and thorough. But . . .'

Rory waited.

'Cold,' John said at last. 'It's not like the old days when we started the office and we were full of dreams about what we would do. Rich clients and a top-flight company, and on Thursdays we did free advice. D'you remember? We called them the ragged clinics. All sorts of problems we had in, and most of them solved by a letter on headed paper. Cheap to do and I really felt we were doing some good. Little Robin Hoods!'

'Good days,' Rory said.

There was a short silence.

'Any chance of you coming back?' John said tentatively. 'Even in a wheelchair, old boy? There's a lot of men worse hurt than you around the town. You see some dreadful sights. Blinded men, men in wheelchairs, men without legs. We've got a one-armed clerk. We could build a little ramp. You could have a downstairs office.'

Rory was silent for a moment. 'Wonder if I could.'

'We need another man, Stephen was speaking of a part-timer. We're overworked but we can't find the right chap. The one we had in mind was too sick. He'd been gassed, poor fellow. His lungs have packed up.'

'Wonder,' Rory said.

The gong sounded dully from the foot of the stairs, resounded louder and louder, and then went quiet.

John rose to his feet. 'What about it?' he said.

Rory grinned lop-sidedly. 'Damn – yes!' he said. 'Start here. Get a telephone. You call me. Send clerk round. A little work. Later on. Come to office. Part-time. I can do it.'

John Pascoe put his hand on Rory's shoulder. 'That's grand,' he said. His voice was soft. 'Get things back to how they were. We can make things right again. Having you back in the office would be excellent. Maybe we could start the ragged clinics again. There's a lot of people hit hard by the war, pensions unpaid, compensation owing, unending marital work. There's still work for you and me, eh?'

'Christopher,' Rory said.

For a moment John Pascoe looked grave, thinking that Rory was speaking of his son.

But the dark eyes gleamed. 'Keep seat warm for Christopher,' Rory said. 'New partner.'

John gripped his hand and felt the answering pressure. 'Another Winters in the office,' he said. 'Pascoe, Winters, Winters and Son.'

Rory released him, and John went to the door. 'D'you take your lunch up here?' he asked.

Rory shook his head. 'Tell them – wait,' he said. 'Come down today.'

John took the message downstairs and Lily clapped her hands and rang for Coventry to carry Rory down the stairs. Nurse Bells fled up to the sickroom to get him ready, and Browning laid another place at the table. Muriel and Stephen exchanged one silent look of displeasure but in front of John Pascoe there was nothing they could do.

Coventry came into the dining room carrying the tall man in his arms. Rory was wearing a dark grey suit and his old school tie. He looked distinguished. Even bundled in Coventry's arms he looked like a man of authority. Coventry placed him gently in the chair at the head of the table and arranged his feet side by side before heaving the chair in place. Stephen watched impassively as his father claimed his seat at the head of the table – where Stephen had been seated as head of the family, for three years. Muriel took her seat at the far end of the table and nervously fluttered her napkin. Stephen sat beside her, as far

459

from his father as he could possibly go. His mother and he were silent.

Lily pulled out her chair on Rory's right and John Pascoe sat beside her, opposite Stephen.

It was tomato soup and then cottage pie for lunch, Lily noted with pleasure. There was no meat to cut and no gristle for Rory to chew. She asked him in an undertone if he wanted his napkin tucked under his chin and did it for him, lightly, as an everyday act. John Pascoe broke the chilly silence with a discussion of a planned new hospital on the seafront for men who had been gassed during the war. There was a committee formed to raise funds.

Rory's right hand, rigorously under control, went from bowl to mouth with spoonful after spoonful of soup. Lily gave him a quick encouraging grin.

When the cottage pie came in with green beans and carrots, Lily spoke to Browning. 'Mr Winters will have his vegetables sliced,' she said easily.

Browning nodded, served the rest of the table and then took the vegetables outside. She came back with them sliced into easy forkfuls. Lily nodded.

Muriel and Stephen said nothing.

Lily and John Pascoe talked easily about the seafront hospital, and about the benefit of sea air. Rory said a word from time to time and Lily and John paused to listen to him and respond. Muriel and Stephen were silent, as if strangers had forced their way into the house and brought with them unknown freedoms. Pudding was stewed apple and thin custard with thick skin. Rory did not spill a drop. They took coffee in the drawing room. Coventry appeared from the back stairs and carried Rory to his old seat by the fireplace. Stephen sat on the sofa with his mother. Lily perched in the window seat, watching for Christopher and Nanny Janes setting off for their afternoon walk.

Stephen set down his cup of coffee and said he was ready to go back to the office.

'And your father's located the missing files!' John said blithely. 'Isn't that a relief! He's going to do a bit of work for us – time we got him back in harness I think, don't you?'

Stephen's smile was shocked. 'Are you well enough?' he asked his father. 'You certainly can't work with clients. They won't understand a word that you say.'

Rory nodded. 'Paperwork,' he said. 'Send clerk round. I'll make myself understood.'

'But surely . . .'

'Lily can help.'

Stephen shot a brief silencing look at Lily. 'I don't know what the doctor will say,' he said. 'Surely you shouldn't rush it, Father. And Lily has her singing, and Christopher to care for.'

Rory grinned at Stephen. 'I'm well,' he said in a tone which permitted no argument. 'Ready to work.'

Stephen was white around his mouth. 'As you wish, Sir,' he said tightly. He stalked from the room without bidding any of them goodbye. He brushed past Lily and opened the front door and ran down the steps without his hat or his coat. Coventry came scrambling from the back door, wiping his mouth with the back of his hand and pulling on his cap.

'Thank you for a lovely lunch,' John Pascoe said courteously, bowing over Muriel's hand. He kissed Lily gently on the forehead and patted Rory on the shoulder. Then he joined Stephen, waiting in the car.

'Lovely lunch,' he said as they drove off. 'How charming your wife is with your father.'

Chapter Thirty-one

Stephen brooded over the changes in his life, saying nothing. A telephone was wired in to Rory's room and John Pascoe supplied him three times a week with routine legal queries from clients which needed easy replies. Smedley, the one-armed clerk, called at number two, The Parade, every Monday, Wednesday and Friday, to deliver work and to take down Rory's replies. He was a patient man and would listen carefully to Rory's speech, understanding almost every word.

For the first few weeks Stephen monitored every letter, hoping that his father would expose himself as irreparably damaged. He thought he would find a letter of nonsense, of disconnected rambling thoughts. But his father's dictated letters were succinct, legally and grammatically perfect. Smedley denied doing more than providing linking clauses in the sentences. 'Your father is perfectly clear,' he told Stephen. 'He has a fine mind.'

John was openly delighted that his old friend was well again, and pointed to the easing of the office work now they had their partner back. He was full of plans again, speaking of the possibility of opening a free legal clinic. Once a day he rang Rory and once a week he came round to the Winters's home and had lunch with him. Stephen could say nothing.

He could not complain aloud, but he felt that his father's return to work had reduced him once more to the status of the junior partner. He was once again the young Mr Winters. He could not say that with his father in touch with office affairs he felt constantly on the defensive, as if his father might catch him out in some error. He feared the comparison between his own begrudging pedestrian style and his father's bright sympathetic grasp of facts. He could not say that it was a misery to him that his father was recovering and growing in strength, and that he could foresee the day when Coventry would drive them both to work every morning, home at lunchtime and then home again in the evening; and the quiet easy journeys alone with Coventry would be lost. His privacy in the back of the big Argyll car would be gone. His silent comradeship with Coventry would be destroyed. It would no longer be *his* car and *his* driver. They would both belong to his father, paid by him and commanded by him and Stephen would once again have nothing more than the mean status of the younger son.

The office would once again be his father's domain, Stephen would fall from being the bright leading light of the place to the least favoured son of a talented man. Rory's easy charm would win the clerks and the receptionist to his side as it had already won Smedley. His disability would earn their pity, his courage would earn their admiration. Watching his fight back from paralysis and his return to life they would forget Stephen's battle to come home from the deathly trap of the Ypres salient. They would forget that Stephen, not Rory, was the hero.

It was worse at home. Nanny Janes complained that Christopher's routine was repeatedly interrupted by Mr Winters, who would send for the baby whenever he heard him crying. Nanny Janes could not blame Lily, who was generally out of sight when the order was delivered by Browning, or Sally, or Nurse Bells. But privately she believed that the mother and the old man were working together to undermine her authority in the household and that the baby was sent for by the old man to reunite him with his mother, against the proper disciplinary system. The chauffeur, Coventry, was undoubtedly on their side. He was always there to fetch in the pram when Christopher should have been left outside. He was always quick to run up the stairs and carry old Mr Winters down to the drawing room for tea with Charlie and Lily, and then Mr Winters would send for the baby and Nanny Janes dared not refuse him. Lily she could intimidate by will power and the threat of a complaint to Stephen. But Mr Winters was the senior male in the household, he was its head. Now he was well again she supposed that he was her employer. Her well-learned habits of deference meant that she dared to bully Lily, but she was helpless against a gentleman.

Stephen planned what he would say to his father, planned to request icily that the older man leave the nursery alone. He knew how to hurt, he thought he could imply that Rory was an old maid, meddling where he was not wanted. But Rory's sharp intelligent look at him when he spoke of Christopher silenced him at once. Rory knew that Stephen did not love his baby and Stephen thought guiltily that Rory knew why. He feared that his father knew that Stephen had always been jealous of his brother, and that jealousy was alive all over again, even though his rival was nothing more than a blond-headed moppet of three months, gurgling and smiling in his pram. Stephen knew what he could say to put his father in his proper place: back to silence and loneliness. But he feared his father's acute response. He feared him too much to speak.

Muriel was as silent as her son over the changes in their lives. If she resented her husband's presence opposite her at the lunch and dinner table she never said. She shuddered once when Rory's hand misjudged the distance to his mouth and he spilled his food. She shot a swift pained look at Stephen, but she made no complaint. Muriel was too obedient a wife to voice her distaste and her fear at her husband's recovery. Her training as a lady had been too thorough for her ever to speak disagreeable truths aloud. If it had been left to her and Stephen, Rory would have died in that stuffy room, attended by the best of nurses, supervised by the finest specialists and surrounded by the most expensive goods that money could provide. They would have spared no expense or trouble to make his last days comfortable. They would have prepared for him an impressive funeral with carriages of mourners, principal and secondary, and a heap of flowers later delivered to the hospitals. Both Stephen and Muriel would have been sincerely grieved at their loss and consoled only by the orderly charm of the funeral, the repast and the will.

What neither of them could bear was his slow repellent crawl back to health. Neither of them could bear his half-state of part-paralysis. Sometimes his hands shook and he could not control them. At every meal time Lily tucked his napkin under his chin like a baby. Privately and only to themselves Muriel and Stephen saw him as a cripple. He disgusted them.

But Lily was happier than she had been since her marriage. She sang: in the drawing room as practice; on the stairs unconsciously; and in the bath for joy. Rory was getting better, Muriel had ceased to criticize, Stephen was reduced to a silent uneasy presence and Nanny Janes had lost her iron control over Lily and her son. Lily could have Christopher with her whenever she wished. She simply had to pretend that she was fetching him for Rory, and Nanny Janes had to do as she was bid. As the days grew sunny and hot in mid-July, Rory asked to be wheeled out in the afternoons at the same time as Christopher and Nanny Janes took their walk. After a couple of afternoons a new routine was established. Charlie would arrive after lunch as Coventry returned from taking Stephen to the office for the afternoon. Coventry would lift Rory into the wheelchair and push him along the seafront while Charlie pushed Christopher's pram and Lily strolled between pram and wheelchair, holding her son's little hand and chatting to her father-in-law. The utter vulgarity of Charlie Smith strolling down the promenade, pushing a pram, was glaringly apparent only to Muriel. The distaste she felt at seeing Lily blithely strolling beside her son's pram and chatting to Rory in his wheelchair was shared only by Stephen. But they could not speak of it.

At tea time they all returned and then the doorbell would start ringing. Lily's friends from the show at the Kings would call in for tea to fill the slack time between the afternoon matinée and the evening show. One afternoon the chorus girls descended in a chattering noisy bunch, another time Madge Sweet and her boyfriend, a saxophonist from the Trocadero Club, called. Often Charlie would play, Lily would sing, Teddy would play tenor sax and the haunting seductive summons of the saxophone would drift up the silent stairs of number two, The Parade and out through the open windows to the street.

'It's nigger music,' Muriel said in an angry whisper to Stephen before dinner one day. 'I half expected a crowd to gather and throw pennies through the window.'

'I'll speak to her,' Stephen promised. But that evening at dinner Rory had said he enjoyed the music that afternoon and would Lily make sure to ask Teddy again.

Muriel and Stephen exchanged a look of silent resentment, and said nothing.

Muriel had thought that Lily's stage friends would clash with the ladies and gentlemen of the charity concert set who had started to visit Lily at home. She had maliciously anticipated a social freeze from Lily's new circle, and had gone so far as to caution Lily that she could not mix her theatre friends with the social world. Lily's look of blank incomprehension had whetted Muriel's appetite for social disaster. The girl had refused to be warned, but if she tried to put Lady Drew next to Madge Sweet at the tea table there would be serious social consequences and Lily would never sing at a charity concert again. Smugly, Muriel waited for the steady flow of callers in good cars to stop.

But she was wrong. The rigid divide of her girlhood between gentry and the rest had been eroded by the war, and the ladies and gentlemen of Hampshire society were delighted and amused by the company they met at Lily's tea table. The chorus girls made them feel daring and Bohemian, Lily's unaffected charm smoothed over any social solecisms, and number two, The Parade was fun in a city where the cost of the war was not yet forgotten and where the future – uncertain in Europe, uneasy at home – was widely feared.

Charlie was a relaxed and charming host, passing plates and sometimes even pouring tea. He would play the piano if anyone asked, he was invaluable with contacts and friends spread across the city and even to London. If you wanted to rent a hall, or throw a party, Charlie knew the best place, the most fashionable band. If you wanted to dine somewhere quite different then Charlie knew of a new place just opened and would scrawl a message on his visiting card which would get you the best table. If you wanted to see a show in London Charlie knew which were on the crest of fashion and which were closing. The ladies who organized garden fetes and concerts for the war-wounded found Charlie invaluable when a wretched man let them down over the marquee, or when a grand piano could not be found for hire.

His behaviour to Lily was that of an affectionate brother. When she sang at the piano she would rest her hand on his shoulder, when the tea tray went out and cocktails came in he would stand behind her chair. If Lily had been less popular there would have been ill-natured gossip, but none of the ladies ever did any more than whisper behind a gloved hand in the privacy of their car on the way home: 'I'm sure he's in love with her, he never takes his eyes off her.' To which the reply would always be: 'Oh! Bound to be! But she's very much the wife and mother.' And the ladies, going home to their elegant manor houses in the Hampshire countryside, would allow themselves a little sigh of regret that they did not have a man like Charlie, handsome, slightly dangerous, single, to come to tea with them.

Charlie said nothing. He watched Lily blooming under the warmth of new friendships with a smile. They had their private times together: walking on the promenade they would sometimes drop behind the wheelchair and talk of the Midsummer Madness tour, or of Lily's singing engagements. Lily would tell him whether Christopher had spent a good night, and they would speculate about the possibility of him teething. Lily would rest her hand on the pram handle beside Charlie's hand and they would gently touch. She missed her mother still and it was only to Charlie that she ever spoke of her.

'She was a fine woman,' Charlie would agree. 'How proud she would be now! And how she would have loved Christopher!'

He would tell Lily about his work, about the hundred daily clashes and crises of a flourishing theatre. He found that she was an astute advisor; often she thought of a solution to a problem which had been worrying him for days. They worked together on increasingly difficult pieces of music and Charlie realized that Lily's career as a concert hall singer could extend further than the charity-concert circuit of Hampshire if she wished. He kept an eye open for classical events and he mentioned to Lily that she should study church music and oratorios.

When they were preparing for a concert Charlie would come in the morning and again in the afternoon. Best for him was the day of the concert when they would perform and often stay out for dinner together. Once or twice Stephen joined them but the third time he refused. He was bored by the music and dozed in the church. He trusted Charlie to bring Lily home on time and he did not care if they stayed out for dinner after the performance. Coventry drove them, a silent chaperone, and sometimes would leave his cap in the car and join them for the meal. At the end of the evening they would occasionally tell Coventry to drop them at the seafront and they would walk home watching the waves breaking gently on the shingle, as the long white line of the moon on the water followed them to the quiet shuttered house and their silent parting.

Lily and Charlie's love affair, never closer than the touch of a fingertip, never discussed between them except for a soft 'I love you' from Charlie when he left in the evening, deepened and widened into a familiar joy that summer. They were comfortable together with the ease of old friends, and they kept their mutual desire locked safely away. Only once during the months of loving Lily and watching her did Charlie wake one night with a burning pain in his groin as if he could love her like a man. He threw on some clothes and walked all night and all the rest of the day until the pain in his body was gone. That night he drank at the Trocadero, steady concentrated drinking, until the pain in his mind was gone too. The steady twinge of heartache – sometimes delight in her, sometimes grief that he could not have her – he lived with; as other ex-soldiers lived with the absence of a limb or with the loss of sight or hearing or taste.

Lily never complained of Stephen, and though Charlie watched with the anxious attention of a man in love, he never saw any sign that Stephen felt anything more than indifference to Lily. He had been afraid of Stephen's temper, and he knew himself to be in a state of continual readiness to take Lily away if Stephen ever struck her again.

'I couldn't go,' Lily said simply once. 'What about Christopher?'

'I'd kidnap you both,' Charlie said grimly. 'I couldn't tolerate him hurting you.'

'He won't,' Lily said certainly; and over the months of the summer Charlie saw that it was true. Stephen had sunk from rage into passivity as everything in his life conspired to reduce him, to weaken him, to make him into a nothing. In sour silence he watched the conversion of his house from a place of silence and disappointment to one of the brightest, most entertaining homes in Portsmouth. By the time he came home from the office they were drinking cocktails and he always had the feeling of a gatecrasher at an elegant private party. The ladies were disposed to be very charming but Stephen could never flirt with women of his own class, he felt ill at ease with anything warmer than the icy frigidity of his mother. The chorus girls were more to his taste but as the summer wore on and the unseasonal darkness of Stephen's mood deepened, he did not want to play and flirt with them. They were nothing more than whores; he might have bought their time but he would never have courted them.

Stephen felt the small gains he had made when he had come home from the war to a darkened house, steeped in mourning, were steadily eroded by the illumination of Lily's easy joy. The hall table became crowded with good-quality visiting cards engraved with names and titles of people Stephen did not know. Lily borrowed the car more and more often to visit people neither Stephen nor Muriel visited, who lived out of town, in the manor houses of Hampshire. Divided between resentment and snobbish ambition, Stephen ordered a little Morris car for Lily so that Coventry and the Argyll would remain free to take him to and from the office. He did not acknowledge, even to himself, that he disliked the thought of Coventry driving Lily around, while Lily called and took tea, and gossiped and had fun. Stephen wanted Coventry to stay with him, like him: in silence and darkness, looking back to the flat lands around the Somme.

He felt himself cuckolded. Cuckolded by his wife's blameless happiness. Stephen had done nothing to make her happy. He had done much to frighten and grieve her. But Lily was young and buoyant, she quite failed to recognize the silence redolent with unhappiness of number two, The Parade. She opened windows, she summoned guests, she broke the rules of raising a child into loneliness and indifference. She left the running of the house entirely to Muriel – as she had agreed to do. But despite the inedible food, despite the sour wine, despite the poor wages, despite the sombre furniture and the dark curtains and wallpaper, in that midsummer of 1921 a sweet sea breeze ran through the whole house and infected everyone with groundless optimism. Everyone but Stephen.

He went on long drinking bouts with Coventry, as if he might find in the depths of drink some way back into the sunlight which shone so easily on his wife. Coventry, uncritical, unspeaking, would drive the two of them to the hard streets of the town, around the dockyard gates. They would park the car beneath a streetlight and leave it there while they wove their way through the dark maze of the backstreets. Under the arches of the railway bridge there were tattooists, drawing designs for drunk sailors. There were all-night cafés where you could buy coffee or tea as strong and sour as they used to have in the trenches, with a tot of secret rum poured on top for an extra threepence. There were makeshift refuges where homeless, pensionless survivors of the war huddled together for warmth and tried to sleep. Stephen used to stare into the darkness of the shelter, smelling the familiar smell of men huddled close, wondering if they had found in their animal companionable warmth an escape from the loneliness and despair that gripped him.

Stephen and Coventry would find their way to ill-lit bars where working men, sweaty from the nightshift at the dockyard, or frowsy from all-night drinking, would gather and drink beer with spirit chasers. Tense as a prize-fighter, Stephen would order beers and single whiskies and sit quietly at their table and scan the room for trouble. If the landlord was burly, and the customers quiet, the two men would drink up and move on. There was a shabby pub in every street and sooner or later, when Stephen was so drunk that his irritability could not be contained, they would find what they were looking for and a fight would start. Often Stephen and Coventry were on the periphery, first as bystanders and then as guerrilla fighters, sliding into the centre of the crowd for a punch, a kick to an unprotected belly, and then sliding back out, unscathed. But more and more often in those hot summer nights, it would be Stephen at the very centre of the fight. He would brush someone at the bar, knocking the drink from his hand and refuse to apologize. He would interrupt another man's conversation and sneer at him in his lah-di-dah officer's voice. He would refuse to pay for his drink and spit in the glass so the landlord would lift the flap of the counter and surge around, fists swinging. Or more and more often he would taunt men with sound bodies that they had found some coward's way of escaping the trenches. He would call them girls and conchies. He would call them yellow and communist. He would tell them that better men than them had died in France so that they could keep their noses in the trough at home. He would shout at them that they were swine and that he was a hero, a bloody hero.

As Stephen grew more dangerous Coventry fell further and further back, scanning the crowd. When Stephen started a fight Coventry would be behind him, his quick eyes looking all around, watching for a knife to be pulled, for the quick crack of a broken bottle. When Stephen was in the centre of milling fists, his face alight with unleashed malice, Coventry would still be reserved and watchful on the fringe. Only when Stephen threatened to sink under the weight of other men, or when someone was coming up behind him, would Coventry move forwards and trip the man, and knee him sharply in the kidneys as he sank down. He would fight his way through a crowd towards Stephen, jabbing a punch into an unprotected back, a hard fist behind a man's ear so he fell knocked out cold, or doubled up by a swift dishonourable kick to the balls. Stephen knew intuitively when Coventry was behind him, and Coventry's touch on his belt was his signal to back out of the fight, still exchanging blows, while Coventry led the retreat to the door. Often they timed their escape to within minutes of discovery; they would be out of the door and walking down the road, catching their breath, as the MPs or the civilian police came running towards the pub past them. Once they were struck a passing blow from a truncheon, once they were threatened with arrest as they were bursting out of one door as the police came in the other. But mostly they disappeared before the arrests were made, and then for the next week or so they would steer clear of that area altogether.

The violence purged Stephen. He fought, not like a gentleman, not even with the straight anger of a working

473

man; he used his skills as a trained boxer but he set aside all the rules he had ever been taught at school. He used his knees, he used his feet. If he had a glass in his hand he would knock off the top of it and flash it, in and out, like a dagger. Generally he cut nothing more than cloth. Once he struck at a man's face, and guessed, by the bitter horrified scream, that he had cut his eyes. If he knocked his opponent down he would kick him at once, hard-shod, in the soft vulnerable belly, or in his curved back. Once a man went down on his back, and Stephen, in a sudden rush of joy, raised his boot and stamped on the man's face, hearing the sweet textured sound of the crushing of his nose bones, the collapse of the septum. Coventry laid hold of him then and drew him back. Stephen was trembling like a youth after orgasm. Coventry had to put an arm around his back to hold him up.

'Damn legs are all weak!' Stephen exclaimed breathlessly. 'Oh God, Coventry! Did you see that! Did you hear it?' He let out a little sob, he licked his lips. 'Oh God! That was so good. That was so good.'

They could hear a whistle and the sound of running feet. Coventry drew Stephen into a darkened doorway and they turned their faces into the shadows. The police ran past them, truncheons out. Stephen leaned back against the door frame.

'Cigarette,' he said.

Coventry took out a packet of cigarettes, put two in his mouth and lit them, then passed one to Stephen. In the brief flare of the match his face was neutral, noncommittal.

Stephen inhaled deeply and then blew the smoke out. 'Christ,' he said. 'That was the best.'

Coventry noticed that Stephen's hands were still shaking with pleasure, his eyes dilated. They stood in silence until they had finished smoking and then they trod out the butts and walked quietly to the car. Behind them was the

474

jangling bell of an ambulance. Stephen chuckled at the sound.

The car was parked some streets away. There was a policeman standing beside it. Stephen spotted him at once and they both fell back, moving like one man, into the dark alleyway. They turned at once and began to groom each other, straightening each other's ties, Coventry wiping a fleck of blood from the corner of Stephen's mouth, Stephen rubbing a smudge on Coventry's collar.

'You're OK,' Stephen said. 'Me too?'

Coventry nodded. He reached into his pocket and pulled out his folded chauffeur's cap. He shook it out flat and brushed it off. Then he placed it on his head and he and Stephen strode confidently out of the shadows towards the policeman, Coventry at a deferential half-pace behind his master.

'Evening, officer,' Stephen said pleasantly. 'Everything all right?'

The policeman saluted. 'Yes, Sir,' he said. 'This your car, Sir?'

'That's right,' Stephen said pleasantly. 'No trouble, is there?'

'Nothing at all, Sir. We were afraid it had been stolen. Not often you see a car like this around here.'

'Thank you,' Stephen said. He slid a crisp ten shilling note out of his pocket and held it at the ready. Coventry unlocked the car and opened the back door, holding it for Stephen.

'Very vigilant,' Stephen said. 'Carry on.'

The man saluted again. Stephen flicked the note out at him. The man hesitated. 'I couldn't, Sir,' he said. 'Just doing my duty.'

Stephen winked at him. 'For a little treat,' he said. 'We all like little treats.'

The policeman glanced at the darkened streets behind

475

them and guessed that in one of them was a brothel where Stephen had been.

'Oh yes, Sir,' he said. He took the note and tucked it away. 'Very good, Sir,' he said. 'Goodnight.'

Stephen waited until the man had gone round the corner and then climbed into the front passenger seat. Coventry got in beside him and took off his cap.

'Let's go home to Hayling,' Stephen proposed. 'Have a brew. It's been quite a night.'

Coventry nodded and drove the big car along the coast road and down the sand-blown lanes to where his little houseboat stood half-surrounded by lapping waters.

Stephen went inside while Coventry fetched water from the standpipe. When he came back Stephen had the lamp lit, and was setting a match to the fire.

They were silent as they brewed the tea and then Coventry poured Stephen a mug, sour and oversweet, and Stephen wrapped his hands around the hot enamel sides and sighed with pleasure. 'That was the best ever,' he said. 'This evening – it was the best ever.'

Coventry did not nod, he was watching the flames. Stephen sensed his reserve.

'Something wrong?' he asked. He glanced at Coventry. Still the man did not look at him.

Stephen reached out a hand and gripped Coventry's shoulder. Unwillingly the dumb man turned his face to his master. His eyes were sombre. Stephen shook him gently, lovingly. 'Don't you forget,' he said. 'Don't you forget. We've done an awful lot worse than that. We've done an *awful* lot worse than that.'

Stephen drove himself home in the early hours of the morning and crept into the bedroom as dawn was breaking. Outside the sea was up and the waves were soughing on the beach. A blackbird was singing.

Lily stirred as her husband came in and leaned up on one arm. The peach shoulder strap of her nightdress slid down her arm showing the smooth line of her breast and neck. As soon as she saw it was Stephen she sank back to the pillows and shut her eyes, completely indifferent.

Stephen undressed quietly, so as not to disturb her, and slipped between the sheets beside her. The memory of the man's face beneath his shoes came back to him as he closed his eyes and waited for sleep. He heard again the extraordinary pleasurable crunch of the breaking nose, and the hoarse scream of pain. Stephen sighed with pleasure and put his hand out to touch Lily's smooth warm shoulder in the darkness.

She rolled over and moved away from him. Stephen wriggled across the bed and took her shoulder in a firmer grip. He could feel excitement mounting at the thought that she might resist him. He had hardly touched her in weeks, he had been so unmanned by his father's return to health. But now, with the perverse thrill of the fight fresh in him, Stephen thought that Lily might resist him and give him adequate reason to force himself on her.

She was a lady, he reminded himself. No-one could say otherwise; as cold as ice, she hated lovemaking. She usually endured it, but in these early hours, when she had been sleeping, after weeks of neglect, she might think herself justified in refusing him, and then he would be justified in forcing her.

He gripped her shoulder hard and pulled her towards him, pushing her on to her back. In the pale light of the morning which showed through the curtains he could see her big dark blue eyes looking at him with absolute indifference.

'Oh, very well,' Lily said in the bored drawl of the Hampshire society ladies. 'I quite thought you'd given it up.'

She took her nightdress in one careless hand and hitched it up to her waist. Her hard unforgiving gaze never moved from his face. She spread her legs, still staring at him, waiting for him to heave himself on her and take his legal rights. Her face was flinty, her eyes blank.

'Christ,' Stephen said, all desire dissolving in an instant. 'Christ, Lily.'

'What?'

'Well, it's hardly lovemaking . . .' he said feebly.

'It's not love at all,' Lily said precisely. 'It's your right. You do it if you want to. I don't care.'

Stephen felt his erection shrivel. He drew back from her and released his grip on her shoulder. 'Ladies permit it,' he said weakly. 'You should allow me to do it without comment.'

Lily shrugged. 'I don't care. It means nothing. It means nothing to me. You can do it or not, as you like.'

Stephen pulled one of the pillows towards him and hugged it. 'Christ, Lily,' he said again.

She turned a face to him that was as stony as her words. 'What?'

'A man likes a bit of warmth, there ought to be a bit of love between us. We're married, we've got Christopher, you're my wife . . .'

Lily listened, her face unchanging.

'We're married,' Stephen said again. It was almost like the cry of a child, calling in playground promises and favours.

'Yes, we're married,' Lily said wearily. 'And I do my part of the bargain. I've said you can have me if you want. You don't expect me to *enjoy* it, do you? You don't expect me to invite it?'

'No,' Stephen said quickly. She was a lady; she could not enjoy it. 'Of course not.' But even as he spoke he had a sudden recollection of Juliette and the warmth of her heavy breasts through her shirt. Her easy smile and the smell of her sweat, that summer, when he had fallen in love for the first time.

'All right, then,' Lily said. She turned her back to him and closed her eyes. She lay in silence. Stephen could not tell whether she was asleep or awake. He lay beside her, hugging the pillow for comfort. Not even in the trenches had he felt so desolate and alone. He had bent and broken Lily until she had become his bride and then his wife. He had raped her, and forced a child on her so that she would leave the theatre and be utterly in his power. But now, at the pinnacle of his control, now she was married and powerless and bound to him for ever by the law of the land, and by her love for his child, she could turn to him and tell him to lie on her or not, that it meant nothing to her.

Stephen blinked, and found that his eyes were filled with tears which ran down his cheeks and blotted on the pillow. He had lost his power at his office, he had lost the easy familiar loyalty of his clerks. He had lost his power at his home, his father once more sat at the head of the table. And the wife he had married to save him from nightmares and loneliness had moved so far away from him that he could not even hurt her, let alone touch her.

Stephen lay sleepless all night. He did not even doze. His life spread before him like the enlarged map of the Western Front which his father had pinned on the dining room wall. Half an inch gained here, half an inch lost here. Every appearance of progress – all those little marching flags – but in reality, nothing but empty ground and a strange harvest of weapons and rotting corpses.

Stephen left Lily to sleep in the morning. He went down-stairs in his dressing-gown and ordered a breakfast tray for the two of them. Muriel glanced at him and his slippered feet as he went past the drawing room door. She looked slightly scandalized, as if the sight of her own son's bare legs were improper.

He sent Sally to carry the tray, and he sent Browning in to Nanny Janes with his apologies and instructions to bring Christopher upstairs to Lily as soon as he was dressed. Then he followed Sally up the stairs to his bedroom and took the tray from her at the bedroom door, nodded to her to open the door, and went in.

Lily stirred and sat up in bed, bemused. 'Gracious, what's the time?'

'Nine o'clock.'

'What's happening? Aren't you going to the office?'

Stephen put the tray on the bed and poured Lily a cup of tea before he answered. 'I'm not going in today.'

'Aren't you well?'

'I'm all right.'

There was a silence. Lily was perfectly composed, sipping her tea. 'Would you open the curtains please?' she asked. 'I want to see the sky.'

Stephen drew them back to let the warm summer sunshine flood into the room. He did not know how to speak to Lily. He expected her to be grateful for breakfast in bed. He expected her to sense a new turning in their relationship. But she was taking it with total indifference.

The sky was a bright innocent blue, it was a lovely day. Already the bathing machines were drawn up on the beach and half a dozen donkeys were waiting to give rides at the foot of the pier.

'I've got a little surprise,' he said, almost as one would speak to a little girl.

Lily looked at him, not like a little girl at all. 'What?'

'A treat.'

Even now she showed no animation. 'For me?'

'For you!' Stephen said engagingly.

480

Lily raised her eyebrows. 'What sort of treat?'

'How would you like your own little car?' Stephen asked. 'A car of your own, which you could drive yourself. A little runabout for you. You could zip off to your concerts and shows, and when Christopher's a bit bigger you could take him out for the day and so on.'

Lily nodded. 'That would be useful,' she agreed.

Stephen buttered her a slice of toast and handed it to her on the plate. Lily took it gravely with a word of thanks. He watched her eat it.

'Lily . . .'

She wiped her mouth with a napkin and looked at him. 'Yes?'

'I want it to be right between us,' Stephen said in a rush. 'Lily. I want it to be right.' He had never been taught the words for the communication of emotion. He was speaking a tongue as foreign as when he had told Juliette that he loved her. It had come easier to him in French than it did to tell his wife in English that he wanted their marriage reborn into love and tenderness.

'I don't know what you mean,' Lily said. 'What do you want us to do?'

'I don't know! I want us to be c . . . c . . . close together. I want us to spend more t . . . t . . . time together. I want . . . I want . . . I want you to l . . . l . . . love me,' he said very low.

'I'm your wife,' Lily said. 'Of course I love you.'

Stephen, knowing this did not follow as a matter of course, knowing this was not true in their case, shot Lily a look of painful appeal. 'Please,' was all he could say.

Lily pushed back the covers and slipped out of bed to put the space of the room between them. She opened the wardrobe door and gazed at her clothes, but she did not see them.

'I feel so damned lonely,' Stephen confessed.

Lily hesitated. There was something in his voice that broke through the year of resentment. Then there was a knock on the door. Both of them stiffened and Lily snatched up her dressing-gown. Sally came into the room carrying Christopher. Lily crossed the room at once and took him from her with a little cry of greeting. Christopher burst into a broad smile and a gurgle of pleasure at the sight of his mother.

'I thought we could take him out today,' Stephen said. 'You and me, and Christopher. We could go out often. We could go out every afternoon. I could leave the office early. We could spend some time, the three of us, together.'

Lily's face brightened with hope. 'We could dismiss Nanny Janes. If we're having Christopher so much, if we're together as a family, we wouldn't want her.'

Stephen stiffened. 'No,' he said. 'The boy must be brought up properly. Nanny Janes stays.'

The joy fled from Lily's face as if he had slapped her. She gave him a small hard smile. 'Nothing changes at all, then,' she said, and turned her head back to her son. 'If you won't let me have Christopher, then nothing has changed.'

Chapter Thirty-two

Coventry drove Stephen, Lily and Christopher out into the country that afternoon. Stephen held the child inexpertly once or twice before returning him to Lily. They drove through the deep sunken lanes that had been no more than cart-tracks when Stephen left for the war. The verges at the roadside were rich with midsummer flowers. The Hampshire countryside was all green and creamy white. The hawthorn was in flower and the hedges were full of the thick blooming heads of Queen Anne's lace. Big moon daisies turned a thousand faces to the car as it drove past, brushing against the grass, sticky with pollen. Bouquets of ragwort gleamed brassy yellow at the roadside. The smell of the white elderflower blossoms filled the car with a sickly sweetness that made Stephen take out his handkerchief and hold it across his face, covering his mouth and nose. Only when he saw the critical sharpness of Lily's glance at him did he realize that the smell could not possibly be gas, that he was behaving like a fool. He forced himself to put his handkerchief back in his pocket, though his hand trembled.

Coventry, serene behind the wheel of the Argyll, drove through the warm lanes as if he were on the wooden corduroy roads laid through the mud to headquarters. He drove indifferent to weather and to the rich heady smells of summer. He watched the lane ahead of him, seeing everything, touched by nothing.

They had brought a picnic tea. Outside the tiny village of Rowlands Castle they pulled off the road and Coventry spread a tablecloth in the shade of trees and laid out plates with scones and jam and cream, sandwiches and cake.

Lily put Christopher on his back at the edge of the tablecloth and let him kick and look at the sky between his fists and feet. She took dabs of jam and cream and tea on her fingers and let him suck them, laughing as his face screwed up at one taste and then another. Stephen watched them, trying to share their pleasure, trying to feel as if he belonged with them. But mostly he was aware that though the wood was adequate cover, an officer who wanted to survive would have dug in the moment they arrived and sent out a scouting party. It was a thick dark wood, like Mametz had been before the shells had stripped it down to tortured naked stalks. He could not be easy in a place so like Mametz wood, where they had climbed over dead bodies to reach the German lines, struggling to get forward and meet their own deaths.

When they finished tea, Coventry packed up. Lily handed Christopher to Stephen while she brushed crumbs from her frock. Christopher beamed at the strange face of his father, and then he blushed red and scowled hard. The baby suddenly stank worse than a latrine.

'He smells!' Stephen exclaimed in distaste. 'He stinks!'

'Oh, really!' Lily exclaimed. 'He needs a nappy change, that's all.'

Stephen held the baby at arm's length, his face frowning with disgust. Lily snatched the child from him. 'For heaven's sake, Stephen! You must have seen worse than this! You can't have been at Ypres for two years and not seen worse than this!'

He shot a look of intense dislike at her, that she should so casually invoke his war, as if it could be compared to peacetime, as if it could be compared to anything.

'He stinks like a cesspit,' he said coldly. 'I suggest you see to him, if you know how.'

Lily turned her shoulder to him and spoke to Coventry. 'Christopher's basket is in the boot,' she said. 'Can you bring it to me, please? And some warm water?'

Coventry fetched the things and together they laid the baby down on a little square of towelling. The basket had a bowl and a sponge, a little towel and a small piece of scented soap. Coventry put these things at Lily's right hand, and poured a little hot water from the tea kettle into the bowl. He spread out the new nappy and a pair of rubberized drawers. Lily stripped Christopher with easy competence.

Stephen drew away and lit a cigarette to ward off the smell. The baby's nappy was a nauseating goo of pale yellow-brown. Stephen stared in fascinated disgust. Christopher's legs and little round buttocks were dirty with faeces. Lily held his feet like a chicken ready for trussing and wiped him, first with paper, and then with the sponge. She washed around his penis and his rosy tiny scrotum. Stephen gazed at the two of them in a sort of horror: at his son's innocent babyish maleness, and at Lily's confident handling of him. As if she were some kind of red-handed nurse, as if she were not a lady at all. Stephen was appalled that Lily should lower herself to be so intimate with the child. It was worse than servitude, what she chose to do. It was disgraceful that she should do it and feel no shame at being watched.

When Christopher was washed clean and she had bundled the soiled nappy in on itself, Lily lifted him up with one hand and slid the folded clean nappy under his back. When she let his legs go Christopher kicked and giggled, his little penis jiggling with the movement. Lily dried him and powdered him, making sure none of the delicate skin was left damp, then she folded the nappy around him and pinned it, with her hand inside to feel for the sharp point of the pin coming through the towelling.

Then she pulled his little feet through fresh drawers, and through his white lawn bloomers, and the baby was clean again.

Lily looked over her shoulder at her husband. He was staring at her as if he had seen her behave shamefully. He looked at the baby with open hostility. Lily gathered Christopher close and asked: 'What's wrong?'

Stephen pinched out the ember of his cigarette and threw it away. 'Nothing,' he said tightly.

'You're staring,' Lily said. 'You looked funny.' Her hand was spread at the back of Christopher's head as if to shield him from his father's hard gaze.

Stephen shook his head. 'It's nothing,' he said again. 'Shall we go – or is there anything worse he can do?'

Lily stared at him uncomprehendingly. 'He's just a little baby,' she started.

'I don't want to discuss it,' Stephen said tightly.

He held open the door for Lily and she handed Christopher to him to hold as she climbed into the car. Stephen held his son at arm's length and looked into his innocent open face. The baby smelled sweet, of powder and soap and fresh linen. He cooed beguilingly at Stephen and waved small tightly clenched fists. His blue eyes were open very wide as if he were surprised. Stephen could not feel tenderness for his baby. He had seen his nakedness and smelt the stink of him. It was too much like the smell of the mud. The little naked body was too much like the stripped corpses. Stephen could not disentangle images of life and death. He stared at Christopher as if the baby were some threatening enigma, and he could not smile at him even though the baby kicked and cooed.

Lily held out her arms. Stephen handed over the baby, and walked around the back of the car to get in the other side. Coventry was putting the basket of nursery things in the boot. Stephen saw his face as he bent over. It was gentle, tender. The shut-in shut-out mute expression had melted away. He looked as he had looked that warm summer of 1917 when they had taken leave, and gone haymaking on Perot's farm. Coventry looked alive to feeling again, he looked tender. He looked ready to speak.

It was Christopher who had worked this magic, because Coventry could handle the child. He could touch him, soiled or clean, and feel the flow of tenderness pass from his gentle fingers to the baby. Stephen stared at the man's face and Coventry straightened up and faced his master. At once the warmth left his face and the old mute indifference took its place.

'All right?' Stephen asked. He was suddenly aware of the cruel inappropriateness of the question. It was all wrong for Coventry, and all wrong for Stephen, and it had been since the trenches had brutalized them, since the little farm had disappointed them, and since their own violence had corrupted them, fatally and permanently.

Coventry nodded, and held the door open for Stephen. They reversed quietly out of the little glade and on to the lane, then Coventry turned the car for home.

They were on the little road between Havant and Portsmouth when Stephen suddenly exclaimed, 'Hang on a minute!' and then tapped Coventry's shoulder and said, 'Stop.'

Coventry slowed and pulled the car over.

'What is it?' Lily asked.

'A "For Sale" sign, on a little farm. Drive back there, Coventry. Let's have a look at it.'

'Whatever for?' Lily asked. It was getting late, Christopher would soon be hungry and tired.

'I'd like to see it,' Stephen said vaguely. 'Looked a pretty place.'

Coventry turned the car and they drove back the way they had come. The sign was hand-painted, mounted on a post at the edge of a field raggedly planted with some leafy crop which Stephen did not recognize. A little track led off the road past a barn towards a small cluster of buildings. 'Let's go down,' Stephen said. 'Drive on.'

Coventry slipped the car into gear and they went slowly forwards, bumping on the ruts. Outside the barn was a tractor half-covered by a tarpaulin, with the engine missing. A rusting harrow was partly blocking the track. The way the track made a little dogleg corner around it showed that it had been there for some time.

The farmhouse itself was thatched, a silvery grey thatch greening with moss at the eaves, which overhung the windows like vegetal eyebrows. The front door was overgrown, clearly never used. The back door was a stable door, the bottom half fastened, the top thrown open. A pane of glass in the kitchen window had been broken and replaced by cardboard. As Coventry stopped the car in the cobbled yard a skinny collie ran the length of a chain and yelped as it was brought up short. The yard was slick with slurry. Coventry got out of the car and opened Lily's door and then Stephen's. Lily merely glanced at the wet cobbles, and did not move, but Stephen went to the back door, looking around him as he walked.

The frantic barking of the dog summoned a man who came around the corner of the barn, wiping his hands on his thick working trousers. At the sight of the big car he straightened up and came forward slowly, his gaze flicking suspiciously from Stephen to Coventry, smart in his grey uniform.

'Yes?' he asked in a slow Hampshire drawl.

A woman came to the half-door and leaned fat arms over the top, watching the newcomers in silence. She took in every inch of Lily's long tea gown, and the baby's white smock. Lily stared back at her.

'Saw your sign,' Stephen said. Unconsciously his voice

was louder, clearer, as authoritative as he had been when he had given orders every day. 'Your sale sign. We could be interested. We'd like to take a look.'

The man nodded and smiled, showing damaged yellow teeth. 'Landowners, are you?' he asked.

'I've done a bit of farming,' Stephen said defensively. 'During the war, in Belgium. I've worked on a farm.'

The man nodded. 'I can show you around,' he said pleasantly. 'Would your good lady care to step inside? She can have some tea.'

The woman at the door smiled ingratiatingly at Lily and swung the door open. She was wearing a thin print frock with a ragged cardigan on top. A stained apron was tied around her broad waist. 'Step in!' she said.

'I'll wait here,' Lily said simply. 'Thank you.'

Stephen hesitated but then he let Lily stay in the car.

The farmer led the way towards the dairy. 'Beautiful milkers,' he said shortly. 'You'd know good beasts when you see them, I daresay. Beautiful milkers.'

The thick-coated cows were standing wearily in their stalls, their udders full, waiting for afternoon milking. Two had open sores in the matted ginger coats and the back leg of one animal was trembling unstoppably. The farmer stood before her, shielding her from sight, and gestured at the others. 'It's a core,' he said. 'The core of a dairy herd. Were you thinking of dairying, Sir?'

'Possibly,' Stephen said. 'D'you get a good price for milk?'

The farmer raised his hands as if expressing a demand for milk which a million cows could not fulfil. 'Portsmouth so near!' he said. 'And the Navy needs! I have a contract with a local dairy, they collect every morning. I could sell my milk ten times over.'

They walked through the barn, ignoring the dirty stalls and the slurry between the cobbles and thick in the drains.

There was a hay barn at the back with a number of ragged bales badly stacked. If Stephen had looked closely he would have seen more weeds than grass in the bales, but he had stepped back and was looking at the roof where nesting sparrows twittered and an old swallow's nest clung precariously to the back wall.

'It needs patching,' the farmer said, following his gaze. 'I've got the corrugated iron to do it, I could get it done tomorrow.'

'Good show,' Stephen said vaguely. He was listening to the sighing sound of the trees behind the farm. They sounded like the trees at the Little England farm. 'Got an orchard?' he asked suddenly.

The farmer beamed at him. 'Wonderful crop of apples!' he exclaimed. 'Your lady wife would love the blossom. It's this way.'

He led the way to the back of the house where once there had been a little flower garden, now overgrown and rank with nettles. Tall spires of foxgloves painted the green with white and mauve. Beyond a tumbling-down wall was a small field with a couple of goats cropping on tethers. Gnarled apple trees, thick with age, their boughs bending with little spotted rosy apples, whispered softly in the breeze. Beyond them was a field of cut hay, shorn pale green, beyond that the cows' pasture, and beyond that a little wood and the hills.

'How far does your land go?' Stephen asked softly.

'Just past the wood,' the farmer said. 'A very fine stand of timber. I've never cut it. You would know how much wood like that would fetch. I was saving it for my boy.'

Stephen turned and looked at him. 'Your boy?'

The man shrugged. 'Went down on the HMS *Hampshire* with Kitchener,' he said briefly. 'We're getting too old for the farm now. We want to sell it and move near my daughter. She lives near Bristol. It's a young man's life, farming. A wonderful life. Were you in the Navy, Sir?'

'Infantry,' Stephen said briefly. 'Good soil, is it?'

'The very best. Not too heavy and not too light. All the farmers around here'll tell you the same. Rich and easy. You can grow anything on it!'

Stephen glanced back at the farmhouse and the thick nettles thriving in the garden. 'What about the house?' he asked.

'Freehold,' the man said. 'You can see it in the Doomsday Book. Freehold, and always has been. You own a bit of English history with this house.'

Stephen nodded, impressed. 'And what sort of state is it in?' he asked.

'Perfect,' the man said simply. 'No gimcrack improvements. No brickbuilt extensions, no cheap partitions. It's as it was built, and you can't say fairer than that. If you want to change it, that's your right. If you want to put in a bathroom and an extra bedroom or so – the fabric of the house is all sound. You've got the freedom to do it. But there's been no cheap alterations that you won't care for. It's the genuine thing. An old-fashioned English farmhouse. There's many who would give their eye teeth for such a place. I've had more offers than I can count from people wanting the house alone. I'd consider selling the house and the fields separately – but I'd prefer to sell it as it is: as a going concern, as a farm.'

Stephen glanced at the roof. 'Needs re-thatching,' he suggested.

The man shrugged. 'If you want to put a bonny new thatch on it I can tell you the man who'd do it for you, for half the price you might expect. And you can thatch it with your own straw for free.'

'I thought thatch was reeds,' Stephen expostulated faintly.

491

The man shook his head. 'Not Hampshire thatch,' he said. 'You can thatch it yourself, with your own straw, and know you've done a good job. You'd live off the land here, Sir. I take it that's your intention?'

Stephen flushed suddenly, as if with desire. 'The place where I worked,' he said urgently, 'it was like nowhere else in the world. The quiet of it, hidden away, and safe. This place is like that. It might be like that again for me. I was planning on buying a farm after the war, farming it myself. But I got caught up in business, and my father was sick, but now . . .'

He broke off; his eyes followed a flock of wood pigeons wheeling over the derelict fields to roost in the overgrown wood.

'All the shooting you could want,' the farmer said. 'It's the fat of the land here.'

'A simple life,' Stephen said. 'Absolutely unchanged by the war. The same as it's always been.'

The farmer, whose experience of post-war farming was of unobtainable workers and high wages, poor prices for produce and the falling value of agricultural land, nodded encouragingly. 'You couldn't get further from your business worries here, Sir,' he said. 'Or further from the war.'

Stephen drew in a deep breath. 'I'll see the house,' he said.

They walked together around the side of the house. The collie snapped at their heels. Lily was still sitting in the car, Coventry standing beside her with his cap off in the sunshine. The farmer's wife observed them both in interested silence over the half-door.

She stepped back as the two men came towards her and opened the bottom half of the door.

'Shall I put the kettle on?' she asked indifferently.

Her husband nodded. 'Take a cup of tea out to the lady,'

he said. 'You'll have to make allowances, Sir. We're just simple people.'

Stephen nodded. 'I understand,' he said. 'Where I was before . . .' He broke off as he saw the big scrubbed table with the bench on one side and the wheelbacked chair at the head of the table, the old-fashioned smoke-blackened range and the cracked red tiles underfoot. There was a clothes rack hanging at the ceiling with a pair of flannels draped on it and a ham in a net dangling from one end. There was a zinc sink with a pump and handle over it. A door with a fingerlatch led off the kitchen into a tiny cramped hall before the bolted front door.

'Parlour,' the farmer said, opening the door to the right and motioning Stephen in.

It was the best room of the house, opened only for weddings and funerals. Everything was coated in a fine haze of grey dust. There was a weighty sideboard and three stiffly upholstered chairs. There was a cheap modern table with drop-leaves in lightweight wood. There was a heavy cakestand with six cake plates in diminishing sizes. The curtains were a crushed dark velvet, permanently drawn against the damaging sunshine and faded in long symmetrical stripes. The room smelled stuffy and hot.

They went back into the hall. 'We just use this as a store room,' the farmer said, opening the door opposite them. Stephen peered in. There was some unrecognizable piece of machinery stripped down and lying in pieces on the floor, there were some crates with punnets piled on top of them, there were a couple of packing cases and a large drying rack.

'And upstairs?' Stephen asked.

The farmer led the way out of the room, closing the door carefully behind him. 'We don't use the front door,' he said. 'Except on occasions. I expect you and your lady would open it up. The front garden's pretty as a picture when the roses are in full bloom. A real cottage garden. You've just missed the best of the roses, they were early this year.'

He opened a small wooden door set high on the first step of a flight of stairs and led the way upwards. Stephen, remembering Perot stamping up the stairs undoing the braces on his trousers, followed the man's boots. He had a tremendous sense of peace, of homecoming. He looked behind him for Coventry to see if he felt the same, and remembered with a twitch of irritation that Lily had kept Coventry by the car.

There were three upstairs rooms in the same configuration as the downstairs space: one on each side of the house that matched the store room and parlour and one large room that matched the kitchen, looking out over the fields.

'Now this would be your nursery,' the farmer said, opening a door at the front of the house. It was piled high with junk: enamel bowls with the bottoms holed, a washstand with the china basin missing, anonymous tea-chests, a bookcase empty of books, a bedstead on its side, a pile of carefully darned linen.

'The main bedroom,' the farmer said, indicating the room over the parlour.

The room had windows over the front garden and backwards over the fields. It smelled hauntingly of cow dung. A large double bed and a matching wood wardrobe took up much of the room but could not overwhelm the view of fields and woodlands and the gently rising hills. From the front-facing window Stephen could see the blue of the horizon and the glint of sea.

'It's beautiful,' he said.

The farmer double-checked, as if to see what Stephen was describing, and then realized he was looking at the unprofitable fields and the distant hills.

'It is that,' he confirmed. 'And that's our land, almost as far as you can see. It's a great thing that, to be able to look out of your window on a morning and see your own land stretching away. Not many businessmen can say that.'

'No,' Stephen said with deep feeling.

'And this is another bedroom, with enough space for you to put a bathroom in,' the man improvised rapidly.

The walls were less stained with damp because of the chimney from the kitchen range which bulged along the wall. There was a single bed and a small chest of drawers with a little flyspotted mirror.

'You could make it into a big bathroom,' the farmer suggested. 'Or a bathroom and a bedroom beside it. It's a big room. One sweet, they call it, don't they? It's the size of the kitchen downstairs, don't forget.'

Stephen nodded, still dazed by the view from the windows, hazy with his sense of returning to a safe haven, of finding Little England again, untouched and undamaged, despite the war, despite the time when he ran his own madness into the kitchen and spattered the clean walls with fistfuls of blood.

The man led the way downstairs. There was a pot of tea on the kitchen table and Lily was sitting stiffly and silently, drinking from a china cup with Christopher on her knee. Coventry was standing in the doorway, his cap under his arm. It was to Coventry that Stephen spoke as soon as they came into the kitchen.

'It reminds me of there,' he said. 'Doesn't it? Isn't it exactly like there?'

Coventry smiled slightly and shook his head.

'It *is*,' Stephen urged him. 'The house is even built the same, or nearly. And the fields, and the whole atmosphere . . .' He broke off.

Coventry smiled his distant smile.

'You *do* remember,' Stephen said. 'Isn't it like that . . . that place?'

Coventry smiled again and nodded slightly, as if he were agreeing from mere politeness. Stephen did not press him any further. He drew back the wheelbacked chair from the table and sat down. Without speaking, the farmer's wife put a mug before him and poured tea. Stephen checked her before she could add milk. He added four spoonfuls of sugar and drank it black and strong. Lily glanced at him in surprise. When she poured him tea at number two, The Parade, Stephen had milk and no sugar at all.

Christopher kicked his little feet and cooed, the farmer's wife went back to the range and leaned her broad hips against it. The farmer drew out a chair and sat on Stephen's left.

'Would you be interested in buying?' he asked.

'Yes,' Stephen said simply.

Lily jumped at that and looked to Coventry but he was watching the red tiled floor beneath his boots. He looked deaf as well as mute.

'Yes, I would,' Stephen said. 'Is anyone else interested in it?'

The man nodded. 'My neighbour would buy the fields tomorrow. He would rent them off you, if you ever thought of not farming yourself, but just owning land. And there are scores of people who would buy the farmhouse on its own. City people from Portsmouth. They're attracted by the price because we're in a hurry to move. We want to join my daughter, in Bristol.'

Stephen nodded. 'Have you accepted an offer?'

The farmer nodded. 'Nothing definite,' he said. 'I've been tempted, but I want to sell it as a working farm. To someone who will keep it as a farm. Someone like yourself, Sir, who knows good land when he sees it. Someone who would buy it as an inheritance for himself and his son.'

'What sort of price?' Stephen asked. He was breathing a little fast, Lily noticed. She was watching him as if she had never seen him before. She could not imagine what fancy had taken hold of him. She thought he must be planning to buy the farm for a client, or as some business investment. But there was some brightness, some wildness about Stephen that she had never seen before.

The farmer looked at Stephen carefully, assessing Lily's clothes, the chauffeur, the Argyll parked in the stable yard, the fine lawn of the baby's smock and the perfect embroidery.

'It would be four thousand pounds for the whole farm,' he said. 'That's with all the stock, that fine herd of cows you saw, all the machinery – that's a tractor and a thresher, harrows, ploughs, you won't need to spend another penny to move in tomorrow. All the furniture in the house, even the curtains at the window. Four thousand pounds lock stock and barrel.'

Lily gasped. Even Stephen looked dashed. 'That much?' he asked.

The farmer nodded emphatically. 'I could get half as much again selling separately,' he said. 'But I'm not prepared to do it. It's a working farm, it deserves a man to farm it. Our boys died for places like this. It's a little bit of England, it is. I feel that they died to keep it safe, and it's my job to pass it on to the next man.'

Stephen nodded, his eyes never leaving the man's face. 'I am that man,' he said suddenly. 'I'll buy it from you.'

The farmer hesitated. 'It's a fair price . . .'

'I know it is.'

'With all the stock.'

Stephen nodded and stretched out his hand. 'Let's shake

on the deal!' he said. 'Four thousand pounds for the whole farm.'

The farmer reached his hand out across the table. 'Four hundred pounds down, and the rest on completion,' he said quickly. The two men shook.

Chapter Thirty-three

Lily was silent until they were in the car and driving back up the bumpy track.

'I didn't know you planned to buy it,' she said. 'I thought you were just looking around it. Who is it for?'

'For me,' Stephen said. 'For us.'

'What?'

'It's what we need,' he said urgently, and then the words came spilling out. 'It's what we've needed from the beginning. We needed a place of our own. I shouldn't have taken you to live in my mother's house, we should have had our own place, to organize how you liked. Well, we can get that right now. It'll be the most wonderful place for Christopher to grow up in, he'll have a real country childhood. Now that my father is better, they don't need me at home. They don't need me at the office either.

'I never wanted to be a lawyer, Lily. I always wanted to do something else. And ever since Belgium I've wanted to live in the country. I wanted to be a farmer. I could see then what I really needed, the sort of life I wanted to live. It's like a vision, Lily. It's like a vision. I should have done it the moment I was demobbed. But it's not too late. We can start again. It'll be the very thing for us.'

'I can't live there!' Lily exclaimed. She had felt an instant repugnance for the dirty yard and the worn kitchen. 'It's filthy.'

Stephen waved the objection away. 'It needs a good clean, and a bit of money spent on it. But it's a sound little house and wonderful land. You heard what he said. We'd make it our house together, Lily. It would be a fresh start for us.'

Lily held Christopher tightly to her. 'We aren't like that,' she said. 'We're not country people. For heaven's sake, Stephen, I don't know one end of a cow from another! I come from Highland Road, Pompey, and I trained as a singer-dancer. I can't go and live in the country. I wouldn't know what to do!'

Stephen laughed. 'You don't *do* anything!' he said delightedly. 'That's the whole thing about it. You just live. We'll just live, Lily. We'll live simply, like simple people in a simple way. You don't like Nanny Janes. Well, we won't have her there! We'll just live there, you and I and Christopher, like ordinary simple people.'

'No cook?' Lily queried. 'No parlourmaid? No tweeny? No gardener?'

Stephen shook his head, beaming. 'No-one! Oh! I expect we'll have a couple of men at harvest-time. But we'll do the work ourselves, Lily. We'll be simple people. We'll make our lives the way we want them to be, not the ways that have been forced upon us.'

Lily shook her head. 'You keep talking about simple lives,' she observed. 'There's nothing very simple about getting up at six in the morning and having to make your own breakfast. You can think that farming is all fine weather and pretty fields but you wouldn't like it in winter.'

'I'm not a fool,' Stephen said sharply. 'And I've worked on a farm, which is more than you have done.'

'I've got up at six every day of my life, which is more than *you've* ever done!' Lily snapped. 'And you'll never convince me that life is better if you do your own washing.'

Stephen stared at her in dislike. 'I am doing this for us,' he said. 'So that we can be together. So that we can have

500

a home of our own. So that we can send Nanny Janes away.'

'This is nonsense!' Lily said impatiently. 'We can have a home of our own in Portsmouth. We don't have to bury ourselves at the back end of a bog! We can send Nanny Janes away today! We don't have to give up a cook and two maids as well!'

Stephen was so angry that his stammer was choking him. 'Y . . . y . . . y . . . you're ag . . . ag . . . against me,' he finally got out.

Lily nodded recklessly. 'Yes, I am,' she said. 'And so will everyone be. You'll have to find some way to make that horrid man give you back your note for four hundred pounds, Stephen. It's just not possible that we could live there. If I'd known you were buying it for us I'd have stopped you then and there. I just didn't dream of it. I thought it was for a client or someone.'

'Y . . . y . . . you'll n . . . n . . . n . . . not stop me,' Stephen said, struggling for speech.

Lily turned her head away from him and looked determinedly out of the window. 'I won't even discuss it,' she said with finality.

Stephen stared at the back of her little hat.

'I'm doing this for you,' he said again, willing her to turn around and smile at him with the easy open-hearted smile of Juliette Perot, willing her to see the place through his eyes, as a haven, as a place of safety where they could forget the war and the uneasy compromises of the peace.

Lily turned and looked at him with anger and hatred in her face. 'I won't even discuss it,' she said again. 'It won't happen, Stephen. You are mad to even think of it.'

He glared at her, his anger rising to match hers. He wished very much that they were at home in the privacy of their bedroom so that he could have slapped her determined face and made her cry. He wished that she was a man so he could plunge a clenched fist into her belly, kick her in the groin. For a moment he thought of Juliette Perot as he had last seen her, her arms flying upwards like a puppet as the bullets lifted her off the man's lap and flung her against the wall. All women are whores, he thought with bitter clarity. All of them. You do what you can for them, you risk your life for them, and then you find that at heart they are all whores and cheats.

Lily turned her little head away from him and looked out of the window. A daisy on her hat nodded its certainty that he was wrong, that she was right, and that she would win.

'Enemy,' Stephen whispered very softly, so low that only he could hear the word. Christopher turned and looked at him. His face was clear and empty of expression but Stephen saw Lily's scornful dark blue eyes in his little round face. 'Enemy,' he whispered again to the baby.

They were late home. Lily did not pause to apologize to Muriel but swept upstairs to change her dress. She took her clothes to the bathroom so that she should not be half-naked in front of Stephen, and as he pulled on a fresh shirt and fastened the studs before the mirror he despised her for the tease she was. Withholding the sight of her underwear as part of her displeasure, and then at other times letting him lie on her as part of their marital contract.

'Bitch,' he said softly to the mirror.

Lily came into the room in an apricot evening dress with a pale shawl around her shoulders. She slipped her feet into her little satin shoes and went quietly to the door. She glanced at Stephen before she went out, as if expecting him to speak. When he said nothing she went out of the room and ran down the stairs.

Since Rory had been dining with them, the family had

renewed their pre-war habit of meeting in the drawing room for a drink before dinner. As Lily came in the room she saw John Pascoe and his wife Winifred with Rory and Muriel. Rory smiled at her, and John rose to his feet.

'I am sorry we were late home,' Lily said, shaking hands. 'I hope you have not been waiting.'

Muriel glanced at the clock. 'I was afraid something might have happened, but I knew nothing could be wrong with Coventry driving.'

'We stopped at a farmhouse,' Lily said.

Browning handed her a small glass of sweet sherry on a silver salver. Lily was given a glass of sweet sherry every evening. She disliked the sugary taste almost as much as the heavy numbing effect of the alcohol. She felt that she exhaled sherry fumes for the rest of the evening. But if she refused a drink then she was asked if she had a headache or if she were unwell. There was no drink except sweet sherry for women. There was no dry sherry in the house, and only men were offered spirits.

Stephen came into the room and greeted the Pascoes and his parents.

'At a farmhouse?' John Pascoe asked. 'For tea?'

'We had a picnic tea,' Lily said, skirting the topic. 'Just outside Rowlands Castle.'

Stephen waved Browning aside and poured himself a large whisky. 'Anyone else?' he asked heartily.

The two older men shook their heads. Rory watched thoughtfully as Stephen added a very little water.

Browning came into the dining room and whispered to Muriel.

'Shall we go in?' Muriel asked.

Coventry appeared and wheeled Rory down the hall to the dining room, positioning his chair at the head of the table. Stephen sat on his mother's right at the far end, John Pascoe on her left. Winifred sat between Stephen and Rory, and Lily sat opposite her, close enough to Rory to tuck his napkin under his chin and slice any extraordinarily tough pieces of meat.

It was cream of mushroom soup with a few leathery pieces of floating mushroom, roast mutton with mashed potatoes, roast potatoes, limp broccoli and hard peas, and shape for dessert. Lily took her slightly soiled napkin from its ring and spread it on her lap with the familiar choking feeling that always came with Muriel's formal dinners.

Rory's hands were bad tonight. He could not manage his soup without spilling.

'Shall I spoon for you?' Lily asked in an undertone.

Rory, one eye on his wife's glacial disapproval, shook his head. 'Bether not,' he said. He had lost control of the muscles of his face too. He was having difficulty with words. His head twitched slightly from time to time. Stephen looked studiously down the table towards his mother, or across at John Pascoe, anywhere but at his father.

'You had lovely weather for your picnic,' Muriel said. 'It's been as warm as the south of France today.'

'And now the crowds will be dreadful for August,' Winifred said with a sigh. 'I envy you your house all winter, but when the crowds come I am glad of our privacy. It's so crowded on the seafront, and every year it gets worse!'

'And the pier!' Muriel exclaimed. 'They are permitting more and more entertainment, and of the most unsuitable kind. All it does is lower the tone and encourage the sort of visitor who can do the resort no good. I have written to the council but I get no satisfaction at all.'

'It quite makes one think about moving house altogether,' Winifred said. 'They should think of that when they increase the rates and then squander them on amenities for trippers. It's what the residents require that should be their concern.'

Stephen looked up and smiled. 'We have some news about moving,' he said easily. 'We looked at a farm today and I have paid a deposit on it. We are going to move into the country, a little place, just between Havant and here.'

'My dear!' Muriel exclaimed. Her hand went to her pearls and she dropped her spoon in her bowl. 'A farm!'

There was a short silence.

'This is rather sudden, isn't it, Stephen?' John asked amiably.

'Actually no,' Stephen said. 'I had a couple of leaves on a little farm in Belgium, well behind the lines, and I got bitten by the bug then. It's a great life. I wanted to come home and farm. But when I got home you were short-staffed at the office, and Father was ill, and I never really thought about it again. But now with Christopher growing up, and the office settling down, and Father well again – there's no reason that we should not settle in the country.'

Winifred glanced at Muriel's appalled face, scenting tension. 'Is it far?' she asked.

'Just before Havant,' Stephen replied. 'A snug little place, a mixed farm, a good herd of cows, hay meadows, some crops. I daresay the soil is good enough for fruit. You can see the sea from the bedroom windows. It's a very pretty place, and a good price. The family lost their son in the show, they're pulling out and want a quick sale. I think I'm lucky to get it at the price.' He shot a quick glance down the table to his father. Rory's head was still, his trembling hands resting on the tablecloth. His whole attention was fixed on his son.

'Very lucky indeed,' Stephen asserted a little louder.

'What do you think of it, Lily?' Muriel asked. It was the first sentence she had spoken since Stephen's news. She was alert at once to Lily's reserve. 'You can't want to live in the country, surely! All your friends are in town, and all your singing engagements. I should have thought you would have hated it.'

Lily turned a pale mutinous face to her mother-in-law. 'I don't like it,' she said simply. 'The farm is dirty and falling down. The house is tiny. The roof has great holes in it. There's no bathroom or running water.'

John Pascoe gave an embarrassed laugh. 'Better think again, Stephen,' he said pleasantly. 'Can't make a home without the little bride's consent! I'll tell you what, I have a friend who is an agricultural surveyor. I'll get him to have a look over it. He can tell you a fair price for it and then you can proceed as the two of you wish. There's nothing so risky as being a gentleman farmer, you know. It's a pricey hobby at the best of times. And the way the country's going this is no time to play with your capital.'

Stephen tried to smile but his face was too tense. 'The deal is done,' he said. 'I've shaken hands on it and paid a deposit. I've bought it. I am a farmer already, not a gentleman farmer. I am a farmer. I own a farm.'

Muriel rang the bell suddenly and noisily and Browning came in and cleared the soup plates though no-one had finished eating. She put the leg of mutton on the sideboard and Stephen, with a triumphant glance at Rory, rose to carve the meat, as the master of the house. Browning carried the plates to the table. Stephen deliberately gave Lily a large portion with a thick slice of pale flabby fat. He returned to his seat and Browning took the vegetables around and then served wine.

Stephen had one glass, and then another.

Muriel watched him. 'I remember now!' she suddenly exclaimed. 'You used to play farms with Christopher. You had some lead animals and a little die-cast farm with a farmhouse and a lead farmer and his wife.'

'Oh yes,' Stephen said.

'How you two would squabble!' Muriel reminisced. 'And

then you would throw the animals across the room and Christopher would say that you would never be a farmer because you had no patience!' She smiled at the recollection. 'And you said that you didn't care because you didn't want to be a farmer in any case, that farming was for people who could do nothing else, who hadn't the brains to go into the law, who knew nothing better than to lean on a gate all day and watch a herd of cows!' She laughed lightly, one eye on her son.

Winifred smiled. 'Young men often get these fancies,' she said. 'Nothing comes of them.'

Stephen opened his mouth to argue but then nodded to Browning for another glass of wine.

'My brother was going to run away to sea!' Winifred said. 'I think he would have found it a good deal too uncomfortable! He works in a bank now.'

'It's not even a very nice farm,' Lily volunteered. 'The yard is all pot-holed and dirty. The cows had marks on their coats. There was a dog chained up and it was all sore around its throat where the collar rubbed.'

Muriel smiled encouragingly at her. 'We'll talk him out of it!' she said with a roguish smile. 'No man in the world can stand against a mother and a wife when they are in agreement!'

'I should think not!' John Pascoe laughed, trying to overcome the uneasy atmosphere. 'I should think not indeed!'

Stephen pushed back his chair and sat back. He nodded for another glass of wine. 'I'm afraid it's too late for that!' he said again. 'The deed is done! The farm is mine! All the arguments in the world can't stop it.'

Winifred's bright gaze went from Muriel's flushed face to Lily's pale one. She gave a soft excited laugh. 'Oh dear! Quite a scene!'

Stephen shot one hard look at her and drank from his

glass. Lily pushed the fatty meat to one side of her plate and put her knife and fork together.

'What do you think, Mr Winters?' Winifred as`ed.

Rory raised his heavy head, formed his lips ready for speech. His mouth opened, he drew in a breath. 'No,' he said simply. His family was silent, waiting for him to say more. His jaw moved, the muscles sluggish to obey, then suddenly he found the power to speak. 'I cannot allow it,' he said simply; and the decision was taken against Stephen.

Stephen and Coventry got quietly drunk in one of the old pubs at the waterfront by the old fortified walls. Stephen was as silent as Coventry, staring into his glass of beer, the whisky untouched to one side.

'They won't be satisfied until they destroy me,' he said softly. 'All of them. Lily's with them now too. They don't want me, they never wanted me. They want Christopher. Now they've got another Christopher I mean nothing again. What I want, what I need – all that means nothing to them.'

He sipped from his glass of scotch and then downed a gulp of beer. 'Damn them to hell,' he said. 'I won't forgive them this. Everything I've ever wanted came second to Christopher. They sent me out to the Front because he had gone. They sent me to a rotten school because he was at a good one. I had to go into law because he wanted to try for the Foreign Office. Someone had to work in the firm and he wasn't going to do it. Who should be the one then? Why, Stephen! No-one cares what happens to him!

'And now I find a place I want to live, and a life I want to lead, and they're all at me, nibbling away at me until I could scream. And my own wife – my damned own wife – smiles at my mother as if butter wouldn't melt in her mouth and says the cows are dirty and she doesn't want to live in the country!'

Stephen suddenly kicked out at the table, spilling the drinks and sending the glasses crashing to the floor. The landlord, who had been rinsing glasses behind the bar, looked up, lifted the flap and moved purposefully towards them. 'That's enough now, Sir,' he said.

Stephen hesitated for a moment, squared up to the man, and then, seeing his bulk and his slow progress forwards, dropped his fists and let his shoulders slump. 'What's the use?' he demanded. 'What the hell is the use of anything?'

He turned and went out into the dark noisome yard outside. Coventry thrust his hand deep into his trouser pocket and handed the landlord a fistful of coins. 'Thank you, Sir,' the man said ironically and closed the door behind them.

Stephen was leaning against a wall, his face turned up to the night sky. 'They think I'm done, but I'll get them,' he said. 'They think they'll get their own way, bend me to their wishes, but I'll get them. I can get them. I know what they want. I know what's precious to them. They can be hurt, I've seen people hurt. I've seen things that these shirkers wouldn't believe.

'I care for nothing now. Juliette is dead and Lily's ganged up against me, hanging over the cradle night and day. Everyone's in love with Christopher and no-one allowing me what I want.

'Well, I won't have it. If they stand in my way I'll show them. They think that they can stop me, well, I can make them wish that they had given me everything I ever wanted. I can give them nightmares – like they have given me. I can give them nightmares that last all day – nightmares like I have. Nightmares that will last all my life if I cannot have my farm and get away from all of this.'

Coventry took him gently by the shoulder and turned him towards the street. The car was parked only a little way away. Stephen slumped in the front seat. Coventry glanced at him uneasily, as if Stephen were an officer again, whose orders might mean death in a moment, whose whim had to be obeyed.

'I shall give them nightmares that last all day,' Stephen said again. His head lolled on to his chest and in moments he was asleep.

Chapter Thirty-four

Ironically, the next day, while Stephen was still heavy with his hangover and sulky, the salesman for Morris Motors telephoned him at his office to tell him that the Bullnose Morris he had ordered for his wife had arrived.

Stephen told the man to take it round to number two, The Parade at midday. Coventry drove him home for lunch and the two of them looked over the car with approval.

It was a neat little silver-grey car with a folding hood of grey canvas on wood. It had the attractive rounded bonnet and radiator of the Bullnose Morris with the temperature gauge in a glass dial mounted on the top of the bonnet so the driver could see easily the red needle moving from freezing to boiling.

It had a self-starter, which was essential for Lily, who would be driving to concerts and tea parties on her own. It had three gears plus reverse. It had simple controls with a tiny red-painted accelerator and two large pedals for the brake and clutch on either side of it. There was a fat horn on the driver's side and a good-sized wing mirror. There were windscreen wipers and electric lights. It was the very latest model and cost Stephen a cool £525.

Stephen sent Coventry up the steps to ring the doorbell and summon Lily out into the street. She came out into the sunshine slowly, not expecting a treat, remembering Stephen's ill-concealed anger from the night before. But he was smiling and waving to her to come to him, and his broad gesture took in the little car.

'I told you,' he said. 'I told you I would buy you a car. Actually, it's arrived early. D'you like it?'

Lily beamed. 'It's lovely,' she said. The salesman opened the driver's door and helped her into the seat. 'Does Madam know how to drive?' he asked politely.

'Oh yes,' Lily said confidently. 'I drive my husband's Argyll sometimes. But tell me what the switches are.'

He pointed to the two matching switches. 'This is the starter switch. You have to retard the spark by adjusting this lever.' He moved the lever on the steering column. 'Is Madam familiar with retarding the spark?'

'I think Madam can just about grasp it,' Lily said.

He nodded. 'Then the switch turns . . . so. The second switch is for the lights if Madam is driving after dark.' His tone implied that Lily would be much better off at home at nightfall.

'This is the speedometer, and at your feet are the usual pedals. There are three gears, I think you will find them light and easy to use. And the handbrake is here.' He hesitated. 'On hills it is advisable to leave the car in gear to avoid accidents, and if leaving it for any length of time I prefer to put bricks beneath the wheels.'

'Bricks,' Lily repeated.

'Should there be any trouble with starting the car with the electric switch then you may use the crank handle, which is stored in the handsome tool box on the running board.'

'Crank handle,' Lily repeated.

'And finally, please observe the calonometer. Easily seen from the driver's seat, it will show you when the car is running at the correct temperature and when it is in danger of overheating. If the needle points to the red, pull over, and let the car cool down. Add cold water to the radiator only when the needle is back inside the normal temperature or gone to cold.'

'Don't worry about it, Lily,' Stephen said. 'Coventry will see to all that. D'you want to give it a run?'

Lily smiled politely at the man. 'May I?'

'Of course, it is Madam's car, I am merely delivering it,' he said politely. 'But perhaps I can demonstrate the car for you, and perhaps your husband will show you again how to drive it later on.' He turned to Stephen. 'One can't be too careful with the ladies. Their temperament does not suit them for things mechanical.'

Lily smiled. 'I think I should like to try driving it now,' she said politely. Stephen got into the front seat beside her. Coventry watched them from the garden gate, smiling at Lily's well-concealed irritation.

'Are you sure you would not feel safer initially with me?' the salesman asked. He lowered his voice to address Stephen. 'The ladies' natural nervousness sometimes makes them drive very slowly. One has to be patient.'

'I think I can manage,' Lily said.

'Now remember!' the salesman said archly. 'Retard the spark! Turn the switch! Select the gear, and gently, gently, gently let in the clutch. And don't feel you have to go fast. We understand. You are bound to want to go slowly at first.'

Lily flicked the retard lever, turned the engine over, revved it hard, let in the clutch and scorched off down The Parade in a cloud of blue smoke and dust. The salesman leaped backwards to save his toes. 'My hat!' he said faintly. 'She *does* know how to drive.'

Coventry leaned on the gate and laughed silently.

Lily drove Stephen down to the Eastney Barracks and then back again. They went into lunch in favourable accord and Muriel and Rory, waiting for them at the lunch table, wondered if the quarrel was ended.

No-one asked Stephen if he was going to bow to his father's interdict and give up his plan for the farm. Lily took Charlie for a spin in her new car in the afternoon. Rory sat in the drawing room and watched the people walking by the Canoe Lake, and Muriel went out for tea with Jane Dent. No-one had the words or the confidence to tackle Stephen.

Stephen went to see his bank manager to raise a mortgage on the place. The man was pessimistic. Stephen offered his quarter share of the business as security, and his expectation of inheriting number two, The Parade when his father died. The bank manager was respectful but could not hide his belief that four thousand pounds was an extravagant amount of money for a farm while land prices were tumbling, and that a trained lawyer who had never been near a field except for picnics was not likely to make a profit from a farm which even the vendor admitted was run-down.

Stephen came home from the meeting with the bank manager tense with temper. His father, smiling placidly, was in the drawing room. Stephen refused tea and went straight to the dining room to pour himself a drink.

'Where's Lily?'

'Out in the car.' Rory spoke the words carefully, one at a time.

'And Mother?'

'Out to thea.'

Stephen nodded. He sat in the window seat. On the Canoe Lake people were boating. A pair of children were skimming the water carefully with shrimping nets, hoping to catch crabs.

'I've just seen old Hardwick at the bank,' he said carelessly. He sipped his whisky. Rory watched the level of the glass and his son's tense face. 'Damn fool won't help me at all,' he said.

Rory nodded.

'I can't raise a loan for the farm without someone to

stand as security,' Stephen said. 'At least not with Hardwick. I suppose I could go to another bank but I'd rather stay with him, of course.'

Rory nodded again.

'I was going to ask you,' Stephen said. 'Ask you to act as guarantor, you know. For a loan for me to buy the farm. A mortgage on it really.'

Rory sighed.

'You may not *like* the idea,' Stephen said. 'But I've set my heart on it. I'd carry on working at the practice. Lily and I need a place of our own. I want to live in the country. I have a right to my own life.'

Rory met his son's sharp look. Stephen turned away and poured himself another whisky. 'I've done enough, surely!' he exclaimed. 'Two years at Ypres! Wounded! Mentioned in dispatches! I've done enough to deserve the place!'

Rory looked at him with a gaze full of pity. 'You've done enough,' he said gently. 'But the farm's no good.'

Stephen looked at him with impatience. 'But I want it!' he said. 'I've set my heart on it.'

Rory shook his head. 'It's a dream,' he said, mouthing the words carefully. 'You can't farm. Lily don't agree. It's no go.'

'I tell you it's a good working farm! I've wanted to farm since I came back from Belgium. You don't know what it would mean to me to build a farm up.' Stephen was breathless, trying to convince his father, trying to convince himself. 'There are things which happened over there which have to be put right . . .' he said. 'The farm where I went that night, the women, the deaths, and the little baby stuck in the cradle with a knife – it was b . . . b . . . b . . . bad, I want to ch . . . ch . . . change it. I want to forget it.'

Rory looked at his son with deep pity. 'Nothing changes it,' he said slowly. 'You did what you did.'

Stephen's head jerked up, his face was white. 'What

d'you mean?' he demanded. 'What d'you mean – what I did? What d'you think I did? What are you saying? I tell you the Germans massacred those women and we went in and cleaned them out. It was an act of war. I was mentioned in dispatches.'

Rory was alert, listening to Stephen's rapid anxious speech.

'What d'you mean?' Stephen asked again.

Rory shook his head. 'Only . . . past is past,' he said. It was an effort for him to speak to Stephen. He was pale with the struggle. 'War is over.'

He leaned over and pressed the bell-button at the side of the fire. Browning came at once and, at his gesture, fetched Coventry to carry him upstairs to his room. 'Rest now,' he said wearily. He smiled gently at Stephen. 'Sorry about the farm,' he said.

That night Stephen dreamed of the farm Little England. It was there he had learned for the first time that the Belgian countryside was lovely. Arriving at night, marching to the Front in a haze of fear, had blinded him to the place. But at Little England he had time to stop and look around him and see a place that was not just a setting for war, but a place that people worked with love.

The land had been fought over for hundreds of years. The Romans had fought the German tribes all over it; Stephen could dimly remember passages of translation from school. The Spanish had fought there for some reason, Stephen could not think what they were doing, so far from home. And of course Marlborough and then Wellington had marched all over the place – and won. Stephen could see how the rolling slow contours would suit a cavalry charge like Marlborough's, like the Iron Duke's. Horses would just fly across those smooth rounded fields, and there was no cover for the infantry at all.

'Poor bloody infantry as usual,' Stephen had said, leaning on the gate and looking westward across the flat fields, where the sun was setting in a dusty haze of scarlet.

It gave him a sense of distance from his fear of the war to know that although this soil had claimed thousands, even millions of lives, it had always been farming country. The Perots could trace their ownership of the farm back to the eighteenth century and beyond. A Perot had been working the land when Marlborough had come riding in – and then ridden home again. Stephen felt that he could be a part of the land, one of the peasantry who watched the armies ebb and then flow. He felt free of his uniform and free of his allegiance and free of his fear. A Perot had been watching this horizon throughout all the battles and they had meant little in the end but temporary disruption. Stephen, watching the sun go down over his Juliette's fields, felt himself at one with the men who stayed at home and let the armies do their bloody business and then disband.

He toyed with the idea of staying at the farm after his marriage to Juliette. The Perots were old, they had no sons. They would welcome Juliette's husband as a worker. They would welcome him as the son they had never had. Stephen, starved of affection from babyhood, thought of the way Madame Perot rested her hand on his shoulder when she served him his dinner, and how old Perot would slap his shoulder when they had completed a task. Stephen smiled at the thought of telling his parents that although they had sent him to his death he had found a life so rich and so contented that he would never come home again. Not only would he never fight again for King and Country, he was prepared to lose his King and Country for the greater joys of a few acres of arable land, a small trout river and a little wood of sound trees.

He loved the skies over the Flanders plains. The land

517

was so flat that the horizon stretched forever, he could even see the gentle curve of the earth. Storms would darken the horizon and roll slowly with great towers of clouds towards the farm. There was always time to pack up the tools and get under cover before the first drops of rain began to fall. And then, sheltering in the barn, there would be Juliette, smiling and warm, and splashed with raindrops which she would let Stephen kiss away from her face and neck.

Every hour he could spend away from the trenches or from the camp behind the lines he would ride over to Little England to see Juliette and to work as her father ordered. His fellow officers stopped teasing him about his Belgian bint after Stephen had sharply told them that he and Juliette were planning to marry. There had been a shocked silence, for the Belgian girls encountered by the officers were generally working whores in brothels. But Stephen's look had been so fierce, and his temper was known to be so uncertain, that no-one ventured another comment.

After a while, it was regarded as rather romantic that when the rest of them took a day's leave lying on their cramped camp beds or getting angrily drunk in the *estaminet*, Stephen and his batman would hitch a lift, or borrow a couple of horses, or commandeer transport, to get themselves out to the farm they called Little England. Stephen never invited anyone to go with him, and for those left behind it became a place of mystery – a place where there was peace. A place where the world had not changed, where plants and crops still grew, where the land beneath your boots was green and fertile and not a slough of mud.

Stephen stirred in his sleep beside Lily and sighed. His dream changed and shifted. Half a dozen half-seen, dreaded images slid into his dream. He saw again the surreal picture of the dead horse blasted by an explosion so it hung, like some demented fruit, from the branches of a tree. A mangled chest, a rolling head. Stephen moaned and Lily half-woke, and put a hand on his shoulder and shook him gently.

Stephen turned on his side and went deeper into sleep. He suddenly heard someone shout, shout loudly at him.

'Winters! I've just heard. They've broken through. They're past your place, Little England. The 4th fell back a day ago. The line is this side of the farm now, and they're still retreating. The Germans will have gone through Little England.'

Stephen's breath came faster as he remembered the cleansing leap of rage, and at the same time his deep longing for Juliette. The whole of the Allied army was in chaos. Brigades were split from their communications, platoons were lost in the withdrawal. The big push had come not from the English and the French but from the Germans, who were suddenly rolling forward in an unstoppable advance. The stalemate of the trenches was smashed and the armies were moving rapidly. The English were falling back to the coast in a desperate retreat to get home, the French frantically grouping and regrouping in an attempt – which anyone could see would fail – to save Paris. Unbelievably, after the years of stuck warfare and the fields sown so liberally with bodies of the dead, the British were losing, and were in rapid retreat.

Not Stephen. There was nothing for him in England, least of all as a returning reluctant soldier in an army that had lost. There were nightmares and a dull office job. There was the cold silent house and a crippled father. There was his mother's unbearable grieving for Christopher and her scant joy in his survival. Stephen rejected that future for himself and swore that he would rescue Juliette or kill her murderers. He did not wait to report to his CO; he simply started running, back down the road, in the darkness, and then down the little lanes towards Little England.

It was a while before he even realized he was not alone. Four men had come with him, and Coventry. He led them at a rapid pace – running and then walking to catch their breaths, and then running again. He was reckless of scouting parties; he did not even fear the main German advance. He was too angry to think of his own safety or of anything except getting to the farm and protecting it with his life.

They ran down the lane and Stephen felt the cold haft of his knife slipped into his hand by Coventry. The lights were on in the little farmhouse. He halted his men and gestured them to be silent. He crept around the back, moving like a shadow in the darkness. He meant to steal up to the window and peep in, to see if the place was occupied by Germans, and how many there were, and what the odds would be. But when he heard the rich delightful laugh of a woman's voice his anger suddenly overtook him and he kicked in the door, knowing that Juliette was already dead and the Germans and their whores were defiling her home, the home he had thought would be his.

He was firing as the door flew open, and the men behind him were firing too in a great explosion of bullets which stormed into the room as they rushed in behind them.

He saw Juliette as she rose from the German's lap, her face a mask of surprise and terror. She turned towards him as a bullet thudded into her belly and her chest and flung her, arms outstretched like a thrown doll, into the wall at the side of the range. As she fell her head lolled into the open range and her hair frizzed and sizzled and her face burned red and then black and the kitchen was filled with the smell of cooking meat. Perot's wife had been at the sink; a bullet took her in the back. She was crawling across the floor towards Juliette when Stephen bent down and put a bullet behind her ear. The German seated at the table with his jacket undone and Juliette on his lap was killed outright. His body was a mess of red blood and red wine from the smashed bottle on the table.

Old Perot stumbled up the stairs from the cellar and Coventry whirled and put a bullet neatly between his eyes, a real marksman's point. They could hear a scream from the other Perot girl upstairs, and the stumbling sound of a man half-falling in haste down the wooden stairs. Two of Stephen's men sent a hail of bullets up the stairs and they heard a scream and then his falling body.

They ranged through the house then, like avenging tyrants. There were three other German officers, who had been quartered at the farmhouse for three days. There were two other women with them. They were shot where they lay, one young boy so exhausted by the rapid advance over the last few days that he barely woke as Stephen raged into the room and shot him and the woman in his arms.

When they had finished, and come back to the kitchen, Stephen found he was trembling with a deep sexual joy at releasing his anger against the war itself, in the house where he had dreamed, like a cuckold, of peace. He pulled Juliette by the feet away from the fire where she lay and he longed to unbutton his flies and violate her dead body, as a final humiliation. She had kissed him and let him touch her, and he could have had her as the dead German had probably had her, but he had treated her according to his code as an English gentleman and held back.

He laughed and his laughter was like the sharpened edge of a bayonet at the thought of the fool he had been, riding out to see his love, slaving on her father's farm, like some knight in a storybook, while all along he could have had her for the asking because she liked him, and because she had no interest in his plans, or England, or his house in Portsmouth. When the German officer had arrived and spoken to them kindly and paid in advance for requisitioning the farm, she had liked him too.

It was then that he heard the baby.

It was a sleepy little cry, from the parlour at the front of the house. It belonged to Juliette's sister, Nicole, whose husband had disappeared quietly when conscription came in. Stephen felt the cool satisfying haft of the knife in his hand and went quietly, softly, as if he did not want to frighten it, into the parlour.

The baby was in a hand-carved crib, the edges of the wood rounded and polished with generations of use. It was a boy baby. Stephen had been wrong there too. Perot did have an heir. He would never have set aside his legitimate Belgian grandson for an incoming foreigner. Stephen looked at the little boy, whose blue eyes stared up at the strange face hanging over the crib. The baby reached out two little hands, his toothless smile beamed out and his feet kicked in welcome.

Stephen leaned over the crib and put the knife with gentle care in the baby's yielding belly. The baby's face changed and a gurgle of blood came from its mouth. It died almost silently. It was as if Stephen had put it quietly to sleep.

He went back into the kitchen possessed of a deep peace. The exhilaration of the revenge had passed. Not even the sight of Juliette with her fair hair and her pretty face all burned away could arouse him to either anger or grief.

'Now then,' he said to the men. 'Line up.'

He smiled at them, as if promising some kind of treat. They had been all over the house, they had seen the food and the good pieces of linen and the little pieces of silver. They were expecting permission to tear the place apart, to take whatever they wished as a souvenir of the night's work. They lined up obediently. They had been obeying orders without question for years. The sudden plunge into savagery was not enough to break the pattern.

Stephen reached behind him. One of the Germans had left an automatic rifle propped against the sink. Stephen had it at his shoulder in one smooth gesture and then he gunned down his four men and they fell almost all at once. One groaned, and tried to scrabble forwards, and Coventry stepped up and shot him neatly in the back.

Stephen and Coventry dragged the bodies of the English soldiers out of line and scattered them around the ground floor: two in the kitchen, one in the parlour, one in the hall. It would have fooled no-one in search of the truth of what happened that night. But there was no-one to ask questions. Stephen's uncorroborated account of what had taken place became exaggerated in the telling and re-telling and then became one of the few stories of courage and initiative that could be issued by the retreating army to boost their status at home. Stephen's CO reported it, journalists embroidered it. The atrocity details fired the anger of civilians safe at home. Stephen and Coventry's defence of Belgian women and children made a good story. They were decorated for courage. Within a few days the Germans had become bogged down in their advance and the war was on the turn.

Stephen whimpered in his sleep and turned over. 'Juliette,' he said quietly, longingly. 'Juliette.'

Chapter Thirty-five

The next day John Pascoe, without saying a word to Stephen, went out to the farm and spoke with the farmer. He came back with Stephen's note of hand for four hundred pounds and left it on Stephen's desk while he was out at lunch, without a word of explanation. The older man was embarrassed at his role in the business, but Rory and he had agreed, after that difficult dinner, that Stephen's note of hand would have to be recovered and the deal broken. They could not spare Stephen from the office, they could not afford to buy him out of the partnership. They could not pay him a bonus that would cover the purchase cost of the farm and they were certain that the tired salt-stained land would never earn enough under Stephen's ignorant management to repay a heavy mortgage. In any case, Hardwick had refused to lend Stephen the money and Stephen had no other resources.

They knew that Stephen was in the grip of some foolishness over the farm. Both of them had seen symptoms of neurasthenia or shellshock in the boy. Both of them had watched his drinking, his late nights and his dark unexplained bruises with silent concern. They had thought that the marriage would be the making of him but for some reason the pretty little wife he had chosen was not able to keep him at home. She was blooming, and the child was a credit to her. But young Stephen seemed to be growing more morose and more difficult every day. Rory did not want Lily to be taken away from the town and away from her friends. He did not trust his son to be alone with her. He had not forgotten her screams that Sunday afternoon. He did not know what marks the war had left on his son, and he did not trust him.

None of this was spoken. John and Rory were old friends; the partnership went back to their earliest days. Rory was finding speech difficult, and it was, between them, quite unnecessary. On parting, after that tense dinner party, Rory grasped John's hand and said slowly, 'Sort out this damn business,' and John replied: 'Leave it with me.' Nothing else was said.

John handled the farmer with weary competence. He summed up the value of the farm as something like two-thirds of the asking price. He knew little about stock – but enough to identify sick animals when the cows limped into the dirty milking parlour. He did his business at the kitchen table and saw, as Lily had seen, the slop pail under the sink filled to the brim with mouldering scraps, and the greasy cobwebs looped in strings above the range. He told the man, briskly, that Stephen had been shellshocked since the war and that the man must have taken advantage of him to close a sale without letting Stephen take legal advice. He told him firmly that there was no money of that amount available to Stephen. And he opened a briefcase full of imposing documents and offered some small compensation in return for the note of hand and the breaking of the deal.

The farmer, who had in any case woken in the morning thinking that the whole visit had been an agreeable dream, took ten guineas for his trouble and considered himself well-paid. John Pascoe took the note and motored back to Portsmouth with an enjoyable sense of a difficult job well done.

He expected no thanks from Stephen. He expected the silence to hold, so he was surprised when Stephen tapped on his office door and put his head into the room on his way home in the afternoon.

'Was the chap all right?' Stephen asked casually.

'Oh yes,' John Pascoe replied. 'I gave him ten guineas. I think he knew he was taking advantage, I think he knew it wouldn't be allowed.'

Stephen's broad smile didn't reach his eyes. 'Oh, really? What did you tell him? That my father wouldn't allow it?'

John shifted a little uncomfortably in his seat. 'Oh, not exactly,' he said. 'I may have laid it on a little thick. I told him you were a war hero and all of that. I said that you'd got carried away at the sight of the farm, and that he shouldn't hold you to it.'

'Told him I was dotty, did you?' Stephen's mirthless grin grew wider. 'I'll say one thing for you, John, you don't do things by halves.'

'Not dotty,' John said uncomfortably. 'Of course not.'

'No,' Stephen said. 'What would you want with a dotty partner?'

'Well, it's over now, anyway,' John said. 'But I do see what you saw in the place. It was a charming idea. Perhaps later on – perhaps a weekend cottage somewhere.'

Stephen frowned slightly. 'D'you know,' he said, 'I never thought of that. That would be an excellent thing to do. No farming, I don't leave here, I stay living at home with my mother and father and my wife and my son. But at the weekend, if I'm not needed for anything, I could be allowed to go to a little cottage in the country and pretend that I was in Belgium again, at the farm which meant everything to me.'

'Some fellows get on very well,' John said hesitantly. He was unsure of Stephen's mood. 'A nice little place in the country.'

Stephen shot him a glittering smile. 'I think it would be the very thing!' he said. 'And so good for Christopher!'

John nodded. 'Lovely for him,' he said.

'And that's the main thing, after all,' Stephen said. 'As long as Christopher gets the very best of everything. As long as Christopher is happy. As long as we all remember to put Christopher first. Well. I must be off home! See you tomorrow. I'm in court all morning with the Priestley case. I'll go straight there. I'll be in my office in the afternoon.'

'Certainly, and good luck with the Priestleys!'

Stephen smiled again and waved and closed John Pascoe's door. John sat for a long time saying nothing, his mind quite blank. Somewhere at the back of his consciousness was the thought, which he had never had before, that perhaps it was easier for those – like his own son – who had never come home, who had never had to make a life in a country that was changed beyond all recognition and that had cost them so very dear.

He sighed and picked up the telephone and dialled the Winters's home number. Lily, walking through the hall on her way to the drawing room, picked up the phone.

'Hello, my dear,' John said. 'I have a message for Rory. Is he there?'

'He's upstairs,' Lily said. 'He's a little overtired today. I shouldn't call him to the phone. Can I take a message? Or do you want to call back at dinner time? He might come down for dinner.'

John hesitated. 'I can ask you to give him a message,' he said. 'Just between you and me, my dear, we were both concerned with Stephen's plan to buy the farm and I've sorted it out. The farmer returned Stephen's note. The sale is cancelled. Just tell Rory that it's all off, there's no need for him to worry.'

He heard Lily's little sigh of relief. 'I'll tell him,' she said. 'You're an angel, John!'

He gave a little complacent chuckle. 'All in a day's work!'

he said. 'We can't have you worrying! And we couldn't have had you buried in the country! I don't know what the boy was thinking of!'

'He said it reminded him of a place in Belgium,' Lily said. 'Somewhere he used to go on leave. I suppose it mattered to him because it was a peaceful place in the middle of war.'

'Well, for heaven's sake – it's peace now, isn't it?' John exclaimed. 'He doesn't need a refuge now!' He recollected that he was speaking to Stephen's wife. 'I do beg your pardon, my dear. Now, if you can tell Rory that it's all settled, we'll say no more about it.'

'As usual,' Lily said sapiently. 'Whenever there's anything in this house that we don't like, we say no more about it.'

In the background John could hear the front door open. 'Oh!' Lily said in a quite different voice. 'I have to go! I'll deliver your message! Goodbye now!'

She put the phone down and faced Stephen as he came heavily into the hall.

'Sorry to interrupt,' he said with icy courtesy.

Lily shook her head with a smile. 'It was nothing,' she said.

'Was the message for me? The message you had to deliver?'

Lily shook her head. 'No.'

'Oh? Is it for my mother?'

'No.'

'For Father?'

Lily glanced around the hall but there was no distraction. 'Yes,' she said. 'A message for your father.'

'How odd,' Stephen said. 'From my office?'

Lily nodded. 'I'll go and tell him now,' she said. 'He's not been very well today. He didn't come out for a walk. If he's not asleep I'll tell him now.'

'I'll come up with you,' Stephen said pleasantly. He slipped his hand around Lily's waist and they climbed the stairs together. Lily had a momentary, foolish thought that it was like being under arrest, being marched somewhere. She could not see how to escape giving John Pascoe's message in front of Stephen and she knew that Stephen would dislike the knowledge that Rory and John had worked together to subvert him.

Lily tapped softly on Rory's door, hoping that he would be asleep and there would be no reply.

'Mmmm!' he called. His voice was strong and clear but the betraying muscles around his lips and mouth and throat would not shape the words he needed.

Lily opened the door and slipped in, Stephen following. Rory smiled at them both but his dark eyes were wary.

'Good afternoon,' Stephen said genially. 'I am sorry to hear you're off-colour. Perhaps you've been overdoing it?'

Rory shook his head slowly, the muscles in his neck straining with effort. 'I'm well,' he said finally.

'Lily took a phone message for you,' Stephen said. 'Didn't you, Lily?'

Both men looked at her. Lily flushed as if she were keeping some clandestine secret.

'John Pascoe telephoned,' she said. She put on her Duchess voice and kept it steady. 'He said to tell you not to worry, and that it's been sorted out.'

'How very odd!' Stephen said. 'What does he mean? D'you know, Father?'

Rory tried to nod, but the muscle in his jaw started to tremble.

'He must have said something else, Lily,' Stephen said gently. 'What matter was this? What was it all about?' He looked from Lily to his father as if he could not imagine what they were withholding. 'You must have a clearer message,' he said. 'This is meaningless! I had better phone

John back! If my father is worried about something then we had better put his mind properly at rest.'

Lily and Rory exchanged a trapped look.

'Unless it is just me who does not understand?' Stephen asked. 'Perhaps it is me who is misunderstanding here? Just me who would need a clearer message?'

Lily shrugged. 'I know nothing about it,' she said. 'I'm going to change.'

'It's about the farm, isn't it?' Stephen said suddenly. Lily's guilty face told him at once. 'Oh! If that's what it's all about then I can tell you all about it. There's no need for this foolish and childish secrecy. I can tell you all about it.'

Rory moved his hand in a quietening gesture, as if begging Stephen to stop. Lily said, 'It doesn't matter, Stephen. It *was* about the farm. It was a message to tell your father that John had cancelled the sale and not to worry. That was all.'

'Did he tell you how he did it?' Stephen asked. 'Or did you all plan it together, perhaps? Perhaps you all got together to work out what you should say? It was really quite brilliant. I congratulate you, all three of you! He told the farmer that I was dotty. From the war. Not fit to take decisions. Probably better off in a home. Perhaps my affairs should be in trust, d'you think? Who cooked that one up? Was it you, Lily?'

Lily shot an anxious look at Rory and then shook her head. 'I didn't know anything about this,' she said. 'I didn't want to buy the farm and I didn't want to live there. But I didn't ask your father or Mr Pascoe to do anything.'

Stephen nodded and slid his arm around her waist. Lily stiffened but he drew her to him. 'You loyal little darling,' he said softly. 'But you have it all the wrong way round. You don't have to express a wish before someone will grant it for you. You don't have to fight and struggle and demand to get what you want, my darling! You just have to open those blue eyes of yours and someone will do it for you.'

Lily let him hold her, but she turned her face away. Stephen looked towards the bed. 'And you, Father, what a pair of old rogues you and John are, to be sure! I shall take care never to go against your wishes again! D'you know for a moment then I thought I might live the life I wished? I thought that since I had gone to Ypres, as you wished, and come back against all the odds, and worked in your office for three years, that I might do as I wanted after all this time! But not with you and John at the helm, eh? You run a tight ship, Father, I admire you for it.'

Rory heard the bitterness in his son's voice and heaved himself up on one elbow. 'Sorry,' he said. 'My boy . . .' He reached a hand out towards his son. Rory's overloaded brain gave him the wrong word, precisely the wrong word for the case. He stretched his hand out further and his eyes looked at Stephen with pity and with love. 'Christopher.'

Stephen gave a low sob of a laugh, turned on his heel and went out of the room. Lily stepped forward and took Rory's hand. She patted it gently. 'Never mind,' she said. 'You acted for the best. He'll get over it. And at least we do have a Christopher now.'

Stephen left early for court the next morning, his wig and his gown in a small bag. Coventry drove him there and parked nearby to wait for him. Lily watched Christopher being wheeled out into the garden and heard Nanny Janes's heavy tread as she went upstairs to tidy the nursery. She slipped on a jacket and went outside.

The wind was blowing in off the sea and she could smell the salt in the air. The late summer roses, creamy and thick, were nodding their heads and opening their petals under the warmth of the sun. Bedding plants in scarlet and white blazed in the circular flower bed in the plumb centre of the garden, birds sang loudly, and as Lily sat and rocked the pram and smiled in reply to Christopher's contented gurgles, she watched the housemartins swooping low and rapid across the sky.

Christopher was dozy, his eyes closed and Lily let the pram rock to a standstill. A little breeze caught the wooden gate from the garden to the garage and courtyard at the side of the house and it banged softly. Lily went to lock it, but the key was missing. She pushed it shut, and wedged it with a stone so that it should make no noise which might disrupt Christopher's sleep. She went back to sit on the bench and turned her face up to the sunshine as Sally came running out of the kitchen door.

Lily put a finger to her lips and went to greet her. 'Telephone, Mrs Winters,' Sally whispered. 'It's Mr Smith.'

Lily glanced at Christopher, sleeping soundly, and then up at the nursery window where Nanny Janes moved to and fro, occasionally glancing down, observing Lily's interference with proper discipline.

Lily went up the steps to the verandah through the French windows, into the dining room, still smelling heavily of fat from Stephen's cooked breakfast, and picked up the telephone in the hall.

'Sweetie, I have to go away for a couple of days,' Charlie said. 'It's the Palace Theatre, London. They just rang. Their MD has been taken sick and they've offered me the chance of the job for a week. I'd be mad not to go.'

Lily felt for the back of the chair near the phone and sank down into it.

'A week,' she said.

'It could turn into the season, I suppose. It was a very brief phone call, I didn't have time to discuss everything. I said I'd take a train up this morning, and see them this afternoon.'

Lily nodded. 'That's wonderful news.'

Charlie chuckled. 'You're a little trouper,' he said. 'It's not wonderful news for us, I know. But it's a big break for me if I take it.'

'Of course you must take it,' Lily said. She heard a tiny tremor in her voice and took a deep breath and ironed it out. 'Of course you must take it.'

'If it came right for me, and I was earning, earning a good deal of money, then a lot of other things would be possible,' Charlie said. 'I could buy you a house of your own. I could send Christopher to whatever school you wanted. You could leave Stephen.'

Lily glanced guiltily around the hall. There was no-one there. Muriel was in her bedroom, Rory was in the laborious process of being dressed for the day, Nanny Janes was in the nursery and the maids and Cook were in the kitchen.

'I don't even think about it,' she said.

'Well, I do,' Charlie replied. 'And this might be the way forward.'

There was a little silence.

'Will you stay in town tonight?' Lily asked.

'If they're desperate, I'll have to. I don't know what's wrong with the other chap. If he can't work at all, they might want me to start right away. If that *does* happen I'll call you at once, sweetheart. And I'll come back on the last train Saturday night and see you Sunday. We'll sort something out then.'

'Yes,' Lily said forlornly.

'If you want me to stay, then say it,' Charlie said tightly. 'But I can't go on like this with you, and you can't go on in that house. If you want me to stay then I'll stay, but I'll only be here to help you leave him. Things have got to change, Lily. It's destroying all three of us.'

Lily nodded. 'I know.' There was a little silence. 'I'm not ready to leave yet,' she said quietly. 'There's his father and mother to be considered as well. And I have to know that I could keep Christopher.'

'Only if you're prepared to divorce him for cruelty,' Charlie said. 'I took some advice. If you're prepared to testify that he's cruel then you'd get a divorce, and you'd be able to keep Christopher. Especially if you could show that you had independent means – if I endowed you with some capital.'

'I can't do that.'

Charlie breathed out, trying to restrain his impatience. Lily held the phone close to her ear. More than anything in the world she wanted Charlie's arms around her.

'Don't be angry,' she said. 'I want to do the best. I want to do the best for Christopher.'

'I know,' he said. 'And I'm not angry. I'm – oh! – impatient! Unhappy! I want something to change! I want something to change dramatically! I want to snatch up you and Christopher and take you away and have everything different! Like a fairy story!'

Lily smiled. 'I want that too,' she said. 'I want that day at the sea again. When I was in love with you so much that I could hardly breathe! And we went swimming, and we had tea at that little post office, and I wore Madge's trousers, and you had that motorbike.'

'I remember,' Charlie said. 'D'you know, if I was on my deathbed that would be the day I would remember? A perfect day. A *perfect* day. I don't think I've ever been happier.'

There was a little silence. Lily thought, irrelevantly, that only lovers use the telephone to say nothing. 'Only you could ring me up and then just breathe at me,' she said.

'I like to know you're there,' Charlie replied. 'I could happily spend all day on the phone to you, just so I know where you are, and what you're wearing, and how you're looking and what you're feeling.'

'I'm in the hall,' Lily said. 'Sitting on the chair. I'm wearing my blue and white striped dress with the little jacket. I wish I was with you.'

'What about that mad farm idea?' Charlie said. 'What's happening about that?'

'Oh, Rory spoke to John Pascoe, and John spoke to the farmer, and he returned Stephen's note, and the sale is off. It's all off.'

'They cancelled his agreement?' Charlie asked.

'Yes.'

'Poor chap,' Charlie said. 'They don't give him a lot of chances, do they?'

'I couldn't have stood it,' Lily said.

'I know. But he wanted it. It was something he wanted. And they didn't even let him have that. He had no right to force it on you, but . . .' Charlie broke off. 'It's a bit thick!' he said lightly. 'For a chap to go through what he went through, and then come home and have to toe the line still. It's just a bit thick, that's all.'

Above Lily's head Muriel's bedroom door opened and closed again, and Muriel started coming down the stairs.

'I have to go,' Lily breathed into the telephone.

'Someone there?'

'That's right.'

'I'll go and get my train then. I'll ring you from London. I'll tell you what's going on. Don't get anxious, I'll see you soon.'

'Break a leg!' Lily said in the old theatre tradition. 'I hope you get it! You deserve it!'

'Give my little boy a hug from me. I shall miss him this afternoon.'

'I will. Goodbye.'

'Goodbye.'

Lily put the telephone down and pushed the upright instrument to the rear of the table, on its linen mat, as

Muriel liked it to be. From the road outside she heard a car door slam, a car start up, pause at the T junction at the side of the house, and then drive off.

'You're pale,' Muriel said. 'Not bad news?'

Lily smiled. 'Not at all! That was Charlie! He has an audition in London this afternoon at the Palace Theatre. Wonderful news.'

Muriel put her hand gently on her daughter-in-law's shoulder. 'Perhaps it is for the best,' she said quietly.

Lily blinked quickly on a rush of sudden hot tears. 'I know,' she said. 'I'm very pleased for him.'

Muriel hesitated, afraid to say more and yet wanting to cell Lily that she understood. She chose to say nothing. Could you drive me into Southsea?' Muriel asked. 'I wanted to collect a dress from Mrs Mates. I forgot that Stephen was keeping the car all day.'

Lily nodded. 'Of course,' she said. 'I'm not doing anything this morning. Now Charlie won't be here for my lesson this afternoon I'm free all day. And I love an excuse to show off my Morris!'

Muriel opened the door and went in to the drawing room. 'I'll only be a minute with Mrs Mates and then we could call in and see Sarah Dent for coffee, if you would like. She's just around the corner.'

'Certainly,' Lily said pleasantly. 'I'll get my hat.'

She glanced out of the drawing room window. 'And my umbrella!' she said. 'It's going to pour! I'll get Christopher brought in and tell Sally to take the pram into the kitchen. Look at that sky! It's clouded over so quickly. I was in the garden only a moment ago and it was beautiful sunshine then!'

Muriel rang the bell for the tweeny as Lily went from the hall, through the dining room and out on to the verandah. Already, large drops of warm rain were starting to fall. Lily started for the steps to the garden and then stopped short.

The little garden was quite empty.

The pram, and Christopher, were gone.

Chapter Thirty-six

Oh!' Lily said. 'Sally must have already brought him in.' She went back to the dining room. Muriel was in the hall, pinning on her hat. Sally was coming up the back stairs from the kitchen.

'Have you brought Christopher in?' Lily asked.

'I'm just going, Mrs Winters. I've only just this minute been asked.'

Lily looked at Muriel. 'The pram's not there,' she said stupidly. 'Has Browning brought him in?'

'Browning's in the kitchen, doing the ironing,' Sally said. 'We thought he was to be left to sleep.'

'It's raining!' Lily said irritably. 'Not even Nanny Janes says he has to sleep outside in the pouring rain!'

'I didn't know it was raining,' Sally said with injured dignity. 'You can't see the sky in that kitchen.'

'Oh!' Lily exclaimed with irritation. 'Where is Nanny Janes?'

The nursery door opened at the top of the stairs and Nanny Janes came down.

'Nanny Janes!' Lily called up to her. 'Did you bring Christopher in?'

'I am coming down to ensure that he is brought in,' Nanny Janes said with quelling dignity. 'It is starting to rain.'

'He's not there,' Lily said blankly. 'He's not in the garden. The pram has gone.'

'Impossible,' Muriel said. 'Cook must have brought him in. Or Coventry.'

Breaking all the rules of proper behaviour, Lily ran down the stairs to the kitchen and burst in without knocking on the baize door. Cook, who was sitting with her feet up on the brass fender before the range and gossiping with Browning, bustled to her feet.

'Have either of you brought Christopher in?' Lily demanded. 'Brought him in from the garden, just now?'

The two women looked blankly at her. 'No, Mrs Winters,' Browning replied. 'He's having his morning nap.'

Lily tore past them, wrenched open the back door and went out into the garden. She had a momentary foolish thought that the pram would be there, and Christopher kicking his feet, or starting a protesting wail at the rain. The garden was empty.

Lily ran to where the pram had been, opposite the little stone seat. The begonias danced and bobbed as the raindrops fell on their petals. Lily looked all around the garden as if the pram could have been mislaid, or pushed out of sight.

She went to the garden gate which had been banging in the wind. The stone which she had wedged in place had been pushed away by the gate, which clearly had been opened from the outside. There was a deep groove in the earth where the stone had been pushed back. The gate banged as Lily looked at it, uncomprehending.

She ran to the gate and tore it open. Beyond it was the courtyard, and her car parked neatly to one side; beside it the open garage where the Argyll was kept. She peered into the garage in case someone, some passer-by, had seen the pram in the rain and interferingly pushed it into shelter. The garage was damp and cold and smelled of oil. There was a dark patch on the floor.

Lily turned away and ran across the little cobbled courtyard. The big double gates to the road stood open, hooked back. Lily took two or three steps, first to the right, and then to the left. Apart from rain, which was coming down harder, dancing on the tarmac, the road was completely empty.

Nanny Janes under a big dark umbrella with Muriel beside her came out through the garden gate. Lily turned to them a face as blank and white as a lost child.

'Where is Christopher?' she asked. 'What has happened? Where is he?'

'My dear . . .' Muriel began and then she broke off. She looked at Nanny Janes.

'I think we should return to the house and telephone Mr Winters,' Nanny Janes said solemnly. 'He will decide what should be done next.'

Without a word Lily turned and ran towards the sea, to The Parade and the promenade. There was no-one in sight. No-one boating on the Canoe Lake, no child lagging behind to rescue a little model boat. No-one feeding the swans. No-one hastily pushing a pram away.

Lily ran across the little road. There was a man lounging in the small cabin beside the upturned boats. A sign over his head showed the prices for boat hire.

'Have you seen someone with a pram?' Lily demanded, falling over the words in her anxiety. 'Someone pushing a pram away from that house? A dark blue pram? A big pram?'

'Today?' the man asked.

Lily stamped her foot in her impatience. 'Just now! Just now! A few moments ago!'

The man shook his head slowly. 'I can't say I have,' he said. 'But I wasn't looking out for anyone. I wasn't watching in that general direction.'

Lily swore under her breath and ran towards the seafront and the raised promenade. She climbed the steps and looked along the shingle beach. It was empty. There was no-one strolling near the waves, no-one taking the air. The rain was coming down more heavily, sweeping in great curtains off the sea. In the distance she could see two women running, hand-in-hand, for shelter. But there was no pram, there was no Christopher.

Lily shaded her eyes against the rain. Looking as carefully as she could in both directions she could see nothing except the rain-washed promenade and the empty beach with waves curling and sucking on the pebbles. The great scuds of rain blew in and blinded her, but Lily stood, straining her eyes to see better until she was certain that the promenade and the lower road were empty.

She gave a quick decisive nod and ran back towards the house. She turned to the right along The Parade and ran the length of the block before she stopped and stared before her. There were a few detached houses overlooking the strip of grass before the sea. Further down there was a small tennis club with two grass courts empty in the rain. Lily stood still and scanned the road carefully for any movement. There was no-one walking. There was no-one pushing a pram. There was no-one running, with their arms wrapped tightly around them, holding a precious bundle. Whoever had taken Christopher had not gone that way.

Lily turned on her heel and ran back past the house in the opposite direction. There was a baker's cart going away from the house. Lily ran alongside it and shouted up at the driver. He stopped the horse and stared down at her. She looked wild and dangerous. The rain had plastered her hair to her scalp and she was red and panting from her run. Her eyes were desperate.

'Have you seen a pram?' Lily demanded. 'A blue pram? Just now? Coming from number two?'

'You've never lost your baby?' the man demanded. 'What happened?'

'Have you seen a pram?' Lily repeated, her voice rising higher into a shriek. 'Have you seen anyone with a baby?'

'You wouldn't think it possible!' the man exclaimed. 'Taken from the street, was it?'

'Please!' Lily said brokenly, and suddenly the tears spilled down her cheeks, hot and salty, unlike the cold sweet rain. '*Please* just tell me if you have seen anyone.'

The man shook his head. 'No-one,' he said. 'You'd better tell the police. Is your husband not at home?'

Lily shook her head, turned from the cart and ran back to the back gate of the house. Sally was there, standing in the rain, wringing her hands.

'Mrs Winters!' she said.

'Have you found him? Oh Christ! I was so afraid!' Lily demanded, suddenly flooded with gladness. 'Where was he? Who found him?'

Sally shook her head and Lily saw the tears in her eyes. 'No!' she said. 'Where can he be?'

Lily shook her head and ran northwards, away from the house to the end of the road. The streets were deserted. The town was quiet, only the rain gurgling in gutters and trickling down drains replied as Lily, suddenly losing control, screamed out, as loud as she could: 'Christopher! Christopher! Christopher! Where are you?'

Sally caught up with her at the corner and took her arm. 'Come on, Mrs Winters,' she said. 'Come home. They've telephoned for Mr Stephen. He'll come as soon as he can. Come home. Your baby's not here.'

Lily turned a haggard face to the tweeny. 'Then where is he?' she demanded. 'Where's Christopher?' Panic swept over Lily and she twisted and struggled in the woman's grip. 'Christopher! Where is he? Where's my baby?'

Sally dragged Lily home. The rain was getting heavier and the thunder rumbled threateningly as they neared the house. The road and the wet-roofed houses were lit by an ominous yellow light. The storm was far out to sea but coming nearer. They could see the crackle of lightning low on the horizon.

'Oh God!' Lily said. 'Where is he?'

The front door was open and Muriel was standing in the doorway, looking out into the rain.

'Come in, dear!' she said as soon as she saw Lily. 'Come out of the rain, there's nothing you can do!'

Lily ran up the steps and took her mother-in-law's arm in a hard grip. 'Why?' she asked. 'Why d'you say that?'

Muriel drew her into the hall, reckless for once of the polished floor and the expensive rugs. 'I just mean that you won't find him running around, dear. Nothing more than that. Try and compose yourself.'

She turned to Browning. 'Take Mrs Winters upstairs and help her change her dress,' she said. 'Lily, you're wet through.'

Lily shook her head impatiently. 'It doesn't matter. It doesn't matter. What can we do?'

'I've telephoned Stephen. A clerk from his office has gone to fetch him from court. He'll be as quick as he can, I told him it was an emergency. I'll telephone the police now. I don't think we should wait for Stephen to arrive.'

'Phone them!' Lily said. 'Phone them!'

Muriel pulled her into the drawing room and pressed her down into a chair. 'Stay here then,' she said. Over her shoulder she spoke to Browning. 'Fetch a towel at least for Mrs Winters to dry her hair. And I think she had better have a glass of something. Fetch her a small glass of brandy from the dining room.'

Lily shivered convulsively.

'You'll catch your death of cold!' Muriel scolded.

'Phone the police,' Lily said. 'Please.'

'I'll do it now. But you stay here, inside the house.'

Lily nodded. Muriel left the room and Lily listened to

her painstaking request to the operator to put her through to the local police station, and then her inquiry being passed from whoever answered the phone, to the sergeant on duty, and then to an inspector. Finally Muriel came back into the room.

'They're sending someone round at once,' she said.

Browning and Sally came in together. Sally handed Lily the towel and she sat holding it crumpled in her lap, her hair dripping cold water down her neck. Browning handed her the glass of brandy. Lily sipped at it but did not feel the burning warmth.

'I'll phone Charlie,' she said quietly.

'Won't he have left?' Muriel asked. 'Wasn't he going to London today?'

Lily's face quivered. 'I forgot,' she said. 'He'll have gone already.'

The four women waited in silence.

'I do think Stephen might have come home by now!' Muriel exclaimed impatiently. She went to the window to look out. The rain was beating against the panes. On the seaward side of the octagonal tower the view was blurred by the flow of the rainwater.

'I should tell Rory,' Muriel said. But she made no move to go upstairs.

'Where's Nanny Janes?' Lily suddenly demanded. 'Where is she?'

'In the nursery,' Sally volunteered. 'She's having a tidy up.'

Lily looked blank for a moment and then she laughed, a thin frightening laugh. 'A tidy up!' she exclaimed. 'She leaves my son in the garden and someone steals him and she goes and has a tidy up!'

She laughed again, louder and harsher, and then a gale of laughter took her and swept her and she was screaming with laughter, helpless with hysterical mirth.

Muriel shook her shoulder. 'Lily, stop it!' she commanded.

Lily shrieked, shaking her head and then put her hands to her head and pulled at her wet hair. Her voice rose higher and higher.

'Stop it!' Muriel exclaimed. 'Stop it!'

Lily's scream went on, she glared up at Muriel dry-eyed, shaking and screaming.

Muriel drew her hand back and slapped Lily hard across the face. Lily's scream was cut short. She recoiled from the blow and hunched herself into the chair, staring at Muriel.

'You do no good to give way,' Muriel said. 'Try and remember your position. Your husband will be here soon. The police will be here soon. This is no time to exercise your emotions.'

Lily shrank even smaller into the chair. She was trembling violently from cold and from distress. Muriel's face was unyielding.

'Go to your room and change your dress,' she said sternly. 'It helps no-one for you to over-dramatize the situation like this.'

Sally moved to help her and Lily rose from her chair mechanically, taking her arm. The tweeny guided her from the room and took her upstairs. Muriel followed. She watched Lily's feet going up the stairs ahead of her. One of the straps at the back of her dainty shoes had cut into her heel during her panic-stricken run up and down the seafront and she was bleeding. She had not even noticed. A few drops of blood, like the spoor of a mortally wounded animal, followed her up the stairs.

'When you have brought Mrs Winters back to the drawing room, take a cloth and mop the hall and the stair carpet,' Muriel said to Sally. 'You must use salt and cold water on the bloodstains or they will never come out.'

545

She stopped at Rory's door as the two younger women continued up the stairs to Lily's bedroom.

Rory was sitting up in his chair at the window, watching the rain. He turned his head as Muriel came in, and looked at her anxiously.

Muriel went to his side and took his hand.

'Lily?' he said. 'Scream.'

Muriel's face suddenly lost its hardness and she knelt at Rory's chair and buried her head into his arm. 'It's Christopher,' she said, as she had once said years ago when the telegram boy had come whistling down the street. 'It's Christopher. Someone has taken him from the garden. The baby's gone.'

Rory was so still that she looked up, fearful that he would have another stroke at the news. His mouth was working.

'How long?' he asked.

'Less than an hour,' Muriel said. 'Lily went to fetch him in when it started raining.' Already it seemed as if days had passed. Already Lily's casual stroll to the garden to fetch her son seemed like a snapshot from an older, easier time. 'The pram was gone and the baby.'

'Police?'

'They're coming.'

'Stephen?'

'He's at court today. I telephoned the office and spoke to John. He's sent a man round to court to fetch Stephen out. Coventry was waiting there. He'll bring him home.'

Rory's hands and arms gave a deep shuddering tremor and were still.

Muriel sat back on her heels and smoothed the skin of her cheekbones and under her eyes. 'No point giving way now,' she said sharply to herself. 'I shall have to set Lily an example. No hysterics, no tantrums, no tears.'

Rory looked at her with pity in his face.

Muriel rose to her feet. 'I shall keep you informed,' she said coldly, as if he were an importunate stranger and not her husband, and the grandfather of a lost child. 'I shall go downstairs now and meet the police. I shall stress that this is a matter of the utmost urgency. I shall hold the fort until Stephen gets home.'

She nodded determinedly and then went towards the door.

'Muriel!' Rory found the name in time to call her.

She turned and waited.

'Be gentle to Lily,' he said clearly.

Muriel hunched her shoulder. 'She will have to learn to draw on inner reserves,' she said. 'She may not have been born and bred a lady but she has to live like one now. She will have to learn to rise to a crisis, not collapse at the first hint of distress.'

Rory hesitated, but then the doorbell rang.

'Excuse me,' Muriel said with infinite courtesy. 'I imagine that is the police now.'

She closed the door quietly behind her and went to the stairs. The bedroom door above slammed and Lily came pattering down the stairs, her hair damp and dishevelled, barefoot, her legs bare. Muriel barred the way.

'I shall deal with the police until you are properly dressed,' she said determinedly.

Lily ran against her, and pushed her with her hands. 'I'm going down,' she said fiercely.

She ducked under Muriel's outstretched arm and fled down the stairs. She nearly fell at the foot of the staircase but the police sergeant, who was standing at the bottom, caught her as she tripped.

'Have you heard anything?' she demanded.

Muriel, following more slowly, looked at the three men. There was an older man in civilian clothes, the inspector. There were two uniformed policemen with him, the

547

sergeant and a constable who stood at the door. The older man replied, 'Nothing, Miss. We came at once. I am Inspector Walker, and this is Sergeant Watts. You are?'

'He's my baby,' Lily said distractedly. 'Have you started searching for him?'

'I will alert all officers when I have taken a description,' the inspector said. 'I need your help for that, Madam. Try to be calm.'

Muriel spoke from halfway up the stairs. 'You must excuse my daughter-in-law,' she said coldly. 'She is overwrought. Browning, show the officers into the dining room.'

The parlourmaid led the way into the dining room. Lily followed them, Muriel coming after. They took seats around the table as if a meal might be served.

'Please look for him at once,' Lily said urgently. 'He was wearing a white embroidered smock and he has a blue pram. A big blue pram. He can't be far away, it's only just happened. If we all went and looked now . . .'

The sergeant took out a notepad. Muriel took a seat at the head of the table.

The inspector looked at her. 'May I have your name, Madam?'

'I am Mrs Rory Winters,' she said. 'This is my daughter-in-law, Mrs Stephen Winters. The missing child is my grandson Christopher, a baby of four months.'

She spoke slowly, waiting for the sergeant to write everything down. 'My son, Mr Stephen Winters, is a lawyer. He is at court at the moment. I trust he has been alerted and is on his way home.'

'I know Mr Winters,' the inspector said. 'And I know his father, of course.'

'Please,' Lily interrupted. 'When will you start looking for him?'

The inspector turned to her with some sympathy. 'As

soon as I know the picture I shall inform the local force and all neighbouring police forces,' he said gently. 'You tell me: what does the baby look like?'

'He's very beautiful,' Lily said. 'He has fair hair. It's growing in little curls. He has deep blue eyes. He's very placid. He smiles and laughs all the time.' She started choking on a sob and found she could not speak. She shook her head dumbly at the inspector. 'It's nearly time for his feed,' she said. 'How will they know what to feed him?'

'We'll get him back for you,' the inspector said. 'Now tell me again what he was wearing.'

'A little white smock,' Lily said carefully. 'Embroidered with smocking stitch at the front with white. His initials CCW on the left-hand hem.'

'And the bedding in the pram?'

'A little white embroidered pillow,' Lily said. 'A pair of white pram sheets, two white pram blankets, and then the pram canopy which is dark blue. The canopy was on.'

'Anything else?'

Lily shook her head. She could feel herself crying inside, a feeling she had never known before, not even at the death of her mother. She felt as if she could cry for ever and never be rid of this swelling fear and grief.

'And the pram. What make was it?'

'It was a Silver Star deluxe,' Lily said. 'In deep blue with a blue hood and canopy. Silver spoked wheels and brakes.'

'And what was the last time anyone saw the baby and the pram?'

'In the garden,' Lily said carefully. 'I was sitting with him. I came in to take a telephone call. I saw that it was starting to rain and I went out to fetch him in. The pram was gone and the garden gate had been opened. It must have been –' She broke off and glanced at Muriel.

'About ten o'clock,' Muriel said. 'No later than quarter past.'

'So the baby had been alone how long?'

'About fifteen minutes,' Lily said very quietly. 'I was on the telephone. I had been sitting watching him a moment before. And Nanny Janes was watching him from the window.'

The inspector nodded to the sergeant. 'I think we've got enough for a description,' he said. 'May the sergeant use your telephone?'

'In the hall,' Muriel said. She rose to her feet and opened the door and pointed it out.

'I forgot something,' Lily said suddenly. Both men looked at her. 'Something else he was wearing,' she said. 'He had little white knitted bootees, made out of lambs' wool.' The thought of Christopher's firm little feet released Lily's flood of tears again. 'Little white bootees,' she said, choking. 'With white silk ribbon ties.'

Chapter Thirty-seven

The inspector, the sergeant and the constable searched the small garden for clues. There was nothing to show that a pram had ever been there. Lily tried to show them exactly where it had stood on the wet grass, but there were not even wheelmarks to show for it. It was as if the pram, and her baby, had never been. Lily showed them the stone by the gate and how the gate had been pushed open. It was just a little stone, it would have taken very little effort to move it.

They searched the cobbled courtyard and the street outside, looking for footprints, or wheelmarks, or the ends of cigarettes. They found nothing.

Stephen came home while they were searching the street outside the garage. Lily was watching them from the dining room. She turned to him from the rainwashed window and ran towards him.

'Oh, Stephen,' she said.

Stephen put his arms out and Lily let him enfold her. He held her lovingly and gently and Lily let herself cry against the comforting warmth of his shoulder. Muriel, coming in to the dining room, saw Stephen's face, calm and contented at last, as Lily cried, heartbroken, against his chest. 'Stephen, where can he be?'

Stephen patted her back and spoke over Lily's head to his mother. 'What do the police say?'

Muriel shrugged. 'Nothing as yet. They have alerted all the local forces. Whoever has taken him cannot have gone far. We called them within an hour.'

Stephen nodded. 'Taken from the garden?'

Lily looked up and held his coat lapels. 'I only left him for a moment,' she said urgently. 'I just went in to the telephone. I would have been sitting and watching him sleep otherwise. Nanny Janes was in the nursery and she watches him from the window. I was only gone a moment.'

Stephen covered her hands with his own in a comforting grip. 'It's all right, my darling,' he said gently. 'I know. No-one is blaming you for a moment. It's not your fault. We'll get him back and we'll be laughing about this tomorrow.'

Lily shuddered and shook her head. 'I can't imagine laughing ever again,' she said.

The policemen came back through the garden, their eyes still on the ground, and mounted the verandah steps. Muriel opened the door to them and indicated the door mat for their wet boots. They both wiped their feet very thoroughly as she watched them, before stepping inside.

'You'll be Mr Stephen Winters, I take it,' the inspector said. Stephen, one hand still holding Lily's, nodded his head.

'Have you found any clues?'

'I'm afraid not. But with the ground so hard and the sudden rainstorm, it was only ever an outside chance. I should like to ask you some questions, Sir.'

'Of course,' Stephen said. 'Mother, Lily, go and sit in the drawing room. Have a cup of coffee and ask them to bring a pot in here for us.' He glanced at Lily, noting her dishevelled hair and bare legs. 'Go and get changed, dear,' he said. 'Smarten up a bit.'

Lily moved as he bid her and Muriel gathered her towards the door.

'And try not to worry,' Stephen commanded. 'This could all be over in ten minutes.'

Lily cast a look back at him as if he were her only hope.

Stephen smiled encouragingly at her and then switched his attention to Inspector Walker. 'A bad business,' he said grimly, all optimism put to one side now that the women were out of earshot. 'D'you think it's a professional job?'

The sergeant flipped open his notepad.

'Do you have any enemies?' the inspector asked. 'Anyone in your professional life? Someone whose defence failed, perhaps?'

Stephen shook his head. 'We do very little criminal work,' he said. 'A man in my position is bound to rub up the wrong way against some chaps; but no-one springs to mind.'

'Ever been threatened?' the inspector said. 'Maybe from the war? Some old scores after conflict in the regiment? They weren't always easy times, especially for young officers.'

Stephen looked at him quickly. 'What d'you mean?'

The inspector shrugged. 'Any shirkers in your battalion who thought you sent them out on patrol too often? Any complaints come to mind? We're picking up a lot of men even now, years after the war, who can't forget.'

Stephen shook his head. 'They were grand chaps,' he said. 'Every one of them would have laid down his life for me.'

The inspector nodded slowly. 'Nearer home then,' he suggested. 'Any members of your staff? Anyone sacked recently, anyone bearing a grudge from the office? Any unhappy maids? Any difficulties?'

Stephen wrinkled his brow and then shook his head again. 'I can't think of anyone. Mother knows more about the running of the house than I do, but everyone we have has worked here for years. The maids, the cook, the gardener, my batman. They've all been with us for ever. And they all love Christopher. It couldn't be one of them.'

'Any suggestions at all?' the inspector asked.

Stephen shook his head. 'We're the envy of all our friends,' he said. 'We have a happy house, and my staff at the office are all happy. Why, some of Lily's friends practically live here! They adore Christopher. Her accompanist is like a second father to him. He's always taking him out for walks with Lily and playing with him. It's a very happy household.'

'Who are your most frequent visitors?' the inspector asked.

'You'd have to ask my wife or my mother to be sure,' Stephen said. 'Madge Sweet, Mrs Sarah Dent, Lady Blakelock has called several times recently. Charlie Smith – he's musical director at the Kings – he comes almost every afternoon to play the piano with my wife. John Pascoe from the office and his wife, some friends of my wife's from the theatre. We see a lot of people.'

'Anyone upset recently? Perhaps any of the ladies recently lost a child?'

'Good God, no!' Stephen said vehemently. 'I can't think that it would be anyone we know. Why, someone like Charlie Smith would lay down his life for the baby! Ask my wife! He loves him like his own child! I can't imagine it being someone we know.'

'Are you acquainted with your neighbours at all? People who overlook the garden?'

'We say "good morning",' Stephen said. 'Nothing more really.'

'We'll start doing some house to house calls this afternoon,' the inspector said. 'My feeling is that either it is someone who is near enough to the house to know the routine – an acquaintance or a neighbour – or else, and this is much worse, a passing stranger who took the baby on impulse.'

'Why worse?' Stephen asked. 'They both sound absolutely bloody.'

'Worse because harder to trace,' the inspector said. 'But you're right. It's two bad options.'

There was a brief silence.

'Telephone calls,' the sergeant said quietly.

'Oh yes,' Inspector Walker said. 'You may receive a telephone call or a note demanding a ransom or giving information about your son. We have some very strict rules about the handling of such calls.'

Stephen nodded.

'If it is a telephone call then you are to keep the person talking as long as possible and get from them as much information as possible. Check with them that the baby is well, for instance, ask them what he is eating, ask them if they have clean clothes and so on. Everything you can hear – make a note of. Listen for background noise, listen for an accent. Listen for any information you can pick up. And if you can, write a note to someone else to alert them to the caller and get them to get a message to us. For the first twenty-four hours I think we'll keep a constable on the premises. He'll know what to do.'

Stephen nodded again.

'Do not make any private arrangements to pay,' the policeman said solemnly. 'Whatever threats they make against the child, you endanger his life the moment you agree to keep it secret from us. Your safest and your best course is to trust us to get your child safely home.'

'You think it might be a kidnap for ransom?'

'It's possible. Your family are well known, and your wife is often in the newspapers. Someone could well have thought that you would be good ransom victims.'

The inspector paused for a moment. 'Alert your servants to any messages which might come. Make sure they take a note of any errand boys who come to the back door, and watch which direction they take when they leave here. Anyone delivering a note should be brought into the house at once, and the constable will deal with them. I'll have the constable answering your front door for the first couple of days. Any note or demand which comes must b_' passed on to us at once. You put your child at risk if you delay.'

'I agree,' Stephen said. 'We'll play this as you say. You're the CO here.'

The inspector nodded. 'Will Mrs Winters understand?' he asked.

Stephen thought for a moment. 'My mother will do as she is asked,' he said. 'But you've seen my wife. She's very highly strung and her nerves are not reliable. I couldn't trust her not to act on her own, especially if she thought any of her friends were involved. If she thought any of her close friends were implicated I can't say what she'd do. She's impulsive, and she adores the child.'

'We'll keep an eye on her,' the inspector said. 'I'll try to explain the importance of keeping us fully informed of any developments.'

Stephen rose from the table and went to the door. 'It's such a damned coincidence!' he exclaimed, turning back to speak to the inspector. 'Lily called in to the phone, and the baby taken in those few moments. It's such an impossible thing to happen!'

The inspector nodded. 'That's what made me think of neighbours who overlook the garden, or a passing stranger,' he said. 'Who was on the telephone?'

'I don't know,' Stephen said. 'You'll have to ask my wife.'

They called Lily downstairs. She had gone to sit with Rory. Muriel's controlled silence over the coffee cups was too much for her. She stole up to her bedroom and put on her stockings and combed her hair. Her face in the mirror was white and aghast. She could not meet her own eyes in the reflection for fear of their blank horror. She crept downstairs to Rory's room, dismissed Nurse Bells and sat in the window seat where she could see the road in all directions. She kept watch, as if the little blue pram would trundle home of its own accord. Rory, seated beside her in his wheelchair, put out a hand and clasped hers in a comforting grip. They said nothing. There was nothing for them to say.

Browning came to fetch Lily and showed her into the dining room where the inspector was seated behind the table. Lily wondered where Muriel would order lunch to be served, and what she would do with the sergeant and the constable. The inspector could eat with them, Lily thought, Muriel would class him as a gentleman. But how would Muriel get around the difficulty of the two other men? Could a sergeant eat in the kitchen like a visiting servant?

'Are you listening to me?' Inspector Walker asked.

Lily jumped. 'Yes,' she said.

He thought she looked like a child herself with her eyelids red and swollen from weeping and her nose red and shiny. Her hands were shaking and when he looked closer he saw she was trembling all over.

'Are you cold?' he asked.

She shook her head.

She was in shock then. He looked at her more carefully. She was not the woman to handle this sort of crisis. They would have to keep her well away from the telephone or the door if the kidnappers attempted to make any kind of contact. They would have trouble keeping her under any sort of control if the baby was not returned within a few hours. She looked brittle and near hysteria.

'Excuse me one moment,' he said.

He stepped out of the dining room and went to the drawing room. Stephen and his mother were sitting in the room in low-voiced conversation. They looked up when the inspector knocked on the door and put his head around.

'I'm sorry to disturb you,' he said. 'I'm just interviewing Mrs Winters and she seems to me in rather a bad way. I was wondering if you had thought of calling your doctor. She may need something for her nerves later on today – and if this goes on overnight . . .'

'Of course,' Muriel said. 'I should have thought. I'll call him at once. She was always highly strung and she has been enormously distressed by this.'

The inspector nodded and went back to the dining room. Lily was staring into space, seeing nothing. Her hands, laid loosely on the table before her, were trembling and trembling.

'Just a few questions,' the inspector said. 'Who comes to the house most often, Mrs Winters?'

'Charlie Smith, Madge Sweet, Jane Dent,' Lily said in a thin distant voice.

'And who are these people? Charlie Smith, for instance?'

'Charlie's the musical director at the Kings Theatre. He's an old friend of mine from when I was on the stage. He is my accompanist when I sing. He teaches me the piano.'

'He comes here – how often?'

Lily looked blankly at the inspector. 'Every day I suppose. Won't you go out and look for Christopher?'

'Whoever has him will have taken him to their home by now,' the inspector said gently. 'So he's out of the rain and safe and dry. We'll find him quickest by working out who it might be who has got him. D'you see?'

Lily shook her head. 'It's no-one we know,' she said. 'Who could do such a thing?'

'Well, that's what we have to find out,' the inspector said gently. 'Have any of your friends recently lost a baby, perhaps?'

Lily shook her head.

'Or have any of your friends been angry with you? Have you any enemies who would want to hurt you?'

Lily looked reproachfully at the inspector. 'Nobody could hate me so badly,' she said. 'Everyone knows that I love Christopher more than anything in the world. I'd rather die than lose him. Nobody who knows me could do this to me. Nobody who knows Christopher could separate us.' She choked on a sob. The sergeant shifted uneasily in his chair. Even Inspector Walker felt himself uncomfortably moved by Lily's naked grief.

'Let's think this through,' he said gruffly. 'What time did you put him out this morning?'

'Nanny Janes puts him out,' Lily said. 'And then I go down and sit with him. She put him out at nine o'clock. I sat with him until he fell asleep, and then Sally called me to the telephone. It must have been about half past nine or quarter to ten. I talked on the phone and when I had finished I saw that it was about to rain. The pram was gone. It was about ten o'clock.'

'Who was on the phone?' the inspector asked casually as if it were of little significance.

'Charlie Smith,' Lily said.

'Does he usually ring in the morning?'

'No. He usually comes round to see me in the afternoon. He was ringing up because he's going to London today. He was ringing to tell me.'

'You talked for a long while.'

Unaccountably Lily blushed deeply. 'Yes,' she said. 'He was telling me about this job he may get in London. I was interested.'

'He kept you talking for about half an hour then?' the inspector confirmed.

Lily shot a quick surprised look at him. 'Yes,' she said. 'But that's not unusual. We often talk for a long time.'

The inspector hesitated. 'I am sorry,' he said. 'I must have misunderstood. I thought he usually came to see you. I thought it was unusual for him to telephone you in the morning.'

'It is,' Lily said. She was slightly flustered. 'But once we're on the phone together we do often chat for a while.' She hesitated. 'There's nothing *suspicious* in that.'

'No,' Inspector Walker said. He gave her a small smile. 'Of course not. Is he an old friend of the family?'

'I worked with him when I was on the stage,' Lily said. 'Before Christopher was born. He met my husband when Stephen and I married. He's a family friend now. He comes round most afternoons. We often walk out with Christopher on the prom.' She broke off, choking, and then swallowed. 'I'm sorry,' she said.

The inspector nodded. 'Where does Mr Smith live?'

'Off Palmerston Road,' Lily said. 'Excuse me, Sir, but are there men looking for Christopher, now?'

He nodded. 'Yes, there are,' he said. 'What I have to do is to see if you, or anyone in this house, can think of any reason why your child should have been taken. That's my job and you can help me do it.'

Lily frowned in concentration. 'I can't think of anyone,' she said. 'I really can't.'

'Is there any member of staff that you don't get on well with?' the inspector asked. 'This is your husband's family, isn't it? Anyone *you* wouldn't employ if you had the choice?'

'Only the nanny,' Lily said very quietly.

'Oh?'

'My husband insisted we had a nanny. I never wanted one. She knows I don't like her. I'm sure she doesn't like me. But she was upstairs all the time. She couldn't have had anything to do with it.'

'Did she have proper references? D'you know where she came from?'

'Oh yes, all of that. But the children she was caring for before she came to us had died. That's one of the reasons I don't like her.'

'Are you saying she is negligent?'

Lily shook her head. 'No. It was an accident. I just think she is . . .' She searched for the right word. 'Cold,' she said. 'Uncaring.'

The inspector nodded. 'Was it her job to supervise the baby?'

Lily thought for a moment. 'I'm not really supposed to be in the garden with him,' she said honestly. 'Nanny is supposed to have him all day and I am only supposed to see him at tea time. But she knows I go out to see him, and Rory, my father-in-law, often has him brought to us so I can see him during the day, or walk with him in the afternoon.'

The inspector frowned. 'You're not *supposed* to see him during the day?' he repeated.

Lily looked embarrassed. 'They think I spoil him,' she said. 'He's to be brought up by the nanny. I'm only allowed to see him at set times.'

'So the child was her responsibility at the time he was taken?'

'Yes,' Lily said. 'Yes he was, really. She watches him from the window as she tidies the nursery.'

The inspector nodded. 'I think that's all for now then, Mrs Winters. I would prefer it if you did not answer the phone for today, even if it is a friend asking to speak to you. If the people who have taken your son get in touch we want to make sure that we handle the phone call in the right way.'

'D'you think they might telephone to give him back?' Lily's pale face was suddenly alive with hope.

'They might very well, or they might write a note asking for money. Either way, this should be handled by the constable or by your husband. Please let your husband open all your letters, and don't take any phone calls today.'

Lily nodded. 'I should like to speak to Charlie when he rings,' she said. Her mouth quivered slightly. 'I need to speak to him.'

'Would you object to my listening to the call?'

Lily looked surprised. 'No.'

'Do you expect him to telephone again today?'

'He'll phone from London, to tell me if he gets the job.'

'When?'

'This afternoon.'

Inspector Walker nodded. 'Thank you,' he said. 'It's just routine. We always monitor all telephone calls in these circumstances.'

'Does this happen often then?' Lily asked. 'Someone takes a baby and then brings it back?'

'Sometimes,' the inspector said. The hope in Lily's face made him uncomfortable.

The clock on the mantelpiece chimed twelve. Lily looked up and got to her feet, thinking of Christopher's lunch. Then the sudden realization that he was not in the house hit her like a blow and she staggered.

'I suggest you have a lie down, Mrs Winters,' the inspector said gently. 'If you think of anything you want to tell me I shall be here all day. I will keep you in touch with whatever happens.'

'Thank you,' Lily said stiffly. She went slowly from the room, walking awkwardly, as if her feet hurt. The two men were silent until the door closed behind her.

The sergeant turned the page and looked at the inspector.

'A little list,' the inspector suggested. 'Just a little

provisional list, and then we'll interview everyone else in the house.'

The sergeant waited, pen poised.

'The nanny, whom the mother dislikes. The nanny's previous employer – whoever that is – the mother whose child died. Mrs Stephen Winters herself – to get the nanny sacked. Mr Charlie Smith – for interest's sake, his name seems to come up first. Any girlfriends of Mr Winters the husband. Any men from his platoon. Wasn't he in some forlorn hope and got half of them killed? What about the dead men's families? Anyone from his work. Any unhappy clients.' He paused. 'That's all I can think of, for now.'

'Not a lot of love lost between the mother-in-law and the young Mrs Winters,' the sergeant observed.

'Not a lot of love lost between any of them,' the inspector said grimly. 'But still, I wouldn't know. Perhaps they feel it, but don't show it. That's what they say, isn't it? The stiff upper lip and all that?'

The sergeant nodded. 'Who next?'

'The loving mother-in-law: Mrs Winters.'

Chapter Thirty-eight

Muriel took interrogation as an affront. She had moved the inspector's headquarters from the dining room to Stephen's study, so that the dining room table could be laid for lunch; but then found she was offended at the man taking the chair behind the desk and leaving her to sit before him, like an applicant parlourmaid.

Inspector Walker took her through the short list of all her friends who regularly called at the house, and through her acquaintances among the neighbours. If he thought Muriel's life sounded lonely and barren there was no sign of it on his face. He noted the unspoken depth of her feeling for her grandson, and her coolness towards her daughter-in-law and invalid husband. He asked her about the staff of the house and she spoke of them with unflinching confidence. Most of them had been with her since Stephen was a small boy.

'And what about Mrs Winters's friends?' he asked easily. 'A wide circle of friends she has, I see.'

'My daughter-in-law was a professional singer before her marriage. Many of her friends still visit us,' Muriel said.

The inspector noted a slight tightening around the woman's neck and shoulders.

'Especially Mr Smith,' he prompted gently. 'She tells me.'

Muriel stiffened. 'He teaches her the piano, he is her accompanist and a friend of the family,' she said firmly.

'I am not sure that your questions are relevant.'

'I'm just trying to get an overall picture of the household. Your daily routine and so on. Mrs Winters spends every afternoon with Mr Smith, does she not?'

Muriel looked at him frostily. 'She practises her music every afternoon, yes.'

'And he is fond of the child?'

'I have no idea.'

There was a brief silence. 'Mr Winters now, Mr Stephen Winters, does he work late?'

'My son is always home for dinner at seven.'

'He's very close to his child, I assume? Spends a lot of time with him when he can?'

'Yes.'

'Takes him out at the weekend, pushes the pram along the seafront, that sort of thing?'

Muriel sighed and then spoke very carefully. 'We have a fully trained nanny who works every day except for Thursday afternoons. There is no need for Stephen to push a pram.'

'And, forgive me, Mr and Mrs Winters, newly married, they're perfectly happy, are they? No stress and strain, very common with young couples?'

'Of course not,' Muriel said, at her most icy.

The inspector nodded. Muriel's face was pale with indignation but there was something about her eyes, the tiniest quiver at her eyelid, that made him disbelieve her. 'A normal birth, was it? Mrs Winters had the baby at home?'

'She chose to have the baby at the hospital.'

'Mr Winters was there, was he? He drove her in, I suppose?'

'He was away that evening. Our chauffeur and –' Muriel paused for half a guilty moment ' – and I went in with her. She came out the next day.'

'The chauffeur?'

'Coventry – that's a nickname. His proper name is James Stokes. He was my son's batman all through the war. The men nicknamed him Coventry because he is mute, and the name has stuck.'

'He uses the car on his nights off, does he?'

Muriel blinked at the change of tack. 'No. He either spends the night here in his rooms over the garage, or he goes to his home on Hayling Island.'

'Doesn't drive down to Old Portsmouth? Down to Portsea?'

Again there was that flicker around Muriel's eyes. 'He does not have private use of the car,' she said eventually.

'So he drives Mr Winters out in the evening, occasionally?'

'Yes.'

'And where do they go?'

Muriel rose from the chair. 'You must excuse me, Inspector. I have to see my husband before luncheon. Will you and your men be requiring some sandwiches and a pot of tea, perhaps?'

The inspector rose too. 'That would be very kind of you,' he said. 'But we won't inconvenience you. I'll leave Sergeant Watts here while the constable and I go for our dinners. We'll relieve him later. If there are any telephone calls or letters I would prefer it if you would let him answer. If the kidnappers try to contact you it will be safer for the child if the call is taken by us or by Mr Stephen Winters.'

Muriel nodded. 'Very well. The sergeant may wait in here. If the telephone rings in the hall he will hear it. Is the parlourmaid not to answer the front door?'

'No. Sergeant Watts can do it, or the constable.'

Muriel hesitated. 'It will look very odd,' she said unhappily.

566

The inspector nodded. 'Yes,' he said apologetically. 'But in the circumstances . . .'

Muriel nodded grudgingly and went from the room. The inspector dropped back into the padded leather chair and beamed at the sergeant. 'I'm off to my dinner,' he said. 'We'll do the staff and the neighbours when I get back.'

They drew a blank at the neighbours' houses. No-one had seen anything unusual, no-one had been watching from the window. Inspector Walker sighed. In the poorer streets of Portsmouth the place would have been alive with gossip and speculation. People were forever leaning on their garden walls and minding each other's affairs. Solving a crime in the backstreets was no more difficult than drinking many cups of tea and listening to the chat. At the better end of Southsea people lived on islands of snobbery alienated from each other by a thousand rules of conduct. Many people whose rooms overlooked the Winters's garden did not even know their name.

The inspector turned his attention to the servants. First he asked to see James Stokes, the chauffeur known as Coventry. But when the man came into the room, looking grave with his chauffeur's cap under his arm, Stephen Winters came in with him.

'He's mute,' he said, nodding his head towards the chauffeur. 'I thought I might be able to help.'

'Thank you,' the inspector said. 'Stokes – do you take the car down to Portsea on your own at night?'

Coventry shook his head.

The inspector looked into the open face and the light brown eyes. 'Were you born mute?' he asked.

The man looked back at him as Stephen answered for him. 'It was the war,' he said. 'We had a direct hit on a gun emplacement. Coventry was trapped for two days, no-one knew he was in there. He had to shout for help. When we finally got him out he had lost his voice.'

'Seen a doctor?'

Coventry smiled his slow patient smile and shook his head.

'Several,' Stephen said. 'They say it's neurasthenia. They don't know anything.'

'The car's been seen several times in the backstreets. Old Portsmouth, Portsea, places like that. Would that be the two of you, out on the town?'

Coventry neither nodded his head nor shook it. He stayed silent and motionless, waiting for Stephen to speak.

'We go out for a drink from time to time,' Stephen said easily. 'You know how it is, Inspector. Family life at times can be a little . . .' He paused and smiled engagingly. 'Especially living at home with parents. Sometimes I feel the need of a little relaxation.'

'In backstreet pubs?' the inspector asked baldly.

'Somewhere informal.'

'And you drink together, as friends?'

Stephen hesitated. 'Some of these places are a bit rough,' he said. 'It's as wise to have someone to watch your back. Coventry was my batman during the war. We've been in worse places together.'

The inspector nodded. 'I know your war record,' he said briefly. There was a slight movement from Coventry, of unease? of dissent? Inspector Walker paused but could not read the swift glance between the two men. He sensed their unity, the bond between them.

'Where were you this morning?' he asked gently.

Coventry nodded towards Stephen.

'He took me to court and then waited,' Stephen said. 'I didn't know how long I'd be, so he waited outside for me.'

'You were parked outside the court for all that time?' The inspector spoke directly to Coventry.

Coventry nodded.

'I went out at about, oh, ten, and collected some papers from the car which I needed. Then I went back into court again. My clerk came and told me there was a flap on at home at about half past ten, or a quarter to eleven, and I came straight back.'

'Anyone see you there?'

Coventry shrugged.

'You could ask,' Stephen said easily. 'We parked where we always park, that little road at the side of the court. Half a dozen people must have gone past the car. Someone might remember it. But as I say, I know he was there at ten o'clock.'

'Thank you for your help,' Inspector Walker said to Stephen. 'I'd like a few words with Mr Stokes on my own.'

'Very well,' Stephen said pleasantly. 'He's not much of a hand at writing. That's why I sat in. You may find progress is rather slow. Call me if you need translation – I shall be sitting with my father. He's taken this rather badly.'

The door closed behind him and Coventry was alone with the inspector and the sergeant.

'Very close to Mr Winters, aren't you?' the inspector asked.

Coventry nodded with a little smile.

'I envy you both,' the inspector said. 'It is a great thing to form a friendship like that during war and find the bonds last through peace as well. Do you like his wife also?'

He was expecting a hesitation, or some gesture which might betray jealousy, or dislike. So he was surprised by Coventry's open-hearted smile and the vigorous nod of his head.

'Oh?' he asked.

Coventry pulled the pad towards him and took up a

pencil from the holder. *'Tawt her to drive,'* he wrote.

'Taught her to drive?' the inspector queried.

Coventry nodded, his smile broadening. *'Very good,'* he wrote. *'Choice her car.'*

'You chose it for her?'

Coventry nodded again. *'Morris,'* he wrote. *'Good make.'*

The inspector sat back, a little baffled by the man's sudden animation. 'You're very fond of her,' he stated.

Coventry nodded his head.

'The baby must have been a bit of a change for her, after a stage career. Must have set her back a bit?'

Coventry said nothing; his face was neutral.

Inspector Walker felt mildly irritated by having to guess at the man's feelings. It was like a children's game with only the clues of 'hot' or 'cold' to aid the seeker near the target. Lily's possible resentment of the baby was obviously 'cold'.

He tried a more simple approach. 'D'you have much to do with the baby?' he asked.

Coventry's smile was unmistakably one of pride and pleasure. He nodded.

'Drive them out, do you?'

Again the smile.

'And I think Mrs Winters said you take the pram in and out of the garden and up the steps?'

Coventry nodded and mimed pushing a pram.

'Oh, you push the pram for walks as well, do you?'

Coventry nodded and pointed to the upstairs room where Rory Winters was resting.

'With the older Mr Winters?'

Coventry nodded.

'And the young Mrs Winters?'

Coventry nodded again, and gestured with his hand as if to imply the existence of another.

'Mr Stephen Winters?'

Coventry shook his head and mimed playing a piano on the smooth surface of the desk.

'Mr Charlie Smith,' the inspector said slowly. 'You all go out for walks together. You pushing Mr Winters, and Mr Smith pushing the pram and Mrs Winters comes too.'

Coventry nodded confirmation.

The inspector sat back in the chair. 'You took her to hospital,' he remarked idly. 'When the baby was due.'

Coventry nodded, and then he leaned forward and made the piano-playing mime on the desk again.

'With Mr Charlie Smith?' the inspector asked carefully.

Coventry nodded.

'Just the two of you?'

Coventry nodded.

'Not the older Mrs Winters?'

Coventry shook his head.

'And not Mr Stephen Winters?'

Coventry's mute face closed up at that question.

'Mrs Lily Winters must be very fond of Mr Smith?' the inspector suggested.

Coventry looked cautious. He nodded shortly and folded his arms as if to hug secrets to himself.

'She's lucky to have such a faithful friend,' the inspector volunteered.

Coventry nodded.

There was a short silence.

'*Are* they on good terms? Mr and Mrs Winters?' the inspector asked bluntly.

Coventry's face was as blank as if he were deaf as well as mute. He looked as if he could not hear the question, nor comprehend it. He shrugged as if to imply that the relationship was a mystery to him.

The inspector looked at Coventry's brown eyes, which were suddenly shielded and almost opaque.

'Did anyone see you this morning, parked outside the courtroom?' he asked.

Coventry glanced away, as if to recall. He wrote on the pad: *'Newspaper boy – bawt paper,'* and pushed the note over to the inspector.

'Thank you,' Inspector Walker said. 'You've been very helpful.'

The sergeant came in when Coventry left. He closed the door behind him and raised an eyebrow at his chief.

'Well, well, well,' the inspector said thoughtfully. 'We're uncovering a scandal if not a kidnap suspect. A husband who likes to take a drink on the wrong side of the tracks, and a wife who goes out for walks with a piano player. But no motive for a kidnap.' He thought for a moment, drumming his fingers on the desk. 'I'll see the nanny,' he announced briefly.

Nanny Janes kept him waiting, and she was stiff with disapproval when she finally entered.

'I hope this is not an inconvenient time,' Inspector Walker said apologetically.

'I was tidying Baby's wardrobe,' she said icily.

'I am sorry. I do need your help, Miss Janes.'

She inclined her head and sank into a chair.

'When did you last see the baby?'

'As I have said, I glanced from the nursery window and saw his mother sitting with him and keeping him awake at about a quarter to ten.'

'Did you see her go into the house?'

Nanny Janes shook her head.

'And did you look out again after that?'

'No.' She hesitated.

'Why not?' the inspector asked gently.

'Mother had obviously taken charge of the child,' Nanny Janes said through compressed lips. 'I had enough to do with tidying the nursery and supervising the tweeny's cleaning.'

'Mrs Winters tends to interfere, does she?' the inspector prompted.

Nanny Janes swelled a little in her chair. It was clearly a sore point. 'I think the young Mrs Winters is unaccustomed to life in a large household,' she said. 'She cannot handle the servants and she does not understand how a child should be brought up.' She hesitated. 'I am accustomed to a rather bigger household. In my previous employment I had my own nursery maid under my direction. Here I have to supervise the tweeny.'

The inspector nodded sympathetically. 'Why did you leave your previous employers?'

'The children died,' Nanny Janes said unemotionally. 'They were drowned in a yachting accident.'

'Dreadful.'

Nanny Janes nodded as if conceding that the death of twin four-year-old boys might indeed be seen as dreadful, but that she was made of sterner stuff, a professional.

'Were the family much distressed?'

'Mother went quite mad,' Nanny Janes said temperately. 'They had to have her committed. The father was much distressed too. He had insisted on taking them sailing. I believe they closed up their house and went abroad.'

'What was their name?'

Nanny Janes hesitated. 'I am sure they would not wish to be troubled,' she said discreetly. 'It is hardly connected with them.'

The inspector curbed his impatience. 'This is a kidnap inquiry,' he said. 'It could hardly be more serious. I will want to contact them.'

'Sir Charles and Lady Harcourt, Harcourt Hall, Wisbech, Cambridge,' Nanny Janes said begrudgingly. 'But I hardly think it is relevant. What possible connection could there be?'

The inspector shrugged. 'I don't know at this stage,' he said. 'I'm just checking everything. If you were doing my job – who would you think took the baby, Miss Janes?'

She shot him a sly downcast look. 'It's not my place to speculate about my employers,' she said.

'Mrs Winters? Mrs Lily Winters?'

Nanny Janes shrugged. 'An unhealthy anxiety about her child, so she can't leave him alone for a moment. And a wide circle of friends ... irresponsible wild people ...' She trailed off. 'Who knows what they might think of? As a joke, maybe? As a way of getting even.'

'Even with whom?'

She shrugged again. 'With respectable people. With me, with Mr Winters. I can't say. But some of the visitors to this house would never be allowed beyond the tradesman's entrance of a respectable residence. Some of Mrs Winters's friends are little better than gypsies. I am not surprised that something like this has happened. They are a wild set of people. A baby has to have routine. Routine and no interference.'

The inspector assumed a look of puzzled anxiety. 'Do you think,' he said slowly, 'do you think that Mrs Lily Winters is so flighty, and so interfering, that she might have asked one of her friends to take the baby from the garden so that it was out of your care, and away from her husband's rules?'

The gleam Nanny Janes shot at him was assent. 'I really couldn't speculate,' she said primly. 'It's not my place.'

The inspector interviewed every member of staff. He checked and double-checked their whereabouts at the time of the kidnap, and what they had seen. Then casually, at the end of the interviews, he asked them what they knew of Lily's friends, and in particular, Charlie Smith.

To his surprise Charlie was a popular visitor. All the household staff liked to hear his music, they all liked to hear Lily sing and welcomed the sound of her laughter when she played with her baby in the drawing room and Charlie joked with her. Nanny Janes was the sole dissenting voice.

Browning would say nothing about the marriage of Stephen and Lily. But Sally, the tweeny, was less trained and less discreet. She confirmed that they quarrelled. She had seen Lily in tears more than once. She said the house had been as quiet as a grave since Mr Rory Winters's stroke, but Lily had brought a new lease of life to the whole house. Her friends were gay and fashionable and brightened the place up. In her opinion, Mr Stephen Winters was a dry old stick who didn't know that a bit of fun and a bit of music brightened up the place.

None of the staff could believe that any of Lily's friends, including Charlie Smith, could have had anything to do with the kidnap, and Sally went so far as to be impertinent to the inspector. She accused him of being blind as a bat if he couldn't see that Charlie Smith loved Christopher like he was his own dad. The inspector nodded at that, and looked thoughtful, rather than offended.

Upstairs in her bedroom Lily slept in a deep drugged sleep though the afternoon sun shone brightly through the yellow curtains. Dr Mobey, summoned by Muriel, had been shocked by Lily's brittle calm. When he asked her what the police were doing she had used language that no lady should know, let alone use. He gave her a dose of strong opium-based sleeping powder and ordered her to rest. Muriel confirmed his diagnosis that the girl was near hysteria.

'No self-control,' she said to him as they stood in the drawing room.

'A terrible thing to happen to a young mother,' he offered, closing his bag.

'The worse the event, the more one should rise to it,' Muriel said firmly. 'Not collapse in a heap.'

The doctor nodded. He had admired Muriel's courage over the years, through her loss of her favourite son and the paralysis of her husband. She was a fine woman, the sort of woman who had held the Empire together by uncompromising standards in impossible situations.

'You're an example to us all,' he said gently. 'If the strain starts to tell, you know where to find me.'

Muriel smiled at him, her brave shell-hearted smile. '*I* shan't need to be put to bed,' she said. 'I think I'm made of sterner stuff!'

'I know it,' he said. 'They're lucky to have you.'

'Will you have a cup of tea?' Muriel asked, a little pink at the compliment.

'I have to leave. Duty calls I'm afraid. If she is still distressed when she wakes she can have another dose at bedtime. It'll be easiest for you all if she sleeps through this, I should imagine.'

'She's certainly no help,' Muriel said sharply. 'She's been in tears ever since the child first disappeared.' She paused, and then her innate sense of fairness asserted itself. 'The difficulty is that there really is nothing that one can do. The police are here, talking to everyone, but they seem to be no further forward. There are no clues in the garden, and my servants are all absolutely reliable. It's difficult to know what should be done.'

'Leave it to the experts,' the doctor said comfortably. 'And you do what you've always done: hold the family together. They'll look to you in this crisis.'

Muriel nodded. 'Thank you,' she said, knowing it was true.

He snapped the locks on his case and picked it up. 'I shall call tomorrow morning and see how you all are,' he said. 'Rory at least seems to be taking this reasonably well.'

Muriel followed him out to the hall. 'He dotes on the baby, of course,' she said. 'But he's been calm. We just have to wait.'

The doctor shook her limp hand and put on his hat. Muriel nodded to the constable who stood by the front door and he opened the door smartly.

'Good day,' Dr Mobey said. He raised his hat and then went down the steps to his small black car, and drove off.

Nothing happened for the whole long afternoon. On the other side of England, in Cambridgeshire, a police constable went to interview Nanny Janes's previous employers and found the house closed and shuttered. The family had left the country and the caretaker did not remember the nanny at all. 'A long-shot,' Inspector Walker said briefly when the Cambridge duty sergeant telephoned to report that it had been a wild goose chase. 'Sorry to trouble you. Was there any local gossip about Lady Harcourt?'

'She had some kind of crack-up after the death of the boys. But she recovered and now they're touring in Europe.'

'No question of her being insane? Vengeful?'

There was a long silence from the other end of the telephone. 'Against her husband?' the sergeant queried. 'It was his boat.'

'Against the nanny? I'm investigating a kidnap here and the baby was in the nanny's charge. I just thought, maybe if her ladyship traced the nanny . . .'

'I never heard that Lady Harcourt blamed anyone. It was a clear accident. I've got the coroner's report here.'

'A long-shot,' the inspector said again. 'But as nannies go she's been remarkably unlucky with her charges.' He put down the telephone and drummed his fingers on the surface of the polished desk. 'Remarkably unlucky,' he said.

Stephen sat in the drawing room, reading a newspaper and sighing heavily with boredom. Muriel sat opposite him. She had taken up her old hobby of petit-point. Stephen was irritated by the neat small movements of her sewing, by the pointlessness of her labour. She had started sewing when Christopher had gone off to war. It was as if she could not completely deny the nervous agitation of her body but had to hide it in this little fretting activity. After his death she had laid the embroidery frame to one side. Stephen knew, without asking, that she had never sewn away the hours of his dangerous days at Ypres. By then she was busy with her husband, and anyway, the worst possible blow had already fallen.

But now, with another Christopher missing, she started to sew again.

At four o'clock they had tea. Muriel went upstairs to visit first Rory, and then Lily. 'My two invalids,' she called them to herself, despising them both for weakness. Rory was working on papers from the office but he did not wish to come downstairs until dinner time. He was pale and tense and the tremor in his hands was worse. His speech was not impaired. He had talked to the inspector earlier in the day. His bedroom, facing over the sea, meant he could volunteer nothing. He had not heard the garden gate, nor running footsteps. He was useless to rescue Christopher from whoever had taken him, and he knew it. His smile when Muriel popped her head around the door was painful.

Upstairs Lily had been in a drugged doze, but when

Muriel opened the bedroom door she raised herself up on one elbow, her hair all bedraggled and her face stupid with sleep.

'Is he safe?' she asked.

'There's no news,' Muriel said. 'It's four o'clock. I wondered if you would like some tea?'

Lily made a face. 'My throat's dry,' she said.

Muriel compressed her lips on her irritation. 'I daresay that's the sleeping powder,' she said. 'Shall I ask Browning to bring you up a cup? And some sandwiches? You had no lunch.'

'I can't eat,' Lily said. 'But I'd like a cup of tea.'

Muriel nodded. She went to the door and then paused. 'I think you should get up for dinner,' she said firmly. 'You don't help Christopher by lying around in bed, you know, Lily.'

At her son's name Lily's eyes brimmed instantly with tears. She shook her head at Muriel as if there were no words to answer the older woman, as if her pain was speechless. Despite herself, Muriel was shaken by the bare agony on Lily's face. The young woman was ugly with grief, her face robbed of its clear lines and sunny contours.

'Well, you should get up,' she said defensively. 'Or you won't sleep tonight, and then you'll be complaining of insomnia.'

Lily nodded humbly, turning her face away. 'I'm sorry,' she said. 'I'll get up after I've had a cup of tea.'

Muriel nodded and went downstairs, feeling obscurely better for having made an attempt to bring Lily up to scratch, but hiding from her memory the picture of Lily's face – anguished at the very mention of her baby's name.

At six o'clock the telephone rang. The police constable, a new man appointed for the evening shift, hovered around Stephen as he answered it. Muriel stood in the drawing room doorway. Inspector Walker, who was on the verge of leaving for the day, opened the study door and waited, intent. From above they heard Lily's door open and the sound of her running feet coming down the stairs.

'Hello,' Stephen said. 'Oh, Charlie! Hello! No, we're all at sixes and sevens here.' He glanced towards the inspector who shook his head urgently and waved a hand. 'Hang on a minute,' Stephen said. He covered the mouthpiece with his hand. 'It's Charlie Smith,' he said. 'He's back in Portsmouth.'

'Could you ask him to come around at once?' Inspector Walker asked. 'But don't mention the baby.'

Stephen raised an eyebrow. Lily arriving in the hall went to take the telephone, but the inspector shook his head. They all froze as Stephen spoke casually and confidently into the telephone.

'You still there, old man? We've got a bit of a flap on here – no, she's fine – but I'd be glad if you could come round. No, I'll tell you when you get here. In a few minutes? Oh, you're at the station now? Well, good show. See you in a moment.'

He put down the telephone. 'He came in to Southsea station so he's walking round,' he said. 'D'you want to see him on your own?'

Inspector Walker nodded. 'Please have him shown into the study,' he said.

'Just a moment,' Lily said. She was a little slurred and languid from the drug. 'Why can't I talk to him?'

Inspector Walker smiled at her gently. 'Just routine procedure,' he said. 'It keeps me straight if we do it by the book.'

'You don't think he did anything,' Lily said slowly. 'Not Charlie.'

The inspector looked at Stephen, who took Lily by the elbow and led her firmly into the drawing room. 'Best to let the inspector do it his way,' he said. 'For Christopher.'

At her son's name he could feel a shiver pass through her. The thin bones of her arm seemed to quake in his hand. 'Sherry,' Stephen said. He thrust Lily gently into a chair and rang the bell for Browning to bring the drinks tray. 'We've all had a hell of a day.'

They sat in uncomfortable alertness, their drinks in their hands, until they heard Charlie's rapid footsteps coming down the street, his familiar rat-tat-tat at the door, Browning opening it, and then the closing of the study door.

'I want to see him,' Lily said. Her lower lip quivered like a child about to cry.

'When the inspector's finished with him,' Stephen said. 'Of course. But shall we have dinner now, Mother?'

Chapter Thirty-nine

Charlie recoiled when he saw the inspector behind the desk, the sergeant at his side. The police constable silently closed the study door behind him.

'Good God, what's this?' he demanded. 'Where's Lily?'

'Mrs Winters is quite safe,' Inspector Walker said slowly. 'Won't you take a seat, Sir? There are a few questions I need to ask you.'

Charlie remained standing. 'About what?' he asked.

'I am afraid a crime has been committed in this household and we need your help,' the inspector said levelly.

Charlie flushed a deep scarlet and then went pale. 'I am sorry,' he said. 'But I cannot help you until I know that Mrs Winters is all right.'

'I have said that she is safe.'

'Do I have your word?'

'Indeed, yes.'

'Is she in the house?'

'Yes.'

'Can I see her?'

'After we have concluded our conversation you may certainly see her.'

'Is she under suspicion?'

The inspector hesitated for a long moment, his mind whirling around what Charlie Smith might fear Lily had done.

'She is not,' he said slowly. 'What is it that you fear, Mr Smith?'

Charlie's colour returned. 'I have your word for it, that whatever is going on, that Lily is not affected by it?'

'She is neither the victim nor the perpetrator of any crime as far as I believe,' the inspector said slowly. 'What is it that you fear has taken place?'

Charlie hesitated, and then he drew out the chair before the desk and sat down. He took out a cigarette. 'I feared there might have been some violence between her and her husband,' he said very quietly.

The inspector nodded as if the information were of little interest. 'There has been violence in the past?'

Charlie nodded.

'Bad?'

'He slapped her once, and I believe he has forced himself on her,' Charlie said tightly.

The inspector kept his face impassive. 'It is nothing of that nature.'

Charlie lit his cigarette and pocketed his lighter. 'What, then?' he demanded briefly.

'I should like you to answer some questions first, if you please.'

Charlie nodded.

'What have your movements been today?'

'I was telephoned early this morning by someone I believed to be calling from the Palace Theatre, London. They asked me to go up to town at once for a meeting. They told me that their musical director was sick and asked if I would replace him.'

'At what time was this telephone call?'

'About quarter to nine.'

'And what did you do, Mr Smith?'

'Leaped out of bed, dressed, called Lily to tell her I wouldn't see her today, rushed for the train, got to London, kicked my heels while they tried to work out what had happened, and then discovered it was some kind of hoax.'

The inspector nodded slowly. 'By whom?'

Charlie shrugged. 'God knows,' he said. 'We all went out to lunch on the strength of it, I saw a couple of chaps I know, and we had a few drinks, and then I came home on the four o'clock train and called Lily from the station, and here I am.'

There was a long thoughtful silence.

'This morning now,' the inspector said. 'What time did you call Mrs Winters?'

'This morning? At about quarter to ten.'

'A long telephone call, was it?'

'About twenty minutes.'

'I see. Did you telephone anyone else at all? Before you went to the station and caught the train?'

'No, I went straight away. I cut it a bit fine but I just caught the half past ten train to London.'

'Have you kept your ticket?'

Charlie flushed. 'I have to confess,' he said, 'I dashed out of the house with not a penny in my pocket. I had nothing but my cheque book. I had to run for the train anyway, and at the other end they weren't checking tickets. I travelled up without a ticket, and I didn't buy one. In London I went to my bank and cashed a cheque. I have my return ticket.' He reached into his pocket and put the ticket on the desk.

The inspector took it up and put it down again. 'Did you speak to anyone on the train? There was no ticket collector, I take it?'

Charlie shook his head. 'I was on my own in a compartment, the whole way.'

The inspector nodded. 'Is there any way that you can prove that you caught that particular train? That you did not catch a later one, for instance?'

Charlie thought for a moment and then shook his head. 'I can't *prove* I was on it,' he said. 'Does that time matter particularly?'

'Yes,' the inspector said. 'It matters most particularly. Are you in love with Mrs Winters?'

There was a stunned silence.

'I am very very fond of her,' Charlie said levelly. 'There's nothing between us. Her husband is a friend of mine also.'

'Your landlady tells us that this morning, on the telephone to someone – presumably Mrs Winters – that you said that you wanted something to change. That you wanted to snatch her and Christopher up, and take them away.'

Charlie inhaled a deep breath and then blew out a thin plume of smoke. 'I think you had better tell me what this is all about,' he said.

'Do you deny advising Mrs Winters to leave her husband? Do you deny offering her financial support if she divorced him?'

There was a long silence. 'I *do* think Mrs Winters should leave her husband,' Charlie said eventually. 'He has been violent to her in the past and I think he could hit her again. There has been no love affair between us, and there will be none. I would certainly do my best to support her if she decided to leave him. I love her and respect her. I am not her lover. I cannot be her husband.'

'Because of your wound?'

Charlie recoiled slightly. 'You *have* been busy, haven't you? I thought there were rules of confidentiality governing medical records?'

The inspector did not answer. 'Because of your wound, Sir?'

'Yes.'

There was a long silence. When the inspector spoke his voice was gentle. 'Is there anything you want to tell me,

585

Sir? I think we should get this straightened out as soon as possible, don't you? It's not worked. It's gone wrong. Let's get it cleared up and we can all go home.'

Charlie stubbed out the cigarette in the silver ashtray. 'We're at cross purposes,' he said briefly. 'I don't know what you're investigating. Everything I've told you about Lily is true. I can't help you any further.'

The inspector nodded. 'I should like you to come to the police station with us, Mr Smith. There are a few things I would like to discuss further.'

Charlie hesitated. 'Do I have a choice?'

The inspector shook his head with a grim smile. 'If you refuse to come with us I will put you under arrest.'

Charlie blinked. 'What the devil is going on here? I insist on knowing what has happened!'

'I'll tell you at the station.'

Charlie shook his head. 'Actually, inspector,' he said, 'I think I'd rather be charged and have a right to my lawyer, and a bit more information, than carry on chattering to you while you consult my private medical history and snoop around my landlady. Charge me, if you think you have evidence to make it stick – or I shall go to Lily now and she will tell me what's happening.'

The inspector nodded. 'Charles David Smith, I am arresting you for the kidnap of Christopher Charles Winters. You need say nothing, but anything you say may be taken down and used in evidence against you.'

Charlie's mouth dropped open. 'What?'

The inspector was silent.

'Christopher's been kidnapped?'

'Yes.'

'Not by me!'

'That we will endeavour to discover.'

The implication of the charge suddenly hit Charlie and he leaped to his feet and steadied himself with one hand on the back of the chair. The police constable loomed silently between him and the door. The inspector said nothing.

'Can I see Lily? She must be absolutely frantic.'

'Not at the moment, Sir, I'm afraid. We'll need to go down to the police station and take a statement from you, and so on.'

'Look,' Charlie said with rapid earnestness. 'Just stop here a moment. It's *not* me. You can search my lodgings. I don't have him hidden there. I *have* been in London all day, you can confirm that. I'll give you names. I wouldn't have taken him without Lily's consent. I would *never* have taken him without her consent. But don't you see – while you're arresting me, the baby's somewhere else!'

'For Christ's sake don't bother with me. I'll come to the station, you can parole me, I'll do anything you say – but find Christopher. It's not me – so someone else has got him. You should be looking for someone else!'

'You'll come to the station with us now?' the inspector asked.

Charlie nodded. 'Please,' he said. 'Don't stop looking for him.'

'I take it we don't need to handcuff you?'

'No.'

'On your honour?'

'On my honour! Will you give Lily a message for me?'

'Yes.'

'Tell her to be brave. Tell her I'm sure it will be all right. Tell her I'm thinking of her all the time. Tell her that she's in my heart, she's always in my heart. Will you tell her that?'

'Yes.'

The inspector nodded at the constable who slipped from the room and went round the corner to fetch the car. Then with the inspector on one side and the sergeant on the other, Charlie walked slowly from the room, through the hall, out of the front door and down the steps to the waiting car. The inspector closed the door on them and went back into the house.

He sat for a while in the silent study. It was growing dark and shadowy. He fiddled listlessly with the paperknife, thinking of the strange painful triangle of Stephen, Lily and Charlie – and the other people around them: the mute chauffeur, the crippled father, the cold mother. And finally – the missing baby.

If the baby was dead there would be nothing to keep the young Mrs Winters in this loveless house. She and Charlie had talent, love and a circle of friends who would not despise a divorcée or even a couple living together without marriage. The little baby had stood between Lily and freedom. He wondered if Charlie were ruthless enough to hire someone to steal the child and toss it in the sea weighted with pebbles while he courted the mother on the telephone. There was no way of telling. Every man who had been to the Front had come home with a strange new ruthlessness, as if everything they had ever known of love and tenderness had been shelled and bombed and sniped out of them in night after night of fear and despair.

He reached for the bell and pressed it. Sally – who was regarded as sufficiently lowly to wait on the police – appeared from the kitchen, wiping her hands on her apron.

'Could you ask Mr Stephen Winters if I might see him for a moment?' he asked.

'He's having his dinner,' she demurred.

'Even so.'

She nodded and in a moment opened the study door for Stephen to enter. He held a napkin in his hand. A gust of overcooked cabbage came into the room with him.

'I am sorry to disturb your dinner,' Inspector Walker said briefly. 'I wanted to tell you that I have made an arrest and we will be continuing our inquiries from the police station. I shall keep you informed at every development.'

'You've made an arrest?' Stephen hesitated. 'You don't mean Charlie Smith?'

The inspector nodded.

'But that's impossible!' Stephen said. 'He's a friend of Lily's, he's a friend of the family. He likes Christopher! Where would he take him? Can you get him back?'

'I don't know where the baby is,' Inspector Walker said levelly. 'I shall be trying to discover that tonight. I will keep you informed.'

'Why should Charlie do such a thing?'

'Again I am uncertain as to his motives. We are working in the dark. But I had to ensure that he was out of contact with his friends in London and Portsmouth while we corroborate his story. Now I must go.'

Stephen went with him to the front door. The police car had returned, and was waiting outside with the engine running. 'But you think he did it,' Stephen asked. 'You think he has Christopher hidden somewhere nearby?'

The inspector shook his head. 'I hope to discover that,' he said. 'I wish you good evening, Mr Winters. I will telephone without fail tonight, to tell you of our progress. Please, try not to worry too much, and tell your wife that we are doing everything we can.'

Stephen made a small gesture of helplessness and watched the inspector walk down the steps and get into the front of the car. A sickly fat slice of moon was hanging over the pier, ghostly white.

'Call us soon,' Stephen said. He looked pale in the moonlight and his eyes were dark shadows. 'I think none of us will sleep much tonight.'

The inspector nodded, then the driver put the car in gear and drove off.

*　　*　　*

Lily looked up as Stephen came back into the dining room. 'What's happening?' she asked. Her voice was high and nervous. 'Where's Charlie?'

Stephen glanced at her plate. She had eaten none of the steak and kidney pudding; the grey wedge of suet pudding crust was congealing in the thick gravy. The vegetables, mashed and roast potatoes, and boiled cabbage, were untouched. She had drunk two glasses of wine, far more than she usually had. She was as pale as a man in a dressing station, bleeding internally. Her eyes were black from the drink and the sleeping drugs. 'Where's Charlie?' she asked.

Stephen went to her and took her small cold hand. 'Something very disturbing has happened,' he said. His voice was gentle. He glanced over at his mother. 'Would you get Lily a glass of brandy, Mother?' he asked.

'Why?' Lily demanded. 'Stephen, please just tell me!'

'Something very odd has happened,' Stephen said again. Muriel placed a balloon glass of brandy at Lily's right hand. 'Charlie is being interviewed by the police. They suspect him of kidnapping Christopher.'

Lily's pale face went whiter still. 'It's impossible,' she said in a whisper. 'Why should they think that?'

Stephen put the glass in her hand. 'Have a sip, darling,' he said. 'You're awfully pale.'

He glanced over at his mother. Her face was hard and blank. Rory watched them all, the uncontrollable muscles in his hands shaking.

Lily sipped the drink and put it down. 'I wanted to see him,' she said. She sounded like a child crying for a playmate. 'I wanted to tell him about it. I wanted to know what he thought.'

'They want to know as well,' Stephen said ironically. He corrected himself at once. 'I'm sorry, darling, this is a shock for me too. I don't know why they suspect him.

590

Inspector Walker said they would call me from the police station when they had more information.'

'But where is Christopher?' Lily wailed suddenly. 'If they've arrested Charlie they must think Christopher is somewhere! Why don't they find Christopher first, and never mind who took him! It's night-time. He should be in his nursery, he should be in his cot. He should have had his bath by now!'

Her voice rose higher and higher and then she burst into sobs. 'What if the people who have him don't know what he wants? What if they haven't any milk for him? What about his supper? Who's going to look after him?'

Stephen picked her up easily from her chair and nodded to his mother to open the door for him.

'I'll take her upstairs,' he said.

Lily clung tightly to him, sobbing and sobbing into his shoulder. 'Send up Browning with that powder the doctor left, would you, Mother? She needs calming.'

Muriel nodded and rang the bell. They could hear Lily's high frightened crying going up and up to the top floor and then the bedroom door closed and the house was silent again.

Muriel took her place at the head of the table. Sally came to clear the plates. She served the pudding in silence: apple pie and custard. Muriel served three large portions and Sally put Rory's plate before him, poured custard for him and left the room.

'I think Stephen is coping marvellously,' Muriel said.

Rory looked at her with his deep-set dark eyes.

'But Lily is a real difficulty. I shall ask Dr Mobcy to prescribe her something stronger when he comes tomorrow.'

'Why arrest Charlie?' Rory asked.

Muriel thought of the long low-voiced phone calls, and Charlie's delighted play with Christopher. She thought of the faithful unswerving love between him and Lily. Charlie had taken her to hospital when Stephen was too drunk to stand, Charlie had brought her home triumphant and laughing with the baby in his arms. She thought of the drawing room filled every afternoon with ragtime music, and Lily singing so joyfully with her hand on Charlie's shoulder and Christopher gurgling on the sofa.

'It must be some awful mistake,' she said stoutly. 'As long as they find Christopher soon!'

Lily fell quickly into a drugged sleep, but she tossed and turned all night and woke at midnight screaming. They had to give her more of the drug, and this time she struggled against it, begging them not to put her to sleep. Stephen held her arms twisted behind her back while Muriel forced the glass between her lips and Lily had to swallow or choke on the drink. But at three in the morning Stephen woke and found the bed empty. He dragged on his dressing-gown, checked the bathroom, and then hurried downstairs. Lily was not in the drawing room, nor the study. He checked the bolt and chain on the front door, but she had not gone out into the street. He heard a noise from the dining room and hurried through.

It was the opening of the French window in the dining room which he had heard. Lily was going out on to the balcony and down the steps into the garden. She was walking slowly, as if there were something wrong with her eyesight. One hand was on the iron bannister and the other was stretched out before her. Her nightdress gleamed eerily white in the light of the setting moon. Stephen followed her out into the cool moonlight and swore at the shiver down his spine.

'Lily!' he called softly, for fear of alerting the neighbours. 'Lily, for God's sake, what d'you think you're doing?'

He thought for a moment that she had gone quite mad. She was searching the garden. She was searching the garden for something quite small. She looked under the seat, she peered into the flower beds. She thrust her face between the rose bushes and the thorns scratched like cats at her skin and clung to her hair. And all the time he could hear her high soft wail: 'Christopher! Oh, Christopher! Where are you?'

He took the final steps at a run and caught her in his arms and pulled her away. She turned her face to him and Stephen started back in superstitious fear. Her eyelids were closed. She was blind.

'Christ!' he exclaimed and abruptly let her go.

Lily staggered and her eyes flew open. She stared blankly at him and then looked all around the garden. Then her face, which had been madly serene, crumpled with grief and she opened her mouth and screamed. 'Oh God! Tell me it's a dream, Stephen! Tell me it's a dream!'

Stephen leaped forward and clapped a hand over her mouth, nervously looking up at the sleeping houses.

'For God's sake, Lily!' he said. 'You'll wake the whole neighbourhood! No, it's true, dammit. Now come inside, darling.'

She resisted him, tugging his hand away from her mouth. 'I dreamed Christopher was stolen,' she said. Her face was anguished, she was pleading for him to tell her she was wrong. 'Christopher stolen, and Charlie arrested for taking him. And I didn't know where he was, and I was looking for him and looking for him and looking for him. I searched the whole house, it was terribly dark but I looked in every room. Everyone was asleep or dead, I went everywhere.'

Stephen shuddered again at the thought of Lily's blank-faced stare at his sleeping mother, at Nanny Janes.

'I went into every room,' Lily said in a vague frightening

sing-song voice. 'I looked under the beds and in the wardrobes. No-one stirred. They were all dead. I looked everywhere, but I couldn't find him. Then I looked in the garden. I've searched everywhere, Stephen. Where is he?'

Stephen put a firm arm around her shoulders and marched her towards the steps. He forced her up them, into the dining room and thrust her into a dining chair. He poured her a glass of brandy and made her drink it. When two red spots appeared in her white cheeks, he had one himself, and took the chair opposite her and held her hands.

'You must try and be brave, darling,' he said with infinite patience. 'You really must try and get a grip of yourself or you'll crack up, Lily. I know, I've seen it happen. It's true. Christopher's been kidnapped and Charlie's arrested for the crime. The inspector said to tell you that he's doing the best he can to find Christopher. The very best he can.'

Lily's face showed no expression. Her hands clasped his lightly in return, but huge tears gathered constantly in her eyes and rolled down her cheeks until her face was wet and the table between her hands was splashed. Stephen watched with a disbelieving curiosity. He had not known that a woman could grieve so much. He had not known that a human being could feel so much. The trenches had hardened him so swiftly that he felt pain only in his dreams. Now he watched his wife's silent, unstoppable tears, and knew that she had loved Christopher in a way that he could not begin to understand.

'Time for bed,' he said gently.

He took her up the stairs and she went obediently, like a little girl. He mixed her another of the doctor's sleeping draughts and she sipped at it. But still the big tears rolled down her cheeks and dropped to the sheet. She did not seem to notice.

Stephen arranged the pillows behind her and she lay

back. When she closed her eyes as she was bidden, the tears still welled up underneath the closed eyelids and trickled down each side of her face. Stephen put out the bedside light on her side, but kept his own switched on, so that he could watch her as she fell asleep. She lay very still as the drug took effect but even when she was breathing regularly, and was deeply asleep, she still wept. Stephen, locking their bedroom door to prevent her sleepwalking again, wondered if she would cry in her sleep, in silence, all night. Cry and cry for the loss of her baby, without knowing where he might be.

Chapter Forty

Stephen was prepared to be tender with Lily in the morning, but she was no longer the weeping wraith who had haunted the moonlit garden. She awoke brittle and irritable. She took only twenty minutes to dress in a long navy skirt, a blue blouse and an unflattering long navy cardigan. She would have no breakfast but a cup of black coffee. She asked Coventry to drive her to the police station. She was going to see the inspector.

Muriel, tested to the very edge of good manners, said that Lily had much better stay at home, see the doctor, who would be calling soon, and wait for news.

Lily looked at her with hard blue eyes. 'Christ only knows what they think they're playing at,' she said blasphemously. 'I'm going down there to find out.'

Muriel looked to Stephen.

'I'll come too if you insist,' he said. 'You'd much better stay at home, Lily. Mother's right.'

'My baby has disappeared. My best friend is arrested for his kidnap. No-one knows where my baby is. What the hell d'you think I'm going to do? Take up embroidery like your mother?'

'Lily!' Stephen exclaimed. 'There's nothing to be gained by being rude to Mother!'

Lily shot a swift mutinous look at him, and did not apologize. She went quickly to the front door and opened it. Coventry had the car outside. She went down the steps and sat in the front seat, beside him. She was not wearing hat or gloves. She looked like a common woman hitching a lift.

'Really!' Muriel exploded and then compressed her lips. She said nothing more.

'I suppose I'll have to go too,' Stephen said. He called to Coventry to wait and then picked up his hat and ran down the steps and opened the front car door. 'Come and get in the back, Lily,' he said. 'You're making a spectacle of yourself.'

'Can we *just go*?' she demanded.

Coventry slipped the car into gear and drove them to the police station. Lily rode in angry silence. As soon as the car stopped she strode into the police station and demanded to see Inspector Walker.

He came from a back room to greet them at the desk. 'I was coming out to your house a little later,' he said. 'I'm afraid we have no idea yet where your son is being kept.'

'Is Charlie here?' Lily demanded.

'He's under arrest, yes. We've been questioning him most of the night.'

'Are you going to release him?'

'Not yet,' the inspector said cautiously.

'You've got the wrong man,' Lily said baldly. 'And while you're bothering with him, Christopher is with someone else. They might even be getting away with him.'

'I don't think so,' the inspector said. 'I know he's your friend, Mrs Winters. But I think we have the right man here. Why should anyone else take your baby? How could a stranger steal a child from a walled garden? It has to be someone who is close to you and your family. It's an unpalatable fact, but you have to face it. If it is *not* Mr Smith, then it is certainly another friend or a faithful servant. All the circumstances point to it being someone who knew the routine of the house. Someone who even knew that you were inside on the telephone.'

Lily shook her head. Stephen made a soft exclamation.

'Would you step into my office, Mrs Winters?' the inspector asked. As Stephen moved forwards too, the inspector made a little gesture. 'In private, if you don't mind, Mr Winters.'

'Right-ho – I'll wait here, shall I?'

They nodded at each other, as men who understand that women have to be managed, then Lily followed the inspector into his office.

'Firstly I have a message for you from Mr Smith,' the inspector said, taking his seat behind his desk.

Lily looked at him and the clutter on his desk. She took in the dark green filing cabinet in the corner full of records of dreary crimes, the clouded glass of the window behind his head and the stale smell of an overused office.

'He asked me to tell you that he was thinking of you all the time, that you are in his heart,' the inspector said.

Lily did not even blush. 'Yes,' she said. Her voice was firm.

'You asked me why I think Mr Smith took your baby,' the inspector said quietly. 'I did not want to tell you in front of your husband, but I must ask you to deal with this calmly and sensibly.'

'Yes,' Lily said flatly.

He hesitated. The doubt that a young mother could take anything calmly and sensibly was written on his face. But he went on. 'I believe that Mr Smith hoped to persuade you to leave your husband by taking your baby away. I think he hoped that you would then join him and the baby, and start divorce proceedings against Mr Winters.'

Lily's angry glare could not have been assumed for effect. 'This is ridiculous,' she said.

'We know that he spoke of divorce to you,' the inspector said patiently. 'We know that he was anxious that you should leave Mr Winters. We know that he is in love with you.'

Lily never wavered. 'All that's true,' she said. 'But it doesn't mean that he would take Christopher. Where would he take him? How could he take him while he was talking on the telephone to me? Why haven't you found Christopher if you've got Charlie?'

'We believe he has a confederate who has the baby in hiding,' the inspector suggested.

Lily was watching him intently. '*Another* kidnapper?' she asked.

The inspector nodded. 'There are women who would do it for money,' he said. 'If there was enough money on offer. Someone who had been hired to enter the garden when you were on the telephone to Mr Smith, who knew that he could keep you on the phone for those important minutes. She takes the baby, she hides the baby, and when Mr Smith comes home from London he tells you what he has done and he persuades you to run away with him to rejoin your child.'

Lily was frowning, following the plan. 'Run where?'

The inspector shrugged. 'Couldn't the two of you get work in America? Or Europe?'

Lily nodded. 'Yes, we could. But that doesn't explain where Christopher is now? Who the second kidnapper is? Why Charlie would put me through such agony? Now that he's arrested, he would surely tell you where my baby is?'

'You could ask him yourself,' the inspector suggested. 'He won't tell us. We've checked his story – he did go to London, but we don't know which train he caught. He was there by midday, but that leaves plenty of time to get his confederate into hiding and to confirm that his plan had worked. He won't betray his partner to us. But he might tell you.'

'Of course I'll see him,' Lily said.

The inspector pressed a button on his desk, the door to the next office opened and Charlie came in.

He was dressed in shirtsleeves and trousers. They had taken his shoes away and he had only socks on his feet. He looked tired and there was dark stubble on his chin. When he saw Lily he put out his hands as if to hold her, but she stayed back, scrutinizing him as if she were seeing him for the very first time. 'Did you take Christopher?' she asked baldly. 'Like they say you did?'

Charlie recoiled from the question and then gave her his old crooked smile which hid his hurt. 'Come on, Lil,' he said. 'Use your brains. Of course I didn't.'

For a moment she hesitated, then she smiled at him and suddenly the inspector saw, for the first time, that she was a beautiful woman. Her smile came out like sunlight. 'No,' she said. 'Of course you didn't.'

She turned to the inspector and he saw the joy in her face drain away. 'Then where is he?' she asked. 'You're spending all your time on Charlie. You're not hunting for Christopher. You've got it all wrong. Christopher is somewhere out there, without even a change of clothing, and nothing for breakfast, and you're not even looking for him.'

Charlie was watching her, his face dark. 'Bear up, Lil,' he said very low. 'Use your brains for Christ's sake. Someone you know has got him. The inspector's right. It's someone who knows you. You *must* think!'

'That'll do,' Inspector Walker said. He nodded to the constable, who took Charlie by the arm.

'I'm coming,' Charlie said shortly. 'Keep your chin up, Lil. Break a leg.'

The door was shut behind him before she could say goodbye. Pale with anger, she turned to the inspector.

'I'm going home,' she said. 'I'm going to go through

every single person I can think of until I find my son.'

The inspector put a hand out to her. 'Don't take my word for it,' he said. 'Think of Mr Smith's friends. Think if anyone would do this for him – perhaps even without him knowing. If you trust him so much, just think if someone would do this for the two of you, without your knowledge or consent. The key to this is in your hand, Mrs Winters. Don't let your anger cloud your judgement. You think what Mr Smith would gain if you left Mr Winters. You think who might help him, or who might do it for him.'

Lily paused for a moment. 'I'll think,' she promised. 'Do you have men out looking now, looking for his pram?'

The man nodded. 'All the men I can,' he said. 'This is a top-level inquiry. But don't forget, Mrs Winters, if it was a kidnap for money you would have had a ransom note by now. It's not a passing opportunist kidnap. A chance kidnap doesn't take a baby from a walled garden, hidden from the road. It's someone who knew the routine of the house. Someone who knew the baby would be out there on his own. Someone *you* know.'

Lily nodded, her face bleak. 'Then I'll find them,' she said.

Stephen was waiting on the bench outside, smoking a cigarette in defiance of the regulations. He stood when Lily came out, pale and determined, ugly in her dark navy skirt. He gave a resigned sigh.

Lily walked past him and out to the car. The inspector laid a gentle hand on Stephen's sleeve. 'A quiet word,' he said.

Stephen paused.

'She confronted Mr Smith and he persists in his denial,' the inspector said. 'She accepts that it must be someone who knows the routine of the house. I have to warn you, Sir, that I am feeling very anxious about the baby's safety.'

Stephen's eyes narrowed and he took a draw on the cigarette. Ahead of them, Lily got into the car. The two men looked towards her. She was out of earshot.

'It is possible that Mr Smith's accomplice took the baby and murdered it,' the inspector said quietly. 'You have to prepare yourself for the very worst, Mr Winters.'

Stephen nodded. 'I was at Ypres,' he said shortly. 'You got used to the worst, there.'

The inspector nodded. 'That's what I thought,' he said. 'That's why I thought I'd tell you now. So that you can prepare Mrs Winters.'

They glanced at the car again. Lily was leaning back against the seat, her eyes shut. She looked utterly exhausted. She looked old.

'Why would Charlie Smith do such a thing?' Stephen asked. 'He'd have to be mad to even think of it.'

'I think he was more attached to your wife than she knows,' the inspector said. He had a sense of having to tread very carefully. 'He may have thought that with no baby to keep her, he might have been able to persuade her to leave you.'

Stephen shot him a swift incredulous look. 'Have you told Lily this?' he asked.

'Just now.'

'Did she deny it?'

'She doesn't believe him guilty.'

There was a brief silence. Stephen pinched out the ember of the cigarette and dropped it to the ground.

'May I ask what you think of my theory?'

Stephen shook his head, a man bewildered. 'I suppose so,' he said hesitantly. 'I suppose it might be so.'

'You think Mr Smith capable of kidnap, or even murder, to obtain your wife?' the inspector confirmed.

Stephen's mouth closed on a hard, sad line. He looked the inspector straight in the face. 'I knew he loved her,' he said. 'But I thought he knew it was impossible. I accepted their friendship – I'm a modern man, I wanted Lily to be happy with her friends around her. There's a streak of ruthlessness in him, I was aware of that. He got himself out of the war, you know. He never speaks of it. I knew he wasn't top drawer, not quite the gentleman he makes himself out to be. But murder . . .'

There was a short silence.

'D'you think he could do such a thing?'

Stephen's face was shocked. He nodded slowly. 'Yes, I suppose he could,' he said. 'I really fear that he could.'

Lily opened her eyes as Stephen got in the car and Coventry started the engine. 'What was he saying to you, all that while?'

Stephen shook his head. 'He was telling me his suspicions of Charlie. I can hardly take it all in.'

'He's got the wrong end of the stick,' Lily said abruptly. 'Charlie couldn't hurt Christopher. Not if his own life depended on it. He's got the wrong end of the stick altogether.'

Stephen looked at Lily thoughtfully. 'Or else you have.'

They drew up outside the house. Lily got out of the car without waiting for Coventry to open her door. She marched up the steps and leaned on the doorbell. It pealed insistently inside the house, but Lily did not take her finger from the button. Sally threw the door open, wiping her hands on her apron. Muriel was hurrying down the stairs.

'Lily! What on earth! Is the bell stuck?'

'No,' Lily said shortly. 'I just wanted to come in. I'm in a hurry.'

Muriel shot one swift anguished look at Stephen. 'Well, really! Did the inspector upset you? Is that what the matter is?'

'No,' Lily said. 'I'm busy. Muriel, I need your address book. I need to talk to some of your friends. May I have it?'

'I hardly think . . .' Muriel began.

'What is this all about?' Stephen demanded. 'What's wrong with you, Lily? What did the inspector say?'

'He said nothing!' Lily said impatiently. 'He said nothing which made any sense at all. It was what Charlie said that struck me. He said that *I* must know the real kidnapper. So I'm going to go through all our friends, all of them, until I know who it is.'

Muriel flapped an angry hand at Sally. 'Don't you have something to do, Sally? Standing around in the hall all day with your mouth open?'

Lily went to the telephone and pulled out her address book which she kept in the drawer of the little table. 'Can I have your address book, please, Muriel?' she repeated.

Muriel glared at Stephen. 'I'll go upstairs to fetch it,' she said slowly. 'Meanwhile, perhaps you two should have a little talk.'

She went briskly up the stairs and Stephen and Lily were left in silence in the shadowy hall.

'Now look here, Lily,' Stephen said. 'You're upsetting Mother, and you're upsetting yourself. You're doing no good to anyone. The police have it all in hand. If they want your address book, or Mother's address book, they only have to ask. What d'you imagine you can do – trying to do their job for them? You'll only put people's backs up, and upset yourself. Now calm down and come into the drawing room and we'll have some coffee and sandwiches. You didn't have any breakfast, and you didn't have any dinner last night either. You'll be ill if you carry on like this.'

Lily lifted the earpiece and held the telephone to her mouth. She gave a local number to the operator and looked up at Stephen while the telephone clicked through to a connection. 'I'm going to find Christopher,' she said. '*You* go and have coffee and sandwiches, if you want. I'm going to find my baby.'

'Lily, for heaven's sake!' Stephen broke off when he realized she was not hearing him. She was speaking into the mouthpiece. 'Madge,' she said abruptly. 'It's Lily. I need you to answer some questions. Do you promise to tell me the truth?'

There was a muffled squawk.

'I'll tell you all about it later. Now tell me. Where were you yesterday morning between half past nine and ten o'clock?' Lily made a note on the telephone message pad. 'Can anyone confirm that?' She wrote, 'In bed. Landlady.' 'Thank you,' she said. 'No, I can't talk now. I'll talk to you later,' and broke the connection on Madge's insistent voice.

She dialled another number. Stephen stepped back into the drawing room and listened to Lily speak to one friend after another in this new hard businesslike voice of hers. When they were unclear as to where they had been, or had no-one to confirm their whereabouts, she insisted that they explain to her what they were doing, and whether anyone might have seen them. She grilled them like a sergeant major, he thought resentfully. They were all suspects to Lily now.

His mother came slowly into the room, her address book under her arm.

'She's going ahead,' she said, nodding to the hall.

Stephen nodded.

'This means *everyone* will know,' Muriel said. 'It'll be all over town by lunchtime.'

'I know.'

'Do you *want* me to give her my address book?'

Stephen shrugged. 'Hardly,' he said. 'But how can we

refuse to help her? She thinks this is the way to find Christopher.'

'She is letting us all down,' Muriel said icily. She handed the address book to Stephen with a gesture of resignation. 'She is an embarrassment.'

Stephen took the book. 'I can't see how we can stop her,' he said. 'When she finally draws a blank I suppose she will stop.'

'That could take all day,' Muriel said. 'Is she to stay there, hunched over the telephone, shrieking at my friends all day?'

'The situation could change,' Stephen said.

Muriel raised an eyebrow.

'We could get some news. Or Charlie could confess.'

'Do you think it is Charlie?' Muriel asked. 'I simply cannot believe it.'

Stephen nodded slowly. 'The inspector is convinced of it. He says that Charlie had some mad idea of stealing Christopher and then persuading Lily to leave me, once Christopher was out of the way.'

Muriel's cold face froze yet further.

'Did he take liberties?' Stephen asked very quietly. 'While he was here supposed to be teaching her the piano? Did he take liberties?'

'I knew he was in love with her,' Muriel said. 'And I'm afraid,' – she hesitated on the betrayal but Lily's hard insistent voice from the hall forced her onwards – 'I'm afraid Lily encouraged him.'

Stephen flushed a deep red of anger. 'Then *all* this is her own fault,' he said. 'All of this distress could have been avoided if she had toed the line with that – that – that damned bounder.'

Muriel sat down in the window seat and looked out at the grey sea and lowering sky. 'She always kept him at arm's length,' she said. 'I'm certain of that.'

Stephen swore under his breath and strode out into the hall. Muriel half-rose as if to stop him, but then let him go. 'He was her choice,' she said under her breath. 'They're married now. They'll have to work it out themselves.'

She heard the telephone bang as Stephen snatched it from Lily and put it down on the table with a crash.

'Before you tell all of Portsmouth that your boyfriend has kidnapped your child, there are one or two things you should know,' he said. 'That the inspector, and my own mother, have both told me that Charlie Smith is in love with you, and that you've been making a fool of me, in my own house, behind my back.'

'I never,' Lily said.

'Don't interrupt me,' Stephen said, his voice deep with rage. 'Don't *think* of interrupting me. My own mother tells me that you've encouraged him. How far has it gone? How far have you encouraged him? Is he your lover, eh? Is he perhaps Christopher's father and you've palmed me and my family off with a bastard, and now his real father wants to take him back? Is that what's happened? And is all this grief of yours, and your driving down to see the inspector and your so-called sleepwalking, all a big act, a big act from a little actress to get Charlie Smith off the hook, and yourself off the hook?

'We all know he did it. The police, my mother, me, we *all* know he did it. What we don't know is whether you were in it too? Did you open the garden gate, not shut it? Did you hand the baby over to another girl of his? Do you know *exactly* where Christopher is, while we're all going out of our minds with worry!'

'No!' Lily screamed. 'No! No! No! Charlie Smith *does* love me, and I love him, but we were never lovers, and we never will be. Christopher is your son. *You* of all people should know that! It was you who forced me time after time until I conceived and had to give up the theatre.

Charlie would never hurt me, he would never take my baby away from me. And I would *never* be parted from Christopher. You're mad to think so! You're mad to suggest it! All I want is to get my baby back! I want my baby back!'

She broke into frenzied sobbing, and Stephen stepped forward, took hold of her shoulders and shook her in his anger. At once she flew at him with her hands flexed like claws, flew at his face and slapped him and scratched him, screaming: 'I'll kill you if you say such things! I'll kill you, Stephen!' and then tore herself from his grip and rushed up the stairs. They heard her bedroom door slam.

'Good God!' Stephen said. He pulled his handkerchief from his top pocket and held it to his face. She had drawn blood. When he took his handkerchief away and saw the red of it, he went pale.

Muriel appeared in the drawing room doorway. 'Dr Mobey is here,' she said. 'His car has just drawn up. Go to your study, Stephen, he mustn't see you like this.'

'He'd better see Lily,' Stephen said. 'She's hysterical. She's out of control.'

'I know,' Muriel said grimly. 'I heard it all.'

The doorbell rang. Stephen turned and went into his study, closing the door. Muriel stood still while Browning toiled up the back stairs, straightened her cap in the mirror, and opened the front door.

Dr Mobey came in with a smile. 'How are you all?' he asked.

Muriel took him into the drawing room, and ordered Browning to bring coffee. 'The strain is beginning to tell,' she said. 'My daughter-in-law's friend and accompanist has been arrested for the kidnap of Christopher. But they don't know where the baby is being held.'

'Good God!' The doctor was genuinely shocked. 'The

chap who played with her, at the concert I went to? Your "do" in aid of the distressed officers?'

Muriel nodded grimly. 'It appears that he thought she might leave Stephen if he had Christopher safely out of the house.'

Dr Mobey looked stunned. 'And she?' he asked cautiously.

Muriel's face was haggard. 'She led him on,' she said shortly. 'I am speaking in confidence, Doctor.'

'Of course, of course.'

'My son even doubts whether Christopher is his child. The mother may even have been party to a plot.'

Dr Mobey reached out and took Muriel's hand. It was icy cold. He chafed it and scanned her tired face. 'What rotten luck,' he said softly. At his sympathy a little colour flowed back into Muriel's sallow face. 'What rotten luck. Shall I see her?'

'She's crying in her bedroom. She was sleepwalking last night, and hysterical again today. She has eaten nothing. I don't know that we can manage her here. She just quarrelled with Stephen and she was violent.' Muriel compressed her lips into a thin line. 'This whole situation is becoming quite unmanageable.'

Dr Mobey nodded. 'I see, I see.' He paused. 'Would it be your wish, if I could find a suitable place for her, for us to take her into safe keeping somewhere? Until the baby is found and your son can decide what is best? If she will not eat or sleep it is probably my duty to ensure she is properly cared for.'

'An asylum?' Muriel asked, shocked.

'A rest cure,' Dr Mobey said gently. 'For ladies with overstressed and overactive nerves. There's a place towards Southampton where all the London ladies go when they are overwrought. The very best of care, a large country house, and the most up-to-date of treatments.

Electricity shocks, water treatment and fresh country air.'

'I don't know,' Muriel said hesitantly. 'We cannot safeguard her here, but . . .'

'Is Stephen at home?'

'I'll fetch him.'

Muriel went from the room and Dr Mobey heard her swift explanation. Stephen came in; he had not wiped his face and the doctor could see the four long lines scored by Lily's fingernails down his cheek. 'Good God,' he said.

Stephen managed a slight smile. 'Just a scratch,' he said ironically.

'This cannot go on,' Dr Mobey said. 'I take it that this was an unprovoked attack?'

'I had accused her of infidelity,' Stephen said. 'I share the blame. I was angry and intemperate.'

Dr Mobey took Stephen's chin in his hand and turned his face to the light. 'Maybe so,' he said. 'But this is not the reaction of a sane woman. Not the action of an innocent woman.'

'Tell him about the address books,' Muriel prompted.

As Stephen explained, and told the doctor of Lily's visit to the inspector, he nodded. 'I'll see her,' he said. 'And then I will bring a colleague of mine. If he confirms my diagnosis we can have her admitted to Green Lawns.'

'Are you sure that's the best thing?' Stephen said. His face was pale and strained, the scratch marks standing out as livid accusations against Lily. 'Shouldn't we try to keep her here if we possibly can? She's just heartbroken over Christopher. She doesn't know what she's doing. And if she had any part in encouraging the kidnap – well – I think she'd just lose her mind.'

'Green Lawns is the place for her,' Dr Mobey said firmly. 'I assure you, Stephen. It's a most attractive house and gardens. And you cannot keep her at home if she is behaving like this. What if she were to attack your father or your mother? It's a risk I cannot allow.'

Stephen nodded. 'I hadn't thought,' he said apologetically. 'I am sorry. I am a little overwrought myself.'

'No wonder!' the doctor said. 'Now, I suggest you go to a bathroom and put a little iodine on that cut, and I will go up to your bedroom and speak with Mrs Winters.'

'I have some iodine in my bathroom,' Muriel offered. The three of them went up the stairs. Muriel and Stephen stopped at the first landing and watched Dr Mobey go up to the second floor and tap gently on Lily's door.

Chapter Forty-one

'Who is it?' Lily demanded.

'Dr Mobey. May I come in?'

'I don't need a doctor.'

'Perhaps you don't. But I should like to see you, if I may.'

They heard the key turn slowly in the lock and Lily stood in the doorway.

'Here I am,' she said grudgingly.

'And looking well enough, too. Have you any news of your baby, Mrs Winters?'

Lily's face was cold and hard. 'Nothing new,' she said. 'Just new ideas of who to blame. But no-one has found him. No-one is looking for him.'

'Come come now, I think the police are looking for him, aren't they?'

'No.'

'But they have arrested a suspect, haven't they?'

Lily lowered her voice. 'They've arrested my friend,' she said quietly. 'My best friend. And they're trying to prove he did it. And now they're saying that I had something to do with it too. I can't understand it. I can't understand why they're saying that. I keep thinking and thinking. Because I know who did it. I must know, somewhere in my mind, who did it. It must be someone who knows us, who knows me. Someone close to us. But I can't think who would take my baby from me. I can't think who would do it.'

She snatched herself back from the edge of tears. 'I'll

discover it,' she said rapidly. 'The name. I keep thinking and thinking. I was going to telephone everyone I know, everyone Muriel knows. But they wouldn't let me do that. They don't want me to do that. But as I was phoning I knew it wasn't someone from the theatre or from the Palais or even someone from Highland Road. It's someone mad. I know whoever did it was mad. And I'm the only one who knows. And somewhere in my mind there's a name. The name of the mad person who has taken Christopher. And I'll keep on and on thinking, until I can get that name. And when I find out who it is, I'll kill them.'

There was a little silence. 'You're very overwrought,' Dr Mobey said gently. 'I'm going to make you up a little drink to help you sleep, and then you're to go to bed for the rest of the morning. You can get up for some lunch, and you must eat something, mind! I hear you're skipping meals and that's no good at all! After lunch you're to have another rest. And we'll leave all this thinking to the people who do it for a living – eh? To the police. And to your husband. We'll get them to do the thinking for you, Mrs Winters. You leave it to them.'

Lily's hands formed into claws again and Dr Mobey flinched, remembering she was violent. 'You're another one then,' she said bitterly. 'You're another one who wants Christopher lost. Another one who doesn't care if we never find him. I won't sleep. I won't sleep till I get him back. I have to *think*. I can't think if I'm asleep. He's been gone twenty-four hours and I have to get him back. I've got the key, the inspector himself said. I have the key to the secret. In my mind.'

'Come into your room and sit down then,' Dr Mobey said gently. 'Shall I ask them to bring you up a cup of coffee? Or tea?'

Lily went into the bedroom. The bed was unmade, her dressing table a mess of hairbrushes, spilled powder and open lipsticks. The wardrobe door was open, a couple of dresses drooping from the hangers. Dr Mobey took in the untidiness in a swift assessing glance. 'And we'll get you tidied up,' he said gently. 'You sit there and think, and I'll go down and order you some coffee. And when I come back, I'll bring another doctor to see you. He's good at helping people think. He'd help you.'

Lily sat obediently in the chair he indicated. She hugged her knees to her chest and stared out of the window. She looked like a child banished to her room for some small misdemeanour. She hardly heard him as he talked, and she did not see him palm the key of the door as he went quietly from the room. Lily did not turn her head.

'Who?' she whispered to herself. 'I must think.'

Stephen and his mother were on the landing. Stephen's scratches were highlighted with the buttercup yellow of the iodine. 'Downstairs,' Dr Mobey said in an undertone.

When they were inside the drawing room with the door shut he handed the key to Stephen. 'I thought it best that we should have this in our possession,' he said. 'She had locked herself in when I first went up.'

Stephen took it with a nod.

'With your consent I shall phone a colleague of mine to come and have a look at her,' he said. 'She seems to me to be dangerously overwrought. She needs sedation and skilled nursing. I don't think you can care for her properly here.'

'I don't want her to go,' Stephen said. 'It's just that she's so anxious – I'm sure she's not really dangerous. If she would only rest and eat something she would be all right.'

Dr Mobey shook his head. 'As you say – if she would rest and leave the worrying to the police she would be well. But I'm afraid that's the last thing she can do. She's a powerfully maternal woman and right now she's a lioness with a stolen cub. She doesn't know what to do with herself. I'm afraid I must insist.'

Stephen raised his hands in a reluctant gesture of assent. 'Very well,' he said. 'But she must have the very best of care.'

'I guarantee it,' the doctor said. He went into Stephen's study, and telephoned his colleague, and then the Green Lawns home.

'Bad news on one front,' he said, returning to the drawing room. 'Green Lawns can't take her until tomorrow. She'll have to spend tonight here. They'll send an ambulance for her tomorrow morning at nine o'clock prompt. I can hire an experienced nurse to stay with her here for this evening. My colleague, Dr Ramsden, is coming at once. I was lucky enough to catch him at the hospital before he does his rounds.'

'He's a hospital doctor?'

Dr Mobey made a grimace. 'Nervous illness,' he said. 'He found his practice very much enlarged since the war. He's now a very busy man. Shellshock victims, neurasthenics, neurotics. The effects are long-lasting, and for many, quite incurable.' He smiled at Stephen. 'They don't all have your constitution, I'm sorry to say.'

Stephen returned the smile. 'It was a dreadful time,' he said. 'Many of the chaps should never have been there in the first place, they didn't have the temperament. Some can take the pressure and some cannot.'

'How's that chauffeur of yours?'

'Coventry? He's unchanged. They could never find any thing wrong but it's my belief he took a piece of shell in his throat which severed the cords. He still can't speak. I think he never will.'

'We could ask Dr Ramsden to have a look at him, while he's here.'

Stephen shook his head. 'I wouldn't waste his time,' he said.

'Anyway, Coventry isn't here,' Muriel interrupted. 'He took the car and went, as soon as he had brought you back from the police station. He had the car last night too and he didn't come home till this morning.'

Stephen nodded. 'I said he could,' he said. 'He was so distressed about Christopher that he wanted to drive around and see if he could spot anything. I think he was searching most of the night. He wanted to have another drive around today, just in case he saw the pram. The police have everyone out looking, but often it's the lucky chance that solves something like this. Coventry wouldn't be denied. He's a loyal chap. One of the best.'

The doorbell rang, and they fell silent, waiting for Browning to answer it. She put her head around the drawing room door and spoke to Muriel. 'It's that police inspector again,' she said. 'Am I to show him into the study?'

'Yes please, Browning,' Muriel said. 'Mr Winters will come to him at once.'

Stephen got wearily to his feet. 'Just a minute, old man,' Dr Mobey said gently. 'Permit the family doctor and an old friend to delay you a moment?'

Stephen smiled patiently. 'Yes, Dr Mobey?'

'Take a cup of your mother's excellent coffee, and a drop of brandy in it, and a couple of these biscuits. The body is an engine, remember. It needs stoking if you're going to make it overwork.'

Stephen smiled. 'A superannuated boiler this morning,' he said. He rang the bell for the brandy decanter and took a generous measure in his coffee cup. He paused to eat the biscuits and then he went from the room.

At the study door he hesitated. The inspector was not alone. He could hear Lily's high strained voice through the wood of the door. She must have seen the police car

616

draw up and pattered downstairs and slipped into the study before Browning had even opened the front door.

'I've been thinking and thinking,' he heard her say. 'I can't get it straight in my head. Will you tell me again, how it happened?'

Stephen opened the door a crack, the well-oiled hinges making no sound.

'I think it was someone who knew the baby was put out at nine every day, someone like Mr Charles Smith,' the inspector said slowly and patiently. 'I think someone else, an accomplice, was waiting and watching the garden. When they saw you go in for the telephone call – or when they knew the telephone call would come – they slipped in the garden gate, they wheeled the pram out of the garden, and then they walked quickly north up the road, away from the sea. By the time you were back out in the garden, they were several roads away. By the time you had called the police and we had started searching they were in hiding.'

'I heard a car,' Lily said suddenly.

The inspector said nothing.

'I heard a car,' Lily said again.

'When was this?' His voice was suddenly sharp and interested.

'When I was in the hall. Mrs Winters had asked me to take her into Southsea. I heard a car drawing away. The noise that a car makes in first gear. It went' – Lily gestured southwards, to the sea, with her hand – 'that way.'

'Perhaps a delivery van, a baker's van, calling at the kitchen.'

'No.' Her voice was suddenly sure. 'It was a car, a car like ours. It made the same sort of noise as our Argyll. It was a limousine engine. I heard the car door slam and it drove away, it paused at the junction and drove off.'

Stephen went swiftly into the room. 'Good morning again, Inspector,' he said pleasantly.

Lily turned a white face towards him. Her hair was unkempt and ragged, her eyes were rubbed and red. The navy blue cardigan was half-off one shoulder. She looked distraught, like a drunk or a madwoman.

'I heard a car,' she said.

'Just now?' Stephen asked kindly. 'Yes. That was the inspector coming to see me. You heard his car and you came downstairs, didn't you? You were quite right. That was his car.'

Lily frowned. 'Not then,' she said. 'When Christopher was taken. I heard a car.'

Stephen hid a little sigh and kept his face gentle. 'Well, tell the inspector anything you want to, darling,' he said. 'And then you'd better go back to your room. Browning was going to bring you some cinnamon milk.'

'I don't want to sleep,' Lily said warningly. 'I won't be given anything to make me sleep.'

Stephen shook his head reassuringly. 'You shall have nothing that you don't want,' he said kindly. 'Do you want to go up now? While I see what the inspector has to say?'

Lily turned again to Inspector Walker. 'I *did* hear a car,' she said. 'They took him in a car.'

The inspector nodded. 'I'll check on that, Mrs Winters,' he promised. The sergeant made a note in his little book. 'I'll check on it without fail. No-one saw the pram and that may be why. It could have been loaded into a car. I'll check on it, don't worry.'

'You don't know where he is?' Lily asked. Her eyes, fixed on the inspector, were huge and black in her pale face. 'You *still* don't know?'

'We still don't know,' he said. 'But I promise you we are looking all the time for him.'

Lily nodded and went from the room. Stephen watched

her go up the stairs to her bedroom and then went back to the inspector and closed the door.

'I'm afraid she's taking this very badly,' he said. Unconsciously he touched the scratch on the side of his face. 'Our family doctor thinks that she should go to a convalescent home for nervous women until this is all over. He thinks we cannot care for her properly here.'

'Did you have a quarrel?' the inspector asked, thinking of Charlie Smith's allegations that Stephen was violent to his wife.

Stephen shook his head. 'Hardly!' he said. 'I'm not the man to take out my worries on my wife. She got hysterical and slapped my face because I was trying to stop her telephoning every one of her friends, and every one of my mother's friends, to interrogate them. She seems to think that we are all in a conspiracy to kidnap Christopher. She cannot accept that Charlie is responsible. My mother has told me that Lily was encouraging him. I'm afraid they were having an affair and it's got out of hand. I think Lily cannot bear her guilt.'

'No car then?' the inspector queried.

Stephen raised his shoulders. 'How can one tell? Charlie Smith doesn't have a car, and I don't believe he has any friends with limousines! If Lily can make herself believe she heard a big car drive off, and if she can persuade us all that the pram was loaded into a car, then she can go on believing in Charlie's innocence. I can see that she'd rather think it was a strange kidnapper in a big car, than believe it was a friend of Charlie's hiding and waiting, and Charlie getting her to the telephone on purpose.'

The inspector shook his head sympathetically, one eye on Stephen. 'A terrible mess,' he said.

Stephen shrugged, his face bitter. 'I'd be more shocked about the affair if it were not for the baby being missing,' he said. 'With Christopher gone –' He broke off.

'Nothing else matters right now. That's the most important.' He shrugged. 'We're expecting another doctor to come during the morning to see Lily. An expert on nervous d'seases. He won't disturb you. He just needs to see her.'

The inspector nodded. 'Are they going to certify your wife, Mr Winters?' he asked curiously.

Stephen flushed. 'No!' he exclaimed. 'Of course not. Nothing like that! It's just that you need the opinion of two doctors to send her to this rest home.'

'Will Mrs Winters consent to go – while her baby is still missing?'

'I think she must,' Stephen said frankly. 'She flew at me this morning, she insisted on having my mother's address book. She was sleepwalking last night, and she got hysterical during the day. I think she must get some help. I've seen chaps in the trenches crack up, and they were in better shape than she is now. Whether she wants to go or not, I think we have to take the medical advice.'

The inspector nodded. 'I am very sorry,' he said. 'This must be an unbearable strain for her.'

'Yes. And since she is partly responsible . . .'

The inspector nodded. 'Perhaps it would be better if she had some professional care,' he said.

The inspector had a list of Charlie's friends and contacts in Portsmouth, and throughout the morning the police constables on the team turned in brief reports on the whereabouts of every single one for the crucial hour around ten o'clock. Inspector Walker and his sergeant sat at Stephen's desk at number two, The Parade and classified each report into a pile of those with a foolproof alibi and those without. Since they were nearly all theatre or club people most of them claimed to be in bed and asleep at that time of the morning. Wearily the inspector detailed his team to go and double-check with landladies and neighbours that Charlie's friends were indeed late risers. They worked until midday and then he heard the Argyll draw up at the back gate and turn into the garage yard.

There was a noise from upstairs. Lily was running down the stairs calling for him. 'Inspector! Inspector Walker!'

He swiftly left the study, nodding to the sergeant. There was a tone of utter panic in Lily's voice which was oddly infectious. 'Get ready!' he said to the sergeant, though he did not know what to fear. He remembered the deep scratches on Stephen's face and the doctors who thought Lily was going mad. Lily came whirling down the stairs and nearly cannoned into him, standing at the bottom.

'I heard it!' she said. Her face was alight with urgency. 'It's exactly the same. Exactly the same. It's our car. It's *our* car that took Christopher away.'

She was panting with distress. She clutched the sleeve of his jacket and shook him roughly.

'Steady on, Madam,' the sergeant said.

'It's our car!' Lily said again. 'D'you understand what I'm saying, Inspector? I just heard our car drive into the yard and I know it was the same sound. It's our car that took Christopher away.'

The doorbell behind them pealed suddenly and Lily leaped up three steps with a gasp of fright. Browning came slowly up the back stairs and Muriel appeared wearily from the drawing room.

'That will be the doctor,' she said. 'Inspector – could you?'

A discreet gesture of her head indicated that she wanted him and the burly sergeant out of the hallway.

Inspector Walker took hold of Lily, who seemed likely to run upstairs again, and drew her into Stephen's study. The sergeant followed and stood before the window. Lily hesitated by the door, holding it half-open as if she might run at any moment.

'Sit down, Mrs Winters,' the inspector said coaxingly. 'There's no need for you to be anxious. I'm very interested in what you have to tell me. But please don't be overwrought.'

Leaving the door half-open, Lily came forward and sat on the chair before the desk. In the hall they could hear the murmur of voices as Stephen greeted the new doctor. Lily did not turn her head.

'I told you this morning I heard a car when Christopher was taken,' she said, speaking rapidly. 'But just now I recognized the noise of the engine. It's our car. I realize that now.'

'Wait a moment,' the inspector said. 'You didn't even remember the car at all until this morning. What makes you so sure now that it was your car now?'

Lily shook her head and took a handful of fair hair and pulled it hard, as if she would drag her memory out at the roots. The inspector watched her, warily, ready to call for help. He glanced at the sergeant to check that he was ready to catch Lily if she should run for the window and the lethal panes of thick glass.

'I don't know,' she said. 'I was so full of dread when I saw the garden empty it was like a photograph, it burned into my memory. But before the photograph is the noise of a car door slamming, and a car driving off. And just now, when I heard our car, I knew it was the same one. You *must* believe me, Inspector. It was our car which took Christopher.'

He nodded to placate her. 'But who d'you think was driving?'

There was a long silence. It stretched and stretched as if Lily could not bear to face the logical conclusion of what she was saying. Finally she spoke. Now she had both hands gripped in her hair, the skin of her face pulled tight and painful. 'It must have been Stephen,' she said in a whisper,

622

as if she were afraid that he might hear. 'Stephen or Coventry. Or both of them together.'

'But why would your husband steal his own baby?'

Lily's eyes were black with the horror of what she was saying. 'Because he's mad,' she said in a whisper. 'Because I called the baby Christopher and he hated Christopher's name. Because I wouldn't let him have the farm like he wanted. Because I love Christopher so much and he knows I will never love him. Because he hates me, and wants to destroy me. Because something happened in that farmhouse, in the war, that sent him mad.'

The inspector and the sergeant exchanged a brief shocked look. 'You must arrest him,' Lily said, suddenly clear. 'You must take him and *make* him tell you where he has hidden my baby. I don't care what you do to him to make him tell. I must get Christopher back. Neither Stephen nor Coventry can care for him. Neither of them knows how. You must take Stephen to prison now! And you must force him to tell you where Christopher is.'

The door behind Lily slowly opened and a strange woman in a pale grey uniform walked in, followed by Dr Mobey, and another man. Behind them was Stephen, his face haggard.

Lily whirled around as she saw them enter. 'Who are you?'

'I'm Nurse Priors,' the woman said quietly. 'I've come to take care of you.'

Lily screamed 'No!' and went to run towards the inspector, but the woman was too quick for her. She folded her in a hard relentless embrace and nodded at the strange man. 'Now! Dr Ramsden!'

From behind his back the new doctor brought out a hypodermic needle. Lily bucked and heaved but the woman was too strong for her. Dr Mobey supported the nurse and dragged Lily's arm away from her body and held it steady, the pale skin of her inner arm exposed, the blue vein vulnerable.

Dr Ramsden slipped the needle into the vein and squeezed the plunger. Within a moment Lily stopped struggling and her muscles went slack. The nurse dumped her into a chair, straightened her lolling head and took her pulse. They were silent while she counted the heartbeats and then she looked up. 'Quite satisfactory,' she said. 'Shall I take her to her room?'

'It's at the top of the house,' Stephen said. 'I'll carry her, my poor darling.'

He picked her up gently. The inspector, watching his face, saw an immense tenderness. Lily's head lolled like a sleeping child. In her drugged repose he saw the innocent prettiness that had made Stephen love her. Her bony anxious anger had melted away. She was like a sugar doll in her husband's arms. He carried her from the room.

The three professional men exchanged looks.

'I take it that none of this is any use as evidence,' Inspector Walker said finally.

Dr Ramsden shook his head. 'In my opinion, the young lady is suffering from what we call a paranoid neurosis. She thinks the world is conspiring against her. She is especially suspicious of those who love her best – in this case, her husband. She's young. Once this dreadful experience is over she should recover.'

Dr Mobey shook his head. 'A dreadful thing to happen,' he said. 'I've been attending this family for all my professional life. I can hardly believe that this should occur.'

'D'you think she heard a car?' the inspector double-checked.

The two doctors shrugged. 'She may have done,' Dr Ramsden said. 'I could not say that she had not. But the identification of the car as her husband's car is a symptom of her mania. She is accusing him of kidnapping their child. She is unable to distinguish between the truth and her own worst fears.' He nodded. 'If her lover has indeed stolen the baby then she has even more reason, in the logic of her madness, to believe her husband is the criminal. She wanted you to arrest him, didn't she? And force him to confess? These are classic symptoms.'

'I'll still check on the car,' the inspector said stubbornly.

Dr Mobey nodded. 'Whatever you think best,' he said. 'The sooner the child is found the better for all concerned.'

'If it *is* found,' Inspector Walker said grimly. 'I am very concerned for its life.'

Chapter Forty-two

When Lily awoke she did not know at first where she was. It was dark and she was hungry, and trembling in every limb as if she had been sick with a fever. She blinked and saw that above her head was the familiar ceiling of her bedroom, the pendant light, the bedposts. She swallowed; her throat was tight and dry, her eyes gritty. She rubbed her face and sat up in her bed.

At once she was swamped with despair so great that she nearly cried out. It was like a wave of grief hitting her as she remembered that Christopher was missing, and that no-one would look for him.

She got to her feet and staggered as the floor heaved and pitched beneath her. She leaned on her dressing table and then slumped on the pretty stool and stared at her shadowy reflection in the mirror. Slowly she was beginning to remember what had happened. She could remember going downstairs and telling the inspector that she recognized the engine note of the car. She remembered the woman in grey coming towards her. But then she had a nightmarish recollection of the strange woman throwing her arms around her and holding her, and wild terrifying dreams of hunting for Christopher and being pursued. She had dreamed she was in the trenches, in Stephen's nightmare landscape, and somewhere, amid all the stiffening bleeding bodies, was Christopher. She could hear him crying but she had no way of knowing how to find him. She turned dying men over, she pushed corpses to one side, and scrambled over injured groaning men, calling 'Christopher! Christopher!', searching for him.

She rubbed her face and stared at the mirror. She switched on the little light and saw herself. She was pale and haggard. Her drugged sleep had put lines in her face and dark bruises of shadows under her eyes. Her hair was limp and greasy, her face shiny with sweat and tears. The navy cardigan was crumpled and the skirt was creased. Lily stared at herself with unseeing eyes.

'He's got him,' she said quietly. 'The mad bastard has got him.'

She got up and went to the door, walking slowly as her muscles reluctantly obeyed her. When she turned the handle but could not open the door she thought it was stuck and that she was still too weak. But when she pulled it once, twice, she knew that they had locked her in.

She slapped on the panel of the door with the flat of her hand and then she knocked gently. 'Hello?' she said. Her voice was cracked and thin. She thought for a sudden foolish moment of terror that the whole household had moved away. They had stolen Christopher and hidden him, and now they had locked her in her room and cleared out. She would starve up there. She would thirst and then die, and no-one would ever search for Christopher. No-one would ever find him.

Lily banged on the door more loudly. 'Let me out!' she said. Her voice was stronger with use. This time she made a noise that people in the house could hear.

On the other side of the door she heard footsteps and then the noise of a key in the lock. 'Step back from the door, Mrs Winters,' a cool authoritative voice said. 'Step back and sit on the bed, please.'

Lily, like a little mechanical doll, obeyed; and was sitting on the bed when the door opened and the strange woman in grey came into the room and shut the door firmly behind her.

'How are you feeling?' she asked.

She seemed to think it quite normal that she should walk uninvited into Lily's bedroom and inquire after her health.

'Who are you?' Lily demanded. 'I want to see my husband.'

The woman smiled slightly. 'I asked you how you are,' she repeated.

Lily felt her grip on reality shifting and eroding. 'I'm all right,' she said uneasily.

'I expect you'd like a drink and something to eat. Throat dry?'

Lily nodded.

'D'you need the bathroom?'

Lily nodded again.

'I shall take you to the bathroom,' the woman said firmly. 'But don't try to go downstairs. We don't want to go downstairs this evening. Just to the bathroom and back again. All right?'

Lily found herself nodding, too puzzled and frightened to argue. 'I want to see my husband,' she said quietly.

'All in good time,' the woman said. 'Bathroom first, yes?'

Lily got up and the woman took her by the right arm and helped her walk across the room. She opened the door and guided Lily to the bathroom. At the threshold she stepped back and closed the door on Lily. The key was missing from the lock. Stephen's shaving things and razor blades had gone from their usual place.

Lily sat on the toilet and then washed her face and hands. Her skin felt tired and dry. She felt as if she were eighty or ninety years old. She wanted a bath but she could not face the effort of running it. She was aware of smelling of sweat and a strange dank smell of fear. She took a flannel and wiped her throat and her breasts, but she had no energy to wash properly. She cleaned her teeth and rinsed the stale drugged taste from her mouth. She felt deeply weary.

When she opened the door the woman was waiting for her on the landing.

'That's better,' she said encouragingly. 'Now back to your room and I'll bring you up some supper, and then an early night.'

'What time is it?' Lily asked.

'Nearly bedtime,' the woman replied. She guided Lily through the door and sat her in the little bedroom armchair.

'I asked what time is it?' Lily repeated.

The woman smiled at her. 'It's been a very long and difficult day,' she said. 'You stop worrying, I'll bring you up a nice tray of something, and then you can have a good sleep.'

'Have they found Christopher?' Lily asked dully. She knew they would not find him until they asked Stephen or Coventry where the baby was hidden. And no-one but her would ever ask Stephen or Coventry.

'They'll find him soon,' the woman said. 'Now, will you sit there like a good girl while I fetch some supper?'

Lily nodded, feeling her will slip away under the woman's determination.

The nurse went out of the room. Lily heard the key turn in the lock without surprise or even resentment. She was apparently imprisoned, and this woman was her gaoler. She thought fleetingly of Charlie who was the only person who would rescue her from this, and then realized that he too was locked up. Slowly, through her exhausted mind she traced the path that had led her to being imprisoned in her own room. Charlie was arrested, she was captive. The inspector had not believed that the car

629

used in the kidnap was Stephen's car. No-one was going to rescue Christopher.

Lily forced herself up from the chair and went to the door and listened. The house was silent. She tried the door handle. It turned but the door did not open. She was indeed locked in. She went to the window, moving slowly as if she were wading through deep water. It was a sash window with a bolt in the middle of the frame, locking the top window to the bottom. Lily stood on the window seat and tugged at the lower window until it shifted. She pushed it up. It made a sharp grating sound. She froze, expecting to hear the woman's return, fearful of her. But the house was as quiet as if they were all asleep. Or as if they had all, indeed, gone away.

Lily leaned out of the window. She was three storeys up. Below her was the perilous drop to the well-cut front lawn and the basement wall. She would break her neck if she fell. To the left of the window was a solid ornate drainpipe, and below her window was Rory's bedroom. Below that was the drawing room. Rory's window spilled yellow light through a gap in the curtains. Lily glanced behind her once more, as if the bedroom door might have magically opened and spared her this ordeal. She was still hazy from the drug, neither miracle nor nightmare would have surprised her. She said quietly, 'Christopher', as if his name were a prayer, and slung one leg over the window ledge, and then the other.

She perched on the ledge, feeling unsteady and fearful. The drainpipe was just out of reach, she would have to push off and stretch out for it. Only a sudden fear that the woman in grey would come back and push her, push her out of the window, off the ledge into nothingness, forced Lily forwards. She thrust out with one foot against the wall and reached with her arms for the drainpipe. She made it. She clung to the drainpipe like a monkey, but her grip was not strong enough, her muscles were still slack from the drug. She could feel herself, remorselessly, unstoppably sliding downwards. Her hands, her arms, the skin of her thighs burned as she slid, but then her scrabbling stockinged feet found a bracket bolting the drainpipe to the wall and she stood on tiptoes on the little metal bars and looked sideways.

She was just a few feet above the level of Rory's window. With a soft sob she slid a little further and gripped tight. Again, the window sill was beyond her reach. She would have to stretch out to it, but this time there was nothing to grab. Lily looked upwards. She could not climb back up. She looked down and knew that she could not hold on for the long slide to the ground.

She stretched out, feeling her fear precipitate her into a sense of floating irresponsibility. She almost laughed from sheer terror. Then she launched herself from the drainpipe towards the window sill and felt the bricks and mortar suddenly scratch her palms as she grabbed the side of the window and lurched inwards, to the pane of glass.

She perched precariously on the narrow ledge and peered through the gap of the curtain. Nurse Bells was just settling Rory to sleep, Lily recognized the routine. The glass of water put within his reach, the electric bell pinned to the bedcover, the final 'goodnight' and then the switching off of all the lights except the little one by his bed. Lily made herself count from one to thirty, slowly, and then she tapped on the window, sidled into the gap of the curtains, and waved.

Rory was sitting up cushioned by pillows. At the noise of her tapping he stared towards the window and his face grew suddenly alert as he saw her, and then recognized her.

Lily mouthed, 'Help me!', through the glass.

Rory pulled himself upright in the bed and looked

towards his wheelchair. He reached as far as he could, but his hands could not grip it. His legs, still paralysed, stayed immobile in the bed. Lily could do nothing but watch him, and feel her own muscles tremble with the strain and with the cold. In a little while the strange woman in grey would be back in Lily's bedroom and then she would know that Lily was trying to escape.

Rory made a final heave and got one hand on the arm of the wheelchair, and drew it towards the bed. He got it as close as he could, and then clicked on the brake. Using both arms he heaved himself towards it and then lurched towards the seat. The chair rocked back as he fell into it, but did not tip over. He twisted himself around into the ordinary sitting position, released the brake, and wheeled it towards the window.

Lily found she was biting her lips with anxiety. Every moment that went by increased the chances that the strange woman would come for her. Lily had an irrational fear that the woman would come after her, down the drainpipe, and push her off the window ledge. She moaned very quietly and then fixed her sharp teeth into her lower lip to silence herself.

Rory was heaving himself from the wheelchair to the window seat. He moved like a merman, with useless fins for legs. He pulled himself along the window seat and then reared up to reach the lock. His anguished face and Lily's were very close, on either side of the glass.

His long weak fingers struggled with the lock. Lily could see the start of despair in his face, so close to her own. She nodded frantically, urging him to keep trying. She could see the muscles on his neck straighten and knot as he struggled with the latch. At last it moved and Lily saw the delight and relief on his face. He dropped back down to the window seat and she could see him shudder at relief from the strain. He rested for only a second and then thrust his fingers through the metal loops for raising the window.

Lily nearly forgot her peril and stepped back off the ledge. She wavered slightly and then the cool updraught of sea air prompted her to cling to the side of the window as Rory raised the bottom half. Lily dropped her head and shoulders and rolled in.

'What . . . ?' Rory demanded.

'I've got to go,' Lily said. 'I know where Christopher is. Give me ten minutes and then ring for someone to get you back into bed. I'll see you when I get back.' She was halfway across the room before she glanced back at him. 'Thank you,' she said. 'I love you, Rory.'

She opened the door and listened intently. She could hear the murmur of talk from the drawing room, but the hall and landing were empty. Nurse Bells had left for the night; the staff would be in the kitchen. Lily, soundless in her stockinged feet, crept down the carpeted stairs.

The clock in the hall showed that it was twenty past ten but Lily had no sense of time. She watched the crack of light under the drawing room door as if she could forbid the door to open. As if she could keep Stephen safely in the room by sheer will power.

She slid past the drawing room door as quiet as a ghost, and opened the dining room door and stepped in. It was so like her dream of the night before that for a moment Lily thought she was dreaming again. Perhaps the woman in grey, and the trenches, and the fear of falling and now the dining room were all part of the same terrifying dream.

The French windows opened easily and Lily crept down the steps to the garden. The moon was hidden by cloud, the garden was filled with shadows. Lily paused, wondering if now she would find the pram and Christopher sleeping easily inside it. She glanced towards the stone

633

garden seat. It was pale and cold and empty. She ran past it to the garden gate. It opened without a sound and Lily slipped through and over the cobbled yard to the garages.

The Argyll was there.

Lily checked for a moment, shocked out of her certainty. She had been sure that Coventry would have taken the car over to Hayling Island. She had been sure that he had taken Christopher on that very first morning to the little houseboat at the water's edge. She had been sure that he would be there with her baby now. But if Coventry was in his room over the garage and the Argyll was parked in its usual place then she had no idea where her baby might be. For the first time since Christopher had gone missing, it occurred to Lily that he might be dead.

Lily opened the door of her own little car. Whatever had happened to her baby she had to get away from the woman in grey, and from the doctors who would drug her, and the police who would arrest her. She would never know what had happened to her son unless she could escape from the house now.

Coventry kept the petrol level topped up, the car was ready for her to drive. She pushed the lever to retard the spark into the start position and turned the switch. The engine started at once. She pressed the accelerator and put the car in gear. It moved forward, and she drove out of the garage yard and northwards, away from the house, away from the staring windows.

She drove as fast as she dared along the streets which were sometimes lit with bright electric lights and sometimes shadowy blue from gas lighting. The roads were empty. When the town was left behind her and Lily was on the main coast road going east, she put her foot down hard on the accelerator and watched the speed of the car creep upwards. On the top of the bonnet was the little glass temperature gauge. As Lily drove faster than she had ever gone before she saw the needle turn around from cold to warm and then slowly towards hot.

She dared not go any slower. She knew that the woman in grey would have raised the alarm by now, Stephen had the Argyll in the garage and Coventry might be in his room or in the kitchen. Stephen might call the police, or he might hunt for her himself. Her worst fear was that he would know, intuitively, where she was going. He would take his bigger, faster car, and follow her. All the way along the coast road with the sound of the waves sighing as the tide came in over the mudflats and the fog rolled in on their grey crested backs, Lily watched her wing mirror for the telltale lights of a pursuing car.

She turned over the little bridge to Hayling Island and gasped in fear as the steering wheel bucked in her hands as she took the right angle turn to the south too fast. The little car held the road and she forced it across the narrow bridge. The timbers boomed as she accelerated, and then she was on the other side and the marshes, ghostly with mist, were behind her. The road running south was twisty and Lily did not know it. She was forced to go slower and slower after she had nearly brushed a corner taking a turn too fast. She had an increasing sense of panic at the thought that the turns of the road which were slowing her down would not delay Stephen, who knew this road well, but they would hide his headlights so that she would not know he was behind her until she heard the rush of his car and suddenly saw the blaze of the full beam of his headlights.

Lily gave a little gasp of fear and pressed her foot down on the accelerator as far as she dared. The road was nearing the sea again, she could see the strips of mist flickering in her headlights and hear the ominous bellow of the light-ships out in the harbour. She came to a T junction, half obscured by blown sand at the southernmost point of the island, and turned right. The road was little more than a bumpy track. Lily threw the little car at drifts of sand and ditches, and clung to the steering wheel as they r cketed along. There were no lights behind her, the road was dark, lit only by starlight and by deceptive veils of white sea mist. The foghorns grew louder, the sand on the road deeper and more dangerous. Lily was forced to slow down and then she saw the little inn and the pier for the ferry passengers and she swung the car to the right and parked it.

Ahead of her were the three houseboats. There was a light shining through a little tear in a blackout blind of the furthest boat. It was painted with black waterproof varnish, unlike the other white-washed pair. A curl of smoke was coming from the chimney, matched by a sea of mist washing and moving around the stern and the prow as if the houseboat were afloat and about to set sail. Someone was at home.

Lily, still barefoot, crept across the shingle, wincing in discomfort from the sharp stones. She stepped on to the ladder which led to the little door and crept upwards. The door was not locked. She put her hand on the latch and it yielded easily and swung open.

In the lamplit room before her she could see Coventry hunched in the fireside chair. At the back of the room was the big blue pram. It was quite empty.

Lily stumbled into the room, her legs buckling beneath her.

'My baby,' she said simply. She was beyond fear. The sight of the empty pram had told her that her search was over and her life was now worthless. She was too late. She had thought her way through the maze of madness too late. All she had found was an empty blue coach-built pram and the hand-embroidered white sheets. Her baby had been dead for days.

'My baby,' she said again. Her voice was devoid of any feeling.

Coventry stood up and came towards her, his face warm with tenderness.

'Here he is,' he said. His voice was croaky and harsh. But the words were clear. He held out the little bundle he had been nursing. As Lily, disbelieving, received him, Christopher stirred in his sleep and then nestled into his mother's arms.

Lily held him and felt the warmth of his little body, the firm lightness of him. She bent her face to him and inhaled the sweet inimitable smell of her baby, she caressed his small clenched fist. She buried her face in his neck and felt her whole body melt with tenderness and with a sense of restoration so powerful that she was suddenly young and strong again.

'Christopher,' she said.

'He wanted him dead,' Coventry said quietly. 'He told me to take him and drown him. So I took him and hid him here instead. I didn't know what to do for the best. I didn't know what was the best.'

Lily raised her head from Christopher's warm sleeping form and was about to question him when she heard, at some distance, the quiet well-tuned noise of the Argyll's engine. It came closer, drew up behind Lily's car and the engine was switched off. Lily and Coventry froze, their eyes locked, as they heard the car door slam and Stephen's confident steps across the gravel and up the steps, one – two – three – four. He pushed the door open and came into the room.

Lily would not have recognized him. His face was bright and alive as she had never seen it before. In his hand was an officer's revolver, held casually with an experienced grace. He looked like the man who had led his men for vengeance, on a forlorn hope. He looked like the man who

637

had learned to look death in the face and laugh at it as an empty threat. He looked like a man superbly adapted to fight a man's war. He looked like a man who could never live at peace.

Stephen beamed as he saw her, and then he turned towards Coventry. 'Didn't I tell you?' he asked, his voice warm with laughter. 'They're all damned whores. Every one of them, as tricky as a barrel of monkeys.'

'Go,' Coventry said very, very softly to Lily. 'Go.'

Like a bird watching a snake, Lily took one sideways step to the door, never taking her eyes from her husband's smiling face.

'Got any tea?' he asked Coventry. 'Got any biscuits?'

Coventry made a small inviting gesture to the fireside chair and Stephen stepped forward into the room. Lily pressed back against the wall to let him pass. She had a sudden realization that he could hardly see her, he could hardly see her and the baby. He simply was not there in the little room with the sea lapping outside and the fog-horn calling through the mist. He had slipped away and was once more the man they had forced him to become in the trenches, a man beyond feelings, beyond fear. A man whose principal pleasure was his friendship with his batman, whose joy was a cup of stale tea, and whose habit was daily murder.

Lily took another silent step towards the door.

'Kettle's on,' Coventry said comfortably. 'Want some rum, Captain Winters?'

'As a chaser,' Stephen said. 'I don't like 'em mixed.'

There was a small step up to the door. Lily had to move into the room to skirt the angle of the open door. As she stepped forward Stephen turned his head a little towards her. Lily froze again. The revolver in his hand was shiny and well-oiled, he held it as one might hold a favourite pen. It fitted his hand.

'Go,' Coventry said, his voice a whisper.

Lily felt for the door jamb behind her with her free hand, her other hand clutching Christopher to her heart. She stepped backwards, up the little step, and felt under her bare feet the cold wood of the outside staircase. Even then she hesitated, for just a moment; fearing for Stephen, fearing for Coventry, fearing for them both and for the madness that the war had forced on them.

'Go,' Coventry said softly. 'We know our duty.'

She closed the door and crept down the steps. She felt that at any moment that Stephen might erupt into madness, he could be down the steps and barring her way in two strides. She crept bent-kneed over the shingle, bruising her feet and stumbling on the wet stones. She got into her car and put Christopher on the passenger seat beside her. He stirred in his sleep and opened his eyes, as blue as her own. She turned the switch to start the engine.

The engine turned over but it did not fire. Lily gritted her teeth and tried again. She knew that the sound of the engine might be the very thing that broke Stephen's fantasy of being back at Ypres in a God-given lull from the shelling. If he remembered where he truly was, and what she knew, he would come after her and the baby with the loaded revolver in his hand.

She switched the car right off, and then tried it again. The engine turned over for a moment and then died. The arrow of the temperature gauge on the bonnet was pointing to red, the car was overheated and the sea mist was penetrating the engine, soaking the points and the plugs with cold damp air. Lily had her foot down hard on the accelerator, flooding the engine with too much petrol. She gave a soft sob, moved the spark lever to the start position, paused, and then turned on the engine again.

The engine suddenly fired, Lily pressed the accelerator, took off the handbrake, slipped it into gear and eased forward. She switched on the headlights and glanced fearfully over her shoulder. Even now, if Stephen came down the steps and jumped into the Argyll, he could catch her. There were long stretches of deserted road between here and home. There were a thousand places where his more powerful car could overtake and then block her way. There was that little shaking bridge over the sea where he could ease forward and nudge Lily's smaller lighter car towards the edge and then through the frail wooden rail into the deep fast-flowing current.

Lily drove carefully forward. There was an open gateway at the end of the estuary where she could rejoin the track. But at the very bend at the edge of the beach the wheels stuck for a moment in sand and the engine stalled.

In the silence the foghorn was very loud. A couple of sea birds called into the darkness.

And then Lily heard it – very clearly – two revolver shots. First one . . . and then the other . . . very sharp, echoing over the dark water and scaring the roosting sea birds up in a screaming pale cloud which circled the little harbour once, twice and then slowly settled again, calling and preening, crying and scolding. Then there was silence; the complete silence of absence, the silence when someone has gone. Lily knew then that Coventry had done his last act of service for the man he loved.

The war for both of them was finally over.